PHILIP .... g *The Mulberry* .... *nency, King of the Badgers* and *Scenes from Early Life*, which won the Ondaatje Prize in 2012. He is a Professor of Creative Writing at the University of Bath Spa and lives in south London and Geneva.

Praise for *The Friendly Ones*:

'He deals in life as it is, without melodrama, but not without horrors … It's a novel like a wild garden, full of unexpected pleasures, unlooked for views, surprising encounters. Hensher is a master of the big scene, but also of the revealing snapshot. Sometimes today even clearly talented novelists don't seem interested in trying to show us how people actually think, feel and live. Hensher does all this, and does it with sympathy and intelligence. Years ago he wrote a marvellous novel, *The Mulberry Empire*, set mostly in nineteenth-century Afghanistan. I thought it unlikely he would ever do anything better, but he has'
Scotsman

'It's the book you should give someone who thinks they don't like novels; sit back and watch them laugh and cry and become obsessed with the history of East Pakistan. This powerful book marshals dozens of convincing characters, each distinctive voice tinting the third-person narrative, cross-fading place and time. Hensher makes all those other weavers of intergenerational, politically charged tales look like babies, frankly. Here is surely a future prizewinner'
The Times

'Marvellous … Zipping between Oxford and Devon, Sheffield and Dhaka, Hensher's immersive, cartwheeling narrative follows the history of two neighbouring families in a quiet suburban street and asks reverberating and powerfully resonant questions about what makes a family, a community and a country'

Daily Mail

'*The Friendly Ones* is a long novel, able to provide the special satisfactions – narrative digressions, fully realised minor characters – no shorter book could manage' *Telegraph*

'As an exploration of race and integration, Hensher's novel is well-observed and often incisive … with sustained concentration and a satirical gaze, he examines the markers of status that underpin the beliefs of so many in this story' *TLS*

'*The Friendly Ones* is not a novel to be rattled quickly through. It's a story that demands a degree of care and attention from the reader. Not least so as to be rewarded for one's effort with the full appreciation of the minutiae that make this novel more than the sum of its parts … Hensher proves himself a tenderly attentive and generous creator' *Independent*

'Beautifully written and intelligent … *The Friendly Ones* is about two families and how people with very different histories can fit together and redeem each other. It's mesmerising'

Attitude Magazine

'Hensher's eleventh novel is his biggest and most ambitious yet: old-fashioned in its storytelling, with sly nods to *The Winter's Tale*, but shot through with tenderness and peopled with an unusually rich cast of characters, from druggies and dropouts to doctors and MPs' *Mail on Sunday*

'A panoramic, Dickensian novel of family life, teeming with vitality and exuberance. It has much to tell us about the way we live now, and celebrates multiculturalism in the face of Brexit naysaying'   *iNews*

'At the heart of this kind and profound book, though, is something serious: Hensher's sense of how deeply the histories that neighbours keep from each other run, how unthinkable are the experiences of violence and betrayal that some people endure, how terribly families are torn asunder by their different allegiances, and how hard it is, in the end, to make peace with that'
                                                                    Financial Times

PHILIP HENSHER

THE FRIENDLY ONES

4th ESTATE • London

4th Estate
An imprint of HarperCollins*Publishers*
1 London Bridge Street
London SE1 9GF
www.4thEstate.co.uk

First published in Great Britain in 2018 by 4th Estate
This 4th Estate paperback edition published in 2019

1

A catalogue record for this book is
available from the British Library

ISBN 978-0-00-817565-8

Printed and bound in Great Britain by
CPI Group (UK) Ltd, Croydon

MIX
Paper from
responsible sources

FSC
www.fsc.org
FSC™ C007454

This book is produced from independently certified FSC paper
to ensure responsible forest management.

For more information visit: www.harpercollins.co.uk/green

For Zaved Mahmood, of course

If I lived in a cave and you were my only visitor,
what would I tell you that the walls had told me?
That people are unfinished and are made between
each other ...

JACK UNDERWOOD,
'Second'

... amid the millions of this great city it is difficult to
discover who these people are or what their object can be ...

ARTHUR CONAN DOYLE,
The Hound of the Baskervilles

BOOK ONE

THE LITTLE SPINSTERS

CHAPTER ONE

I.

Towards the end of the afternoon, Aisha got up and stood at the garden window. The arrangements for the party had been in place since the morning – the hired barbecue, red and shiny under the elm tree, the festoons over the bushes, the torches lined up along the shrubbery. Over the fence, the old man was up a ladder against a fruit tree. He had been sweeping fallen white blossom from his lawn, and now had found something to do where he could see his neighbours better. Inside the room, the Italian was continuing to talk. Her mother and father were still listening.

'Really?' Nazia said inattentively. She could not see this one as a son-in-law. He was bald; his brown sweater hung, unravelling, around his dirty wrists. His party clothes were underneath. Aisha had been an eager, encouraging member of his audience until early yesterday evening, and then, quite abruptly, had wilted into silence and bored disinterest, passing him on to her parents, like a pet she had passionately wished for before finding the task of caring for it too much.

'In Sicily, we often have such parties,' the Italian was saying. 'But it is too hot, in the summer, to have parties during the day where food is served. We wait until nine or ten o'clock in the evening, and then we eat cold food, perhaps some pasta. We would not grill meat like this, in the open air.'

'Really?' Sharif said, in his turn. A bird was singing in the elm tree, a loud, plangent, lovely note, as if asking a question of the garden. Underneath, the light fell through the leaves, dappling the lawn, the shiny red box of the barbecue, the white-shirted help, now talking quietly to each other, raising their eyes quizzically, serious as surgeons.

Nazia had felt she had done everything that she could have for Aisha's Italian. They had taken him out to an Italian restaurant in Sheffield on Friday night, said to be very good, where he had poked suspiciously at his plate and explained about Sicilian food. They had gone out for the day into the countryside on Saturday, where Sharif had got lost and the stately home had failed to impress. She had cooked a real Bengali meal last night that Enrico couldn't eat, and had said so. This morning, Aisha was supposed to take him for a walk in the neighbourhood, through the woods, but her change of heart yesterday had done for that. 'Oh, Mummy,' she had said, throwing her hands up, when Nazia had suggested it after breakfast. 'Don't be so dreadfully boring. I can't think of anything worse. We'll be perfectly happy just reading the paper.'

They had been in the square red-brick house almost four months. It was perfect, resembling a child's first drawing of a house, with a square front, a door with brass knocker, windows to either side, and a chimney on both right and left. The purple front door had been changed to imperial blue, the kitchen modernized, the fitted carpets removed and the parquet flooring re-polished, the avocado bathroom altered to white: everything had been done under Nazia's direction and control, but there had been no official opening.

Aisha had been mentioning her friend Enrico for some months now, another student on her MPhil course at Cambridge. Nazia and Sharif had agreed that they would be welcoming and open, however confiding or confrontational Aisha became in mentioning her friend. Aisha had said she would bring Enrico to visit them one weekend. It would be a perfect opportunity to have a lot of people round. They had agreed this without consulting Aisha. 'Oh, Mummy, for God's sake,' Aisha had said, when she had heard. 'Enrico doesn't want to meet the aunties and hear about all their babies. I can't

imagine how you could inflict that on him.' But this was an
ordinary sort of complaint, not a storming-out, a door-slam-
ming, a refusal to join in, and everyone knew how much fun a
party could be. What they would have done with Enrico if they
hadn't been able to excuse themselves, to make sure the preparations were in order, Nazia could not imagine.

The Italian was leaning forward as if to make an important
point, but he was still talking about the details of his country.
'My mother and father always go away in August, to the same
place in Tuscany they have gone to for forty years. A spa town.
Many Sicilians go to the same spa town, and go at the same
time. There would be no point in holding a party in the summer,
in August, at home in Sicily.' Italians were expected to be
good-looking. But Enrico sat with his pale fat hands, like wet
skinned fish, his black, chaotic hair about the bald dome. With
his squashed, irregular and expository features, he looked like
someone who should have been apologized for. Nazia knew that
people could have different effects in different places. Enrico, in
the damp cafés and libraries of fog-bound Cambridge, explaining about things to Aisha, showing her how the world was and
how it could be put right: that was fascinating. For a moment
she saw him, his face glowering with righteousness in a cloud of
tea-steam, tearing at an English cake and bringing it in crumbs
and fragments to his mouth, and Aisha opposite, listening. The
Enrico in her head wore a scarf and a brown duffel coat and
woollen gloves. He was not a person for home or family, but
one to make a compelling case in public places and temporary
rented rooms with another person's ideas of wallpaper, a speech-
maker with bold, urgent gestures. Aisha stood at the window,
having renounced her Italian for the moment. There would be
a slow, sour conversation on the train tomorrow.

'Is that in Sicily, too?' Sharif said politely.

'In Sicily?' Enrico said. There was a tone of mild astonishment in his voice, as if he had not been talking about Sicily, as
if it were extraordinary and in slightly bad taste to have raised
the subject at all.

'The place you said – where your parents go on holiday.'

'No, no, not at all,' Enrico said. 'I think I said it was in Tuscany.'

'Really?' Sharif said. He smiled, but fell silent. It was his way when he felt snubbed not to engage further, to let the other person do all the work from that point onwards. He could have explained that they had been on holiday to Umbria only two years before, where he had learned to say '*Buon giorno*' and '*Buona sera*'. The Italian did not notice, and started to explain.

'Who is that man next door?' Aisha said suddenly, not turning round. 'He's been up that ladder for ages.'

'We haven't really met the neighbours,' Nazia said to Enrico. 'We've said hello – we apologized about the builders. Is he talking to the twins? He has an odd name – I can't remember what it was, but it was really quite odd.'

'They're talking to him,' Aisha said. 'I think I'm going to go and fetch them in.'

'Has Aisha shown you round the garden?' Nazia said to Enrico. 'We're not gardeners at all. We're having to get a gardener in to do all the work. He had to come twice last week. But it is nice. Are you interested in gardens, Enrico?'

But Enrico was not interested in gardens, and could only remember that in Sicily there was a lemon tree in his parents' garden and some jasmine, which smelt too strong for him in the summer: it made him sneeze.

'Oh, jasmine,' Sharif said, calling himself back to the conversation, and remembering something himself. His tone was so fond and rich that Nazia looked at him expectantly. But he fell silent again. Nazia's heart filled with love for her husband, lost in his association of ideas. Aisha left the room and, in a moment, was walking across the newly trim lawn towards her brothers, the twins, now talking across the fence with her parents' neighbour. Nazia fervently hoped that she was going to get five minutes alone with her daughter before she left with the Italian the next morning.

2.

The house would do for the rest of their lives. There were rooms for all three of the children, and a playroom, or second sitting room, they could make their own, although Aisha was no longer living at home. 'It's a lovely garden, too,' Nazia had said, as they drove away, leaving the happily waving estate agent on the pavement next to his car.

'Gardens take upkeep,' Sharif had said, but indulgently, as if they might after all develop an interest in gardening. 'Your grandfather's garden was so pretty. I always wonder that his skill never descended to any of you.'

'Nana had no skill in gardening,' Nazia said. 'If his garden was pretty, it was because the gardener kept it like that. Twelve rows of flowering plants, and when they stopped flowering, out they went. Not like the English, nurturing dead twigs in hope.'

'Well,' Sharif said, 'it was pretty, whoever was responsible.'

'Your father's garden in Dhanmondi was nice too, and that was down to the gardener, I would say. We can have a gardener, too.'

'And a cook, and a butler, and a khitmagar ...' Sharif had said.

'Just a gardener,' Nazia had said. She was overwhelmed with possibilities. They had not been born in this country; they had been born in East Pakistan, East Bengal, Bangladesh – it had changed its name several times in their lifetimes, whether they were there or not. The thick-oaked avenue was a place to settle in. She thought with some licensed amusement of the green, underwaterish flat over the tobacconist's shop they had lived in all that first winter, as students. The silverfish wriggling across the squelching carpet, them all hunkering down around the gas fire, its blue flames hissing behind a burnt ceramic grid, and Aisha in her cradle, snuffling through the damp.

To others it might have looked like the steady ascent of a celestial ladder, into glory and wide acres. But Nazia dreamt of her and Sharif aboard some rickety wheeled vehicle, driving faster and faster, coming to a halt only by veering off the road into a field of soft ploughed mud, where they now rested, dazed. It had been only twenty-five years.

The avenue had been built and rebuilt over time. The houses were old, behind heavy stone walls, some more fanciful than Nazia and Sharif's. They had been inside one or two of the houses; a package from Dhaka of some books had arrived when they were at work, and a neighbour opposite had taken it in. (Samu's brother, living in the old Khondkar house, was so help-ful – Nazia's sister-in-law's brother-in-law, you had to say in English, and just one word in Bengali.) They knew from expe-rience that some neighbours would be friendly, and some would not. The man next door had spoken to them a few times. He was a very keen gardener: he spent his time pruning, and trim-ming, and mowing the lawn; he had a small greenhouse, a kind of lean-to against the kitchen wall of his house where he had been seen transferring seedlings from one pot to another, and then, last week, taking them out and installing them in the flowerbed. His house was Victorian, the stone blackened and the gateposts adorned with rampant beasts, now covered with lichen and blackly unidentifiable. At the top of the house was a round turret with what must be a round window-seat, and, at the back, an outbreak of castellations. They had thought he lived on his own until Wednesday, when an ambulance had arrived, and an elderly person, a woman with a white shock of uncombed hair, had been carried out on a stretcher. It was odd that the man had not mentioned he had a wife, during their three or four conversations over the garden fence.

He was a doctor, a retired one. They had not quite caught his name at first. He had four children in different parts of the country, married, divorced, and two still unmarried. The road was rather full of doctors at or near retirement, he had told them, and certainly the four or five neighbours Nazia had passed the time of day with had owned up to being anaesthe-tists, surgeons, paediatricians. She had not made the mistake of mentioning anything to do with her own health, of course, in response, or mentioning that her brother Rumi had been a public-health specialist and GP in Bombay these last twenty years. Sharif was less enthusiastic about striking up conversations with strangers, even strangers you lived next door to, but he was interested in the outcomes of Nazia's conversations, as she stopped, often, to admire the springtime burst of life in the front gardens of numbers 124, 126, and the house that must be 139, the house labelled Inverness Lodge on the gatepost. The bursts of cherry blossom and apple blossom, pink and white, up and down the avenue were an opportunity to Nazia to introduce herself. Soon, she would be telling them about the fruit trees that were in the garden of her father-in-law's house in Dhanmondi. But that house was sold, and a block of flats was being built, and the fruit trees only existed in her conversation, these days. She had no idea what Dhanmondi looked like, these days. The whole of Dhaka.

3.

Outside, in the garden, Aisha and the twins and the retired doctor next door were discussing a tree in their garden. It had dark, glossy leaves, and in recent weeks the twins had noticed that it was starting to bear fruit. Among the leaves now were clusters of solid yellow fruit about the size of dates, just starting to soften, at the bottom end of each fruit a kind of pucker, like a navel. The tree was eight feet high, against the latticed fence. The garden must hold other secrets and surprises, and other plants, which had looked like scrubby crawling weeds, were now beginning to produce buds and flowers and blossom, and might, too, in time produce fruit. It was all a mystery. Aisha hadn't even walked down to the end of the garden yet.

'I don't know if you can eat them,' Aisha was saying, quite sociably. The twins had that polite aspect, their hands behind their backs and their heads slightly cocked, that they liked to perform before ridiculing their victim. 'They might be ornamental only, I know.'

'Oh, yes,' the doctor said. He was on his ladder, cutting back the branches of the apple tree that ventured over the fence, and talked down at the three of them. 'You can eat them. It's not every year that they ripen, though. I remember the hot summer of 'seventy-six, the fruit started early and kept on coming. Of course it was only half the size it is now. You're in luck.'

'I've never seen a tree like that before,' Omith said, and his twin Raja offered the idiotic opinion that it might be a mango tree. Omith and Raja had been born in 1976, just up the road in the Northern General Hospital; they had seen a mango tree no more than half a dozen times in their lives, and never in the country they had been born in.

'No,' the doctor said mildly. 'I don't think you could get a mango tree to grow in a garden in Yorkshire. It's called a loquat. Some people call it a medlar, or a Japanese medlar. They're not like the medlars we have here. You've got to wait for them to ripen and then go rotten, almost, before you can eat them. These look more like kumquats, you see, but with a much thinner skin.'

He reached across the fence, perilously leaning on the top of his ladder, and easily plucked one of the fruit. They thought he would eat it, but with a quick, testing gesture, he threw it precisely at Raja, who dropped it, picked it up, peeled it with a scholarly concentration, but then, instead of eating it, handed it to his twin. Omith ate it, dutifully.

'There's a big stone,' he said, plucking it out and flinging it to the ground. 'But it's really good.'

'Are your parents having a party?'

The long table with plates and cutlery on it and five bowls of pickles, bread, raita; the polished barbecue, borrowed for the afternoon; the chairs scattered around in threes and fours and fives. Was there some reproach in the doctor's tone? Should he have been invited?

'It's mostly a lot of aunts and uncles and cousins,' Aisha said. 'My dad's family, mostly. All the English ones are coming, apart from Aunty Sadia whom we've never met. Well, maybe twice, but I can't remember her, I was too little. She lives in Nottingham but she won't be coming. There's a new baby called Camellia, too.'

'What a pretty name for a baby,' the doctor said abstractedly, cutting at a branch.

For a moment they all ate loquats, with absorption. The flesh underneath was fresh and soft, and with an acidic quality; it bit like a lemon at the tongue; it made you want another one. Aisha spat the smooth solid stone into her hand; it was surprisingly big for a small fruit. She tossed it into the soil of the border, and snatched a fruit from the hand of Omith, who had just finished peeling it.

'Well, thank you so much,' Aisha said. 'It was a pleasure to meet you.' She tried to lead the boys away. But Raja protested, and went on picking the fruit from the tree. Someone had arrived: there was the noise of people being greeted; the two hired help now were starting to bring out dishes and glasses in an efficient way. Aisha smiled at the doctor, and took another fruit from Raja. She remembered Enrico, being subjected to family inspections and greetings. He was the man she was going to ... but, no, the romantic thought trailed away as the general idea of the man for her gave way to the specific image of Enrico, balding, snuffling on about himself, his island at the bottom end of the continent. She would rescue him, but only in a moment.

4.

The arrivals were Uncle Tinku and Aunty Bina; they had come from furthest away, from Cardiff, and so of course were earliest. They were getting out of their car, a polished dark blue BMW, Tinku in a tweed jacket and tie, Bina in a silver jacket, holding a foil-covered dish. Dish and shoulders and car and arms splashed with mid-afternoon sunshine. She was as definite in her elegant surfaces, her swift gestures of greeting, as a garden bird. Bina was scolding her son in the back of the car and hailing Sharif and Nazia in turn; the son was deeply engaged in a book, and was not paying any attention to his mother.

'We are here, sweet-chops – come along, put the book away and say hello – brother, sister – just a tiny thing, a very few, few sweets I thought you might like – now, you'll feel much better if you get out …'

'Is the boy unwell?' Sharif said from the porch, as Nazia went forward and greeted her sister-in-law and her husband, taking the dish from her.

'What a beautiful house! I love the district. You are so lucky to live in such a beautiful place. And the view as you come into the city! I always thought Sheffield was a beautiful place, but from this side – No, he is quite well, he only insisted on reading a book in the back of the car, and Tinku said he would be quite all right, reading in the back of the car on the motorway, it was only small windy-bendy roads that did the damage. And now look at him! Where is Aisha? She was coming, wasn't she? Are we the first to arrive?'

Little Bulu, a six-year-old with giant hands and feet, tripping over himself, the colour of an old and mouldering pond, as if decaying from within, tried to shake his aunt's hand. But he did not remove the book, a novel by Enid Blyton, from his hand, and she settled for a short embrace. And here were some more guests – the Mottisheads and, close behind, Ada Browning with her married daughter.

'Go into the kitchen, Bulu,' said his mother, 'and get a glass of water. You'll be quite all right in ten minutes. Poor little boy.'

'And this' – they were entering the house, Bina first and exclaiming over everything – 'is Aisha's friend, Enrico, who is visiting with her.'

'Daddy's portrait! Look, Tinku – they have Daddy's portrait up, here. I quite forgot about it. Where was it before? And what a lovely colour you've painted the room. This green – what is it? – does it have a special name? Sage? Sage green. How lovely. So nice to meet you! Mottishead. What an unusual name. Have you been to Sheffield before? We are early, Nazia, I can see. I am so sorry, you live here. Why did I think – Bulu will be better before most people arrive, however. A blessing. And are you at Oxford, too, like clever Aisha?'

'She's at Cambridge,' Tinku said, smiling. 'Not Oxford. A very different sort of place.'

'I am studying this year at Cambridge,' Enrico said. 'I am studying international relations.'

'That's what Aisha is studying, how nice!' Bina said, as if it were an extraordinary coincidence, rather than the way in which her niece might have met the man in the first place. 'She was always so, so clever. Nazia, there is more in the car – I thought my husband was bringing it behind me but he has forgotten it. Some mangoes. They are Alphonse – in the boot, Tinku, quick, quick. Have you ever tried Alphonse mangoes, Mrs Browning? You must – they are *sublime*. And where is Aisha?'

'I am studying in Cambridge,' Enrico said. He was standing in the hall, as if to prevent them from moving through into the sitting room and through the French windows into the garden. 'But I come from Sicily. Have you been to Sicily?'

Bina had spied Aisha in the garden, and now squeezed past Enrico with cries of joy. Tinku had gone outside again to fetch the mangoes; Bulu was drinking water in the kitchen. 'It is a beautiful island, and the best climate in the world,' Enrico was saying, as he trailed disconsolately behind a new arrival. He had not changed, and the clothes he had worn to read the paper all morning looked caught-out next to the party clothes of the guests.

'And the boys!' Sally Mottishead responded, flying out into the garden, glittering in the afternoon sun. 'Look, you two! I remember you being born! Ada!' For the moment Enrico was left alone; brilliant light fell on his dull surfaces and sank into brown or perhaps grey or perhaps a poisoned green; unhusbanded, unescorted, unentertained, unseen.

Nazia had planned the food for this afternoon with some care, not worrying about the confusion that was the inevitable result. There would be tea at first, and with tea some savoury snacks – there would be samosas, and falafels, and fried onion bites, and pickles, of course. But there would be some English things too, the sorts of things that went quite well with a Bengali tea, the Cornish pasties that Sharif had always liked to eat, and then even the pork pies that Aisha had eaten once by mistake and then gone on eating, with the English pickle and then with the Indian pickle. She had become quite a connoisseur of pork pies, and of piccalilli, and if people didn't want to eat it, then they needn't. There were sweets, too, from the shop in the Ecclesall Road, gulab jamun and sandesh and jelapi, and a chocolate cake and a cheesecake with redcurrants on top – the children liked that – and two big bowls of fruit to peel and eat and pick at.

Nazia thought that the barbecues would start producing food later on; they had been hot for an hour now, and once all the aunts and cousins had arrived and taken nibbles, there would be some grilled lamb chops and chicken breasts and slices of aubergine and courgette and halved tomatoes. She could not remember everything; that was what the caterers were there for, in their white shirts and beautifully pressed dark trousers, to keep the tea coming and not to forget anything that they had decided to supply. And as the afternoon went on, the tea that went with the pork pies and samosas and Cornish pasties and cake would give way to long drinks, squash and American fizzy drinks and perhaps, for the men, even a beer. 'We are not in

Bangladesh now,' Sharif had said sonorously, before observing that the Italian Aisha had brought would probably think nothing but tea very strange, or imagine that they were deeply religious, or something of the sort. The Italian that Aisha had brought and was now neglecting was peering at the assortment of food as if he had never seen anything so awful in his life.

Nazia went over to where the twins and her daughter were talking to their next-door neighbour. They were picking fruit from the tree, peeling it and eating it with absorption.

'We were so worried about your wife,' Nazia said to the doctor next door. 'I do hope she will make a recovery.'

'Oh, she's perfectly all right,' the neighbour said, and he must have seen some questioning anxiety, not about his wife but about the children eating the fruit as Nazia raised her hands. 'Don't worry about that. Loquats. Perfectly edible. Mike Tillotson was always giving unlikely things a go. No, my wife – I'm sure she'll be out of hospital shortly. Thank you for asking, much appreciated.'

'We aren't gardeners,' Nazia said. She had persuaded the gardener to place rows of red, yellow, pink and purple flowers against the house: when they were finished, they would be thrown away, but they looked wonderful today. 'I love the garden, but I couldn't identify anything in it, really.'

'Mike Tillotson tried to plant bamboo – that lasted three years and then died of root rot – and a bird of paradise flower, and that didn't take at all. The olive tree's still going over there. I would never have believed you could grow an olive tree at this latitude. He talked at one point about a mango tree.'

'My father-in-law had a mango tree in his garden. Sharif will tell you – he used to love it as a child,' Nazia said.

'Oh, yes,' the doctor next door said, not very interested. 'And then there was the jasmine – that has good years and not such good years. It'll be flowering in a couple of weeks.'

'Which is the jasmine?' Nazia said. The children had wandered off with a handful of the yellow fruit. She was keeping an eye on the staff's preparations: they were solemnly

arranging the cold food and peeling the clingfilm from the top
of the salad bowls. It was all very well, this old man being
friendly; she wished these retired people with nothing to do
would choose their moment better. And now it was clear that
Bina and Tinku and puking Bulu had not arrived too early,
because through the door now were coming half a dozen engineering PhDs that Sharif must have asked, and Steve Smithers,
and surely that was cousin Fanny, said to be driving from
Manchester ahead of her parents and brother?

'It's the one just by the wisteria,' the man next door was
saying with a tone of mild incredulity. 'You must know which
is the wisteria, my dear. It's the one –'

'Oh, you must excuse me,' Nazia said rudely, and with a
smile turned towards the new arrivals. 'Bina! Sister! Was that
Fanny I saw? Where is she?'

'She was here a moment ago,' Bina said, waving the back of
her hand at her face in an ineffective cooling gesture. 'Where
did she disappear to?'

'There she is!' clever Bulu said, pleased to be able to supply
the answer to the riddle. 'She went upstairs with Aisha.'

There they were, the two cousins, framed in the window of
the bedroom upstairs, looking down and waving. Of course
Aisha had been the first to see Fanny, and had whisked her off
to get all the answers to all her questions, and catch up as much
as they could before Fanny was absorbed into the aunts and
cousins. She probably wanted to tell her about the Italian, now
standing with the caterers, lifting and lowering slices of pork pie
and shaking his head. He was like an antibody sourly reacting
to the flow of the party. Nazia wished she knew what she could
do with him. But there it was; and now Fanny and Aisha were
drawing back from the window into the darkness of the room
to talk. 'Two gardeners once a week,' Nazia said, in response to
a question of Bina's. 'At five pounds an hour.'

'Five pounds an hour for two gardeners!' Bina cried. 'In
Cardiff, that would be impossible, impossible. In Cardiff, we
can't get gardeners for less than –'

'Five pounds an hour each,' Nazia said firmly. 'Look, here's the vice-chancellor – how nice of him to come. Excuse me, Bina.' She was so fond of Bina, and hoped very much that Fanny and Aisha weren't going to stay upstairs gossiping for hours, as if they were still little girls.

5.

'Have a fruit,' Aisha said, inside, giving Fanny a loquat to peel.

'What the hell is that?' Fanny said.

'God knows,' Aisha said. 'Try it – it's all right. It grows in the garden. I've just picked them.'

'So this one,' Fanny said, putting the unpeeled loquat down on the talc-dusty glass top of the dressing-table. 'Is he The One, then?' She picked up and dumped down again the silver-backed hairbrush, a green-tufted gonk and Aisha's Cindy doll. The bedroom was not where Aisha lived and slept any longer, and she had preserved a few fossils of a previous life here; the books on the shelves were not the detailed histories of genocide she worked with, or mostly not, but A-level economics textbooks, an English classic or two and fervently worn copies, fifteen years old, of a twelve-part series about a pony detective. The Cindy doll on the kidney-shaped dressing-table, which Fanny and Aisha had dressed and involved in long fantastical adventures, had survived too as a souvenir of a single and remote experience, like a dangerous illness; Fanny picked it up and put it down again.

'Is who the one?' Aisha said, and then, in a sing-song voice, 'Who in the world can you be talking about, Fanny?'

'Don't call me Fanny,' Fanny said. 'Everyone calls me Nihad, these days. Mummy doesn't know why people laugh when she talks about her Fanny. They're driving behind me, very slowly. Should be here before nightfall. Bobby wanted to come with me, but I insisted.'

'You're such a cow,' Aisha said. 'You could be the last woman in England to be called Fanny. It would be quite distinguished.'

They were only second cousins, and had always lived fifty miles away from each other, on either side of some range of hills that most English people thought of as an insurmountable barrier. But they were also only three weeks different in age; the aunts and cousins and uncles had shuttled backwards and forwards, that autumn of 1968, visiting Aunty Rekha's second baby in Manchester, in their neat little semi-detached in Cheadle, then back again to Sheffield where Nazia's first baby was living in a flat over a newsagent's shop. (All this was Nazia's favourite story. Aisha could retell it without effort. It was almost as if she herself had been there.) Rekha and Rashed had been very kind to their cousins, cousin Sharif finishing off his engineering PhD with not a lot of money, and had passed on all sorts of baby clothes; they had said they were passing on baby clothes, Nazia had explained afterwards, but baby Fanny was exactly the same age as Aisha, so they must have bought an extra Babygro and given it as a present, along with little donations of money that had, Nazia always explained, been very handy at the time. Of course they hadn't seen each other when they were very tiny, after Nazia and Sharif and baby Aisha had moved back to Bangladesh, or East Pakistan as it then was, and had stuck it out in Nana's house in Dhanmondi all through the war in 1971 and the troubles afterwards. But when things really changed in 1975, they had decided to come back to England, and Aisha and Fanny/Nihad had been seven years old; they had seen a lot of each other, and had been best friends always. For fifteen years they had talked about The One; he was Adam Ant, he was Marcus Cargill over the road, he was the Duc de Sauveterre, he was Mr York, who was a student teacher in French at Aisha's school (she found out where he lived, or lodged, and they played in the playground opposite for almost four hours until he came out and she could say, 'Hello, Mr York – this is my cousin Fanny.' There had been a row when they got home and had missed lunch and tea and the police had almost been called). They had made up stuff about even Aunty Sadia's son Ayub, though neither of them had ever been allowed to meet Aunty Sadia because of what Uncle Mahfouz had done in 1971, and they weren't even very sure how old cousin Ayub was or even if he definitely existed. Still, he had been The One for a while. He had also been the son of the manager of the hot, tree-dappled camping ground in the Cévennes and the owner himself of the large manor house in Umbria where they had gone on holiday only two years before, just after they had finished their degrees. It would be nice to do it before they started the next phase, have a proper holiday in Italy, their parents had suggested. Aisha was going to Cambridge to do an MPhil before trying to get into the UN or Amnesty or something like that, Nihad/Fanny to do her law conversion course in Guildford after the degree in English she'd insisted on. The owner of the yellow-stone farmhouse in Umbria had, surprisingly, been no more than thirty-two or -three, grizzled and tanned but a real Duc de Sauveterre, *gorgeous*, they had agreed. He had made up for the plague of little scorpions that infested the house; he, irresistibly, had been seen outside the kitchen door of his own house, just down the hill, shirtless and oiling a shotgun as if grooming a dog in his own dumb, adoring perfection. 'I feel,' Nihad had said quite solemnly, one night in the big bedroom they were sharing during that holiday, 'that for you, it might not be the Signor with his gun and his pecs and his house with the hundreds of scorpions. But it might very well be an Italian.'

'Mummy would have a fit,' Aisha had said, giggling at the thought of the Signor.

Now, together, they looked out of the window at Enrico. He was on the lawn, raising his hands together, talking to a caterer who had just put down four teacups and was trying to excuse himself. By the fence, the twins, Bulu and Uncle Tinku and, for some reason, Aisha's father's co-author Michael Burns and his wife were eating the new fruit from the tree, and the next-door neighbour was explaining something. Why couldn't Enrico go and talk to them?

'I met him in a seminar,' Aisha said. 'He took me for a cup of tea afterwards.'

'What are his pecs like?'

'Oh, if you –'

'What was the seminar about? The one you met him at?'

'About Pakistan,' Aisha said. 'And military law. I have an awful feeling he thought I was Pakistani or something. He found out I wasn't, though. He was the only one who had done any of the reading we were supposed to. Anyway.'

'I heard baby Camellia was coming this afternoon.'

'Can't wait,' Aisha said.

6.

'And here is Sharif-uncle,' Dolly said to her baby Camellia, coming along at a steady pace – she must be two now, and in a party dress rather than the padded-solid H-shaped control garment they remembered from last time. She looked at them suspiciously, and turned her face into her mother's thigh, clutching for safety. 'And cousins Raja and Omith, you've never met them before, but they're your special twin-cousins. Oh, Camellia, don't be like that. She was perfectly all right ten minutes ago, chatting away, talking about her twin-cousins, she knows all about you, boys, asking if there would be cake. No, Camellia, don't pull like that at Mummy – and what on earth?'

Dolly was shy with those outside the family circle, but dictatorial towards those she had grown up with or seen born; she had made an effort with her husband, Samir, although as the son of her daddy's oldest colleague, she had really always known him. The sight of her altering at a stroke from bold instruction to inward-twirling wallflower as Samu came in was the favourite story of her brothers and cousins; as the story continued, it took a few months, perhaps even a year, before she started telling him what to do in the same way that she did with everyone else. Samu was quite cheerful about it, but he must sometimes have wondered who it was he had married. Now Dolly, dressed up for a family party in a dark blue sari with a silver edge, was finding her behaviour hard to calibrate. Was the neighbour within the social group or outside it? He was on the other side of the fence up his ladder, and therefore might be ignored; but he was apparently on speaking terms with the others. Dolly's behaviour depended on this judgement: if she could not ignore this unfamiliar presence, she would search like baby Camellia for a thigh to hide her face in, would fall silent or, more probably, go off to somewhere safer where she could boss Samu and her big brother Sharif.

'Everyone here!' she said boldly. 'Fanny and Aisha – is that Aisha's friend? We heard about him – and the Manchester lot on their way, and where is Bina, and Sharif has made such a lovely party, look at all that lovely food – and … No Mahfouz and Sadia. No, of course not. I don't know why I thought …'

'And this must be baby Camellia,' a voice said. 'I've been hearing a lot about you, young lady.'

The question was answered; the voice belonged to the old Englishman up a tree. For a moment Dolly and Camellia turned in on each other, clinging. But then she remembered herself, and said who she was. 'You must be their neighbour,' she went on, and the twins giggled.

'Yes, we've been here for over thirty years,' the man was saying. 'My daughter was the age of your little one, there, and I remember my son was only six months old – we had two more soon afterwards. Got children of their own now. Some of them. It was a hard winter, that first one – we were the first in the avenue to install central heating. An oil boiler. The garden was really quite abandoned, overgrown.'

'These are so good!' Dolly said, ignoring the man and turning to her relations. 'But the stone is big. Camellia, do you want one? Do you? Peel one for her, Raja, but take the stone out first.

Small pieces – it's too big for little girls to have in their mouths. Do you like it, darling? Is it too sour?'

'Hello,' the Italian said, coming over and holding his hand out. 'I am Enrico. I am the friend of Aisha, staying for this weekend. I am from Sicily but studying at the University of Cambridge.'

But Dolly could only giggle and hide her face behind the fold of blue and silver cloth.

7.

In some ways Nazia thought it would be best to ask Sadia and Mahfouz to one of these gatherings. She missed Sadia – she could admit it to herself. They had been such friends back in the 1960s, when they'd come back from Sharif's PhD, and Sharif's big sister had been such a help with everything, living so near in Dhaka. Without Sadia, there was something unexplained about Sharif: he just had two little sisters, Bina and Dolly, but he hardly behaved like the protective older brother. She had always had to talk him into doing things, into moving house because they needed an extra room now that there were twins, into moving back to England from Bangladesh after everything changed in 1975 and it was clear there would be no future in the country for people like them. It was the same decision that Sadia and Mahfouz must have made at the beginning of 1972, upping sticks and turning up in England (as they had discovered after a year or more). But they had had a different reason: the opposite reason. What was missing from any explanation of how Sharif was, with his lazy manner, his feet out in front of the television, his pensive silences and slow smiles, as if they were students in need of forgiveness, was the presence of that oldest sister. Nazia missed her. Sharif would never allow himself to, and now nobody else would be able to understand if they reached out and made contact with Sadia. They hadn't seen them since Mother died. Nazia didn't believe that Tinku and Bina especially would be able to understand if they had walked in this afternoon with dear little green-faced Bulu, and found Sadia there under their elm tree, eating lamb chops with her husband, Mahfouz, the murderer and the friend of murderers. There was no excuse for what Mahfouz had done. As Tinku said, in a proper world, he would have been in prison or hanged. But there it was. Nazia could not forget that she had always liked Sadia. She was not a murderer.

'What are you thinking?' Bina asked. 'You shivered just then.'

'Oh, there's so much to do,' Nazia said. 'A new house. I just haven't the time or the energy.'

'It is so so lovely!' Bina said. 'You have a real gift for making a nice home. I wish –'

'Oh, you say such kind things, sister,' Nazia said distractedly. 'I must go and say hello to Aisha's friend Caroline's mother. Excuse me.' Did she have that gift? The man next door, the marginal and somehow disturbing presence at their party, perhaps had that gift. There was a curious smell about him she had noted, wafting across the fence; it was not the smell of gardening, of old clothes and soil and some sweat; it was not the smell that might be a possibility, the smell of medicine. She remembered he was the doctor next door, as the Tillotsons had put it when they sold the house to them, but he was also retired. The smell was characteristic, she could tell, a smell of slight sweetness and decay. He was not in the party, and was not invited to the party, but stood aloof on the other side of a fence, genially chatting to anyone who came near. The smell she noticed was the smell of ease, of settlement. Nazia thought she would never reach that point of settlement, and in thinking that she and Sharif had found the house that would make them settle, merely because they were now in the largest house they had ever lived in, was to deny their history and their nature. Sharif had gone to England to do his PhD; he had returned to Dhaka; and after the military had taken over, they had come back to England and a professorship for Sharif at the university. Everyone they knew, or were related to, had made similar moves, from one side of the world to another, alighting in rented or leased houses, throwing parties to celebrate their arrival. They were unhoused beings, spending money on new curtains from time to time.

'But you look so sad!' Bina said, to keep Nazia a moment longer. 'What is it? Everything is perfect – the food, the weather, everything. What is it?'

'Oh, nothing,' Nazia said. 'I was only thinking that the people you do all these things for – they are the ones who never appreciate any of it.'

Bina made a wave of her hand, an amused, dismissive, gracious wave, like the Queen at the end of the day on a Commonwealth tour. It was the same wave she had been making to Nazia for decades, ever since Nazia had married her big brother Sharif. She had made it in gardens in Dhaka, in libraries, in rented flats in Sheffield, wherever they had happened to be when they met and Nazia wanted to make some sort of point, as she so so often did. And then she turned and tried to join in with Dolly, who was explaining to the child that 'He's a retired doctor – very suitable – and I hear his wife is in hospital. Four children. And grandchildren. I don't know what his name is. Nazia-aunty probably knows. We are so worried about our neighbours. No retired doctors for us. The problem really is …'

8.

On the terrace, Tinku and Sharif had pulled up a chair for Aisha's Italian friend and, almost at once, Tinku had started an argument. The vice-chancellor was sitting, astonished; Sharif, too, watched, comfortably, enjoying it. Aisha had drilled it into her parents that they were not, repeat not, to start being Bengali and confuse having a friendly conversation with starting an argument. They were not for any reason allowed to discover what the Italian's political beliefs were on a subject, in order to put the opposite point of view with maximum force. They were to behave like civilized people and say to their guest, 'That's very interesting,' and move on to neutral subjects. She had been very firm on the principle of not behaving like Bengalis, and Sharif and Nazia, with heavy hearts, had agreed. Sharif felt they had been tiptoeing around with pathetic subservience, saying, 'How interesting,' every three minutes since four p.m. on Friday afternoon. He had had to make up for it by having a truly monumental discussion with Nazia about whether or not it was important to preserve the coal-mining industry in Britain, which started before bedtime on Saturday night, and resumed as soon as they woke up until it was time to go down for breakfast, after which they both felt very much better, and neither of them had said, 'That's very interesting,' at all. Nazia had just got an exercise bike: she had discovered that she could do twenty minutes with no trouble at all, if Sharif came in and started in on whether Bangladesh should be expelled from the Commonwealth.

Aisha had not been allowed to extend her instructions to her aunts and uncles and cousins. 'That,' Nazia had said, 'is too much.' So Sharif was watching his little-sister's husband, uninstructed, unseam the Italian from the nave to the chaps with a lot of enjoyment and interest. Tinku's chosen subject was Italy.

'There is a lot of corruption in Italy,' Tinku had begun, and by now he was on to the *fons et origo*, as he liked to say in his University of Calcutta way, of the problem. 'If you base everything on who you are related to, or who you know, or that you can give somebody a favour in return for them doing you a favour, then how can this become a modern country?'

'There are many problems with Italy,' Enrico said. 'But there are many problems with every country.'

'Not insuperable ones,' Tinku said. 'Not ones where the problem starts in the home, starts at birth. I have read a lot about Italy, and I think everyone agrees that this is the problem.

You are taught that your obligation is to your mother and father, then to your brothers and sisters, then to your aunts and uncles, then to your cousins, then to people called your cousins, then to people you are told to think of as your uncles … The future is in being made to submit to merit, and to discover merit through examination. Not in having uncles.'

'There are many cultures with this problem,' Enrico said. He moved his hand as if to pick up the beer that Sharif had poured for him, and then, as if refusing to join in, pushed it away a little on the teak garden table.

'Ah, you are looking around you,' Tinku said joyously. He had proceeded by a very familiar method, Sharif recognized: he had laid a trap in the argument by describing an opposing position in terms apparently applicable to his own. If he had been talking to a Bengali, the Bengali, if he had fallen for it, would have said, 'But you! What about you! You describe yourself when you speak!' But an Italian would allude with indirect grace, as he fell head first, graciously, into his opponent's trap. Sharif sat back. It was the first time that Enrico had been led in conversation to start talking about something other than Sicily. It had been done by talking about Sicily, interestingly. 'You are looking around! You are thinking that a Bengali has no right to point the finger and say that your way of obligation is not the way! But this is the point. We come together and we talk and eat and drink and then – we go away. Tell me, have you ever obtained a job because of someone your father knew? Or your mother?'

'No, I am certain, no, not at all,' Enrico said.

'But, Enrico,' Aisha said – she had come out of the house with Fanny, was standing in the French windows, her arms folded, taking interest in the conversation, 'tell us how you avoided military service. There is still military service in Italy, you know.'

'Ah, that was so terrible,' Enrico said. 'I had to go to military camp for one week. I thought I would die, it was so terrible. One of the men there, he was a peasant, a goatherd, he could not be understood in the language he was speaking. And the first night they were lying there in the barracks and talking, talking, talking about the terrible, horrible things they did to their girlfriends as a last thing before they went to the army. I thought, I must come away from this, I cannot stay here for two years. I am an educated person and I do not belong with these people, and I telephoned my parents. But then it turned out that when they examined my chest with an X-ray I had suffered from pulmonary, is that correct, from scar tissues on my lungs from a disease in childhood, and so I could not be considered as fit for military service, and I left after six days. It was a matter of health.'

'But, Enrico,' Aisha said. 'You told me your father remembered that he knew a general in the army, and that he phoned him.'

'Well, that is not the same thing at all,' Enrico said. The vice-chancellor spluttered with pleasure at this move in the argument, like a checkmate. Tinku and Sharif were sitting back, with the beginnings of smiles, as of a barrister about to say, 'Your witness.' Tinku said nothing: he was going to let Enrico carry on and bluster. 'There are many other cultures where there are such connections, and worse. How can there be equality of opportunity,' Enrico went on, winding himself up to the killer point, 'when your opportunities in life are dictated from birth, by what caste you happen to be born into? There is no opportunity for your *untouchables*.'

Enrico now reached forward and took his beer. Sharif and Tinku exchanged a worried look. Was it a theatrical worried look? Or were they sincere? When the argument is won or lost by a single error of the opponent, how sincere is the triumph, and how much is the triumph performed? They left it to Aisha, who at least should be allowed to indicate how little her boyfriend had discovered about her, while lengthily explaining about Sicily.

'We don't have castes,' Aisha said. 'You're thinking of Hindus. We don't have a caste. We're not Hindus. You're probably thinking of India, too. We're not from India.'

Enrico appeared confused: his eyes went from face to face, and each of them looked downwards, performing an embarrassment that none of them probably felt. They were people dedicated to moving forward, dynamically, never resting, but they paused quietly, demonstrating what stilled embarrassment might look like if you performed it when other people found themselves in trouble.

9.

The twins were the only ones still left at the fence, and the old man up the ladder had stopped talking. They had eaten twenty loquats each and, without consulting or setting each other a challenge, were going for thirty. It amazed Raja and Omith that other people ate so little, could refuse food. They watched their aunt, their sister too, eat half a piece of cake with a fork, so dainty-dainty, like a bird pecking with its little beak at crumbs, then set her fork down, push away the half-left cake on its plate; they watched this spectacle incredulously, since they had finished their cakes ten minutes before. 'Don't wolf,' people would say to Omith or, especially, to Raja – he was the real gannet, as a teacher had once called him in the dinner hall. Don't wolf: but how could you not wolf when food was so little and hunger was so enormous? 'You really will spoil your dinner,' their mother used to say when she came in, and there they were, making a sandwich home from school, with their favourite mix, Marmite and sandwich spread. But they never had spoiled their dinner.

They knew that Mummy would have their guts for garters if they went over to the table and made a start on what they really fancied, the samosas and pork pies and pickles. And the kitchen was full of people chopping and preparing things and bustling about: there was no way you could get into the fridge to make a sandwich to tide you over. Raja and Omith were absolutely starving. They had no idea what it might be like not to be hungry, almost all the time. They stood by the tree, and picked, and peeled, and stuffed the loquats into their mouths.

'These are good,' Raja said. 'I really like these things.' He popped another one into his mouth.

'I really like them,' Omith said. 'I'm going to eat these things all summer. I've never …'

But he trailed off now, because Raja was making a strange noise from the throat, trying to speak without success. Omith asked what it was, but Raja made glottal, ugly sounds; and bent over violently, as if to make himself sick. On the patio, the others had seen, and were standing up. Omith's hands fluttered; decisively, he pushed his twin. But the choking continued, and now Raja's face was darkening, filling with blood.

'Cough, Raja, cough,' Omith said. Raja made flapping motions with his arms; he was trying to cough. Omith hit him on the back, gently and then harder. There was no response. The caterers had been starting to cook the meat, but now were watching with curiosity. It must look as if Raja and Omith were fighting, but now Omith remembered something from school. He got behind Raja – he cursed himself for not remembering, not paying attention – and his hands joined together in a double fist, pulled heavily into the pit of Raja's stomach. Mummy was running towards them, and, strangely, the old man from next door, climbing nimbly over the fence. Omith was punching into the stomach. So this is how your brother dies, he heard his mind horribly saying, and Mummy screaming, and knowing that nothing was happening, that he was just punching into the stomach and Raja was making an awful choked skriking noise, a noise of a throat in mud, and twitching and flailing, and then quite suddenly Raja went limp, his head falling to one side.

The old man from next door was quite calm. 'Put him down,' he said. 'There, on his back. Go and bring me a sharp knife – there must be one at the barbecue. Wipe it. Go on. And a pen,' he said, turning to Aisha as her brother ran. 'Just a biro would do. Take everything out, just the tube. Quick – good.' Omith was back already, with a steak knife. The old man took it from him, running his finger along the blade. He knelt down, muttering, 'I'm a doctor,' in some kind of response to all this screaming, and reached out his hand for Aisha's pen. She had found one in her bag, a new one, and tried with shaking hand to take off the lid, the stopper, to pull out the ink tube. The old man's hand was patient, but steady, demanding; it was in that horizontal calm waiting that his professional standing was apparent. Aisha finally succeeded, and handed it to him. Before they could quite understand what he was doing, he had placed the tube in his shirt pocket, and with his left hand felt urgently at Raja's throat. His hand stopped; held; and with a single gesture the other hand cut between his second and third fingers, into Raja's throat. Raja made no movement as his flesh was sliced. The biro was taken from the upper pocket, and the old man – the doctor – plunged it firmly into the incision. There was a sound of whistling; you could feel the air re-inflating Raja. But Aisha was already leading her mother away to a little crowd of comforters. The flurry of action was over. The old man reached out, and pulled himself up with the aid of Omith.

'He should be all right now,' he said, to nobody in particular. 'Has someone called for an ambulance?' (Sharif was doing that, inside the house.) 'The hospital will sort him out. I've done it once or twice before. Dramatic, but it leaves no ill effect.'

'That was –' Omith said, coming down to his brother. Raja was going to be all right, but he would come round with blood trickling down his throat and a biro stuck in his neck. He would want Omith to stay with him.

The others were crowding round, appalled. 'It's best if you sit down,' Tinku said and, placing his arms around Dolly, who was giving small piping noises of despair and helplessness, tried to push her in the direction of the patio. 'Don't – there's nothing you can do here, Dolly. Come along.'

The doctor was feeling Raja's pulse, perhaps for the lack of something better to do, perhaps to go on seeming professional. 'It looks frightening, I know,' he said. 'You've been taught the

manoeuvre. It usually works, but if it doesn't – well, you saw
what to do. You have to decide you're going to do that very
quickly. I suppose it was one of the stones from the loquat tree
he swallowed.'

'It must have been that,' Omith said.

'Well, now you'll be more careful eating them,' the doctor
said. 'If it ever produces fruit again. The Tillotsons put it in.
They loved it. I would say you've been lucky. I'm retired as a
doctor – I was a GP. But you never forget these things. I once
removed an appendix. That was the limit of my surgical experience. This was child's play. I retired five years ago now. There's a
young fellow in my place – you might know him. Dr Khan.'

'Where is that?' Omith said, with a sense of feeling dizzy.
Raja had ordered him about all their lives, and that might have
gone in a minute. His brother had nearly died and was still
lying there faint and exhausted, his hand warm in his brother's;
this old man was talking to him about himself. Tinku and Bina
were standing by, looking down as if awaiting instructions. It
was for Omith to listen to the doctor talking.

'Where is it?' the old man said. 'The surgery? On the
Earlsfield road, just where it curves towards the top. We made
a successful surgery out of it. I hope Dr Khan's doing us proud.
If you happen to see him, tell him Dr Spinster sends his best
regards. My wife's not at home. She's in hospital herself.'

But now Sharif was coming out of the house, and Tinku was
going over to find out what news of the ambulance. Their
mother was being comforted – restrained almost – by Aunty
Bina. It was for him to stay here, with the doctor, and his
brother, and in a moment the ambulance would come.

'There are grandchildren now, of course,' the doctor was
saying. Had he lost interest in Raja? He let the wrist flop down.
'Quite normal. My daughter has four, and my elder son has
one. The younger two children don't have any as yet. They're
coming up today or tomorrow. To see their mother, of course.
It is serious but not final, not yet. Have you ever thought of
becoming a doctor, young man?'

It was as if the old man had not quite known who he was talking to, and with that last sentence had taken a look and realized who Omith was; he had spoken in a hearty, encouraging, routine way, as doctors must to any fifteen-year-old who shows the slightest interest. But Omith had shown no interest. He wanted to design computer programs with Raja. The old man had just decided that he ought to speak to someone like Omith like that. The party was dissolving; people were tactfully leaving without demanding anyone say goodbye to them. And now there was a light flashing somewhere nearby, on the other side of the castellated house, reflecting from some high leaf, and two paramedics in uniform were coming around the side of the house with their box of tricks. This was the proper stuff, not a biro and a steak knife now lying on the ground with his brother's blood on it. In confusion, too, coming round the ambulance, bearing dishes wrapped in clingfilm, were the Manchester lot, concern written on the faces of Rekha and Rashed, their son Bobby and, with impeccably poor timing, like the worst storyteller in the world, his wife Aditi carrying the secret she had been waiting to divulge, her pregnant belly. Omith felt that this conjunction of stories, however ill-timed, was what they had been waiting for, and as the old man started to explain what had been done, he stood up, too, eyeing the ambulance men as they set to work, sure that in a moment they would turn and tell Dr Spinster off firmly for what he had done, for what he had failed to do. The party was over. The festoons hung, unenjoyed, unfulfilled, from the trees above the uneaten food. He had quite looked forward to some aspects of it. His mother was rushing forward to embrace Aditi, to tell her everything.

IO.

For some reason, Enrico was still in the seat where he had been arguing, and in a sulky, ignoring stance. Had he not seen? Did he think this sort of thing was normal? Aisha looked out from the sitting room where most of the rest of them were sitting. The party was over; Mummy and Daddy and Omith had gone with Raja in the ambulance. Aisha had offered to stay, to see people off, to give them a cup of tea before they had to go. It was a great shame, but there it was. Now the remnants of the party were in no great hurry to go; they were, rather, in a mood to cap each other's tales of lives put at risk and saved by timely intervention. They were enjoying each other a great deal. Mummy and Daddy would be at the hospital all evening, she supposed, but they would be coming home at some point. If all the aunts and cousins were still here when they came back, it would really be too much. And then there was the question of what to do about Enrico.

He sat outside, drinking what must be a third bottle of beer, his back in its tattered brown sweater eloquent with resentment and complaint. She wished he would go home. But he would not: he was staying with them. His back spoke to her. It explained that Enrico felt they had failed in their duties towards him by leaving him outside, by showing inadequate interest in him and, worst of all, by correcting him on a matter of fact. All that would have been far more irritating to Enrico had Raja actually died. She looked at him and really felt that she could ask him to take a train back to Cambridge this evening.

'What's up?' Fanny said, coming up and slipping her hand into the crook of Aisha's arm. 'Poor old Aditi. No one's paying her the slightest attention after all. She was planning to be the star, too.'

'You kept her secret so well,' Aisha said.

'To be honest,' Fanny said, 'I half forgot. She's such a bore. Now what?'

'Oh, someone ought to go and pay the caterers,' Aisha said. 'It seems such a waste.'

'We can pack it up and parcel it out,' Fanny said. 'And take it home and eat it for the next week or two. Lucky that old man being a doctor.'

'At the end he said, "Well, now I suppose I should climb back over the fence," and we all said nothing. This is after Raja had been taken off and there was nothing else for him to do. But then I realized what he meant, and said, "Oh, no, you must come through the house. There's no need for you to be climbing fences." And that turned out to be what he meant, could he come through the house.'

'They just want someone to talk to, people that age.'

'He's got a wife and four children, the man next door.'

'Well, I don't know, then.'

'They are just so weird. I don't understand them.'

'Who?'

'People. Where's baby Camellia?'

'God knows. Not my business.'

They looked out together at the garden, at Enrico sitting with his back to them, at the caterers now packing up and parcelling out. Next door, there was the noise of the French windows being closed, and further away, the sound of a mother calling to her answering, querulous teenage son. The afternoon had started beautifully, but now was darkening. There were a few spots marking the flagstones. The cousins stood and watched with some enjoyment as it began to rain in earnest.

CHAPTER TWO

I.

There was another man next door. Aisha remembered that the old man had said he had grown-up children, and this one could be one of those. She was going to stay on. She had explained to Enrico that she would be hanging around until Wednesday at least, to make sure of Raja, and he might as well get a train back to Cambridge on Sunday night. Enrico had looked doubtful, in his party shirt underneath his tatty old sweater, but Aisha had assured him that the trains were good until quite late on Sunday night. There was a train to Birmingham every hour, at five minutes past, then a short walk over the platform and a fast train to Cambridge, all night until at least eleven. In fact she had no idea. By the time he was at the station and on a train to Birmingham, it would be too late for him to do anything about it.

It wasn't until she heard the impatient rattle and tick of a black cab outside in the street that she realized how keen she was to get rid of Enrico. The poor man, she found herself thinking. He was sitting there with his coat on, his small bag by his side on the floor, and it only takes the sound of a taxi for them to leap up and say, with relief and thanks, 'That'll be for you.' It was herself she was shaking her head over, leaping up and smiling brightly. Fanny smiled, gorgeously, slowly, pulling herself up without much enthusiasm, and the two of them took Enrico to the door.

'I've very much enjoyed myself,' Enrico said, scowling. 'Please thank your mother and father for me.' He made a sort of gesture towards Aisha, but she had a sandwich in her left hand, a piece of pork pie in the other. Although the rain had retreated to the spattering stage, Aisha was not going to venture out from under the porch, and the handshake he had in mind turned into a sort of shrug, performed by two people leaning into each other.

'I'm so sorry they couldn't be here to say goodbye themselves,' Aisha said formally. 'And I'll see you in Cambridge in a few days' time.'

'I don't think that's Enrico's taxi,' Fanny said, drawling. 'Someone's in it.'

The cab had pulled up outside their gate, but Fanny was right: there was a man in the back of it. His shape was hunched over, counting money or gathering bags.

'Why don't you take it anyway?' Aisha said. She took a bite of the pork pie. 'One taxi's much like another.'

The man got out. He had two suitcases with him, old brown leather suitcases. He put them on the pavement and stretched, a wide, relieved sort of stretch. He looked up at the heavy sky, feeling a drop of rain. There was even some enjoyment in his face at being rained on. At first Aisha thought he was going to walk up their drive, but that was impossible. He was coming home, not visiting a stranger. That was in the way his arms fell after the stretch. There had been other homecomings. She saw the stranger's relieved face, and it was with a sense of something being talked over that she heard the Italian's voice beginning to complain. That face, bemused, round, the eyes big and startled and blue: it was like a long-ago familiar piece of music that you caught in a public place and paused, listening intently to its cadence. She could not go on chewing. The stranger's expression, warm and humorous, regretful, even flirtatious, went over the three of them, and he turned away. The taxi had got the house number wrong – they were hard to read from the road – and this man with the two suitcases walked twenty paces, and into the house next door. It was a strong, assessing, somehow disappointed face moving away quickly from what it had considered.

'I'll go now,' Enrico was saying.

'See you later,' Aisha said. She smiled brightly, and surely she smiled in his direction. But there was something strange in the way she did it: he looked at her first curiously, then, as if with understanding, with the beginnings of fury. He walked down the wet gravel drive, hunched as if it were still bucketing down. He did not look back.

2.

Leo had forgotten what the trains on a Sunday were like, and had managed to get on the wrong one. He had found himself at Doncaster and having to change. There had been nothing to eat on either train, and he had even thought about getting a sandwich when he arrived at Sheffield. The girl who had sat opposite, with the Louise Brooks bob, the heavy boots and the delicate ankles, she had agreed – it was a scandal, she was starving. She'd got off at Chesterfield.

Under the porch of the house next door, three Asian people stood, saying goodbye to one of them – no, two and a white man. It had been raining hard. He wondered what had happened to the Tillotsons. His father, when he opened the door, looked surprisingly chipper, and was even rubbing his hands together.

'Good, good,' he said. 'Parked your car on the road, have you?'

'No,' Leo said, coming inside by pushing past his father. 'It wouldn't start this morning. Some mechanical thing. I took the train in the end.'

'You could have got someone to come out,' his father said. 'That's what they're there for.'

'I'm just doing what Mrs Thatcher was telling us to do the other day,' he said. 'Save the planet. Go by train! We're all going to die.'

'I don't suppose taking the train from London to Sheffield instead of driving is going to put that off very much,' his father said.

'You seem cheerful,' Leo said.

'Do I?' his father said. 'Come through. That would be most extraordinary. I suppose I did something rather clever, just an hour ago.'

'Oh, yes,' Leo said, discouragingly. They said that when you returned to your childhood home it seemed smaller. The house was the same size, and in any case, he'd last been here at Christmas. His father had succeeded in shrinking, however. He was determined that he was not going to let him begin by explaining how clever he had been. There had been enough of that. His father should look outwards, and think of other people, and not sing his own praises for once.

'You know the people next door moved out,' he said. 'The people who bought it, a nice family, Asian, they were having a party for all their relations. Visiting, visiting, not living there. And one of them was eating something too fast and got it stuck in his throat. And luckily I could do something about it. He'll be fine. It all comes back to you when it needs to. I dare say they'll always be grateful for me leaping over the fence like that, just at the right time.'

'Like speaking French,' Leo said.

His father gave him an interrogative look, as if there were something superior and dismissive in what he had said.

'Is there anything to eat?'

'Oh, I dare say,' his father said. 'I eat at six, these days. Your mother's left the pantry stuffed with the usual and there's all sorts of goodies in the freezer. It never changes.' He went off into the sitting room where the *Sunday Telegraph* lay folded on the arm of the chair. Had he changed newspapers? Leo could have sworn he used to read the *Sunday Times*. When he'd said, 'It never changes,' he'd meant, of course, that your children came home, dumped their suitcases on the floor, and started demanding food. It was true that Leo had done exactly that. But it was not quite the same. He discovered this by going into the kitchen, and then into the pantry. The kitchen was bare; a single mug and a single plate stood, washed, on the side of the sink. The pine table in the middle had a scatter of breadcrumbs, the remains of something on toast, all that the old doctor thought he would make for himself.

To go from the kitchen into the cool, windowless pantry was to go into the ruin of his childhood. In the past, when he had come home or when he had lived here, there had been six of them – the old ones, Leo, Blossom, Lavinia and Hugh. Quite often a boyfriend or a girlfriend, too, turning up and needing to be fed. Sometimes Leo, at fifteen, had come in here and dithered, pleasantly, unsure whether he would go for a biscuit or for the full sandwich, for a piece of cheese and pickle – one of seven or eight different pickles – or for a piece of cake. What must the shopping have been like? Speculative, unplanned, just getting food in for whenever anyone felt like diving into it. Now it was depleted, like the middle point of a siege: one tin of beans, a jar of pickled onions with the label half slipping off and translucent with spilt juice, cloudy and menacing within, a jar of peanut butter for the children. Leo reached up and took the cake tin from the top of the fridge. There was a dried-up and stony block inside that might once have been half a walnut cake. Christ on a bike. Only in the fridge were there a few things: a small steak, some bagged tomatoes and small potatoes, a block of Lancashire cheese and an open jar of pickle, the lid lost. The contents of the pantry did not show that his mother had got the usual in. Hilary was shopping for himself, these days.

'No news, then,' Leo said, coming into the sitting room with the best he could do, some crackers with cheese and a smear of peanut butter and a couple of very doubtful pickled onions. He had found, too, a bottle of beer in the cool corner of the pantry.

'No developments on that score in either direction,' Hilary said. He put his newspaper down, folded it, set it aside. 'I went over after lunch. She's in a ward with some dreadful old folk.

One Alzheimer's woman wandering round all night, wanting to know what all these people are doing in her bedroom, shouting. I've asked that your mother be moved to a private room, but there's none available just now.'

'Can't you pull rank?' Leo said.

'Well, I could,' Hilary said. 'But I don't know that it's worth it. You'll see her tomorrow. Gaga with morphine, alas.'

It had always been one of his father's guiding principles, he remembered: pick your battles. If you're going to have to stand your ground over the withdrawal of palliative care tomorrow, don't have a row about the shepherd's pie not being hot today. For a moment they sat in silence. The light was fading, but only the small lamp by his father's chair was lit; some paperback book was on the table, his place marked neatly with a bookmark.

'They seem quite nice,' his father said, in a conciliatory way.

'At the hospital?' Leo said, puzzled.

'Next door,' Hilary said. 'Our new neighbours. Asians. Very nice. A pair of boys and an older girl at university. I think she said Cambridge. They were all visiting this afternoon, though, aunties and cousins and all, coming over for a party in the garden. That sort of person, they keep in touch with every one of their family, having them over at the drop of a hat. Live with them, too – there's always an old mother in the spare room, sewing away, not speaking much English.'

'How many are they next door?'

'Oh, I'm not talking about next door. There's only four or five of them, less than us. Practical, professional people. Speak better English than you do. I meant the families I used to see when I was in practice – nine or ten of them, living on top of each other, you couldn't understand how they were related to each other, happy as clams. Baffling.'

'It's the culture, I expect,' Leo said.

'Of course it's the culture,' Hilary said shortly. 'I don't think anyone would suggest it was biological necessity.'

'I see.'

Hilary looked at him. He might have registered for the first time just which child it was who had arrived. 'Can you get time off work like this?' he said. 'Don't you have hotels to write about? Tell the readers how luxe they are? Counting the sausages at breakfast? That sort of thing?'

'That sort of thing,' Leo said. 'I'll have to take their word for the number of sausages at breakfast, though. I just go down for the day.'

'What a wonderful way to earn a living,' Hilary said.

Leo smiled graciously. He had made a decision, long ago, and with renewed force on the train coming up to Sheffield, that he would not respond to Hilary's disgusted comments on his job. Of the four of them, it was only Lavinia, his younger sister, who had anything resembling a job that Hilary thought worth doing, and that not very much: she had left her job as a marketing assistant for Procter and Gamble and was now working for a medical charity. Lowest on the scale was Hugh, just out of drama school, scrabbling for parts in this and that. Blossom had four children and a colossal house in the country: she was excused, with all the glee at Hilary's command whenever he spoke about her. Leo did not do the job that the elder son of a doctor should do. He knew that. He worked for one of the daily newspapers that Hilary never read and, between subbing the copy of grander writers, was permitted from time to time to go round the country, visiting hotels and restaurants and writing a paragraph on their pretensions. How he longed, sometimes, to be allowed to spend the night at one of these places, and be rude about it afterwards! But the hoteliers told him they were aiming to introduce a new level of luxury to Harrogate, and he went home from a long day taking detailed notes about thread counts, and wrote, 'The Belvedere Hotel is going to introduce a new level of luxury to the already excellent Harrogate hotel scene.' It was the job that the recently divorced son of a doctor did.

'How's Catherine?' Hilary said, as if he had closely followed Leo's train of thought into the deep morass of his failures. 'I always liked Catherine.'

'I always liked Catherine, too,' Leo said. 'Catherine's absolutely fine. She's staying with Blossom, in fact, as we speak.'

'Blossom said she was going to come up soon, but I can't imagine when,' Hilary said. 'I told her she didn't need to bring the children – there's a difference in coming if you have to bring four children.'

'It takes some organization, I expect,' Leo said.

His father stood up; jounced his fists in his pocket; went to the window and looked out, pretending to be very interested by something in the garden. Finally he made a casual-sounding comment.

'I was thinking the other day,' Hilary said, 'what would it be like to have your family – all your family, the grown-up bits as well – all of them around all the time?'

3.

'It must be terribly hard for your father,' Leo's mother used to say, 'to spend the whole day telling people exactly what to do. And then come home and find out that he can't do the same to us. We don't follow doctors' orders, do we, darling?'

Whenever Hilary said something of great import, something he had been contemplating for days and weeks, he brought it out casually, sometimes walking towards the door or turning away while he spoke. Leo supposed that it was the habit of an old GP, getting the right answer to an important question about vices or symptoms by asking it in passing. In just such a way, he had chattily said, 'Oh, another thing – I don't suppose you're drinking much more than a bottle of vodka a day?' or 'Still taking it out on you, is he, your husband?' just as the patient was getting up to leave his consulting room. His children had got wise to it, of course, and the words 'Oh, by the way ...' or 'I don't know whether it's of any importance, but ...' had long put them on guard. Only Hugh could imitate it convincingly, the way Hilary's voice querulously rose in light, casual enquiry, like the happy, imperfect memory of an old song.

But this was not an enquiry: this was Hilary observing that he didn't know what it would be like to have your family, the grown-up bits as well, around you all the time. He was not – could not be – casually suggesting that all his children uproot themselves and come and live in his house. It could only be a general observation, yet Hilary had brought it out exactly as he brought out the one significant statement of the hour, with a careful lack of weight, his voice rising a jocular octave. What would it be like to have your family, your grown-up family, living around you all the time? Leo said, 'Ye-esss,' and then, 'Well ...' and then a delaying 'Erm' that threatened to turn into a hum. He was examining the statement from all sides. Finally he had to respond. His father had fallen silent, waiting, head slightly cocked, for the answer.

'It would be nice,' he said. 'But it's not very practical nowadays. I suppose people elsewhere marry and move in and work alongside each other. We probably wouldn't get on, anyway.'

'I always thought it was odd that you threw in the towel so early.'

'Threw in the towel?'

'With Catherine.'

'Oh,' Leo said. 'We're much better off now.'

But his father shook his head irritably, and Leo understood that he was thinking about their separation and divorce from his own point of view.

The marriage had been failing for ever – sometimes Leo felt that what had separated them permanently, put an end to whatever joy there had been, had been the long, painful and ugly preparations for their immense wedding. For eight months before the wedding, there had been something to talk about in absorbing and horrible detail, every aspect of it. They had gone

on fucking – that was the thing, the way they'd fucked cease-
lessly, three times a day, four, the feeling that here he'd met his
match. But before the wedding you couldn't help seeing that the
fuck came at the end of a big argument. Disagreement about a
choice between napkins – surprising personal remark – serious
row – apology – fuck. Catherine had been swept up in the intri-
cacies; Leo had gone along with the process and the reconcilia-
tory fuck; and then, three days into the honeymoon, sitting on
a beach in the Seychelles, facing the theatrical sunset, she had
turned to him and he, unwillingly, to her. They had seen that
they really had nothing more to say each other. He had got a
good deal from the Seychelles Tourist Board for flights and
accommodation and a couple of excursions.

So the marriage had failed from the start. Before long, Leo
had turned up in Sheffield on his own, and told his parents he
and Catherine were going to separate, and then divorce. 'A trial
separation?' his mother had cried, half rising from her chair, but
his father had shaken his head irritably. For Hilary, the crisis
had come at that moment when, in fact, Leo and Catherine's
marriage – their divorce, rather, it was so much more permanent, dynamic and long-running – had gone beyond the new
lacerations of contempt and insult and into a curious cosy zone
where the whole thing was the topic of despairing, rueful,
shared jokes, mock generosity about awarding custody of the
household's colossal Lego collection, the occasional absurd,
almost ironic fuck, with Leo not bothering to take his socks off,
and the important question of who would have the more
successful divorce party when it was all done. Catherine had not
come to break the news. It was for Leo alone to see the collapse
of his mother's face, his father turning to him with what looked
very much like irritation. He had quite enjoyed it, actually.

'People stay married all the time,' Hilary said.

'Don't they just,' Leo said. 'Do you mind if I turn the lights
on?'

'Do as you please,' Hilary said. He watched him closely as he
moved about the room, turning on the two standard lamps, the

other table lamps; there was a central light, a brass construction, but no one ever lit it: it cast too brilliant a light over everything. 'No one else planning a divorce, I don't suppose.'

'Not that ...' Leo began, but Hilary didn't expect or need a response.

'I rather thought – I don't know, but I rather thought' – his voice went up in that querulous, amused, treble way again – 'it might be my turn.'

'Your turn?'

'My turn to get a divorce,' Hilary said.

'That would be interesting,' Leo said.

'After all,' Hilary said, 'it's now or never, you might say.'

'No time like the present,' Leo said. 'You might even find it an interesting way to fill the time, you and Mummy.'

'Oh, I haven't told your mother yet,' Hilary said. 'I'm just going to present her with it when it's all ...'

'What?'

'When it's all ...'

'When it's all ...'

There were questions that, in the past, Leo's father had raised with him in exactly this way, at exactly this time of day, when there was nobody else in the house. When Leo's life had run away from Oxford, the conversation about his future had begun here – they had, surely, been in the same chairs. Hilary was sitting and, in his light-serious voice, talking about getting a divorce in the same incontrovertible way. Hilary gazed, half smiling, patiently, into the middle distance, waiting for Leo's slow understanding to catch up.

'Are you serious? You're not saying ...'

'Am I serious?' Hilary said. 'About getting a divorce?'

'A divorce from Mummy?' Leo said.

'A divorce from Mummy,' Hilary said. He sat back; he might have been enjoying himself. 'Why wouldn't I be serious?'

Leo stared.

'I should have done it years ago,' Hilary said. 'Actually, I was going to do it five years ago. Perfect time. You'd all left home.

Then you waltz in with your news. That was that. Couldn't possibly have two divorces in the family at the same time, would look absurd. So there you are. It has to be now, really.'

'You're not serious,' Leo said.

'I wish you'd stop asking me if I'm serious.'

'But Mummy –'

'Oh, Mummy,' Hilary said, in a full, satisfied voice: it was the voice of parody, but also of warmly amused affection for something almost beyond recall. 'Well, I'll tell Mummy myself. You can leave that to me.'

But that was not what Leo had meant. He did not see how he could point out what he had wanted to say. The urgent point that first presented itself to Leo was that the situation would solve itself: that a man who wanted an end to his marriage could, in Hilary's position, save himself the trouble of a divorce by waiting six months and burying his wife. It was only in a secondary way that the humane point cropped up, that his mother might, at the end, be spared something. Silence had fallen between them. His father, surely, had never said what he had said.

'You shouldn't even say such a thing,' Leo said.

'Oh?' Hilary said. 'Why? Is it forbidden now?'

'You're …' Leo waved in the air.

'I'm?' Hilary said. 'Or we are? Are you trying to allude to something unmentionable? Oh – I think I see. You think divorce shouldn't happen after the age of, what, seventy? Or sixty? Or is it the length of marriage that's in question? One isn't permitted to think of divorce after forty years of unhappiness? The thing I don't believe you quite understand is that I am still a free person, able to take my own decisions, and your mother has a degree of freedom, too. I am under no illusions. She deserves to have a future without being shackled to me. There should be an end to this – this punishment.'

'But she's dying,' Leo said, forced into it. He looked away.

'Well,' Hilary said. 'Well. Yes. That's why there's some urgency about the matter.'

'You must be mad,' Leo said. With that he hit, apparently, the right answer. His father sank back in his chair, almost smiling. He had been waiting for exactly this. He might have started the whole conversation to lead Leo to say that he was mad.

'You might like to reflect whether you have ever changed anyone's course of action by calling them mad. Worth thinking about, that one. And here comes Gertrude,' his father said, with sardonic pleasure.

Gertrude must have been approaching for some time, and now she stood in the doorway. Her scaled neck reached upwards, swaying to and fro: she placed first her left foot, then her right foot, on the carpet, with almost angry determination, as if making a point. No, she appeared to be saying, not this, but this, here, here, you see, and her right foot stomped down. It should have banged with the determination of Gertrude's movement, but there was no sound, and Gertrude walked forward to inspect what was going on. Did she know who anyone was? Had she recognized Leo and come forward with her greenish-grey, flexible but hard features bent downwards in angry disapproval to inspect him at close quarters? Gertrude had been here for ever; she had been bought when Lavinia was born to give the older children something to take an interest in. Sometimes Leo, greatly daring, had called her Gertie, but, somehow, never when she was in the room; her look of firm inspection and silent disapproval was too much. Now she came forward in her silent stomp, the almost agonized way her fat little legs held her up in the air. How did she pass the days? Was the arrival of Leo the cause of unbearable excitement, or just another flittingly trivial occurrence in the smooth passage of seasons from waking to sleeping and back again?

'Dear old Gertrude,' Hilary said, with relaxed warmth. 'Here she comes, dear old thing. I gave her some hibiscus yesterday. My goodness, she enjoyed that. Come to say hello to Leo, have we?'

'Blossom never carried out her threat, then?'

'Hm?'

'Wasn't she going to take Gertrude off for a life in the country with the kids?'

'No, thank God,' Hilary said. 'I took advice and it turned out to be not such a good idea.'

'Oh, I remember,' Leo said. 'There was some talk about them being eaten by badgers, wasn't there?'

'Not in front of Gertrude,' Hilary said. 'Don't you listen to what the awful man says, Gertrude.'

But Gertrude paid no attention. She lumbered forward in their direction, the whole expanse of hallway and sitting room behind her as she came. She was ignoring the talk of badgers as if it were a lapse in taste, and coming forward with patient insistence, her head turning disapprovingly from side to side, like that of a dowager in a nearly empty room. In a moment the humans, apparitions in her slow world, would flicker out like candle flames and be gone. What mattered were the things that were there more often than she was: walls and tables, floor and carpet and the box itself, the beloved box.

4.

When Leo got up the next morning, there was a note on the kitchen table – one of his father's thrifty pieces of paper, a complimentary piece of stationery from a pharmaceutical company torn into quarters. It said that Hilary had gone out, and suggested they meet at the hospital at the beginning of visiting hours, at two. His father had forgotten, of course, that Leo had no car.

The house was not unfamiliar, but estranged from Leo. In the bathroom, the range of soaps and shampoos had narrowed to what his father had chosen for himself – an amber-transparent slab of Pears with its smell like nothing else, a father-smell, and a supermarket budget brand. Dressed, he went with interest from room to room, having nothing else to do, and though he knew everything, recognized everything, it was now a part of his blind past. The house was, as it had always been, in a state of mild decay: things had gone wrong, sometimes months ago, and had been left as they were, a clock stopped, a burst cushion thrown irritably behind the sofa, a bookshelf collapsed onto the shelf of books below. Where steps had been taken, they were, as always, inadequate and impatient. The doorknob to the sitting room shook in the hand; when Leo looked at it, he saw that it had fallen off and been reattached with a nail rather than a screw. Everything was familiar, and seen for the first time in an age. When he lived here he would not have seen those jade fingerbowls edged with engraved silver: they had always been there. The blue carpet, the vase lumpy with Japanese fish, the William Morris curtains in the sitting room, Gertrude's box in the kitchen, the view of Derwentwater in pastels on the wall in the entrance hall – he had lived among them for years and had hardly seen them. Now he saw them, with a flavour, even, of reminiscence. These things were what had happened in his childhood.

But the house, too, had altered. The distancing had not happened solely in his head, from his change of dwelling and experience. Between the unmoving objects, the treasures chosen and bought and placed with care, the lives had begun to shift. Leo had glimpsed this the night before when, in the pantry, he had understood what happened when his father went up and down the supermarket's aisles, thinking about nobody but himself and what he might like to eat over the next few days. Now, going through the house, Leo felt that it had lost a quality of crowded possession.

The telephone in the hallway began to ring. That was what it had always been like – some urgent professional call for his father. Perhaps now it was his father, calling with some important information, but he let it ring and in a while the caller hung up without leaving a message. The telephone ringing in an empty house – a house empty of father and mother and sisters and brother – and Leo cocking his head as if one of them

were about to hurry forward to answer it. The Trimphone
warble was specific, and now he went from room to room,
recognizing what in particular it reminded him of. Those three
or four years before he left home to go to Oxford, what his life
had mainly been devoted to was cunt.

   He must have fucked a girl in almost every room in the house
– even on the polished dining table, wobbly and not as much
fun as it had promised. The kitchen table had been more solid
– Barbara – and, of course, the armchair where he had begged
that Chinese girl with the beautiful smooth skin to sit and part
her legs and let him kneel and taste her. 'Let me taste you,' he
had said – he could almost laugh at it now, and she had certainly
stared. Six months later he would have said, 'Let me taste your
cunt.' She was one of the first he had had. It had been in the
sitting room because he hadn't known how to ask her to come
upstairs. Carol, her name was. And in his room, too, the first
time had been Jayne, with the *y* and the untrimmed pubes, the
wonderful smell she had blushed to be complimented on, the
light floating of hair on arms and legs – she was a nice girl,
adorably unkempt, the youngest of four sisters. She had had
every make-up tip, every look tried out on her bullied features
every day since she was six. And the look of bewildered amusement, the fascination on her face when it had come to it! She
had averted her eyes only when she had seen the stupid poster
of the tennis girl scratching her bum that had been above his
bed for ever. To his astonishment, she had cried afterwards. She
had been so tender and happy and even sympathetic towards his
gormless gratitude, and when she started crying he'd comforted
her and told her he'd always love her. Downstairs the phone had
been ringing, and he'd ignored it, gazing into her face with the
sincerity of a love with no end. He'd taken the poster down a
few days later – he wanted nice girls like Jayne to see the point
of him, not just nasty girls who wanted to tell him he was
gorgeous, a dreamboat, a hunk in miniature. They couldn't
believe he was only fifteen before taking their bras off and pushing his head down between their tits. Not just them. And

Victoria – not Vicky, Victoria – and her red hair and the way she had sneered at him on the walk home from school, and called him 'little boy' and said he was like a dog bothering her and all her friends. Look at the little man's Adidas bag. He thinks he's really something, look at him! And one day he had said to her, 'Why not come round and find out how little I am?' And she had walked on with him disdainfully, like someone carrying out a bet, her friends calling rudely after them. He had sworn she was going to walk with him to the front door and then carry on, not looking back; but she hadn't. Victoria with her red hair had walked up the drive with him and had come in – with his beating heart he hadn't believed it until the front door was shut behind her. She led him upstairs and into a bedroom. It had been Blossom's room. Victoria had looked up at one point and said, 'You don't sleep in here, for God's sake.' He hadn't realized before then that her strutting contempt was mounted to hide the fact that she was never quite sure she had understood. A life of being ridiculed by her brothers and father for being slow on the pick-up. It was filled with pictures of ponies, Blossom's room.

He remembered all of those girls – after Victoria, they had come round to him, the female half of the species. He'd known, after Victoria, what the secret was – not to beg, not to apologize, just to *know* with perfect certainty that the girl, the woman you had brought within your orbit and decided to fuck, was going to want to fuck you. They were already persuaded or they were not going to be persuaded. After Victoria he never had to wear anyone down; he did not pester, was always aloof, his gaze moving steadily over the surface of an irresistible girl as if he had hardly registered her. When his parents and his sisters and his brother were out of the house, for three years, his life and the house he lived in were alive with cunt. That was how it was. Once on the stairs, even.

And then when he had come back from Oxford after that disastrous four months. He had had to try it out. The outrageous line had failed in Oxford. Even the level gaze had failed in Oxford. It had been greeted, once or twice, by its challenging partner, a level gaze in return. He could not understand it. It was as if they all knew what it was he had said. And soon it was his gaze that shyly dropped, in a college bar facing a girl who knew that, two years before, she wouldn't have been let in here, across a table in a seminar room, in the faculty library. The women had scented blood and, instead of going after him, had laughed and turned and gone elsewhere. The way Oxford had misread him, and that last night in January with that man Tom Dick outside his room with half a dozen drunk cronies, hammering on the door at three a.m. and shouting, 'Shy boy! Shy boy!' Had he ever been a success with women? He had returned to Sheffield in failure and misery at the beginning of February. It had been a month before he had raised his gaze in a bar, and made sure it did not quail, waited for his gaze to stay level and draw a woman to him. It had worked again, as it had not worked in Oxford. He had brought the woman home; she had stayed the night. She was called Lynne. It was a month after that that he had met Catherine. That had been a triumph, too. Framed by a life of accustomed triumph, by the ability to get whatever he wanted, however, there were those four months in Oxford.

He was at the foot of the stairs. He ought to phone Lavinia – no, Hugh, no, Lavinia – and find out whether their mad father had said anything to either of them about divorcing Mummy. Lavinia would be in the office; Hugh would be at home, and quite possibly still asleep. He thought. This was always the dark part of the house, the wood panelling and the lack of windows seeing to that, but also, outside the front door, the heavy growth of wisteria casting a shade over the porch. There was a figure outside in the gloom. It might be peering in, or just deciding whether to ring the doorbell. Leo came to his senses. He opened the door.

'I think it must be your father,' the small person said.

'I mean,' she went on. 'I came round to say thank you – it must be your father I was going to thank.

'It is your father – I mean, you're his son, aren't you?' she said. She was very young, her tiny hands fluttering a little as she talked. She had known that it would be him answering the door and not his father. She had started talking, unprepared, as soon as Leo had opened the door, her eyelids half closing defensively, and had begun to explain things starting with the wrong end.

'Yes, that's my dad,' Leo said. 'Did you want him? He's down at the hospital with my mum.'

'Oh,' the woman said. 'Only to –' She flapped, not knowing what else to do.

Leo hung on to the side of the front door. She had given some thought about what to wear: the grey skirt and paler grey sweater were new, and the burst of orange in a little silver and plastic brooch her only concession to a colour she had been told she ought to wear more of. It was the brooch that made Leo decide he ought to help her out. 'You live next door, don't you?' he said.

Perhaps she thought she had already explained, had ventured into detailed conversation. 'I'm Aisha,' she said. 'I'm not living next door – I'm just visiting for the weekend and a day or two more.'

'Come in,' Leo said. 'I can do you a cup of tea and perhaps a biscuit, but more than that – anyway, come in. It's nice to meet you. You're in the –'

'Everyone says it's the Tillotsons' house,' the girl said. 'I never met the Tillotsons. I expect they're sitting somewhere everyone describes them as the new family living in the Smiths' house.'

They were in the kitchen now.

'Your dad is astonishing – a genius. Yesterday. He was straight over the fence and putting Raja right in no time at all. My brother, Raja. Mummy hardly had time to scream, even. Your dad was as cool as a cucumber. Raja's back home now, with nothing to show for it but a gauze bandage round his neck. His brother keeps on at him to take the bandage off but he only wants to see the hole in his neck.'

'You'd have to ask my father,' Leo said, smiling, 'but I don't think he should do that. Probably.'

'I haven't been in here before,' Aisha said. She looked around her at the kitchen. She might have been observing it with the weight of evidence and experience, comparing it as Leo had to the kitchen he had known, groaning under the weight of six adults or near-adults with bellies to fill. 'I haven't been in any of the neighbours' houses – well, only as far as the hallway of one. I'm Aisha – I'm so sorry I didn't introduce myself.'

'Aisha,' Leo said. He had got it the first time. Then he realized what she meant, and said, 'I'm Leo Spinster. I don't live here either.'

'Well, there you are,' Aisha said. She almost glowed. She might have prepared all this, and at the last, when it came to getting it out, found that there was something on her tongue that was keeping her from saying it in the right order. 'Your kitchen's nice,' she said. 'It's so nice to come somewhere just next door where, you know, that oven's been there for ever, and the kettle and the toaster.'

'The toaster doesn't work,' Leo said. 'It wasn't working at Christmas and it still isn't working.'

'You should see our house,' Aisha said. 'Mummy's gone mental. Every single thing is new – well, not quite everything, but she said she's not going into a new house with all the old things. She's got a fridge that opens the wrong way because of where she wanted to put it in the kitchen. She's got her own money, the houses in Wincobank she lets out, and she's spending like a Rothschild on new stuff just now.'

Leo's face must have responded somehow to this; he had, he understood, been wandering about the house touching things in wonderment and alarming fulfilment, picking up objects that had always been there: a piece of rock crystal on a shelf, not seen through years of dull observation, had possessed the deep shock of a truth recognized immediately, as if for the first time. He had picked up object after object, turning them round and inspecting them in the familiar light of the empty house, letting them lead to the memory of one fuck after another.

'Not even the bloody clock's telling the time,' Leo said. 'Nothing works in this house.'

Aisha looked up at the Swiss railway clock that hung over the stripped-pine door to the hallway. She flicked her wrist upwards for Leo to see; she wore a man's heavy watch. Now Leo looked at the clock, he didn't know why he'd thought it had stopped: it was ticking solidly, reliably, just as it ever had. It was twenty to two.

'What time is it?' Leo said. 'I didn't put my watch on this morning.'

'Twenty to two,' Aisha said. 'Have you got to be somewhere?'

'I thought it was about ten o'clock,' Leo said. 'I'm supposed to be at the hospital. Oh, God, I was supposed to book a taxi and everything.'

'Which hospital? I can take you. Mummy's not using her car. Don't you drive?'

5.

Aisha told him to wait there, just at the end of the drive, and dashed off – scampered, you could almost say. Leo could meet them all another day, she called over her shoulder. Mummy's car was a red Fiat, a little run-around for town. Aisha briefly opened her front door, shouted something, and slammed it without waiting for an answer. She jumped into the car and, with a reckless burst of speed, reversed through the gates and onto the street. She rolled down the window. 'Hop in,' she said. 'Other side. Come on, quick.'

'It's very kind of you,' Leo said. With the act of driving, Aisha had taken on an air of capacity and system; the sense that she was doing things out of order, of staring and nearly giggling and not knowing what came next had quite gone. He got in. 'Where have your parents come from?'

'Bangladesh,' Aisha said. 'Or do you mean just now? Hillsborough. They've moved from Hillsborough. Which one did you mean?'

'Did you go to school there?'

'In Hillsborough? Yes, mostly, but then I got taken out and I did my A levels at the high school. My mum wanted me to go to Oxford. It's all right, you can ask where my family come from, being brown and all that.'

Leo had, in fact, retreated in an embarrassed way at the thought that he had been asking an English girl where her family came from. He gave a shy grunt.

'Look at that woman,' Aisha said. 'She's really going for it, isn't she, with the Cornish pasty? Go on – go on – can you get it all in in one go? Can you? My God, the things you see in Broomhill on a Monday afternoon.'

'I think I was at school with that woman,' Leo said.

'Surely not,' Aisha said. 'You were asking – I was born here, but then they went back to Bangladesh. That's where we come from. Daddy was doing a PhD in Sheffield, in engineering, and he was married to Mummy and she came over and I was born here. All I can remember is the blue door we had by the side of a shop and the Alsatian that sat in the shop downstairs. When he finished his PhD we all went back. I don't know why he didn't stay – it was a terrible time over there. And then after 1971 Daddy said there was a duty. He had to stay and work at the university in Dhaka, the university needed him and, really, the country was going to need people like him. He says it now and it's like a big joke that anyone would ever need someone like him, but Mummy says that that's what people used to say, back in 1971. Duty – they used to sing songs about it, probably.'

'What happened in 1971?'

'Oh, I'm sorry,' Aisha said, concentrating on the road. 'I forget not everyone talks about it all the time over breakfast, lunch and dinner. Bangladesh happened – there was a war of independence. It was part of Pakistan and then there was a war and it became independent but very poor, which is how it's stayed since. Lots of people were killed, you know. I had an uncle who was killed. I just about remember him. We talk about 1971 like you'd talk about 1066 if it happened twenty years ago.'

'I don't really know anything about it at all,' Leo said. 'I went to India once with my wife, before we got married. I thought it would be romantic.'

'It's sometimes quite romantic, I believe,' Aisha said. In the little rectangle of mirror, he caught her eye; it flicked away. 'I've not been, apart from once to Calcutta where we were changing planes and Daddy thought we'd stop over for two or three days to see things. Where did you go?'

'Rajasthan. Temples and palaces. There was a night in a really expensive hotel, a palace on a lake, but apart from that it was terrible backpacker hostels. My wife got awful food poisoning – she thought she was going to die or have to be shipped out.'

'What happened to her?'

'Well, she was fine in the end, no harm done.'

'No, I meant ...'

'Oh – we're divorced. Is that what you meant? Her food poisoning and some camels and the traffic – that's what I remember about India. I must go to Calcutta,' he said, in a rush.

'That wasn't romantic, I don't think,' Aisha said. 'I remember little bits about Bangladesh when I was little, but it's all confused now. We've only been back once since Mummy and Daddy left definitively. They came over in 1975 – they said enough was enough. The twins were born here. They were born in the Northern General, actually – I remember going through the snow to visit Mummy with some flowers and seeing the pair of them for the first time. It was really the snow more than the twins I was excited about.'

'Your family's all here, then,' Leo said.

'Yes, they all came over in dribs and drabs,' Aisha said. 'Most of them after 'seventy-five, though Mummy and Daddy were the first. No, I tell a lie. Aunty Sadia and Uncle Mahfouz came over here before then. Do you have any war criminals in your family? I've hardly met Aunty Sadia or Uncle Mahfouz, apart from maybe when I was about two years old and had no judgement.'

'How glamorous, having war criminals in your family,' Leo said.

'Well, I don't really know what they're supposed to have done,' Aisha said, 'but we're never allowed to meet them and Daddy always says that if everyone got what they deserved Uncle Mahfouz would have been shot by a firing squad years ago, or hanged, or put in the electric chair. Everyone, I mean the aunts, they all say that nothing could ever bring them to have Mahfouz or Sadia in the house again, which is unusual. They never agree with Daddy about anything. Here we are, the Northern General Hospital. How are you going to get back?'

'You've been very kind,' Leo said. 'I hope you didn't have anything important to do.'

6.

The hospital wing he found his way to, with many confusing blue signs, had a new brick frontage with a choice of steps or wheelchair ramp, but inside, its narrow corridors and metal windows revealed it as what it was, a conversion of army huts, thrown up rapidly during the war. It had the powerful disinfect-ant smell that all hospitals had, a sharp twinge of annihilation – there was no real question of cleanliness in the smell, just a sense that things, quite recently, had gone too far.

All about were families of visitors, a small gang of decrepit patients in dressing-gowns and slippers heading outside for a smoke, a child or two carrying a bunch of yellow chrysanthe-mums and there, in the middle of the hall, an old woman in what must have been a communal wheelchair, abandoned and fretful, sitting with her expectant gaze in the middle of the space, waiting to be collected or returned, like a volume of a dictionary in a public library. Leo reached his mother's ward thinking that he too should have brought some yellow chrysanthemums. Grapes.

His mother was sitting up in bed in her nightie, a shawl round her shoulders. Her right arm was in a thick plaster, her fingers poking out of the end, like curious animals. She looked clean and pink, her hair in an unaccustomed greying shock round her face, and she broke out in a delighted smile to see him.

'Nobody tells me anything,' she said. 'What are you doing here?'

'Came to see you,' Leo said. 'I thought you'd be a bit bored.'

'Your father was here a moment ago,' Leo's mother said. 'Did he know you were going to come?'

'He should have,' Leo said lightly. 'I got in last night. We arranged to meet here. What's up?'

'Oh, he does madden me,' she said. 'He's just gone out for a cup of tea, I think. Fancy not mentioning that you were on your way.'

'Probably wanted it to be a nice surprise for you,' Leo said, wondering. 'But what's that? What have you done?'

'Oh, I don't know,' she said, raising her heavy plastered arm with some effort. 'It's so absurd. I can't imagine how it happened. I thought I just banged it, just that, and then there was this awful pain, and your father looked at it and told me I'd broken it. You wouldn't think you could break an arm that easily. Did you …'

But then she went off into a fit of vacancy, and Leo remembered that she must be on a heavy dose of morphine.

'I got up here yesterday,' he said. 'Late last night or I would have come over. I met the new neighbours!'

He wasn't quite sure, but Celia refocused, smiling in a woozy way, and nodded. Out of her window was a courtyard, and in the middle an ornamental cherry tree. There was a bench on the far wall; a man in a tweed jacket was sitting on it, reading a book.

'Plenty of people have been coming,' his mother said. 'Plenty of people. It was Catherine and Josh yesterday. They brought those flowers.'

Leo thought it unlikely that his wife and son had been to visit yesterday, but he nodded encouragingly.

'She's a lovely girl,' Celia said. 'Of course, it's mostly been your father. He's been very strict with the hospital, telling them what needs to be done, keeping an eye on all the treatments. I think –' she broke off and almost sniggered '– I think they're actually a little bit frightened of him. It's good to have some-body strict and professional in charge of your care. He's a good doctor.'

'I would have brought you some flowers,' Leo said.

His mother seemed surprised at this. 'Have you come very far?' she said, in a sociable manner. 'I do hope it wasn't too much trouble. It's been lovely to see you. Thank you so much. I truly appreciate it.'

'Mummy, I've only just got here,' Leo said. 'I'm here for a few days to look after you.'

'Oh, that's nice,' his mother said. She appeared to focus, and now she lit up with real pleasure at seeing her son. 'You haven't come up just to see me? I'm quite all right. I'll be out of hospital in a day or two.'

'Well, I'll still be around then. Are you hungry?'

The question appeared beyond Celia. She wetted her lips experimentally, and passed her tongue over them. But then she cast her eyes downwards, shaking her head, as if she were a small girl with something to hide.

'Have you ever been in hospital?' Celia asked in amused, society tones. 'Like me? Look – this is my husband.' Leo wondered who she thought he was. There was no Daddy: the way she was speaking to him was as a grand guest at a party offering warm platitudes to an unimportant stranger. But she was a little more acute than he had given her credit for, because in a moment there was a peremptory knock on the door that Leo had shut, and his father came in with a bag from Marks & Spencer's food hall.

'Got here, then,' he said heartily to Leo. 'I forgot – you don't have a car. But it didn't seem to stop you. Well, how's the patient?'

'I'm quite all right, thank you,' Celia said. 'The pain is under control.'

'Well, it will be if you keep pumping morphine into your system at that rate,' he said. 'She's no idea what's going on. She's been given a device with a button she can press. Once every six minutes. She's pressing it constantly, as far as I can see. She'll be lucky if they don't take it away.'

'How am I, Doctor?' Celia said.

'I'm not your doctor,' Hilary said shortly.

'I mean Hilary,' Celia said. 'I know perfectly well who you are. We've been married long enough.'

'Yes, indeed,' Hilary said. 'Leo doesn't want any more nonsense.'

'Well,' Celia said, 'I'd be quite happy if ...' but she trailed off, not quite following what she should be saying in response.

'Yes, dear?' Hilary said, and that *dear* was something Leo had never heard before from him. Never had Hilary addressed anyone near to him as *dear*; it was a vocative from a sitcom, a ludicrous performance of old woman and old man, a word that Hilary would never have used to the face of any of his patients. The only use he had ever made of the word, as far as Leo could remember, was dismissively, on returning from a day in the surgery, and remarking that there had been nothing but a lot of 'old dears', nothing much wrong with them, and God knew what he was doing wasting his life in this way. But now he had said *dear* to his wife, and the word was savage.

'And all because she can't pay attention and falls head over tit,' Hilary said.

'Did she fall over?' Leo said.

'I didn't fall over,' Celia said. 'I didn't. I didn't.'

'You've started her off now,' Hilary said.

'I went over because someone pushed me. I don't want to say who it was because that would get them into a lot of trouble.'

'I wasn't even in the house when it happened,' Hilary said.

'Be that as it may,' Celia said, with a matching flavour of grandeur. 'Be that as it may, there have been things in that house that led up to this. You should understand that as part of your investigations. When I think – I could have married anyone. There was Alastair Caron. He was a friend of my brother's from school, he was very interested. He was a banker in the City. No messing about with sawing bones and sticking his fingers up men's bottoms for a living. Or if there were doctors there was Leonard Shaw –'

'Oh, for God's sake,' Hilary said. 'Not Leonard Shaw again. We're really never going to hear the last of Leonard Shaw.'

'– and he was charming, charming, a lovely man, and I was stepping out with – with him and he had a friend, an awful, pathetic friend, and once when Leonard Shaw had to go abroad, to Paris or Rome or Brussels I think, I forget, I can't remember. Once when he went abroad he said to me that his pathetic friend Hilary was stuck there in London and he didn't know anyone, and would I drop him a note some time and take him out to the cinema?'

'This, I may say,' Hilary said, 'is not at all how things really were. But let the morphine have its say.'

'*The King and I* was on,' Celia said. 'It had just come out. This is material to your investigations. But the awful, the pathetic friend of Leonard Shaw said he wanted to see this – you know, with corpses and shooting – this *film* about *gangsters*, and the dead head of a horse in someone's bed, and –'

Celia gave a sudden gulp, a whinny inspired by the dead horse and by pain in equal measure. Her fingers scrabbled; no one had repainted her nails in their usual deep red for days. She plummeted with her thumbs on the button, and in a moment the look of alarm on her face was smoothed away.

'It's just the drugs talking,' Hilary said, with every air of satisfaction, of being proved right. 'As you might have gathered
from the total confusion about dates. I think you were old
enough to see *The Godfather* when it came out, weren't you?'

'I wondered about that,' Leo said.

7.

Lavinia had had it up to here – with Sonia, her lodger, as well
as with Perla, her cleaner and Perla's so-called sons and daughters, whose names she had never caught. She needed to employ
Perla to cope with the chaos that Sonia left round her, and
Sonia's rent money went to supporting Perla, who came – or her
'son' came in her stead – twice a week, every Monday and
Friday. Pretty soon the rent money would be going towards
paying mental-health professionals to sort out Lavinia's head
after having to deal with Sonia's chaos, Perla's neediness and lies,
and the bloody son whose name she had never caught.

The flat in Parsons Green was hers; a little fretted balcony ran
along the front of the first floor, right along the L-shaped drawing room. When she had bought it, she had seen possibilities;
the same woman had lived in it for twenty years, and encrusta-
tions and odd ways of doing things had made the flat peculiar,
difficult to sort out, a bargain. One of those possibilities – and
Lavinia always prided herself on seeing possibilities, in people
and places as well as in property – was that there would certainly
be at least one spare bedroom. That ought to bring in six
hundred pounds a month, and any lodger she acquired – she
remembered thinking this from the start – could pay her rent
money into the Visa account, then nobody would ever catch up
with her. That struck her as sensible.

Sonia had turned up, thanks to Hugh. She had lived with
him at drama college. According to Hugh, she was no trouble
at all, kind and quiet – *heaven*. Those things were relative, it

appeared. If, among the drama students, she had been easily overlooked, living alone with a charity administrator of (Lavinia had to admit of herself) slightly set ways, she proved herself clearly a drama student: flailing, noisy, tearful, irregular in her hours and needful of statements of love at all times of the day and night. (It was a Brazilian lawyer called Marcelo whose dastardly treatment had created this need, according to Sonia.) She was, too, rather fascinatingly resourceful with irregularly detailed tales of how her grandmother had come over from Jamaica on the *Windrush*. She had undone all Lavinia's good work with regard to Perla and her son.

Lavinia had made it absolutely plain that Perla was not to bring her son along, and not to subcontract the cleaning of her flat to him, either. She didn't believe that he was Perla's son: he could have been only ten years younger than her, at most. She didn't know how long it had been going on. She had had the afternoon off, and had come back one Friday at lunchtime without warning – one of Perla's days – to find a moon-faced man in his mid-twenties sighing over the ironing in her kitchen. She had asked who he was; he had said that he was Perla's son. Where was Perla? She wasn't there. He had giggled nervously. She had had to go: she needed to work for Mrs Putney. (That was what Lavinia pieced together; the word 'Putney' had had to be decoded.) The man, his face greasy with worry, pitted with the remnants of a savage history of acne, tried to go on ironing, but Lavinia dismissed him. It took some time to make him understand. He didn't know 'Mrs Putney's' phone number; in fact, Lavinia thought he hadn't understood that Putney was Perla's customer's place of residence, not her name.

On Monday she stayed at home until Perla arrived, and told her that she had employed her and that she was not to give her key to anyone else. Not even her son. They were in the L-shaped sitting room as Lavinia spoke to Perla; Perla's anxious face, her thin coat, her hands already clasped in supplication. Lavinia did not look, but she knew that outside, on the street, there was a man no more than ten years younger than Perla, waiting underneath a tree, kicking his heels, skulking, one might almost say, waiting for Perla to give a signal so that he could slide in and take over her task, let her go on to subcontract her job elsewhere. Was Perla the English-speaking agent of a vast subcontracting army of recent illegal immigrants, the one whose papers and verbs were more or less in order? Lavinia had made her point. She couldn't sit there while Perla was supposed to be there, not twice a week.

That had been a year ago. Without enquiring into it, Lavinia had made the optimistic and positive assumption that Perla had, indeed, instructed her 'son', that from now on, she was going to do all the work, that Miss Spinster preferred her to do it. She would not be a cynical person. She would expect the best from everyone, even Sonia, and she would definitely hold the possibility in mind that Perla might be a lot older than she looked – the broad practised innocence of her face might do that – or that the son, skulking beneath trees with his big hands and his bad teeth, might be a lot younger. It was all possible. Anyway, she didn't check it out. She had to say that Perla did what neither Sonia nor Lavinia was prepared to do: clear up the chaos of Sonia's living quarters and the chaos that Sonia created whenever she ventured into bathroom or kitchen for face wrap or toasted cheese.

It had been only the week before that Sonia had remarked, 'Perla's so sweet.' They had coincided; they were watching the television news. Sonia could hardly go two minutes without offering some irrelevant titbit from her life.

'Were you at home today?' Lavinia said.

'I was feeling rather grim this morning,' Sonia said placidly, 'so I thought I'd give the agency a ring and tell them I'm not well. It's been ages since I had a day off sick. Everyone else does it all the time. I'm due a sick day. I need to relax. I'm Jamaican.'

Lavinia thought that sick days were days when you were ill, not days when you felt you could do with a day off, even in Jamaica. But she understood that the rules of the theatrical agency where Sonia worked, having given up on the idea of

making a living as an actress, were not quite the same as everyone else's.

'And Perla was here, was she?'

'She's so sweet, she really is,' Sonia went on. 'She told me that
I was a truly good person, a person with a truly kind heart.'

'What had you done to make her say that?'

'What, me?'

Lavinia waited.

'She asked me something – oh, I know. She said would it be
OK if her daughter came to do the work because she had to buzz
off somewhere, to Mrs … to Mrs – I can't remember her name.
Anyway, so I said yes so she said that I was a truly kind person.'

'Sonia, I've told her she's not to let anyone else do the work
in her place.'

'She said I'm a kind person,' Sonia said. 'You've no idea what
those people at that office think it's all right to tell me.' She
pulled her knees up to her chest, and pressed her bare feet
against the cushions on the sofa; her toes made that kneading
gesture against the silk a kitten makes.

'I don't want anyone but Perla cleaning the flat,' Lavinia said.
'I told Perla that ages ago.'

'Your brother phoned, too,' Sonia said. 'He said could you
call him back.'

'Oh, OK,' Lavinia said, but Sonia was waving a piece of
paper in the air, not looking at Lavinia, concentrating on the
television news. Lavinia reached over and took it. In Sonia's
handwriting it said, 'Your Brother called' – a scruffy, tattered
piece of paper, folded over several times.

'He said it was really urgent,' Sonia said. 'At least, when he
called he did.'

'I'm playing detective here,' Lavinia said, giving up, 'but did
he call today?'

'No,' Sonia said, astonished, her eyes wide, her hands making
a shrugging gesture. 'No, I told you, it was a couple of days ago.
It was when Claude was round or I'd have asked your brother
how he was.'

Lavinia picked up the phone. There was no point in investigating Sonia's beliefs about her behaviour. But Hugh, when she got through to him via a confused flatmate she didn't recognize, shrieked and was full of a glorious story about what he'd said and what he'd done and about being thrown out of Pizza Express last night before he'd even finished his Veneziana. But in the end they established that he was not at all clear that he had, in fact, phoned her. They started again. Hugh wanted to get Lavinia's opinion on a new set of photographs for his folder, more brooding, more serious, less comic-sidekick-who-could-advertise-soap-powder and more –

'King Lear?'

'King Richard the Second, please,' Hugh said, making Lavinia laugh at the specificity of his ambitions. They established that neither of them really knew how Mummy was but, as Hugh said, Leo was up there in Sheffield. If there was anything serious about Mummy being in hospital with a broken wrist, he'd definitely be in touch. Lavinia put the phone down with slight puzzlement.

'Not Hugh,' Sonia said, her attention burningly fixed on the Channel 4 news. 'Was that Hugh? It was actually your *brother* who called. From Sheffield. I thought I said.'

Lavinia didn't explain that Hugh, as well as being Sonia's ex-flatmate and friend, was also capable of being Lavinia's brother, or that it was possible to have more than one brother. She phoned her home number – the number she had been taught to say out loud all her childhood, whenever nobody else was by and the telephone needed answering; and it was answered, this time by Leo.

'I didn't get your message,' Lavinia said. 'What's up? How's Mummy?'

'How were the two of them last time you saw them?'

'Who – Mummy and Daddy? It would have been Christmas. No, I went up in March. They were all right. They've always been like that.'

'Rowing, you mean. Were they rowing?'

'They always row, Leo. He called her an idiot several times and she burst into tears and slammed the kitchen door on him. You know the sort of thing. He was just sitting there and saying, "Oh, charming." She didn't call him a prick this time. How is she? Physically, I mean.'

'Broke her arm,' Leo said. 'They're keeping her in. It broke too easily, or something – she hardly even fell, she said, and it went.'

'She's old,' Lavinia said. 'Old people are always breaking things.'

'They think it's metastized – is that right? It's metastasized. Well, they're keeping an eye on it. It can spread to the bones and then they start breaking for no good reason.'

'What does Daddy say?'

'He's keeping stuff to himself. I talked to another doctor. Once it's got into the bones it'll finish her off, but incurable doesn't mean terminal or that she's got weeks left. You don't need to rush up here.'

'I'll come as soon as I can. They're not keeping her in, are they?'

'Not indefinitely. This is the thing, though. Daddy's said to me something really terrifying. He says he's going to divorce her. He says it's his last chance to, I don't know, make things plain so she's not dying in some sort of illusion about how their marriage was. He's serious.'

'He *can't* be serious,' Lavinia said. 'What's she saying when he says all this?'

'She's up to her eyeballs in morphine,' Leo said. 'She's not making a lot of sense, apart from being just as beastly to him as he is to her. He's going to tell her, though – at least, he says he is. He told me on Sunday night and he's talked about it every day since then, going into all the details, what happens, who handles it, whether she's got to appoint her own solicitor. It's given him a real interest in life, frankly.'

'What do the others say?'

'I haven't told them,' Leo said. 'I didn't want Blossom turning up in her Jag to put everything right.'

She put the phone down, and immediately Sonia began to warble something about the Rain in Spain. She might have been suppressing it while Lavinia had been talking.

'And he couldn't sing at all,' she said gleefully. 'What a strange decision, to go into that particular line, if you can't sing.'

'What are you talking about?'

'Rex Harrison died,' Sonia said. 'Didn't you see? They had a lot of people on the news saying what a wonderful person he was. Hilarious. He was ghastly, famous for it. Still, you know – the Rine in Spine,' Sonia went on, dropping disconcertingly into terrible stage Cockney for some reason. 'Did yer muvver caw yer farver a prick, I mean for reaw?'

'Maybe just the once,' Lavinia said. 'I wish you wouldn't –'

8.

And the next day, Leo found that his father had gone out again in much the same way, on a trivial errand to buy something to eat from Marks & Spencer. He went out at the front of the house, and there was Aisha, watering the front garden next door with a hosepipe, wearing a dazzling pair of white trousers and a sailor's blue striped top, casting aigrettes of glittering water over a pink-flowering azalea, a white-flowering rhododendron. It would be a pleasure to take him, she said. It was the least she could do. He could not read the expression in her eyes: she was wearing an absurdly glamorous pair of Jackie O sunglasses, covering half her face, like a panda's eyeshields. There was, after all, nothing else she had in mind to do today, and in any case, there was something she had to do over that side of the city, something she'd been promising to do, had been putting off for weeks. The clothes she was wearing were quite impractical for anything resembling gardening, but she smiled at him and, given what she was wearing, Leo could not find it in himself to refuse her generous offer of a lift to the hospital.

MUMMY'S TIME WITH LAVINIA

This would have been in 1968, perhaps 1969, but Lavinia could not have been much older than that. Because it involved Dr Mario. If she had started school, it could only have been a few weeks, so Lavinia could only have been four or five. Surely they remembered Dr Mario? Some of them did, indeed – Blossom groaned about the memory of him, and Lavinia's father said, in an uninterested way, that he remembered something of the sort. But Hugh had been too young to know anything about Dr Mario. Why was he called Dr Mario? Well, reliable grown-up men who you told all your secrets to, or felt you could guard your secrets from, were generally called Doctor. Call for the psychotherapist. Why was he called Mario? Because, Blossom explained to the kitchen table, he was going to marry Lavinia when they were grown-up, or perhaps just when they had run away. Doctor marry-oh. Is that psychotherapist on the way?

'I can't understand how a doctor's daughter can make such a fuss about meeting new people,' Mummy always said. It was true. Lavinia just didn't like it when new people came in. It was always best to go off with Dr Mario and pay no attention.

Dr Mario always listened to Lavinia. He was always there when she wanted to say something and he thought she was the most important person in the world. Not everyone was like that. Everyone else never listened to Lavinia like they never listened to Daddy. 'Pay no attention,' Mummy often said, and sometimes she meant pay no attention to Lavinia and sometimes she meant pay no attention to Daddy.

'I guess it was really just about – well – about needing attention –' Lavinia started to explain, but Blossom cut her off.

'Much as I love these caring and sharing –'

'The psychotherapist's on his way,' Leo said. It wasn't so often they were in the same place, round a kitchen table; they were not going to waste it in embarrassment and delving.

The psychotherapist might explain, too, why Dr Mario was extremely tall and a curious, attractive shade of pale green in bright lights. He was so tall that he had to bend to get through doors, and occasionally scraped lights with the top of his head. It was intriguing that the two elder children had managed without a Dr Mario of their own. None of Blossom's children had acquired one, and she now knew from the child-development books that a Dr Mario was most likely to make his appearance in the nursery of an eldest child, or a single child, not a younger. Blossom hadn't had one – Blossom supposed she was just too unimaginative a child – and Leo had only had one in the shape of a very detailed and confessional relationship with a rabbit, stuffed with straw, called LaLa. Why had Lavinia acquired an invisible seven-foot green man with a doctorate? What was wrong with her?

Dr Mario, like LaLa, heard everything but, unlike LaLa, evolved plots and possessed ambitions of his own. Sometimes these requests were granted, like waiting for Dr Mario to put his best shoes on and join them in the car while they were setting off for a day in the country, a visit to Granny Spinster, even a trip to the fishmonger and greengrocer. Sometimes they were negotiated over and reduced; Dr Mario wanted to sleep in the same bed as his friend Lavinia, and it was with a queer feeling of criminal indecency confidently averted, Celia admitted years later, that Celia suggested their seven-foot pale green guest would be just as happy sleeping in the sitting room, and promised to help him put a comfy cushion on the floor for his long head to rest on. Sometimes they were bluntly denied. They knew that the story must have happened some time in 1968 or 1969 because it was then that Lavinia went to school for the first time, a place where Dr Mario was utterly forbidden to follow her. In a year or two, Lavinia would return from school to hear the mild observation, greeted with storms of tearful protests but soon to be fulfilled permanently, that Dr Mario didn't seem to be around the place so much. Perhaps he had moved away altogether.

But before that there was a day in 1968 or 1969 when Dr Mario decided that the time had come to run away from home. Didn't Leo remember any of this? Lavinia had gone in a matter-of-fact way to Mummy, who was sitting in an armchair reading a book, and had told her about Dr Mario's decision. 'I see,' Mummy had said. 'That seems awfully permanent. Couldn't you and he go away for the afternoon, see if you like it once you've moved away? And then if you think it's nicer here, you could come back.' But Lavinia was determined – well, Dr Mario had made his mind up, Lavinia thought it was just best to go along with it. 'When will you be leaving?' Mummy had asked, but Lavinia was surprised. She was leaving with Dr Mario straight away.

Dr Mario had decided to leave the Spinsters' home with his friend Lavinia and get a job. She had talked the subject over with Dr Mario and they had decided that, of the possible jobs grown-up people did – they could be hospital consultants, or GPs, or radiologists like Tim, or nurses, or train drivers, or paediatricians, or receptionists, or professors, or oboists, or teachers, or policemen, or headmasters, or dinner ladies, or oncologists, or ambulance drivers – of all these jobs the best was train driver. Dr Mario wanted to get a job as a train driver. Lavinia did not know exactly where the train drivers went, but she knew that the main station was in the middle of the city, and the middle of the city was down the hill. So she and Dr Mario left the house, walking briskly next to each other, and Mummy waved them goodbye from the doorstep with baby Hugh waving goodbye too, or being made to wave goodbye by Mummy holding his little wrist and shaking it. It was a good job that Lavinia was with Dr Mario. If she had been on her own she might have been scared.

They walked downhill from their house, underneath the quiet trees. The sun was shining above, she could tell, but the leaves were so thick that only the shadow of green fell upon her. At the end of the road, you could turn left, and that went up to Crosspool and the shops and the school with its black wall and the word GIRLS over the gate, though anyone, girls or boys, could go in. It wasn't like the old-fashioned times. Or you could turn right, and that went downhill and, Lavinia thought, if you turned left when you got to the Fulwood road, you would reach Broomhill and after that carry on and reach the centre of the city. They turned right.

There were two old people coming up the hill towards her: a lady in a hat and a strange fluffy yellow coat, and a person that at first Lavinia thought was a man. In this sunshine you could see the whole shape of the second person's head through their hair. It was as if they were bald but with a thin little cloud clinging to their scalp and anyone could see through it. Lavinia did not know either of these people, and she felt very nervous that she had now got to a place where people did not know who she was or where she lived. One of them looked at her: the one who was definitely a woman. Lavinia thought she was going to say something to her, and she swung her arms and carried on as if they weren't there at all. In five minutes, striding briskly and bravely, Dr Mario and Lavinia reached the bottom of the road, and were facing a busy flow of traffic. Lavinia was almost sure that here you were supposed to turn left and walk down the hill, and then you would reach Broomhill. But the road first went down and then went uphill again. She was not certain, and turned to Dr Mario to see what he thought. But Dr Mario was not there. He had gone. All at once Lavinia felt that she had been playing a game, a stupid game, that none of it was real, that Dr Mario was just something she had made up that could not help her against the smell of petrol and the flash of shining metal and the incurious, unhelpful gaze of the women passengers driving past. She had made a terrible mistake.

But then all at once there was Mummy, just standing alongside her as if she were waiting for a moment to cross the road. She looked right, and looked left, and looked right again, just as the Tufty Club said you should, and then, with great surprise, said, 'Lavinia! How lovely to see you! I was just thinking – I would love a cup of tea or a glass of squash on a day like today. I know just the right person who would really like to have us round, and her house is just over there. Would you like to come with me and have a glass of squash with Pauline?'

Pauline taught music – she taught the piano, which Lavinia might learn when she was a little bit older, but also the flute and recorder. Her husband was a musician; he had once played the violin in the Hallé Orchestra but he had suffered from nerves. Now he played in the Edward Carpenter Quartet and taught, but only older, special people. Their house was wonderful. There were musical instruments lying around to try out, and two whole pianos, and wonderful pictures on the wall that you could look at, and afterwards you found you were making up stories about the pictures, and best of all, there was a piece of paper that Beethoven had signed with his own name. That was in a special frame. You had to know who Beethoven was or you wouldn't think it mattered at all. Pauline was so happy to see Lavinia, and she made Lavinia exactly the sort of squash that grown-ups didn't know how to make – how Lavinia liked it, with so much squash, almost a quarter of the glass, that Daddy, if he saw it, would normally say something like 'Do you have enough water in your squash?' Pauline asked her to say *when*, and she only stopped when Lavinia said *when*, and she poured the water into it from a special clay bottle that sat on the piano, a grey china pot with the face of a wicked dwarf, all bulging eyes and warty nose. Lavinia completely forgot that she didn't like meeting new people, and perhaps Pauline wasn't a new person, really. And afterwards Pauline let Lavinia try to play the flute. You blew across it as if you were blowing across the top of a milk bottle. It was hard, and for a long time Lavinia couldn't get a noise at all, and then suddenly it rang out, just like a flute on a record. 'Well, there you are,' Mummy said.

Quite soon it was time to go home, and Lavinia took Mummy's hand. They walked together up the hill, and all the time Lavinia was telling Mummy about the adventure she'd had. Mummy was laughing and once she lifted Lavinia up and gave her a kiss – Mummy smelt so nice, and her clothes were always so clean, her hands warm and dry. Just as they were turning into the house, and before Blossom and Leo, holding baby Hugh in the crook of his arm, could get up from where they were sitting on the lawn in front of the house, underneath the cherry tree, Mummy said something to Lavinia that she would never forget: she said, 'Well, Lavinia, you'll always remember today, won't you, all your life?' It was true. She knew that. She would. It must have been 1968 or 1969, the day that Dr Mario went and she knew that Mummy, after all, would always be there.

CHAPTER THREE

I.

Aunt Blossom's house was like a house in a cartoon. The things that Josh had only seen drawn hastily, on the funny pages of Daddy's newspaper, were here made real. There was the lake with swans, there were guns in the locked cupboard where nobody was allowed, and there were rooms with names from books. Once he had forgotten this, and at school had said that his aunt Blossom had a china pug that sat by the fireplace in her morning room: the class had stared, had half laughed, the teacher, too (Miss Hartley), had stared. Afterwards his friend Andrew had asked him what he had meant: a room for morning. What happened to it in the afternoon? And after that Josh had made sure that Aunt Blossom's house was confined, in his mind, to the ranks of houses in books, to Netherfield and Thrushcross Grange and Toad's house and Bludleigh Court: the flushed warm brick of the front before the gravel circle, the azalea-lined drive, the terrace above the lake and the sweep of the lawn down to it. Aunt Blossom ought to be good at inhabiting it, and she did her best, but it seemed to Josh that she was not quite convincing. Her head held up and her shoulders back, she was nevertheless like an actress who was going to play a role in six months' time, and had decided to live in the part until then. Was that unfair? She was the smallest of them, small as Daddy – even Thomas was almost as tall as her now. She had to make herself felt.

But the house was the real thing. The woods to one side, hiding the houses of the village; the washed-pale stone, the peeling wallpaper that nobody noticed or commented on, the sofas with the torn green silk and the fascinating horsehair bulging out; all this retreated from reality into a fantasy of Josh's and, by repeating a formula, he could sometimes convince himself he loved it, when enough time had passed since they had gone away, Josh silently screaming in the back of the car. Aunt Blossom's house had a morning room, a drawing room, a library, a dining room – Granny's house had a dining room, as well as a conservatory, which Aunt Blossom didn't have. But Granny's dining room was not like Aunt Blossom's, a room from a cartoon, with Aunt Blossom and Uncle Stephen sitting at either end of the long polished table, the cousins in the middle around the silver candelabrum with the Japanese nanny, practising their Japanese and boning their breakfast kippers with two forks. In the middle, too, were Josh and Mummy, both humbly limiting their breakfasts to Coco Pops and toast with strawberry jam. The cousins had told him many times that the Coco Pops and jam were got in especially for him and his mummy, and collected dust in the buttery between their visits. That was another room: *buttery*.

The food at Aunt Blossom's was sometimes OK but sometimes frightening – they ate things that had been shot, things that were bleeding, things with bones and innards and eyes still looking at you. Josh didn't believe that anyone liked these things, plucking lead shot from their teeth or wiping blood from their mouths. They ate them because they thought they ought to. Even at breakfast the food could be frightening. The cousins had finished with their kippers and their kedgeree, a kind of fishy risotto but nastier, and were now piling marmalade onto their plates from a glass bowl with a glass spoon. The Japanese nanny was eating something of her own confection, something white, puréed, babyish; with her other hand she was feeding baby Trevor pieces of toast, cramming it in between the baby's sneezes and coughs. The two eldest cousins, Tamara, who was Josh's age, and Tresco, who was two years older, fourteen, old enough to have his own gun, were speaking to each other in

Japanese, mostly ignored by the nanny. Their sentences barked and yelped at each other across the silverware; Josh felt pretty sure they were being as rude about him and Mummy as they could manage in Japanese. Underneath the strange no-go-ho-ro-to yelping of their secret language, Josh could hear the usual twittering yawning intonations of his cousins; they didn't sound like the Japanese nanny at all when they spoke her language. The third cousin, Thomas, gazed at Josh as if not quite sure what he was doing here; when Josh was not there, he was the one they 'teased', as they put it, with his prole's sweet tooth and his grasp of Japanese that was (Tamara said) all that could be expected, frankly, of a seven-year-old. The baby, Trevor, sat dully with toast and marmalade all over her face, waiting for more food, and thought her own thoughts. Josh believed that Trevor was the most evil of all of them.

'It's going to be fine today,' Uncle Stephen was saying. 'What's everyone's plans?'

Josh looked, agonized, at Mummy. Her cereal spoon paused for a moment; she very slightly shook her head. She didn't want him to say anything. Josh thought of the book he had started reading yesterday, permitted by the heavy rain; he thought of Bevis, running down a hill to build a dam across a stream, to catch frogs and fish for trout with his bare hands. How exciting *Bevis* was! He longed to stay inside in a quiet quarter and read all about his adventures, and let his cousins rampage around outside, catching trout for real. Beyond the grounds was the Wreck, with the disgusted village children kicking at stones and stomping on frogs. That was more terrifying still.

'I don't want to see you children inside until luncheon. It's far too nice a day to be mouldering about inside,' Uncle Stephen said, from behind his newspaper. 'I'm looking particularly at you, Joshua.'

'Josh doesn't like *mud*,' Tamara said, quoting something Josh had said once, years ago, when he had not wanted to sit down in a water-meadow at her command. 'He can't bear it. Thinks it's awful. He *won't* want to come out today.'

'Nonsense,' Uncle Stephen said. He lowered his newspaper; looked over his glasses, down his nose at Tamara on the other side of the table. He was talking, nevertheless, to Josh. 'It's a beautiful day.'

'Ho-to-go-so-mo-to Josh,' Tresco said.

'To-ho-ro-mo-so Josh go,' Tamara said. The Japanese nanny raised her eyes to heaven, shook her head, whistling in frustration. 'It will be a little muddy, I think. But mud never killed anyone, not that I heard of.'

'Josh *wants* to go out,' Aunt Blossom said. She was a warm, interested presence at the far end of the table; she was smiley and caressing; she always got everything wrong. 'Do you think there's no fresh air in Brighton? Josh probably knows a good deal more about fresh air than you do, living right on the English Channel.'

'We'll go into the woods,' Tresco said. 'May I take my gun, Papa?'

'Of course not,' Uncle Stephen said. 'Find something else to entertain you.'

'What a lovely way to spend a morning,' Mummy said. 'Just messing about in the woods. I can't imagine anything more fun. I'm sure you're going to find something intensely dramatic.'

Uncle Stephen lowered his *Daily Telegraph*, stared at Mummy. 'Intensely ... dramatic?' he said. 'Catherine, what an impressive thing to say. What an awfully ... *Brighton* thing to say. You make it sound like ... like ...'

'Oh, you know what I mean,' Mummy said, in the way she had when she had said the wrong thing. But Josh could not see what she had said wrong. It appeared to him to be about the best thing that anyone could say about what might happen, once he went with his cousins into the gloom of the purple-edged woods; the world that lay beyond the lawn, beyond the ha-ha, at the end of the wilderness, the world in the woods that Uncle Stephen had bought two years ago and was still deciding what he would do with it. He wanted to go back to Brighton, where you could say 'intensely dramatic' if you felt like it.

2.

'What news from Sheffield?' Stephen said, setting down his paper with a rustle and a sigh.

'No news,' Blossom said. 'I spoke to Daddy last night. He is extraordinary. I asked him about Mummy, and he said just, "Oh, fine, fine," and then started telling me this immense story about the neighbours. I can't work out whether we should go up there or not.'

'Please, let's not go up there a moment before it's strictly necessary,' Stephen said.

'I love Granny and Grandpa,' Tamara said. 'I love dear South Yorkshire, and Sheffield I love best of all.'

'Oh, shut up, you ghastly little snob,' Blossom said. 'You really are the bally limit.'

'Who are the new neighbours?' Catherine said.

'Daddy was telling me all about them,' Blossom said. 'They had a party, or something, and, my goodness, somebody nearly died but didn't.'

They had lived in the house in Devon for seven years now. 'Made a packet in the City,' had been Stephen's explanation for it, 'always wanted to come down and vegetate in the country' was his wordage. Where had Stephen grown up? Oh, in the sticks, out in the borderlands, in the Home Counties, in Bedfordshire – the explanation and the wordage here differed. Blossom knew where he'd grown up, in a neat house with half a horseshoe drive and red, upward-pointing gables in Edgbaston; in the upstairs bedroom, blocking the view, was the back of his mother's dressing-table, blue and gilded. It was a lovely house, where his parents had been happy and where they had still lived when Blossom had married Stephen. It was not clear why an elegant suburb of Birmingham needed to be concealed from view in this way. Nowadays the parents lived in a square white Regency villa just down the road in a sea of brown chippings, like a boiled chicken in a sea of cold Edgbaston gravy. Stephen had bought it for them, and they lived in three rooms out of thirteen. Fewer and fewer people knew or remembered that Stephen had grown up anywhere else.

This house had come seven years ago. It had a satisfying manorial address – Elscombe House, Elscombe, Devon – which suggested the seigneur and the peasants at the gates, the annual garden fête and the squire venturing out on Christmas Eve to commend the church choir. The moment had not, somehow, come for the issuing of invitations to an annual fête; it had been a mistake not to go to church and not to go to the Lamb and Flag in the village; help had been hard to find and, once installed, fast to resign. The children's rooms were an abandoned disaster area. Soon Blossom was going to start importing help, like builders and groceries, from London, and to hell with what they thought beyond the gates.

The grounds were perfect, wild and grand, as far as they went. That was not so very far. A generation ago, much of the land had been sold and built on. The major-general and his sister Lalage, at the end, had sold rather more, before concluding that they might as well sell the whole lot to some cad in the City. Elscombe House now ran up to a wall dividing it from a new estate in yellow brick of retirement couples and young families. The best that Stephen had been able to do was to repurchase three acres of woodland that had been sold but not built on. Just beyond the newly built low wall at the far end of the copse – more a gesture of separation than an enforcement of it – was a recreation ground. The woods had been the property of the village children, for their own dark games and secret purposes; now it was the property of the four children of the big house. This change was purely legal, enforced by a wall anyone could climb over. Only the most abjectly law-abiding of the village children had stopped going into the woods because of the change of ownership, and if they called it 'the woods', older people in the village called it Bastable's Beeches, after a long-dead gamekeeper. Ownership was not so easily transferred. The older children and Stephen had their guns. That was an important part of living in the country. But the grounds had been trimmed and abbreviated and squared off and sold to such a degree that there were really only one or two directions in which you could point the gun, not into the newer parts of Elscombe village or towards the house itself. It had been open to the public three days a week in season; not any more. Blossom believed the plasterwork in chinoiserie in the long gallery was rather admired by the sorts of bods who admired that sort of thing.

'Norman said there was a family of adders in the woods,' Blossom said neutrally. (Norman was the new gardener.) 'Be a little bit careful for once. Don't go trying to collect an adder in a jar.'

'Plenty of little toads,' Stephen said. 'Bring those back. Make friends with them. See an underlying affinity. Is it tomorrow you have to be off, Catherine?'

'I was supposed to hand Josh over to Leo. But he's in Sheffield.'

'I would just go straight up the M25,' Stephen said. 'It used to be hell, having to cross London, take half the time getting to Cricklewood. Just go straight across to the M25 down the Great West Road, up and over, Bob's your uncle. The Bristol motorway, the London circular in a clockwise direction, the Leeds motorway northwards. Robert,' Stephen said, entering a whole new world of sonorousness, 'is your father's beloved brother.'

'Catherine's not going to Sheffield, darling,' Blossom said. 'Enough of the walking road map. We're talking about –'

'Oh, I see,' Stephen said, then pulled a funny, told-off face for the benefit of the children.

'– wretched Leo, my wretched brother.'

'It won't be so bad,' Catherine said. 'I don't mind a bit of a drive.'

'Please may we get down?' Tamara said. 'Josh has finished his Coco Pops, so may he get down as well?'

'Yes, you may,' Uncle Stephen said. 'I don't want to see any of you until luncheon. My God,' he said, 'there's no danger to England. As long as there's been boys in England, there's been woods and mischief and mornings spent getting muddy. And houses like this. Look out there, Catherine. I don't suppose much has changed in that view since 1600. And the boys and girls getting out there to shoot and trap and run and hide and make battles in the mud. My children, doing what I did, doing what their children are going to do, in the same house, on the same land. Nothing's ever going to change.'

The motorway ran against the purple hills, twenty miles off; the grazing was let; a small kiln and workshops against the river lay half empty, a sign permanently up on the B road. In the breakfast room of the house, a man stood, explaining about Englishness. He went on speaking, jingling his change in his pocket, like a trotting horse, and behind him the children stood one by one and left; their mother left; Catherine left; and the Japanese nanny, finally, stood up and went. Stephen let his peroration go on, though he could sense that the room was now empty. It didn't matter. After a while he stopped jingling, fell silent, content. Soon the New York markets would open.

3.

It had been just like this when she had been married to Leo. Blossom, Leo's sister, had descended from the start with cries of incredulity about what Catherine was proposing to do – to have two rather than three tiers on the wedding cake, to do without a honeymoon, to take a job in the local council answering the phone, to work in the private library in St James's Square. Catherine and Leo had taken the firm decision not to tell Blossom about her pregnancy for as long as possible – it was only that it meant keeping the news from the rest of the family, and especially from Leo's mother, that made them tell her five months in, to a torrent of smiling advice, offered with a shaking head and a gesture towards her own successes. That torrent had never yet dried up. The one thing that Blossom never tried to set Catherine right about was her divorce. Over the phone, there had been a full, satisfied silence before cries of joyous pity rang out; the news confirmed her nosy enquiry of a month before. Blossom was her great friend, of course, but she and Josh came to stay mostly for Josh's sake: his friends in Brighton were timid, bookish, quiet, and his cousins would surely be good for him. This was their third weekend at Josh's Uncle Stephen's. She hoped he would not pick up an adder. She believed they were mildly poisonous.

Catherine felt that she was always resting in the interstices here at her sister-in-law's house. In much the same way that, since her divorce and the so-surprising, pressing invitation – the first of five – from Blossom to come and stay, not any time but on a particular date, and to bring the little one too, there was always something intermediate and uncertain about the positions she found herself in. Was she a guest that Blossom and Stephen longed for, found excellent company, enjoyed being in the house? Or was there some underhand and contemptuous motive, unknown to and unspoken by even them? She had felt like discussing it with Leo on the phone or at those sad handovers, asking him what place he thought she occupied in Blossom's life. She had a good idea, however: she knew that he would think she was invited for the sake of the retelling, so that Blossom could subsequently say to Leo, just in passing, 'Oh, we had your ex-wife and little boy to stay last week. They are so charming, I must say.' The pleasure of causing pain and rendering Leo's life inadequate quite outweighed the difficulty and tedium of having Catherine and Josh as awkward presences in the house for four or five days. At some future but not at all remote point Catherine and Josh would surely be evicted from Elscombe House by her sometime sister-in-law's husband and her sometime nephews and nieces, bearing shotguns and laughing as the sometime relations stumbled, suitcases in hand, down the gravel drive.

Breakfast finished, and the children were shooed off, going upstairs – Tresco said, over his shoulder, in a dismissive way – to dress for the woods; the Japanese nanny followed, carrying the now rather large Trevor (a girl) and puffing up the stairs towards the nursery. Catherine stood at the foot of the wooden stairs, resting her hand on the carved heraldic beasts forming the stop at the bottom of the banisters. She had been here too long: she wondered, as her mind formed the word, whether 'banisters' was not a word Blossom would consider common in some way. The bedroom was forbidden during the day, apart from moments when it was necessary to change clothes and quietly to drink a little vodka from the bottle she had brought; in any case, there was nowhere to sit, apart from a hard cane chair. She could read her book, but she had already finished it; there was nothing to read in the house, apart from the dutiful books the children ought to read and the forbidding leather-bound antiquities that had gone to make the library, bought with the house by Stephen. What did people like her read in a house like this? There was no place for a person like her in a house like this. She stood at the foot of the stairs, wondering whether she could justify going out for a walk to the village. The pub would not be open yet.

'I've got some dull letters to write,' Blossom said, having followed the girl clearing the breakfast table out into the hall, berating her all the while. 'It's no pleasure. Come and sit with me and we'll chat. Stephen's in his study all day, manipulating investments, I suppose.'

Without waiting for an answer, Blossom continued on her way, following the skivvy through the green baize door underneath the stairs that led to the old kitchen. There were meals to order, tasks to assign, purposes to fulfil. Catherine tried to remember which was the morning room – the little square yellow one, she thought, at the back of the house with the ugly china pug in it.

There was a rumpus from the first floor, and down the double staircase, proceeding underneath the Burne-Jones stained-glass window, the children thunderously came. The two middle ones, Tamara and Thomas, were first, and dressed unexpectedly,

Tamara in a full-length white lace ball-gown, a First Communion frock in a Roman Catholic country. She had pink ribbons in her hair. Her brother Thomas was dressed for the same occasion, in blue velvet knickerbockers and a foaming white shirt to match his gleaming white stockings; he was wearing a pink bow-tie, not very expertly tied. But Tresco and Josh, behind, confident and shamefaced by turn, they were dressed just as they had been at the breakfast table.

'Going somewhere?' Catherine asked Tamara.

'Don't tell Mummy,' Tamara said. 'There's a good Aunty Catherine.'

'We're just going to the Wreck,' Tresco said. 'Goading the proles.'

'I see,' Catherine said. 'Well, don't shoot any of them. You won't be popular if you wade through the woods in that dress, Tamara.'

'There's something called a dry-cleaner's,' Tamara said. 'Poor little Thomas. He hates his Faunties – he simply loathes them.'

'They made me,' Thomas said, his face screwed up with rage as they processed past their aunt; their usual way into the grounds was through the drawing room and its French windows. Catherine caught her son's head and rumpled it as it passed. He looked back: shame, fright, secrecy all melded in his look. They would find an excuse not to come next time they were asked.

'It's rather nice to see them all getting on, the cousins,' Blossom said, emerging from the servants' quarters. 'There's no accounting for children and whether they'll get on with each other. I always tell my children it's just not on to be fussy about food, to like this food or that food, and it's not on to like some people and think you don't like others.'

'Oh, I don't know,' Catherine said, following Blossom towards the morning room. 'I think you're allowed to like some people more than others.'

'If you're grown-up you are,' Blossom said. 'Good morning, Mrs Bates. Everything all right? Good, good. If you're grown-up you're perfectly permitted to have likes and dislikes about people or food or anything else. I'll make a confession to you – I absolutely can't bear desiccated coconut. I can't bear it. But I'm sure that I wasn't allowed to say that I wouldn't have this or I wouldn't have that when I was a child. And it was exactly the same with people. Get on with everyone and the world will be a much easier place. That's my motto.'

'Leo's absolutely stiff with likes and dislikes, what he won't eat, and who he gets on with at work and who he can't abide.'

'Well, there you are, then,' Blossom said illogically. As so often, when she talked grandly but vaguely about her past, she seemed to have an invented, imaginary life in mind, one with ponies and acres and grandparents with Victorian principles. She had forgotten, perhaps, that Catherine had been married to her brother, and knew all about the reality of the doctor in the suburb of Sheffield and his self-pitying, indulgent wife with the hands fluttering as she spoke. 'We're all so fond of Josh – he's such a nice little boy. And so fair-minded, as you say. How is he at school?' She plumped herself down behind the writing table. On it were any number of curiosa: a set of miniature furled flags, a miniature reproduction Buddha in marble, some Japanese porcelain dishes – corporate gifts that had ended up here. The better ones were in Stephen's study. Catherine pulled the armchair out of the direct sunlight. It was still a little bit like a job interview, the way Blossom had situated herself.

'He likes it,' Catherine said. 'He seems to be thriving there. It's a lovely atmosphere – you can't help feeling how friendly everyone is. There's a proper feeling of helping out and thinking of everyone.'

'Oh, Brighton,' Blossom said. 'I can well imagine. It sounds absolutely lovely. I know those schools, putting everyone's welfare first, making sure no one's left behind … I sometimes wonder, though.'

'I know it's not much like the sort of schools we went to,' Catherine said.

'Or Tresco's school,' Blossom said. 'To be honest. It's a terrific school, you know. They're introducing Mandarin as an option.

Have you ever thought about what Josh could be doing? My children can be little swine, I know, but they're constantly vying to outdo each other, speak better Japanese than each other, run faster, survive a day in the woods without anything to eat or drink. Do they have sports day at Josh's school?'

'Well, sort of,' Catherine said. 'It's called the Summer Festival. There are races, or there were last year, but they arranged it so there were all sorts of things that the kids could be good at in their own way. Someone won a prize for the happiest smile of the year.'

Blossom lowered her head. The sound she made could have been a cough or a suppressed snort. She concentrated for a moment on the papers on the desk – letters, mostly. She shuffled them, squared them off, plucked one from the pile and placed it on top, squared the pile again. She looked up and gave Catherine a brave, watery smile, as if beginning all over again. 'I should have done all this yesterday, I know,' she said. 'I've been thinking and thinking about the kitchen garden – I just can't make up my mind.'

'The kitchen garden?' Catherine said. Around the unpicturesque back of the house there was half an acre or so where, once, vegetables had been grown. The half-acre had been abandoned to its fate long before Stephen had bought the house. The major-general and his sister Lalage, the twin white mice to which the family had been reduced, had retained the kitchen garden, which in an Edwardian heyday had fed a family a dozen strong and a small army of helpers, carers, serfs and labourers with asparagus, beans, potatoes of waxy salad varieties as well as the floury mashing kind, tomatoes, turnips, lacy clouds of carrot tops, cucumber and lettuce; there had been a long, crumbling brick wall of soft fruit, raspberries, blackcurrants, whitecurrants, redcurrants, apricots trained against it, a full half-acre of once beautifully tended vitamin C, running up to orchards of apple and pear and plum, and the hothouses where grapes had once been grown. All that had been abandoned by the time of the major-general's withdrawal, and that of his mouse-like sister Lalage. (How had he ever commanded anyone, with his bright, inquisitive eye, his neat and fey, almost girly moustache?) The shape of the garden remained, but the major-general and Lalage had cleared a couple of beds, and grown a few sad roots and a couple of tomato plants and lettuces. Beyond that, the tendrils and shoots and wild-flowering mass of vegetation climbed and clambered, untrimmed and unprotected; the vines pressed against the glass of the greenhouse, many panes now smashed. Stephen had instructed the gardener, Norman's predecessor-but-seven, to get it in order, but he had taken most of an autumn to do nothing but strip it bare, or almost bare: the apricot tree had survived, espaliered against the wall, and now spread there, its branches unfurling over the blank domain. The flowerbeds in the front had been more urgent, and their care had proved a nearly full-time occupation for Norman, the new gardener, and his seven predecessors. 'Really,' Blossom was practised in saying, 'we ought to have three or four gardeners, not just one. We're never going to get anywhere. Now, the kitchen garden ... I would love to do something with it. I can't think what.'

'You could do exactly what it was meant for and grow vege-tables in it,' Catherine said. 'I always think there's something so lovely about a really well-kept allotment, even, with neat rows of things. And you could have a lot of exotics. Plant an olive grove. Make English olive oil.'

'The children are using it as an awful sort of pet cemetery. I found a little array of crosses down there next to Moppet's grave – it turns out to be Thomas's gerbils and some dead birds that they found in the woods and christened posthumously for the sake of the burial service. I hate to think how the gerbils met their end. Olives wouldn't grow down here. The trees might, not the olives themselves. What about a rose garden?'

'So much work,' Catherine said. She had had the bright idea, when they moved into the house in Brighton, of growing yellow roses up the back wall. The pruning and trimming, and the array of murderous insect life that had to be fended off with sprays and drips and feed had been exhausting. Jasmine grew there now, which nothing much killed.

'Perhaps you're right,' Blossom said. 'I do think the children – they're growing up wild, I know, but they have a sort of confidence. I worry about Josh.'

'Josh?' Catherine said, taken by surprise.

'He's so charming and delightful, but he's just so – what's the word I want? – *different*. No. Diffident. He doesn't put himself forward, he goes along with things. It does him so much good, being in a gang of ruffians, running riot through the woods instead of being alone with a book. I really wonder …'

Blossom set down her pen and looked, with a frank, open, rehearsed expression, at her sister-in-law. Catherine had experienced this expression before when, for instance, Blossom had asked her whether things were quite all right between her and her brother, whether she might like to come and spend time with them in the country, whether Josh might have any idea at all (the gaze still fixed on Catherine, quelling any motherly gesture of defence) who it might be who had spilt most of a bottle of ink on the Turkey carpet in the sitting room. It was an expression that got its own way. Catherine looked instead at the life-sized china pug that sat by the fireplace, impertinently quizzing the world.

'I really wonder, and I think Stephen wonders, too, whether we could do a little bit more for Josh.'

'You do so much for Josh,' Catherine said. 'And for me, too.'

'Let me explain,' Blossom said. She placed the cap on her Mont Blanc pen, a present from Stephen two Christmases ago. He had got it from Harrods for a four-figure sum. There was a diamond set in the top of it. In time it would become the pen that Blossom had written all her essays with, the pen she would have inherited from some namelessly patrician great-aunt, the sort of pen that the family who owned Elscombe House had always had to write bread-and-butter letters of thanks and instructions in the morning room before luncheon. Now

Blossom set it down. She clasped her hands between her knees. She began to explain.

4.

'We shan't shoot the proles,' Tresco said. 'We've promised Aunty Catherine – we've promised your *mummy*, Josh.'

They paraded across the lawn in front of the house. Tresco first, Tamara second, lifting up the skirts of her ball-gown. She had her Dr Martens boots on underneath, and tripped delicately, as if to a minuet in her head. Thomas came third, disconsolate in his Faunties, and finally Josh. No one had suggested that Josh wear anything in particular; he had been spared the full knickerbockers-and-frilly-shirt treatment inflicted on Thomas. He felt there was something sinister about this neglect, not kindness. They were heading to the woods, where in practice the worst things happened. Tamara had once crucified a vole there, using an industrial stapler, and left it hanging on the tree as a warning, she said, to the village not to come into their private domain. Last summer they had fetched out their catapults, a gift from Uncle Stephen's father, and had tied Josh to a tree. They had said they were going to play Cowboys and Indians. It was a game Josh had never heard of anyone playing outside books, and he had known something dreadful was going to happen. For half an hour, they had fired acorns at Josh's face, in silence broken only by knowledgeable, acute advice on catapult technique from Tresco. He had thought it would never end. Then, on some kind of agreed signal, Tamara had freed him and roughly wiped his grazed face of tears, mud and leaves, then announced that he, Josh, had passed the initiation with flying colours. Josh had not regarded this with much excitement. The initiation had made no difference. The cousins went on thinking up more and more events that might count as initiation ceremonies, and when knowledge was shared out between them, Josh was not often included. For the rest of time, he was going to be forced by his cousins to squat on the edge of a pit and told to shit into it, to prove something or other. He had no idea why Tamara and Thomas were wearing their party clothes into the wood, or what was about to happen there.

Tresco observed that there was nobody about. The woods had belonged so recently to the village – to the *proles*, Josh practised in his head – that it still possessed an old name. Bastable's Beeches, like the children in *The Treasure Seekers*. He did not share this association. And then they started to have a lovely time. They ran off after Tresco into the little hollow, and poked sticks into the burrow where the badgers might be bringing up their babies. They went to the muddy bit where there was still a good four-inch-deep puddle, and took turns jumping into it from the tussock, Tamara's ball-gown flying into the air, the mud splashing all over her skirts. They looked for the adder using Thomas's head in the undergrowth, like a battering ram. They weed against an old oak, Tamara bending over almost into a crab position, pissing into her skirts more than on the ground. They dared each other to eat a toadstool still hanging around from last winter, and they threw stones at the old hut with the roof falling down. They managed to smash one of the remaining panes of glass in its one window.

It was a lovely time, Josh told himself. They hadn't seen any wildlife at all and they hadn't made him eat anything and they hadn't tied him up. An expression of seraphic calm was on the faces of Tresco and Tamara, as of the desires of little drunks being fulfilled. It counted as a lovely day, even to Josh. They hadn't been near the Pit at the far end of the wood, the one that Tresco and Tamara had last had a shit in two days ago, squatting over its lip, the one where everything lay in black confusion, of rubbish and poo and what dead animals they could find. The bodies were thrown here, though their burial took place some-where else – the respectable theatre of the adult ceremonial took place under the approving look of the adult windows, in the kitchen garden with empty boxes as coffins. He dreaded the Pit most of all, but today, after all, was a lovely day, not like one of the bad days so far: they had not gone anywhere near it.

The suburb ran right up to the edge of the forest, and a sad concrete and tattered grass expanse opened up beyond the wall that Uncle Stephen had built. It was the Wreck. Only recently had he understood that it was not a Wreck like a disaster, but short for Recreation Ground. 'Recreation' was one of those words like 'Amusements' over the door of a dark seaside hell of blinking machines and staring old people feeding coins into empty upper sockets, pressing buttons and pulling levers; it described what wasn't there. What was there was duty and miserable escape, sodden carpet and torn grass. He wanted to be on this side of the wall, in fact, in Uncle Stephen's woods that he'd paid for and deprived of a name at all.

Something struck the side of his head with a blow; a cold wet thwack, a torn lump of soil and grass. 'You berk,' Tamara said. Her face was flushed pink, her eyes wide with excitement. 'You unutterable berk. Standing there staring into space. I bet you were writing a poem in your head, weren't you, about the forest and the babbling brook and the fucking wood sprites?'

'We've got loads of fucking wood sprites in the fucking forest,' Thomas said, plucking at his Faunties with gross, clutching abandon.

'Or we did before Tresco shot them with his fucking rifle,' Tamara said, gambolling off, lifting her skirts and skipping with fury. 'Ow – I've hurt my ankle. No, I'm all right. I'm not going to sprain my ankle, not today, no fucking way.' She ran off in the direction of the wall.

'She's such a fucking moron,' Tresco said. 'She's no idea what wood sprites even are. I swear to God she thought we were talking about jays or magpies of something. They're mythological fucking beasts,' he called after her. 'Before she starts asking Mrs Arsehole if she can make a wood-sprite pie or something. Well, go on, do your stuff.'

Thomas's face took on an evil, set expression. He ran off after his sister. His white tights were falling down; the froth of shirt

and the front of his Cambridge-blue velvet jacket were thick
with mud where Tamara had pushed him into the puddle,
twenty minutes before.

'Here we go,' Tresco said, his voice lowered and intense,
egging himself on. 'Here we go. Here we go. They go first, then
we come as a lovely surprise. Yeah?'

Josh said nothing, but Tresco must have seen that he didn't
know which way was up, as they said.

'Today's fun and games. You'll like this, Josh. It's called Get
the Proles. You watch. It's going to be fun.'

There was nobody about but, fifty yards away, Tamara and
Thomas, their spattered white and blue garments winking
through the trees, but Tresco now hurled himself behind an oak
like a commando and, squatting down, ran to the next one. He
pulled a woolly hat out from his pocket and stuffed it over his
shock of white-blond hair. He might have been concealing
himself from a sniper. They dashed from tree to tree, Josh
following. Ahead, Tamara and Thomas had reached the wall.
Were there kids playing in the Wreck? It looked as if there might
be. The proles. Tamara and Thomas paused, faced each other,
and Tamara gave Thomas a sweet smile, raised the skirts of her
ball-gown with a pinch of either hand. Thomas scowled, then
made an effort and gave a smile that lasted no more than two
seconds. He had been instructed. Tamara began. She gave a
dainty skip, then another, then a twirl, a bow. Thomas said
something – perhaps 'Do I fucking have to?' – then gave in, and
made his own dainty skip, a second, a twirl, a bow.

Tresco and Josh had reached the edge of the woods. They
would not be seen by the kids in the Wreck; only Tamara and
Thomas, giving their courtly dance behind a wall in ball-gown
and Faunties, only they would be seen by the proles. It occurred
to Josh that in this part of the wood, they were quite close to the
Pit. Tamara and Thomas bowed at the same time, advanced,
took each other by the crook of the elbow and rotated; Tamara's
left hand rose above her head and twiddled, as if at a magnifi-
cent and embarrassingly beribboned tambourine. Over there,

the kids sitting around on the swings and the slide weren't playing any more, if they ever had been. They had noticed the palaver the kids from the big house were kicking up. They had seen something maddening: two posh kids, one wearing a big posh gown like a wedding dress, the other wearing frills and fucking knickerbockers, prancing like shit. Tamara lifted her ankles, delicately waggled her feet. Thomas's knees leapt up almost to the foaming linen of his chest. The proles had seen them. They were watching.

5.

Blossom's hand, its ring with the ruby as big as a pomegranate seed, went across the desk, spinning the Rolodex, as if thinking on its own. Blossom looked, open, sincere, happy, at her ex-sister-in-law.

'What would you think,' she said, 'if we made the arrangement with Josh a touch more permanent? Do you know anything about Apford? The school? Tresco's school?'

There must have been something that Catherine gave out, some physical withdrawal, some veiling of the eyes, because Blossom in a moment said, 'I'm really only thinking of Josh's welfare,' in a mildly reproving way.

'And in the holidays?' Catherine said lightly.

'Of course we would take care of the fees,' Blossom said.

'Yes,' Catherine said. 'It's incredibly kind of you, it really is. I can see that. I need to think it over.'

'Well, don't take too long,' Blossom said. She turned to her desk. 'It's a complete waste of time, writing letters, and three-quarters of them are nothing but thank-you letters, but there you are.'

For five minutes Blossom wrote steadily. Catherine could feel her face was flushed. Nothing that she wanted to say could be said. Blossom was thinking of Josh's best interests. Catherine was thinking only of her own. After a while, Blossom looked up and, as if surprised that Catherine was still there, said, 'It's a lovely day – don't let me be selfish and trap you inside like this.'

'I might go and read a book,' Catherine said despairingly, thinking of vodka.

6.

There were seven proles in the Wreck. It was school holidays for them as well. They were three girls and four boys, one quite small. They were wearing the sort of clothes that proles wore. They weren't shiny shell suits, but jeans and T-shirts with some sort of writing on them. One was wearing the top of a tracksuit, a red one with stripes, as if they were ever going to do any exercise. There was another who had a pair of cream chinos on and a blue polo shirt. That was quite like what Josh was wearing. That was the funniest thing, really – that the proles in the village would look at Josh and think he was posh, that they wanted to dress like him.

The proles were sitting on the kids' roundabout and chatting, about a hundred and fifty yards away. Another was on the swings, swaying gently back and forth. They were deep in conversation. A bark of a laugh came from one of them. Tamara and Thomas skipped to and fro, but they hadn't seen them; the power of a ball-gown and Faunties and pastoral frolicking went over their heads. Or perhaps they had seen their wealthy neighbours and had no interest in it – that would be too bad.

'What's going on?' Tresco said, squatting behind the tree where he couldn't be seen. 'Hey – you need to put a bit more welly into it. Go on. Up and over, dosie do –'

'I'm doing the best I fucking can,' Tamara said, out of the corner of her mouth.

The proles had noticed Tamara and Thomas, skipping and dancing around each other. They had stopped where they were, and were casting looks at the edge of the forest. But in a moment they turned away again, definite that the posh rich kids weren't worth their attention. Perhaps it was a decision; perhaps they were unable to see the spectacle behind the wall, remote from jeans and Wreck and trainers and semi-detached houses in yellow brick. 'Not working,' Tresco said. 'Wish I'd brought my gun.'

'I can't believe it,' Tamara said, pausing and puffing with breathlessness.

'I've got an idea,' Tresco said. 'They've not seen Josh, have they?'

'I don't want to,' Josh said. 'I won't make them do anything. I'm not putting on Faunties or anything.'

Tresco took his branch – a two-foot club – and poked Josh hard. Josh stumbled upright so as not to fall into the mud. 'Go on,' Tresco said. 'Just go and wave at them or something. No one expects you to do anything *intensely dramatic*.'

Tamara and Thomas started laughing. Josh felt tearful; he had forgotten that, sooner or later, the cousins would move on from being vile to him to being vile about Mummy.

'Oh, for fuck's sake,' Tamara said. 'If you don't come up here now, this second, I'm going to come and drag you out.'

It would not work, Josh was sure; all he had to do was go and stand at the wall and be ignored in the same way that the proles were ignoring his cousins. It was as easy as that, and then the cousins would get bored and go and find something else to do. He stood up properly, and went to the wall where Tamara and Thomas had been dancing. Tamara, a firm look on her face, took him with a solid grip and pushed him forward. She raised her arm and pointed at him, grinning like a mud-spattered loon in a ball-gown. By their side, Thomas continued to caper.

'Do you know what Josh does?' Tresco said. He was talking half to Tamara and Thomas, and half for Josh's benefit. Over their heads, the music of disdain in what Tresco was saying floated, across the Wreck, to be caught by the proles. 'Josh touches things. He's always touching things. Have you seen that? When he comes into a room, he can't stop and sit down, like a Christian, until he's been right round, picking up this and that, putting his hand on the Staffordshire dogs and the photos on the piano. Do you reckon he does that at home? Or is it just when he's taken out? Do you think it's a Brighton thing? They can't stand it, the seniors. They bite their lips. They try not to say anything about Josh having to touch everything. I saw him once bend down and touch the tassels on the Turkey carpet in the drawing room. I bet they think he's bringing his Brighton ways into the house.'

'Stand there,' Tamara said to Josh. 'Just like that.' She took Thomas by the hand, firmly, and walked back a few paces. The proles were standing now. They had seen Josh. One of them shouted something, and then the biggest of them was sprinting towards the wood, maddened, leading a ragged troop. They had endured and accepted Tamara in her ball-gown, Thomas prancing in his Faunties, but the sight of Josh, dressed just as they were, standing behind the stone wall within the purchased woodland acres, had been too much to bear. Their howls were terrible.

'Run,' Tresco said. 'Fucking run!'

They ran, Josh jumping after Tamara, her skirts clutched in her fists. She was going towards the end of the woods where the Pit was. Thomas was already far ahead of them; Tresco had not moved an inch. The proles were over the stone wall now, and their howls within the estate. Somewhere behind them, through the trees, there was a confusion of movement and stumbling; somewhere behind that was Tresco. He must have armed himself somehow because quite suddenly there were shrieks of alarm within the roar of rage – a pitchfork, a gun? Josh stumbled, was grabbed by Tamara. He had almost fallen into the Pit. And here came the proles, with Tresco behind; he had smeared his face with mud, was clutching a terrible weapon; a glint of metal on the end of a pole, a kitchen knife. The littlest of the proles turned as he ran, placating with his hands, screaming, and one of the others seized him – was it the child's sister? She tripped, stumbled, and two, three of them fell exactly as Tresco had wanted them to, into the mud and shit and filth of the Pit. As if nothing at all had happened, Tresco slowed to a walk, hoicked the pole underneath his arm and turned away. At the same moment, Josh found himself seized from behind, by Tamara. She had a plan for him. It was Thomas who started to bind his wrists; Josh surrendered himself to it. It would be easier. The morning's task was over. Behind them, as they started to make their way to the house, the sound of some prole puking, or so Tamara jauntily observed. It was the sight of Josh they couldn't stand, in the end.

7.

'You won't believe this,' Blossom's voice called from the great hall.

She was trying to find out where Catherine was, and Catherine called back, 'Yes?' from where she had removed herself to, the dining room. She had worked out that nobody came here in the mornings. It had a pleasant view out towards the woods that divided the house's grounds from the village.

'You won't believe this,' Blossom said, coming in, papers in one hand, her glasses in the other. 'I've been tracking down my brother. He's definitely in Sheffield. In the meantime, the arrangement about meeting you and poor little Josh – he'd never heard of it. But listen. When I tracked him down in Sheffield he was full of such alarming news I really think I'm going to hotfoot it up there. I could perfectly well take Josh with me.'

'It's not your mother, is it?'

'It's always Mummy,' Blossom said briefly. 'She's not dying, or not imminently. Gracious heavens, what on earth have those awful children of mine been up to?'

A scene of apocalypse was approaching the house across the lawn. Their faces were smeared with mud and filth; their clothes, once party clothes, wedding uniforms, pageboy and miniature princess, were torn and smeared with earth or worse. They wore expressions of sheer joy, waving sticks that might have been meant for spears in a celebratory greeting. It was not directed at them, but at someone fifty feet to the left. Stephen must have seen them and opened the study window to call to them. Only at the back, trailing in his ordinary clothes, was there a dissentient presence; behind Thomas Josh came, his shoulders shrunk and beaten. Catherine saw with a shock that he was being pulled by the others; his wrists were bound together and he was being dragged along by a rope, or perhaps merely a thick string.

'How adorable,' Blossom said. 'They've been playing captives, and Josh is on the losing side. He'll be the pirate king or something. Conquered by the imperial forces, or by savage natives, one of the two. It'll be his turn to rule and conquer next.'

'Poor old Josh,' Catherine said, attempting lightness in her tone. But something in the way she said it made Blossom turn to her, a half-smile of amused dismissal quickly forming. Poor old Josh, she was clearly thinking. A little bit less of that, a little bit less encouragement of Josh to stick in his ways and run from ordinary little-man savage pursuits that any child, surely, would like.

'I have no idea,' Blossom said, with dry amusement, 'how – or if it's even possible – to get mud and blood out of pale-blue velvet Faunties. I could simply kill Thomas for putting it on to romp around in the woods. They were for the Atwood wedding, those Faunties. They very sweetly asked Thomas if he'd be a pageboy.'

Across the lawn, like a cavalcade of shame, misery and death, came the children, panting, filthy and prancing. Their teeth glittered like those of carnivores, fresh from a pile of flesh and blood. They waved to the man upstairs, the father of three of them. He was yowling into the end of the morning over the lawns, lands, woods and gardens he had made the money to possess, singing his children home from a triumph, somewhere out there in the shadows of the woods.

MUMMY'S TIME WITH LEO

This would have been in 1969, or maybe 1970. It was just a bag
– that was all it was – and ten shillings. What was it then that
kept rattling around his head years later, occupying brain cells
that could have been used for preserving other facts instilled at
school, how to draw a box with perspective and what the chem-
ical symbol for beryllium was and how the passive went in
German – the consequences of the playground event that kept
him in dread for weeks, just sitting there like a useful lesson for
survival learnt at school? It must have been 1969 or 1970, but
definitely it must have been after school, because that was when
　　Here
　　Here over here
　　Dave it's to me
　　Run and grab it there there's a
　　Stuart Stuart Stuart
　　Grab it then it goes to Stuart that kid from Crookes is
　　Grab it grab it then
　　The kid was standing there looking at what was in his hands.
It was his sports bag – a black plastic one like everyone's, with a
sports-shoe logo on the side. He looked up in rage – it was that
kid Gavin who was in Mrs Tucker's class – and pushed Leo,
hard, with his bag in his fists. It was almost a punch. Leo was
sweating, though it was a cold day, the air puffing into steam
from their mouths even now in the late afternoon. Around
them the others loosened their scarves and dropped their own
sports bags.

'You did that,' Gavin said to Leo, pushing him again. 'You
did that. You little dwarf, you bloody did that.'

'Sod off,' Leo said. But Gavin was pushing his bag into Leo's face and the others were looking concerned, grave, worried as trainee oncologists in a small circle. The bag was torn at the handle, a raw gash of cardboard under the smooth black plastic surface.

'You bloody did that,' Gavin said. 'You're going to pay for that, you dwarf.'

'Piss off, you crater-faced TCP addict,' Leo said. But he had done it – he had felt the handle tear under his grip as he pulled at it, hardly knowing whose bag he was tugging at. Gavin, the dour kid who always wore a shirt two days running, who sat in front of him in French and never knew the right answer, the kid with the worst acne in the year, the one they'd tried antibiotics on. He'd torn his bag.

'It's nothing to do with me,' Leo said. 'It was torn already.'

'You did, though,' Stuart said. 'I saw, you know, Leo. You really tore it.'

'Everyone was grabbing it,' Leo said. Then he remembered why everyone had been grabbing at it – that boy Gavin, he'd taken Andy's copy of *The New Poetry*. Everyone had seen him do it; it was because he hadn't had his own copy this week and hadn't had it last week and not the week before that. He'd lost it – Mr Batley had pointed it out and Gavin had said he'd forgotten it. And this week Mr Batley had said it again and Gavin had said it again and then at the end of class, after sharing Paul's copy, he'd turned round and, when he thought no one was looking, he'd just picked up Andy's copy and put it into his bag. That was why they were chasing after him and why he'd taken his bag and why it was torn now. But everyone had forgotten that, apparently. They weren't bothered about A. Alvarez and his anthology of urgency and suffering.

'I don't care,' Leo said. 'Don't be so pathetic.' He went off, striding out of the school gates and up the road. It really was pathetic.

But the next day there was spotty Gavin, waiting for him when he came into the classroom, and again thrusting his bag into his face. 'You're going to have to pay to have that mended,' he said. There were seven or eight kids sitting around. Of course she was there – She: she was sitting on top of a desk with her two friends and pretending not to notice that he'd come in. That was always the way in the half-hour before the register was called, kids sitting around. Gavin was right up against him, pushing his bag and his concerned, angry-red, pus-weeping face into his, leaning over him, his fists clenched. 'You tore it. You're going to pay to have that mended. It's going to cost you ten shillings.'

'I'm not paying for something I never did,' Leo said. 'Don't be so pathetic. And what did you do with that book you stole from Andy yesterday?'

'It's you that's pathetic,' Gavin said. He went back to his desk.

But from the next day Leo lived in different worlds. In one, the main one, no one knew or cared about a torn bag; they had forgotten or never knew. They did not even see the way that Gavin came up to him, hissing. At home, it was as if a world of anger sat at the end of the drive outside the gates. In that other world, Gavin and he were bonded together by the vile and righteous demand, never shifting, never negotiating, just insistent on its correctness. I want that money, you dwarf, it said. Two or three times in the evening Mummy said, 'You're very quiet, Leo. Are you all right?' The little ones, Lavinia and Hugh, they stopped their constant chatter to each other; they looked at their big brother; they were interested.

It took a week before Gavin started saying that new thing. He was slow on the uptake in class. He must have taken some days to work it out. One day, when he came up in his usual way, he said, 'You owe me ten shillings. And if I don't get it by the end of the week, I'm going to come and ask your mum and dad for it. I know where you live.'

'They'd tell you to sod off,' Leo said bravely. From the outside, it must look as if he and Gavin were just in an urgent, serious, friendly discussion in the corner of the playground, scuffing away at the gravel underneath their feet.

'They wouldn't say that to me,' Gavin said. 'They're dwarfs too.'

'I'm not giving it you,' Leo said, and walked away. But all that week, it was Gavin at the beginning of the day and at the end of it; the horrible voice, the horrible face, raw with blood-sore swellings, sometimes actually bubbling up with blood or yellow pus; sometimes when Leo was alone, he thought he would dare anything.

That Thursday night, they were all at the table when the doorbell went. Leo knew exactly who it was. The soup spoons paused, halfway to the little ones' mouths. Daddy continued talking as if nothing had happened. Mummy just said, 'Oh, God,' and dropped her spoon. 'If that's a patient ...' she went on, walking into the hall, because it had been known for desperate patients to look up the doctor they liked in the phone book. She opened the door and, from the table, Leo could hear the familiar voice. For the first time he realized how much bravado was in it. The story it was recounting was so familiar to Leo that he could hardly tell whether he would have been able to understand it from here. Certainly the others just went on as if they would hear about it sooner or later; Lavinia was poking little Hugh with the corner of the tablecloth, and Daddy was asking Blossom whether she could go to the library on Saturday to take Granny Spinster's books back. In a moment Mummy put her head in. 'Money,' she said to Daddy.

'How much?'

'Ten shillings.'

'In my wallet. Should be a note in there. Or I had a new ten-shilling coin today. Have you seen the ten-shilling coin, Hugh? Be good and Granny might give you a nice shiny one for Christmas.'

'Just a debt I'd forgotten about,' Mummy said, coming back in. 'Have you finished, Blossom?'

Leo thought there would be an inquisition of some sort, but after dinner Mummy didn't mention it. Nor was it something she was brooding on. The ten shillings had been handed over and now, during the school day, Gavin positively avoided him. All the embarrassment was his now, and he faced the world with some defiance, not speaking to Leo at all. It was a few days before Mummy mentioned it, and she hadn't been saving it up. It was simply that it only then occurred to her.

'What was that,' she said, 'the other night? That awful spotty boy.'

'I tore his bag. He thought I ought to pay for it to be mended.'

'Poor boy,' Mummy said casually. 'He hasn't had much luck in life, I would say. Do you think – Oh, damn …' She went down the side of the sofa after the thimble she had dropped, found it, raised the needle and thread critically to the light. 'That sort of person. My motto is always *pay them to go away*. Ten shillings and then it's done. It's awful, I know.'

'I didn't have ten shillings,' Leo said.

'Oh, well, there you are, then,' Mummy said. 'I don't suppose that boy is ever going to paint a great picture, or save a life, or build a bridge, or write a book … People who do stuff, they're never like that. Do you think they had spots and moaned like that, the people who – the people who wrote the Book of Ecclesiastes?'

There must have been something startled in Leo's expression. He had never heard his mother allude to the Book of Ecclesiastes before. Where had that come from?

'Oh, you know what I mean,' Mummy said, laughing, rather shamefully, as if she had alluded to something truly embarrassing. 'I would always pay someone like that to go away. Can you thread that one with the red cotton, Leo?'

It was 1969 or thereabouts, the year that Leo learnt you could pay people to go away. It was the year when he learnt, too, that his mother thought that was a way you could deal with people. It was many years before he really considered which of these discoveries had shaped his life more – the idea that you could do it, or the knowledge that his mother comfortably believed it.

CHAPTER FOUR

I.

Blossom was no sooner in the house than she said, in her new, booming voice, 'Is that boy Tom Dick back in Sheffield?' Behind her, the two boys were stumbling out of the car, pulling heavy suitcases. Leo gave his sister a brisk kiss on the cheek, and bobbed quickly, arms open, to embrace Josh. There was not much bobbing required, these days, and for Blossom's boy Tresco, none at all – he was as tall as Leo. Blossom was wearing a white blouse with a brilliant velvet scarf knotted about her neck – Georgina von Etzdorf, Leo believed. Had she put on some weight? Or it might just be a new hairdo, falling to her shoulders. It was a flatter, closer one than Blossom's accustomed chrysanthemum of hair, made big with Elnett. He didn't recognize what Josh was wearing – a blue shirt rolled up to just below the elbow, and chinos with pink espadrilles. Apart from the colour of the espadrilles, it was what Tresco was wearing.

'Tom Dick,' Blossom said again. 'I thought I saw him on the street as we were driving through Ranmoor. No mistaking him.'

'Not as far as I know,' Leo said levelly. He separated himself from Josh, who had rather thrown himself into his father's arms; he gave him a rumple round the head, a pat on the shoulders. 'I haven't seen him for years. Because of his height, you mean – that's why you thought it was him?'

'Frankly somewhat surprised to see him here, but perhaps – Just leave them there, darling, we'll take them up when we know where Grandpa's put us. I would have thought he was off in Paris or New York.'

'I really couldn't say,' Leo said.

But you couldn't snub Blossom: she was too inured to it. It wasn't worth it, either. Blossom was going to get things going where Leo had just stared at them, then buried his face in his hands. She looked about her as if something was missing.

'Where's Grandpa?' Tresco said. 'Isn't he here to say hello?'

'He's at the hospital giving your granny a hard time,' Leo said. 'Do you want a cup of tea?'

'Gasping for one,' Blossom said. 'Look, boys, put them in the room that's got the pony posters in. The one next to the bathroom. Or your spare room, Leo, what do you think?'

'Not in my room,' Leo said. 'I don't know where Daddy thought he was going to put everyone. We'll sort it out later.'

His heart plummeted to think of his son and nephew going into his room and seeing, perhaps, what lay on the bedside table: a fat envelope with sheet after sheet of a letter inside. He wondered if it were best simply to say to Blossom that he had woken that morning to find a love letter lying on the mat. It had been pushed through the door at some point between him and his father going to bed, and him finding, around a quarter to seven in the morning, that he couldn't sleep any longer. He couldn't remember the last time he had had a love letter. Perhaps he had never had one.

2.

It had been on the mat when he stumbled downstairs, an envelope with his name on it. Opening it, he had assumed disaster. The parts of his life that would supply catastrophe to him were so many that he overlooked for the moment why his employer, his ex-wife, his son's school would have decided to deliver whatever bad news they had by hand in the middle of the night. Leo opened it – it was his habit to take a deep breath and open anything fast and start reading, to get it over with. His heart beat: in his dressing-gown he could feel himself beginning to sweat. For some moments he did not understand what he was reading – the handwriting was neat, purposeful, educated and pleasant. The statement of love came soon, and then it seemed to him that he had opened a letter not meant for him. In ten minutes he had understood what he had opened. He pushed it into the pocket of his dressing-gown. Upstairs, there were the noises of an old man unwillingly rising: a groan; a fart; a shuffle and a yawn that went through the gamut. Leo composed himself.

He had had letters of love before. Girls had sent them – they liked to send them when it was all over, he remembered. Catherine had sent one or two, but there was something dutiful about her letters, a sense that if she was marrying this man she had better choose to invest in him, do things properly. They were still around somewhere. A letter out of nothing was unfamiliar to Leo, and, here and there in the next few days, he would take the long composition to a solitary place and go over it. He was convinced that one day he would be rather proud of getting this, and prouder still of his decent, dismissive and respectful response to it.

At the moment, however, the overwhelming reaction he had to it was embarrassment, and it seemed to him that this letter, alone among all professions of love, spoken or written, had succeeded in creating a swift emotional response that was utterly authentic, that could never have been faked to please anyone. In the past women had said that they loved him, and he had said that he loved them back: he knew how to make it authentic, with the eyes wide and the mouth open; he knew even how to fill his heart with love so that it looked right. Sometimes he had said that he would always think of them, but he just couldn't – he didn't know how – and once or twice he had managed to cry. It was easier to make yourself cry than to make yourself laugh.

But now, a divorced man, a failure, with a son, Leo sat in the middle of the afternoon in his parents' house and looked at the words the girl next door had put on paper, and it seemed to him that no confession of love had ever succeeded in summoning a feeling with half the terrible authenticity of the embarrassment he now felt. He could hardly look at the sentences: Aisha saying she had known she loved him when she saw the watch he wore, too loose for his dear thin wrists. Were his wrists thin? Or dear? His eyes shut. And when they opened again there was Aisha's missive, promising that one day she would look out of her window and see him in the garden, except that then it would be his garden and his house, and the garden and house he shared with her. Had he read it correctly? She was young, so young: she had thrown herself on his mercy and he would let her down very kindly. He would not even quote what she had said about the beauty of a man's face striking like an axe at the frozen heart.

'What's that?' his father had said once, coming uninvited into his room. 'What's that you've got there?'

'Nothing,' Leo said. His father sighed, turned, left. Perhaps that was how his parents' marriage had begun: with a confession of love that rested on nothing.

And love? What was love? Leo looked out of the house he had always lived in, its windows and doors, into the street and into the garden behind, and he understood. The thing about love between adults: one confessed it, and the other allowed it, endured it, refused it or let the other down gently, decently. It was a test of character, how politely you refused another's love. Hand outstretched, a smile, a shake of the head, a kiss on the cheek. She was so young, this girl, and Leo, he had been through everything.

He felt that he might want to share the letter with his sister Lavinia, but only with her. She knew all about love, and about guarding it. The rest of them would never know how gently he had let down the Indian girl who lived next door to his mother and father.

3.

The postman in December always arrived later than usual – all those cards; sometimes he didn't get there until half past ten or eleven. Leo, at eighteen, had been waiting for the postman before going to school. School either mattered now or it didn't. The postman would be carrying a letter offering him a place at Hertford College, Oxford, or one containing a polite rejection. He wasn't going to delay the news because he needed to hear what Mrs Allen was going to say about *Antony and Cleopatra*.

It was a Tuesday. He was squatting by the door, where he could see the postman's approach. The envelope fell, crisp, white, bearing a red crest, and Leo tore at it.

'Well?' Mummy said. She had been waiting too.

It said exactly what it was supposed to say, and after half an hour of celebrating, of phoning Daddy at his surgery, even, Leo thought he should phone Tom Dick. But there was a strong possibility that Tom Dick wasn't celebrating, and he thought that he might, after all, go back on his word and find out what had happened at school, later.

He didn't see Tom Dick that day. He was impossible to miss. The next day they were in a French class together, and from the way Tom sloped in, Leo decided to lower his eyes and be as tactful as possible. But Miss Griffiths, the first thing she said was 'I hear congratulations are in order, Tom, and Leo, too,' and Tom Dick said, '*Vous auriez pu m'abattu avec une plume*,' which was joke French for 'You could have knocked me down with a feather.' He grinned, self-consciously, not engaging Leo's gaze at all. After the lesson, Leo caught up with him. 'When did you hear?'

'Got the letter yesterday. You?'

'Same. What did you get?'

'Two Es. And they're giving me an Exhibition.'

'Fantastic. Congratulations.'

'Well, congratulations to you,' Tom Dick said.

What was he supposed to think of Tom Dick? He hadn't been quite sure what he was supposed to say at the beginning when the head of the sixth form had said to him, 'And the other boy who'll be taking the Oxbridge entrance with you – it's Thomas Dick. Do you know Thomas?' Of course he knew Tom Dick. He was six foot seven inches tall. He seemed perfectly nice. He was in Leo's French set for A level, but otherwise was doing German and history. They weren't friends exactly – how could they be? It would have looked ludicrous – but Leo could see that Tom Dick was a solid, hard worker of a kid. He had a book of idioms that he added to, pencil in hand. The A-level French group had gone to Reims in the spring; they had practised their French in visits to champagne manufacturers and in lists of questions that Mr Prideaux had put together for them to ask in patisseries, of stationers, of ordinary members of the public in the streets of the handsome city. The patissiers stared, and admitted they had never quite thought why that particular cake was called a *religieuse*. On the Thursday night Leo had gone to a bar with two girls, less serious than him, and had drunk Calvados; Tom Dick had bought and annotated newspapers. Leo could put together a flamboyant argument, could make the case for this or that being the case in Pagnol or Mauriac. Tom Dick could just get the sentences right, learning and producing showy and frankly ugly subjunctives in the *passé simple* – '*Que je l'eusse su*,' he had said once, requiring even Miss Griffiths to pause and roll her eyes and work it out mentally before saying, 'Very good. But you would startle a Frenchman if you ever said that out loud.' *Le Noeud de vipères* was the same, a matter of list-making and significant points, principal characters, important themes, the subjunctive in the *passé simple*.

The Oxbridge classes had taken place in the sixth form terrapins that sat in the playground. The Christian Union had been turfed out of the smallest classroom, where they usually met to talk about God on Wednesday lunchtimes, and instead Leo and Tom Dick met there with Mr Hewitt, the head of the sixth form. He had been getting boys and girls into Oxford for years now, he said – one every other year, on average. They had a good relationship with Hertford College, so it would make sense to apply there. The rest of the time, he gave them old Oxford entrance exams to do, with much speculation about what the examiners would be looking for. You cannot weep for the heroine while admiring the zoom shot; societies, like fish, rot from the head; 'He is very clever, but he will never be a bishop' (George III on Sydney Smith). Discuss, the questions finished.

Was Tom Dick a friend of his? It was Miss Griffiths' favourite joke, in a French class, to go through the class names and call the next person Harry; often, talking about the Oxbridge entrance, that had been him. You could see that Tom Dick had heard this one before, and that he didn't like being shackled together with anyone for classroom purposes, and the purpose of an old joke. Perhaps Leo ought to have liked it even less.

Tom Dick was not a friend in the sense that his friend Pete was a friend. Afterwards, Leo thought that he and Pete loved literature as much as any human being had loved literature, those two years. Pete obsessed about D. H. Lawrence; he chanted him to the skies, and, when his memory faltered, he and Leo could produce endless amounts of D. H. Lawrencey shouting. On the first day of spring, the wind blowing and the sun blasting into your face like fury, there they were, in the middle of the street, shouting, 'Come to the flesh that flesh has made! Unravel my being and drag my soul, yes, my body and blood and soul, to the wet earth, and fire me up, O Fate …'

They could keep it up for hours.

Pete was his friend. He could have reconstructed Pete's bedroom from memory, the hours they'd spent there. He'd converted Pete to Blandings Castle but not to Jeeves – Pete said that the Blandings cycle was touched by a sense of the infinite, by Life, and outside the window the Empress of Blandings was waiting, savage, to devour everything. Wodehouse didn't know this, but it was so. That was Pete's phrase, learnt from Lawrence, and he said it about everything. *It was so*, and that was the end of the debate. Leo loved Pete's mind: he had the most original ideas about everything. Once they took a trip into the centre of Sheffield to look at an electricity substation. The cliff of blank concrete soared above them in the rain, a spiral of frosted glass to one side its only link to the world. Beautiful brutality, Pete said. It made you feel that the only thing man ever did in the world was to punch a hole in its being. It made you feel, that was the thing. They stood in their cagoules, the rain frosting over Pete's little round NHS glasses, the cars running past the electricity substation and the old cardboard-box factory. Probably they thought the pair of them were doing anything but what they were doing, admiring beauty and – after twenty minutes – chanting D. H. Lawrence at the great concrete wall on the other side of the road.

'Why don't you put in for Oxbridge?' Leo said once, in the pub where they thought they could get away with it. Pete was untidy, scowling, pugnacious, and he kept his hair in a short-back-and-sides: he didn't hold with sideburns and big hair and anything that would come and go. It made him look older than he was, though not always old enough to get a drink. He could have been in employment, even.

'I'd love to,' Pete said. 'But it's not for me.'

'I don't see that,' Leo said. 'It'd be for you if you got in.'

'There's no hills,' Pete said. 'I couldn't be doing with no hills. Oxford – no hills. Cambridge – definitely no hills. It's Leeds for me. That'll suit me all right.'

'I thought you said you needed to test yourself in life,' Leo said.

'I've tested myself,' Pete said. 'I don't need to test myself until I fail and then understand that I've failed. There's a world out there. They're just men and women, writing their tests and seeing if you're going to fit in. You and Tom Dick.'

'He's all right, that Tom Dick,' Leo said bravely.

'It's just strange when someone as tall as that starts speaking French,' Pete said. 'German you could understand. German's a language for tall people. French, no.'

'Spanish?'

'Dwarfs. Definitely. No one over four foot eleven sounds normal speaking Spanish. Short and packed with sexual energy. That's the language for you – you and your family.'

I wish it was you in the little room, talking about Oxbridge essays, Leo thought about Pete. I wish it was you. But it was Tom Dick and that was the end of it. And then the letters came and they were released from each other, or shackled to each other. It was hard to say.

That summer, it was so hot; a summer they were still mentioning with relish fourteen years later, one everyone would remember, always. The waters at Ladybower Reservoir had sunk and sunk, and you weren't allowed to wash your car or water your garden with a hose. People went out there in their dusty cars to see what had been revealed by the water's fall, the remains of the village that had been destroyed to create the reservoir. Derwent village; the stone walls, the outlines of dead houses sunk deep in drying mud, deep and cracking. Leo lay in the garden, trying to read what the college had advised, a book by John Ruskin called *Praeterita*. He had thought he knew all about Victorian literature, the subject of the first term's study, with Dickens and Thackeray and the Brontës and Tennyson. It had not occurred to him that the Victorians wrote anything like this. He couldn't understand it. They were twenty men and women seated respectfully in a hall, writing steadily at desks; that was how he understood it. Next door sat an old woman in black called Victoria, and her two prime ministers, Gladstone and Disraeli. They were dead by now; their numbers were hardly likely to be increased as time went on. Here was a book called *Praeterita* and, next to it, waiting horribly, a book called *Sartor Resartus*. He lay on a beach towel under the tree in the garden, hearing the remote rise and roar from inside as Lavinia and Hugh followed the Olympics from Montréal on the television, the curtains drawn against the bright day. Lavinia and Hugh usually liked to suck lemon ice lollies while watching sport; yesterday they had watched weightlifting, entranced, for hours. If he could get them to go out tomorrow – perhaps to the Hathersage open-air swimming-pool – he might ask Melanie Bond to come round.

People came round all the time. When the doorbell went in the middle of a rising roar from the television, Leo could almost see Hugh rising grumpily to open the front door to let Pete in, most often, or Melanie, or Sue, or Carol, or perhaps even Simon Curtis or Nick Cromwell. Sometimes when the ancients came back from work, there was a party going on in the back garden, Pete declaiming from the top of the rockery to the bewildered Tillotsons next door. But now the figure that came through the kitchen door behind Leo was six and a half feet tall.

'I thought I'd come round,' Tom Dick said, seating himself on the low brick wall round the flowerbed. 'I wasn't far anyway.'

'Where do you live?' Leo said.

'Nearby,' Tom Dick said. 'Is that your brother and sister watching the middle-distance races?'

'That's the first thing I'm glad never to have to do again now I've left school.'

'What, the middle-distance races?'

'No, sport,' Leo said.

'Oh, sport,' Tom Dick said. 'Is that what you're having to read?'

'Do you want something to drink?' Leo said.

'Yeah, that'd be – just some squash,' Tom Dick said. Leo went inside and made it. From the kitchen window, he could see Tom Dick, unobserved, turning and looking in an inquisitive way at the flowers. He tore off a leaf from the hydrangea then another; placed them together and lifted them up towards the sun. He tore them carefully, once, twice, three, four times, then separated them and compared, it seemed, the rips. All the time his feet were jogging on the spot. It was so hot, and Tom Dick was wearing a flannel tartan shirt and jeans and what looked like his school shoes. Leo had been wearing shorts for six weeks now, and nothing else; his legs and chest were as deep a brown as they would ever go. He watched Tom Dick, his pale face wincing against the sun, holding the leaves up.

'How are you getting there?' Tom Dick said. 'To Oxford.'

'My mum and dad are driving me,' Leo said, surprised.

'Oh – yes – mine too,' Tom Dick said. 'I passed my test last week.'

'Congratulations,' Leo said.

'But they've still got to drive me down,' Tom Dick said. 'They've got to drive the car back or it would be stuck in Oxford.'

'I'm taking my test next month,' Leo said.

'It's brilliant, being able to drive,' Tom Dick said. 'I went out yesterday, drove all the way to Bakewell with the windows open.'

Quite abruptly, Tom Dick stopped, raised his hands in bafflement. For the first time he was going to talk to Leo, and then he had remembered something, three sentences in, and stopped himself. In a few minutes, Tom Dick had said something about it being nice to see Leo, that he'd see him in Oxford, he supposed, that he had to make a move. He finished the squash in one; he held the glass awkwardly; set it down on the ground. His mother must have said that he ought to go and see the boy who was going to the same college as him.

'Who the hell was that?' Hugh shouted from the sitting room, the little prodigy. Someone was throwing themselves over hurdles, or chucking a javelin, or something; Lavinia was clapping her hands in breathless excitement. Quite at once it came to Leo that Tom Dick had told him a lie; he had said that his mother and father were going to drive him down to Oxford, but that could not be true. Tom Dick lived with his mother alone, Leo remembered. His parents had divorced, years ago. His father lived in Scotland. If he thought about it, he could remember Tom Dick saying, '*J'habite avec ma mère, à Fulwood, mais mon père habite Édimbourg d'habitude.*' It was clever of him to know that the French had a word of their own for Edinburgh. Leo wouldn't have.

The ancients drove him. The brown Saab was OK, Leo felt. It was the car of a respectable GP, antique but workable. No one was going to sneer at it. And the ancients, too, they had made a fist of it, not dressing in a ridiculous way in suit and tie, like some people's parents, not just turning up in what they'd wear to garden in. (They'd known and, after all, Leo had been fretting about whether to instruct Daddy in particular to wear a tweed jacket at the very least. They'd known about university and what Leo would be thinking about the people who brought him.) He'd been given a room in the main part of the college – not on the ground floor, like Charles Ryder in *Brideshead Revisited*, but under the eaves. His name was painted on the board on the ground floor, and again on the board by his door. The second year who had been assigned to show them the room formed a smiling bond with Hilary, who knew all about it.

'Isn't it just – lovely?' Mummy said, looking out of the window.

'That's obviously the most important thing,' Daddy said. 'That you study somewhere Mummy thinks is lovely. Of course Cambridge would be lovelier, according to Mummy.'

'I wish your father would …' Mummy said. But she wasn't quite clear of what she wanted. Hilary was going to goad her, of course, and comment on her saying that the college ought to be lovely where her favourite son was going to study. All the same, he was pleased, today, too. The row – the proper, full-scale row – could take place on the way home when Leo would know nothing about it, never hear until Christmas that Daddy had seriously threatened to abandon Mummy in the car park of a service station in the middle of nowhere.

'Isn't that – what was his name? That very tall boy? Wasn't he at school with you?' Hilary was looking down at the quadrangle. 'What's he doing here? Look at him, doesn't he look a complete package? He looks so serious, the way he's standing. Do you think he had to bend down to get through all these tiny medieval doors? I'd like to see that.'

'He got in,' Leo said. He came over. Tom Dick was there with an anxious, small woman in a piecrust-collared blouse and an aquamarine suit. Tom Dick was wearing what he had worn when he'd come round, a tartan shirt and a pair of jeans with, now, school plimsolls. His mother had dressed up. She was only five feet two or three at most; they made a conspicuous pair. They were carrying a cardboard box each; the mother was limping somewhat.

'Oh, that's nice,' his mother said. 'Having someone here you know the first day. He's a nice boy. Isn't he?'

'I don't remember hearing anything about anyone else getting in at all,' Hilary said. 'Is that it, then? Do you know where to go? You don't want us to unpack everything and put your books on shelves in alphabetical order, I don't suppose. Ce – stop staring out of the window. Leave Leo to what he's got to do. I'll treat you to a cup of tea in an Oxford teashop if you play your cards right.'

Then they were gone. Leo almost congratulated himself – he had come quite close, he felt, to having an argument with his father, and had walked away from it in a grown-up manner. That was the thing to do. Leo was to reflect – not then, but at some point weeks later, when everything had gone wrong – that he had spent almost every day of his life with his mother and father. You could probably count the days he had seen neither, and the number would be less than fifty. It hadn't appeared to be an important moment, their going just at that point, leaving him in a sculptural landscape of brown cardboard boxes and a cheese plant balanced on top, like a De Chirico interior. What had happened was a strange thing, the sudden vision of his parents as if they were complete strangers, as anyone would see them, his father warm and jocular, taking his mother's hand in a courtly way as they left. They had flung themselves into the world again; Leo had been delivered to this place and had shut the door. For a few moments he could hear the click of his mother's footsteps as she went briskly down the wooden staircase, and even something that might have been a word or two, exchanged bravely, a little laugh. He was, at that moment, thrilled and excited that the parents had finally gone. Out there was a library that had a copy of every book in the world – in this college there were people who had read and understood every book in English literature, whom he was going to meet. Downstairs, waiting for him at the Fresher's Mingle that started at six tonight, was a whole new exploratory world of cunt.

Next to him at the Fresher's Mingle was a boy, and Leo might as well start with him. He was glad that he'd made the decision about what clothes to wear, and had put on a pair of jeans and a shirt – that looked about right. One or two poor saps had put on their interview suits. The boy who had come in at the same time as him and had taken a glass of sherry was in jeans, too.

'Hello,' Leo said. 'I'm Leo. Are you starting here?'

'Am I starting here?' the boy said, with a theatrical spasm at being addressed with a question. His movement was like a fountain driven sideways by a burst of wind.

Leo smiled.

'Yes, I am,' the boy said. 'Is this normal? Do we meet everyone like this?'

Leo wasn't quite sure what the boy meant. 'What are you studying?'

'PPE,' the boy said. He smiled, an open, big smile, but not particularly aimed at Leo.

'I'm Leo,' Leo said, persevering just for the moment.

'Well, it's very nice to meet you, Leo,' the boy said, 'and I'm sure we'll meet again some time and have another interesting conversation.'

He walked away. Leo caught the eye of two girls who had been watching this; they seemed familiar. They covered their mouths, giggling.

'That was tough,' one of them said, a girl with untidy black hair wearing green slacks. 'He looked quite normal, too.'

'Probably one of the geniuses,' the other one said. She had red hair, straight down, and granny glasses; her macramé waistcoat was from another time altogether. 'I'm Clare and that's

Tree. I remember you, you were at the interview, looking nervous.'

'I'm nervous now,' Leo said. 'I'm really nervous.'

'Oh, why?'

'This is the cleverest room of people I've ever been in,' Leo said, for something to say.

'Well, you've found us, which is something,' Tree said – Tree? Oh, Teresa.

'I know,' Leo said. It was going quite well.

Then a man arrived – he was dark and unshaven, a mop of curly hair about his ears. 'Here, you,' he said to the girls.

'Oh, not you again,' Clare said. 'He's on my course,' she said to Leo. 'We found him staring at the same noticeboard we were staring at. And then he came up to charm my mum and get me to make him a cup of Nescafé. You're supposed to meet new people, Eddie, not hang around with the ones you've already met.'

'I'll meet this chap, then,' Eddie said. 'I'm Eddie. Who the hell are you?'

Eddie's voice was raucous, posh, confident, but he did not seem to be daunting the girls. He was the sort of man you would expect to meet on your first day in Oxford. Leo introduced himself.

'I'm sick of meeting people I knew at school,' Eddie said. 'I thought I'd get away from them by coming to Hertford. Isn't it hell?'

'I don't know anyone from school,' Tree said tranquilly. 'I'm the first person who came from my school to Oxbridge, as far as anyone knows or could remember.'

'And I went to Bedales,' Clare said. 'So it's a total mystery how I came to be able to read and write.'

The evening was like that. As he went round the room, the energetic conversations he had were with people who, he could see, were dull; the ones who wanted to talk to him about what A levels he'd done and what grades he'd got. The sticky, difficult ones were with people who were sizing him up, not very successfully. They didn't ask what his father did for a living, and once he brought it up anyway – he was a doctor's son, there was no reason for anyone to look down on him.

There was another question that Leo had not anticipated at all. A girl with a half-open mouth and a cocked eyebrow asked him first. 'What did you do in your year out?'

He hadn't had a year out, and said so with a smile and a shrug. She had an odd, eggy smell, this girl, and he didn't particularly care that she gave a short, dismissive laugh and replied that she supposed he was keen to get at it, couldn't wait for university. 'So what did –' Leo began, but she had turned away, shrieking as she recognized someone from school. And then, in the way of things, someone was answering the same question there, just behind him and, apparently, above his head.

'I taught English in India,' a male voice was saying. 'It was amazing. It took a day to reach the village. I don't think they'd seen ...' and there was something familiar about the voice. Leo half turned, and there was Tom Dick, talking about his year out in India. It was the same voice as six weeks ago, but the vowels had changed, and the volume, too. Tom Dick was talking confidently to a small group of girls and a clever-looking boy, dark, saturnine, energetically nodding. Tom Dick's summer, stuck with his mum, had been transformed into a year out in India.

'How amazing,' a posh girl with big hair was saying, a girl almost as tall as Tom Dick. 'I went to India last year, with Mummy and Daddy. We went to Rajasthan. I adored it. But the poverty – didn't you find the poverty awfully upsetting?'

'That was what I was there for,' Tom Dick said. 'It was frightful. But one coped.'

'Where were you?' a boy in the group was saying, but Tom Dick could all at once be said to become aware of Leo, a foot away. With that he became aware of himself. His high face was in the room, talking energetically with lies, rat-a-tat, to entranced faces a foot below his own. Was that what you did? Leo moved away. Once, later on, they turned and moved at the same time, and found themselves facing each other. Leo asked if Tom Dick was all right, observed that it was good to see him, and Tom Dick made a shocked, embarrassed grunt in response, twice. They might have been spies on a shared mission in a crowded room.

The next morning Leo left his room early, and went out to walk the streets. It was a beautiful day. He went into the porter's lodge, and read the notices on the board – here they were informal notices; the ones about work were on the subject boards behind glass. There was something called Daily Info – a large yellow sheet, close-printed, with details about film showings, cinemas called the Penultimate Picture Palace and Moulin Rouge, lonely-hearts adverts as well, which Leo read with interest. His mail would be in a pigeon hole; he looked in the wall of pigeon holes at Sk–Sz, but there was nothing for him. He left the college, and walked down past the Bod, as he was practising saying, past the beautiful circular library building and down the little pathway by the side of the church. The sky was a malleable blue, the stone everywhere the yellow and texture of soft fudge. He was going to like this. Later in the morning, there would be a meeting of the English students – undergraduates, he corrected himself – in one of the dons' rooms. He wondered if they were supposed to take *Praeterita* and *Sartor Resartus*.

An elegantly shabby figure was stumbling towards him, wandering from side to side across the broad pavements of the high street. It was the boy from last night – Eddie, the girls had called him. Leo smiled broadly at him, in greeting, raised his hand and finally, with certainty, said, 'Hi.'

The boy stared at him, paused. 'Do I know you?'

'We met last night,' Leo said. 'In Hertford.'

'Oh, God, yes,' Eddie said. 'Hi, hi. Sorry. Rough night. Just going back for a few hours' sleep.'

He stumbled past Leo in the general direction of their college. Leo had gone to bed at eleven or a little later; he had finished the evening with a dull pair of mathematicians called Mike and Tim in the college bar, sitting in the corner listening to them explaining Dungeons and Dragons. It had been

perfectly nice; he had not thought there was an option for any
of them to go out and not come back until eight in the
morning.

There was a principle there, and the principle was this: you
don't refuse something that has been willingly opened to you.
Leo would not refuse the hand of friendship, or question it.
That was what he would do, not say, 'Do I know you?' to someone who greeted him, not dismiss people. When something was
openly offered to you, the gift of friendship, a greeting, a smile,
you should smile and accept the kindness that someone had
offered, making themselves vulnerable.

It was not like him to come up with principles of behaviour.
It was the significance of the day – his first day – that had done
it. But there was a class at ten – a class or a meeting. He was
going to go to it, and for the first time, he would be there to be
introduced to a world that knew everything. Before now, the
paths that he could have taken towards knowledge had come to
an end, and you could see the end from where you stood. A set
book led to twenty books in the school library; and those led to
two hundred books in the central library; and that was good
enough for most people, especially since you would never meet
anyone else who had read what you had read. Now he felt as
though the doors were being flung open onto sunlit downs
where minds, like lambs, gambolled and grazed in herds. The
doors of the Bodleian were still shut and locked. It was too early
for anything but breakfast. He wanted to go to the library now,
this second, and begin to read a book he had never heard of.
They were all in there.

4.

'Where has your uncle gone – Daddy, I mean?' Blossom said.

The two boys were in the kitchen. For the fourth time in ten minutes, Tresco had gone to the fridge, opened it, peered into it and shut the door again. There was nothing in there – nothing but what Blossom had fetched back from the supermarket that morning, when she had shopped for meals, not for the idle little snacks that Tresco was after. Josh looked at his aunt. The way she had put the question confused him, and he said nothing. 'Where did your daddy go, Josh?' she asked again.

'I don't know,' Josh said. 'He said he had something to do and then he went out.'

'He didn't go out with Grandpa?'

'No,' Tresco said from the larder, his voice muffled. 'Grandpa went out earlier. He went out in the car. I think Uncle Leo went for a walk, or maybe he was going to catch a bus somewhere. Doesn't your dad have a car?'

'I don't know,' Blossom said, exasperated. 'I really give up. If anyone wants me, I'm in the bath.'

Josh raised his eyes at that, watched his aunt go. It was half past one. Josh had lived an irregular and unpredictable life; he did not always know where he was going to be sleeping in a week's time. But the adults in his life took baths at the same time of day, before breakfast, or at any rate in the morning, before they got dressed. Tresco came out of the larder. He looked enviously at the empty plate in front of Josh, the orange-smeared remains of the beans on toast he had made himself. Josh made himself look back.

'One of Mummy's baths,' Tresco said eventually.

Mummy overheard this. She was going upstairs, her face lit in flashes of blues, reds, purples, the sun falling through the stained-glass window above the stairwell. They could perfectly well go and see the patient later this afternoon, but just now, Blossom felt that she deserved a touch of

pampering, and solitude. One of Mummy's baths, she heard
Tresco say from the kitchen, and it amused her to have one
long-standing and recognizable habit. She crushed the word
eccentricity as it rose in her mind. People like her did not
have *eccentricities*: that was a middle-class, a wilful word
from the place she had come from. Blossom sometimes had
a bath in the middle of the day. She felt she needed one;
needed solitude and the locked door and time to be alone
with hot water and her thoughts.

She had brought her verbena soap and her cucumber sham-
poo, and rather wished she had brought some decent towels.
The towels here were bald and rough, the same old white towels
Hilary and Celia had had for at least twenty years. But the bathroom was, as she had always thought, a beautiful room; an
irregular shape because of the turret above; the washbasin sat in
the circular recess, the bath under the long, frosted window. It
was deliciously hot in here – it caught the sun in the mornings,
and the heated towel rail, a newish indulgence of Celia's, hadn't
been turned off for days. Blossom locked the door; in a tearing
hurry, she shucked off her pale blue dress, her white sandals, her
knickers and bra. Naked, she opened the hot tap, pushed the
plug into the hole; she stood before the mirror and looked at
herself. The roar of water, the juddering of the old boiler
surrounded her. She was safe and alone.

Four children, she murmured, not even saying the words out
loud as her lips moved. Around her neck was the dear little
chain and pendant her husband had bought her when the first
of them had been born – Tresco, she worked out in her solipsis-
tic nudity. He was downstairs; he was a letter T between her
breasts, the points marked in tiny diamonds. And then the
other children had come – three more Ts, marked with the same
chain and pendant, should they ask. She liked it. The room was
filling with steam; the mirror beginning to cloud. It was a long
mirror, floor to ceiling. Her father had always said that you
should know what your body looked like, and the foot-square
mirrors in other people's bathrooms had always struck her as

shameful. Now she wiped the clouding mirror with her forearm and stepped back.

What was it, that pale thing clarifying itself into a shape? A body; she could look at it as if at –

She looked at it, making sure of the analogy. It was not an object she could analyse remotely, but it was not *her* either. When she looked at her body, it was as if she had turned her eye on a no doubt beautiful acquisition that had been in the same position in her house for years. And now she moved her hands over it, feeling as her used and hardened palms slid down her still soft sides how her children must feel when an adult, hardened in the edges they reached out, touched their marshmallow softness of cheek. In the mirror, there was the body you had after forty-odd years and four children; it was good for that, but the breasts were different in shape – the feel of the skin underneath the hardened hands now had a grain like the grain of leather. She raised one breast in her hand, its liquid weight, its skin giving up; she lifted one leg and examined the oldest parts of her outer crust, her worn and wrinkled kneecaps, the thick yellow skin of her heels. How old was she down there, at her exhausted joints?

One day Stephen was going to leave her. Not today, not this year, but one day. She did not look as she had once looked, and she had seen Stephen's face in the bedroom at nights, caught his expression in the looking glass over the top of a book he was pretending to read. Money would go where it wanted to go, and Stephen would dye his hair and allow himself to be taken to nightclubs. She hoped that it would not happen until Thomas was a little older.

The bath was full; she closed the tap.

And the mirror now was misting over again, with drops of steam running across her pink and white reflection, like the trickle of sweat down her side. Her shape and her colour were beautiful, she had always known, and they were still beautiful, the subject of astonishment that she was the age she was. Over her soft bottom and thighs she went, and back up again, both her hands running up her sides and into her armpits, making shapes like a curlicued vase. She adored herself.

(Downstairs, in the kitchen, the boys were discussing it, and Tresco had just said, 'It's just one of Mummy's bathtimes,' and Josh had looked at his cousin, struck by something in his voice, to discover with amazement that Tresco's face had crumpled, his expression that of a hurt little boy. 'Mummy and her fucking baths.')

The body and she were alone together; out there was her life, and the people who felt it all right to come and ask her where they had put their best dress, or why that fucking useless boy, Norman, was it?, hadn't turned up when it was supposed to be today that he … The mind returned to the world outside. She turned it off like a tap. This was her moment of the solitary. *Pampering*. She loved to stand and look at her body and list its properties, to identify its inwardnesses and its losses, the scars and the long passages where the skin, when pinched, could only return slowly, thoughtfully, to its original flatness. She took a step forward; she wiped the steam-clouded glass; she opened her mouth and counted her remaining teeth. Three wisdoms were gone, a molar.

But if anyone saw her yawning into the looking glass like this they'd think she was a total and utter loony, fit for the bin, a prize chump all round.

The voice of sense and business had sounded like a gavel. She was going to have her bath. She wanted to think about what she was going to say to Mummy about this stupid divorce business. There was no point standing there and staring at herself in the nuddy all day long. There was some chance, as well, that when she was done, she'd find that Leo had come back and could fill her in. She wished it wasn't Leo: he had always been quite hopeless at this sort of thing. But now she unhooked her pendant, bundled her dark hair into a sort of bun with an old hairgrip from the bowl on the lavatory cistern, and slid with purpose into her long, hot bath. The boiler hissed. From downstairs she could hear the voice of her boy, the confident sound it made, as if calling through the woods it owned. There was sweat down her face, and steam condensed, too, and after a while she found that the salt liquid running from her eyes seemed to be tears. It was her age, she supposed, the habit of crying when no other bugger was around.

5.

Immediately afterwards, and on the diminishing occasions when somebody said to Leo, 'But I don't think I ever understood – why did you leave Oxford?' he would say, 'I don't know, but it was just impossible.' He had an idea. It was because he'd said the wrong thing to a girl, and the wrong thing had affected not just her but everyone for miles around. It acted like an old-fashioned map on the Paris Métro: a button was pressed, quite innocently, to a remote destination, and the lights had lit up, showing the crowd the full route. Leo had been ordinary, dim, overlooked, nothing special, and what the crowd had been waiting for. Someone to blame. After that he would never say, 'I want to taste your cunt,' to a woman; he had always said it enthusiastically, with tender and assumed naivety, and once in Sheffield, in a wood-panelled back room in a pub, a woman had grasped his hand, holding a pint of Guinness, and said, 'That's the nicest thing anyone's ever said to me.'

He was in quite a good room, there in Hertford; it was under the eaves, but pleasant. The second night he was there, the whole evening, the room was full of someone else's music. He didn't know what it was. It kept on until after two. In the end he slept through it. The room underneath him, he thought, but when it started up at ten on the third night, he thought he would be brave and go and make a friendly comment to his neighbour, and went downstairs in stockinged feet. An unfamiliar face answered the door. He was Geoffrey, he grudgingly offered, when Leo introduced himself, and Leo realized that there was no noise of music coming from the room at all. Behind Geoffrey Chan – his name was painted above the door – there was institutional space; a poster of a South American revolutionary; two green mugs and a kettle on a bookcase with a dozen books in it. Geoffrey Chan wished him good luck. He wasn't going to make trouble. And the noise was coming out of the room on the floor below, belonging to Mr E. Robson. There was a sweet smell that Leo identified as marijuana.

In fact there were only five people in the room, and the boy turning in astonishment to him was Eddie who couldn't remember his name – he must be the owner of the room. He recognized the others: the posh girl from the other night with the smell of eggs and the half-open mouth, and Tree, who did English, and her friend Clare. Tree had sat next to him at the seminar yesterday, and had said she hadn't a clue what they were supposed to be doing – she was all right, he had thought, but seeing her here made him wonder. The fifth person in the room was Tom Dick. He stared at Leo; he looked away.

'Would you mind turning it down a bit?' Leo said. 'I'm trying to do a bit of work upstairs.'

'I thought it was someone else upstairs,' Eddie said. 'A ching-chong Chinaman. Who the hell are you, then?'

'I'm two floors up,' Leo said. 'It's really loud.'

'Daddy said my best chance to get in was by applying for theology,' the egg-scented girl was saying, ignoring Leo. 'I'm not awfully bright, not like my sister Louise. So I did what he said and it worked. He said, "Lucy – just get the summer job at Harvey Nicks for two months, selling perfume or whatever, go to Oxford and get a degree in theology, then you can, I don't know –"'

'That's a new one,' Clare said to Eddie. 'Before long you're going to be getting people who don't even live on this staircase. You're terrible, Eddie, you really are.'

'You've not been in the college five minutes and straight away you're getting us a frightful reputation,' Tom Dick rattled off. He did not look at Leo as he spoke. His voice had changed and the way he said words. Leo had never heard anyone seriously say 'orff' for 'off' before, and it appeared to him that Tom Dick had not done it convincingly.

'Hello, Tom,' Leo said. 'How's it going?'

Now Tom Dick did look at him, with an expression of pure dislike and vengeance. 'Oh, it's you,' he said. 'How's it going with *you*? No, no, Lucy, you're doing it quite, quite wrong – the way you do it is –'

'Turn it down, Eddie,' Tree said. 'You need to be a bit reasonable.'

She smiled at Leo, the one person in the room who was prepared to acknowledge that he had come in at all. Eddie leant over and lowered the volume on his stereo – a black plastic affair with a rigid plastic lid and separate speakers. Captain Beefheart: Leo was oddly proud to have identified *Trout Mask Replica*. Pete had been obsessed with it, all last year. But he was hardly through the door, not even closing it behind him, when the five of them inside burst out laughing. 'I've just got to tell you,' Tom Dick's new posh voice insisted, 'I simply have to make it utterly and completely clear ...'

The work was what he was here to do. It progressed in a world quite separate from the quicker processes by which five people were so intimate that they would lie around together with *Trout Mask Replica* playing, as if they had known each other for ever. He was not sure he had really become anyone's friend yet, and in its place was the yawning aversion of a gaze that had happened when he went into a neighbour's room to complain about the noise.

The next day was the first day of lectures, and after breakfast he found himself walking towards the faculty with the others. It was a beautiful morning – again that shimmer of the clash of colours, the dense yellow of the stone against the deep October blue of the sky. There was Tree; she gave him a sidelong look, a half-smile.

'We're going to the lecture on George Eliot, are we?' she said. 'I've not read much beyond *Middlemarch*. I read that because

Mrs Kilpatrick said it was the best novel ever. And I read *Silas Marner* but that was a right load of old rubbish.'

'What's that Eddie boy like?' Leo said.

'Oh, you're there, are you?' Tree said. 'He's a dickhead, really. I don't know why everyone says he's such a laugh and a hoot. He got us up to his room and then he played us this terrible music, one record after another. Do you know that Thomas? I didn't know you knew him from before, from school.'

He was going to say that Tom Dick was a terrible liar: that he hadn't had a year in India; that he had never been called Thomas in his life; that that was not what his voice had sounded like until, at most, five days ago. 'Yes, we did the entrance exam together. He was at my school.'

'I thought you said your school was a comprehensive or something,' Tree said.

Leo gave her a sideways assessment. Her eyes were cast down, her face demure; she hugged her books to her chest. Her hair, which he had thought untidy and tangled, was in fact beautifully chaotic, that sweet disorder. Only somewhere in her mouth was there the suggestion of amusement.

'Well, he said he didn't really know you at all. He's a funny boy, that Thomas. Lucy thought she knew someone who knew his parents but it turned out not. So what have you read in the George Eliot line?'

That, it turned out, was the question of the lecturer, almost at once. What Leo had read in the George Eliot line – the point was not its extensiveness, but the sincerity, the shock of recognition that the mass of words had come down to. He had read on after *Daniel Deronda* not in a spirit of completeness or duty, but only wanting to find in *Felix Holt* and *Scenes from Clerical Life* the same force of recognition and understanding that he had experienced in the face, exactly evoked, of Gwendolen Harleth. That was the book that had struck him with violence, and ever since, he had wanted to look out into the world to see a stranger's face full of anger and discontent, to say to himself *Was she beautiful, or was she not beautiful?*; and in the meantime to devote himself to the means of understanding, to books and literature and the words on the page. The lecturer began by asking who had read what books by George Eliot, and asking them in order of likely popularity. In the large lecture hall, devoid of natural light, with a middle-aged man rubbing his hands, he felt that the whole question of a life's work, of an insight that might lead to recognition, a century later, had been reduced to the opportunity to perform as good little boys and girls. He knew that, despite everything, George Eliot and he himself and anyone she would have wanted as a reader had more in common with Gwendolen Harleth than with what was happening here, good little boys and girls. Had they read *Mill on the Floss ... Middlemarch ... Silas Marner ... Daniel Deronda ... Adam Bede ... Scenes from Clerical Life ... Felix Holt*. And what was the real, the ultimate test? The number of hands being raised had steadily diminished, and as he rubbed his hands and said *Romola*, only two or three hands were raised. Good little girls and one boy, sitting in the front row. But that was not the ultimate test, to have read it all: the ultimate test of literature was to have set it down in mid-flow and to have thought, after a dozen words that were like fire, that here was something that struck through to you, a mind that understood. The lecturer, pleased and satisfied, started explaining about the nonconformist religious traditions.

'I've got to go and buy a toothbrush,' Tree said, when their lectures were done for the morning. 'I'll see you back at the ranch. I've been brushing my teeth with a toothbrush, I thought there was something strange about it, and I realized this morning, I got a postcard from my sister Karen, I'd taken hers by mistake. I packed the wrong one.'

'Well, it's yours now,' Leo said. They walked down the steps of the English faculty; she gave a bright, tight little wave to the others, a despairing shrug to the last of them.

'Oh, I couldn't do that,' Tree said. 'Cleaning your teeth with a toothbrush you thought was yours and using one you know for a fact isn't the right one. That's different. So I'll see you later.'

'I've got to go and get something in any case,' Leo said. 'I'll walk with you.'

'Oh, right,' Tree said. 'You hadn't read anything, then.'

'What's that?'

'You hadn't read anything. When they said, who's read what by George Eliot, you didn't –'

'Oh – no. It was embarrassing. It was like being back at school. I've read some George Eliot.'

'Oh, right.'

'You know …' But Leo was thinking what it would take to produce an account of that moment. He had read that sentence in *Daniel Deronda* which had made him think that somehow he had been observed, and the way he responded to that – 'It was just a bit embarrassing.'

'Not as embarrassing as everyone thinking you've not read a word of George Eliot before turning up, and it's all Victorian literature this term. I loved *Middlemarch*. I thought that Rosamond Vincy had a point, though. I don't know what she did wrong, wanting her husband to make a living and be reasonable to people she knew.'

'I know what you mean,' Leo said. 'What did you do for A level?'

'I see what you're saying, Leo,' Tree said with amusement. 'But I loved the books we did for A level – it wasn't just a test to get through. Do you know what we did? We did *The Rape of the Lock*. Most people couldn't stand it, couldn't see the point of it, but I loved it. I still love it. It was just so clever and, you know, the things it said. I had no difficulty learning the quotes for that – they just stuck there. Like a song. *The light militia of the lower sky.*'

'You love literature,' Leo said. They were in a narrow lane between high stone walls; diagonal columns of light struck solidly across their path. There was silence around and, above, the deep blue of the late-morning sky.

'Of course I do,' Tree said. 'I've always loved to read. It's the best thing ever. *And maids turned bottles, call aloud for corks …*'

'Call aloud for what?'

'For corks. It's a bit rude, you see. That's *The Rape of the Lock*. Didn't you do that?'

'No, I never did,' Leo said. 'We did John Steinbeck. That wasn't so good. It's going to be good here.'

'Of course it is,' Tree said. 'It's going to be fantastic.'

'One of these days,' Leo said lightly, 'I'd really like to taste your cunt.'

It was an unfamiliar street, but as he pronounced the last word it appeared to him that it was not just an unfamiliar but a wrong street, a street in which he had found himself with no warning or explanation. The girl he was walking next to continued walking, sedately, her books and notebook under her hand, as if he had said nothing at all. He felt sure he had said the same thing in the same circumstances, and a woman had in response talked back with indirect amusement, accepting the offer without saying so, or sometimes dismissing him but without much hostility. People had said to this rumpled girl with the beautiful teeth and the wry, shrugging manner something that amounted to what he had said. There was no need for her to say, 'Actually, I think I'm going to head off here. See you later,' and walk briskly down a side street, not looking back.

He could not take it in his stride, what he had found himself saying, or the response that was no response, like a final step on the staircase disappearing under the foot. The world around him shivered and trembled, and as he thought of it, he had to shut his eyes against the world. That afternoon he devoted himself to Browning, not in an armchair but sitting at a desk, reading one monologue after another, making notes as he went. The desk faced the wall, and he found he could concentrate. Only sometimes did Browning's energy, his cryptic shouty manner, pass into another room where the meaning subsided into blankness, and Leo found himself once again knowing what it was like to say *I would like to taste your cunt* to a woman he had hardly met, mistakenly thinking they might have been flirting, and for her to dismiss him briskly. She had no reason on earth not to tell everyone. She came out of the episode really quite well.

And at suppertime he found himself sitting not so far from Tree, and she was sitting as she always was with Clare, but also with Tom Dick and Eddie and that egg-breathed girl called Lucy, the one who had got in by doing theology. He could not hear what they were saying, apart from one moment when Lucy's braying voice cut through the noise of the hall, saying, 'But I don't understand – what on earth did he think –' and a little later, 'How disgusting and pathetic,' and that was it. There was no doubt about it. He could hear that the conversation had begun with them listening intently to what Tree had to say, and she was making light of it, but by the time the soup had been taken away, Tom Dick was at the rapt centre of attention, telling them all what he knew. He was squaring this somehow with his account of his history, the suggestion that he had gone to a different sort of school from the one Leo had gone to, and that nevertheless Tom Dick knew all about what Leo was like from – what? Youth orchestras? Sports teams? Was he saying that Leo's mother was his family's housekeeper? Impossible to guess, but he was doing it. They were all rather gripped, and some people in the seats surrounding them, people who, surely, were in the second or third year, had started leaning in and asking fascinated questions, their elbows propping up, their fingers making decisive and principled points. Only once could he hear what Tom Dick was saying, and surely he was meant to hear. The pudding had arrived, and Tree had pushed hers away. Tom Dick stopped talking in his lowered, muttering way, and said, with brisk clarity, 'Those shy people – they can say anything. And if you're not going to eat that, I'd love to taste your –' But there was a burst of laughter, immediately followed by a burst of scolding for Tom Dick and the boys who had laughed. Lucy was rubbing the shoulders of Tree, making exuberant noises of scolding and pity, saying, 'It's not at all funny, it's not funny at all, poor you, poor Tree, poor thing,' and putting her in her place. Leo knew he shouldn't have said what he'd said, but he now felt that he'd politely given Tree a bold possibility as an equal. She'd turned it down as women sometimes turned down the offer, but the consequences of her refusal were to reduce her within her group to the girl from the comprehensive. Now she was the clever, pretty, helpless girl with the northern accent, the one they had to be kind to.

'Are you going to eat that?' the boy sitting opposite Leo said. He hadn't touched his pudding, and everyone else had finished. The boy was sharp-eyed, alert, a flop of black hair over his Asian face. 'I'll have it if you aren't. I'm starving still.'

'Here you go,' Leo said and, with a difficult entanglement between legs, feet and long bench, pulled himself out and walked briskly to the door. With a bit of luck, people might think he was feeling ill.

Now he was the fresher whose idea of flirtation was to ask a girl whether he could lick her cunt, or in some retellings if he could finger her, or in a version that took only two days to emerge, to say to the woman, 'Can I smell your cunt?' and for her to give the prompt response, 'I hope not – I had a good wash only this morning.' It happened in the street, at the freshers' bop, at a lecture on Dickens, in a sandwich queue – any number of places. The girl screamed, or slapped him, or reported him to the authorities, or shrugged and coped with it as women always had to. The thing that never altered was that it was Leo. He was the man who had said that thing to a girl, and in the rapid establishment of friendships in waves of warm, amused laughter, he was the one who was left holding the turnip in protest and puzzlement. One day he turned up at his weekly tutorial to find that, as Mr Bentley briskly and amicably explained, he wouldn't have a tutorial partner from now on, since Mr Allsop – a devout member of the Christian Union and the Tolkien Society – had decided he wanted to be paired up with Miss Britten in future. Mr Allsop had not been much of a social connection, but he had been somebody to talk to from time to time, to ask politely how things were going with the Matthew Arnold essay. If Tim Allsop had been told that Leo asked girls if he could lick their cunts, then everyone knew.

From time to time Leo found himself walking towards Tom Dick, whose name these days was Thomas. Perhaps in Hall, or perhaps outside, walking round the quad, once or twice on the staircase going up to Eddie's room on the second floor of Leo's staircase. Tom Dick had won a game that Leo had hardly known he was a contestant in. Each time, he would look down towards Leo; they came towards each other and, without saying anything, he brightened his eyes to a terrible gaiety, drew back his shoulders, bared his wet teeth in something that might be a smile, or a parody of a smile, or the beginnings of laughter. It was for his friends to avert their eyes; Tom Dick was always surrounded by his friends, laughing at his sallies, impressed by his hands folded behind his back and his elaborate stories of life in India and life in the absurd ruin of a house in Yorkshire. Every year had a scapegoat. The gazes of others turned elsewhere. They understood that it could have been them.

Above all, in his room alone, trying to get on with what he was there for, the books and with literature, he found his mind returning in a transfixed way to the sentence he had spoken to her. It was like the return of the mind to a sentence in *Daniel Deronda*, worrying away at it, unable to believe that the sentence that had said so much might have disappeared. The sentence he had said to the girl had indicated what he was, and what he might become. The sentence – this sentence and that sentence – was always there. This sentence: *Was she beautiful or was she not beautiful?* This sentence: *One day I want to taste your cunt.*

'Your father's done something awful,' his mother said. There had been a note in the pigeon hole in the porter's sloping hand – *Pls call your mother*. He had been writing letters each week to his mother and father. There was plenty to tell them, even if you left out what they probably wouldn't understand. He had passed the time of day with people, and he said hello to people when he saw them – it was not hard to put up a good face. It was only three years, after all. He spoke to them occasionally, on the

phone, but the payphones were at the bottom of a staircase, and
he knew that anyone waiting could hear what you were saying.
There was always someone waiting. So his phone calls, once a
week or so, were brisk and cheerful, and over in five minutes.
He phoned his mother, as requested.

'Here we go,' Leo said heartily.

'He's put his back out. I don't know how he did it. It's never
happened before. He's had to cancel his surgery all this week.
It's very inconvenient. I've got to go in there every ten minutes
to listen to him making his awful jokes and pretending to be
cheerful.'

'I bet,' Leo said. 'Is he mobile?'

'No – I said I was having to go in there every ten minutes.
He can't do anything. He's upstairs in bed with his knees drawn
up pretending to be cheerful and in reality complaining about
absolutely everything. Ordering me around like a … *doctor*. I'm
ignoring most of the orders, as you can imagine. He can just
about get to the loo. He says it's sciatica rather than a slipped
disc, but in my opinion –'

'He's the doctor,' Leo said.

'Yes,' his mother said peremptorily. 'Ordering me around like
his receptionist. But the point of this – shall I call you back?'

She called him back.

'As I was saying, the point is that, aren't you supposed to be
picked up a week on Saturday? Was that the date? Well, obviously, I can't leave your father in the state he's in,' Celia said.
'You know what he's like. But then rather a marvellous thing has
happened. I was down at Sainsbury's with Hugh and there, in
the detergent aisle – Do you know who I mean by Edna and
Keith? Keith, his surname – Keith Archibald?'

'No, not at all.'

'Keith was a nurse in the hospital where your father did his
training. He's long retired now. Edna, poor woman, she's very
nice-natured but, your father always says, a little bit simple.
They're very happy and pleasant, a very nice couple. Christians.
Keith was a pillar of the Northern General Christian Staff

Association. They've come to our rescue. It's their Christian duty, apparently, to help out their neighbours wherever possible, and this time we're their neighbours, and they don't mind driving down in their car, picking up your stuff and driving you back to Sheffield. It's ideal.'

'Mummy,' Leo said, but he didn't know what, if anything, he would be remonstrating about. In ten days, he would be picked up by two people called Edna and Keith, Christians, and anyone who saw them arriving would think they were his parents. Celia explained the arrangements, saying at the end that of course they would talk again; he could talk to Keith or Edna nearer the time too. He put down the phone. He winced at his own snobbery.

That was towards the end of term, in week seven. At the end of that week, there was a party. There was no avoiding it. You had to hear about it, in seminar rooms or in the dining hall or in the common room, reading the newspaper. There were invitations in the pigeon holes, dozens of them, photocopied on pink or blue paper – the same colours that Daily Info was printed on, with an amateurish drawing of someone meant to be Eddie in a bathtub with a bottle and a spliff, his eyes X'd out to show that he was incapacitated, drunk and high. Everyone knew about it – as a great joke. Eddie had invited everyone. There was a dress code; it was supposed to be a great secret, the substance of the dress code, but everyone knew about that, too. People Eddie liked were told that they had to dress in white. People Eddie had decided he didn't like had been told that it was a Black Party, head to toe black. There were four people who, everyone knew, had been told they had to dress entirely in red.

'It was Thomas Dick's idea,' Clare was heard to say. 'I do think it's simply brilliant. I can't wait.'

Was there anyone he had not invited? People had been invited who had never met him, or didn't think they'd met him. It would be happening downstairs. Even Mr Bentley had been invited, though he said at the beginning of one seminar to Tree, who asked directly, that he wasn't sure – he would make an effort to look in. What was Mr Bentley invited to wear?

Leo smiled faintly. He tried to make a good, amused, clever point about Clough – he'd really enjoyed Clough, in fact. He looked patiently forward, waiting for the end of any conversation that wasn't about Clough. Presently it came to an end. He got up, tried to engage one of the others in conversation – had he seen him going into Browns in the covered market yesterday? Did he think Browns was the best? – but without much success. He left the seminar room. They were talking about the party, which was going to happen in two days' time. He'd got a shed-load of beer in. Daddy's credit card, but who cared?

He determined not to pity himself. There had been parties before, in Sheffield, he hadn't been invited to. That had been absolutely fine. He had done something else. It was not true that this party had been mounted for the sole purpose of not inviting him, of inviting everyone but him. He thought of the pronoun in Cherokee that Mühlhäusler had talked about in his Wednesday lecture last week: the first person plural excluding the person spoken to. *We-but-not-you are going to have fun on Saturday night.* That was perfectly all right. He thought about it, and concluded that, since the way to and from his room could only lead past Eddie's, he would not make himself conspicuous by going out. He envisaged his wretched smile, edging past the beautiful people in white, in black, even in red here and there, scuttling up the stairs. They should not know that he was there at all.

At six, some shrieks up the stairs; the intimates had arrived. A champagne cork popped.

At six thirty, music began; thunderous, rich, unexpected. The party was beginning with recordings of opera – was it Wagner? Out in the court, people raised their faces to the first-floor window, laughing. Many of them were already in white, a procession of virgins, lurching with bottles.

By seven the crowd noise from downstairs had dissolved voices and words into a sound, as of the sea. On top, in sudden bursts, shrieks and attempts by the rugby club to sing along.

A little later, the applause of feet in boots on the wooden stairs, up and down, coming right up to the landing outside Leo's room. He tensed himself. He had shut and locked the outer door to his room, indicating that he was either out or not to be disturbed. It was called 'sporting the oak'. There was nothing to indicate that he was in the room, unless they went outside and saw a chink of light between his curtains. But the rowdy ascent was some sort of race; the sprint up the stairs happened six or seven times, with cheering, and then the popping of more champagne corks, a kind of chant.

After an hour or so, the music changed: some kind of pop with drums and a screaming singer.

After eleven, a couple stood and had a conversation in the court. There was some acoustic peculiarity, and Leo found he could hear everything they were saying with the precision and intimacy of a paranoiac. He knew what people like that thought about him, if they thought about him at all. They were enjoying themselves. He should not think badly of them or of what they were saying about him, with hilarity.

By midnight, he had read nearly four hundred pages of *Martin Chuzzlewit*.

At some point after midnight, or perhaps after one, a long and prolonged argument between someone who might have been egg-smelling Lucy, certain of her rights, and a weary-sounding porter took place on the stairs. The music, which had turned to something like Yes, was lowered.

In a while, a girl's voice rose in complaint or hysteria, and answering it, Tom Dick's voice, but amplified somehow, through some megaphone. Up the stairs the voice came, and it was chanting something in French. '*Si vous jugez*,' it said. '*Si vous jugez – vous serez souvent trompée*,' and the *trompée* was full of delight in itself, plumping down on the word at having found precisely the right one. '*Trompée. Parce-que ce qui paraît n'est presque jamais la vérité, la vérité, la vérité …*'

It was unfamiliar to Leo, but he understood it well enough. He had sat for long enough at school listening to this voice painfully negotiating subjunctives to understand the words it was now producing in drink and disdain. And now the voice said, still through the megaphone, 'I know. I know. I've got a marvellous idea. It's marvellous. Listen listen listen. Let's have some fun. Let's just have ourselves some fun.'

Leo's hand had been gripping his book firmly for some time now. He realized that he had taken in nothing of *Martin Chuzzlewit* for dozens of pages, his hand turning them in a mechanical rhythm. But now the voices downstairs hardened into a two-syllable call, voices joining in and stomping. What was it? He tried not to listen, but there it was. '*Shy boy. Shy boy. Shy boy.*' They were coming up the stairs, half a dozen people by the sound of it, and still chanting, '*Shy boy shy boy shy boy.*' They were hammering on his door – it was banging through both locked doors. He had not thought that was what people had concluded about him, that his withdrawal and solitude was down to a pathetic shyness. The judgement of everyone around him had gone from grateful contempt for him saying the worst thing you could say to a girl to hilarious contempt for him as someone who could not speak to anyone. *Shy boy. Shy boy. Shy boy.* In ten minutes or so they went away – it was Tom Dick and Eddie and voices he did not recognize. The music downstairs had long been turned up again.

He didn't sleep until five, and woke again at eight. There was no point in not going to breakfast. Besieged, he had had nothing to eat the night before. He was not going to pity himself. He was going to get on with life, and do well in his degree, and read all the books he had wanted to read. He was going to walk past the Beckettian detritus on his staircase, the bottles and bodies and torn waste of the morning after debauchery, a man continuing his duty in a landscape that would not support it. He almost put a tie on.

He sat on his own in the dining hall. There was hardly anyone in apart from the rowing squad, back from an early-morning practice and getting through a mound of bacon. To his surprise, a tray was placed opposite his, and someone sat down. It was Geoffrey Chan. It had not occurred to Leo that anyone else in the college could have suffered from the party downstairs last night, rather than enjoyed it. Geoffrey Chan came to the point.

'If I had a record player,' he said, 'I would put it on full volume, this morning, the most unpleasant music I could think of, and get it to repeat for several hours, and go out for a walk.'

'I don't know that anything would be enough,' Leo said. 'I'm sorry. It was bad enough for me, two floors up.'

'Yes,' Geoffrey Chan said. He set down his spoon in the muesli and, with his second and third fingers, chewed at an itch at the base of the thumb on his other hand. There was something excessive about the energy he did it with, like a dog gnawing at fleas in its toes. 'It was very bad.'

'They didn't invite you,' Leo said.

'Oh, no,' Geoffrey Chan said. 'They didn't ask me. They don't know me, in fact. Everyone in this college, if they gave any thought to the matter, they certainly think that I'm studying maths.'

'Maths?'

'You know – because of. No. I'm actually a historian. You wouldn't know if you weren't actually in my year and in my seminar group. Or I suppose if you were a mathematician. You'd know I wasn't a mathematician then.'

'That's tough,' Leo said.

'Around four a.m.,' Geoffrey Chan said, 'I came to the conclusion that I could, in fact, just leave this place and go back home. I didn't need to stay here. My mum and dad are only sixty miles away. And that was a great comfort at four a.m. But I don't think it's going to happen. Do you eat that crap? The baked beans?'

'They'd be very disappointed, too, your parents,' Leo said.

'Oh, yeah,' Geoffrey Chan said. 'There'd be plenty of that. They came from the old country. They knew about Oxford a bit, but not the stuff about parties and jazz and cocktails and champagne and all that shit. And the lying.'

'The lying.'

'Oh, yeah. You know when they tell lies – they say their uncles are dukes or that they went to Swiss finishing schools. They wouldn't have known about that, my mum and dad. They just think it's the best place you could go to as a student. My parents, they've only been in this country twenty years. They're not going to be OK with their son walking out on something like this. It was just a nice thought at four in the morning, the thought that you could give up.'

'Best not to give up,' Leo said. He marvelled that he was able to have a conversation at all, that Geoffrey Chan was talking to him in an ordinary way.

'No,' Geoffrey Chan said. 'But at least those arseholes weren't running up and down stairs to shout abuse through my keyhole. I think if that happened to me I might really give up. I hope one of them had an overdose or something. That would make me chuckle. I suppose they were taking drugs.'

'Thanks, Geoffrey,' Leo said. He had to get up and put his tray back, leave the hall. He couldn't cope with Geoffrey Chan's sympathy. There was only six days to go.

6.

In her parents' new house, Aisha waited. She worked. She waited. It was only Dr Capper's last class that she would be missing if she didn't go back to Cambridge, she had concluded, and that would not be vital. She had brought her notes up, and could get on with the writing of her dissertation.

Initially, once told of this, her mother had said 'Fine. Excellent.' But some kind of conversation had taken place subsequently – of course Daddy knew about dissertations – and she came into Aisha's room in the morning to ask whether they would not be expecting her back in Cambridge. 'This is work, I hope – not some kind of holiday.' But Aisha gestured at the notebooks open on the desk. She looked, at any rate, as if she were hard at it. Her mother asked what she would like for lunch, and Aisha said that anything would be fine. She had thought about it, and it seemed to her that by now she must be safe from the party leftovers. Next door, Leo Spinster was walking around the garden, poking at a plant or two. He was wearing a blue jacket. Aisha thought it might have been denim.

The next day her cousin Fanny called. There was only one telephone in the house, and Aisha was very conscious that her mother and Raja were listening – Raja was still at home because of his throat. Fanny was trying to discover what the state of affairs was between Aisha and Enrico, but since Raja kept getting up and walking past, Aisha was determined to be as unhelpful as possible. After a while, Fanny gave up: she told Aisha a long story about her boyfriend Matthew buying her a bunch of yellow roses.

If there had been nobody around to listen, Aisha would have said this to her cousin Fanny: that nobody in the house had any idea what it was like, being in love.

In the evening, Aisha thought she heard Dr Spinster singing while doing the washing-up. She half rose from her seat. In fact it was Leo. 'What is it?' Nazia said to her daughter. 'Had you forgotten something?'

Whole days passed in which Aisha wrote only forty or fifty words. One day she sat in the study at the back of the house and, for hours, watched her brother Raja juggling. He had learnt in Italy on holiday, and now he was making sure of his skill again, juggling first with two balls, then when he was confident of repeating the parabola, three. He tossed the balls, proper leather green and red juggling balls, from one hand to the other. Over the fence was Leo Spinster. At the end of the Spinsters' garden Dr Spinster was doing something complex with secateurs to a fruit tree. Leo called over the fence to Raja, and then, quite carelessly, took three of the loquats from the tree and began to juggle. For a moment Leo and Raja were both juggling with three things on either side of the fence; Raja remembered himself and, out of something like politeness, dropped the balls, shook his head. Leo was gratified: he appeared to be offering advice.

A letter from Enrico arrived. It thanked Sharif and Nazia for what it called a lovely weekend, although Sharif's name was wrongly spelt. He hoped to see the whole family again very soon. Nazia opened and read it, mouth pursed. Although two weeks late, it was, she mentioned to Aisha, a very polite letter. There was nothing wrong, Aisha assured her in return. 'He says that he had a splendid time which he will never forgive,' Nazia said, showing Aisha the line with some amusement. Aisha smiled with restraint before going upstairs to carry on working on her dissertation. The family next door were nowhere to be seen. They must have gone out. They were probably at the hospital where the mother, Aisha recalled, was dying of bowel cancer.

One day Aisha realized that she had written only fifteen words the day before. They were 'We hope to return to this important matter in due course, in its proper place.' She determined to stay inside all day, writing. The dissertation had interested her: the prosecution of war criminals and their Bengali collaborators after 1971. It was six days since she had put her letter to Leo Spinster through the letterbox next door. She had no idea what he had thought of it.

At some point during the day, Fanny telephoned. Aisha took the telephone into the dining room, shutting the door so that nobody would hear. Fanny told her that her mother, Rekha, had discovered all about her boyfriend Matthew. (They had been together for four years now.) 'Mummy just wants to know if I've gone too far with Matthew,' Fanny said. 'It's so unreasonable.'

She spoke to Leo's elder sister; they found themselves at the postbox together. Aisha had contrived a walk, though she really had nothing that needed posting. The sister was called Blossom, as she introduced herself.

'Those must be your boys,' Aisha said.

'One is,' Blossom said. 'The other is actually my brother Leo's. Didn't he mention? You were so kind, driving him to the hospital that time.'

Aisha smiled; she made a small performance of the grateful immigrant, taking one hand in the other, left in right and then right in left. She made a note of Blossom's pearls, surely too large to be real. She had never met anyone called Blossom before. She considered pointing out that she had driven Leo to the hospital three times, not just once.

'But he can thank you himself,' Blossom said. 'Here he is.'

They had reached the gate of the Spinsters' house, and Leo was standing there with a letter in his hand – with the letter in his hand, indeed. He might have been waiting for Aisha. Blossom waved inconsequentially behind her, leaving Aisha at the gate with Leo holding her letter. She stopped; she looked him in the face.

'Are you going to the postbox?' he said.

'I've just been,' she said.

'Let's walk,' he said. 'Would you mind? It's not every day – your letter. I got your letter.'

'Yes,' Aisha said. Already she hated him. She wished she had never laid eyes on him. He was smiling in an unfamiliar but practised way, and chopped at his wrist with the side of the envelope. It appeared almost as clean as when it had been put through his door. He hadn't read it more than twice.

'I don't know what I was –' Aisha said.

'It's very flattering for someone on the verge of middle age like me to get a letter like that,' he said. He was probably in his early thirties.

'You don't need to say anything,' Aisha said.

'But I think I do need to say something,' he said. 'I know it's not the thing, but I really need to give you some advice.'

'I get the point,' Aisha said.

'It's not about me turning you down,' he said. 'Which I am doing, by the way. But there are plenty of men out there who would get a letter like this and –'

'I don't know that I would write a letter like that to a man who – to plenty of men,' Aisha said.

'You don't know what men are like,' he said. Aisha could feel her lips pressing against each other with the effort of not saying anything; her right hand was gripping her left elbow. 'You're really very young, you know. You might not have seen as much of life as you think you have.'

'I've seen plenty of life,' Aisha said, not able to stop herself. She had got Leo Spinster completely wrong. He was someone who talked like a vicar on the radio.

'I know it feels like that,' Leo said. 'But you haven't, you really haven't. I know what Oxford and Cambridge are like. You feel that you could run the world from there. I went there for a term and two days and I couldn't stand it any more.'

'Why did you leave?' she said.

'I don't know,' Leo said. 'It was just impossible.'

'What time is it?' she said, more for something to say than anything else.

'What, now?' Leo said. 'I don't know. I haven't got my watch on.'

He looked away, embarrassed. It was too much for so small a failure, but the letter in his hand, she recalled, had talked about his watch, how it banged around his thin wrist. She had somehow struck at his emotions with that, and he had remembered it.

'I want you to promise me something,' Leo Spinster said. It seemed to her that he wanted to stay in control and, having rehearsed this conversation, he was at an advantage. She had rehearsed other conversations, but not this one. 'I want you to promise me that you will never, ever write that sort of letter to a man again, unless you're actually engaged to him, in fact. It was ardent, it was passionate, it was a beautiful letter, Aisha –'

'Don't say that,' she said. What she meant was that he had used three adjectives that nobody ever used; he had rehearsed what he was going to say.

'– but it won't do. It just won't do. I'm really sorry, but I want to help you not to make a mistake like that in the future. OK?'

'OK,' she said. That evening, before going to bed, she only wrote in her diary that she had fallen asleep on the sofa in the afternoon. She had had a strange dream about Aunty Sadia and Uncle Mahfouz. They were teaching at Oxford in the dream, she confessed to her diary.

7.

The last Saturday Leo spent at Oxford, two Christians called Edna and Keith arrived and, by anyone who saw them carrying boxes down the stairs, were taken to be Leo's parents. He was watching out for them. Keith had left a message with the porter's lodge to say that they expected to be there between ten and ten thirty – meanly, Leo reconstructed the full message Keith had left from the wearily abbreviated summary. He put in all the 'Traffic permitting' and 'I'm hoping there will be parking available in the vicinity' and all the other things that porters had heard a thousand times. He deplored this in himself. He made the allowance that Keith, too, would want to set out nice and early to avoid the worst of the morning rush. From half past eight he sat at the window, looking down into the quad. His father had said he had met them in Sheffield, but Leo was not at all sure he would recognize them.

At five past nine he recognized them. He did not think he had ever seen them before, but their demeanour was obvious. They hovered in the lodge, and one of the younger porters pointed at the door to Leo's staircase. Edna was wearing a tangerine coat, woolly and scrupulously cared for, at least fifteen years old, and a best hat; Keith was wearing a suit. It was Edna who stepped brightly forward and started to take the most direct route to Leo's room; it was the porter who stepped forward sharply and called out. Half a dozen kids, loafing about, reading the notices, enjoyed Edna throwing her hands to her face and scuttling off the grass. They were wondering whose parents these could be, almost the first to turn up.

Leo felt horror and shame, of course, but in there, too, was a sense of no longer belonging, and of pity and sympathy for this kind pair. He had not made any connection with Oxford: he did not belong here, and even the Bodleian had started to acquire its own terrors, was no longer a place just for the piling up of books. He had tried but failed. And then there was home. Once there had been a network of friendship and obligation and society that had connected him to Edna and Keith, who, after all, despite her tangerine woolly coat, lived just down the road. Now he was not so sure. The horror and shame that had come over him in a wave was Oxford's doing: he would not have felt that three months ago, not in quite the same way, and it had succeeded in making him understand he no longer belonged to Sheffield, either. Someone who came to collect him would put on their best hat and a suit. Where was he to make his life? The answer came swiftly: *London.*

In the minute before Keith and Edna knocked at his door, Leo submitted himself to everything that could be worst in him: to snobbery and coldness, to feeling ashamed of who he was and who other people conceived of themselves as, to gracelessness and thanklessness. He felt that he could quite easily say, at some point this morning, 'Thank you so much for making all this effort – I'm sure that my parents and I are most grateful.' Say these things for no better reason than that somebody who despised him was standing by. He could construct the scene exactly. The absurdity and the cruelty of his own personality rushed in on him like a collapsing wardrobe. He submitted to the temptations of unkindness when Edna and Keith were not there, so that they might be purged from him. They were good people, in their best clothes, with their cringing gait. There was no other way to think of them.

He offered them a cup of coffee; they stood, smiling, looking about them.

'It's a lovely room,' Edna said. 'You must be lucky.'

'Edna and I, we've never been to Oxford before,' Keith said. 'It looks beautiful, even in this weather.'

'Oh, you must come down and see it properly,' Leo said. 'I'd be very glad to show you round, any time.'

'Well, that's very kind of you,' Edna said, and it was true, Leo had sounded much more lordly than he had hoped to.

'I don't know if you remember us,' Keith said. 'I used to work with your dad, years ago. We always got on very well, me and your dad. It was nice to see him again – he hasn't changed a bit.'

'He's always been the cheerful one among the doctors, Keith always says,' Edna put in. 'Your father, he's what people used to call a card.'

'It's your dad's back that's playing up?' Keith said. 'It can be terrible, I know. I don't believe in all this bed rest. I had it once and just worked through it. It was tough at first but by the third day, you'd never have known it was anything but tickety-boo. When I heard from your mum what'd happened … Well, you see, Edna and I, we're Christians, and we believe in doing good for our neighbours, doing good cheerfully.'

Leo was overcome with embarrassment; the kettle was boiling, and he occupied himself with some business with teaspoons and mugs and a pint of milk. He hoped – it was all packed away – he hoped they didn't take sugar? They didn't, with a small hesitation from Edna.

They might as well get it over with, and in five minutes, they started taking the boxes downstairs. There was Eddie, standing at the door of his room, staring at Edna, who was carrying a tiny box, all feminine flutter and weakness. There was Lucy, who smelt of eggs, standing in the porter's lodge with her parents – two six-foot posh people, the man with a salt-and-pepper beetling brow, the woman like Willie Whitelaw in drag. There was the rowing team, who stopped their fight on the first-floor window when they saw Leo and Edna and Keith to stare and comment. Edna and Keith hardly seemed to notice: Edna kept up the chatter about how she almost preferred it when Keith was out at work, not always with his feet under the Hoover. At one point Tree came out of the staircase opposite with a cowed-looking woman, ginger and fat, and said, in a loud, practised voice, 'Just as long as we set orff before eleven, that's all I ask, Mummy –' her voice and accent quite changed from what it had been eight weeks before. She looked straight through Leo; she took in Edna and Keith; she looked away as if he had disgraced not just himself by possessing such parents but the whole bunch of them. Wretchedly, Leo said, 'I do think it's most awfully kind of you to step into the breach like this.' But Keith hadn't heard him. Out of the mail room had stepped Tom Dick with a couple of his posh cronies.

'It's Tom, isn't it?' Keith said. 'Hello, Tom.'

Tom Dick stared, his attention taken. He appeared to be hesitating before acknowledging.

'You remember me – Keith, and this is Edna, my wife. Tom, we used to sing in the same choir as your mum. From Sheffield!'

'Oh, yes,' Tom said. 'I remember.'

'Your mum still in that lovely bungalow?' Edna said. 'I remember going round with Keith for a cup of tea – I don't think you can have been in, probably kicking cans round the precinct like all the boys your age.'

'If we'd known you were here …' Keith said, setting down the box he was carrying on the floor. His hair was wet with sweat. 'And in the same college as Leo here? That's ever so nice, it must be. Your mum's not coming down, is she? If we'd only known, we could have offered to bring your stuff back to Sheffield as well.'

'That's perfectly all right,' Tom Dick said, clearly aghast. 'I don't think Mummy will be down for hours yet.'

'Leo's dad's not very well,' Edna explained, 'so we offered to come down and pick him up. I know your mum's a nervous driver, too, so –'

'It's quite all right,' Tom Dick said. 'Very nice to see you.' He bundled his cronies off. As he went, he caught Leo's eye in passing; there was an expression of malevolence there, a sense that

Leo had blown his story wide open and would pay for it. As long as Tom Dick lived, he would never forgive Leo. Leo, understanding that, felt as if a burden had been lifted from him, that he had no need any longer to feel anything like shame. They loaded the boxes into the back of their yellow Capri and nothing mattered any longer.

'I know I ought to know,' he said, there in the open air, where anyone could hear him, and snigger, 'but what church is it you go to?'

After Christmas, Leo returned to Hertford College, Oxford, driven by his mother. His father, upright in the front seat, cursed at every jolt in the road. He stayed until Tuesday afternoon, three days after arriving. Then he packed a suitcase with his clothes, went to the railway station and took a train home. After two more weeks, his sister Blossom arrived at the college and, with her new husband Stephen, loaded all the dim possessions in Leo's empty room into boxes, and returned to Sheffield.

The next time Leo went to Oxford, he visited seven hotels in four hours, and afterwards wrote, 'Oxford has always been well served by typically English hotels with a degree of discreet luxury, and the Lawrence House Hotel adds a touch of continental refinement to the famous university town's hospitality.'

MUMMY'S TIME WITH BLOSSOM

Mummy said straight away that she would come down to London immediately. She didn't hesitate one bit. Blossom would always be grateful for that. This would have been in 1974 or -5 – it must have been 1974, come to think of it. Blossom could remember making the phone call from the old office in Bread Street, where she sat outside Mr Cannonside's room to field his calls and type his letters. When Blossom phoned up Mummy in tears, having to tell her that Piers had changed his mind, they weren't going to get married after all, it was best if they stopped seeing each other, Mummy had known exactly what to do. She was as good as her word: she was in London and waiting outside Blossom's flat in Earls Court by the time Blossom got home.

Funny – Blossom never wondered what she had had to do to abandon husband and three children still at home at the drop of a hat. At the time she was just grateful, and took it as what mothers would always do, running to the aid of the one most in need. When Blossom considered now what she'd had to undertake, even with a small army of paid helpers, to look after *her* remaining three children and a husband while she came up to Sheffield, she was genuinely impressed by the promptness of Mummy's response in 1973, or was it 1974?

The flat in Earls Court was horrid; damp and smelly, with carpets that actually sucked at the soles of your shoes with moisture, and a flat next door that was home to a perpetual cycle of between six and eight visiting Australians, all of whom had boyfriends or girlfriends squeezing in and playing their awful music at any hour of the day or night. She took the flat, sharing with a girl called Annabel (who had gone to school with Caroline who worked on the floor below) because it was close to Piers in South Kensington. She could pop over at any hour of the day.

Well, all that was over, and instead here was Mummy, standing on the doorstep, a couple of Sainsbury's bags at her feet. She looked concerned, exhausted, but wrapped in a kind of fulfilled excitement. She stood between the shabby white pillars at the porch that had once indicated an ambition towards gentility. When Blossom turned the corner into the long, curving road, Mummy raised her hands in a poor-you-darling way Blossom immediately recognized, and came down the steps towards her elder daughter. It now occurred to Blossom, telling the story at the kitchen table, that her mother could only have been forty at the time.

'Poor you,' Celia said. 'Poor old, poor old Blossom.' She embraced her daughter, and only then did she let Blossom fish in her bag for the keys to let them both in. 'Your father – don't tell your father,' Celia said. 'He spends the whole day long telling people what to do, and he's usually wrong. We're going to sort this out. Just you and me.'

Afterwards, there had been a lot to mull over. It had all ended well – no point in keeping up any suspense: everyone round the kitchen table listening knew perfectly well Blossom had gone on to marry Stephen and have four children with him. Would Mummy have done the same for any of her other children? Whatever Blossom thought, the other three had agreed that she would not have done. Blossom had too much at stake.

She had declared very early on that she wasn't, after all, going to university. She wanted a different sort of life, and she knew how to get hold of it. When her friends at school were agreeing that the important thing was to live a good life, where people mattered, not money, Blossom kept quiet. She wanted a life where the neighbours did not get about in a green Citroën 2CV with a sticker on the back saying *Atomkraft? Nein Danke*. She happened to know that none of the Tillotsons spoke German anyway. Her father kept moaning – but Mummy was on her side. Whatever Daddy said about education, Blossom knew it wouldn't matter in the end.

Blossom had devoted two years to Piers. If she did not marry him, she would have to find someone else of his sort, who would not mind that she was the cast-off of a colleague in a broking firm in the City. A second one could be found; a third would be much harder.

(Of course Blossom did not put it to herself in this way, and she did not talk about it to Mummy like that.)

So Mummy came down to hold Blossom's hand and make her a bit less weepy.

'That's not my Blossom,' Mummy said, when they were both sitting on the sofa. Blossom had changed so much since Tuesday night, when Piers had asked her to step out with him for a drink after work. He had taken her to a grim pub by the Inns of Court where only solicitors' clerks went. It was dark and stained nearly black with decades of cigarette smoke; a sour, bosomy landlady hung over the bar-top complaining with her two regulars, bulbous veiny old drinkers, retired from their labours in the law, drawn back there daily. Blossom had known as soon as he mentioned the name of the pub that Piers would know nobody there to witness her tears.

'What did he say, exactly?' Mummy said, when they were safe on the sofa drinking a cup of tea. Blossom would have preferred a gin and tonic, but she saw the virtues of Mummy's suggestion. He had said they were terribly young to be making these sorts of plans. The landlady, true, had raised her bosom from the bar with a kind of hydraulic effort; she stared; she had heard that last sentence and later, when the pair of them had departed, she would repeat this line to her customers with satisfaction, and feign incredulity. Piers forged on. It might be best if they had some time apart. Blossom might come to think that, after all, she might prefer someone of her own background.

Mummy didn't know what that might mean. As far as she knew –

'Oh, Mummy, you know exactly what he means. His uncle Cumbernauld owns half of Northumberland. That house his parents live in and that flat they bought him and the house in Devon, rolling acres, Mummy – I was just a fool to think he hadn't noticed that ... that he didn't know that he was better than me, than us.'

'Different, darling, not better. We don't say better.'

But Piers had gone to the races only days ago with his chum Stephen, and last night his friend Mark's papa had asked the pair of them to dinner at White's one night and afterwards they had dropped a hundred each at backgammon. That was honestly the sort of life he'd been living since school, apart from the last couple of years with Blossom.

'What's so hurtful,' Blossom said, dissolving into tears, 'is that he obviously thinks he could do so much better than me. That awful Stephen and that awful Mark, I can just see them saying I might be all right for Edgbaston or Hendon but for Henley or the other sorts of places ...' Then an awful voice came out of Blossom. She had never been a mimic, could never have done a ridiculous teacher at school, but she opened her mouth and for her mother did what Stephen or Mark or all of that lot would have said to Piers: '*You can do a bit better than that, I should have thought, old chap.*' They did say *old chap*. They truly did.

At that point Mummy should have said what she was being cued to say, that nobody was too good for her little girl. It was so clear what a mother's duty was at this point, but Mummy said something that was, in fact, rather interesting and made Blossom stop crying.

'Of course he's too good for you,' Mummy said. 'That's what a marriage consists of – one person deigning to settle down with someone, even though they could really do much better.'

'What do you mean?' Blossom said.

'Look at me and Daddy,' Mummy said. 'We've been married for, what, twenty-five years? And all that time I've known perfectly well – I'm too good for him. I could have done much better.'

Blossom had no idea what to say: this observation was so far from what she might have expected, so deep within the territory of the unsayable.

'Daddy quite likes it, I think,' Mummy said. 'He puts up with a touch of insecurity for the sake of knowing where we stand.'

Blossom stared.

'I could have married any number of people,' Mummy said. 'Some of them were very eligible indeed. But I went for your father.'

'But, Mummy,' Blossom said. 'That's not at all like me and Piers. He's looked at me and decided that I wasn't up to the mark. And now he's dumped me like a bag of old washing. He's not going to marry me.'

'No,' Mummy said thoughtfully. 'But someone else is. They're going to see that you're sad and a bit of a victim, and put up with being insulted, and they'll think they could enjoy a marriage based on that. That was my mistake.'

'I thought –'

'The chance of being horrible to your wife or husband,' Mummy said. 'It looks so tempting. I can rule the show! I can order them around! I can get my way! And it's only after months or years of that that you realize – all the power is with the one who's saying submissively, "I'm so sorry." The one who's making that silly apologetic smile, he's the one who is giving the one in charge the permission to run the show. It's like a trap that you don't see coming. If you're raising the whip, you have absolutely no secrets from the other person. The one who's cowering and apologizing – that's the one with the secrets, that's the one with the power in all of this. Just promise me one thing – you'll never give everything of yourself to the other person, ever again. You'll let him beat you, call you an idiot, and you'll put your head down and say, "I know, I'm so sorry, darling." And you've won.'

'Mummy, it's over,' Blossom said. 'He's not going to come back, however submissively I act.'

'No,' Mummy said. She got up and went into the kitchen. 'This one won't. But the next one is going to stay. Are these really your mugs?'

'The mugs?'

'And those plates – they're awful, Blossom,' she called. 'How could you buy them? Come and look at this – it's some sort of transfer, the design, and it's coming off already.'

So the next day Blossom telephoned the office the very first thing to say that she was too unwell to come in – she supposed that the word had got round about Piers, but hardly cared at all. Mummy had slept in Blossom's room – she had proposed sleeping on the floor, but the carpet was frankly moist, and in the end she and Blossom had squeezed up together. They didn't glimpse Annabel. Mummy and Blossom had gone to bed before she came in, and heard her clanking around in the kitchen preparing a glass of her usual nightcap, Alka-Seltzer; heard her in the morning stumbling around in her bedroom, the kitchen and bathroom and hallway saying, 'Oh, God,' a good deal before leaving and slamming the door. Then they could get up. Mummy didn't want to meet the flatmate.

And after the phone call to the office had been made, off they went to Tottenham Court Road, to Heal's and Habitat and all the other homeware shops. It started with mugs, a set of four with an elegant brushstroke of Japanese calligraphy on the side. That was really sweet of Mummy. But then there were plates to buy, and a set of six knives and forks, and two really sharp kitchen knives, a small one for vegetables and a larger one you could use even to carve a chicken. 'You should look hopeless, a little,' Mummy said firmly. 'But everyone should be able to cook a chicken.'

'Oh, Mummy,' Blossom had said, feeling pleasantly hopeless at this exact moment. Had Daddy told her that she could spend all this money on Blossom? Then Mummy said something truly astonishing: she remarked that it had taken her only one night to discover what Blossom ought to have concluded long ago, that she urgently needed a new bed. 'I can't afford one,' Blossom said humbly. The landlord's bed, sagging and with the beginnings of a crack down the centre of the mattress, was simply an awful bed she'd got stuck with. Of course a new bed could be bought: she supposed she had never thought she deserved it.

But in ten minutes, after both she and Mummy had lain down on a series of mattresses in Heal's, Mummy was talking about delivery dates and handing over her new credit card. Blossom was incredulous, and only Mummy saying casually, 'Pay me back some time,' made her give way. The bed was more than three hundred pounds: she could not imagine how she would ever have got to the point of paying for it herself. As for the scene at home when Mummy told Daddy that he would have to shell out for a new bed for Blossom – she understood that now, completely. In a short and unpredictable fit of weeping that overtook Blossom just after the pair of them had left the shop, she came unavoidably to the conclusion that it would be quite impossible ever to imagine how that degree of contempt could ever be transported into any marital relationship of Blossom's. 'Come on, baby girl,' Mummy said, smiling and stroking Blossom's arm, sympathetic and warm but also picking at the dark hairs on her forearm. Blossom, through her tears, recognized that as Mummy's way of making a judgement. She would wax her arms; she would have a bed that she could sleep beautifully in; and she would discover just how much she could lower her head penitently, exerting all her power over a man who believed he was controlling her. She would practise it with Annabel, the next moment of domestic discord she experienced.

Mummy went back the next day, having done her work, and within six weeks, it must have been, Blossom was saying, 'Yes, I know – it was really too bad of me. I'm really terribly grateful to you for being so honest with me.' Only this time she was saying it to Stephen, Piers's awful friend, who, it turned out, had grown up in a suburb of Birmingham. She lowered her head before Stephen's suddenly bewildered expression and felt the mastery of the subordinate. She would not argue with him;

she would accept that he was quite right; she would win him. Blossom would walk, open-eyed, into the victim's role, and before long she would be running the show.

That Heal's bed was still perfectly good. It was in one of her guest bedrooms, in fact. It was only the next time Blossom came home that she looked at her mother, and her father, and her brother, and understood how they all looked to the outside world. They were standing outside; Daddy was locking the door and was about to unlock the Opel. Blossom's new white Mini must have been parked next to it. They were about to drive off to see Granny, and Mummy was holding the little ones, hand in hand, dressed in their Sunday best. They all looked so strange. Blossom saw that now. When Lavinia and Hugh grew up they would be the same, because Blossom knew she was four foot eleven, and Leo was five foot one, and Daddy was five foot exactly, and Mummy was five foot two. They were all going to be the same height, all of them, the little Spinsters. After that day, Blossom never cared about it ever again.

CHAPTER FIVE

I.

There was always the Sainsbury's at Fulham Broadway – a cathedral-like space under girders, tranquil, strip-lit, and (if it were a person) faintly smiling in the aisles. But Lavinia thought she would save herself twenty minutes and ransack Abdul's round the corner. Abdul and his family, Kashmiris with a twenty-four/seven that stayed open sixteen hours of the day, could not be trusted with fruit and vegetables – the limp curtsy of his broccoli, the soft, bruised give, like cotton wool, of his Granny Smiths. You would not venture into his freezer cabinet or trust the unusual brand of tinned tomatoes he stocked. But Abdul – a nice man, who was stockpiling a fortune with this emergency fall-back shop in Parsons Green – had a very good line in crisps and sweets and chocolates and fizzy drinks. Lavinia found he would do very well for her drive to Sheffield with her brother Hugh. They had always enjoyed loading up the back seat with lurid crap, the e-numbers howling from the sunshine roof. Today, she bought a pair of Caramac bars, some Curly-Wurlys, a box of Quality Street and another of Roses, pickled-onion Space Raiders, half a dozen packets of Monster Munch, a fistful of Black Jacks and Fruit Salads, and some bright green fizzy drink from a maker known only to Abdul. He took her incredible shop through the till without raising an eyebrow; she wondered what his other customers could be like.

Outside her house, she delved into her bag repeatedly. She had left the house key on the kitchen table. Sonia was at home, in bed, however, and her room was at the front of the house. Lavinia called out, at first quite gently and then with more force, but it was no good. She was still standing there when Hugh's car drove up and he got out. Lavinia explained.

'Oh, it'll be like waking the dead,' Hugh said. 'Don't you have a spare key with anyone?'

'Yes,' Lavinia said. 'I've got one with you.'

'With me?'

But the key, if it was still with Hugh, was in his house in Battersea, half an hour away. He wasn't at all sure it was still there, either.

'But it's better than standing here, screaming in the street at eight o'clock on a Saturday morning,' Lavinia said. 'My neighbours will be furious.'

'Let me try,' Hugh said, and called, quite gently but with an actorly penetration of tone, 'Sonia … Sonia … Sonia …'

And that did the trick. The crumpled and half-drawn curtains in Sonia's room rippled and then were pulled back. Sonia had heard Hugh's voice, and had responded to it. The full-length window in her room gave onto a little balcony – Lavinia was never sure whether it was quite safe to stand on it. Sonia was draped in a floral pink duvet, pulled around her bosom, her hair rumpled; her legs emerged like those of an aspiring actress who had once seen a Jayne Mansfield movie. Black women should always wear brilliant pink, Lavinia believed: Sonia was a striking vision in the Parsons Green street. She opened the window with one hand, and stepped out.

'Ere,' she called down. 'What the fack are you doin ere, darlin? What the fack, eh?'

'Is she talking to you?' Lavinia said to Hugh.

'I think she must be,' Hugh said. 'She's so common.'

'Ere you are,' Sonia cried. 'You want to see my tits or what, darlin?'

'Why is she talking like that?' Lavinia said.

'Like what?' Hugh said. 'Oh God, she's going to – Sonia, put them away.'

Sonia had dropped the duvet to her waist and was shaking her breasts around – plump and neat, they were her best feature apart from her ankles, she had once confided to Lavinia.

'Sonia, I don't have my keys,' Lavinia said, calling up to the first floor where Sonia now turned her bosom round from left to right to the admiring empty street. Her smile was dazzling. 'Let us in, will you?'

'Awright, darlin,' Sonia said. 'Only – woss in it for me?'

'A great big kiss on your big black bottom, you awful old thing,' Hugh said. 'Now let us in.'

2.

Hugh's face: so nice, so strange. He was the only one of them who looked like that. His eyes were sad and funny at the same time, triangular and downward pointing, just like a puffin's, the only one whose face crinkled when he smiled. He had smiled just now, putting her into the passenger seat.

They had hoped to be on their way out of London by eight thirty, and in fact were only half an hour shy. Across the river they went, a broad shining slice of air and water and emptiness in the crowded city; Lavinia and Hugh loved the river, and she said it again, how much she loved it. The western suburbs of London grew softer; harder; more opulent; shabbier. A market-town shopping street was succeeded by a dual carriageway with pedestrian bridges. At the corner of one street, three women in hard-crusted perms, like the Queen, and stout belted pastel dresses laughed at something their friend, the vicar, had just said. Behind them a suited figure moved about within an estate agent's, ready for opening. A man at the lights jogged on the spot, just where the suburb gave onto the sweeping carriageway; over the other side was a council estate but, then, the luscious common with its trees like Constable powder puffs. He jogged patiently, and just then another figure, also in shorts and a

T-shirt, joined him at the lights, paused, jogged, exactly in synchronicity, right and right and left and left. They ignored each other. The car drove by.

'You're driving southwards, Hugh,' Lavinia said fondly. Like Hugh she had no particular interest in road routes; at some level they both wanted their trip to go on for ever, there in the car with the both of them. 'It's not southwards, the road to Sheffield.'

'But you'll hit the M25 whichever direction you go in,' Hugh said. 'It's a circular, it goes right round. So then I'll take a right turn. I've worked it out, it's a right turn. And then, sooner or later, you'll hit the turn-off for the M1.'

'What's this car?'

'Lavinia, I've had it for four years. You just don't notice cars.'

'That's a complete lie,' Lavinia said. 'I notice cars.'

'If you notice cars, tell me this – what sort of car has Blossom got?'

'I remembered your car as red. Non-car drivers, you see.'

'That's exactly it,' Hugh said. 'If you're not interested in something, you just don't see it. When are you going to learn to drive?'

'I don't need to.'

'Oh, honestly. Did you see that? What was it?'

'Was it a badger? I couldn't see. It was pretty squashed, though.'

'Poor little darling. A badger in Putney, fancy. And now it's dead, poor little darling. I thought it was bigger than that. If I saw a badger I wouldn't drive over him, I just couldn't. I'd stop or drive round him, let him get on his way.'

'They're big things to drive over, too.'

'That would be awful, the bump … I'd have to stop and cry, I know I would. Look! Look!'

Over the road, there was a large sign, indicating that this was the route towards the M25. Its confident scale was reassuring, and both Lavinia and Hugh now felt that their journey was well planned, full of intention and purpose; also felt that, in starting by travelling southwards, they would not get to their end point too quickly. They liked their times in the car together.

'Did I ever tell you the thing that Mrs Tucker told us once in RE at school?' Lavinia said. 'About the ducklings? She said she was driving down a country lane once and a great big lorry was behind her, inches behind her, she said. And she turned round the corner and there was a line of ducklings behind their mother, crossing the road, and she had to carry on – she couldn't stop or the lorry would have gone straight into the back of her. She had to drive on and straight over all those ducklings.'

'Well, that stayed in your mind,' said Hugh.

'I have an awful feeling, knowing Mrs Tucker, she told that story and then said we should understand she was not devoid of human feelings but was not a generous person in the slightest. And appeals to her sympathy, or whatever it would be, were a complete waste of time.'

'She was nuts,' Hugh said. 'Did anyone do RE? O-level RE?'

'No idea,' Lavinia said. 'Do you want a Monster Munch?'

'A what?'

'A Monster Munch. They're crisps. You must have had a Monster Munch.'

'Don't think so,' Hugh said. 'What makes them monster-y?'

'They've got a monster's sort of face on them. Go on, I'm putting it in your mouth. With my fingers.'

'I – I – I couldn't see! I was looking at the road. That's horrible. What did you get those for?'

'Oh, I've got worse in the bag,' Lavinia said. 'I got them from Abdul's. Here, I'll give you another. Careful. And then you can have a look at it. Can you see it, Hugh?'

'When Africa stops needing your attention you've got a great career ahead of you, explaining things slowly to mental patients.'

'Like you in that musical, you mean,' Lavinia said. Hugh had had a minor part in the fourth recast of a West End musical. In it, *Hamlet* was reset in the context of a dog show. Hugh had been a King Charles Spaniel. 'When I came to that matinee

there were coachloads of mentals in the stalls. You were definitely doing your lines more slowly.'

'Is that supposed to be a face?' Hugh asked. 'Eyes, mouth –
I'm not impressed.'

'Oh, Hugh,' Lavinia said. 'There are hundreds of thousands
of children starving in Africa, and you turn your nose up at a
nutritious bag of Monster Munch.'

They had always loved settling in the car and driving off
together, Hugh driving Lavinia. She had been the curious failure. Blossom had learnt to drive and Leo had learnt to drive.
But Lavinia's seventeenth birthday had come and gone, and she
had made a brushing-off gesture if anyone mentioned it. She
had not learnt to drive. She had got into Oxford and, unlike
Leo, had stayed in Oxford. (She had stayed in Oxford because
of Leo but, afterwards, she had wondered what the hell his
problem had been. It was true that it was her first experience of
education where people didn't hit her because she was called
Lavinia, or just say, 'Is there a lav in 'ere?' But it had seemed
OK to her.) It was her second summer back that Hugh had had
his seventeenth birthday, back around Easter, and had spent
the next four weeks learning to drive with an intensity of
concentration that surprised even his mother, or so she told
Lavinia. And then when she had come home at the beginning
of the summer he had been – she made allowances for the
imaginative power of memory, here – he had been standing
outside the beautiful big house leaning with one elbow on the
roof of a car. Had it been blue? Or yellow? Or black? What
colour were cars?

Dark blue, she thought.

Anyway. He was leaning with one elbow on the roof of the
car and a huge, brilliant, naughty smile. In his hand was a set of
rattling keys, like an insistent and exotic percussion instrument
that would make itself heard through a large orchestra. He
shook them. Behind him in the porch was Daddy, the jovial
presence, his arms around Mummy, and Blossom and Leo,
proud of their little brother. That could not have been the case,

since both Blossom and Leo were certainly married and living
lives away from Sheffield by the time Hugh was seventeen. But
that was what she remembered. They were giving their blessing
to Hugh and his car and his ear-wide shining smile, full of illicit
possibilities. He was a nice-looking boy, her brother. That talk
about him becoming an actor, it might not be all rubbish.

She had put her suitcase into the boot of the car, without
even really greeting Mummy and Daddy and the big ones, and
off they had driven. The whole summer! It was the summer
Charles and Diana had got married; the summer after Granny
Spinster had died – that was how they could drive wherever
they wanted: they'd got three thousand pounds each from
Granny Spinster. They went to the ordinary local places, to
Chatsworth and Bakewell, as if they were old folk enjoying a
nice day out. Then they had daringly got onto a motorway and,
Hugh screaming with terror, gripping the steering wheel, they
had driven all the way to Leeds, had a cup of tea and come
straight back again. Was it then that he'd said, 'You can just
drive anywhere,' and, that summer, they'd got into the car and
driven down, out of Sheffield, down eastwards and downwards
until they'd seen a sign to Harwich. Granny Spinster's three
thousand pounds! It wasn't until they had almost reached the
ferry terminal that Hugh admitted he'd translated a thousand
pounds of Granny Spinster's money into travellers' cheques,
thinking he might well do this some time soon. Where were
they? There in the bag, along with Hugh's passport and Lavinia's
passport. He'd put them both in when they set off. They had
driven through towns bright with bunting. There on the board,
there had been Esbjerg. Where was Esbjerg? It had a polar-bear
feel. They had bought the tickets. For ever afterwards, Lavinia
had loved getting into a car with her little brother Hugh and
being driven by him; for ever afterwards, she was sitting in the
passenger seat eating some bizarre salted liquorice, wearing
clothes that they'd had to buy in a Danish service station (not
having packed), driving across the flat, windy grasslands towards
the birthplace of the composer Nielsen, a composer they had

never heard of, whose collected symphonic works they invented and sang in two-part counterpoint, shrill and rumbling, hardly wondering whether there was any money left. Granny Spinster's three thousand pounds!

It must have been on that trip that Lavinia had said to Hugh, 'Don't you hate meeting new people?'

'Why should I?' he'd said. 'You mean if they look at us and laugh because we're all so tiny? No. Of course not. If anyone did that, they wouldn't be the sort of people I'd want to meet.'

She'd always remembered that afterwards; tried to live by it, not to be frightened at the idea of meeting anyone new.

When there was a hundred pounds left they said goodbye to Denmark and went, regretfully, homewards. They just made it, the petrol sputtering out as they turned into the Sheffield road they and the ancients had always called Home. What sort of car had that been? Lavinia had no idea. It had cost Hugh another five hundred of Granny Spinster's money. Maybe it had been blue.

'Show us yer fackin tits,' Hugh said. They were paused at a set of traffic lights, a strange sudden manifestation of stern control halfway down the riverine flow of the dual carriageways. A woman in a sleeveless black dress, struggling with the task of lighting a cigarette, waited.

'That's not nice,' Lavinia said, with a swerve of the head. 'Do you mean her?'

'*No*,' Hugh said. 'I absolutely didn't mean her. Or you. I was trying the line out.'

'Show us yer *fackin tits*,' Lavinia said, trying it out. 'Why does she talk like that?'

'I expect it's because she was brought up by people who talk like that,' Hugh said. 'What do you mean?'

'Sonia,' Lavinia said. 'I was talking about Sonia.'

'Yes, I know,' Hugh said. 'I was talking about Sonia too, show-us-yer-fackin-tits Sonia. She talks like that because that's how she talks.'

'I meant – why does she talk like that *to you*?'

'She doesn't talk to me any differently from how she talks to anyone else,' Hugh said. 'Have we finished the Monster Munch?'

'I've got some Marathon bars,' Lavinia said. 'Aw that fackin rabbish she bleedin tawks. She only talks like that to you.'

'Oh, what crap,' Hugh said. 'That's what she sounds like.'

'Not to me,' Lavinia said. 'Are you telling me –'

'What does she sound like when I'm not there?'

'Like you and me. She just talks normally. It's just when you're there that she goes all *Minder.*'

'Are you telling me that all the time I've seen Sonia, every single time, from the first time we met, every time she opens her mouth when I'm around, she's been putting on a funny voice?'

'Looks like it.'

'She's good at accents,' Hugh said – an actorly piece of admiration that Lavinia let go.

'Are you telling me …' Lavinia said, but he had told her. Did she want him to tell her again? The joy of it came over her, and her conviction that some time, soon, she would smuggle Hugh into the house, place him quietly on a chair in her bedroom and wait until Sonia was home; she would let Hugh eavesdrop on Sonia talking normally, and after an hour, even half an hour – enough to convince Hugh that this was what she ordinarily sounded like – he should emerge shyly from his hiding place. What would Sonia do?

'She'd try to carry it off,' Hugh said.

'Carry it off how?'

'She'd …' Hugh thought. 'She'd laugh – no, she wouldn't laugh, that would be acknowledging something. She'd just turn round and talk to me. But in the way she always talks to me, the *ere darlin show us yer* … She'd have to. And then it would be up to us.'

'Are we ever going to get on the M25?'

'We're on the M25 – we've been on it for twenty minutes,' Hugh said. 'I'm only hoping we're going the right way round.'

In a while Lavinia pulled off her little black cardigan and rolled it into a ball. There was nothing to see on the M25 and she had got up too early. She put it behind her neck and closed her eyes. Soon she was dreaming – she supposed she was dreaming. She was in a car with her brother Hugh, and they were on a long journey somewhere. They were laughing and talking all the time! The sun was shining outside, and in the back of the car there was someone who she couldn't quite make out. In the end Hugh – not her – turned round and told the back seat to pipe down and shut up, and then she turned round after him, and they weren't in a car at all. They were in a large bus, and what was behind them was row upon row of identical dark schoolchildren. They started to sing a song, but as that was the one thing Lavinia could never abide in dreams, she woke up.

3.

'Would you ever get divorced?' Hugh said.

'You have to get married first,' Lavinia said, mildly confused, blinking herself awake. 'I don't see any chance of that.'

'Yes, but,' Hugh said, 'you wouldn't ever, ever, ever get married in the first place if you thought there was the slightest chance of getting divorced, if it was even in your mind as a possibility.'

Lavinia thought, or she made the gesture that looked like thinking. Hugh's fervent and flushed expressions of belief needed reassurance.

'No, of course not,' Lavinia said. 'I wouldn't marry anyone I thought there was a good chance of me divorcing.'

'But Mummy and Daddy,' Hugh said.

'Oh, Mummy and Daddy,' Lavinia said.

'We should have gone up two weeks ago,' Hugh said.

'They'd been married fifteen years when we were born,' Lavinia said sensibly. 'Daddy was in his forties, Mummy was nearly forty when I turned up. They weren't like they must have been when they got married.'

'Oh, I bet they were,' Hugh said. 'I bet they were always exactly the same. I bet Mummy was saying romantic things beneath her veil, saying how much she loved him, but then making fun of him somehow, saying it was typical, and I bet Daddy was just shrugging and going off in search of a new person to charm and entertain.'

'And tell what they should do,' Lavinia said. 'Was I asleep?'

'And snoring like a demon,' Hugh said.

'I had a lovely dream,' Lavinia said. 'I dreamt I was in the car with you, going somewhere, and then I woke up and I really was in the car with you, going somewhere.'

'How unambitious of your *id*,' Hugh said, in a lordly, technical way.

'But he's very certain of it, according to Leo. He's definitely going to divorce her. You think nothing much has changed, why not just go on as usual?'

'He hasn't said anything to her.'

'He doesn't love her. He's never loved her. He's going to tell her he doesn't love her and she's going to have her freedom before she dies. Otherwise –'

'Otherwise nothing,' Hugh said. 'Do you think the M25 goes on for ever? How long have we been on it?'

'There's the sign,' Lavinia said. It was to the M1 and the North. 'Hugh, it's the sign for the turn-off.'

They had been driving in the right-hand lane for some time – certainly since Lavinia had gone to sleep. Hugh went on cruising, his eyes flicking up to the mirror.

'Hugh, you've got to get in the left-hand lane,' Lavinia said. 'Hugh.'

'I know,' Hugh said.

'You're going to miss the turn-off,' Lavinia said, and the junction itself was now approaching. They were two lanes away from where they could diverge from the M25, and in a moment of panic, as if Hugh hadn't heard what she had been saying, she reached out and placed her hand on the wheel. She hadn't meant to pull at it, but before she knew it she had –

'Christ!'

– she had given the car a little tug, and it was edging into the middle lane. An uproar of hooting and flashing came from behind them, very close. Hugh pulled the wheel firmly back, and they moved into the right-hand lane again. A black BMW slid past on their left. Rage and fist-shaking had possessed its interior – a shaved-head bald man and, in the back, two scared-looking children, their hands raised to ward something off – and then it was gone. She glanced at Hugh: he was white, his teeth biting his lower lip. Behind the BMW there was a gap, and Hugh signalled, moved into the middle lane, signalled again, moved quickly between white vans into the left-hand lane – another uproar of hooting and light-flashing. They were on the turn-off to the M1 and the North before they knew it.

'Christ, Lavinia,' Hugh said, after ten minutes. 'You nearly killed us back then.'

'I'm sorry,' Lavinia said. 'I just panicked.'

'There was no need to panic at all,' Hugh said. 'It was all perfectly under control. If we'd missed that junction we could probably have taken the next one.'

'I'm sorry, Hugh,' Lavinia said.

'Just promise me never to do that ever again.'

'I promise.'

'OK, forget about it.'

But how was it that Hugh could drive a car – could do adult things at all? She knew what it was that had made her reach out and adjust his path – it was the same thing that had made her, at three, reach out and hold his hand and help him to toddle along without falling, or to listen to his lines in the school production of *The Crucible*, her holding the book and helping him out, down at the bottom of the garden. From time to time she needed to reach out and make sure he was on the right path. She put it like that to herself, and now examined the sentence as she had framed it. Where did the need lie? In him, or in herself? Because, not for the first time, he had passed her into adult concerns and capacities – it was astonishing to her to

discover that, at fifteen, he had a girlfriend who was quite serious about him, and a little later, to realize that they had slept
together. It was as if he weren't tiny at all. They both had houses
and lodgers, but it was Hugh who had gone through the business of helping her find a house and explaining a mortgage, and
had had to supply her with a lodger – she wouldn't have known
what to do. He had known what to do, however: the house he
inhabited in Battersea, he was the last remaining tenant from
the fivesome who had originally rented it, and now the collector
of rent. Whenever someone moved out, he charged the replace-
ment ten pounds a week more than before. He had confided to
Lavinia that he made a useful sum of money every week by
doing this – by now, at least sixty or seventy pounds. She had to
accept that he had mastered adult life and she had not; should
accept, too, that from time to time she had the habit of reaching
out from her own seat, unable to drive but with the compulsion
to place a hand on the steering wheel and tug. One of these days
she would kill both of them. It was in a spirit of experiment, to
establish where exactly that *need* lay that she said, in a cheerful
voice, 'I'm going to have a Curly-Wurly – do you want one?'

And she felt no surprise at all that he said, clearly having
given it some thought over the last hour or so, 'No. I'm fine. I
don't think I really want to eat any of that crap, actually.'

4.

They drove on in silence for a while, in the tranquil flood of the
motorway traffic. Lavinia tried to think of something to say, to
bring Hugh back, but nothing came to mind. She knew
everything about his life, after all: she knew that rehearsals
started for *Bartholomew Fair* at the National in a week's time;
she knew that the run of *Hay Fever* had finished a week ago,
since she had gone to the last night. He was lucky not to struggle to find work; if he wasn't a colossal success with his name in

lights, he made a living and was pleased with it – even with the two days last week, providing a voiceover for a TV documentary about the Boer War.

'I'm going to stop at the next opportunity,' Hugh said, after a while. 'I could do with a break.'

'This is the one where we couldn't find the car once, went round and round the car park, and then in the end Leo said he thought we might be in the car park on the wrong side of the motorway.'

Hugh wouldn't let himself laugh – Lavinia had done wrong too recently for that – but he made an amused sort of grunt.

'Is it too early for lunch?' Lavinia said.

'No, no,' Hugh said. 'It's twelve now. I tell you what – we won't stop at Crappy Corner. I'll get off the motorway at the next junction and we'll find some charming little pub in a market town. How about that?'

'A charming little pub in a market town. Sounds perfect,' Lavinia said. But that sounded sarcastic, which she didn't mean. 'I'd love that,' she said, but she somehow couldn't make herself sound like herself.

'Well, we're going to do that in any case,' Hugh said. If he was cross there was nothing to be done about it.

In five miles a junction appeared, signposted to Northampton. 'A charming little pub in a market town,' Lavinia said, and this time she meant to sound sarcastic. It was her brother's view of life, and now she could see that something in him had hardened; the actor in him looked for what was vivid, what was easy to get across the footlights, what could be projected, and what that consisted of was what he and the audience already knew about. A charming pub in a market town. At those words, you could almost see what Hugh meant. That was all that an actor needed, to grasp what he already knew and what his audience already knew. But Hugh had lived all his life in two cities; he had lived in Sheffield and he had lived in London. His knowledge of charming pubs in market towns was slight. She felt that all he needed, as an actor, was a knowledge, quickly acquired, of how life was assumed to be, how life was in other actorly renditions. Just at that moment she hated her brother, his charming shallowness, but in a moment she understood that he had proposed something banal, something invented, which reality would shortly fail to supply. The charming little pub in a market town was detailed in his imagination – in his specifications, rather – with a landlady of a certain sort, and food, and a quiet, dusty interior, and flowers and horse brasses and regulars ... On stage, in a play, the words could be left as they were, but out here reality would intrude, testily, and fail him. Her brother had acquired the charm of their father; acquired, too, the limits of that charm.

Now they were in an English country landscape – the English country landscape that consisted of a grey road with signposts, curving through some land. A line of pylons crested the hill, and four trees in a copse, far off. The driver of a container lorry had pulled to the side of the road, and now was walking round his load in a puzzled way: they would never discover what it was that had presented a problem.

'Would you ever live in the country?' Lavinia said.

'I'd love to,' Hugh said, 'when I'm old, in a sweet little cottage, very cosy, low ceilings, with roses growing outside the door and a path to the front gate. And geese in a pond out the back.'

'A thatched roof?'

'Maybe. I don't know. I always think there would be things living in a thatched roof. What the hell.'

'Or in a market town?'

'Would I live in a market town? Let's see. Yes, that might be nice too. Are we talking about retirement? I want snowy white hair and a walking stick and a trilby –'

'Nothing much wrong with you, though.'

'No, nothing at all. I just want a walking stick. And the house, let's see. A big square Georgian house with a square front garden, very plain, a path between two lawns, little lawns. A cherry tree, do you think? I'm not sure. But there's got to be a cat in the front window, a nice marmalade cat, and a notice about the church fête tied to the front railings …What's all this?'

'Oh, nothing,' Lavinia said. 'I think it was all too much for me buying that bloody flat. I can see myself still living there when I'm ninety.'

'You can come and live with me in my big square house. Don't you worry about that,' Hugh said. 'And here we are. How about that?'

He had been following some confident route in his head, and as they had been talking he had taken the car directly into the centre of some market town – Towcester, had it been? – and there, all at once, was a sort of square, a public building with an ambitious tower, a white-painted hotel, and outside it, an empty parking space. Lavinia gave up. Hugh's mind followed what it already knew, painting familiar pictures, and then, before you knew it, the cliché was there. The world arranged itself at Hugh's convenience. She, on the other hand, could walk down the whole length of Oxford Street, muttering, 'There must be a toilet *somewhere*.'

The day had grown hot. The wide hallway of the hotel was dark and cool, a vase of white flowers on the table by the door and flagstones underfoot that were dark and shining with age. It was very quiet. Hugh took off his sunglasses and went ahead into the bar to the left, a clean space of wood and shining brass. 'No one around,' he said.

'There are menus,' Lavinia said helpfully.

'Looks OK. Hello? Hello?'

A man appeared from behind the bar; he had been polishing glasses in the pantry. He surveyed Hugh and Lavinia; they must look like a handsome London pair, perhaps, with Hugh's white shirt and pale trousers, Lavinia's sleeveless summer tunic. 'What can I do for you?' he said.

'Are you doing lunch?' Hugh said.

'Should have thought so,' the man said. 'Haven't seen much today, but can do you a spot of lunch.'

They ordered. The menu was unpromising, but probably better than the service station. The barman was garrulous after the first professional chill.

'What brings you here, then?'

'We just dropped off the motorway, actually – wanted to have a break. You know how it is.'

'What's that?'

'We're driving up to Sheffield. From London. We were on the motorway?'

'The M1,' Lavinia put in.

'Oh, that thing there,' the barman said. 'I know about that. It ripped up the land in my mum and dad's time. Never did anyone any good. Getting about faster and faster.'

'I know what you mean,' Hugh said. Lavinia thought she might giggle, but sat there solemnly, thinking of her lunch.

'That's why it's so quiet here,' the barman said. 'We only survive on the business that comes in Saturdays. And Tuesdays, of course.'

'Today's Saturday,' Hugh said. It was a quarter past one: they were the only customers in the place.

'Well, there you go, then,' the barman said. He leant on the bar; he plucked a toothpick from the little bowl of olives; he started to pick at his molars. The place had seemed clean at first, comfortable and polished, but now Lavinia wondered why they had thought that. The cuffs on the barman's shirt were frayed, stained, a rim of black. There had been a sharp whiff of twice-worn clothes when he had brought their drinks over. She wondered who his mother and father were, in whose time the motorway had been built. He had the air of the son of the failing hotel.

'I'll go and have a look, see what's happened to them lasagnes,' the barman said. But he didn't move. 'We've got a new cook in. Can't keep a chef for two months in this place. This one's from ... Where's that place? My mum found him. Probably comes cheap.'

'Well, that's the most important thing, after all, isn't it?'

'Rajeeb, he's called,' the barman said. 'Nice bloke ... I'll go and have a look.'

This time he went.

'Let's just ...' Hugh said, but the course of action escaped him.

'Haven't paid for the drinks,' Lavinia said.

'We could leave two or three pounds and just run,' Hugh said.

'It'll be fine,' Lavinia said bravely. 'I'm sure it'll be fine. Do you remember those hotels when, you know, we were going off on holiday and –'

'Stopped for lunch,' Hugh said. 'A wonderful place I just happen to remember.'

'Those wonderful places,' Lavinia said. 'They were always wonderful places. They're all gone now, I suppose. Or hanging on like this.'

'Daddy setting off at seven, Mummy with the map trying to make sense. I know. They don't still – well, no, they don't. Obviously they don't.'

'No,' Lavinia said.

The barman reappeared with the food. 'Watch out,' he said, as he set the dishes down. There was that whiff of human again and, too, something of a suggestion of deodorant, some hours ago. 'Plate's very hot. Rajeeb's managed to – Well, there you go. Got everything you need? Enjoy it.'

'The plate's very hot,' Lavinia said. 'But the lasagne –'

'Not so much,' Hugh said. 'Microwaved. Heats the plate first, then the food if it gets round to it. Shall I get Rajeeb to do it some more?'

'It's fine,' Lavinia said. 'You were saying. Has anyone said anything to you? About Daddy wanting to divorce Mummy?'

'I'm ignoring it. It's not going to happen. I think the most important thing is how Mummy is, which everyone seems to be ... Oh, I can't work it out – Mummy's really dying. She really is. We should have gone up ages ago.' He levered his fork underneath the brick of lasagne, one forkful removed; he raised it six inches, raised an eyebrow, and flipped it like a pancake. It fell heavily onto the plate, splattering a little.

'What I think – Hugh. Stop it. He just wants attention, I would say. You know what Daddy's like at a party. He can't bear just standing by. Mummy dying, it's like the worst thing for him. I mean –'

'Nobody's looking at *him*,' Hugh said. 'Well, of course. The dramatic announcement. The important thing! The race against time! Will Hilary be true to himself? Centre stage, the man of principles. I can see it.'

'I almost feel like turning round and going back home,' Lavinia said. 'I just don't want to do this. I'm really not going to have an argument with him. I'm just not.'

'I suppose,' Hugh said, 'the one bright point is that it's much better for the drama if he just tells us he's going to divorce her. If he tells her too, it's all over.'

Lavinia tried to follow.

'But,' Hugh said, 'if he never tells her – if everyone knows he's not going to tell her – then it stops being dramatic. We lose interest. It's an empty threat. He's got to tell her and he's got not to tell her. It's a curious one. I agree. I'm not going to have an argument with him either.'

'I like your workshop manner,' Lavinia said. 'I really feel as if I'm paying attention to what Daddy might do for the first time in years. I wish –'

'Oh, everyone wishes that,' Hugh said. 'You wish it was happening to someone else, or that you could put the script down and walk out into the sunshine. I know what you were going to say. We'd better get a move on. Are you going to eat any more of that? It's awful.'

And there, a figure in the doorway behind the bar was watching them, in a chef's white jacket, a dark mobile face. It must be the promised Rajeeb. He had come here somehow; he had taken an opportunity; he was watching their casual refusal to do anything with his work. He would be gone soon. He was indifferent. But there was not much future here. Lavinia watched her brother go up to the bar and lay down a ten-pound note and a five-pound note – he was going to be contemptuously indifferent to the actual bill. Fifteen pounds would cover it and then they were out of here. She scrabbled for her cardigan and scurried after Hugh, but as she left she caught the eye of the chef. He had seen her, and looked at her. He scratched the side of his face as he took her in, casually, with a good deal of interest. The sight of the Englishwoman in a bad hotel almost running had taken its place in the long catalogue of what his eyes had seen, one impression of the world after another, going back years, never shared, never to be guessed at. She would never know anything about him; if she ever came back here, she knew he would be gone and have left no trace. From time to time his face would come back to her. She knew it would. For years.

5.

The grown-ups had gone to see Granny. She was in hospital and she was very ill. Josh had been left in the house with Tresco, and Aunt Blossom had told them to entertain themselves – to behave – to keep themselves busy. Downstairs Tresco was moving about. You could hear him. It was like being upstairs and hearing a burglar or some dangerous suspicious animal sniffing about. There he went, from the room at the back to the room at the front, from the room where they ate into the kitchen ... The door to the little room, the sort of buttery, that had a squeak to it, and it squeaked now as Tresco opened it. How should Tresco entertain himself? How should he be good? Soon, Josh knew, Tresco would exhaust the possibilities of picking things up and setting them down again, of the immense thud that must have meant him falling backwards onto the sofa in Granny's drawing room, of the strange contents of drawers in a strange house. He would be finished with downstairs and he would come upstairs to where Josh was. It had happened before. Josh had one weapon that he could use against Tresco, if things with him got too bad. He hugged it to himself, the sentence he knew and had never spoken. It was like that bit in *The Magician's Nephew* when the witch destroyed a planet with the Unspeakable Word.

The grown-ups had taken Josh to the library a week ago. They had found an old library card of Granny's in one of those drawers, and Aunt Blossom had taken him to the big white square library in the city centre. She had wondered, on the way, why there weren't books enough for Josh at home. But that was one of the questions that didn't need an answer – a rhetorical question, Josh explained to himself. He wondered why rhetorical. That was good, because he did not have an answer. There were books at Granny and Grandpa's house, here and there, on odd shelves and left in piles underneath beds, in an abandoned state in a cupboard in the spare room. Of course he hadn't read all of them. But they weren't really for him, and sometimes when he had started on one, drawn by a lovely title – *The History of Mr Polly* or *The Matador of the Five Towns* – he had not got far before feeling these were not books meant for him, and perhaps not books meant for anyone to read. Today he was reading the last of the books that he had got from the library, and he was getting towards the end, slowing down, not wanting to finish it and to look up. The book he was reading was *David Copperfield*, and he was hoping that Little Em'ly was going to be all right. When he had brought his pile of books back, Grandpa had turned it over, there on the kitchen table, and said, 'Queer lot of old-fashioned stuff. There's a set of Dickens kicking around somewhere. Never read it myself.' Aunt Blossom had raised her hands as if to say, 'But what can you do?' and Tresco had made the gesture of a gun and shot Josh. Daddy hadn't said anything. He never said anything much to Josh but he had understood.

Tresco was coming upstairs: right foot, left foot, right foot, pause. His feet on the stairs were deliberate and threatening. You could not mistake them for anyone else's. That was what Tresco meant by his tread, the unmistakable approach. It was the opposite of silent tracking. Josh's eyes remained on the page where they were, *fairly striking out from time to time, as if he were swimming under superhuman difficulties.* And Tresco was standing in the doorway, staring at him.

'Keeping busy,' Tresco said. 'Busy busy busy. You like *reading*, don't you? Keep on *reading*. Go on. What a good little boy.'

Josh said nothing.

'They're coming today,' Tresco said. 'Aunty Hugh and Uncle Lavinia. They're all coming and then all the uncles and aunties, they'll be here. Aunty Hugh and Uncle Lavinia. Do you hear what I call them? You know why I call them that?'

Josh mouthed *no*, his eyes still on the page. He knew why Tresco called Uncle Hugh and Aunty Lavinia that. Tresco went on explaining the joke because it was the cleverest thing that he had ever thought up by himself. Disdain and terror mingled in the audience whenever Tresco began to speak.

'I call them Uncle Lavinia and Aunty Hugh,' Tresco went on, 'because that suits them. He's such an old aunty, fussing away, and he's an actor – he likes putting on make-up and pretending to be brave. And Uncle Lavinia's coming too. Have you seen her? She's got a moustache, she looks like a man, she's got short hair like a man, she's definitely an uncle –'

'She doesn't have a moustache,' Josh said.

'She definitely does,' Tresco said. 'She's like Matron at school, she's definitely got a moustache. She's a man, she's a man, she's a man.'

'Go away,' Josh said. 'I'm trying to read.'

Tresco stared – you could feel it without even raising your eyes. 'That's so out of order. I've got as much right to be here as you do. Don't you ...' Tresco said, but then he had a better idea: he picked up a hardback book from the shelf by the door and flung it, hard, at Josh. Josh leant back; it missed him by miles. The book lay on the floor, torn.

'I'm going to say you did that,' Tresco said, twisting and raising his arms in an archery shape. 'I bet you wish you knew what I know.'

'Is it that Uncle Lavinia's a man and Aunty Hugh's an old woman? You've done that,' Josh said. There was a fierce exhilaration in him in choosing to speak to Tresco like this.

'It's not that, you pillock,' Tresco said. 'It's something you really want to know. You know Granny and Grandpa, right? Do you know why we're here?'

'Have you only just worked that one out? They think Granny's going to die,' Josh said. 'What did you think we were here for?'

'She's not going to die,' Tresco said. 'She's going to die but not for a while yet. I'm bored of this place, but Mummy says we've got to stay. You know why?'

Josh lowered his eyelids, the nearest he could come to shaking his head.

'Grandpa's decided he wants to get divorced from Granny,' Tresco said.

'Don't be stupid,' Josh said. 'That's just making stuff up.'

'It's true,' Tresco said. 'Mummy told me. She thinks he's gone mental.'

'That's not true,' Josh said.

'You know what else is true that I bet you don't know about?' Tresco said. 'You're not going back to that school you go to in Brighton. You're going to go to my school. Starting in September. I heard Mummy on the phone.'

'That's not true either,' Josh said. 'Mummy couldn't afford to send me to your school, and even I know you've got to take an exam to get let in for nothing. I haven't taken an exam. So I'm not going. QED.'

'Yes, but what you don't know is Mummy – my mummy – she's so fed up of having someone like you in the family, she's talked Daddy into paying for you to go to a proper school. We're paying. So you'd better be grateful. What we do to bugs. Ah, yes. First the bugs line up in their rugby kit in front of the fifth-formers. Then there's confession, when anyone who knows one of the bugs, they come forward and they tell everything they know. *That's going to be me.* That happens in the jakes, what they call lavatories at school. You say toilets, I believe. You'll see. And, oh, what fun it is when we put the bugs through their paces and especially the Confessional Bugs. So QUED.'

'I don't believe you,' Josh said. 'My dad wouldn't let them do that.'

'Nobody's asking your dad,' Tresco said. 'Haven't you worked it out yet? Before she was ill, Granny decided everything. Now it's my mum. No one asks your dad what he thinks. They'd ask Grandpa what he thinks first, and they wouldn't pay any attention to him either. No, you're going to school where I go. What fun we'll have.'

'They wouldn't send me to a school like that. And it's QED, not QUED, you moron.'

'You wait and see,' Tresco said, his voice thickened and muddled with excitement. All this time, all through his bestial explanation, he had been roaming around the room, picking things up and throwing them at Josh – a cushion, a wooden bowl, three or four books, a carved stone apple. There had been an ominous crack when the stone apple hit the headboard of the bed, though Josh wouldn't investigate until Tresco was gone. 'You didn't think Mummy was going to put up with having a cousin of ours come to stay who went to some pit in Brighton? It's amazing that you can read and write. What's that crap you're reading? Janet and John. Enid fucking Blyton. Give a fairy story to the kiddies and run a fucking mile, that's what your school does.'

'I don't believe it,' Josh said. 'Daddy would have told me.'

'I told you – it's nothing to do with Uncle Leo. This is the school my father went to we're talking about, and Granddaddy too. We're not talking about the school your father went to, any of that. So get it straight, get it into your head. Number one. Granny and Grandpa are getting divorced. Number two, from September, you're in my school and you're two years under me, a bug.'

Perhaps now was the moment for Josh to produce the Unspeakable Word. He looked at Tresco. He said it.

'But you're not going to be there,' he said.

'Ha-ha,' Tresco said. 'The possibility of me not being there – zero.'

'They had to write to Aunt Blossom about a regrettable incident, didn't they?' Josh said. 'It was on Monday, the second of April, when the usual inspection of dorm rooms takes place. On this occasion, we found a bottle of Southern Comfort imperfectly concealed in Tresco's bedside locker and, still more worryingly, a small quantity of an illegal drug. That's what they wrote. With great regret they were obliged to ask your mother and father to collect you without delay. With a view to the welfare of the other boys in their care, they regretted that it would be impossible to accept Tresco, that's you, back for the summer term. Fees paid or due are not remissible. So I don't think they're going to take you back, Tresco, and I don't think they're going to send me there anyway. You're full' – Josh spoke confidently, and it was the first time he had used the expression, heard from Tamara and Tresco – 'of shit.'

'*You're* full of shit,' Tresco said. 'You're – The fuck are you talking about?'

'I saw the letter,' Josh said. 'It was on Aunt Blossom's desk. I read it.'

'Little sneak,' Tresco said. 'Going round sneaking. I'm going to –'

'But I read it,' Josh said calmly. 'You're not going back to that school. I'm still here because Daddy phoned my school and told them that he wanted me here because of Granny. If anyone told your school that, they'd probably say you needed to be a man or something and they wanted you in gym by two p.m. *They would.*' Tresco didn't even try to deny this. 'You've been expelled. I bet Uncle Stephen's hard at work at this exact moment finding a school to send you to in September. Borstal.'

Underneath, in the driveway of Granny and Grandpa's house, there was a splash of gravel, a grey car drawing up. He didn't recognize it. It was Uncle Lavinia who stepped out, and then, on the other side, Aunty Hugh in a bright white shirt,

the car keys in his hand. Uncle Lavinia said something to
Aunty Hugh. They looked up at the window where Josh was
looking down, and waved. He forced himself not to duck back
inside.

'You poor idiot,' Tresco said. 'This is life. It's not fair.
Wilkinson was caught selling that stuff in Study – selling it, not
just smoking it – and they expelled him but his people offered
to pay for a new swimming-pool and they took him back. It's
only an extra year or two's fees and Wilkinson said it's all tax
deductible. Your uncle Stephen's on the phone at this exact
moment, offering to pay for a new cricket pavilion. By the time
I'm done with that place I'll be selling spliffs to the deputy
headmaster.'

'Who's the deputy headmaster?'

'A johnny called Wiesel,' Tresco said.

6.

All the rest of the journey, Lavinia and Hugh had talked with
conscious safety about unreal possibilities. In the small cabin of
the car Hugh had bought, they talked brightly. When Lavinia
was older, she would go out and live in a mansion in a poor
country, a teak mansion guarded against termites with a special
paint only the locals knew about; and with such little money
she would manage to live with servants, under fans, in loose
cool silk robes, eating the local river fish and rice, with servants,
such devoted servants ... and Hugh in his Georgian house in a
market town, square and white and a cat in the window, they
had gone over that. They had been on the road for ten hours,
including breaks, or nearly – Hugh said he could not understand it when people said it was only two or three hours on the
M1 from London to Sheffield. They had delved into or entirely
consumed the Monster Munch, the Caramac, the glowing fizzy
drink only Abdul stocked, the Space Raiders and Roses and

Quality Street; they felt terrible, in urgent need of an apple and some water. It had been nice.

But something was being fended away here, and Lavinia understood what it was, in the driveway of her parents' house. She looked up at her nephews in the window upstairs and waved brightly. She would not think of it. Arriving home was like the end of a happy book, the beginning of Christmas, the world shut out and you in the grip of everyone who had always known you. Daddy talking and Mummy telling you that you didn't have to listen. Hugh had hurried into the house; Lavinia stood and waved. Tresco, up there in the window, said something to his cousin. It was something funny, she could see that, and she enjoyed the cousins and relations making each other laugh.

One day Lavinia was going to marry, but it didn't matter if she didn't. She was quite good now at meeting people, new people. Not as good as Hugh had always been, walking forward already laughing, his hand held out, but good enough. One day – she hoped not soon – Mummy was going to die, but there would always be new nephews and nieces and in time, even great-nephews and great-nieces. Maybe some children of her own, ones that would look just like Hugh, perhaps. Her sister would always be there to give good advice, and her father to try to talk to them like he had talked to his patients. And her elder brother would always be there to tease her gently, and she would never love anyone as much as she loved her brother Hugh. She knew that. Hugh was always going to come first in her life and she was always going to come first in his. They would grow old in tandem, not together, but in parallel, inseparably. There would always, as long as they lived, be days when they sat together in a car and talked and ate Monster Munch, like children, and made their way together across the bare signposted surface of the earth, trickling and crawling, like a pair of cockroaches, living on crumbs without complaint or hope of anything better.

'Here we are,' she said brightly.

'That was always the intention,' Hugh said, hurrying towards the front door. His suitcase was still in the boot. Someone else could deal with it.

MUMMY'S TIME WITH HUGH

This would have been in 1979, 1980 something like that – Hugh ought to know the exact year. It was such a hot summer. Or was it a hot summer? Hugh couldn't be sure. Perhaps he was confusing it with other hot summers. It was that summer when he was hanging out with Alex Dimitriou and Albert Wheatstaff – he wasn't really called Albert, but that was what he was calling himself that summer – and Madge Stace. That was the summer they all knew they were the cool kids. There were other kids in the year who thought they were cool – there was that terrible girl called Debbie who had been going out with boys five years older than her since she was thirteen and was now, at sixteen, having a relationship with Mr Currie the physics teacher, the gingery-bearded one. There were the smokers, there were the kids who were in the Sheffield running squad. But anyone could see that Albert and Madge and Hugh and Alex Dimitriou were the cool kids. Madge even said that it must be the naffest thing ever to want to be cool; she was really happy that they were such a bunch of outcasts and weirdos and that was that. Debbie Kilton, snogging with a thirty-year-old physics teacher from a mournful provincial town, letting a *child molester* (Madge said) finger her: that was what was cool, so they weren't going to be cool.

Hugh had never been cool. He'd been the short kid, that funny-looking kid, whose dad was the doctor, who never got the point of anything in physics or chemistry. 'But surely …' the science masters used to say, exasperated with Hugh's timidly proffered, blotched and crossed-out homework.

The funniest day was when Madge said, 'Let's have a debauched sex orgy on the crags,' and they went round to her house and got dressed up as participants in a debauched sex orgy before going out. It was such a scream. Madge had arrived at school six months earlier; she'd moved from Newcastle with her dad who was a lawyer of some sort. She had a neat appearance; she didn't seem cool; she seemed like the sort of girl mothers approved of. But she made teachers uneasy, with her neat hair and her perfect uniform, unnerving in someone of nearly sixteen. The perfection of her blazer and hair and the neat little knot of the tie, her skirt and dark stockings and polished shoes: it had the air of satire about it as, strangely, her precisely correct but not excessive answers to questions had. 'Call me Madge,' she said briskly, with the sideways glance that Alex Dimitriou said drove him slightly crazy. Alex and Hugh and Albert had known each other, had been pretty good friends, but not unified in a pack like they became that summer. Madge had said, 'Call me Madge,' and a week or two later, to Albert, who then was just called David, 'You don't look like a David to me. No David has what you've got, simply perfect cheekbones and the skin of a milkmaid. David. No.'

That summer of 1979, there was something awful about having a mother called Margaret. Years later, Hugh wondered whether Madge had been Margaret, too, right up to the moment of her arrival in Sheffield. It was not impossible.

'What do you want to call me?' Albert, then David, had said. They were in the quiet study room in the school library; it had been years since anyone had tried to enforce the quiet rule in there.

'I think you're more of … an Albert,' Madge said. And then she was Madge and he was Albert. 'That is irresistible to the imagination.'

'And what am I?' Alex Dimitriou said, his eyes dark and longing, his hand resting, blue-ink-stained, on his open history O-level textbook. They were supposed to be revising the Factory Acts or, as Madge had ruefully remarked, in her case vising them.

'Oh, you're who you are,' Madge said. 'Some people! I can't rechristen everyone. You're Alex! Everyone knows you're Alex! Who else could you possibly be?'

And then at some point in the summer it was Madge who had said they should be cool like Debbie Kilton, and have a sex orgy on the crags. It was brilliant. They went round to Madge's place, a pleasant square stone house with a mental dog called Josephine hurling herself at the front door at the first ring of the bell. Madge had stolen all sorts of old clothes from the jumble-sale bag, stuff from her granny and her mum and her dad, Margaret and Ronald. She said the thing about a debauched sex orgy was that you had to dress up for it. The dressing up is the really sexy stuff, she said, and disappeared with the instruction that Alex Dimitriou was going to have to indulge his feminine side: she really felt like going lesbian this morning with a girl in a dress and a beginning moustache.

Hugh would never forget Madge in a weird floral raincoat and headscarf and orange tights, striking poses on an outcrop of rock, a mascaraed beauty spot by her mouth, shrieking, 'Fuck me, Rosalind.' (Rosalind was what Alex was allowed to call himself once he was in Madge's grandmother's sage-green ball-gown with a white lace neckline.) There were some brilliant photographs lying around in a shoebox somewhere.

So it must have been later that year, when the summer was over and they were back at school in the lower sixth that they decided they would all go in for drama. 'Go in for drama' was how Hugh put it years later; 'put on a play' was how they described it then, like a serious endeavour. It was Madge's idea, but it also emerged from one of those long, fabulous Wednesday afternoons – they were supposed to be doing sports. They ran enthusiastically to the corner of the road, then walked in a calm and conversational way to Madge's house, where they sat and had cups of tea all afternoon. 'We should perform *Macbeth*,' she said, 'not just read it scene by scene in English class.'

'We're going to go and see it at the Bolton Octagon next month,' Alex Dimitriou said.

'It's among the most distinguished of provincial English repertory theatres,' Madge said.

'Maybe not,' Hugh said. He wasn't sure it was a good idea. The idea, however, resurfaced, and resurfaced, and soon they were talking with every appearance of commitment, every Wednesday afternoon. What was it in him? He could not work out whether he wanted to do it or not. Something in him pulled passionately towards it, but he knew he was not the sort of person to show off on stage. What would he look like on stage, five foot nothing? People would laugh. He put off his decisive refusal to take part; after all, week after week, they thought of one play after another, and nothing would quite do. It would never happen.

But when, one rainy Wednesday afternoon, they gave up and caught the bus to Madge's house, she had the perfect solution. 'I don't know why I didn't think of it before,' she said. She had been reading Genet's plays, borrowed them from Sheffield City Library, and first of all she'd thought of *The Maids*, then *The Screens*, before the solution had come to her. 'I can't imagine what we were thinking of,' Madge said, getting off the bus and turning and turning in joy, her immaculate PE gear dry under her umbrella. '*Huis Clos*. What about that, then? With Alex in drag as the lesbian? Not very much drag, Alex. You'd make a lovely lesbian. Go on. You know you know it. Three people have died and they're in Hell. They're shown into a room one after another by a valet. Then the door shuts. They think there are going to be torments, tortures, hellfire, but there's nothing. Then they start to talk. And after an hour they hate each other so much that they try to kill each other, but of course they can't, they can't, because they're already dead, they're already in Hell. It's *divine*. If you forgive the expression. It would be perfect. *L'enfer, c'est les autres.*'

She had the text at home, and they read it that afternoon. Albert was the valet; she would be the fey woman who murdered her own baby; Alex could be the lesbian; and Hugh was the Brazilian pacifist, the cruel adulterer with twelve bullets in his chest. They read, and broke off, and acted bits out with hilarious gestures, especially the murderous bits. They had conversations about what it might mean when the door flew open; whether it was within the power of the damned to choose to be nicer to each other. There was nobody but the dog as an audience and, after the first couple of scenes, an appreciative Albert. It took all afternoon, sitting round the kitchen table with cold mugs of tea. It was after five that Madge's mother came in just as Madge was stabbing a fainting Alex through the heart with an invisible paper knife. 'I see,' she said, and went out again, taking the dog with her.

They had to go home. Hugh felt, walking in his unused trainers in the rain, he had been presented with a terrible destiny. He could feel in himself how much he wanted and dreaded this; how at one point he had leapt up from the table and could feel in the tension in his face how he was trying, there in a suburban kitchen, to *be* someone else. Could see it in their faces, too; that they had laughed and joked and mock-acted, performed parodies of acting as much as anything, but then – he could feel it – there had been something there, just for one second, when it was as if someone else was in the kitchen with them. Sartre was wrong: what Hell was was not to be stuck in a room with these three people for ever. That would be Heaven. Hell was to have that exposed, to perform, to bring Hugh's terror and shyness out to be pointed at, to be laughed at, for someone to say, as he started to stumble over the third sentence of his part, 'But you – what made you think you could be an actor? Look at you!' What was he? Was he the man who hardly wanted to leave the house sometimes, who could hardly say anything in class, could really talk only when he was alone with his sister Lavinia? Or the man who could walk to the front of the stage and stand in a pink limelight, grin, push his shoulders back and rattle off the lines that turned him into a seducer, a robber, a sprinter, a charmer for a couple of hours? His mind filled with the sensible advice of parents, godparents, agony aunts on the subject of wanting to be an actor; on top of that advice, he gave himself some advice, very sensible advice, and it consisted of two words. He was seventeen; he would grow no more. The words were 'five foot'.

But then eight months later, coming to the front of the stage that was only the floor of the studio that was used for music practice and anything of that sort, taking an incredulous bow at the end of the single performance that half the school came to, seeing for the first time that afternoon what was on their faces, a sort of shock, a sort of relief from total and utter absorption, he knew that he had done that. He had done it badly and in a raw beginner's way, he knew. He knew that Madge couldn't act – she was satirizing the whole idea of acting as she spoke the words, distinguishing herself from it and that made it bad; that Alex really couldn't act; that Albert could act so beautifully in the little part of the valet-demon he hardly valued it, would never pursue it. He knew, too, that Alex would remember that afternoon for one thing, being discovered afterwards by Hugh behind the scenery, crying hopelessly with lust unfulfilled, with love for Madge that she had encouraged and led on and finally turned away from with a small smile on her face. Was that what it had all been about, really, in the end? Hugh hated it and it went against what he most wanted to do and yet he had to do it and yet he would do it again. In ten years' time it would be so much better in ways he could hardly guess at. But that afternoon, as he bent, what had made it happen was what Mummy had said to him the afternoon he had come back from Madge's.

She was in the kitchen, chopping onions. 'It always makes me cry,' she said, raising the back of her hand to her eye. 'I'm not overwhelmed with emotion or anything.'

'Where's everyone?'

'Upstairs or watching the telly. You're late back.'

'We were at Madge's. Instead of doing sports.'

'Very sensible.'

'Mummy. We think we're going to put on a play.'

'A play?'

'It's called *Huis Clos*. It's by Sartre. It's about Hell, three people who find themselves in Hell. We read it through and kind of acted it this afternoon. Madge says maybe we could – Mummy. They're all really keen on it.'

And then Mummy did something she might not have been expected to do. She put her knife down on the chopping board, and turned to Hugh with floods of funny unmeaning tears in her eyes, and seized him. 'Hugh,' she said. 'Don't say to yourself, "Oh, it doesn't really matter." You are going to be able to do anything you want. You could stand on stage in your underpants if you felt like it. Do you understand me?'

'Mummy,' Hugh said, half laughing, but in fact alarmed. What was this? Mummy was saying something to him that might be about him, might come from her total understanding of her youngest child, or might just be her saying what she had always wanted someone to say to herself.

'Just don't let anyone tell you that it's not something for you,' Mummy said, and she turned back to her onions.

'I don't know …' Hugh said, but the conversation now seemed ill-formed, too much unsaid underneath the words. His mother was not going to answer any question he had. That was Hugh's time with Mummy. It must have been in 1979 or 1980, something like that. The summer had been blissfully hot. Sometimes, when Hugh told this story, he found himself saying that it had been Lavinia, his sister, who had egged him on. In the retelling, she was clearer in what she said to him that someone could succeed though they were no taller than a child. It often went down quite well, that story.

CHAPTER SIX

I.

It was around then that Hilary started overeating, massive, indulgent, extended feasts, lasting all morning and all evening. Pauses – for television, for conversation with one child or another, to say, 'Good, good,' to the two grandchildren who were still there, for a small potter down to the bottom of the garden – were intervals between the real business of eating. Meals had disappeared. At first breakfast, lunch and supper continued, and between them came the snacks. There was a plate of red Leicester on biscuits, ten of them, and coming with a pile of glowing piccalilli late at night. Half a walnut cake from Marks & Spencer, mid-morning, or even a sandwich when Hilary got back from the hospital in the early evening – ham and tomato, perhaps. Then one day lunch stopped. Blossom had made the sort of pasta and salad that the boys would eat, but it wasn't the food her father was turning his nose up at. Leo and Josh and Tresco were sitting there, waiting for Hilary to come down. Blossom went to the kitchen door and called, and Hilary called back from his study. He wasn't hungry, he'd just had something. He was fine. They ate their lunch constrained by what they couldn't talk about in exactly the same way as usual. (They'd been in Sheffield for five days at this point.) There were yogurts afterwards. The boys washed up the plates and forks and glasses and the pan, and went off into the drawing room, followed more slowly by Blossom and Leo. It was twenty minutes later that the door to the study was opened and Hilary made his way into the kitchen. Blossom got up and went in there. He was absent-mindedly putting together a plate of bread, cheese, grapes, pickle and a slice of cold roast beef from last Sunday. He paid no attention to her and in a moment she turned and went back into the drawing room.

Hilary had given up on meals, those ordinary dividers of the day. The next day, though he ate breakfast in the sense that he woke up, came to the kitchen and started eating, it was hard to say when Hilary's breakfast had come to an end. Food represented by an experience with boundaries was gone. There was nothing gradual about it: one day he was a heavy snacker, who came to the kitchen table or the dining table, too, at the usual times, and the next, after the pasta with tomato sauce, he was a continuous eater. Into the kitchen would come the boys' grandfather. He would walk about, gaze out of the window at where, perhaps, the new neighbours, Nazia and Sharif, were saying goodbye to their daughter, heading off somewhere. He would remark that they seemed a very kind couple. Then he would lean over one of his grandsons – Josh was a softer touch than Tresco – and pluck a roast potato from his plate, juggle it, put it into his mouth, panting at its heat. Half an hour after the rest of them had finished supper, he would be back in the pantry, rifling for haslet.

And then there were the sweets – impossible to ignore, the artificial sugar of the sweet-sour smell around the house, the wrappings that he'd missed and let fall here and there. Hilary had moved on from the sort of doctors' sweets that had some kind of adult presence, such as extra strong mints, and his indulgence now had an indifferent childish quality: jellies, sours, sweets in the shape of snakes and spiders and transparent primary-coloured beetles, lemon sherbets, boiled sweets, flying saucers, even babyish things, like dolly mixtures. He must have bought them as if for his grandchildren, and the result, as Leo commented, was like a huge bag of pick-and-mix from Woolworth's. Some of it *was* a huge bag of pick-and-mix from Woolworth's. The whole day he was sucking and chewing at these things, perhaps only turning to his pork pies and his cheese on crackers when the load of sugar in his blood grew too strong. Blossom and Leo watched their father, and wondered how they were going to explain any of it to Lavinia and Hugh, when they got here. Once, but only once, Leo had turned doctor to Hilary's mirthful self-stuffing toddler, and said, 'I don't know how you can eat all that crap, all that sugar.' Hilary's eyes had turned to him – they were in the study, and a bowl meant for fruit was half full of what looked like cola pips, midget gems, coconut ice and liquorice wheels. His eyes had turned back again. 'It seems to calm me down,' he said, in the end.

If he wouldn't talk to his children, knowing what they were going to want to start talking about, this was the time when, to their surprise, Josh and Tresco found themselves lined up as unwilling audiences to their grandfather's monologues. He had never done it before; they had always been the object of a hug and a push away. Now there were not enough grandchildren around, the two offered only a regular alternation as listeners to Hilary's tales of himself. The two developments went together, the orgy of sweet-eating and the incapacity to stop himself telling stuff, pretending it was an interesting or even a funny story. 'He's always been the life and soul,' Blossom said dismissively, when Tresco actually complained. 'Just get used to it.' But it was more than that. The sound of the house now was a deep voice, two rooms away, holding forth, a rustle of sweet wrappers coming and going and the words, which might have been 'I remember when my mother, your great-grandmother, this would have been ...' It was trying to be good-humoured. No one was interested. They wondered what was going to happen when Lavinia and Hugh got there. Perhaps they would join in with the sweets, at least – everyone remembered how Lavinia liked that sort of thing, and perhaps it had cascaded up the generations, like a vice the old ones had never had time to cultivate.

2.

'Good, good,' Hilary said, getting out of the car. Blossom was driving; Leo was in the back; Hugh and Lavinia were coming out of the house to greet their father. He had been at the hospital. 'Good, good,' he said, embracing Lavinia and giving Hugh a perfunctory shake about the shoulders. 'I'm not driving any more,' he said. 'I'm like you, Lavinia, a non-driver. Blossom took charge. I've given up while she's here – she wouldn't hear any different. Do you know' – they were now in the hallway, Lavinia and Hugh following their father, waiting to say something – 'it's forty-five years since I learnt to drive. It wasn't even legal when I learnt but I went on so much at your grandfather he gave in. I went on cycling, mind – I was mad keen on cycling. The last trip I made, it was a whole week through the West Country with my friend Bernard Greening. We got the train to Bristol and cycled westwards. That must have been the last summer before the war. It was never the same afterwards. We would stop at a farmhouse and they'd put us up for the night for shillings, and they'd be glad of it – and clotted cream for tea, you've never tasted anything so good, not since pasteurization and the EEC, and bacon for breakfast and their home-made sausages. That was the last cycling trip because the war happened. Poor old Bernard was killed in Sicily and afterwards I had my medical training to get through. Good trip, was it?'

(Later, going out to the supermarket with Lavinia, Blossom asked what Hilary had been saying. 'He just started telling me about life before the war,' she said.

'He does that,' Blossom said. 'He's enjoying himself. He's even doing it to Mummy, telling her about how wonderful his life used to be before the war. I would tell him to shut up, but it would be such an awful row afterwards.'

'And Mummy?' Lavinia asked.

'Mummy just closes her eyes and rests,' Blossom said. 'I think it's a change from what he usually says to her. It's more like him boring a stranger at a party than talking to one of us.'

'Or what he might be saying,' Lavinia said. 'He hasn't said anything to her, has he?'

'Not as far as we know,' Blossom said. 'Listen,' Blossom said. 'I had a terrible conversation with Leo. About Josh. I'm not at all sure I've done the right thing.')

'I'm quite enjoying not driving,' Hilary said, coming across Tresco. His grandson was lying prone, supported by his elbows, in the long grass around the elms at the bottom of the garden. He was taking aim with a catapult at a thrush. He hadn't heard his grandfather coming: he had his Discman over his ears – he'd been listening to Beethoven, which was the best music ever. There could be better wildlife and better weapons in Sheffield, in Tresco's view; he had smuggled his catapult in, but had failed to get away with his rifle. And now Grandpa had come along and started talking to him as if he weren't doing anything in particular. 'I suppose you'll be learning to drive soon.' Tresco lowered the Discman resentfully, started to object that he couldn't learn for three years yet, but his grandfather cut him off. 'I suppose it would have been 1935 I learnt to drive. I didn't pass my test, mind – it wouldn't have been legal. I wonder your father doesn't take you off to a quiet part of the grounds and teach you. My father – your grandfather – he said that when the next war came there wouldn't be time for anyone to teach me to drive and probably no petrol either. So he took me up on a quiet road on the moors, beyond where Lodge Moor is now, beyond the hospital. That's a hospital for infectious diseases, or was. It's not much used now but then, back in the thirties, it was an important sort of place. Well, your grandfather took me up there, said to me, "I'll sit with you the first couple of times, and then it's up to you." Your grandfather, great-grandfather I should say, he had an Austin saloon. Doctors like your great-grandfather were the first people to have cars, you know. He said, "Don't be frightened of the motor and you'll find it's nothing to be frightened of." And that's good advice.'

'If you say so,' said Tresco, giving up and humouring his grandfather. He had seen his mother and the uncles do just that.

'And I've driven most days for decades now,' Hilary continued. 'I must be one of the most experienced drivers in the land. And your mother's decided that, after all, she wants to drive me to the hospital, and your uncle Leo, too. That's what happened yesterday. Your aunt Lavinia never learnt to drive, did you know? I was driving long before I met your grandmother for the first time.'

(An hour or two after this, an hour or two after Tresco had lowered his catapult, crossed his forearms lying in the grass, and prepared to let his grandfather get on with things, his uncle Hugh came across him, sourly kicking the dining chairs. 'It's so nice to see a grandfather and grandson getting on so well,' he said lightly. 'That was a charming picture. I was watching you from what you call the drawing-room window.'

Tresco stared at his uncle, incredulously. 'That wasn't a *charming picture*,' he said. 'I wasn't getting on with Grandpa *so well*. He was just talking at me.'

'What was it this time?' Hugh said.

'About how he once ran something over and thought it was a little girl with ginger hair, when he was sixteen or something.'

'Oh, that one,' Hugh said. 'And it wasn't a little girl with ginger hair. It turned out to be a fox.' Tresco disgustedly nodded. To have this story inflicted on you, and for no child to be killed at the end of it – the patience and suffering was still too fresh in his mind for speech. 'I've heard that one,' Hugh said. 'He's told it once or twice before. Is it true what your mother's saying?'

'Is what true?' Tresco said.

'That your cousin Josh is going to live with you?' Hugh said. 'Is that true?')

'Enjoying where you're living, are you?' Hilary said, coming into the kitchen with a ham sandwich in one hand. Lavinia was loading the ancient dishwasher, and stood up, flushed. Hilary set the sandwich down on the counter, and went to the fridge in the pantry. He picked up a toffee from the bowl on the way, popping it into his mouth. It was a quarter to ten in the morning. Hilary emerged from the pantry holding a pork pie. 'Enjoying Fulham, are you? No – Parsons Green, is that what you say? I don't remember Parsons Green, though I know it's got a tube stop. It's changed a good deal, London. I know when I was there – well, it was just after the war I went there for medical training. Your grandfather said I didn't want to stay in Sheffield, do my training here, and he was probably right. You came across better minds in London. It was dreadful, though – I took lodgings, I remember, in Earls Court. It was either there or Notting Hill but Notting Hill was dreadfully run down and poor, and it would only have been a few years later it was taken over by immigrants and went downhill even faster, God bless their souls. London, it was really a single huge bomb site, great piles of rubble and maybe one old house, standing there in a field of bricks like an old tooth, terrible. And you handed your ration card to your landlady and she did her best for you or she diddled you, one of the two. I had one of the diddlers. I was there with my friend Alan Pritchard. He'd gone through the war, too, and was at UCL with me, too, getting a medical degree. Well, Alan Pritchard said one morning to Mrs Ratbag, "This jam's got marrow in it," and she said, "Yes, I know. That'll be because it's marrow jam, Mr Pritchard, my sister Dolly in the country made it from marrows she grew herself and sent it up for me, knowing I had lodgers to feed from the ration. Do you not care for it, Mr Pritchard?" Alan Pritchard, he said, "No, Mrs Ratbag" – he didn't call her Mrs Ratbag to her face, of course. I can't remember her real name. Instead of this, Alan said, "I would like my friend Hilary and me to be served with this orange marmalade on our toast in the morning, thank you." And he produced a jar of orange marmalade. Well, we were all astonished – in 1946, you simply did not see orange marmalade. And Mrs Ratbag just said, "Of course, Mr Pritchard, sir," and beat a hasty retreat. It turned out that his grandmother had a store of it – she'd made an enormous quantity before the war, when there was no trouble getting Seville oranges and sugar, of course. So that's why I like orange marmalade so much,' Hilary said, taking a bite out of his pork pie and going back to his study.

'I wish …' Lavinia said, as someone came into the kitchen. She stood up and turned round to make sure it wasn't her father, but it was Leo. 'Have you been getting a lot of this?'

'Lot of what?'

'Daddy going on about the remote past. He never stops.'

'No,' Leo said vaguely. 'I don't think I have. I saw him talking to Blossom the other day – she said he was telling her about what summer holidays used to be like before the war.'

'I don't know – but, Leo, is what Blossom's saying about Josh –' Lavinia said, but just then her father's voice came, triumphant, from the study.

'Rowbotham!' he called – it was as if he were calling to someone in particular. 'She was called Mrs Rowbotham. That's right. It was definitely Mrs Rowbotham.'

'Has anyone started an argument in there with him?' Leo said.

'I don't think so,' Lavinia said, but a sort of mutter had succeeded Hilary's shout. He was in there rehearsing, or going over something, or just telling for telling's sake. There must be a bowl of acid drops on the arm of his chair.

3.

The road had always been a favourite with driving instructors. It was quiet, and broad. Nervous teenagers could be brought there by their tutors to practise the horrors of the three-point turn and the reversing around corners (into Bradleigh Road) without much fear of their being interrupted by traffic. Those who lived in the solid Victorian villas down the street paid no attention. The A1 Driving School would be gone in twenty minutes. Hilary, in the front drive, washing his car, paid no attention to the Austin Metro that had stopped by his front gate. It was only when a woman got out and came up the drive-way – a tanned, even leathery, face, brilliant blue eyes and a lick of glossy gingery-blonde hair – that he looked up.

'You all right there,' the woman said. 'It's your son I'm after.' She had a strong, perhaps artificial Sheffield accent. 'Your son Leo. I heard he's back home for a bit.'

'Leo's not back,' Hilary said shortly. 'He's just visiting for a few days. He's around, I believe. Go and give him – hey, I know you. You're that girl he used to hang around with.'

'That's going back a bit,' the woman confirmed. 'I'm Helen. We used to go running together. I heard Leo's back home – my girlfriend Andrea told me she saw him mooching down Banner Cross. Well, she said she saw him, she was sure it was Leo Spinster. She was at school two years below us – we've got to know each other since. So I said to Andrea, "Are you sure it was him? What was he doing?" And it was then she said, "Well, he were just mooching." So I knew it must be Leo.'

'I'm sure he was …' Hilary said – he was seized with embar-rassment. A boy next door was standing there, idly following the conversation. 'This is Raja,' he said more briskly. 'Our new neighbours' son. I couldn't tell the difference between him and his twin until two weeks ago. His twin's called Omith. You're not going to be mistaken any more, are you, Raja?'

'What do you mean?' Raja said. 'Oh, this.' He brought his thumb and forefinger up to his throat, bandaged white. 'It's only got to stay on another ten days, Dr Spinster.'

'The boy'll be scarred,' Hilary said to Helen, not lowering his voice or speaking confidentially; he had got her off the subject of lesbianism. 'No two ways about it. It was really a stroke of luck. I was in the back garden, a couple of weekends ago, trim-ming the conifers against the hedge – they're slow growers, but every so often they do need a trim or they'll take over the whole damned place. Raja's mum and dad, next door, they were going to have a party for their cousins, sisters and brothers and everything. I was just up a ladder in my garden, minding my own business. Looked as though it was going to be a nice sort of party. The people who had the house before, they were called Tillotson, never liked them.'

'You didn't like the Tillotsons?' the boy said, from over the fence, with some interest.

'It was a welcoming party,' Hilary went on, gathering some energy as he went on talking. 'Of course their father and mother have been there for a few months now, but they've taken their time in organizing something. The children are in the garden out of the way, and the boys have noticed something. There's some fruit to be eaten, growing on a tree in the back, just there by the fence. It's a Tillotson addition. Like the rest of us, I suppose, it didn't much care for the Tillotsons. It's waited until the Tillotsons have gone altogether before it's prepared to produce any fruit worth eating. I don't blame it in the slightest.'

'Oh, Dr Spinster,' a voice said, from the side of the house next door – an admiring, humorous voice, and in a moment a handsome woman in a dark green skirt and sweater came forward from the shadows, dangling the car keys from her forefinger. She was shaking her head and smiling, and came up to her son, wrapping her arm round his neck. He might be too old for the possessive gesture, but he put up with it.

'We ate forty fruit,' the boy said. Behind him, his father stood in the doorway.

The visitor – Helen – looked unimpressed. She moved her hand up to her glossy head in a smoothing gesture, not actually touching the immaculate hair at all. As if the end of the story had been reached, she said, 'So Leo's inside, is he?'

'Throwing the things down their throats, they were,' Hilary went on. He turned to his neighbour, the woman, and spread his hands in a what-can-you-do gesture. She was enjoying this story, or making a good pretence of it. 'But even teenage boys – well, this one, suddenly, he starts choking, faints. His brother's seen the thing that you do, the Heimlich manoeuvre, the punch in the stomach from behind. But it doesn't work. I knew immediately what I had to do. I haven't been a doctor for forty years for nothing. I'm there straight away. I've got a knife, and open up the airways. That saves him. Then he's off to the hospital and I wouldn't have thought he would ever go near that tree again. Learnt his lesson. You see, the thing is, first aid, it will get you so far. But in a serious situation, what you want is a doctor. For instance, there was once, years ago, I was driving along one Sunday afternoon with wife and kids, when all at once, I saw a woman in near hysterics, running along waving her hands to stop anyone. She had no idea I was a doctor, or there would be a doctor in any of the cars approaching. This would be on the –'

'Helen,' Leo said. He was standing in the front door, his arms stretched up like an ape's in the frame, and grinning. 'What the –'

'Just a second,' Helen said curtly to Hilary before turning to Leo. 'I've come to take you away. The pub's open.'

'The thing was,' Hilary went on, laying his hand on Helen's sleeve, 'the thing was that this woman's husband, he was –'

'Thanks,' Helen said. 'I'm here to see Leo. Come on, lad.'

Hilary was still talking as they got into the car, a note of complaint and resentment creeping in.

'Your mum's in hospital, isn't she? Probably enjoying the peace and quiet,' Helen said, reversing. Somewhere back there, a brother or something was trying to put a jacket on to follow Leo and escape with them; he was being detained by Hilary, introducing him to the charming neighbours. 'I'm sorry. I could never stand your dad. I don't mean any disrespect to your mum, naturally.'

'What the hell is this?' Leo said. 'A brown Austin? What came over you?'

'My mother's got an unacceptable turn of phrase for the shade,' Helen said tranquilly. 'I'm not convinced it wasn't the original name for it, fifteen years back.'

4.

Sharif shut the front door behind them; Raja went upstairs. They might have been counting until he was out of earshot.

'The way that boy walked away,' Nazia said.

'It's just how some families are,' Sharif said.

'His father was still talking,' Nazia said. 'And the grandson, too – Dr Spinster was just saying who we were and who the grandson was. It was very nice of him. And the grandson just walked away before he was finished.'

'Learnt it from his father, I expect.'

'Well, I just don't understand it,' Nazia said. 'And I can't understand why Dr Spinster doesn't do something about it, his own family being like that.'

'I think he's used to it,' Sharif said. He rubbed his nose with the flat of his palm, made the snorting noise he made when they were unheard. 'He went on talking until there was no one left to listen to him. I just don't understand them.'

'Who?'

'People. People in this country, really. If the boys ever –'

'They won't.'

'Now I understand him. Dr Spinster. It's like a rotary engine running on and on without anything to slow it down. No belt, no friction, just spinning on and on. He's talking and they look at him and walk away. He'd do anything to get them to listen. I don't know how things get like that in a family.'

'Someone's told the children they don't need to listen to their father.'

'She wouldn't do that,' Sharif said. 'Nobody would say that to their children. I can't believe it of her.'

'You don't know her,' Nazia said.

The pub Leo and Helen went to was the pub they were always going to go to. It was a 1930s brick roadhouse, built at the edge of the city and clinging to a steep collapse of moor behind. The front of the pub had two storeys; the back had four, a now unused dining room and a deep cellar filling the gap. It had never been very successful: built to catch travellers going to Manchester, or arriving from there, it had discovered that travellers rarely wanted to fill up with one last chance before heading off on the thirty or so miles to the next city, or were so desperate on arriving that they couldn't go a little further. Leo was touched that Helen had come here without asking. They went to the Tyler Arms because that was where they had always gone.

And Jack the landlord was still there. Leo had to suppress an inclination to walk in with artificially rigid arm-swings. This was the pub they'd come to because the landlord would serve even a fifteen-year-old. It was some years later that they realized the pub was so short of custom that it thought it could spot a policeman, and take a risk. In the early seventies, it was more important to impersonate a grown-up. They didn't know the landlord's name was Jack. He just looked like a Jack, and J was his initial in the licence over the door. There was nobody there, in the afternoon.

'Andrea saw you,' Helen said. They were settled with a pint each. 'You remember Andrea? We've been together six years now. She's pregnant – in fact, she was on her way to her six-month check-up when she saw you.'

'How does that work, then?' Leo said. 'The impregnation, I mean.'

'Oh, for fuck's sake, Leo,' Helen said. 'It's none of your fucking business. We just did it with the aid of some sperm, all right?'

'Yeah, but fresh sperm – it's not exactly lying about on the street, is it? What did you do?'

'Leo,' Helen said. 'You can ask whatever questions you like. I am not going to take you through the process in detail.'

'Congratulations,' Leo said. 'You've taken your time. I was twenty-two when Catherine had Josh. He's twelve now.'

'Well, you didn't have to plan and organize like we did,' Helen said. 'Actually, no, we were lucky, we just found a jar of top-quality sperm on the street and thought, That's as good as any. What's up with Catherine?'

'We split up years ago,' Leo said. 'You wake up one morning and you look at the other person, and you think, I don't know about this any more. I had this real moment of generosity. I thought, You could do better with someone other than me.'

'Has she got someone else, then?'

'No. She's not. She says it's tough out there for a woman with a child. No one's interested. It's unfair – women like a man with a kid, left on his own. Other way round – brings out the maternal.'

'This conversation is exactly why I never had the slightest regret in putting men like you behind me,' Helen said.

'I just can't understand why you went lesbian,' Leo said. 'I'd never have thought it while we were together.'

'We were never together, Leo,' Helen said. 'We had it off five times. That was it. Another pint?'

'Definitely.'

Helen, he saw, had a distinctive way of standing at the bar, not masculine but head up and elbows out. She had bought the last round, too.

'It's good to see you,' Leo said, when she came back.

'And you,' Helen said. 'You want to come up to Sheffield more often. We'd ask you to be the godfather to our child, except that obviously we're not going to ask someone who abandoned his own child.'

'I've not abandoned my own child.'

'Oh, yeah? What's going on with your dad? Where's your mum? She always used to be able to shut him up.'

'She's dying, love,' Leo said. He was oddly pleased to be able to say something so abrupt, something that would change the whole conversation. He had noticed this in himself before, the eagerness to carry news, whether some public catastrophe, a bombing or the death of a celebrity, or some family event. He deplored it in himself, the wish to place himself at the centre of events, as the first bearer of news. But he had to tell Helen that his mother was dying.

'I'm sorry to hear that,' Helen said formally. She took a swig of beer; she continued in exactly the same tone of voice. Leo recognized Helen, the way she had of refusing to be embarrassed or put in the wrong. 'I always liked your mum. Is she in hospital?'

'In the Northern General,' Leo said. 'She was supposed to come home, but she's developed an infection – it's cancer of the bowel. She could come out of this and carry on for a while and come home. Or you never know.'

'You're all up here, then,' Helen said. 'Your brother and sister – both your sisters. Your dad, though.'

'Sometimes I wish my mum and dad had married different people. What size children did they think the pair of them were going to produce? My sister's four foot eleven.'

'And you're five foot one,' Helen said. 'On a good day. The grandchildren are all right, though. They're up to normal, the ones I've seen.'

The bar of the pub was unchanged in nearly twenty years. Even the spider plant on the windowsill, dead and dusty, had not been moved, and the horse brasses in a vertical line on the wooden panelling between the two leaded windows made the same claim to hearty gentility. Jack, in his usual brown cardigan, had poured their pints, and now returned to his usual occupation, working with a much-sucked biro at the *Telegraph* crossword, bent over underneath the long run of empty glasses, suspended in their wooden cage above his head. The television was on, and showing some curious sport from where it hung above the dangling dartboard; two men carefully stood on a green expanse, judged, calculated, then sent a ball spinning forward to come to rest through momentum where they had planned or, disappointingly, some distance from where they had wished it to come to rest.

'What fills your days, then?' Helen said. 'Still the old journalism?'

'It's hardly journalism,' Leo said. 'That makes it sound like investigating and reporting. I sit in the office and correct what other people write about exotic places they've been – make them say, "The markets of Asia are famous the world over," whether they want to or not. And their grammar. You'd be surprised. And put it onto the page and think up a headline. "Miss out on Paris? You'd be in Seine!" That was mine. Or my colleague Julie got "Why not holiday in Ireland? You'll be walking on Eire!" They wouldn't have "Total calypso the sun" for a piece about Jamaica – they said it didn't make sense.'

Helen drank again, and if it was possible to take a swig of beer in an unsympathetic and even disapproving way, that was what Helen now did. Leo tried to remember what she did for a living. He had lost track of the days, but surely today was a weekday.

'You're not working for the Crucible, then,' Leo said, not quite able to work out how to ask directly.

'No – why would you think that?' Helen said. 'It's Andrea works for them, does their marketing. I can't stand theatre. I only go there when I have to. I can't think why you thought – Did we ever talk about theatre? I couldn't tell you how much money the Crucible get from the Arts Council – that's how little interest I have in it.'

Helen looked over the rim of her beer glass, now empty, at Leo. She set it down and, quite suddenly, gave a brief dry laugh. 'You're not up to speed, are you, Leo, love?' she said. 'I actually thought – if I just dropped in, how much has Leo been wondering about me? Enough to find anything out?'

'I don't know who I'd ask,' Leo said.

'There'd be someone,' Helen said. 'It doesn't matter. It's not important at all. I work for the university library, as it happens. I love it. I don't see why I should ever do anything else.'

'Nor me,' Leo said bravely.

'Oh, aye,' Helen said, and that, surely, was a deliberate, a performed piece of talk. Leo was sure that nobody they had known had ever said, 'Oh, aye,' in anything but a ridiculous way.

'The thing is,' Leo said, 'Miss Saul who taught German at school – I once bumped into her in Broomhill. Was I taking a year out, she wanted to know – she'd thought I was going straight up. They were so proud of me at school. No, I said. I'd had to leave. Oh, she said, why was that – and I had to explain. You have to explain. And she put her hand on my arm as if I'd suffered a terrible loss. For someone like me to walk away from it just because some idiot – Well, it looked terrible. She looked so upset.'

'I can see that,' Helen said. 'But you wanted to go in the first place.'

'Yes,' Leo said. He couldn't think what else to say. He took the empty pint mugs up to the bar. Jack the landlord raised his head – watery, yellow, bloodshot eyes, as if some ulcer had developed the capacity of sight. His skin was pocked and darkened, as if smoked. He assessed Leo. For a moment Leo was fifteen again, and passing himself off as eighteen. Without meaning to, Leo straightened himself. But no one would ask his age ever again. He would never be fifteen again, or eighteen. That was how things worked. He ordered two pints of beer; Jack observed that it was nice out; Leo paid, noticing that it was about a pound cheaper here per pint than it was in London; and he took them back to the tiny table in the corner where Helen sat, quite upright, entirely sober.

'You'd have done better to stick Oxford out and show a bit less limpet-like loyalty to this job you're doing now,' Helen said savagely. 'At least you'd have had a qualification at the end of it. Tom Dick stuck it out.'

'Yes,' Leo said flatly. 'Tom Dick stuck it out.'

'He's back in Sheffield now,' Helen said, clearly giving up on any idea that Leo might be about to tell him why he'd left Oxford.

'I heard he was back in Sheffield,' Leo said. 'My sister Blossom thought she'd seen him. Still tall?'

'Still tall,' Helen said. She stroked, almost affectionately, the brown glossy anaglypta wallpaper by their table. 'You're obsessed. People might think ... well, Andrea heard from a girl in ante-natal. Her dad was the editor of the *Morning Telegraph*. So he went into newspapers in London, too, but with him, he was more on the administrative side, so to speak. He went in to ask for a job, Andrea's friend heard, and they were very impressed – he's got a lot of stuff on his CV, looked like hot stuff, rapidly rising. And then Andrea's friend's dad said, "Hold on, why's this man with a career like this in London, in Fleet Street, wanting a job in Sheffield all of a sudden?" He's got a glowing reference but, you know, a bit *guarded*. I've written references like that myself and I've expected what happened here, which is a phone call. So before he called Tom Dick in, Andrea's friend's dad, he phoned his friend on the last newspaper Tom Dick had worked on for a discreet off-the-record chat to see what's behind this glowing but guarded reference. He knows everyone in Fleet Street, Andrea reckons. And his friend knew the whole story, and it was that Tom Dick had been caught taking drugs in the office – not even in the evening or at an office party, at ten thirty in the morning before going into some routine meeting. Sacked him straight off. Very puritanical, some of those old newspapers. I expect you know all about it. I'm surprised you hadn't heard the story.'

'We're very tucked away in Travel,' Leo said. 'We don't know even people on the next page to us, let alone suits on another paper altogether. I've not heard Tom Dick's name for ten years, tucked away as we are.'

'You wouldn't get away with snorting cocaine at your desk, then, not at ten thirty in the morning? Thought not. Tom Dick tries to say that everyone's doing it, that it's not something he asks anyone to admire, but he's being made a scapegoat and, look, all these other people – he named names, a dozen people, the paper calls them all in, conducts immediate blood tests, urine tests on them, shows nothing. One of them's carrying on alarming, threatening to sue the paper and sue Tom Dick for making groundless accusations now that the investigation's produced absolutely nothing. Or almost nothing. The boy

fetching and carrying for Tom Dick turns out to be the one
fetching and carrying the drugs as well as more orthodox tasks.
He's high as a kite when they call him in, told him he's lucky
not to be facing a jail term. All this Andrea's friend's dad, the
editor of the *Morning Telegraph*, finds out with one phone call.
Tells Tom Dick he's grateful for his interest but he won't be
taking this any further.'

'It's a small world,' Leo said dismally.

'Thought he could remove himself up here, impress them
with some London and Oxford chat, drop some names, tell
them his father always spoke highly of the other chap's father,
then Bob's your uncle. Didn't work. I think he's living with his
mum again. He's hard up – bought a flat in Docklands at the
first opportunity. Had to sell it – tried to sell it for two years, no
one wants to buy it. Nobody wants to live out there, I reckon.
Lost a packet. I don't think he's really going to get sued for
defamation in the workplace. They knew he wouldn't want stuff
to come out.'

'Oh dear,' Leo said lightly. All this filled him with
happiness.

Helen looked at him suspiciously. Could it be that Helen had
told him this story in a spirit of sympathy for Tom Dick? Did
he think that Leo and Tom Dick, having gone to Oxford
together, had so much in common that his heart would go out
to the six-foot-seven height of Tom Dick, like a warm beacon
of care? It appeared to Leo that Helen's face had, in the last ten
or fifteen years, changed in more than physical incidentals: it
looked at him as if she was not sure that she had ever met him
before.

'You know something,' Helen said, after a while. 'Tom Dick
asked me if I wanted to have sexual intercourse with him. But
he asked me in French. That was after I'd packed you in, when
we were fifteen or so.'

'*Qu'est-ce que vous avez dit en réponse de cela?*' Leo said.

'What do you think?' Helen said. 'Your French.'

5.

At first he had just felt that he wanted a pee. But he had made the mistake of switching the light on in the bathroom. You couldn't find your way without it, but after going back to bed, he found that he couldn't go back to sleep, and reached out for his book, an old Josephine Tey. He had read it before, but he liked it, and for the moment could not remember whether the man who had surfaced claiming to be the heir was going to turn out to be a villain, or not. His eye went over the lines, then the pages. He was fully awake now, but he could not take in the meaning of the words. Perhaps he should try one of those queer dull old books the boy was always reading.

The bedside clock, a travelling alarm clock, said 2:20. If he turned off the light, the luminescent hands would go on telling the time into the dark for a while. He wondered what Celia was doing now: was she moaning with pain, was she being attended to by nurses, was she awake and thinking? Probably none of them: pain management was far advanced nowadays. She would be sleeping and deep in confusing opiate dreams, the massive weightless power of the assertions the sleeping brain made and the scenes swiftly shifting. He could have done with some opiates himself, or at the very least some diazepam to send him off to sleep. There was probably some in the house still – he'd written enough prescriptions for Celia over the years, and she was always putting the little strips down and forgetting about them. He wouldn't go searching for them.

In the past, he had woken in the small hours, for no particular reason. A worry would surge into his docile brain, and bring him to alertness. But then he would not turn on the light to read, or any longer than it took to check the time on the travelling bedside clock; Celia was deep in her diazepam spell, a mound of blonde hair on the pillow opposite, but to keep the clock on would in time wake her. Then he would lie awake, thinking, brooding. Those times had gone. It was only in the last few weeks that he had found himself waking like this again, with serious regularity only since the children had come home.

He tried to self-diagnose. He had always been good with patients, he considered, jollying them along, sharing examples from his experience that he knew would be a help. People didn't want to know that your doctor had never seen this before. If he placed himself in the patient's chair and asked the questions, what came out? Lord knows enough patients had presented with what he was experiencing now.

– So what seems to be the problem?

– I don't seem to be able to sleep. I mean I can't sleep.

– Is it from bedtime, this sleeplessness you're experiencing?

– No, I don't have any difficulty getting off to sleep, but then I wake up at three or four and I can't get back to sleep.

– It's not over-stimulus, then. Are you drinking alcohol in the evenings?

– Not to excess.

– That depends on what you call excess. Do you have anything on your mind? Any worries?

But that question had too obvious and idiotic an answer. An answer, too, that, if he addressed it, would inevitably bring back into the mind the postulated cause of the insomnia, to use a technical term of the sort we doctors are very fond of. All at once the woman this afternoon came to mind, before Hilary and the children had set off to visit Celia, the friend of Leo. Who was she? A woman probably younger than she looked, who had dismissed him, she'd rather talk to anyone else – go away, old man. He luxuriated in the rage and the plunder of his emotions. All he had been doing was telling a trivial story about something interesting that had happened. There was no cause for people to be so rude. The memory of the insult was strong. It was keeping him from sleep on its own. It rose up, but then it dropped away and the subject it was veiling came upon Hilary with a great clang of righteousness. Tomorrow would be the day he would tell Celia they must get divorced.

There was a noise from downstairs. It was not a burglar. It was one of the children coming in late. It must be Leo. Hilary quickly turned off his bedside light. He did not want to speak to Leo in what remained of today, and certainly not to have an argument with him. The boy had gone out at lunchtime, just as they were preparing to go to the hospital to visit Celia; he had left the woman's bad-taste insult behind him. He had not been back by the time Hilary and the rest of them had gone to bed. Hilary lay as silent as he could, his tendons and muscles quite stiff in the dark. There was the sound of the light fizzing on in the kitchen, and the tap pouring out one glass after another. The downstairs toilet was used, and up the stairs, heavily, came Leo's footsteps. Hilary listened; there was a heavy pause, somewhere towards the top of the stairs. He held his breath.

'Daddy?' Leo's voice said. But he would not respond, and Leo did not know that he was awake; his voice was lowered and tentative, expecting only a waking response, not to wake him up. Leo went on, into his bedroom, the door shutting. Hilary lay there in the darkness, and after some minutes, his son's snoring vibrated in the house's unmoving spaces – it was quite a soft noise, the noise of paper riffling rather than what Hilary had sometimes heard from patients in hospital, heavy furniture being moved across a hard floor. In time the house was completely still, apart from the soft sound, and some time after five or five thirty, now that it was light, Hilary got up and went downstairs. He wouldn't mind having something to eat, something on toast, a piece of cake, a slice of the M&S apple pie that was in the fridge, if he wasn't very much mistaken.

6.

When Lavinia came down to breakfast, her father was already at the table. She had been woken by Blossom – she supposed her sister must always be an early riser, what with four children and a house to run and Stephen, quite often, to see off. From the study where Blossom was sleeping had come half a phone call; Stephen, it turned out, was fine, Tamara and Thomas and Trevor were quite all right, though Trevor had had a touch of colic and Thomas had fallen off a wall and punched his big sister. The Japanese nanny didn't know what to do. It sounded much as usual to Blossom, repeating almost everything she was told by Tamara at the other end of the line. It was almost as if she were relaying the news to the rest of them. Lavinia came into the kitchen to find her father sitting, drumming his fingers on the pine table in his paisley pyjamas and striped dressing-gown. Around him were bowls and an empty plate. She couldn't think how long he might have been there.

'Good, good,' her father said, not quite looking at her and, as if he were waiting for her arrival, got up and turned Radio 4 on. The news was just winding down – it must be a minute or two after seven. Without any kind of delay, he began: 'I can't believe that John Gummer.'

'That …'

'That John Gummer!' her father said. 'That's him, on the radio. Talking about Creutzfeldt-Jakob syndrome. As if he knew anything about it! It really is beyond me, how these people get into these positions.'

'These –'

'He runs agriculture in this country. And now he's looking at this situation where cattle have been fed quite inappropriate food, and it's spreading into the human population, and as far as he knows thousands of people are about to die terrible deaths and – John, Selwyn, Gummer. You never trust a person with three names where two would do perfectly well. Like David Lloyd George.'

'Or Nat King Cole,' Lavinia said. She took a couple of spoonfuls of the standing Bircher muesli into her own bowl and added some yogurt to it. It was quite a nice day outside. She determined that she would not sit down.

'Or Patrick Gordon Walker,' her father said, perhaps ignoring what she had said. She was not sure, herself, who Patrick Gordon Walker was, but she was certainly not going to ask.

'Or Martin Luther King,' she added.

'Exactly,' Hilary said. He might have been waiting for exactly this name. 'Things would have been much better all round if it weren't for that gentleman drumming up publicity for everything that crossed his mind. And now John Selwyn Gummer. He's in charge of agriculture. Never spent a day outside in his life. Pallid little pen-pusher. Imagine him telling a room full of farmers what they were to do!'

'What's up with him?' Lavinia said. 'Has he died?'

'Died?' Hilary said. 'What made you think that?'

There was a range of breakfast possibilities, these days, including the Bircher muesli, which, of course, you could customize to your own requirements. Lavinia thought about slicing a banana on top. Out there, the lawn was splashed in the light of the dew. The back garden would probably be even nicer. Yesterday, she had been sitting at the window of the sitting room, quite idly, when a movement had been made, far down the end of the garden. A quick start – a flurry – a sharp stop. Whether it was a bird or a squirrel, Lavinia had seen the movement but not the body that had made it. She wondered what interesting things could be happening out there now.

'Of course,' Hilary said, 'you wonder about the motivation of these people. The ones who want to become politicians in the first place. Revenge on all those people who are more interesting than he is. This one doesn't know a sheep from a goat until it's roasted and sliced up on his dinner plate. But who cares? You see –'

'That's an interesting point,' Lavinia said. She picked her bowl up and walked without reproach into the sitting room. Her father carried on talking as if he were following her. She sat down on the sofa, drawing her bare feet up to the side. Out in the garden, birds were singing. The garden looked delicious and fresh, the lawn just at that lovely point where it could do with cutting. She liked that, just the point of disorder before somebody would say that something really ought to be done. In the kitchen, her father's voice subsided; there was the sound, tranquil, reassuring, superior, of one public figure after another supplying answers on Radio 4.

In a moment, Tresco came downstairs, his plunging impatient feet bounding two stairs at a time, and a big leap at the end. Her father's voice started up again almost before Tresco was in the kitchen, but in less than a minute, Tresco was out again and, like his aunt, straight into the sitting room. He threw himself full length on the sofa and started gnawing at a heel of a loaf with half a jar of marmalade spread over it. Tresco's breakfast was a thing of horror. Lavinia watched it.

'What are you up to today?' she asked.

There was a noise from Tresco that might have been 'Dunno'.

'It depends on Mummy, I expect,' Lavinia helped. There was a massive and contemptuous shrug – a difficult thing to attempt while lying down with both fists around half a loaf of bread. She watched it with interest. In a moment Tresco swallowed the bolus of foodstuff clogging his mouth. One day he would be enormously fat.

'Who the hell is John Selwyn Gummer?' he said.

'A mass-murderer,' Lavinia said lightly. 'According to your grandfather. Is he still on about it?'

'I thought he was talking to Gertrude,' Tresco said.

Blossom came down, already calling for Tresco, who was in the sitting room, and Josh. Where were they? She hoped they were up. In the kitchen, the radio was still running, and someone was talking about the sports – usually their father's cue to get up and go to the lavatory. Where are they? Had they

somehow acquired their own breakfast? They hadn't put poor
kind Grandpa to any trouble, had they?

Blossom's voice, so resonant these days. She was the mother
of four, but so was Granny, and Granny had never seen the need
to raise her voice, had retreated with a book and a cup of tea to
shut the door when discipline was needed or a sense of who was
in control. And, strangely enough, that had worked: the shutting of the door, the giving up – or saying, 'I really give up,' at
any rate – and all at once the quarrel sank. Why did Blossom
call so resonantly? Was it the wide acres she owned and surveyed?
Was it to silence something, the observation that she was really
quite ... tiny? And she was down the stairs and into the kitchen,
still calling, as if her father were not there, calling for Josh and
Tresco. She subsided, and then, at the same level of voice, her
father said, 'They're in the sitting room. They took their breakfast in there.'

'It's just me, Mummy,' Tresco called, then to Lavinia, 'I don't
hang about with Josh all the time. We don't wait for each other
to get up in the morning or anything. Mummy –'

'Good morning, Blossom,' Lavinia said, as her sister came in,
eating a yogurt from the fridge. 'Sleep well?'

'I know,' Blossom said to Tresco. 'Did you hear Leo come in?
What a din. He simply fell through the front door. Daddy's in
a vile mood now. He asked me whether it was about time that
bloody woman went just now. Mrs Thatcher.'

'He was asking me about someone called Bummer,' Tresco
said.

'What are you talking about in there?' came the voice from
the kitchen. It was so easy to forget that their father was there,
in a cloud of bad mood – denunciation and regret. But then she
heard him say something else, to somebody who was in there
with him. 'Oh, there you are,' he said. Josh had come downstairs silently. Nobody really noticed Josh. And now Daddy was
rousing himself, you could hear, and was starting on the
Conservative cabinet again. Let him not be horrible to Josh, not
Josh, Blossom found herself thinking. But then all at once she

heard her father's voice say, 'But I was listening to ...' and instead of the metallic radio voices there was music. Josh, her brother's shy son, had come into the kitchen and had stopped his grandfather's complaints by turning the radio station over.

It must be Radio 3. Blossom stood up.

When Josh had gone into the kitchen, he understood three things. His grandfather saw him only as someone he had seen before and need not bother with. His grandfather was feeding off the radio voices, urbane, heated, complaining, acute; feeding off what they said and turning it black. What the radio was saying was not important to Josh. His grandfather went on talking, talking with a kind of angry joy: his rage had been fed, given subjects. There was no space for anyone else in the room.

Josh saw two things: his grandfather, swelling, almost choking, and the stream of words out of the radio. On the floor was the third thing; it was Gertrude. Gertrude inspected Josh. He was not so stupid as to ask whether Gertrude liked him or not. He did not know if she had even noticed him, in the slow passage of her days across which her family flitted, like flies across a screen. But now, in her kitchen, Gertrude raised her long scaly neck and looked at Josh; her face was confident and cross, like a teacher who knew that you knew what you were supposed to do, and was waiting. Grandfather said something that showed how cross he was as the morning started. It didn't matter that it was Josh who was there to hear it. But Josh did know what to do. He walked across the kitchen to where the radio sat on the shelf above the cabinet where the pots and dishes lived. He pressed the station button to the third one along. It had been on the fourth station. There was a shocked silence.

'Here, I was listening ...' his grandfather said, but Josh ignored him. Gertrude watched him sit down and, in his grandfather's company, begin making his own breakfast. He had switched the radio station at exactly the right time, just before a piece of music began to play. Now it started. It was like a doorbell ringing, the first sound; it was an orchestra playing. Josh poured Coco Pops into his bowl, and added milk. There was a tune, a thoughtful, wandering tune, then something more like a dance. You could feel the orchestra, in rehearsal, smiling as this started, and soon a bell – a bell? No, a triangle like the ones at school – rang. Josh was listening to the tune, which showed no prospect of stopping, just passing from one instrument to another. Sometimes it was hard to find for the moment, but then it swelled from lower down in the orchestra, and there it was. Grandfather had gone quiet; there was nothing to start up his breakfast time complaint in all of this. Was he enjoying it, the way that Gertrude appeared to be enjoying it, her neck swaying from one side to the other?

In the door was Tresco. Josh knew he would come to listen. Music was something Tresco secretly liked; he would never let anyone borrow his Discman, and what he kept playing on it nobody knew. Tresco stood in the doorway, not expecting anyone to say anything to him; the music was growing noisy, but wonderfully so, an orchestra filling the kitchen with a huge tune, and underneath, like swells of sea groaning underneath a wooden boat, the rolls of a deep drum. His grandfather was looking at them, at Josh, and then at Tresco, as if he did not quite understand; he had a sort of nervous fear in his trembling red-blue eyes. Tresco came in and sat down; he made a comedy miming gesture, as if he were a mad conductor bringing this piece to the climax, and behind him were Josh's aunts. They had been summoned, too, by the magic of the music, summoned back to finish their breakfast in the kitchen. It was coming to an end; the orchestra seemed to be floating towards a resting place, and over the top, some frolic yells, repeated, a rude gesture, full of invulnerability and joy. Josh enjoyed those; at the end of this piece, he could see a man making two fingers at his enemies, clustered on a beach, and sailing off. There he goes – there he goes – there he goes. Aunt Lavinia was smiling. She had enjoyed it as much as he had. And now here was Daddy, in his pair of pyjamas, smelling quite – Josh liked to find the right word, and the right word presented itself – smelling quite *pungent*.

'You woke me up,' he said. 'I came in late and I was going to sleep in.'

'We heard you come in,' Blossom said. 'It was deafening, your arrival, falling through the front door.'

'And now you're getting your own back,' Daddy said. 'Waking me up. You and Lemminkäinen. An old favourite, but maybe not at eight in the morning.'

'The *Today* programme doesn't finish until nine,' Grandpa said, with a touch of uncertainty. He looked from face to face, from Josh to Tresco to the aunts, Blossom and Lavinia, to Daddy; he had the nervous look of someone at school who had heard a joke told and had seen everyone else laugh, but who had not quite understood it himself. He would not have been summoned into the kitchen by Lemminkäinen. It was a wonderful sight to Josh: Blossom and Lavinia and Leo and Grandpa and Tresco and, if he was honest, himself. They would look so nice to the rest of the world, the six of them, and not one of them taller than five feet two inches.

Outside, on the front lawn of his grandfather's house, Josh's uncle Hugh bent over in shorts and vest, panting and pink, his dark hair tousled upwards. His sad-funny face; his puffin eyes, like no one else's in the family. He shone in the brilliant light; the lawn was splashed in dew and sun. He was back from his morning run, the last bit a mad-making sprint up the hill, and Hugh was five feet tall, two inches exactly taller than his sister Lavinia.

7.

'Is it Sunday today?' Leo heard Lavinia ask Hugh. He was inside, reading a book; his head was throbbing, the book made very little sense. He had returned to the top of the page half a dozen times. Lavinia and Hugh were somewhere about. He could not tell from their voices whether they were outside on the terrace, upstairs, in another room or even in the sitting room. His head was pummelled against the sofa cushions.

'Is it what today?' Hugh said. But then Leo realized it wasn't Hugh, but Daddy. Their voices were both such performances.

'Sunday,' Lavinia said. 'I've completely lost all sense of time. I don't know when we got here.'

'It's certainly not Sunday,' Hugh said – it was definitely his voice now, and from another room. 'It certainly isn't. There were kids starting to go to school as I was running home. Don't say it's Monday.'

'It can't be Monday,' Lavinia said, her voice rising. 'I've got to phone the office if it's Monday. I promised them I'd only be away for a couple of days.'

'It's Tuesday,' Leo said, his voice slightly raised.

Lavinia and Hugh were silent for a moment: they hadn't known he was there.

'I bought the *Observer* the day before yesterday,' Leo said. 'That's how I know.'

'I should have phoned the office yesterday,' Lavinia said. 'You're supposed to have started rehearsals yesterday for *Bartholomew Fair*. You've got to phone them and explain.'

But Hugh had phoned his agent last week and said that things were worse than he had expected, and he would miss the first four days of rehearsals, no more.

'I didn't think to do that,' Lavinia said humbly. 'You're so well organized, really. I don't dare to phone them now – they'll be furious. When are you going to go back?'

'You'd better go back,' Hugh said. 'You shouldn't depend on me so much for anything.'

'I don't depend on you,' Lavinia said.

'I just think we shouldn't do so much together.'

In the office at this moment – in Leo's office – there would be a message to call a hotel manager URGENTLY because somebody had described his hot tub as a Jacuzzi and said that it was in the garden, rather than in the grounds, of the hotel. There would be a telephone call to make to the restaurant reviewer, who knew quite well he was supposed to file by lunchtime on Monday, who also knew quite well that copy could be got in if it was filed on Thursday morning. Leo's office mate, the editor of the pages, was Rob. He'd been there for ever. He looked up when Leo came in in the mornings in precisely the same unenthusiastic way that he had looked up when Leo had been brought in for the first time a couple of years ago. No – not a couple of years ago. A decade ago. Josh had just been born. He had looked up as if smelling something, waiting for something to be foisted on him. He gave the nod that consisted of a backwards tilt of the head. Rob came to the office in a charcoal pinstripe suit every day, these days. He had remarked that he didn't propose to buy another suit this side of retirement, which, please God, was only months away. But he had said that a year or two back. Somewhere along the line Janice, who was the busy PA to the Foreign editor, had told him that Rob lived in one room in Balham with a wife in the country he hadn't seen since the spring.

Leo had told Rob all about what was going on. The schedule had been passed over to a stringer. There was no shortage of idle sub-editors around who could lend a hand with the page and layout. In any case, Leo happened to know that there was getting on for seven clear weeks' copy in hand, having written most of it. It was surprising that today was Tuesday, and now he felt that before they went to the hospital, he ought to call Rob again. It had been ten days ago or something, the last time they had spoken.

'Travel,' Rob's voice said, at the end of the phone.

'Hi, Rob,' Leo said. 'It's Leo.'

'What?' Rob said. 'Speak up – didn't catch that.'

'I said, it's Leo.'

'Oh. Yes. Leo. Happened to you? Woman down from Admin Friday asking – still ill, is he?'

'I'm not ill,' Leo said. 'It's my mother. She's dying and – well, she's dying.'

'OK,' Rob said. There was one of those lengthy pauses in Rob's conversation that came before an uncomfortable and often punitive statement. Rob was not someone who would swear in the office, and very much disapproved of it in his colleagues. He would make up his mind and inform you of it, and then that was it. 'Said you were going off – thought meant two, three days.'

'Well, I'm sorry my mother's not died yet,' Leo said.

'Not the point I'm making,' Rob said. 'If it was going to be going on for some time, would appreciate it if you'd keep me informed, maybe, you know, come back for a couple of days to help out. How long's it been? Since you, you know, gave us a bell? Woman from Admin says, "I'd like to discuss situation with him." Had to say, "Good luck with that, young lady, no idea where he is. Sheffield, perhaps. Don't know." He's ex-directory, your father. No Spinsters in Sheffield, she discovered. Retired now, too.'

'Well,' Leo said, 'I suppose I could come back to work. Day after tomorrow.' Outside in the garden, Blossom was playing badminton with Tresco; she was bouncing around heavily, her face reddened and her hair flying. Tresco would have been defeating her thoroughly if the game of badminton they were playing had any borders or rules; they had just started up, there on the lawn, without net or lines, and were batting the shuttle-cock at each other. Perhaps for his own amusement, Tresco had manoeuvred his mother round so that now they were playing along the length of the lawn where, five minutes ago, they had been playing across its width. In the sun, the piling up of the flowers in the border, the neat lawn, the figures of mother and son at ill-assorted sport were what had always been there. In his hand, the telephone receiver was still speaking.

'Very good of you,' Rob said. It was impossible to determine whether he was being sardonic. 'And when you come back – stay back? Or just put in a day or two? Woman from Admin. Wants to have a word, I warn you. Calls herself Human Resources these days. Make you sound like a seam of coal in a mine.'

'I'll have a word with her,' Leo said. 'When I come in.'

'And that'll be Thursday,' Rob said. 'Right. OK, see you then.'

Rob was prepared to put the phone down, but he had got the wrong end of the stick.

'No,' Leo said. 'I said I'll try to be back on Thursday. It depends on how things are with my mother. And my father.'

'Father ill, too, is he?' Rob said.

'No,' Leo said. 'Father not ill, too.'

'No need to take that line,' Rob said. 'Might be a figure of fun to you. Trying to bring out a newspaper here. Other chap absented himself without notice, about month ago now. Are you here on Thursday or not?'

'I'll do my best to be back on Thursday,' Leo said.

'I need to know,' Rob said.

'Well,' Leo said. 'If you insist on a definite answer, I'll have to say that I'm not going to be back on Thursday.'

'Right,' Rob said. 'I'll inform the woman from Admin, whatever her name was. She'll put the whole thing in process.'

'The whole –'

'Absent without notice,' Rob said. 'We need to bring the paper out. You're no good to us if you can't tell us when you'll be back. They'll see you all right.'

And then something very strange happened that Leo would not have predicted at all. He would have said, if asked, in any circumstances, what he most feared, that he feared losing his job; he knew that the job was what kept him going, what paid the mortgage on the house in Battersea, what gave him something to do. No one ever had asked Leo what he most feared, in fact. No one had ever really been interested enough. But he had always been clear in his own mind that what he most feared was the loss of employment, of a future in which he would never again correct 'pristine' to 'immaculate' in another's copy, and never again author a printed sentence which told the readers of the daily newspaper he wrote for that the luxury hotels of the Cotswolds were raising their game to levels never before seen. Never seen before. He had thought that that was the worst of all futures before him. He had not thought that that was a future imminently before him when he had picked up the telephone in his father's study, surrounded by Blossom's clothes pouring out of her grip, the balled-up green-and-blue duvet on the single bed, like a sleepless night. He was terribly hung-over. It was important to say it, however.

'Yes,' Leo said. 'I think that's best. I think I've been looking for an out for some time now. It's been good, Rob, and I'd like to say thank you some time, but I don't think I want to carry on. I'll be in touch with the woman from Admin. Thanks.'

'OK, thanks to you,' Rob said. 'Clarifying matters.' The phone went down. Outside, the game of badminton had reached a breathless, panting pause. Blossom was bent over, her hands on her knees. Her son Tresco was waiting, thwacking his racquet against his flat hand. Downstairs there was the soft sound of Lavinia and Hugh affectionately berating each other; the regular patient clarity of Bach or Handel or someone of that sort ticking away on the radio. No one had thought to turn Radio 3 off.

8.

The visiting hours at the hospital were from two o'clock, but the nurses on the ward made no objection when Leo arrived just before one. His mother had been moved into a room on her own at least a week ago, for no reason that had been shared with Leo. This was a permanent arrangement, apparently. He had decided that he wanted to see his mother on his own, before the rest of them could get there. The visiting hours were supervised by their father, who sat by the side of their mother's bed for six hours without much of a break, admitting one child or grandchild after another, finding the occasional space for a visiting friend or neighbour. All that time, Hilary eyed them, listening with half an ear to Celia's confused painkilled ramblings, the feeble offerings by each of the children of things that might be positive and interesting. When Leo was there, he was convinced that at any moment his father was going to inform Celia that they were going to divorce. He kept on talking, making less and less sense, so as not to open a gap of silence. Hilary sat back in the blue armchair that was really meant for patients to sit up in, and folded his arms, waiting.

But today Leo was early. He had left the house without saying anything around twelve; he had caught the bus into the city centre; he had taken another bus from the city centre. He was rewarded by his mother. She was sitting up in bed, tired and pale, but not confused, or with that look of groggy cunning that was the product of morphine. She was expectant and unoccupied, as if she were quite clear that Leo was about to come through the door; her white hair was combed in a way not quite her own, and her face took on some delight as he came in.

'Leo!' she said.

'Hello, Mummy,' he said, and kissed her. He could feel that she winced a little at his embrace, trying not to; she still had her clean smell of lily-of-the-valley and Persil. She was as white as the plaster that held her right arm. 'I thought I'd come a bit ahead of the others.'

'Oh, that's a nice idea,' Celia said. 'You never get a chance to talk to anyone when your father's sitting there, glowering. Go and sit in his chair.'

'It's not his chair,' Leo said. 'It's your chair, really. What news?'

'Nothing much,' Celia said. 'The doctors came round this morning and said they're quite satisfied with things. I suppose they mean I'm not dying faster than they expected me to. They've stopped asking when I'm going to go home, I don't know why.'

'I don't know why you can't be at home,' Leo said.

'I've just dropped off their radar,' Celia said. 'I've gone from being one of the patients they're paying close attention to. Now I'm one of the ones that just sit there and get looked at once a day. If it weren't for your father I'd just pack up and get a taxi home. Your father! Telling everyone what to do the whole time!'

He left that – she could have meant one of several things by it.

'Mummy, I've done an awful thing,' Leo said.

'Oh, what now?' Celia said, but fondly. 'You're always doing awful things.'

'I've left my job,' Leo said. 'You know, my job at the newspaper.'

'Yes, I know your job at the newspaper,' Celia said. 'Well. That's no great loss. It was an awful job. I had to put up with Sue Tillotson saying, "Oh, there's another piece by your clever son in the newspaper," whenever she noticed it, and it was only you saying that readers might like to consider a long weekend in Whitby. Running away again.'

'I'd just had enough,' Leo said. He knew what she meant by running away again. He had run away from Oxford; run away from his marriage; run away, now, from his job.

'That's fine,' Celia said. 'I start to think that it's not running away that's overrated.'

'It's a bit late for that,' Leo said.

'It's a bit late for that,' Celia said, as if he hadn't said anything at all. 'I suppose your father's going to come this afternoon, as usual. Is he bringing –'

'Blossom and Hugh and Lavinia are coming,' Leo said. 'Is it too many? Do you want them to come on alternate days?'

'Once,' Celia said, 'when I was first walking out with your father, this would have been when I was just nineteen or twenty, just after the war, my mother said to me that I shouldn't commit to anything if I wasn't sure, that it wasn't too late to walk away from everything so far. Your granny, she had old-fashioned ideas. I don't know what she meant by "everything so far". I should have told her. It was going to the cinema, and it was going to a coffee bar – that seemed very exciting – and it was going to the opera, once, and it was going for a walk on a Sunday afternoon in the park. It wasn't so very much. I think your father was in digs and you know how very depressing Sunday afternoon can be. I saved him from himself, going for a walk on a Sunday afternoon in the park, and letting him talk about –'

'About how he was going to save the world,' Leo said. 'That's what medical students usually talk about.'

'About how he was going to save the world,' Celia said, in a meditative way. 'No. That doesn't ring a bell. I don't think he did want to save the world. I think he just wanted to be a kind of overseer of statistics. He just wanted to say, "I'm a doctor," when people said, "What do you do?" at parties. You don't remember your grandfather, my father. He died when you were very little. He used to have this awful expression about famines and plagues – we were just starting to hear about famines and plagues in Africa and Asia around that time. He used to look at the photographs or the films and then just say, "Nature's pruning fork." As though it was all planned and it was all for the best, the plague killing all those people who would never amount to anything anyway. My mother, she had a baby who died. I was ten. It was nothing so unusual then – pneumonia in very young babies, it happened. But I remember my mother never speaking about it, just going around the house and staring at things. For years. I think she never got over it. All those preparations being made and she'd decided the baby was going to be her last baby. He was a boy and then he died.'

'I never knew that,' Leo said. 'He would have been my uncle.'

'He was your uncle,' Celia said, 'but he died. And then my mother didn't talk about it and my father didn't talk about it and then nobody talked about it, ever. I wanted to say to my father, "Was that Nature's pruning fork, too?" Your father – I know he thought there was a point there. That's why he became a doctor. Putting the world in order with the right numbers. I should have walked away.'

'Oh, Mummy,' Leo said. 'You don't mean that.'

'When your grandmother said it wasn't too late, that I should walk away if I wasn't sure, I should have listened,' Celia said. 'There was someone else I could have walked away with. I made a terrible mistake, and then the terrible mistake, it's your life. When I look at the world, it's always on the verge, always, of saying something terrible and terribly funny. That's how your father sees the world. And he's always picking a fight and the fight never comes. It's too late for me now.'

'Oh, Mummy,' Leo said. He had no idea what to say, what consolation to bring. The children and grandchildren must have brought some. His own existence must be quite a good consolation, to other people.

'Anyway,' Mummy said. 'Anyway. So you're leaving the job. What are you going to do?'

'No idea,' Leo said. 'But I don't need to do anything just yet – I've got some savings. Blossom asked me yesterday how I would feel if Josh was to go and live with them. Have some stability in his life, she said. He's quite keen on the idea. So that's that. I was a father for a bit and I had a job for a bit. I suppose it could happen again. I'm going to take some time out.'

'Time out,' Mummy said. She winced; something had struck her, painfully. She reached out with the wrong hand, the one not in plaster, for the blue bulb that was attached to her, the morphine bulb, and squeezed. He had caught her at the end of a dose, at her most lucid. Had she held off, knowing they would be coming soon, and hoping to keep herself awake until two? She had not made it to visitors' hour, or only just, but she had managed to see Leo, and to talk to him. In a moment there was a noise in the corridor. It was two o'clock exactly, and Blossom and Daddy came into the room, Blossom with a bag of clean nightwear.

'There he is!' Blossom said. 'Leo snuck off this morning and we had to leave without him. There's an aggrieved note on the kitchen table – you'll have to ignore that. Now. What can I get for you?'

Blossom's practical performance of sympathy and helpfulness took over for a while. She was good at this. Like her mother, she had four children, and there was a sense of reassurance in the way she went about the room straightening books, emptying the vase of five-day-old flowers, replacing the bag of scrunched-up laundry with an empty one, placing the new nightgowns, folded, in the drawer. All the time she made warm and sympathetic enquiries that needed no response. How was Mummy's appetite? Did Mr Simpson – the consultant, Blossom was quick to catch their names – plan to make an appearance today? And then bits of news from home, what Blossom's children were supposed to have sent by way of love to their granny, a smashed mug, the rose bush coming into flower, the sun continuing, but of course Mummy could see that …

Blossom was good at it. It was not like conversation for the purpose of the visiting of the sick, but just a chat and, flopping down rather in the chair, she brought in Leo. He had supposedly gone out with his friend Helen last night. Helen was a lesbian now, how about that? *Pints*. It was what, two, three o'clock when Leo was finally home, falling through the front door – it was the sort of conversation that Leo was able comfortably to join in with, cosily denying the whole thing (and it hadn't been so very awful, just a pizza out and a couple of whiskies round at Helen's and digging out some old LPs, Siouxsie and the Banshees and X-Ray Spex and the Blockheads for old times' sake, till the girlfriend, what was her name, came down hugging a pillow and wondering what all that racket was; they'd had worse nights). If it weren't for Mummy now glassily smiling, disengaging as she turned from Blossom to Leo a moment or two behind the switch of conversational exchange, it would have been quite normal. They might have been visiting their mother in a hotel, not a very good hotel, one that had developed a curious smell and décor, decided to go on using sheets and blankets about forty washes more than was ideal. They could have believed this if it were not for their father, standing there with a patient face. He had worked in such places, and his face declared what they were: they were places of endings. Glowering. His mother had found the right word.

9.

'I think I ought to say something,' Hilary said. His voice was practical, decisive, the voice of a diagnosis being made without chance of negotiation or discussion. 'Blossom. Just shut up, please. I think we all agree that things haven't been right for a long time. I want to put things right now. You know what I mean.'

But they didn't, or they were pretending they didn't. Blossom sank onto the end of the bed, her chatter over.

'Your mother had an affair in 1962 and 1963,' Hilary said. 'It's odd to say it. I don't know whether she knows that I know. We never spoke about it. I know everything about it, I think. She met a man. He was married, too, but they hadn't any children. He was working in the university, a junior lecturer. They saw each other when his timetable allowed it – it must be so easy for junior lecturers in theology to have affairs. You just say, "I'm spending the morning in the archives," or in the Bible Institute, or wherever it might happen to be. And then you meet up with your mistress for two hours. The ease of it!'

'Decades ago, Daddy,' Blossom said. 'Decades. I don't believe it.'

'William Gillieaux,' Mummy said. She was glassy, impenetrable, faintly smiling, her face drawn in pain, and this name had come to her. 'He was wonderful. William. I haven't thought of him in years.'

'That's good,' Daddy said. 'There hasn't been a day – no, let's not exaggerate – there hasn't been a week in the last twenty-eight years or so when I haven't thought of him. I know how they met, at the vet's in the waiting room. I know how they met for a second time, because he saw her in Broomhill wheeling Lavinia in her pram and asked after Gertrude. How was Gertrude doing? That was how they came together, William Gillieaux being invited up to the house to take a look at Gertrude. That's how it started.'

'William Gillieaux,' Mummy said again. What was crossing her mind to smooth out the lines of pain, to bring back some months of happiness and guilt erased? What had William Gillieaux looked like? Was he dark and unshaven, his hair unkempt and swept back, his brow heavy over his dark blue eyes – it was impossible to know. But he was again in the front of Celia's mind, as he laid his hands on her with joy, in the front bedroom of the house, Lavinia asleep downstairs, the 1960s just beginning, out there on the street, and him inside, naked and in Celia's arms and floating in a dream of morphine dependency. There he was.

'I know all this,' Hilary said. 'I know because I found out about it. I saw. I saw. I saw. And I left the house again, very quietly, and came back when I was supposed to come back. I found out who he was. That was the hardest thing. I found out – No, I'm not going to tell you. You're just going to have to wonder who it was of all those friends you told about William Gillieaux who was happy to tell me. That's going to keep you busy for the next few weeks and the next few months and the next few years. Maybe not. No, not the next few years.'

'Daddy, please,' Leo said.

'And I went to find him. And we went out for a drink. It was quite a long drink. He didn't want to come and he didn't want to stay. But at the end I pointed out that he was dealing with the lives of … Well, I'm not going to go over it. I don't want to say everything I had to say. But the interesting thing – I don't know whether you know this, Celia, but just then, his wife was pregnant, too. She was going to have a baby. He told me that. I don't think he had told you that. That was the thing that weighed with him. His wife going to have a lovely little baby with him.'

'Is she?' Celia said. Her face brightened. 'How lovely. That really is good news. I do like it when people have babies like that. I do hope –'

'Are you hoping that William and Ruth – the *Gillieauxs* – are going to bring their new baby in to see you, by any chance?' Hilary said, spitting their surname. 'Because that infant, he'll be nearly thirty by now, I would say. They're probably divorced. Which brings me to my point. Well. So I said to William, "Why don't you have a think about it, and why don't you say goodbye to my wife, and why don't you take yourself off somewhere where we won't bump into you? Or, better still, why don't you just push off without saying goodbye? That would work just as well." And that's what he did. I put in an enquiry and it turns out that he took up a job in Dundee. And after that he went to Australia, where as far as I know he's still at it to this day. Boning the sheilas. It all ended terribly well, apart from for Celia, who must have wondered why it was that one Tuesday afternoon her nice, handsome theologian didn't turn up and never turned up again. I suppose that's why Celia kept on crying and crying all through that autumn and winter. Or maybe it was some other reason. Who knows? Maybe it was something he read in one of those mouldy old books he was always having to read, something about not going to bed with other people's wives.'

'Daddy, this is ancient history,' Blossom said. 'I don't know why you're doing this. It's just cruel. Let's talk about something else.'

'Oh, yes, cruelty,' Hilary said. 'I know all about cruelty. It was my specialist subject for a long time. When Hugh came along, and Mummy, the first thing she said – she'd been thinking about it – she said, "Isn't he handsome? Not like the others, not like the others at all." She knew what she was saying. She cried all through that pregnancy and she cried all through that baby's first year. Hugh's first year. I should have walked out and never come back. That was the place it should have ended, with William Gillieaux. I won the game and there was an awful booby prize. Called being married to your mother. So, Celia –'

'Yes, darling?' Celia said. 'Look, darling. Look! Here they are! Here they are!' And it was Hugh and Lavinia, standing at the door in an apologetic way, the children behind them, not coming in, knowing this would be too many visitors, but smiling and waving as if hundreds of yards away. 'Look, darling! It's everyone – how lovely. Hugh, we were just this second talking about you. Daddy was saying ...'

But what had Hugh heard?

'I was saying,' Hilary said, 'that it's enough now. I think what we're going to do is involve the lawyers. You've got some money of your own that you ought to be able to leave to who you want to leave it to, not just descend on your husband who should have divorced you decades ago. You know what we've got in common, don't you – all of you? Money. And genetics. The thing that's made it absolutely clear that we're all of us under five foot two, between four foot ten and five foot two, adult height. That and an increased propensity to die of bowel cancer because, of course, that's what your mother's dying of but also what her mother died of. I won't put a figure on that increased propensity but it must be substantial.'

'If you say so,' Leo said. It was what had so often shut up his father in the past. It did not have that effect now.

'It affects the females in the family more than the males,' Hilary continued. 'And of course it doesn't affect me at all. I'm going to put everything on paper and we'll go from there. Height, and the way you'll die. It's not the end of the world.'

A nurse was at the door, just in time to see Celia's face move from happy empty welcome to confusion and to crumple in real pain. She was here to deal with them, but her patient's suffering presented itself, and she went to it with urgency. Leo thought he had met this nurse in the past – she was a plump blonde girl, with a moue for a mouth, a face that Hollywood in the 1920s would have loved. But if he had flirted with her, that mattered nothing now. 'There's a reason why we only permit two visitors at a time,' she said. 'I can't have this. Celia can't be hosting a party. Everyone out, and then two in at a time – the rest of you can wait patiently.'

'I'm going,' Leo said. 'I've heard enough.' He went. The rest of them could sort themselves out. He would go home – no, he would go back to the house where he had grown up and then after that he would go home. There was nothing left for him to stay for. The last thing he would ever say to his father was 'If you say so.' Let him think what he wanted to think. Leo was not going to contradict him. The life of the family was over and all he had to do was go home and live the life he could make for himself. A saying about childbirth came to his mind. He walked towards the hospital's exit. A family had gone into that room, yellowish and disinfected and lined with paint that shone like nail varnish; one family had entered, and eight people had left. He would not say goodbye to his mother, even.

10.

At the entrance to the hospital an old man in a raincoat was getting out of a taxi. He was holding a bag and a bunch of yellow flowers; defeated, he gave the impression of visiting a daughter, not a wife. Leo waved at the driver, who was sorting out his money. Like most of Sheffield's taxi drivers, he was a Kashmiri with a thick red beard. Leo pushed past the old man, and got into the open door of the taxi, pulling it shut behind him. The taxi driver turned round, surprised.

'I was just dropping someone off, pal,' he said.

'Could you take me home?' Leo said. 'I'm in a real hurry.'

'You're supposed to ring, to book a car,' the driver said, but then turned his meter on and set off with Leo in the back. Leo gave him the address. 'So are you following the football?'

'No,' Leo said. 'I don't follow football.'

'That match last night,' the driver said.

'I didn't see it,' Leo said. At a street corner, three boys stood; one raised his hand as if in ironic greeting before quickly lowering it. There was a clatter on the side of the taxi. The boy had thrown a stone or a clod of mud.

'Little bastards,' the driver said equivocally. 'It's been a good World Cup, this one. Last night, Schillaci – I thought he was out of spirits in the first half. He's been a star of the tournament so far, but last night he left it until the second half to score. Italy versus Uruguay – just the sound of it. Two former champions meeting each other in battle, a passenger of mine was saying this morning.'

'I don't know about that,' Leo said. 'I don't have any interest in football.'

'It's all about the heritage, you might say,' the driver went on. 'Do the current teams, do they match up to the great teams of the past? Italy – their striker Schillaci, Toto Schillaci, I would say he stands fair to be one of the greats. I didn't know his name until the tournament started, but now he must be one of the most famous men in the world. Same with Roger Milla for Cameroon. Last night –'

'I really don't follow football,' Leo said. 'I really don't have any interest in it at all. I wouldn't have known anything other than the fact that the World Cup was running at the moment.'

'That's strange.'

'I don't know about that,' Leo said. 'It's not so strange, if people don't all have interests in the same things in life.'

'But most English people who get in the back of my taxi, they really like football, they really like to talk about it. It brings people together, the World Cup. Everyone.'

'Well, you've just discovered – Look. My mother's in that hospital dying. She's probably got a very few weeks to live. Just now my father, who's nearly eighty years old, has told her that he doesn't want to go on being married to her. He's never loved her, he says, and now he's determined he's going to try to divorce her before she dies. My family's just falling apart. So no. I don't have much interest in keeping up with the football – World – Cup.'

'Me, I just want a quiet life – I just want to be at home with my kids and the missus, eat my dinner, do my job, don't get beaten up by the passengers, go to the mosque on Fridays, that's all I ask. Most English people like sitting back there and telling me what they think about the football World Cup.'

'I'm sorry. I wouldn't know what to say to you about football.'

'Don't give it another thought, pal.'

The streets of Sheffield unwound. Down the hill: there were patches of green, scrubs of lawn and thin, hopeful trees at junctions, then bare-windowed supermarkets, local shops with self-painted adverts and chain-link over the windows. This was the poor half of the valley. Leo was never going to see it again. The car reached traffic lights at the worn-out bottom of the valley, just before the old stone bridge that carried the road over one of the city's rivers, plunging towards the centre. On the other side of the valley, the hill began to rise, and now the houses were made of stone, not brick, and came in pairs with gardens, not facing the street in a bare, hopeless way. They were neat, the gardens, and sometimes elaborate, with a pergola or a shade at the front, and in the windows of the houses there were net curtains, and in the upper rooms the shadow of the back of a dressing-table. Soon they were in the shopping centre near to home – near to his father's house – and a fishmonger stood there, a bookshop, a café and an ironmonger's. There was a group of teenagers sitting on the back of a bench outside the newsagent's – it was a Tuesday, Leo remembered now. They were eating chips from paper with forefinger-and-thumb amused delicacy; they were wearing the yellow striped tie of King George V School. It was terribly funny to recall that he could, if he wanted, take up his promise and go back to the office, not even on Thursday, as he had suggested, but tomorrow. In the streets outside the florist three women stood, one with a wicker basket even, passing the time of day. Leo had never seen them before and he would never see them again. And then up the hill once more, vast trees now, planted a hundred years ago, buckling the pavements outside the big stone houses, yew trees in the gardens at the front, or Japanese maples, and on top of the walls the stubs, like black teeth, of what had once been iron railings. These were the roads he had walked all his life and he would never walk them again.

The taxi stopped outside the house. Leo told him to wait: he would only be two minutes. He went in, turning off the burglar alarm with its old code, 9389, and upstairs to his old room. He had been living out of the suitcase, and the pile of crumpled clothes sitting on his bedside chair went straight into his bag. There were probably dirty clothes in the wash – he wouldn't hang about finding them. He was out of the house in a minute. He set the burglar alarm again, astonished by his own responsibility and decency. On the other side of the road a man was standing, watching Leo's rapid progress in and out in a transfixed, idle way. Leo ignored him. He could be identifying houses to burgle, or anything. It didn't matter any more. Leo wasn't going to come back here. He had said goodbye to his mother, and his brother and sisters, and his father had done the rest. He put the suitcase into the back of the car. There was one more thing to do, and he told the driver to wait for a couple of minutes. He hoped Aisha's mother, at least, was at home.

But it was her father who answered the door.

'Come in, come in,' he said. 'We're just finishing our lunch.'

Leo followed him through the hallway and left into the dining room. This was where the Tillotsons had kept their piano, and Nazia and Sharif had changed it in other ways, not at all easy to identify – the wallpapers had gone and the house was now painted in plain colours. 'Please, sit,' Nazia said, sitting at one end of the table. 'Would you like to eat? There's biryani, it's very nice,' she went on, indicating a blue-and-white china tureen with a lid on it.

'How's your father?' Sharif said. 'Sit, sit.'

Leo refused: he had a taxi waiting outside. 'He's fine,' he said. 'At least …'

'He seems a bit lost,' Sharif said. 'I never see any of you talking to him. Just walking away and leaving him still talking to himself.'

'He's fine. I wondered,' Leo said. 'I wanted to write to Aisha. I think we left it –'

'Yes,' Nazia said. She picked up a chicken bone from her plate and gnawed at it. She set it down, chewed, swallowed; looked in a friendly but unsupportive way at Leo. 'She went back to Cambridge.'

'She went back before I could speak to her,' Leo said, sitting down. 'I'd like to keep in touch with her.'

'To be honest,' Sharif said, 'I'll tell her, but I don't know that she will really want to get in touch with you. The easiest thing –'

'Her parents live here,' Nazia said pleasantly. 'And your parents live next door. I expect you'll see each other again some time soon. I'm sure you'll want to be coming back. Make a bit of an effort with your father, I expect.'

And now something very strange happened. Heavy steps came down the stairs, and one of the twins came in. It was the one his father had saved; there was a bandage at his throat still. He ignored Leo altogether. His mother stood up; the seat she was sitting in was ceded to her boy-son, and a clean plate provided for him from a pile on the sideboard. The mother stood by her son, almost like a servant, as she served him with biryani from the tureen. This piece of family behaviour, so remote from the way his mother would have behaved if any of her children had come in, was like a pain to Leo. He felt he should not have come into a house where the mother stood for her son to demand an address. He had made a mistake in thinking that Nazia and Sharif were in any way similar to him and his family. What were they doing at home on a Tuesday afternoon, the boy and Sharif?

'I will pass on your request,' Sharif said. 'But I would be surprised if she wanted to write to you. The truth of the matter is that you should not have said those things to her. After she wrote a letter to you. You upset her a lot.'

Leo began to blush; it was those things he had said that he wanted now to take back, to apologize for. He had no idea that she might have shared any of this with her father.

'She wrote a foolish letter and she regretted it very much afterwards,' Sharif said. 'I saw the letter. It was foolish. We all write foolish letters sometimes, and sometimes when we lay ourselves bare like that we deserve to be treated with a little bit of kindness. Anyone would have known what to do. I can only thank you, I suppose, for not taking advantage of her in a stupid way. But if you had spoken to her with a little bit more … But, well, it's all finished with now. She has a dissertation to finish. So you said you're going back to London?'

They didn't get up from the table to say goodbye to Leo, and Nazia did not move from her sentry-duty by the side of her son's chair. They would not. He went to the door and let himself out. The taxi was still there and, over the road, the man who had watched him leave his parents' house and go into Nazia and

Sharif's. The man was tall and haggard. He called something, and it was only after Leo had got into the taxi and told the driver to go to the railway station that the call resolved itself into Leo's name, called twice – *Leo Spinster, Leo Spinster* ... there had been something about the way the emphasis had been fallen in that voice's calling that made the name almost unfamiliar. He wondered who would next shake his hand and hear the sentiment 'Hi, I'm Leo Spinster.' The taxi drove on, now in silence from the front seat. The meter reading was north of twenty pounds by now. In five minutes, Leo understood why that man waiting on the street had been familiar in his general shape. It had been Tom Dick, six foot seven, come to see him. What had Tom Dick wanted? He had stood on the pavement opposite Leo's parents' house for some time. It didn't matter; he wasn't going to find out now. Whether apologies, humiliation, argument, self-justification were being plotted, he was now in another realm of existence. The taxi was almost at the station; the ticket was going to be bought to take him away from here. The family was over. He would go back to London and enter into training for the job he would strive to deserve. Blood; sweeping; shit; mopping; a man no more than five foot tall. The clock on the taxi ticked. He hoped to be of use.

CHAPTER SEVEN

I.

All the way to Penzance, Mahfouz kept feeling that something was about to drop, shamefully, from his inner clothing, from underwear or shirt collar. He got up – and it dropped. He was right. It was confetti. His new brother had rushed up to him at the last, at the railway station, and had shouted, 'Congratulations, brother,' in his ear before stuffing a fistful of confetti down his collar. Mahfouz had not expected that from Nawaz, or from anyone else. And confetti was thrown, was it not, over the heads of the bride and the bridegroom, not pushed hard down the groom's neck? He was not sure.

But Nawaz had arranged everything. It was Nawaz who had decided that a honeymoon was needed for his sister – that he had heard of the perfect place, a long way down at the very end of England, that he knew of the perfect hotel, that it would be best if Mahfouz and his new wife took the train down there – that the best thing would be to take the train to London and then, no difficulty at all, the train out of London again. Nawaz was her younger brother. He was the only one still living at home, the one she still treated like a little boy, muttering into his ear and making him gurgle with laughter. But he had sat with her father and the old uncle and the three severe older brothers in their little house, walking Mahfouz delicately around what they all must have known already as they talked. He had organized the whole thing by saying out loud in the hearing of his sister that it might be best if –

And at the end, at Nottingham railway station, he had leapt forward, his hand in what Mahfouz had taken for a packet of breakfast cereal, and had plunged a fistful of confetti down the back of Mahfouz's new shirt. He had never been so close to his new brother-in-law. His glee-filled, almost furious face pressed up against Mahfouz's; their beards smeared against each other. All around them the ordinary travellers looked away. A ticket collector lowered the tools of his trade, interested to see if action was needed. But Mahfouz had stepped back and they had all said goodbye. All the way to London, every time he moved, he could feel the wet lump of a fistful of confetti. Discreetly, sitting in the first-class seat by the window, he pulled the tail of his shirt free from his trousers and shuffled. He felt the paper fragments drop behind him onto the seat in a single mass. It was so strange that Nawaz had taken this one thing from English weddings.

Then, of course, when the train pulled into St Pancras, he had to push his new wife forward to go ahead. She should not see the mess of confetti he was leaving behind him on the clean leather seat, like the brightly coloured droppings of a large animal.

'What is it, my husband?' she said, but he just told her to walk on. No one saw: at this time on a weekday, the first-class compartment had been nearly empty. In the taxi that Nawaz had insisted on, the one to take his sister from one London terminal to another, Mahfouz could feel more pieces of confetti, stuck in the hair on his shoulders underneath his shirt; and again as they had sat on the bench at Paddington, their suitcases before them, Mahfouz's new wife producing a box of travel snacks and a Thermos of tea to fill the hour before their train left. The travel snacks had been delicious, a treat; her capacity to anticipate and please with food was the first thing he had liked about her. Today, however, he could only feel the confetti about him, damp and uncomfortable. He supposed that that was what English weddings were like, now, two hours out of London.

'Look!' she cried.

'What is it?'

'So beautiful – the little animals. The sheep.'

There were fields of sheep, rising up to the left of the train, and on the hills beyond, a house in stone, a big square house.

'Yes,' Mahfouz said.

'And the little ones, look – there are black sheep and their lambs. Look, husband – they are black, too – oh!'

'Yes,' Mahfouz said. Then he saw that this would not do. 'Have you not seen black sheep before?'

'Yes – oh, yes, but …' She seemed to remember something she had been told, and lowered her head.

'The black sheep produce black lambs,' Mahfouz said. 'It is their nature.'

She went on looking. Her eyes were bright and curious. Perhaps she had not often been taken out of Nottingham. Schools took children out into the countryside, he knew. They had taken his son Ayub out, and his daughter Aaliyah, hadn't they? It was something he could ask his wife when they had been married for some time. He caught himself thinking that he ought to ask Sadia to enquire about what sort of experiences this girl had had. The thought was painful. As a moral duty, to pass through the pain properly, he reiterated it with all the circumstances: *I must ask first-wife to ask about second-wife, first-wife who died last year about second-wife.* Sadia.

'Oh –' second-wife started to say. She stopped herself.

But Mahfouz was not the man she feared he was. He had loved Sadia and now he was about to love second-wife. He was going to be gentle with her, as he had been with first-wife. He would love the sound of her voice, and listen with interest to what she said. She had been about to comment on the view from the train. The river had been widening, with mud-flats and wading birds; the afternoon sun flashed like a sheet of polished metal on the still water, standing in pools, brown and milky. The far side of the river was receding from them; a small cluster of white-fronted houses and a cliff of rock, surprisingly red in colour. The flat spread of water and mud and light: it was like a landscape from his childhood, from those long trips out from the city into the wide rivers and flat green of the country.

'It must be a delta,' he said kindly to his new wife. 'The river gets wider as it gets near to the sea. It spreads out and it floods.'

'Are we at the sea?' she said.

'No, not very near,' Mahfouz said. He smiled. 'The delta can be huge – it can go on for many many miles. I don't know how near to the sea we are.'

But the drama of this nation was smaller than the nation he was thinking of, because now the train gave a grand wide swerve to the right, and there was the sea. A seabird's call, so harsh and near it could be heard within the carriage, announced it, and the cheerful hoot of the train's horn. The horizon, far off across the smooth, green-blue sea under a deep blue sky, was a flat, decisive line. Out there, a cargo ship rested; was it moving out, very slowly, into the world, or returning from it, or poised in its element, like a tethered balloon in air? The world began out there, and there was no end to it. They were so small here, carving a route between the sea and the green-spattered cliffs of rock. There was a narrow beach, and families, some with bright buckets and spades, like pictures in the old books, were camped out on the sand.

'It's even nicer where we are going,' Mahfouz said to his new wife. 'And we are at the sea. I made a mistake.' He knew that was what she had restrained herself from asking. Her eyes turned down to the table, with suppressed pleasure.

On the other side of the aisle was an older couple – English, white people. They looked as if they had made this journey many times before. They sat very upright in their seats; he was reading a newspaper, and she was reading a paperback book. They were both thin, and grey, and their white hair shot upwards in similar ways. They were married, but they had grown alike. They were the kind of English people whom Mahfouz tried not to fear, the faces of authority. They had got onto the train at

Exeter, he thought. The husband had taken a look at Mahfouz and his wife, then checked his seat reservations very carefully. The old woman had not looked at them – had made a clear effort not to look at them. There was no reason for Mahfouz not to be friendly to them.

'A beautiful sight,' Mahfouz said heavily, leaning slightly over the aisle and smiling.

'Yes indeed,' the man said, lowering his paper and giving a brief sharp smile, baring his long yellow teeth. The old woman made no move of acknowledgement, but gave the impression of fixing her gaze on the page, fixing her grip on her novel tighter.

'The country is beautiful down here,' Mahfouz said. 'And the sea, it's so lovely.'

'I'm pleased you like it so much,' the old man said, with a great air of finality, and raised his paper again. Mahfouz had tried, and he had found the response you sometimes found in English people. He turned and smiled at his new wife, who touched his hand gently with her hands in their black silk gloves. Her eyes brightened as if nothing at all had happened, as if she were quite impervious to being shrugged off. Or as if she entirely expected it and had stopped caring. The old man and his silent, frightening wife had been offered the hand of friendship and had been dismissive. It was easy not to want to engage with anything unfamiliar, and if they lived in Exeter it was quite probable that they very rarely, if ever, saw a young woman in public wearing a full veil over her face. Mahfouz hoped that the hotel in St Ives would be kind to them, him and his new wife.

2.

Her brother Nawaz had taken an interest, and had organized all the details of their honeymoon. It was really from him that Mahfouz had understood that it would be quite all right for them to go on honeymoon, that their circumstances were a little unusual, and that nobody would mind if they did something unusual. Their family was quite different in their looks. Most of them were stocky, dark, even plump – her elder brothers were comfortable and lazy fellows who liked their food too much. But towards the end of their family, when it came to his new wife, the fourth child and first daughter, and her younger brother, it was as if the parents had created an improvement. Nawaz and his sister were pale, very smooth-skinned and taller than anyone else in the family; they liked their food delicious, exquisite, and in tiny pieces, taken between delicate fingertips. They had always been special to each other as children, the youngest, their father told him; it would be hard for Nawaz when his sister left home.

Mahfouz had known the family for some years; they went to the same mosque. He had not heard any tales about the girl; it had been brought up once discussions had started that Mahfouz, newly widowed, might like to consider marrying her. The father, uncle and brothers had agreed to meet with him after Sadia had died, and the conversation, even with its awkward admission, had gone well. In the sitting room of his pleasant, airy, modern house, they had even found things to laugh about. A friendly neighbour, who had volunteered to help Aaliyah, Mahfouz's daughter, brought refreshments. Aaliyah had been very nervous. This would have been her first important gathering since her mother's funeral. Mahfouz's son Ayub had talked well about his job, a good, good job, at the council where he helped to rehome people in need. Her family understood more about him than he had expected. There were no questions about his family, about why they were not there to support him at this time. There were

awkward things to admit, after all, about Mahfouz, and about
Sadia's family. It was not just that he was proposing to marry a
girl for the second time. Everything had been understood,
explained, and forgiven, and the neighbour, who had been one
of Sadia's best friends in England, came through with another
plate of food. Mahfouz's lawyer, an old friend, handed over the
neat and comprehensive folder of Mahfouz's affairs; he was
honest, open and affluent. Everything was smiles; only in the
corner a pale, thin boy with a patchy beard and big bony hands
on his knees inspected everything in the room, and did not
speak. 'The youngest,' the father had said. They were putting
their coats on in the hallway, saying goodbye. 'He will suffer –
his sister getting married. No one to talk to! She would not
agree without his consent.' Mahfouz had wondered, before
today, whether the youngest boy would do for his daughter
Aaliyah. The boy was putting his coat on with impatience,
almost with rage. He did not look at his new brother-in-law.
Mahfouz saw, without quite understanding why, that this boy
Nawaz would not do for his frightened, fumbling daughter, so
often in tears at nothing, whose mother had died last year.

The consent for Mahfouz to marry the girl must have
followed, because in two weeks Nawaz was starting discussions
with his brother-in-law-to-be about the details of the wedding,
and what would happen afterwards. Mahfouz was amused. He
had been married before. It was a good idea to marry again. His
children had agreed, and they thought that Mahfouz's new wife
was a good choice. (They had been at the same school, Aaliyah
two years below, Ayub three years above. The only thing that
Aaliyah remembered was that she had started to wear a veil. She
could not remember her before that.) Nawaz was alongside
him, quite suddenly, one Friday as Mahfouz walked towards the
car to drive home, and the friends who had been by him had
melted away, Aaliyah and Ayub now ten paces behind. Was it
arranged in some way?

By the time they reached the car, it had been established
between them that Nawaz's sister was an excellent seamstress,

that she very much liked to sew, and that Mahfouz's wedding gift to his new wife would be a sewing machine of her own. 'And a room to keep it in,' Nawaz said, but that was no problem. The demand had been made boldly; Mahfouz's generosity was in excess of the demand. Before the wedding, Mahfouz had planned to redecorate the whole house, and do something about the small box room that currently held nothing but old furniture and records of the shop's transactions more than five years old. That would do very well. 'There is so much to arrange,' Nawaz said, wringing his hands theatrically by the door of the car. 'I want so much for everything to be perfect for sister. But how can you know what sister would like? If I could explain ...'

And Nawaz was inside the car, in the front seat, buckling himself up and explaining about the honeymoon. In the back seat, Aaliyah and Ayub sat stolidly. They did not have the same relationship of intimacy as Nawaz had with his sister; Mahfouz could almost feel his daughter willing her brother not to take any steps to explain what she would like when she married. He wondered whether it had seemed possible to her, too, that Nawaz might be paired off with her, and whether she now understood that the question had been ruled out of court. Nawaz was impossible.

'There must be a honeymoon,' Nawaz said firmly.

'There will be a honeymoon,' Mahfouz said grandly. There had not been a honeymoon with first-wife, with Sadia. But now there was licence permitting a honeymoon, and he would take his new wife on one. The boy would look after the shop. There were plenty of experienced people there to make sure that nothing went wrong.

'I can suggest the perfect place,' Nawaz said. They were reversing out of the parking space, Mahfouz raising his hand in farewell to an old friend and his family. 'The end of England.'

'The end of England?'

'If you go as far as you can, you reach the very end of the country, and you look out. Ocean. It is very beautiful, brother.'

'Land's End,' Ayub put in.

'Oh, yes,' Mahfouz said. 'Land's End to John o'Groats, I know.'

'A beautiful place,' Nawaz said. 'I know of a fine, fine hotel in the nearest town, which is St Ives, where you could stay in great comfort. And there are restaurants in the town that are some of the best in the world.'

By the time they had reached Mahfouz's house, the matter was settled, and Mahfouz had agreed with Nawaz that it would be best all round if the worry and stress were removed, if they went to Land's End, or St Ives, by train and did not drive. The Ford Sierra could be left in Nottingham, and Ayub could drive it about as much as he liked. From then on, Nawaz was always there, putting forward suggestions on behalf of his sister, showing details of the arrangements, photographs of the hotel, sharing the polite letter back from the management, handing over the train tickets in a folder in a little ceremony. After the first few meetings, the sister was there too. They were trusting him; and a lot of what Nawaz said appeared to be stated for the benefit of that listening figure. Until the very moment that Nawaz had launched at him at the station and pushed a fistful of confetti down his neck, Mahfouz still believed that he might very well announce at the last minute that he, too, was coming on the honeymoon. It was a surprise to say goodbye to the boy.

3.

'My brother is so good to us!' his new wife said, once they were in the taxi at the other end.

'Why do you say that?' Mahfouz said. Around the car the green unfolded, a gash of mud in a field, a black shoulder of trees above the road, a glimpse through a gate of a mound of bright flowers up the wall of a cottage – these things had the force of things seen on honeymoon, things never to be forgotten. Inside the car the driver was English, old, silent; he had not even acknowledged that he knew where the hotel Mahfouz had

named was. From behind, his hair was greasily banded across a
raw red scalp; his clothes, a yellowing cardigan, and the interior
of his car, scattered with ancient biscuit powder and food wrappings, stank of many cigarettes. But the countryside was beautiful, and the windows were open.

'My small-brother Nawaz,' his wife said. 'He remembered
that there was a very good, a luxury hotel here at Land's End. It
was so good of him to bear that in mind. I have never been to
the countryside to stay in a hotel. I have never seen the sea.'

'Have you not looked out of a plane window, when you fly
home?' Mahfouz said. He liked her careful, discreet way of talking, of placing each word in a row. He thought he would come
to like his wife.

'Oh, but we are so close to the sea here,' his wife said. 'Small-
brother said that it was beautiful, I would never forget it. It is
so kind of you to take me on a honeymoon. Is this the town we
are staying in?'

The houses, irregular and surrounded by gardens, fields and
untended land, had thickened into streets, and with a ride over
the crest of a hill, the broad sea was there in front of them. He
had not often seen the sea himself; twice Sadia had persuaded
him to take the children to Skegness, which was the nearest
seaside resort. That was not like this. They were descending into
a busy town, the traffic slow and solid, and walking around were
people with their children in shorts, T-shirts, bathing suits. It
was a beautiful day. Everyone was eating something as they
walked: ice-creams, face-sized glistening lollipops, candyfloss,
even a kebab. They were eating with steady devotion. He hoped
there would be places they could eat in this town.

The taxi stopped. In a moment it was surrounded by bodies
pressing onwards. The driver, without turning, said, 'That'll be
eight pounds.'

'Is this where the hotel is?' Mahfouz said.

'Can't get no nearer the hotel,' the driver said. 'It's down
there, isn't it? Down there straight. Walk on a hundred yards
you'll see it. Eight pounds.'

There was nothing for it. Mahfouz thought of asking the driver if he would wait here with his wife while he went ahead, but that was worse than the alternative. He got out and, with a flourish of stately graciousness, walked round to the other side of the car to help his wife out. The taxi driver sat in his seat. Mahfouz had to walk to the boot of the car and open it himself. All the time he was making sure that he did not look around him at the people walking down- or uphill in their shorts, their swimsuits, their bikinis. They were certainly staring at him and his new wife. He let his wife take his arm, and, his suitcase in his right hand, her smaller and newer suitcase in her left hand, they walked down the hill without speaking, without looking. This is your country, he said to himself. This is my wife's country. This is where we live and where we will go on living. The sea, the houses, the shops, the English sky: this is part of our country, and we will walk through it.

When he saw the hotel he could admit that he had not been sure of his brother Nawaz's intentions. Perhaps he had expected something malicious, an ugly or rundown establishment, a place where a wife would not be taken. But the hotel looked very pleasant; whitewashed, with a tub of red flowers to either side of the green front door, and the name of the hotel, Penmarric, painted in blue on a white signboard. He pushed at the front door, then rang the bell. The door was so immediately opened that the girl must have been standing just by it; she was as young as Mahfouz's daughter, in an apron and a flowered dress that, he guessed, was not her usual style of clothes. Her face was round, very pink and white, and she made a frightened O with her mouth when she saw Mahfouz and his wife. She clung to the side of the door.

'We're full up, I'm afraid,' she said, but Mahfouz explained that he and his wife had a reservation, and produced the letter he had received from them. Hesitantly the door was opened, and they came in. All the time Mahfouz was filling out the form at the reception, faces kept appearing from the back of the house, from what must be the office, the kitchen, the lounge at the front. Finally it was done; they could be taken to their room.

'Beautiful,' his wife said, when the door was shut, the girl handed a small tip. 'This is a beautiful hotel. Thank you.'

It was nice – he looked about him at the room, which had a large double bed with an embroidered bedspread, a white and gold dressing-table, and a bay window looking out onto a quiet side street. He felt it was all a great mistake. They were there for two weeks – how were they to get through two weeks of being stared at, of having nothing easy to say to each other?

'And a little kettle,' she said fondly. 'I shall make some tea, and there are some cakes here, still, that we did not finish on the train.'

'I think now –' Mahfouz said, but a knock came at the door. His wife removed herself into the bathroom.

'Good afternoon,' the lady said. She was plump, her face heavily made-up with powder and a bright red lipstick; she smelt of a sweet, floral scent; she smiled, her head on one side. 'I'm Mrs Harrison – the owner of the Penmarric. I just wanted to say …'

Her head tilted further, as if trying to see past Mahfouz. But new-wife was in the bathroom. There was nothing for her to see.

'Is there anything we can do for you and your wife?' Mrs Harrison said. 'Anything special we should know about?'

'No, thank you,' Mahfouz said. 'I think we will be very comfortable.'

'Good, I'm so pleased,' Mrs Harrison said. She loitered; she allowed her embarrassment to display itself. 'What would you like for breakfast? Not a cooked breakfast? Or just an egg? We could do you some beans and a mushroom? And toast and cereal?'

'That would be good,' Mahfouz said. He thanked the land-lady, without saying that she had reassured them about unclean meats at the breakfast table; he said goodbye to her; he shut the door. His new wife came out of the bathroom. She had removed her veil. With judicious kindness, he looked at her face; he allowed his face to fill with warmth; he did not frighten her. He remembered what his daughter and son had told him, that she had only started wearing a veil two or three years ago, when she was seventeen. He thanked her in a formal way; she made the tea. There were little biscuits there, and she brought out some nuts and two savoury pastries and the cakes she had made, lemon and coconut and chocolate. She had brought pretty English iced cakes. Together they had tea, and ate, and he told her what they were going to do during their honeymoon.

Once she said, 'My brother told me that I should ask you to be kind to me.'

Mahfouz felt his heart fill. Despite everything that had happened to her, she was so young. 'I will always be kind to you,' he said. She had asked something specific, about the way he would behave in the course of their first night. But what he had said, he had meant about the course of their whole life.

Downstairs, the English people were wondering about the man from Nottingham and his wife, her face covered with a thick black veil. He would always remember promising kindness to the new wife; the second-wife. Her name was Farhana.

4.

By the fifth day of their honeymoon, they had fallen into a routine. Mrs Harrison had explained to Mahfouz that there were buses which would take them to local beauty spots, including Land's End. He had somehow thought that Land's End was just by the hotel, perhaps on the outskirts of the town, but it turned out to be a long drive. They took their breakfast in the hotel, a hard-poached egg, cereal and tea; new-wife took the seat with her back to the room, facing the wall, and could not see how the customers of the hotel stared at her deftly eating, her hand, her fork or her spoon rising up behind her veil. After breakfast, they left the hotel and walked through the town to the bus station. It was a pleasant walk, though Mahfouz had the impression that they were becoming one of the curiosities of the town. At the bus station he would reveal to Farhana where they were going that day – a monument, a famous view, a pretty village around a harbour. She was always delighted. The sinking feeling of that first morning was not repeated. Had Mahfouz been kind? Would she ever come to like what had happened to her? She had rallied, and these questions did not recur. Now, she chattered – tales of her childhood, of her aunts in Bangladesh, visited three times, stories of neighbours and of girls at school, riding along in the green English countryside, delighting at a horse at a gate, a field of yellow flowers, a burst of rain from nowhere. It was as if only Mahfouz noticed how the English stared and frowned. Her joy in the world was a wonderful thing, whatever her world had been and whatever it would be.

It was Wednesday that Mahfouz decided they would go to Land's End. He told his wife before they went down for breakfast. She clapped her hands. 'I am so happy!' she said. She had been looking forward to it, so much – she had heard that it was beautiful, and she wanted more than anything to be there at the end of things. 'Thank you for being kind to me,' she said, after a minute or two. 'You needn't have married me.'

He knew what she meant. It was not the kindness of the first night, when they had been together for the first time. She had been offered to him because not everyone would take her. There was the fact that her eldest brother had specifically raised, that when she was fifteen, they had found her kissing a man – it would do no good to say the man's name, and Mahfouz had not pressed the matter. Because of that, she would marry a widower. Mahfouz had agreed. She was a virtuous girl now. And because it was his second marriage, nobody had raised questions about the way things were being done, and the suggestion that they might go on a honeymoon was raised by her brother and accepted by everyone. Even a honeymoon in England, like

English people. He was damaged goods; she was damaged goods; the end result was happiness for both of them.

The bus to Land's End drew in and out of a view of the sea, plunging deep into rich farming country; they sat, boldly, on top of the open bus, Farhana holding tight to her veil as the wind whipped at it. The sun was bright and hot; the wind beautifully refreshing. It was not a full bus, but the dozen or so passengers on the top deck turned to stare at Mahfouz and his wife, sitting at the back. A small boy of two or three walked all the way back, a plastic figurine sticky with chocolate tight in his hand, and stared at Farhana as if she were not human. His mother looked around, saw where he was, and dashed back to scoop him up and return him to his seat. She said nothing to Mahfouz and his wife, and the gesture saved the child rather than protected fellow passengers from being bothered.

But the countryside was beautiful; beyond the thick hedges, the fields spread out, and from time to time, beyond that, the sea with its own texture of depth and constant shifting sparkle. Once they saw a dash of surprise: a rabbit in a field, a white flash. And then a whole crowd of them running in their silly way from the noise of the bus. It was after twenty minutes in the bus that his wife said, 'But, look, the sea!'

Mahfouz did not understand her exclamation. The sea had been a constant presence for the last five minutes to their right; the road had been hugging the coastline. But then he realized what she meant. His wife had seen the sea to the left, too. The land was a thin finger, pointing outwards, and now as it drew to its end, the sea closed in on both right and left. It was a dizzy sensation, to cling to land buffeted so close by the blue sea on all sides; it made him feel that even this solid stretch of rock was vulnerable, unsafe, fragile as pottery. In a few moments, the bus drew up before a single-storey white building: LAND'S END was written on the front.

They went to the café, and had a cup of tea with biscuits, but it was uncomfortable there. Mahfouz would not give way

to the hostile gaze of strangers too easily. The ride to Land's
End from St Ives had filled him with a kind of joy and security.
This was his country now, his nation, and he was happy to
know it. This had always been his wife's nation. She was born
here and she was of its rocky soil, sea to every side. They would
never return home again now. There was no home but this. The
land's fragility had struck him most, but you could think of it,
too, as a land without borders, no one to press up against it. It
was theirs now. All the same, the feeling in the café grew
uncomfortable, and after five minutes Mahfouz said that they
had come to see the End of Land, not to sit inside a café, and
they left. There were terraces with benches overlooking the
grand sight of the sea, far below at the bottom of rocky cliffs,
though these, too, were busy with people. There was a path
with a signpost, for keen walkers, leading away from the very
point of land, up into green downs along the edge of the cliff.
Mahfouz was not a keen walker in the way that the English
sometimes were, but he thought that five minutes' walk in that
direction would take them to a quiet spot where they would be
less prominent. There was a pretty farmhouse, selling pottery,
and a tiny pond with white ducks on it, some sort of polished
brass and red-painted farm equipment sitting unused.
(Mahfouz did not think it was a real farm, on the top of a cliff
two minutes' walk from a tourist café, and the machinery was
as clean as it possibly could be, not soiled with any recent
application, but the spot was pretty all the same.) The flowers
in the grass were tiny, the height of moss, but brilliant in
purple, white and yellow splashes, and in another five minutes
the land was empty; the harsh song of seabirds, the plunge and
curve of rock, the trim grass and heather, the patches of tall,
leaning, bearded grass, the blue of sky and the magnesi-
um-flashing light on the surface of the deep blue of the endless
sea. A yacht with white sails, a rich man's sporting thing, lay
anchored a little way off, its sails fluttering in the faint breeze,
the body of the boat slowly circling at rest. It was far down, but
you could see a pair of young English people, a boy and a girl,

their legs dangling off the side of the boat, their arms on some kind of railing, talking to each other in a casual, familiar, interested way.

His wife delved in her bag and, to his surprise, produced her Thermos flask and its two cups, as well as two of the little packets of sugar-dusted biscuits that the hotel had left out for them; the sparkle of the sun on plastic and sugar in her gloved hand was the same as the sparkle of sun on sea. She must have made the tea while he was taking his bath, when she had finished her prayers.

'Why didn't you mention it, before we went into the café?' Mahfouz said.

'I thought husband wanted a cup of fresh tea first,' Farhana said. 'Are you happy, husband?'

She meant it locally, but when Mahfouz not only said yes but went on to ask whether she was quite happy, there was no mistaking the formal decency of the request he was making. It might have been a legal requirement of their wedding.

'Thank you,' she said simply. 'You are so kind to me. I don't think I deserve it.'

'I don't think I deserve you,' Mahfouz said back, mumbling a little bit, and thinking as a token of his luck, confusedly, of nothing more than the way she had brought out the tea and biscuits, not needing to be ordered about, having thought about what a husband might want or need. But it was all much more than that. It broke his heart to think that she might have remained, unforgiven by the world, at home because of what she had done and what she had long regretted.

'May I ask something?' his wife said after a while.

'Anything,' Mahfouz said.

'It is your family,' she said. 'At the wedding, your uncle Muqtadir.'

'Yes,' Mahfouz said. 'He was living in England when I came here. I lived with him for the first two years – he had a big house, three empty rooms, and no children. We needed somewhere to live. It was very kind of him.'

'Yes,' she said. 'Your uncle, father's brother, and a telegram from brother in Bangladesh, regretting and wishing us well. I hope one day I meet all the others.'

'Some uncles in the village. Brother's children must be grown-up now. Perhaps only that. Not like your family – so many! How many niece-nephews running around!'

'Only eleven,' she said. 'That is the fault of elder-brother Jabbar, but he had four daughters, one after the other, and only then a son. And then one more. Other brothers, not so many – three, two children. And uncles, great-uncles, cousins, girl-cousins. Yes. That is a big family. But one day I want to meet all the others in your family. I want to meet first-wife's family.'

Mahfouz controlled himself. There was no reason to be angry. She was making a request because nobody had talked to her about it. He made himself look out to sea at the anchored yacht, the two young people talking. If they looked up they would be able to see two people on the cliffs, two tiny figures, sitting on the grass, talking pleasantly, too. 'I haven't seen them for some years,' he said. 'First-wife stopped talking to them, and they stopped talking to us.'

'That is so sad,' Farhana said.

He felt he should explain, or give some indication of why she should not ask much more. 'It was 1971,' he said. 'They were on the wrong side in 1971. There were things that could not be forgiven. I don't think we will get in touch with them now.'

'Where are they?'

He thought of telling her to shut up, to stop asking stupid questions, but she had asked so little. If he told her now, just once, in detail, then it would not spoil their honeymoon. If she went on asking, when they were again at home, then he could tell her that the question was finished, the business concluded.

'She had an elder brother called Sharif,' he said. 'He was married to Nazia. They had a daughter – a baby daughter. She is grown-up now. I last saw them when Nazia's mother died, at the funeral. Then she had two younger sisters, Bina and Dolly. Everyone called her Dolly. I can't remember now what her real name was.'

'Bina —'

'Yes, it's a strange name, I know. You have to understand — Sadia's family were not like us. They would just hear a name and think it sounded pretty and then give it to their new baby.'

'It is so sad to think of first-wife's family, not seeing her and then she has died and they don't know about it.'

'Well, that is the way of things,' Mahfouz said.

'So far away, too, in Bangladesh.'

Mahfouz was startled — he had thought that somehow he had stated the facts of the case. 'They aren't in Bangladesh,' he said. 'They all came over here. They are all in England. I am sure. There was another brother. Little-brother died in 1971. And now that is really everything.'

'It is so sad when this happens,' second-wife said. 'When you cannot forgive your wife's family for what they did. It is twenty years ago. It is so sad.'

He looked at her in astonishment. Her eyes were cast down modestly. She smoothed her lap with her black-gloved hands. There was no reason to think that she was being anything but open with him. He was on the verge of saying what was true, which was that they had only done wrong in being against religion, and right, and security. They had not killed anyone. There was nothing in them for Mahfouz to have to forgive, except what they were and what they had decided to be. He would not know how to begin to forgive Sharif for being Sharif, for being humorous and singing about the place, an old Tagore song, a funny old folk song he had just heard, and liking an argument to pass the time, and believing in the Soviets, and believing in Mujib, the leader of all his hopes, and of never praying — some of it was wrong, but what of it needed to be forgiven? He could respond to what Farhana had guilelessly said. He could say, 'It wasn't them that did something wrong. It was me.' He had not done anything wrong. He had acted for the best. But there was

no doubt that in the minds of Sadia's family, of everyone except
Sadia, he had done wrong that could not be forgiven, that never
would be forgiven. He felt their rage and contempt, just beyond
the green horizon. He always had, and he had not informed
them that their sister had died. He did not want them to know
where he lived.

5.

Her brother Nawaz had enquired, and had discovered that there
were two restaurants in St Ives where they could eat. They were
both 'Indian' restaurants, run by Bengali Sylhetis. A friend of
her eldest brother Jabbar knew the owners of one of them, said
they were good people. Mahfouz was greeted as an old friend
when he came in to say hello, was given a cup of tea, introduced
to the whole family, the cooks wiping their hands and pausing
in their work to greet him. He wondered what account had
been given of him. They found him a quiet table near the back
where he and his wife could eat dinner without being stared at,
and where they would not be bothered by the sorts of people
who sometimes came to 'Indian' restaurants to drink alcohol
and make trouble. It was a clean, respectable, modern restaurant, and they went out of their way to cook delicious food for
Mahfouz and his wife. They did not present them with the sort
of heavy dishes, thick with gravy and overladen with chilli,
English people expected. Instead, they made fresh dishes with a
fish like rui, lentils, rice, plain dishes of bitter gourd, a biryani
made with a bird called a guinea fowl that the waiter said was
better than the sorts of chicken you bought in the supermarkets
in England. He was right; Mahfouz made a note. He had always
found the white, pillowy blandness of English chickens a disappointment. The food at the Rajput was perfect, more elegant
and delicious than home cooking but not heavy or too rich. He
had always taken pleasure in food, and he was pleased to see

that his wife did too. They were helpful in other ways: they suggested pleasant places where the two of them might go during the day. The Rajput restaurant was where the two of them felt safest.

It was the Saturday evening, the sixth day that they had been in St Ives, when his wife made her apology. She had not apologized promptly; perhaps she wanted to think about it. But they had only just sat down, and the jug of water and hot towels been brought, when she said, 'I didn't mean to intrude in saying what I said.'

Mahfouz thought he knew what she was talking about, but just smiled and raised an eyebrow.

'When I asked about first-wife's family,' she went on. 'I know that you made the right decision about them. I won't ask about them again. I don't want to embarrass you or ask too much.'

'It's fine,' Mahfouz said. 'I wasn't angry. You were right to mention it. You would always have wondered about it if you had not asked. I should have explained earlier.'

'There should be no secrets between us,' she said. Was she demanding that Mahfouz make a clean breast of everything? It was hard to tell. Perhaps she was offering to tell her husband what he only knew in general terms, that the reason she could only be married off to him was that she had kissed a man, and been discovered doing so. That had been three years ago or more. There was no doubt in Mahfouz's mind that the girl and the woman were quite different people; at least, he told himself so. There was a possibility, however, that had struck Mahfouz and would prevent him from ever asking for clarification.

The father had told him when they were alone, the brothers out of the room, and had told him very openly. But he had not tried to name the man she had kissed. It was over and done with. In Mahfouz's mind there was a possibility – not a certainty, but a possibility that would not go away – that she had been found by an elder brother in the home itself, a man's arms about her, raising her face to the adored face she had known for ever. Nawaz. What preyed on Mahfouz was that it was not a passion that anyone else would know about: it was completely safe, and no one outside the family would be able to mention it because the crime itself was entirely within the family. Her brother Nawaz – everyone knew what he was like, and what he felt for his sister, two years younger than him. Mahfouz did not know; the possibility that this crime, which could never be contained within a legal marriage, had stained his bride meant that he would never make any kind of direct enquiry. If he did not know it for a fact, he would never be called upon to forgive her. Her feelings would change over time and, Mahfouz thought, so would her behaviour once she had had her first child.

She surprised him, then, by saying now, 'But what did you do?'

He did not understand.

'I know it is none of my business,' she said. 'But I would like to know what it is that separated my husband from his wife's family, so long ago. Forgive me, husband. Just say one word and I will be silent on the subject for ever. But what was it?'

What was it?

He remembered, there at the dining table at the back of the restaurant in St Ives, in Cornwall, in the United Kingdom. Music was playing – soft sitar music, he could not identify it. The memory was of three minutes in all, and it would continue to be in his mind for the rest of his life. It was far away and long ago. He had thought of it every day in the twenty years since that day in September 1971, in a country that did not exist then and should not exist now.

The man had been in his face, his face almost against his own. The face was sweating and wide with terror. It clutched with its hands at a woman who must have been its wife. It did not trust Mahfouz and it did not know what else to trust. The face had hissed at him in a dark room, forty silent faces behind it. They were against a door, shut, and on the other side there could be freedom. The face spoke to him. Its voice hissed and whispered and it spoke.

Is it good brother. Is it safe. Can we go brother. Are they gone brother.

Yes brother yes brother.

That was what Mahfouz had said. For one terrible moment he had felt what it would be to let them go on; felt what it would be to say, No. Silence. Stay here. Stay without moving. But he did not go on in that way. He did not yield to temptation. He had said: Go on brother. Walk on brother.

The door opened and they went out. Mahfouz stayed where he was. He did not know what there was downstairs, two floors down. He did not know whether the waiting guns would know that they were not to shoot at him. Soon the men and women had passed. He made a pretence at counting them. Behind the last of them he made a feint to follow, but instead shut the door behind them. Quickly, firmly. He sank to the floor. On the other side of the door there was a scream, a gulp, a swallowed scream. The ones at the back had understood as the door to the safe room had closed behind them. Mahfouz sank to the floor with his back against the door. He pressed his hands to his ears. The noise was so great that he heard it anyway. He shut his eyes. The hesitation he had felt, the moment when he could have said, No. Stop. That would go on with him for ever. He waited for a long time. When he opened the door he had to tread carefully between bodies. They lay in piles, all the way up the stairs. From them came cries and moans, here and there; small frail gestures with the hands, soon stilled by the soldiers who were still there. They lifted their guns at him too; he raised his hands and called the name of their captain, in Urdu. They lowered their guns. The look on their faces was terrible, a look of dread and fear and, here and there, of nothing at all, of a bored man in a minor position about to complain about the labour he had had to undertake.

'What was it? My husband?'

His wife was looking at him with expectation. The food had started arriving: delicious-looking plain grilled meats and fish and vegetables.

'I did what needed to be done,' Mahfouz said. 'It was a different time.'

'I know that you never did anything that was wrong,' Farhana said.

'That's right,' Mahfouz said. He looked up at the youngest of the waiters, now placing down a dish of rice, and smiled at him. He had a nervous, worried face, and was probably still at school. His life would be so different.

6.

The holiday came to an end.

The honeymoon came to an end.

Their last day was more like an embarkation than a departure. On the last but one day the heavens had opened, and it had rained solidly all day long. They had visited some souvenir shops and returned to the hotel. An English board game had kept them innocently entertained in the lounge of the hotel. When, from time to time, a guest or one of Mrs Harrison's employees looked in and saw Mahfouz and his wife playing Ludo, they smiled, but withdrew. In the evening they paid a last visit to the Rajput restaurant. The staff lined up to say goodbye to them and to wish them well.

In the morning a taxi took them to the station on the other side of the isthmus, through the steady drifting grey rain. They were in plenty of time, and settled themselves in the drab little café on the platform. His wife sat at the table with their suitcases to her side. He went to the till and asked for two cups of tea. The woman serving stared beyond him, at Farhana. He no longer minded or worried. It was not a serious issue. This was the first day of the rest of their lives, and he thought of the wonderful time they had had, and of the love for each other that was only just beginning. Out there at the end of England, on the train tracks, the rain was falling. In seven hours they would be home and with each other. Farhana neatly raised her cup to her mouth, beneath her veil. She looked at him; her eyes caught his inspection; she modestly dropped them again. He could not be sure, but it appeared to him that her lovely eyes were shining with what must, surely, be grateful tears.

BOOK TWO

THE FRIENDLY ONES

CHAPTER EIGHT

In June 1990, Hugh Spinster approached a woman in a rehearsal room in Islington, north London, and asked her to come out with him on a date. He made inverted quotation marks around the words 'on a date'. She agreed. He took her to a restaurant, an ordinary pizzeria, and five days later he asked her to marry him. She laughed, but they married in October 1990. She was a costume designer and had been working on a play about Henry VIII in which Hugh Spinster was playing Sir Thomas More.

Hugh Spinster's sisters, Blossom and Lavinia, came to the wedding. Lavinia was brought by her flatmate, Sonia, who had heard about it. Blossom came with her husband, Stephen. She had been told her brother was getting married the day before by her sister, Lavinia. Stephen was in London and close at hand in any case. The wedding was on a Thursday in a City church. Afterwards Hugh kissed his sisters and introduced them to his new wife. They all walked out to the street, and in the middle of the conversation and congratulation, Hugh stuck out his arm and hailed a taxi. He and his new wife got into it and were taken away.

The Christmas of 1990 Lavinia went up to Sheffield to be with her father and her mother, who was at home. She gave them a handsome slipware vase in grey, and enough flowers to fill it. The flowers died. Her father gave her a calendar with photographs of Derbyshire landmarks, and, to his wife, a five-year desk diary bound in red leather with locks. Lavinia had to stay until 27 December, as the trains did not run on Boxing Day. She went back to her house in Parsons Green to find that the boiler had packed up. Her lodger had gone away, and

Lavinia had to wait until the New Year for a heating engineer to come out to mend it. She did not go back to work until 5 January. She had nowhere else to go when the boiler failed.

By February Josh Spinster had been living with his aunt and uncle, and going to the same school as his cousin, for five months. He went up with his aunt and his cousin Tresco to Sheffield at the end of the month. They were given special leave from school for the purpose. His grandfather and grandmother had not divorced, after all, before she died. It was two days after Josh's birthday that they heard. The birthday had been encouraged and Aunt Blossom had made a special fuss of him. There was a party with twenty guests, as it coincided with half-term, and a donkey and a conjuror in the grounds. It was terribly cold, and the conjuror's blue hands kept dropping cards, metal globes, fumbling with five-pound notes that had or had not been torn up. There was nobody at the party whom Josh had known long, apart from his cousins. The other children edged away from him or broke out into fits of half-hearted fighting. When their parents appeared, each of them ran away with hardly a backward glance, barely reciting that they must thank him for having them, they had had a lovely time.

At the funeral of his grandmother, a week later, he saw his mother. The funeral was held in a bright modern church, with pine simplicity and clean-designed abstract windows. His grandfather came in unsupported, saying hello to left and right. He looked surprised when he saw Josh's mother, sitting in the back row.

Lavinia came to the funeral. She arrived the day before and stayed the night. Blossom made an early start, and was there by the start of the funeral at twelve. So were Hugh and his new wife, but they did not stay. Hugh hardly kissed his sisters. His wife made a small sympathetic gesture of the hand, a demonstration that everything was inadequate, a flap upwards, and then she was gone. There was something interesting about the clothes the costume designer had on. She wore an abbreviated poncho in astrakhan over a tight black cocktail dress. They said goodbye to their father and went off, in different directions. Blossom explained, just in front of Catherine, holding on tight to her boy's hand, that none of them had seen Leo since May. Hilary made a brutal backwards-upwards nod, meaning it was no more than he expected of his son.

Once Stephen met Catherine on the tube. It was half past eleven in the morning. Stephen was returning from Westminster, where he had been hauled up before the Treasury Select Committee. He could have taken a car but he thought he would tough it out, face the world, stand with his hand on the rail. He saw Catherine, he said, his former sister-in-law. But Blossom corrected him: she was not his sister-in-law, she was Blossom's sister-in-law. There had never been any term for the relationship between them. Catherine was drunk, falling-over drunk. At first he had thought she was ill, or having some kind of a fit.

Josh was settling down so well. In the photographs of their holidays in Eigg that summer you could not tell the difference between Josh and Tresco and Tamara and Thomas. He had found his place at school – he had his little friends in the Latin set – but his housemaster told Blossom in a long letter that he was making persevering strides with his hockey, too. He was quite a different boy. It was that summer that his voice broke, too. 'How are things in the dorm?' Stephen asked him.

'Fine,' Josh said grudgingly. That was how boys of Josh's sort were.

At the beginning of that summer, they had a letter from the headmaster saying that Tresco would have to be withdrawn from the school after his GCSEs. Stephen had organized his donations to the school in a schedule that would run over the next five years, the most substantial chunk falling on the last payment. He cancelled the payments, responding briefly to the pained letters from the governors that claimed a contractual commitment there. Josh was not removed from the school. Tresco said that he was happy to go to the village school, as he called it – in fact to a school in a large town ten miles away, once famous for lacemaking. He spent the next three months shooting at birds with an airgun. The children of the village were invited into the woods; they met Tamara; they told her what they thought of her.

In late August, the National Theatre began public performances of a new production of *Flower Drum Song*. In it, Hugh Spinster had been cast as Wang Ta. The casting was varied: the heroine was played by a black actress, her father by a Bollywood star. Lavinia went to see it on the third night after the press night, on the first Saturday – her friend Sue from work said in the interval, eating an ice-cream, that Lavinia's brother Hugh was very good, and that you got used to it quite quickly. By then the reviews were out. Hugh had been a revelation. One newspaper said that a star had been born. Lavinia wrote Hugh a card congratulating him, sending it to the theatre. The birthday card that she had sent to his previous address had been returned – he and his wife had moved. In a week she had an effusive but somehow impersonal note in reply, saying she ought to have come back afterwards.

Hugh had moved because his wife was pregnant. They had bought a new place in King's Cross. The terraced house was on a street noisy with prostitutes and drug deals. Nearby a decrepit cinema played repertory favourites, cult classics and ancient porn. There was a Maltese baker nearby. On that, and on the newsagents and shops in King's Cross station, they relied a good deal. Across the road a member of a pop band sometimes left casualties prostrate on the pavement outside his house, agape with heroin. Hugh and his wife said they loved it there.

That spring Hugh's wife lost her baby. There had been talk of *Flower Drum Song* transferring to Broadway, but American Equity cut up rough about non-American actors being imported with the production, and everything was delayed. In the meantime Hugh was going to go into rehearsals for *Kean*, and there was some suggestion about a television dramatization of *The Possessed*. For the first time that year, he was regularly recognized in the street, even by the local prostitutes putting themselves out for a rock of crack. They recognized him from a television advert he had done for an upmarket chocolate manufacturer, for Bacardi, and another for a particularly stretchy vest material, more often seen in cinemas.

Stephen had had an excellent year, and the building works had been extensive, the materials of the best quality. The children had not been told what was going on. On Christmas Eve, a huge family dinner with candles had taken place. Stephen's parents had come to stay from Birmingham, and Josh's mother Catherine, too. An invitation had been despatched to Josh's father. There had been talk of asking Blossom's father Hilary, but then you would have to ask Lavinia. A family belonging to a colleague of Stephen's who lived twenty miles away had turned up. They had two small, cowed children, fussy in what they would or would not eat. They were just like Josh had been until last year. The evening went smoothly. There were drinks in the drawing room; they had gone in to dine in the old style, formally, Tresco pairing off with the vicar's wife and Catherine with Stephen's colleague. After pudding but before dessert, which Blossom served in the library, lit by candles, they filed into the great hall where the stairways were entwined with holly and mistletoe. There the choir from the local church was standing halfway up the stairs. They had been let in and put in their places by Mrs Wicks. They sang four carols, including what had always been Blossom's favourite, 'See Amid the Winter's Snow'. It always made her cry, she confided to Stephen's colleague's wife, Paulette. Piers had married late, but quite successfully. His career had stalled. Stephen had found him a post at Carradine Kronberg Matthiesson really out of kindness, and for old times' sake. He would never know how much Blossom had urged it on Stephen. In a year's time Stephen would probably stand back and let them sack him. After that they would not speak again until the new millennium.

After dessert came the grand revelation. The children were led out onto a path lined by torches to the new stables and their Christmas presents: ponies for Tresco, Tamara, Thomas and

Josh, and even baby Trevor had a very small one. Ribbons had been tied round the necks of all of them, a red one, a green one, a blue one, a yellow one, a silver one. The horses neighed and snorted tranquilly. Tamara burst into tears: she had wanted a grey, and the grey had gone to Josh. She did not want a piebald. But Josh agreed to swap with her, and all was well. 'I think she means skewbald,' Stephen's colleague Piers told his two cowed children, as if merely conveying some information. Catherine reached out and rested her hands on her son's shoulders. In a moment he walked forward and petted what must now be his horse, the skewbald. Paulette was a Frenchwoman. Her outer surfaces were hard and glittering, a Lacroix dress with sewn-in brilliants and a turquoise and scarlet clash across the very full skirt. Her hair was waxed down like beautiful old furniture. When her husband had been explaining for long enough about the colours of horses, and how easy it was for people to make those kinds of mistakes, she raised her eyes and impaled him on her glance. '"Hail, redemption's happy morn,"' he said, and then fell silent. He knew that he was going to be sacked in the next few months.

For months Hilary could never be sure when he opened the front door that he would not find a woman there holding a foil-wrapped dish. Did it happen to everyone who had – their words – 'lost someone'? This siege of widows and divorcees? At first, when they came thick and fast, their expression was stricken, pained, but still managing to smile. The fair-weather ones faded away, or perhaps took a realistic view of their prospects, and in six weeks there were three regulars, turning up with a supportive but strict smile and the dish of lasagne, shepherd's pie, fish pie, boeuf bourguignon or coq au vin. 'Mary's brought you a nice moussaka for your din-dins, Gertrude,' Hilary remarked, if Gertrude was in the kitchen and showing an interest. The three kind ladies tended to ignore this. The rudeness of the recently widowed was factored into their calculations. Of course one could not expect gratitude every time; of course one could not expect Dr Spinster not to give way to the sort of insults that really masked deep grief. They kept on coming.

They had got it wrong, the kind ladies. It was not grief that badgered him, but the precise memory of the things he had said out loud, in those last days, when there was nobody now left alive to remember having heard them.

One of the kind ladies was widowed; the other two were divorced. Hilary liked to ask them, on the days when he could be bothered, how their divorces had been. Adultery, was it? Or unreasonable treatment? An interesting one, that. Or had it just been separation, an agreed time spent apart? And how had it been for them? A relief? Or had it been painful? Interesting. They answered bravely. So much had happened since then, one said, she was really quite a different person. 'I see,' Hilary said, and smiled his own smile, waiting for her to say that she had to get on with things, to get up like an unwilling camel rising to work again.

In the first months, he took himself in hand. The sweets tailed off. For a week or two he kept coming across packets of sherbet lemons, fruit pastilles, wine gums, all the sours and fruits and jellies, each half finished, then stuffed down the side of a chair. They were like the secret half-bottles of vodka an alcoholic leaves about the place. For a while he came across them with cries of delight, hands raised to shoulder height; by the end they were making his heart sink. But finally they were gone. And mealtimes returned – he became rather strict about it, eating his breakfast at eight, his lunch at one, his supper at seven thirty. He placed the radio on the end of the table where a guest, a child, a spouse might be, and ate at a civilized speed. There were other routines. He cancelled the newspaper delivery, and each morning walked down to Broomhill, whatever the weather, to buy the *Daily Telegraph*.

The predatory trio brought made dishes, to perform a display of their skill, but they liked it to be irregular. He supposed they did not want an obligation to settle upon them. So there were trips to the supermarket, too, to buy fruit and vegetables and bread and milk and the business for breakfast, as well as emergency lamb chops and tins of soup. Would a widow – even a retired doctor – hold similar appeal for sad and lonely old men? He examined his feelings. He thought not.

Once a month, he went out for lunch with his new friend Sharif from next door, and his successor at the surgery, Imran Khan, an amusing young man. Funny how they so often shared names with each other, that lot, not even caring if they had the same name as someone famous. Funny, too, how Hilary had become so mixed-race in his friendships. He would say this to the ladies with the foil-wrapped dishes. Some of them blanched because of the expression; one because of the fact. Imran and Sharif thought he was a card; he liked their outings for lunch, usually to a pub in Derbyshire where one of them could drive and Hilary, for once in a blue moon, could drink. Sharif didn't mind having half a pint; he told Hilary that he had never had an alcoholic drink until the age of thirty-two. Now he was making up for lost time, with his half-pint of bitter once a month. Together they chewed through the problems of the world.

The problems of his world? The children were off his hands, with children of their own to worry about, some of them. He could please himself, these days. Get up at four a.m. and listen to Beethoven's Eroica symphony on the gramophone. Anything. The pressure of another person in the house, of wondering what to say to them, of pushing your life into awkward corners and peculiar shapes around their own corners and shapes – all that was over now. In the last year and a half, he had become a truly voracious reader of thrillers. He could get through one in an afternoon, as the light outside faded over the neglected garden.

Anne got married. She was a friend of Lavinia's from work. They had joined the charity at the same time. Their conversations were a matter of discussing what the mosquito-net provision for northern Uganda was like. She had remained where she had started, and now Lavinia was, in some lights, her boss. She was marrying her boyfriend from university, a vet who had his own practice in Wimbledon, dogs and cats and a surprising number of horses. Anne asked Lavinia if she would be her bridesmaid. Lavinia suppressed the thought of how disappointing a tiny adult as a bridesmaid would be to the congregation, when she turned round, and said yes. The wedding was in May. 'I hope you're not superstitious,' Anne said, sitting on the desk in Lavinia's office. Lavinia had not heard that particular superstition, but apparently it meant that, even in the year 1995, it was easier to find dates for churches and register offices in May than June. The wedding was going to be in the country near Dorking, where Anne had grown up. Anne had arranged a lift for Lavinia with a friend of Martin's called Jeremy, who lived in Waterloo. The only other thing, Anne said, laughing, was that Lavinia would be wearing a nice big dress with puff sleeves, in a shiny shade of peach.

But of course Anne was a good sort, and when the doorbell rang on the Saturday morning Lavinia was in a very pale blue dress, an icy, flattering shade. Over a shiny silk floated a layer of fine lace in grey-blue; there were no small girls among the bridesmaids, and so the shape and colour of the dress could be adult, an elegant shift. She had put her hair up that morning, and had taken a little trouble with her make-up for once. She reminded herself, as she always did, that she was not a small girl any more; that strangers were not to be run away from; that she, too, could greet someone unknown with a smile and an outstretched hand. Outside it was pouring down in buckets, a real English spring day, with almost comedy effects of thunder and gusts. The figure at the door under the umbrella bowed, absurdly, smiling, as she asked him in. '*Mariage pluvieux, mariage heureux,*' Jeremy said. Was he a vet, too? She had forgotten.

She made him a cup of coffee – he said he wouldn't risk anything else in his hired morning suit. It was the seventh time in the last twelve months he'd had to hire it. It would really be sensible to buy one, Lavinia cautiously ventured. But the capital outlay! Jeremy said, rolling his eyes. Against fifty pounds a time to hire it! And no discount for – well, Jeremy said, look at me, I'm five feet four. That ought to save something.

'I'm even smaller,' Lavinia offered.

And think, Jeremy said, of the dry cleaning, too – but then he was off on wondering whether the bridesmaids got to keep their outfits, he supposed so. It wasn't at every wedding that they'd want to, but in this case … What was she going to wear on top of it? It was only a short dash to the car, but … Perhaps he would just have a biscuit, there was no danger in that.

Jeremy was a teller of tales, a yakker, a goer-on. He announced himself as that, and some time later as a vicar. He had always looked younger than he was, he was afraid, and actually had got to the point now of having his own parish. And a chamber-music festival once a year – it was their fourth now. The teller-of-tales stuff – well, once a mother of twins, a regular attender, had rushed round to the house at lunchtime on a Saturday in real despair. Her six-year-olds were having a party, and the entertainment had cancelled – his own child was down with measles. She had tried everyone, and in the end she had come round to ask the vicar if he by any chance …

Jeremy, retelling this story at Lavinia's kitchen table, put on a comedy voice of despair. He had important things to do, jam to make, the sick to visit, the Mother's Union meetings to schedule, a sermon to write. (But none of these in reality – just a favourite old movie, *The Way to the Stars*, just then starting on BBC2.) But a mother could always make Jeremy's cold old heart melt. After all, he said, he could probably tell a story, if she didn't mind something out of the Acts of the Apostles. 'Oh, anything, anything,' the mother said, wringing her hands. In the end Jeremy had kept a dozen six-year-olds quiet for half an hour with his memories of *Charlotte's Web*. He changed the spider into a cockroach, for reasons of copyright, he now confided. In the nick of time he remembered that cockroaches don't spin webs – rather crucial in the denouement, in fact. But his cockroach pushed and laboured and overnight arranged a thousand crumbs of bread into the vital message on the kitchen floor before dying of old age. The mothers of Waterloo and Kennington, the word had got out among them. He asked only for a donation to the funds.

The wedding was in a church in a village, not a picturesque church, but a square, practical 1930s church with plain windows and a noticeboard at the back, like a Nuffield institution for the efficient processing of souls. Jeremy had no role in the ceremony. Afterwards, in the marquee in Anne's parents' garden, he had a place at the top table next to Lavinia. Anne had gambled on them getting on well together. He wasn't the best man but, in an unconventional way, had been asked to speak. He told Lavinia this as they sat down, and immediately she wondered that he had no nervousness at all. Actors could be like that – cripplingly shy people in everyday life who nevertheless could fling themselves out there. The time came for Jeremy to stand. He began to speak. In three minutes a woman at the nearest table was smiling, and holding a napkin up, shaking her head, to staunch her tears.

It came as a surprise to Blossom that Lavinia was getting married. She took the phone call in the morning room after breakfast, and came back in to share the news. Tresco was there, of course, loafing about, nothing to do until he decided to take himself outside and shoot things, but Josh and Tamara as well – they had finished their A levels and come home. Thomas was on a pony trek and Trevor upstairs, practising her Japanese with the nanny. She told the three of them. They were going to have an uncle who was a vicar. 'Not an uncle,' Tamara said, with spitting contempt. 'Just the man who's marrying Aunty Lav.' But what did she think the name for that relationship ought to be? The wedding was going to be in November – no time at all. She hadn't heard anything from Lavinia all year. She had supposed everything was all right and now it clearly was all right. Lavinia had been phoning to make sure the dates suited but also to ask an embarrassing question or, rather, two. The first Blossom could answer and did not share with the children. She had an address for Hugh. But the awful thing was – what was Hugh's wife called? Blossom had an idea it might be Francesca – Rosamund – Margaretta – one of those names. No – she was called Carla. There you are. She did not ask Lavinia whether she thought he would come. It was difficult to know what to say there.

But the other question she could not help with, and had to ask the children. Lavinia had wanted to know whether Blossom had an address for Leo. Blossom had tried to say, as gently as she could, that Leo had disappeared because he had wanted to disappear. One day he was going to come back, she was sure, but it would be – well. She wanted to say that perhaps the time would come when six years of silence would not seem like a long stretch. She gave some last cries of delight and excitement. A vicar's wife had emerged from nothing, like somebody having concealed a secret identity. 'Mummy,' Tamara said. 'I'm not going to be here. I'm in Australia then. I can't come back just for Aunt Lavinia marrying a London vicar.'

'Oh, your gap year,' Blossom said, as if just reminded.

Tresco kept himself out of the way after those disappointing A-level results. He would disappear after breakfast with a gun, or spruced up to visit a friend in the village. It was only when Tamara got on a plane to Australia and, two weeks later, Josh went away to university that Blossom looked at her eldest son and realized he would soon be twenty-one, and without any kind of plan in life. There was a trust fund set up. Tresco could go and live in the London flat with his father if he wanted to work there. But he did not. He lived in his old bedroom and shot at things from the window. Some time in March, Blossom agreed with Stephen that something had to be done. She carried out some research, and established the cost of a bedsitting room in the nearest town. She then told Tresco that, from now on, she would charge him that sum of money, weekly, for his food and lodging. He informed her that he would pay her out of his trust fund, and carry on much as before. She had anticipated this ingenious solution, and told Tresco that if the money did not come out of earned income, the rate would be three times as much. By the end of the month, Tresco was working in the garage of one of the girls he knew in the village. He answered the phone and kept the tools in their place. He did some work underneath the cars, and was learning about engines and other mechanical things, his mother explained. His father thought it was funny.

At the end of the summer, Tresco moved into a flat in the village with the garage owner's daughter. Blossom would always remember that. The three things went together, with their demands of incompatible responses from her. Her daughter returned after a year away; her son was living in a slum with a little tart and giving up on life; her husband produced the catastrophe so long expected of him. It was not the expected catastrophe. She had always thought it would be the fact of sex, and she had conceived of it in the most banal terms, a secretary, a girl in the office, a hard-faced Russian woman with a perfect figure and her eyes fixed on any old fool who drifted into a bar in the City with his wallet open. But it was not sex. It was money, and the law. She had always thought Stephen knew what he was doing.

It must have been after the millennium when Carla looked out of the window into the street in King's Cross and saw a short, frail figure on the other side, looking with bashful determination at her. It must have been 2001, because Hugh had that awful haircut and beard for the part as a 1920s socialist in that Bloomsbury epic for Channel 4. Frail figures were ten a penny in King's Cross, though the cinema had gone and the crack dealers had been cleared up.

Hugh came to the window, and said immediately that that was his sister. Carla had met her at their wedding. He went to the door and called Lavinia over, asked her in. He expected her to smile as she took her coat off and say that she'd just been passing on her way to – what, the Maltese baker? But she shook her head in that way she always had, and just said that she hadn't seen him for eight years, perhaps even nine, and – Hugh –

Hugh was no good at these emotional scenes. He fetched a bottle of gin and a bottle of whisky, and sent Carla off to the kitchen for some ice and a bottle of tonic water. They sat down. Tremulously, Lavinia admired the painting behind Hugh. She hadn't seen it before. Hugh explained that it was by Albert Irvine, he was a friend of theirs, of Carla's really – but they must have bought it from him, what, five or six years ago. The tonic arrived and some slices of lemon. Carla set them down, kneeling like a geisha, then got up again, resting with her arms folded in the doorframe as if to check that everything was quite all right before withdrawing once more. Lavinia began to cry. Hugh poured her a gin and tonic, held it out to her. She drank it in two long gulps. Her husband – did Hugh know that she was married now? The invitation two years ago? – her husband didn't know she was here. He was a vicar, he was good at these things.

Hugh understood that, with the decision to come to see her brother in his house in King's Cross, had come a decision not to be veiled in politeness. Hugh always fended things off so. It was not normal, Lavinia insisted, it was not normal at all for Hugh to go away when Mummy died and just not to speak to her again. What had happened to them? Leo just disappearing, Hugh not wanting to speak to them either, what was it?

Hugh had not spoken to Blossom since his wedding; he had not wondered if there was any reason Leo had not come. Nobody knew where Leo had gone, or where he lived. Whatever the reason for Leo to disappear, to wipe himself clear from the family history –

'That's it,' she said. 'That's exactly it. It's the family history. I saw my children in thirty or forty years' time asking if I had a brother, and me saying yes, and he was a famous actor, but then I would have to say that I couldn't remember what his wife was called. I had to check when I sent the invitation. I don't have any children so – oh, Hugh –'

'We don't have any children either,' Hugh said.

Lavinia's face was stricken. Hugh hoped that Carla was not listening. He thought she was downstairs in the kitchen.

'May I?' Lavinia said, making a formal sort of gesture. He did not at first realize what she was asking for, in the manner of a polite guest.

'Of course,' he said, after a moment. 'It's on the first floor, the first door you come to.'

'I won't be long,' she said, and went out, and up the stairs. It seemed an unusual thing to say, and it was five minutes before Carla came up from the kitchen to ask if Lavinia was all right. The noise from upstairs was a familiar one. His sister was apparently having a bath. The huge plunging delicious hiss and roar filled the house. Late at night, he loved to lie in bed after a performance and hear the noise of his wife bathing.

The bath was a beautiful deep Victorian one. Nobody had touched large parts of the house since it was built. The sash windows were still there where so many of the neighbours had, some time in the 1970s, installed aluminium ones; there was a stone butler's sink in the back room behind the kitchen; and a colossal Victorian bath on the black iron legs of a lion. Everything needed replacing – the bath had been stripped and polished and re-enamelled. Now Lavinia was pouring gigantic quantities of hot water into it, was shedding her clothes, losing her tiny physicality in the swimming-pool-like expanse of the bath. Downstairs Carla looked at him, quizzically. What she wanted to know was this: is this normal? Does your family do this?

He could not say, and in a moment Carla said that she would be getting on with things. Lavinia had undertaken this to pose him a question or a challenge. There were people in the world who could get up and go upstairs with hardly a word and take a bath in his house. Carla, for instance. And when he had lived at home he had, surely, got up from a conversation with his sister or his mother, or with any of them, and just gone to take a bath in the old bathroom with the avocado fittings and the stained-glass window.

When Lavinia asked if she could go upstairs, she only really meant if she could go to the loo. But then she saw the bath – a huge, extraordinary affair, it could have held her and Jeremy at either end with their books and no suggestion of entanglement or romance. She turned the tap. It dribbled, then poured, and then, as she turned again, gushed with the release of great waters after a collapse of barriers. There were bath salts to add, and shampoos to raid. They were the sort of people, Hugh and his wife, who gave way to temptation. The shelf above the bath had half a dozen bottles scented with jojoba, coconut, cucumber, lavender, ginger, lime, apple, combined and singly. She slid her clothes off and plunged into the hot water. Her husband had gone on regarding her brother in the same way he always had, never having met him: with a mixture of tenderness and impatience. He felt impatience for Hugh because he had walked away from his Lavinia so; but he felt tenderness for this absent brother-in-law because he was his Lavinia's, and because she held so much of her heart aside for him. When she went downstairs she would find out if he would accept her behaviour still, whatever it was.

It seemed to Hugh that Lavinia had understood she possessed a right but not a custom. Once, she was the one person who, in his house, could have taken a bath without even asking. That permission had disappeared, had been withdrawn from his sister by Hugh. The noise of the water running had now stopped. The sounds of bathtime, of water being raised and dripped and poured, now followed. She dared him, stepping forward into his controlled space. He remembered a day when she was sitting in the passenger seat of the car, and for some reason reached over and took hold of the wheel, pulling at it, wanting to make him turn. It could have killed them.

Presently the bath came to an end, gurgling through the drains. He and Carla usually opened the window so as to disperse the steam, but Lavinia did not know to do that. The sound of the bathroom door being unbolted, and the sound of his sister padding downstairs. She was in the door of the sitting room – by now Hugh was holding a book open – and her shoes were in her hands, her hair combed but damp.

'Sorry,' she said. 'I just felt like one.'

'That's fine,' he said. 'Do you want a cup of tea?'

'Lovely,' she said. 'What are you reading?'

'I should be getting on with my script,' he said. 'I'm supposed to be in rehearsals on Friday.'

Lavinia stuck out her lower lip. 'Well, I'm not here every day,' she said. 'And I'm not staying much longer.'

'Let me just go and tell Carla we're having tea,' Hugh said.

Carla was in the kitchen. She had made a decision, and the decision was about Lavinia's bath: it would not be talked about. She broke into bright chatter about work, about how the raw silk had apparently not turned up at the workshop for the third consecutive day. When Carla joined them in the sitting room, they heard all about Lavinia's husband Jeremy and his parish in Waterloo and the constant ringing of the doorbell by derelicts – Lavinia was even quite funny about it. She had created a kind of secret space for her and her brother, or half-brother, where Carla could never enter. In half an hour Lavinia finished her tea. She picked up her handbag, an old one but a good-quality one, from the sofa, saying that she had meant to bring photographs of their wedding, but another time. That was the only suggestion they might meet again. He was not sure if the ice had been broken, or if intimacy had been tested and now shown to be a lost cause. At the door he acted out the loving brother. He went back into the sitting room and talked about their plans for a holiday. They thought perhaps Brazil, when the run of *Oklahoma!* came to an end.

Blossom and Stephen sold the big house in the country in 2004. There was no point in it any longer. The children's ponies went as well. Blossom had thought that the house and the estate would be theirs for ever, that it would pass down the generations through Tresco and Tresco's children and Tresco's grandchildren. But Tresco was living with his girlfriend in an awful semi-detached house in Hereford made out of bright yellow brick and running a party business. The girlfriend was a nice, capable girl, with short hair and big hands. They were never going to take over the running of the estate. In the end she and Stephen had had it for twenty years, bought it for a song – God, it had been a wreck – and then in the end it was just a house. She didn't care even about giving up the new carp pond. Despite all fears, it had been easy to find someone to buy it. Someone in the City who was making a packet, a partner in a derivatives business with three children. She might have been looking in the mirror twenty years ago. Blossom wondered whether this derivatives partner was going to be had up for criminal practices and barred from ever holding a job in the City again. Stephen kept out of the way.

He had really been very lucky. He had escaped the criminal trial and the custodial sentence that had fallen over some of the others. He had been badly censured, and of course it was terrible to be told that you could never work in the City again. But he was of an age when lots of men retired. She could see the shame, but not the detail of what Stephen had done. She got Josh to sit down and talk the case through, with plenty of 'Oh, wait,' and 'I think the problem with that must have been'. Josh had finished his law degree and his solicitor's training and his articled clerkship with Bowers Jenkins in the City and was now set on a professional course. He was almost enthusiastic about it, like a half-trained puppy, only remembering halfway through that it was his uncle he was talking about. He assembled his face and tried to look on the bright side. She was grateful for Josh. He had tried to tell her what Stephen never would.

They left most of the contents of the house in the house. She heard that the derivatives bloke was opening the place up to the public on Sundays in the summer. Most of what was on show had been built or bought by Blossom and abandoned where it could not be moved. She supposed that was what was meant by 'heritage'. They had moved to London. Now that there were only Stephen and Blossom and Trevor, and Thomas home from Cardiff in the university holidays, there was no need to have anything but an elegant stucco house in a square in Clapham.

You got your money's worth there, and it had a coach house to the side where Tamara could live if she ever came home. There was forty feet of garden. The best pictures, such as the Guercino, came with them and probably about a quarter or even less of what Blossom thought of as *the stuff* – half a dozen Turkey carpets, two small sideboards, some armchairs and beds, small tables. Some things just had to be bought again, like the dining table and chairs. She didn't suppose they were ever going to seat twenty round a rosewood table ever again. How they would fill their days defeated her.

Stephen, after a long period of morose silence, took to going out in the mornings. Books began appearing on the bedside table with an emphatic label on the cover, and she discovered that her husband had joined the London Library. She supposed on other days he was going off for a tramp across the Common or perhaps off to Richmond Park at the end of the District Line from Sloane Square. She deduced his day from the state of his boots, whether they were dusty or thick with mud and left at the kitchen door.

They were strange, the books he was reading. At first they were large historical works, randomly selected with nothing to connect them, lives of Napoleon, histories of the Hundred Years' War, disquisitions on the end of the Empire. But then she was surprised to see a study of Eastern mysticism, and then another, and another. Soon Stephen was reading nothing but books about Buddhism – first about what the religion meant, then about the Buddha, his life. Books started appearing on the bedside table that were not from the London Library, that could not, she swore, be bought in any ordinary bookshop, covers bearing vividly coloured mandalas and promises of self-improvement in forty steps, inside a self-assembled computer typeface garishly shouting. Once she found a black notebook. On the first page, in Stephen's neat, decisive, practical handwriting, was written *The Book of Failure* and on the next, *I consider myself a failure. Failure is something I must learn to possess, to breathe in like air. Failure is my sacred* (crossed out) *gift to myself.* 'Does Uncle Stephen seem different to you?' she asked Josh, when he visited one Sunday for lunch. (If Stephen was devoting his time to the path of enlightenment, she was improving her cooking. There seemed no point in sticking to game in SW4.) Josh thought there was something different about him. She decided to leave the revelation of hippie nirvana to Stephen. She supposed that the regular income from letting the Kensington flat and handling the investment from the capital in a low-risk sort of way (Josh had checked, it was all perfectly fine) would calm him; the Buddha would help. 'Whatever else,' she said, over the phone to Tamara in Australia, 'I'm definitely not going on any meditative retreats. I can't squat any more. I can't even cross my legs when I sit on the ground.'

'My housemate went to one in Thailand,' Tamara said, across the thousands of miles. 'She said they slept on straw mats and had wooden pillows and got up at four to meditate. She said it was *awesome.*'

'Well, your father's not …' Blossom began, but, to be honest, she didn't even know any more. She supposed it was a good thing that her husband, after nearly thirty years, was still surprising her.

There was really no reason for his getting the bus that morning. The company had supplied drivers, or said they had, to get Hugh to the rehearsal rooms in the morning. He took them for a few days. But then he told them, with a sad and embarrassed smile, that he would actually rather not. It was a BBC production of *Little Dorrit*, and he was the star. Strangely, what he wanted in the morning was not comfort and the driver's flattering conversation. He wanted a brisk walk and then the silent crowds of public transport. He worked much better like that, he told Carla. He was never recognized. He could stand there with a baseball cap on, watching the way that a young man stood when he was consumed with happiness, stood in the year 2005, just as he had stood in the year 1855. That morning he had shouted that he was a bit late, he'd see her this evening, and the front door was slammed. He usually said he loved her: had he specifically said it that morning? It was a glorious day. In her mind's eye Carla for ever afterwards saw her beautiful tiny husband, walking along with his face under a baseball cap into the bright morning. His face: those queer triangular eyes, neither sad nor happy, like a puffin's. She saw him, getting on a bus at King's Cross that was inexplicably crowded, looking about him at the interesting London faces.

When Josh heard the news he was sitting at his desk in the City. He read it on a celebrity update page that he was mildly addicted to; he googled his uncle's name, and found, all over the internet, that the English actor Hugh Spinster was among the dead. For some reason he knew straight away that he was the first of them to know. He had a client meeting coming up in twenty minutes with one of the partners – the papers were in a block in front of him ready to go. He didn't think even the solicitors' firm he worked for would begrudge him this. He phoned Tresco first, who would be at home – party planners weren't like solicitors with their nine-to-five. ('Eight-to-eight,' Josh sadly responded.) The baby and the two little ones were screaming in the background. 'Oh, Christ,' he said. 'Does Mummy know?'

Thomas was showing a flat in a new development in Kennington – he kept up the business-like tones. In the end Josh said, 'I'll speak to Aunt Blossom. I don't know if she'd have heard yet. I've only seen it online.'

'If it's not in the paper yet she won't know about it,' Thomas said. 'Got to go. Have you spoken to your dad?' But Josh had not.

'Have you heard?' Blossom said. Her voice was steady. 'Josh just phoned. He's seen it reported on the internet.'

'It was on the radio just now,' Lavinia said. 'I've had it on. I'm at work. I don't know why – I just felt immediately that Hugh – Oh, God, Blossom – like a crack in the universe opening up, it felt like.'

'Were they nice about him?' Blossom said.

'A big hole suddenly being in the place where Hugh always was. Were they nice to him? I don't think they'd quite got as far as –' Lavinia said, her words spilling over each other.

'He didn't suffer,' Blossom said. 'I'm sure he didn't suffer.'

'He wanted to live in a big square house in the country. With a path down the middle of two lawns and a cherry tree. I could have seen him in it and now he'll never be old.'

'Don't,' Blossom said, not trying to make sense of this.

'I haven't seen him for years,' Lavinia said. 'Oh, Blossom. I went round there, five years ago – it was before Russell was born. I was going to tell him about it and then I saw there was no point. So I went upstairs and I had a bath in his house and then I came downstairs clean and I went.'

'Just get a taxi home. There'll be time for everything,' Blossom said.

When Sharif heard, he reached out and took his wife's arm, laying his hand on her forearm in an awkward and unfamiliar gesture. He had been attempting to take her hand, just there in the sitting room where the television news was spooling on. But her arm was there and he had to grasp her, somehow. She felt the strangeness of the gesture and looked round at him. In her face was concern but she had not at first registered the closeness of the news. Only when she saw what must be his wide eyes did she understand. She said the name again, repeating what the television had said.

'Hugh Spinster,' she said.

'I saw him come out of the house this afternoon,' Sharif said. 'I saw him come out and sit down on the chair. I wondered if he was all right. He was just sitting there without moving. I must go over.'

'What is there that you can say?'

'I don't know,' Sharif said. He patted her arm; he tried again and now squeezed her hand. He got up. 'Whatever there is, it must be said. He can't be alone.'

'This will kill him,' Nazia said. 'Kill him. He's nearly ninety.'

'He's in good health. We'll see him through this.'

'Those bombers – those men – the murderers – they were …'

'Say it,' Sharif said, seeing the historical necessity, it might have been. 'Just once and then never again.'

'They were Pakistanis,' Nazia said.

'I know,' Sharif said.

'They were –'

'That's enough now, Nazia,' Sharif said. 'That's enough historical wrongs.'

Sharif left the house. Sometimes when he went round to Hilary's he stepped nimbly over the little fence between their front gardens. Today he walked to the end of his drive, and back the full length of Hilary's. There was no response to the door-bell, but Hilary was growing a little deaf, and often did not hear it if he was in the garden. He shyly pushed open the wooden gate to the side of the house. It felt like a liberty. Deep down he had known the possibility that Hilary would not want to see his brown face. An obligation might lie on Sharif to renounce any connection with the murderers. And they were Pakistanis. They were the people who had murdered Rafiq, the people who had murdered Professor Anisul. That was what Sharif knew and Nazia knew and what Hilary would never know.

Hilary was sitting in one of the wooden chairs on the patio, his hair a white shock, like the splash of a stone thrown into a pond. Sharif coughed gently, and Hilary turned. He looked alert, interested, a little irritated, but that was what he always looked like.

'That was a very discreet noise,' Hilary said. 'How are you, young man?'

'I thought I would pop over,' Sharif said.

'You're always very welcome,' Hilary said. 'Would you like a cup of tea or something? I've just had one.'

'No, nothing,' Sharif said.

Hilary motioned at the chair by him, quite grandly.

'I wondered if you wanted to come over and spend the day with us,' Sharif said. 'With Nazia mostly – I've got to go to the faculty this afternoon.'

'That's awfully kind of you,' Hilary said. 'Very kind.'

'I don't know what to say.'

'That's all right,' Hilary said. 'I was just thinking – he was the one I saw most often of all of them. I don't know what Leo would look like now. But I saw Hugh all the time.'

'When was ...' Sharif said, puzzled, and then realized what Hilary meant. He was delving into his own pain, he could see that.

'On the telly,' Hilary said. 'The last time was last month. He had that part in *Offices and Chambers*. Did you see it? Jolly good. I don't suppose he looks like that in reality – they'd aged him up somehow, with latex and a wig of some sort. He looked older than me. And then one day I got to the end of the episode and turned over and there he was on ITV, looking about twenty-five, selling Sainsbury or something. No escaping him, I said to myself. With a wry chuckle, you understand, a wry chuckle. Do you think they'll take it off now?'

'I don't know,' Sharif said helplessly.

'His poor wife – his widow, I mean. Just turning on the telly to escape a little bit and then suddenly, without warning, ta-da, there he is, holding up a tin of beans in a quizzical manner. Holding it up with his right arm. That arm must be lying in bits halfway across Tavistock Square, a hundred yards from his head.'

'You mustn't think too much about it,' Sharif said.

'I've made a terrible mess of things, really,' Hilary said, but quite calmly. 'I hadn't seen Hugh since before Celia died. I haven't seen Lavinia for two years and Blossom longer than that. They're always very sorry about not being able to make it up. You're very lucky with the boys and Aisha. I wish I knew how it was done.'

'It's just luck,' Sharif said. 'There's no way of knowing.'

'But things change, don't they?' Hilary said. 'Sometimes people decide they don't want to kill everyone because they don't have the same religion.'

'That must be true,' Sharif said. 'And sometimes the religion changes. My grandfather –'

Sharif stopped. There was a noise just behind him, the noise of a tapping on glass, quite urgent. Someone was knocking on the glass door of the patio from inside. Sharif found himself thinking, idiotically, that it must be Hilary's wife, as if all these years he had kept a wife hidden inside, away from Sharif, and now she was trying to attract his attention. Sharif turned and at first saw nothing in the gloom of the room. A movement at the bottom of the glass caught his eye. It was that animal Hilary kept that he called Gertrude. Its head was butting the glass window. It looked like a stone when it did not move, green-ish-grey and encrusted with age. It did not know what glass was. It hit its head against the barrier, retreated, paused, forgot, hit it again with its stony head, and again. Hilary could see as well as Sharif could, but he did nothing.

'What about your grandfather?' Hilary said.

'Oh, nothing,' Sharif said. He had been about to start telling a story about himself, and about his family. He remembered just in time what Nazia had said, that he was not to start talking about himself in the usual way he had.

'Go on, then.'

'It's silly, in fact,' Sharif said. 'My grandfather, he married polygamously. He had two wives. I don't really know which one was my father's mother, he just called them both mother. Big-mother, small-mother, he used to say. That's gone now.'

'It doesn't really matter,' Hilary said. 'Things change, and at the end there is the son of your eighty-eight-year-old neighbour, being scraped from the tarmac by patient workers with knives and dustpans.'

'My grandfather had two wives; but my father and I would never think of that. Things change and things sometimes get better. Come over and sit with Nazia, just today,' Sharif said.

'I don't know about that,' Hilary said. 'Not very good company for anyone.'

'We don't care about that,' Sharif said.

Even a year later, Lavinia could not prevent herself from reading everything she could about what was now called 7/7.

She found herself moving from the coverage of her brother, who was, in death, often considered much more famous than he ever had been in life, to the ordinary folk who had been in the tube trains or the bus. She knew about the things those ordinary people had done on behalf of the injured and the dead; she had heard their voices. Once she went to a meeting of survivors and the bereaved, with Jeremy. It was not a success. At one point a survivor started telling his story – he was a man in a wheelchair, both legs amputated above the knee – and she could hear in his voice the tension and restraint. His eyes flickered round the room. He had survived; there were those whose wives, children, brothers had not. A curious etiquette had evolved here, that the survivors would not describe their success in full if the bereaved victims were in the room. Jeremy held her hand tightly. He was always tender, but he was tender only to her and, in a formal, decent way, towards Hugh.

She tried to explain to him how it was, that a solid feature of the room she lived in had been removed at a stroke, and one felt first of all that the room would collapse – it was a structural feature, surely a load-bearing one – and then saw that it was holding up together for the moment. It was more than she could bear to hear anyone, even Jeremy, talk about religion, in any context. In those first days of love you could find yourself talking with intensity and commitment on almost any subject, gazing into the face of the loved one. It would have been the same if Jeremy had been a microbiologist. Now it was gone. Lavinia almost collapsed, however, when, eight months after the attacks, in a grim February, a card came through the post, neatly marked with a once-familiar hand. It was Leo, offering his sympathy and saying that he was thinking of her. But there was no address on it. The postmark showed only that it had been posted in London W1. Then her other brother was gone again. Poor stupid Russell – bovine, fire-engine obsessed, solidly repetitive, a stranger from the moment of his birth – was bewildered by his mummy. Jeremy knew too well what to do. He had no mood of crumpled grief himself; he had gone into the kind, sad, supportive figure that he impersonated once a week for near-strangers. He had never met Hugh and he had no grief, only concern for his wife; he could not feel the wind that was tearing through the hole left in the universe by violent design. She wanted to apologize.

Most of all she could not stop constructing the minutes before it had happened. Hugh running for the bus, then seeing that there were a lot of people shoving to get on. Something must have happened to the tube that morning. It was always happening. He must have been one of the last on a very full bus. Just by him a man was sitting in one of the disabled seats with a rucksack on his knees. That rucksack would really get on people's nerves in a crowded bus or tube. Was he a tourist, that poor man? He was sitting and muttering into his phone and perspiring there in his seat. The rucksack had been a mistake, the man was coming to understand, during a London morning rush-hour. He was clutching it tight, trying to stop it spilling over onto his neighbour's knees. Hugh had raised his head. He had caught the eye of a girl, a pretty girl from a Chinese family, her hair scrunched up in a sort of perm, and her eyes dropped – she had recognized him from an advert. The muttering from the man in the seat just by him was continuing. It had a fierce quality, the sound under the breath. Hugh couldn't see, but he wasn't quite certain that the man was talking into a mobile phone, after all. The bus was turning off Euston Road, down towards Tavistock Square. Travelling in the morning on public transport in London, you quickly learnt the importance of treating other people with respect and consideration. Hugh very much hoped he wasn't going to be late for the ten o'clock start of rehearsals. He told himself firmly that there was all the time in the world.

CHAPTER NINE

I.

So there we are, small-wife said.

Yes, here we are, big-wife said.

They were in their room. It was the good room that son had assigned them. This was their nice nice room with two beds and it was on the ground floor of the house. Big-wife she had the bed by the wall and small-wife she had the bed by the window. The window it had mango by it. Then it had tamarind by it, in the garden too. Then it had other trees in it, palm and date and tamarind again and another mango and birds in the trees. The wall it had picture on it. Out there beyond the trees and the birds and the garden was the street the district the city of Dacca but they did not go there, the big wife and the small wife. This was their house now and they stayed in it.

Picture said it was river and field and grass and sky. Picture was blue and green and sun. Picture was on clean white wall. So kind of son and wife to them, no need to climb stairs.

So there we are, big-wife said.

So there we are, yes here we are, small-wife said.

This was their morning talk before the light came. Outside the servants worked quietly because they did not wake those who slept. The wives they were awake and they were washed and their white clothes were ready for the day. When they spoke they spoke quietly. It was secret that they were awake and waiting for son's voice, outside in the house.

'Husband says –' small-wife said, her eyes cast down.

'Sister,' big-wife said, suggesting caution.

'Husband said he hopes everything, for everyone ...'

The house belonged to son.

'Sister!' small-wife would sometimes say in her quiet voice. 'I remember ... there was the day when I married husband, and I had to leave the house, the beautiful big white house by the rice fields a half a mile from the riverbank.'

'Beautiful house of father, more beautiful house of husband,' big-wife said.

'And I cried in my gold sari. And husband was so kind in the car. I had never been in a car before. He brought box of sweets from the wedding and when I cried I ate from the box of sweets. And we came to the house of husband and it was in Dacca, a beautiful house with a high wall, and there was big-wife, waiting there to greet me.'

'That was me, sister,' big-wife said.

'And now guns are shooting in the street again,' small-wife said.

'I remember the day you came,' big-wife said. 'Your new son had a bicycle, a bicycle because of it.' She shook her head and said nothing more.

'And now husband says ...' small-wife said. She looked at the corner of the room where the chair was. Dark corner of room, chair in the dark and the dark shadows. Husband had died long back, long long back. But some morning when they woke in the dark husband was. Looked from small-wife to big-wife, back again. Sat there. Once light came to the room then husband faded away slowly.

'Listen,' big-wife said, and she tipped her head on one side.

'It is still dark,' small-wife said. Son could not be up and busy. The day does not start in the dark!

'Listen!' big-wife said, and reached out and slapped small-wife across the face. They sat. Big-wife was silent and small-wife was silent. The noise came again. It was not near but it might get nearer. Gun was firing and another gun and another, out there in the dark last of the dark. Night was thinning and soon the dark would be a shadow cast by the mango tree by the window and soon the sound of son moving about would be heard. Day was coming. They listened.

2.

Dhanmondi, as a district of Dacca, was a quiet, pleasant place to live in 1971. The houses were single-storey, occasionally with a two-storey house for some important family. The streets were peaceful and dusty, with only a few street hawkers and security guards seated outside each gate, falling asleep against the white-painted plaster walls. Some of the guards against strict instructions, would get up to pass the time of day with their colleagues a house or two away before an impatient pip on the horn of a motor would summon them back, scurrying, to open the painted iron gate of the house for a master returning from work.

The white houses were flat-roofed. When they had been built in the 1950s, the developers had had an eye on the future, and on modernity. Modern, too, was the grid pattern of the streets, and the systematic rather than picturesque names. Other people might live in an Indo-Saracenic villa called Rosebud in the Minto Road, but Dhanmondi streets were not named after viceroys. Dhanmondi families lived in houses rationally named, number 14, street 19, Dhanmondi. The houses were of severe angularity, wide-windowed and shuttered without frames, the pillars iron joists, the roofs without ornamental tiles, the gutters without softening curves, the colours white or terracotta. The streets ran parallel to each other or turned at a rigid angle of 90 degrees, forming absolutely regular blocks of eight houses each. It was easy to go from house to house systematically – postmen or canvassers – and be sure that nobody had been overlooked or omitted. Only in the gardens was there some kind of ornament, as trees grew large and shady after fifteen years, with fruit trees, tamarind, mango, fig, as well as bilimbi and the strangling banyan. Flowers in neatly arrayed pots flooded the trees' shades with colour and filled the beds. Ornamental, too, was the lake at the edge of Dhanmondi, delightful for a long circulating walk in the evening, an agreeable argument with an old friend, a gossip, an adda to catch up and listen to the latest. It was an item of faith with the Dhanmondians that their lake, unlike all other lakes, never bred mosquitoes to annoy them.

The house in Dhanmondi had been commissioned and bought by Sharif's grandfather, who had had some ideas of modernity, but whose life had nevertheless been rather different from his son's, or from what his grandchildren's would have become. Grandfather had been the last man in the family to marry two women. He had died ten years ago, having enjoyed only three years in his house. Nowadays his two wives lived together in a room with two single beds on the ground floor, and treated each other like elderly sisters, dressing in white, rising at dawn.

Father was the master of the house. He returned from his chambers or from court, dropping his legal bands on the floor for the houseboy to pick up, went to pay his respects to his mothers, to Mother, and then to speak to the children. These days there were a lot of them, and some had children of their own. Sharif had gone to England with his wife Nazia to finish his PhD; he had returned with a baby, Aisha, who was now three years old. They had a flat of their own, but often dined at Sharif's father's house and, in recent weeks, seemed to have moved back home semi-permanently. It was only five minutes' walk away. Rafiq was seventeen, and studying at school. He would go to Dacca University to study political theory in the autumn, if Dacca University still existed in the autumn. He was a good boy. Then there were the girls: Bina and Dolly were children, and sharing a room because they liked to. The household was interestingly book-ended, as Mother drily observed, with the grandmothers sharing a girlish room at one extremity of the ménage, the girls sharing a more enthusiastically readerly one at the other edge. Sadia was not living at home. She had married over a year ago, in December of 1969, and now lived in the unfamiliar atmosphere of her husband Mahfouz's household, where prayers were said five times a day. It was what she had wanted and what she had got.

It was at the beginning of March that the housekeeping threatened to collapse in a spirit of chaos. It was impossible to be absolutely clear from one day to the next how many people would be sitting down for dinner. Some days it was six or eight; the next it might be twenty. The grandmothers were always there, and the master and the mistress; the two girls were there, too. But Sharif and Nazia were not always there to dinner; they took tiny Aisha with them, they accepted invitations on the spur of the moment. These were exciting times, and they went out with Aisha hidden underneath a large shawl, to sit at a colleague's dinner table or in their salon, to argue and sing and speechify. Sometimes they brought a colleague back to the Dhanmondi house, but only a colleague in some kind of need – Nazia was thoughtful in that way. It was often Professor Anisul Ahmed, who was an old bachelor, married to his subject. His parents Father remembered fondly. Sometimes there was the married daughter, Sadia, and sometimes she came with her new husband, Mahfouz. And then there could be many more, friends and associates of Rafiq. You did not see him from dawn to bedtime some days; other days he would burst in with five or six glowing revolutionaries, all noise and happiness, demanding dinner. Some days stools had to be brought in and the children asked to sit on the floor on cushions. One day Mother gave up and required Nazia and Sharif to wait to eat with Rafiq's noisy fellow students in an hour or so. Professor Anisul had to eat now: he had to be treated with respect. But ...

It was an evening when Sadia had come, and her husband, Mahfouz. Mahfouz had talked about the rallies, about the Movement. His eyes had flickered from face to face. He should not be asked to sit down at the table with Rafiq's friends, but peaceably, with grandmothers and with his parents-in-law, to talk about other things.

Mother smoothed things over daily with Ghafur, the cook. She usually ordered a vast chicken curry, something that could be expanded and thinned out with extra rice if three more guests appeared, and bowls of simple vegetable dishes, gourds and beans and lentils that would stay good for two or three days. Ghafur was under constant instructions to be prepared to make half a dozen omelettes.

Only Sharif and Nazia were at home for dinner, meaning with the girls there were only eight at table. For once this was certain, and Mother had taken the opportunity to send Ghafur out to buy some fish. Ghafur, wonderful resourceful Ghafur, had found some beautiful rui, who knew where from – they would feast tonight. The delicious smell was filling the house. Mother went upstairs to wash and brush her hair, to change into something a little bit elegant.

There was a rally going on today. Everyone knew of it: a summons had come from the political leaders to assemble at the racecourse. Something important was to be said. Rafiq had bolted his breakfast and shot out of the house before eight. That evening, the family had got up and were filing into the dining room at the back of the house, where it overlooked the flower-bed and the mango tree, when there was a rumpus from the front door. Rafiq had returned in time for dinner. Father and the grandmothers paused before carrying on; the girls were shooed onwards by Nazia. Mother detached herself and went to greet her younger son.

He was pulling the old shawl from his face where he had bound and wrapped it. His clothes were dusty and his shirt had a tear in it, but at least he was alone.

'I don't know what we are supposed to do,' Mother said.

'Oh, I don't want food,' Rafiq said. 'If there is food I will eat it, but if there is none – Mother, do you know what happened today? Listen.'

'Wash your face and hands and come into the dining room. You can tell us all.'

'Yes, yes. Wait – who is here tonight? Elder-brother? Is that all? I will wash and come through. Stay with me.'

He dashed into the downstairs cloakroom, shutting the door, but going on talking. Khadr, the boy serving at table, emerged and stood by the door to the dining room, his dark small head on one side waiting for a command. With a fierce gesture of her hands, Mother ushered him back to his place at the table. Rafiq's voice continued, but what it was saying was not clear through the door. His head was wrapped in a towel.

'... to hear that voice, those words,' Rafiq said, emerging. His face was pink and fresh; his hands, at least, seemed clean.

'And your shirt,' Mother said. 'At least go to change your shirt.'

'Must I?' said Rafiq, but he bounded off, and was back from his room in twenty seconds with a clean white shirt on, still talking. 'I thought the day would never –'

'Come along,' Mother said. 'Your father and everyone must be impatient at waiting. Now. Start again.'

'I was at the rally,' Rafiq said, sitting down. 'I went to the racecourse with everyone – we grew in size, the closer we got. We had to walk for an hour and a half, and we thought we would be early, we thought there would be few people there, but –'

'I heard of it,' Father said. 'What did he say?'

'Everything in its proper order,' Mother said.

'When we arrived, we thought it was the largest crowd any of us had ever seen, and so early, hours before anything was supposed to happen. We thought we would be on the very outskirts of the crowd, but then we realized, there were people arriving behind us, a sea of people going on arriving, and in half an hour it seemed to us that we were in the middle of a crowd, we were even quite near to where the speakers would stand. We had food to eat when we were hungry and water to drink and we settled down, young and old, and we talked of what we hoped for. The women and the VIPs were at the front – they had their own enclosure. But the nation! The nation that does not exist yet, it was there! It was there on the racecourse. Father, Mother, the hopes of us all – you cannot imagine.'

'Rafiq, child …' Mother said. She covered her feelings. She stood to give him fish from the plate, a movement of grateful servitude. This was not the moment to speak her fears. Around the table, everyone was quiet, listening to Rafiq.

'He came in the end,' Rafiq said. 'The Friend of Bengal. He came in his white car – it had to carve a way through the crowd. For an hour he was coming through the crowd, we were getting up and trying to see. But then he was there. I thought we would hear nothing but he spoke so clearly and everyone was so silent. It was so important to hear what he had to say.'

'Is it true?' Nazia said. 'Are we a country of our own? Did the Friend of Bengal say that we are ourselves now?'

'No,' Rafiq said. 'No, he did not. And that was a disappointment. But he is making us stand on our own two feet. I think we all know that will come. Remember – it was only two days ago that they raised the flag at the university. The flag of Bangla Desh, flying over the university! Those four men of ours who raised the flag – you know their names. I wish the Friend of Bengal had declared independence, I do, but he is who he is. There are things that must be done first. Father, Mother, I wish you could have heard the speech – I wish you could have heard how he talked of what we have come through and what must be done – I had never ever felt like this before. I heard it, I heard every word. There will be a home for us. He told us that every home must be a fortress in the months to come. Oh, I was there today.'

Rafiq's excitement had stilled the table – even the grandmothers were silent; even Bina and Dolly sat with their eyes wide, taking in their brave brother, his curly hair rumpled, his face pink, almost shouting what he had seen while shovelling food into his mouth. At the other end of the table, Sharif. He had not gone to the rally at the racecourse. He ate sedately, listening.

'And then?' Sharif said. 'The Friend of Bengal will take charge. Yes? Tell me, how much did he talk of us, and how much did he talk of himself? In this famous speech, I mean.'

'What are you asking me, brother?' Rafiq said.

'I have heard him speak before,' Sharif said. 'And I admire him as much as you do, but I wish he would not speak always of himself, how his own rights have been trodden over, how his people and his nation –'

'He is a modest man, Rafiq,' Mother said reprovingly. 'He is not a puffed-up politician.'

'Yes, yes,' Rafiq said. 'Today he was dressed in a white shirt and trousers and an ordinary waistcoat. It was almost what anyone in the crowd was wearing. He is an ordinary simple modest man – you can see that just by looking at him.'

Mother listened carefully, with feelings she could not quite suppress. Tonight – or tomorrow night or the night after that – she would go up to the roof of the house, and order the flag of Bangla Desh to be flown. Like Rafiq, she had wanted to be sure that only elder-brother was here, and not elder-sister, not elder-sister's husband Mahfouz.

3.

There was talk out there of collaboration and defiance, of standing firm or standing against. In the house there was no talk of it. 'It is all the same,' Sharif said, and turned to talk of the engineering students' projects with Professor Anisul, who was there for dinner. 'A sort of cantilevered bus shelter, sir,' he said. 'Of course the great issue is floor area, which would be absurd, but a clever project. He is thinking through the possibilities.'

'But, my dear Sharif,' Professor Anisul said, 'what may be achieved in the real world, not in persuading them to impossibilities?'

'This is not an impossibility,' Sharif said. 'Merely an impracticable suggestion. I believe he knows it is impracticable.'

'Without someone dreaming in a fanciful way,' Mother said, 'what would ever be achieved, Professor?'

She had intended to open up the conversation between Sharif and Anisul, but Professor Anisul merely said, 'My dear lady,' as if no woman could ever have any opinion about engineering projects, 'I do not encourage them in this.'

Bina and Dolly had been looking awestruck at Professor Anisul. They were seated on either side of their father, who had started by reading a story, but now they leaned forward rudely, Dolly whispering in her sister's ear and making her titter.

'In the EPUET,' Professor Anisul said, 'formerly part of Dacca University, we are constantly concerned with the creation of the possible and the practical. When I began as a student, many years ago, at the University of Dacca, in a very similar faculty to where you and I now labour ...'

Professor Anisul regretted, everyone knew, the formation of the East Pakistan University of Engineering and Technology, and the scything off of the Engineering Faculty of Dacca University where he had spent the happiest days of his life. Nazia, who had studied English literature at university, described the topic as his King Charles's Head. How had Professor Anisul come to be such a presence in the house? He had taught Sharif as an undergraduate and for his first postgraduate degree – Nazia imagined sleek, wonderful Sharif swimming out of an indistinguishable cloud of identical fish, Professor Anisul's attention first drawn by a brilliant paper, first realizing who Sharif was, then developing a regard for him, forgetting all the rest of the cloud of fish looking up with pained incomprehension. At the end Professor Anisul advised Sharif that he hoped he would ultimately take up a job teaching at the University of Dacca – 'I think you would maintain the high standards of the existing faculty,' he said morosely – but now, he advised, Sharif should go to the West to study for his PhD. He would arrange a scholarship. This was strange advice from Professor Anisul, who had never studied outside the boundaries of the city of Dacca, but Sharif took it. Professor Anisul suggested the University of Michigan, an institution that had produced an individual whom Anisul had met and got on with like a house on fire. That would have been in 1958, at a conference in Bombay, and possibly the last time such a meeting of minds had taken place. Instead, Sharif looked into the matter seriously, and decided to take a place at the University of Sheffield in England. He married Nazia and they set off in August 1965. They were not entirely without connections there – Sharif's cousin had moved to England, to Manchester, which was not far away. They would be able to see a lot of each other. At the beginning of 1969 they returned with a good job for Sharif at what was now EPUET. The very first task he set for his second-year students was a design for a cot for the baby they had brought with them. The best of them Sharif kept, or at any rate the oddest.

A thought had come to Mother, and now she kindly asked, 'Your poor sister, Professor – I know she lives with you. You must ask her to join us for dinner one day.'

'She died, dear lady,' Professor Anisul said. 'I am surprised you did not know. She died a year and a half ago, quite suddenly and painlessly. It was nearly five years after the death of her husband.'

The grandmothers, sitting almost opposite him, a pair in white, had been munching and listening brightly, their eyes flicking across the table. Now they lowered their gazes; the elder muttered to the younger, the younger to the elder in return. Professor Anisul leant forward and, with all the appearance of cheerfulness, lifted a slice of fish from the serving platter to his own plate.

'Professor,' Father said, 'we had no idea. You must have thought us very remiss for never mentioning her.'

'Professor Anisul has an excellent housekeeper,' Sharif put in, but this was a mistake: it made his mother realize that he had known all about Anisul's sister, and had never thought of mentioning it.

'Excellent and thorough,' Professor Anisul said. 'I wish she would not disappear for days on end, but when she is there, she manages all those important matters such as a clean shirt to wear, food on the table. The mysteries of these things!'

'And when she is not there?' Mother said. 'She should not disappear without a word for days on end, as you put it.'

'That is the curious thing,' Professor Anisul said. 'Eight days ago, she announced that she was going to Gazipur to pay a visit to her sister, and left. In the most extraordinary manner, that is the absolute last I have seen of her. I must confess – in two days' time I am going to run out of clean shirts.'

'You must get somebody new,' Mother said, in a rush – she could see Father concentrating on the matter at hand, and coming close to suggesting an awful solution. 'It must be possible to acquire a new housekeeper at short notice. Or your housekeeper may return tomorrow. Let us not be pessimistic.'

'These are strange days,' Father said, ruminating. 'Rafiq goes to the rally – he hears the Friend of Bengal – he is thrilled. But Rafiq is seventeen years old. There are some who do not care about the country being born, who perhaps see that a city is not a safe place to be in the days to come.'

'It is our duty to stay here, in Dacca!' Rafiq called, his attention drawn by his own name.

'Perhaps,' Father said. 'And perhaps discretion is the better part of valour. If a single woman prefers to remove herself to the safety of her sister's village until things calm down, who am I to condemn her?'

'And yet Professor Anisul has no one to look after him,' Mother said. She seemed resigned to what was about to be said, but it was the child Bina, unexpectedly, who said it.

'Papa,' she said, looking very pleased with herself. 'Could not Professor Anisul-sir come to live here, if there is a war coming? It would be safer and there would be plenty of room.'

'That would be very agreeable,' Professor Anisul said quickly.

4.

'The laces in my shoes are broken,' Sharif said later, to Nazia, when they were on their own. He saw an amused gleam of pleasure in her eye.

'Take your daughter out in her push-chair,' she said. 'She would like a nice walk in the fresh air. It's chilly, mind, out there in the March wind straight off the moors. Take the number fifty-one bus.'

'Oh, yes, the fifty-one bus,' Sharif said, in a sort of ecstasy. 'Is that the one that goes through Broomhill and past the university and down to the town hall? And is the ticket still three-pence, a threepenny bit?'

'That one,' Nazia said. When they were alone, they liked to talk about how their lives would be, if they were back in Sheffield. The four years of Sharif's life there, working in the engineering faculty, making easy friends, going about with Nazia on the top deck of buses, to the countryside and the rolling high purple moors, the great granite boulders tossed about the mountain, which was not, they learnt, a mountain but only a hill, the snow, the solid bland food, the little flat above the newsagent's, and kind Mrs White and her husband, who asked them for dinner up in Ranmoor, and the City Hall, and the Whites' daughter Eileen, who babysat for Aisha and said every time that she had been as *good as gold*, and the carol service they had been to in gloves and coats, and everyone knowing the songs, and Dr Pennyfoot crying, holding her pink angora scarf up to her sweet, fat-cheeked face to hide the tears when she said goodbye to Nazia and Sharif and especially to little Aisha, wrapped up in a padded one-piece, only her dear face emerging stolidly from the construction – Sharif and Nazia liked to talk about the four years they had spent in Sheffield. Sometimes when a really awful prospect emerged, such as the likelihood that one of them was going to have to take a rickshaw to Elephant Road and try to match a pair of shoelaces, they liked to pretend they were still there. 'I'll catch the bus,' Nazia said, 'and then I'll go to Rackham's, do you think?'

'I don't know about Rackham's,' Sharif said. 'If I were you I would stick to reliable quality and buy the shoelaces from Cole Brothers. And then you could pop into Marks & Spencer while you were out.'

'Oh,' Nazia said. 'Marks & Spencer. Marks & Spencer. Marks & Spencer.'

There was a devout and amused silence. Nazia reached out her hand and stroked the back of her husband's arm. Their game was funny, and they both enjoyed it, but it had a knack of falling into a hole of disappointment. It was what Nazia most cherished about Sharif, his spark of comedy, the way his eyes lit up when someone in the room was making himself into a spectacle, even on a minor scale. The night before he had sat and quietly observed as Dolly fashioned her plate of rice into a hill, two hills, making a lake of gravy to go with it, and all the time a serious humming of her favourite song. No one at Father's table had paid any attention, apart from Sharif – the argument between Rafiq and Father about the coming declaration of independence was too energetic. Sharif's bored little sister sculpted and hummed, and waited for all this *talking* to finish. Sharif had sparkled with silent delight at it.

'Your father is going to regret his munificent offer,' Nazia said.

'I don't see what else he could have done, once the conversation reached that point.'

'We could have offered to house him,' Nazia said. 'Here, in the flat above Dr Matin's, where we are returning soon, Sharif.'

'And yet we have not offered to house him,' Sharif said. 'I have heard him observe out loud that he did not know what he was going to do, where he was going to live, three or four times. And somehow I did not offer to house him.'

'It may come to nothing,' Nazia said.

'Oh, no,' Sharif said. 'It will not come to nothing. Professor Anisul must be packing his bags at this moment. I expect Mother is clearing out the room that used to be big-sister's.'

'No, I meant that events may come to nothing,' Nazia said. 'We may walk up to the brink, and then walk away from it. The Friend of Bengal may come to an agreement. Professor Anisul's housekeeper may return from her village near Gazipur, and Professor Anisul return to his house where she can look after him.'

'I don't think that is going to happen,' Sharif said.

They were talking in the salon of their flat, upstairs in a two-storey house in Dhanmondi. For all purposes, they had moved back to Father and Mother's house. From time to time, they visited their flat, and sat, and talked, and once in a while slept there. Downstairs lived a tall and sarcastic surgeon at the hospital, his wife and two children, who let the first floor as a flat; they had modified the building so that an outside staircase now led up to an unassuming door. Nothing about their door made it look like a residence; Dr Matin, almost certainly, was pulling a fast one by pretending it was a storage space, or where his servants lived. But the flat was perfect, with a big sitting room, solid walls, enough bedrooms for Aisha and the next child and the cook, when she was needed, and their bedroom at the back was shaded by a eucalyptus, casting a medicinal tang into the room. It was five minutes' walk to Father and Mother's house, and the five minutes' distance was, Nazia had found, quite perfect. She looked forward to the time when the five minutes' distance was reinstated as a permanent fact of their existence. Her own parents were in Chittagong, and their welfare and interest largely taken on trust.

5.

There had been no word from Sadia for some time now, since the city had been cast into uproar by their leader's speech at the racecourse that Rafiq had heard. But two weeks after Professor Anisul had moved into Father's house, she sent a postcard with one of her servants to say that she and Mahfouz were coming to visit that night. It must have been 23 March.

Sadia had never been like any of the other children – not like Sharif and certainly not like Rafiq. She never argued or spoke back; she lowered her eyes and did what she was told. Mother found it agreeable but disconcerting; she was more at home with her elder boy's losing himself at the bottom of the garden, ignoring all calls for help, or with her younger boy's passionate and enraged responses to authority, stamping his feet as soon as he could stand. She did not believe that Sadia's behaviour was innate. As a baby, she had cried and fist-pumped as much as any child Mother had ever seen. It was as if, afterwards, she had made a decision that it was right to obey authority without question. She was not quite convincing in the role, and the sweet smile she tried to assume was often pursed and pressed in what, deep down, must be rage. Religion was for everyone, and yet, when Sadia took it on with fervour and some commitment, she looked to everyone like a miscast actress in an unsuitable role, making the best of things. Gently Mother remonstrated. The important thing, after all, was for women to gain an education, and to regard the world with interest and curiosity. Sadia had been good at mathematics and physics. They had expected her to be a scientist in a laboratory, not a village mullah's wife. It was only Sadia's age, Father said when they were alone. It took some children like this.

But the fervour did not diminish, and Sadia asked Mother if, when she left school, Father and she could find her a husband. She was not interested in going to university. Mother would always remember that moment like the infliction of a wound, there in the sitting room of the house, the sun shining through the windows onto her daughter, headscarved and round-faced. When the children made impossible requests, Mother normally said, 'Let's see,' or 'I must ask Father what he thinks', but to this she only said, 'No. Impossible.' It took six months and a number of visits from some of Sadia's aunts to persuade Mother to listen to the proposal. The aunts took the view that Sadia would not shift; she would go on insisting; that at any rate if her parents took charge of finding a husband, as Sadia was requesting, they would have some measure of protection against a really offensively orthodox family. In the end Mother had to agree. She went to Father, and endured his shock, disgust and outrage in turn. In three months they had both come to accept it as inevitable. Sadia was only eighteen when a visit took place, in pomp, from a family doctor Father knew and his friend, a supplier of medical goods with his own shop. Father would have preferred the doctor, but it was the supplier of medical goods who brought his elder son with him, a boy called Mahfouz.

Tonight Mahfouz and Sadia were coming to dinner. It was unexpected. For the previous days, there had been regular outbreaks of shouting and even gunfire outside in the streets. Mother had noticed that some of the houses nearby which had been flying the new flag of Bangla Desh had, earlier this week, removed it; they looked bare, solitary, sad as a site cleaned up after a festivity. She had gone up this morning and removed theirs. It would be flown again later.

When Mahfouz and Sadia arrived, they found a household that had been warned to stay off significant topics of conversation. They talked about Professor Anisul's poor sister; they talked about Mahfouz's sister's pregnancy; they talked about the delicious fish that Mother used to cook for them. Professor Anisul embarked on a long explanation of the difficulties of bridge-building over the Padma; Mahfouz did his bit, and listened carefully to the explanation, interjecting occasional well-considered questions. If they passed the conversational baton one to another, there need be no reason ever to embark on an argument with Sadia and her husband. The children watched, bored now that voices at the dinner table were lowered and they knew everyone round it; they knew all about good behaviour, and if Bina did her showy best to inhabit it, smiling to left and right graciously as she was handed dishes, Dolly scowled and kicked and slid with her whole body underneath the table, until spoken to sharply, just because she could.

The evening came to an end: Father went out with them to hail a rickshaw, as if they were the most distinguished guests ever to have come through the door.

'An intelligent young man, your son-in-law,' Professor Anisul said to Mother. 'I don't remember having met him before. He was talking to me about the new projects to increase road capacity across the country. What use are we if we can't move material from one side of the country to another, whether this is a separate country or half of one?'

'They can't know anything about what's being planned,' Rafiq said, at the far end of the salon. 'They wouldn't have come otherwise.'

'Maybe nothing's going to start,' Sharif said.

'The planes from West Pakistan have been full for weeks,' Rafiq said. 'Full of soldiers in mufti. The East Pakistan regiments, they've all been sent off on exercises in the country. Why? Because they don't trust them to follow orders and shoot Bengalis. They're being replaced by Pakistani officers. It's going to start.'

'Mother took the flag down,' Sharif said.

'Did she? Mother, did you? Never mind,' Rafiq said. 'It needs to fly, but –'

'Well, Bina and Dolly,' Nazia said. 'It's all very well saying that we would die for a flag, but it's hard to volunteer Dolly to do the same.'

'I'm sure Dolly would die for her country,' Rafiq said. 'No, I understand, I do. Sadia and Mahfouz don't know when it's going to happen, any more than we do.'

'The Friend of Bengal …' Nazia said, and with a big, uncomfortable, theatrical gesture reached to her side and swept little Aisha up into her arms, brought her over to her lap. Aisha had been nearly sleeping, and kicked out, her fists brought sleepily to her face in protest. Nazia kissed her little head, again and again.

'I'm going out tomorrow,' Rafiq said. 'But I don't think you should. And don't let Sharif go to the university. There won't be anyone there.'

'My students!' Professor Anisul said, overhearing this. 'Education is the most important thing in life!'

Father raised his right finger at Professor Anisul. It was his preface to making a point.

6.

Since Grandfather's time, they had liked to move to the salon after dinner to continue the conversation. The children came for half an hour; then it was time for the little ones to go to bed. If there were guests, Sharif and his wife often stayed a while longer. When Sadia was a little younger, she had sometimes been encouraged to read out loud, and these days Bina and less often Dolly were sometimes asked to. Sadia had liked to read from *Sandesh* – her favourite author was Leela Majumdar – and the tradition had continued until it was their bedtime. You were not supposed to read it – the government had banned the magazine. But Mother had a friend in Calcutta who got it through to them. In the last year or two, *Sandesh* had started publishing detective stories about a genius called Feluda, and even Father enjoyed those. They were written by Leela Majumdar's nephew, or so Mother had been told by her Calcutta friend, and even Father and Professor Anisul had been known to shake their heads and laugh ruefully over the ingenuity of the solution, some overlooked detail that only Feluda had been able to explain to his nephew, Topshe. Then you wondered how anyone, even Topshe, had been able to ignore the clue. It shone out from its surroundings, like a gun sitting on a polished table in a library.

Even though there was a new Feluda story being read out tonight, Bina only had Dolly and one of the grandmothers as an attentive audience. The others had something they wanted to go on talking about. Bina half wanted to hear it, too. It was a great shame and, sooner or later, Bina knew that she would have to go back and read it to them all over again, but there it was. Only one of little-brother's friends had come tonight. With his way of talking over everyone to contradict them, the words spilling over each other in excitement, Rafiq's friend Dev reminded Bina of a naughty boy in her class at little school. Dev sprang up from time to time as he talked, running his fingers through his rough hair until it stood on end. His hands waved before he sank down again into the armchair. He seemed to want a blackboard to write on.

'Yahya is gone,' Dev said. 'Now there is nothing left but to wait. The Friend of Bengal has declared independence of Bangla Desh –'

'The Friend of Bengal has not declared independence of Bangla Desh,' Sharif said, with impatience. 'He was expected to declare it three weeks ago at the racecourse. But he did not. And he has not.'

'The Friend of Bengal has declared independence tonight,' Dev said, holding up the palm of his hand in protest. Rafiq looked at him, his eyes shining. 'I am sure of it. And now the Pakistani has gone and thousands of Pakistanis are here to take his place.'

'Where is the Friend of Bengal?' Father asked.

'I do not know,' Dev said. 'But one thing is certain …'

Over in the corner, a flurry was taking place between the grandmothers. Nazia was keeping an eye on it; they liked to make sure that the little outbreaks of distress or need between Grandfather's widows were quickly solved with the cup of tea that one wanted, the finding of the walking stick that the other needed to get up, the helping hand to walk to the bathroom. They were so small, the grandmothers' needs, but they started with gestures of real distress. One was rubbing her hands, her face a study in anxious worry, the other listening to her tiny voice with no less worry. Bina was continuing to read, apparently not having noticed that she had lost her audience. Nazia went over.

'Grandmother,' she said, 'is there something that I can fetch for you?'

'There are men in the road,' a grandmother said. She was the one whose anxiety was being tended. 'There are strange men in the road.'

The windows of the salon faced onto the back garden, and beyond that only the back garden of the house in the parallel street. It was as quiet as a garden could be. But asked the direct question, the grandmother grew distant, vague, a small smile. 'Is she quite sure?' she asked the other grandmother.

'Husband told me,' the first grandmother said. 'Husband saw them. The men in the road.'

Nazia left it and returned to her armchair. Dev was giving his own account of what Sheikh Mujib had said at the racecourse, and what the now famous Four Students had demanded of him – these were the ones who had raised the flag at Dacca University. When he had finished his by now polished account, Nazia said, quite casually, 'Has anyone been outside the house in the last hour or two? Ghafur or Khadr or anyone?'

Her mother-in-law stared at her, reproving and baffled, but Dev somehow understood that she had come by a piece of information. He got up and left the room, walking towards the front door of the house. He made a gesture of stilling to Rafiq – *sit* or *at ease* or *remain at your position, soldier* – that would have made anyone who saw it understand that, in the last resort, there existed a relationship of command and obeisance between the two. Dev was Rafiq's officer. All student naughtiness was gone. Dev turned off the electric light in the hall as he went. The telephone began to ring and, without hesitating, in the darkness, he picked it up. 'Hello,' he said, and then 'Yes, it's me.' He stayed silent, his head bent, his half-illuminated hand reaching for the pen and pad of paper always kept by the telephone in the hallway. He put down the telephone without saying goodbye to whoever it was. Father and Mother and Sharif and Nazia and Professor Anisul had been drawn to the door of the salon.

'That was Iqbal,' Dev said. 'He is working at the InterContinental – the foreign correspondents are all there.

Carrying bags, the last four weeks. There have been Pakistani troops there. They have torn down all the flags, the flags of Bangla Desh. Are there men in the streets now? Don't turn on this light.'

He swiftly went through the front door in the darkness of the hall, almost closing it behind him. Khadr had been drawn out too; he stood with Ghafur at the door of the kitchen, waiting. They stood in the near-darkness silently for what seemed like minutes. Behind the family, in the salon, a quiet girl's voice could be heard going on: "'… but the trouble with you, Topshe," said Feluda, "is that you will always jump to conclusions. If, like me, you examine all the possibilities, and the situation from every conceivable angle, you will soon discover that the gold snuffbox was far from an innocent object. It was, in fact, placed there by –"'

'Quiet, Bina,' Father muttered, turning back. Out there in the dark between the house and the front wall, Dev was moving stealthily. Nazia suddenly remembered that there was a watering can out there, left on the tiles. She had noticed it that afternoon, when she had taken Aisha out in her arms to admire the jasmine, just now in flower, to greet the chickens. It was a heavy metal watering can, not so heavy that it could not be kicked over by a passing foot to crash on the tiles. Out there it was nearly total darkness; the front of the house was heavily shaded by the strangling banyan tree, its many downward growths forming a screen against what little light came from the road. Dev was walking out into the garden, and could so easily kick over the can. But, she consoled herself, he must have passed it by now. They waited in silence.

The front door opened, quickly, quickly, and the figure closed it behind him, turning the lock so as not to make any clicking noise. He stood in the dark. It was only when he spoke, so quietly, that she could rid herself of the thought that this was a Pakistani soldier, just the size of Dev, who had taken his place and was standing there to carry out his orders. But he spoke and it was Dev. He had been on the longest journey, to the front wall of the house and back again.

'I saw,' he said, his voice lowered. 'There are men in the street. They were running, a platoon with guns, padding as quietly as they could. It is time for me to go.'

'No,' Mother said. 'Tonight, you must stay here.'

Dev did not bother to respond to this.

'I must come with you,' Rafiq said.

'No,' Dev said. 'If you have a working telephone line you are going to be needed here. Keep them all safe and bolt the doors. When I come back I will sleep on the terrace. Look for me in the morning.'

He was through the door, pulling his scarf up over his head and shutting the door behind him. In only a second Nazia heard the noise that she had foreseen but done nothing about, the watering can being kicked over with a crash. She could have warned him. It could not have been more than ten seconds after the sound of the can falling on the terrace that a great industrial burst of sound broke out, it seemed only yards away.

It was only Father who understood how little time there might be. He turned to Nazia. 'Take the girls down to the cellar, and Mother too. Go. Behind the packing cases, sit in the dark. Make no sound, whatever you hear. Go. You,' he spoke to Khadr and Ghafur, clutching themselves as they understood that they had heard the death of the honoured guest, out there in the road, 'you have heard nothing and you understand nothing and these are the people who are still in the house.'

But there was no more. Half the household sat in the salon, in darkness, and half in the cellar for eight hours. At some point somebody tried to turn on a light, but the electricity had failed, or been cut off. They had to assume that the telephones had been severed, too. Towards the end of the night Dolly started crying, for water, but silently, and Nazia comforted her. She had finished crying at the thought of her daughter, Aisha, left sleeping in her room. She hoped husband had had the sense to take her with him. When they went up the stairs, they did not know what they would find. In fact the others had gone to bed, reasoning that they might as well be roused from there to be killed as from the salon. Nazia recognized the characteristic style of assessment of Professor Anisul in this decision. Rafiq, in his nightwear, went out and onto the roof. He came back in five minutes. The city was on fire. Heavy black smoke hung in the air – last night, he explained, they had seen tracer bullets in the sky, black explosions of flak, and the heavy thumps of tank fire, not at all far off. That immense noise that had burst out at one point in the night – it must have come from the HQ of the East Pakistan Rifles in Road Number Two. The women looked at him: down there, they had heard only a general rumble, a continuous one. Rafiq thought that one blaze might be coming from the bazaar, but it was huge, huge. Outside on the road, in the middle, lay a body lying face down. It had been left there by whoever shot it, as some kind of warning. 'It could have been worse,' Rafiq finished. 'They just saw a man running in the road, and shot him. They did not investigate where he had come from. We have been lucky.'

'Rafiq, how can you? That was –'

'We have been lucky,' Rafiq said obstinately, and in his deliberate style emerged the clarity of feeling of the soldier. He was only seventeen. In a moment he turned on his heels and went into the kitchen to find something to eat, some tea to drink. 'Nobody is to leave this house until I say so. The telephone is still cut off, I presume.'

7.

Dolly had been deputed to look after Aisha, and they walked about the house, hand in hand. It was dull and tiresome not to be able to walk outside, not even in the garden, but there was plenty to look at inside. She showed Aisha the photograph of Father, just qualified from university, and Mother and her three sisters in what looked like white, but was really pink and palest blue, so young and pretty. The bench in a park they sat on was

a seat in a photographer's studio. She showed her the ivory
elephant, which made Bina shudder, an elephant carved out of
its own teeth or tusks. She showed her the special dish for
sweets, with the ivy and the irises curving round in silver, and
the picture of the devil with burning eyes in Daddy's copy of
Milton. Dolly was showing Aisha all of this when with a great
flop Aisha flung her fists down, throwing the book on the floor,
and began to grizzle. One of the grandmothers was in the room.
She looked up in surprise.

'Come here, girls,' she said. 'What's wrong?'

It was rare that either of the grandmothers spoke to any of
the children, and the children paid them little attention. They
yawned and slept and ate and muttered to each other and slept
again. Aisha clung to Dolly, and with some difficulty Dolly led
her over to the grandmother. She smelt clean but aniseed-ish,
her hands soft and pale as she took theirs.

'When I was a girl ...' she said. 'Do you want to hear a story?
I can tell you a story, nice nice story.'

They agreed.

'Father was an advocate,' she began. 'And Father had an
important case. Went all the way to London and the Privy
Council and the House of Lords. It happened in Jessore, village
near Jessore. A man in the village was famous. He could eat!
Everyone knew the glutton in this village. If there was wedding
and the glutton was invited, then they had to make more more
food. If there were a hundred guests, then food for a hundred
and thirty. He ate it all!

'Then one day the zamindar heard of this man. He was so
famous! He said, "I am going to challenge the glutton to a
contest. I am going to supply him with more food than even he
can eat." Because zamindar very rich, you understand.

'So the day is named and the glutton comes forth in a new
white kurta. And a whole sheep is roasted and a whole ox and a
cauldron of rice and many many other things. The man he starts
to eat, it is afternoon, perhaps four o'clock, eating so steady
careful. The people in the next village, they hear what is

happening, and they walk and run to see the glutton. One family is about to ride on the donkey but then the father says, "No, no, if we take donkey, perhaps glutton will eat donkey when he has finished with the ox and the sheep." The man finishes the sheep, licks bones clean! Whole sheep! And he starts to eat the ox, calm, patient, steady.

'Now the zamindar starts to worry. Because after the sheep and the ox there is not much that is prepared for the glutton to eat. Zamindar sends out order that another sheep should be killed and roasted. But the village is not so happy about this. Now the glutton has finished the sheep, half finished the ox, has been eating steadily for twelve hours. It is now late at night, but still hundreds of people gathered, watching the glutton eating eating eating, watching rich zamindar looking worried. The elders of the village go off into a house next door, and start to discuss. "This is enough!" some of them say. "The zamindar has proved his point, the glutton has shown his capacity. Enough." But others say that the village is famous now, and the glutton is famous now, and he should go on while he still can. One of them just starts to say that they should talk to zamindar, get him to see reason, when there is big noise from outside and screaming. They rush out.

'The glutton had eaten and eaten and now his body can do no more, and the noise they all heard, it was his stomach exploding. There is the remains of the glutton painted all over the inside of the room where he was eating, the remains of cow and sheep and two-three cauldrons of rice as well, and the glutton is dead. Glutton splashed all across walls, splash, splash, splash, splash, splash. The policeman is there, policeman from next village, and he stands up solemn very solemn. He says to zamindar that he is under arrest for murder of glutton because you cannot allow man to be killed like that.

'Court case follows, very long and many people. Hundreds of people saw the glutton eat eat eat. People cooked for him, all of them witness in court. Grandfather a junior in case. Did zamindar murder him? Was food the weapon? Was it wrong to give the man food when should be obvious will kill him? Or was it man's responsibility, glutton's responsibility for self? Well, finally court decides, and zamindar guilty of manslaughter. Like handing a drunk man a full bottle whisky, judge says. Knows he would drink it, knows that it kill him. There is appeal and further appeal, and then to Privy Council and House of Lords. Zamindar found guilty manslaughter. Famous, famous case and Grandfather junior counsel. In the end zamindar say as he go to prison, docsn't care, was fine fine entertainment.'

The girls had their mouths open; they had been listening. Without meaning to, Bina had cast her eyes around the room when the glutton had exploded and his stomach painted across the walls. She saw steaks, globules of rice, meat and blood and a neat fried aubergine painted across these walls, hurled by the explosion. That had been how it was. Dolly and Aisha stood, their eyes enormous, waiting for the grandmother to go on. But the story was finished. Dolly dropped her niece's hand, and went on her own to think on the sofa, the blue one covered with yellow cushions where Mother liked to sit. Mother was in the kitchen, it sounded like. She was trying to work out how much food there was, and Ghafur was disagreeing with her. You could hear their voices rising, their voices falling, trying like everyone else not to make much noise in Father's house. Bina hoped it would not go on for much longer like this.

CHAPTER TEN

I.

The war was a month old when a new name started to be heard. Almost certainly, in those days, the best thing to do was to behave as if everything mentioned was familiar to you. A new name was mentioned, and everyone nodded, or made no sign, as if they understood completely what was being referred to. So it was impossible afterwards to know who it had been who had first said anything about the Friendly Ones.

The Friendly Ones: its membership was unknown to anyone. It was an organization of citizens who wanted peace with Pakistan. The Friendly Ones would work towards ending the outbreaks of violence and insurrection, and help to return things to how they had been before 25 March. There was one of the Friendly Ones directing this endeavour in every district of the city, and in every village of the nation. How they had come together, nobody knew. But their pamphlets were delivered and passed from hand to hand.

Perhaps it was Khadr, the boy who waited at table, who first mentioned the Friendly Ones. Mother despaired of his intelligence: he could learn nothing and could understand nothing. Almost always, when he set out the chutneys and pickles and bowls of salt and jugs of water in front of each place, he was found to have mixed it all up, and Sharif's preferred chutney sat alongside the slices of lemon that Mother liked to have to hand. Every dinner at table began with a sighing passing of dishes to left and right. One day Khadr was sweeping the floor and looked up to see Sharif. 'It is so good that the war will soon be over!' Khadr said.

'Why? What do you mean?' Sharif said.

'Peace is coming,' Khadr said. 'The Friendly Ones are making sure of that.'

'What?' Sharif said.

'Please, sir,' Khadr said. 'The citizens of the country, they are tired of the fighting and the traitors in our midst, and they have formed together to make a new beginning. They are calling themselves the Friendly Ones. Soon there will be peace again and we will be good friends with our brothers in the rest of the country.'

'Where did you hear this?' Sharif said.

Khadr stopped brushing. He looked up at the ceiling; he hooked his thin forefinger and plunged it deep into his ear. He had become self-conscious because Father had heard him talking and had followed Sharif out into the hallway to listen.

'I think I heard it,' Khadr said in the end.

'Yes, but where?' Father asked.

'Oh,' he said, with relief. 'Oh, Ghafur told me. He had it written down and he read it out to me. Ghafur is a scholar. It was this morning. I do not think Ghafur knew of the Friendly Ones before today. I had known about them for weeks. I said to Ghafur, "How is it that you do not know the Friendly Ones? Everyone knows of them and their good works."'

There was no contradiction in Khadr's claim that he had only heard of the Friendly Ones from the cook that morning, and that he had been able to tell the cook that he had known of them for many weeks. Perhaps even in his own mind he could believe the two things, one after another. Father made no objection, and sent Khadr off to find the piece of paper. It was a pamphlet bearing a photograph of a smiling peasant. It was much-handled, stained, its ink smeared with thumb-prints and grease from the kitchen, but Father read it. There were citizens in this country, almost the whole, who believed that the people around them loved their bonds with the people of West Pakistan. They were not going to be held to ransom by a small group of thugs and badmashes. They were going to form together in a band of patriots, and would organize the people of their neighbourhood to stand firm in a time of anarchy and subversion. The band of patriots had named themselves the Friendly Ones.

Father tore the paper across into two, four, then eight pieces. Khadr shrank back. He had not understood that he had got something so badly wrong. He loved peace! He wanted everyone to be happy! But then Father explained that there were people who hated their country, who wanted it to be forgotten and wiped out, and ruled by madmen from far away. He asked Khadr if he liked the song '*Je rate mor duarguli*'. Khadr stared. The master had never before asked him if he liked a song. But the master asked again and this time Khadr replied, stammering, that he did. The master explained. The Friendly Ones were men who wanted to make sure that no one ever sang '*Je rate mor duarguli*' ever again. The only thing the Friendly Ones wanted to hear in the streets was the Holy Koran, being chanted for ever. The Friendly Ones –

After that even Khadr understood that the Friendly Ones would kill you, and turn away with a regretful smile.

In those days, news travelled from house to house in guarded ways. The telephone had not worked since the twenty-sixth. It had come to be known that the house could be left for a number of hours, but that everyone must return by a given time. Only Rafiq had gone out, returning to say that the body outside had been moved, taken away. It was there when he had left. It had been moved when he returned. He had not gone near it. He had seen many bodies during his excursion. Ghafur and Khadr had gone out, each in a different direction; they had spent two hours buying what food they could, according to Mother's instructions.

The streets were declared out of bounds during certain hours. The children and the women stayed inside. And yet they heard of events. Rafiq went out from time to time – they did not ask where. He returned with some news from his friends. The telephone was cut off but the radio still worked. Events came to them in fragments, often contradicting the last piece of information. For days and days, they heard different reports of the Friend of Bengal – some said he had been shot, others that he was in prison – and of other people. The deaths of writers were announced on the radio, then the fact that they were still alive. Ghafur went out into the markets and met someone he knew from another household and heard that the Pakistanis had killed thousands at the university – had herded them together, shot them. Professor Anisul was mute, for once. Ghafur did not know who had been killed. He might have been told, but the names meant nothing to him. Rafiq returned one day with certain confirmation of the Mukti Bahini's success. That was what he was waiting for, the call for him to leave and join the fighters. From the radio, from an illicit radio station, they learnt that there was now a Government of Bangla Desh – formed in exile, stating policy on behalf of the new independent state. The Friend of Bengal was in prison: he had declared independence after the killings had started. One day they would know everything, but these days news filtered through to them incompletely, with rumours of the Friendly Ones.

The Friendly Ones! Were they running everything? Who was in it? How many members did it have? Did it meet daily, the twenty neighbourhoods of Dacca coming together to talk about the subversives and the traitors on their streets? Did it even exist? The name had floated into the house by means of an ignorant servant, and now they talked about it by the hour. What would they have done, if they were the Pakistanis? They would – Father went on, thoughtfully – they would give themselves a kindly name. The Friendly Ones! The beasts that would watch the house opposite; that would take note of who came and who went; the ones who would pick up their telephone and inform the appropriate person, and then, an hour or two later, watch their neighbour be bundled into the back of a car from behind their windows. Their telephone wires would not be cut.

But who was among the Friendly Ones? Nazia asked Sharif this, when they were alone together in their room. Aisha was sleeping at the foot of their bed. Nazia had managed to go to Gulshan that day. It was where the foreigners lived, and for that reason it had been left alone until now. On her way, she had seen that many of the businesses she had used all her life had chosen to change their signboards. They had been mostly in English until this week; now they were in Urdu. Had an order been issued? Or were they just anticipating matters? Where were the Friendly Ones? And what were their faces?

'I don't believe that we want to know,' Sharif said. 'If there is an organization called the Friendly Ones. And if anyone in Dacca belongs to it – then I know two people who will carry out its bidding.'

'Oh?'

Sharif's eyes were big; he held his wife's face there, on the pillow, like a trainer trying to calm an animal by gazing into its firm-held face. 'Mahfouz could have written that rubbish about the Friendly Ones himself.'

'I hope Sadia keeps her promise,' Nazia said.

There was a flash of evil across her face, startling to experience at close distance, horizontally, on the same pillow. He shifted; his unshaven chin scratched in a nice way against the clean cotton pillowcase. He did not want to ask.

'She said to me that if the country gains independence – if Mujib makes good – if we find ourselves separated from Pakistan and with our own affairs, she said she promised to leave.'

'Moving to Lahore,' Sharif said, 'with the rest of Mahfouz's family, or just him?'

'I don't know,' Nazia said. 'I had the impression that she was talking about giving up on this part of the world altogether.'

'I don't think we should have talked quite so much about Sheffield,' Sharif said. 'That will have put ideas in her head.'

'Doesn't he have an uncle in Britain?' Nazia said. 'I could have sworn *my uncle Muqtadir* came into it somewhere. Where was he? London? He has his own travel agency there, I think. Was it Muqtadir? Or something else?'

'Those people!' Sharif said. 'Always making money with their own little shops and their own little corners and living as they do! How could she?'

'It's what she wanted,' Nazia said primly. 'Now I want to sleep.'

'I want to read for five minutes. I am so bored with all of this, all this stuff that has nothing to do with engineering. I am so bored with talking to Professor Anisul about it, even. I don't want to see them again. Perhaps just to wave them off on the steps of a plane, going far, far away. Let me read. I have a novel by Shahidullah Kaiser. I like him so much.'

2.

Professor Anisul appreciated what was being done for him. He had settled into a rhythm of behaviour in the house. He had not been able to bring everything he might have wanted from his own house. He had not realized before now what comfort he drew from the largest book in his collection, an American atlas of the world. He missed it, and in particular the cosy hour before bed tracing a route across the Soviet Union, or from one interestingly named village in Yorkshire to another. There were other books he had brought, and of course there was his hosts' library, but he had to admit it to himself – the three weeks during which it was thought unsafe to go to his office had been a long and tedious period. At least he had taught young Sharif the complicated version of gin-rummy that he and big-sister had evolved over the course of years. Poor big-sister! She was spared this, at any rate. He had brought his toilet bag, a cycle of clothes lasting ten days, three pairs of shoes and a photograph of sister in a leather wallet, to be placed in a drawer, to be opened up and greeted whenever he felt he wanted to, and nobody was observing him. He had behaved badly towards sister. He had made her marry that man, so much older than her. The man had given her no children – he had only tied her down. And then he had died and her brother had tied her down in his turn. She should have had a life, not just looked after their laundry. She could have become a doctor.

Professor Anisul handed his dirty laundry over every Monday to the housekeeper. He thought that the washing here was done to a higher standard than by his housekeeper. They were so kind to him. Young Sharif's mother had noticed, for instance, that he left the bowl of karela untouched when it was served. He had never liked it. But he noticed that the next time it was served at table, there was an extra vegetable dish. Sharif's wife, who was seated next to him, made what seemed to be a point of serving him with the extra vegetable dish, and asking how he liked it. He liked it very well: it was an aubergine dish, rich and slippery in the mouth.

It was really only the boredom. He got up at eight, washed, shaved and dressed; made his bed. If the night had been noisy, it might be a little later, but he had discovered that he seemed to be able to sleep through what roused the rest of the household. He took his breakfast; then there was the rest of the day to fill. He liked to go round the house talking to his hosts, and often they had time to talk to him. Sharif was good to talk to about engineering and would play the occasional game of sister's gin-rummy. His brother Rafiq was an impatient fellow! He wanted to be off. He was waiting for the summons to come, to leave the house to go off to fight, like a student who wanted to start building bridges on his very first day in the school of engineering. Sharif's wife was kind to him, but her enquiries came to an end, and Sharif's wife stood up and went about her business, satisfied that her obligations were now met. The other women in the house he was not sure about. Sometimes when he was at work at the table, he looked up to see Sharif's mother assessing him. It was as if he might be concealing a secret of some sort. After his colleague and friend Sharif, he thought that the member of the family he liked the best was Sharif's sister's husband. His name had been Mahfouz. He had had a ready,

open smile and his genuine interest in what an engineer did. It
was a shame that he had not been able to visit again, since the
events of 25 March.

He had found an occupation that filled his mornings, at any
rate. He had brought some reference books – Marks's standard
handbook and a big book about material science – and a notebook for sketches and making calculations. In Professor Anisul's
view, there was no really thorough, up-to-date book about
material science. Someone with a lot of time left before them,
someone at the beginning of their career, ought to set about
writing one. He had been able to borrow a slide rule and some
drafting paper of a good size from Sharif. In the mornings of
this strange time, with teaching apparently suspended and with
nothing to do, he was going to occupy himself with a useful
speculative task. He was going to build a bridge.

He said nothing to Sharif about it. It appeared to him that
that young man, excellent as he was in many ways, had returned
from his stint abroad with an idea of his profession that could
be reliable, or could veer off into completely impracticable
fantasy. It was important to have new ideas about the subject,
and to come to the fundamental questions with a mind that was
constantly being refreshed. He would indulge that impracticable fantasy for a few days.

At first he drew an ordinary suspension bridge. That was
what he did every day. Then he began to ask questions that, in
other situations, from other people, he might dismiss as whim-
sical or foolish. Could the pillars of such a bridge be half a mile
high? Could they be made of solid gold? The tensions, on paper,
grew immense; the materials to support such a project extra-ter-
restrial. Then another question occurred to him. Buildings were
made of glass, these days; he knew that whole sides of skyscrap-
ers were glass. Could a bridge be made of glass? What would the
issues be, and could such a bridge ever be constructed to look
invisible, or at any rate transparent, without a steel skeleton?

He worked away at it, chuckling. Young Sharif saw him at
work, and clearly longed to ask him what the project was; but

he said nothing; he continued to calculate, and to make rough sketches of what such a bridge might look like. There was a paradox, or so it seemed to Professor Anisul. The more transparent a bridge was, the more massive did its materials have to be. But how to manufacture a glass block of adequate scale? Could it be made with layers of glass? These things exercised Professor Anisul. In the end, he thought he would take his project of a glass bridge over the Padma by surprise. He designed and built a glass bridge of a size that would be natural for the material. It turned out to be three feet long and two feet high. After that special measures started to be necessary. It was so interesting! Sometimes he looked up with surprise as the servants started setting the table for luncheon. A whole morning had passed.

'Good morning, sir,' the younger son said. He was standing by the side of the table. A friend or something of that sort behind him was standing in the dimness of the hallway. There were two green canvas bags by his feet. Perhaps he was waiting for Professor Anisul's indication that it would be acceptable to introduce him; but Professor Anisul made a general welcoming gesture and, if anything, the friend drew back slightly into the gloom.

'Good morning,' Professor Anisul said. 'You discover me building castles in the air. Or bridges, rather – I am entertaining myself by discovering whether it is possible –'

'Sir,' the young man said. His name was Rafiq, Professor Anisul said to himself – an impetuous, fiery young man He was used to this sort of person. Not everyone would have been so patient at being interrupted like this. 'Sir, where are my parents? I must say something, a word –'

There was Rafiq's mother, emerging from what Professor Anisul knew was the kitchen of the house. It took a lot of organizing, a household like this one. The mother laid her hand on Rafiq's forearm. It was like a gesture of silencing. She glanced at the friend of the boy, but did not greet him; he lowered his head, and that could mean anything – greeting, submission, a formal pretence that she had not been seen and could not be acknowledged. Professor Anisul found the ways that people behaved so strange and inexplicable.

'I have to go,' Rafiq said to his mother. 'It's time.'

'It's time,' his mother said. Professor Anisul did not move. His pencil hovered above the sheet of drawing paper. There was a bridge of glass beneath the point of his pencil; a bridge that could never be built and perhaps would not bear the strains.

Rafiq turned to the friend, there in the gloom. His mother walked to the window and there covered her face with her two hands. The two boys were hoisting their canvas bags onto their shoulders. They opened the door. For some reason he had taken the unknown man to be older than the young Rafiq. But light fell on his face from outside. He could not be more than nineteen or twenty. Rafiq did not turn back. After a second the door was closed behind them.

'Dear lady,' Professor Anisul said.

She gave a heavy gasp, a throttling noise, and walked with swift intent out of the dining room, shutting the door behind her. In five minutes the door was reopened. It was the housekeeper, who made a deep acknowledgement of Professor Anisul. The mistress would appreciate it if Professor Anisul would not inform the master when he returned home that Rafiq had been taken off by the freedom fighters to join the armed struggle. 'You understand,' he said. 'The Friendly Ones may be everywhere. The mistress said she will tell those who need to know, and the others – they do not need to know.'

3.

At first Nazia did not know what she had been woken by. It was some time in the afternoon. She was extended, fully dressed, on their bed. She had got into the habit. There was so little to do in someone else's house, and Mother took charge of everything. If it was possible to go out to the market, she would offer to do that with Ghafur, but it had not been necessary today or yesterday. Now something had woken her up. She swung her legs to the floor where the chappals sat neatly, and gave her hair a cursory brush in the mirror of the old dressing-table.

Professor Anisul was sitting at the table with a calculator and a broad sheet of paper unrolled and spread out, its corners held down by small stones. At the other end of the salon Mother was talking to Sharif's elder-sister. That was what had woken her – the sound of Sadia actually laughing. She didn't think that Sadia had been to the house since the night of 25 March. Sadia and Mother were sitting looking at a photograph album – the one in which Mother kept all photographs of the family, of her father standing stiffly, of Grandfather in his robes and court bands. She was turning the pages for Sadia with absorption.

Sadia looked up, her scarf-wrapped face full of joy. 'Sister!' she said. 'I am so happy to see you.'

'We were so worried about you,' Nazia said. 'We had the note that Mahfouz sent round, two weeks ago, and that was a relief, but –'

'We heard that everything was well,' Sadia said, 'I think from Khadr or Ghafur to someone next door and so on until Mohammed in our kitchen heard you were safe.'

'A great relief,' Mother said formally. But she had just now been turning the pages and laughing with Sadia. It must have been the sight of Nazia that made her think of what she was doing.

'My husband had to come to Dhanmondi,' Sadia said. 'Things seem to be calming down a little – it was terrible in the Elephant Road, the hooligans running riot. My father-in-law locked the gates and we stayed inside and prayed.'

'And that seems to have worked,' Nazia said. She could not help herself.

'My father-in-law says that he has seen this before, and things must go on as normal,' Sadia said. 'So husband today was travelling to Dhanmondi, and he is so kind! He would drop me at

Father's house for an hour, and I should stay and drink tea with Mother. Sister, did you ever see this photograph? Of Grandfather? I think this must be of him at Oxford, so many many years ago, before independence, before anything – look.'

Nazia knew the photograph she meant, as indeed Sadia must do, but she came and sat by her on the sofa. In it, Father was standing with a pole at the end of a flat-bottomed boat. The sun dappled through a tree hanging over the river – dappled black and white and grey. She thought it must be a willow. Grandfather and his friends were wearing shirt sleeves, rolled up to above the elbow, and were smiling broadly. They looked so young. Grandfather had said once that he had met only three or four Englishmen as friends in all his time in Oxford; he had remained in the company of other Indians for those years. (Of course they were Indians then and thought of themselves as that.) Grandmother now was explaining to Sadia that the Sikh in the photograph was another lawyer, and he married an Englishwoman and stayed in England, in Manchester where her family came from. Hardeep – he called himself Harry afterwards, or so Grandmother believed. 'An unusual thing to happen, fifty years ago,' Mother said. 'But there are plenty of brown Englishmen now.'

'My husband's Muqtadir-uncle!' Sadia said, clapping her hands. 'He went to England twenty years ago, he lives in London, he has a restaurant and fifteen people working for him! Sister, do you not have any photographs of your time in Sheffield?'

Of course Nazia did. The album was kept with Mother's other albums in the downstairs study, she wasn't quite sure why, and Mother got up to fetch it. Sadia and Nazia were left alone.

'Oh, sister,' Sadia said, 'it is so good to see you. I missed you so much.'

'We all missed you,' Nazia said, melting. It was true: she had always liked Sadia, despite the decision she had taken in life. 'But your husband's family – they are all very kind to you, aren't they?'

'Oh, yes,' Sadia said. 'They are lovely. But that old man – is he living here? He would drive me crazy, the way he talks.'

'I find something very urgent that needs to be done,' Nazia said, 'if he starts explaining things to us. He needed shelter – he was not looking after himself very well.'

'And Aisha? She was so pretty when I saw her last. In her room? And little-sisters? Sleeping too? I insist that Bina, at least, be woken up to say hello to her sister. And Sharif, I am so sorry to miss Sharif. He must stay safe. I really miss everyone. I wish I had been able to tell you that I was coming. And Rafiq? Where is Rafiq? I miss him so much.'

There was nothing in Sadia's demeanour or voice to indicate that she had now reached the commanded purpose of her visit, but Nazia understood it all the same. She would not tell Sadia what she had come to find out, that Rafiq had left the house to join the fighters. She believed that he was probably a few hundred miles away by now, undergoing training somewhere near the Indian border, or over it. Everyone knew that. Sadia had come to confirm this news.

She was saved from answering, however, by Mother returning with the photograph album covered in a brown woven-cloth binding – it was different from the other photograph albums, and that was because she and Sharif had bought it in Sheffield. They had bought it at W. H. Smith's – what an ordinary shop that had seemed after a while in Sheffield! Of course there were shops in Dacca they loved and had been going to all their lives. But W. H. Smith's would be so perfect for Aisha now, with its perfect little presents, just interesting enough for tiny hands when she had been good – a rubber in the shape of a rabbit's head, a bright orange pencil sharpener, a lovely little picture book with an interesting story about Ant and Bee discovering a rainbow that was really a bicycle tyre. Nazia felt she remembered all of it, and everything always in stock. Mother sat down with a cry of pleasure, and together they began to look at the book. The photographs were not in sequence; the very first one was the most important thing that happened while they were in

Sheffield, a pretty little girl in a white fur hood, tied up with reins on her back, her flushed face so pretty in the padded jacket against the white of the snow. It was only on the next page that there was a picture of Sharif in his doctoral robes with Nazia in a beautiful sari, gold-edged and blue. The colours throughout had faded, become a little yellow and sepia; the park they stood in, the grass was as dry and yellow and dead as a desert, the same colour as their happy yellow faces.

They spent a nice hour, and suddenly there was Mahfouz, smiling, to fetch his wife away. Professor Anisul had paid no attention to Sadia and Nazia and Mother talking over the photograph album. But when Mahfouz was shown into the room, Professor Anisul rose, delighted, with the three of them.

'A pleasure to see you,' Professor Anisul said.

'Thank you, sir,' Mahfouz said. 'I'm here to collect my wife. Is everything well with you?'

'Oh, very well,' Professor Anisul said. 'Everyone is being most kind. After that first night – it was so worrying. But now we all have our lives, not the life we want. We hardly know what dangers lie outside.'

'The dangers are lessening,' Mahfouz said.

Nazia looked at his familiar mercantile face, as if for the first time. His fresh, open complexion; his wide eyes; his wavy hair brushed back, thick and luxuriant; his open hands and his (for the moment) half-puzzled smile. She made herself think one thing: that is what a murderer looks like.

'It is so hard,' Professor Anisul said forgivingly, 'to keep track of all these threatened dangers. Young Rafiq used to explain them to us, but now he has heard the call of duty, left us –'

'Is Rafiq not at home?' Mahfouz said quickly.

'Why, now,' Professor Anisul said, 'he hasn't been –'

'And your father?' Mother said firmly to Mahfouz. 'He is well, I hope? I hope his business isn't suffering with the protests and hartals? Not too much? I do hope …'

She was ushering Mahfouz and Sadia out. But Professor Anisul had managed to tell them that Rafiq had left home to fight. Two of the Friendly Ones, Nazia believed of Mahfouz and Sadia. She could feel the lazy hot gaze of their brother-in-law turning ineluctably in Sharif's direction, too.

4.

And then all at once it was four o'clock in the morning and the whole house, or almost the whole house, was clustered in the hallway in darkness, the door just shutting behind Rafiq and them all embracing him and calling out as silently as they could manage. Mother was even crying, and she was saying she knew he would be back. He smelt terrible, his clothes stiff with old sweat and dirt, his hair thick and encrusted, a great beard spreading out like wildfire, but everyone embraced him – Father and Mother and Sharif, and now Nazia and even Bina and Dolly, giving muted little squeaks. Dolly was saying that Bina thought he had gone for ever when he was gone for two weeks, but she, she knew he would come back, and where had he been? Brother, what is that, those marks, those blisters on your face, your hands?

Mother stopped him replying, and gave Dolly a light slap. No one must know where Rafiq had been or what he had done. Did she want to have to keep a secret when the Pakistanis came?

'I've dreamt so much about a hammering on the door in the middle of the night,' Sharif said. 'And then there it was. I was terrified. But I woke up, and it wasn't a hammering, it was a tap-tap-tap at the window frame.'

'And there you were at the window, returned,' Nazia said, 'safe, asking to be let in. I am so happy.'

'Before anything else, you must have a bath,' Mother said. 'Are you hungry? Have you eaten?'

'I am so hungry, Mother,' Rafiq said. Here was something she could do for him. Ghafur and Khadr and the housekeeper lived in the little annexe at the bottom of the garden; they would not be disturbed if she now went and cooked some eggs and rice for her younger son. 'I want you to wash – you are so dirty! You smell so much! So bad! How did you get here? No, don't say. You walked, or you came with people as dirty as yourself. I am so proud of you. Later, when you are clean and your hair is clean, I will cut your hair.'

'No, Mother,' Rafiq said. 'Are there no barbers in Dacca any more? I will go to them.'

'Oh, Rafiq,' Mother said. 'He is so nice, so, so nice, his face like a cat, his hand going up like that when he yawns. Now it is time for him to wash and then to eat. And then I will cut his hair.'

'But a barber,' Rafiq said. 'Barbers are good people! I will go to a barber far, far away, in Gulshan, a barber who speaks only English and keeps his customers' secrets. Please, Father, I beg you, not a haircut by my mother, not that. Leave it as it is. Is it so bad? Is it so very bad? Cannot Khadr cut hair? Or my brother? He is a structural engineer! Cannot you do this simple thing, big-brother? Then I bow to my terrible fate. Mother, take the scissors in your hands. I bid you, cut my hair.'

A bath was filled, and Rafiq went to it, splashing in the hot water, washing (he afterwards said) his hair four times before it began to feel like hair and not like dry, sticky twigs. He combed and combed his hair under the water until the comb would go through and not stick like a plough in deep mud; he washed himself in the tub, then stood up and soaped himself all over, then took a jug of clean water and rinsed himself off. He dried himself with the two rough towels; the first bore black marks afterwards, the second was clean. He must have gone for two weeks without washing between the neck and the wrists. But he put on the clean shirt and trousers that Mother had laid out for him, and, as his little sisters had begged, let them look at the colour of the bathwater before he emptied it. Bina told Dolly afterwards that as long as she lived she would never see water so black and filthy. If little-brother had had to lie in a ditch, he would not have been made dirtier by the experience; much later, when she studied English literature at university, she read in *Antony and Cleopatra* of Antony drinking from the gilded puddle which beasts would cough at, and she thought of her brother's last bath.

And then Mother had boiled rice and there was bread to eat and some of the chicken dish from last night, she warmed it in a pan, more than anyone could eat, and she fried eggs as well, giving her son three, then three more, and just let him eat. In the kitchen there was little light; just an oil lamp hanging above the kitchen table where Rafiq sat. At first he was silent, eating and eating, pushing the food into his mouth. Father sat by him, watching him with interest and amusement, and Mother standing behind Father when she judged there was food enough before him for the moment. After a while Rafiq began to talk.

'Mother, I have blisters on my hands and my neck,' he said. 'Some are infected. I must clean them before I set off again. It was the Sten guns, firing off sparks. Afterwards, you are deaf, almost deaf for minutes. And the lying in the water! We know about fighting in the monsoon, we know about water, but they don't know anything. It is then that we are going to defeat them.'

'Don't tell us,' Mother said, pleading. But she would never have any information taken from her.

'We were in India!' Rafiq said. 'We have been training, no more. I have killed nobody yet. I picked up guns and I fired them and I held hand grenades and I hurled hand grenades. And all the time we ate what there was to eat – Mother, I am so happy to eat and eat – and we ate off broken shells with our hands, and – Are there more eggs, Mother?

'And tomorrow or the day after we go off to fight. I will stay in my room and draw the curtain and sleep for two days, because soon it is the monsoon, and then it will be the Pakistanis' turn to run and hide. The Friend of Bengal knows it. Our time is coming.'

'Pitter-patter,' Sharif said, from behind him in the kitchen gloom; the small oil lamp over the plate of food half illuminated his brother's blister-scarred face. 'Pitter-patter.'

'Brother, this is not a child's game,' Rafiq said.

'I know,' Sharif said. Then he began to say the poem. They all knew it. Any one of them from Father down to Dolly at eight years old could have recited it. It was what everyone remembered, the days that the rains came, every year. You could smell, from outside, the quality of the air when rain was building up. Soon the rain would fall and the Pakistanis would be gone. Now Sharif started to recite, in his dry, practical, engineer's voice. You would not have thought that such a voice knew very much poetry.

> *'Don't you think it's extraordinary to see*
> *All those different games the clouds play*
> *Like hide and seek, we used so many holes and corners!*
> *And there's that song*
> *Pitter patter drip drop rain and the river overflows –*
> *There was a light in our house*
> *Mother smiling*
> *Thunder and my beating heart*
> *A little boy, a mother's worry, sleeping on his side*
> *Now jumping and the thunder outside in the world's sky*
> *Mother is singing, singing from far away*
> *Pitter patter drip drop rain and the river overflows.'*

'It's time to go to bed,' Father said. His voice was thickened. He turned away from the dim light the oil lamp threw. 'Don't let anyone go into his room, for any reason.'

5.

Of course there had to be a celebration. It would have to be very quiet. Nobody but they would know that they were marking Rafiq's brief return from training, his imminent departure for war. Mother thought that the best thing would be a grand biryani. She sent Khadr out to buy mutton in the market, explaining that everyone was so bored with chicken and fish, she thought she would do what she could. They had tidied up after the night's feast and were all safely in bed long before six when the servants got up, but still Ghafur had commented that there were fewer eggs than he remembered – he could not explain it – and Khadr should buy three dozen more. She thought she could not conceal Rafiq's return from the servants indefinitely; she would not mention it until he got up from his long sleep.

He was sleeping so deeply! He must have been exhausted. Once or twice she went into the room, very quietly, just to listen to his breathing under the sheet. From early boyhood, he had liked to pull the top sheet over his mouth and nose, bandit fashion, before he slept. His hair spilled over the pillow like Rapunzel's. It was really too bad. She would cut it when he woke up. She had never cut any man's hair in her life, but she was sure she could do it.

The house helped out with the biryani. The grandmothers were patiently shelling nuts, and the girls were sorting through the new bag of rice for stones and dirt. Ghafur was slicing onions and mixing up the paste for the meat to soak in. Together with Nazia, Mother directed the carpets to be taken out to the back garden, hung and beaten. She even thought about taking the covers off the sofas and cushions to wash. She wished she had known Rafiq was coming when he came. But it was best that she had not.

He finally made a movement around half past six in the afternoon. He had slept for at least twelve hours. He emerged looking rested and clean, his too-long hair combed and falling to his shoulders. Somehow he had managed to shave his beard off. He wore a clean white shirt and trousers, taken from the drawer in his room. There was no way of keeping him from the servants now, and the family, seated or busy around the salon, made discreet and excited noises of welcome. Bina and Dolly ran up to him, embracing their brave brother, and after them, Aisha did the same. She clung to his legs.

'Mother, I have come for my ordeal,' Rafiq said. 'Fetch the scissors.'

'You look so dear,' Mother said. 'I shall take a photograph of you with your long hair. I wish I had taken one before you had a chance to shave your beard away.'

'No, Mother,' Rafiq said, laughing.

'Very well. It should be done on the veranda, as always,' Mother said. But then she remembered that there could be not the slightest possibility of glimpsing Rafiq. He had to stay inside. Nazia went to fetch a sheet, and placed it underneath a wooden upright chair. Mother fetched her pinking shears. The girls drew up with fascination. They had never seen their brother's hair cut before.

But Rafiq sat down confidently, saying, 'Mother, my head is in your hands,' and she draped a towel around his shoulders and began work. His hair was so long! All that she needed to do, in the first instance, was to go round the bottom of his dear head, cutting two-three inches off the bottom of his hair. The girls shrieked as the clumps fell to the floor, clapping their hands to their mouths so as not to make much sound. His hair was still very long, so she chopped off clumps, higher up, all over his head. When she had finished it looked slashed off, the cuts unrelated and random, as if everyone in a crowd had had a go. But Mother thought she knew what she was doing. Now she took a comb and, working from the bottom of Rafiq's head placed her scissors, snip snip, against the back of the comb. The girls shrieked again.

'It is going to be so short!' Bina said. 'I can see his scalp!'

'This may not be a very good haircut,' Father said. 'We will try to salvage what we can, when Mother has finished. But we may need to shave your head with a razor. There may not be very much to salvage.'

'I go to my fate,' Rafiq said.

'I remember when I was a law student in Calcutta,' Father said, 'I was so poor. I only had ten annas a month to spend on a haircut, and that was not very much. I never saved on laundry and I never saved on soap and I never saved on haircuts or razors by doing without. But I could not afford a good barber. When I was very poor, I had to go to a pavement barber, a man who has only a fragment of a mirror, and the man cuts your hair without your being able to see what he is doing. The thing I most disliked about it was that people would gather round – ne'er-do-wells, stragglers, loiterers – for some free entertainment. I went to a pavement barber called Manzoor. He was a terrible man. I think he was addicted to drink – his hands shook in a way that you never want to see in a barber. I never saw anyone else having their hair cut on his little stool. I knew if I went to him rather than the other pavement barber on the other side of the road I would be able to have rice and dhal for my dinner. But every time I went there, the next friend I saw from Calcutta University, he would always without fail ask what in the name of heaven I had allowed to happen to my hair. It would take ten days at least for it to grow out enough to look less than a public spectacle. Now I look at my son, and I see that Mr Manzoor has a rival.'

'Do not open the door,' the smaller grandmother said.

'This is an awful haircut,' Father said, laughing. 'I'm glad he's going where no ladies are going to see him.'

'Do not open the door,' the grandmother said again.

'What did she say?' Nazia asked her husband, but he had not heard anything.

'Do not open the door,' the grandmother said.

'What is it?' Mother said. It was not often that the grandmothers made a remark for all of them to hear. Now she looked. She laid her scissors and her comb down on the towel she had placed on the table. The grandmother seemed to be in distress. She was plucking away at the shawl of the other grandmother, her little face screwed up like a walnut, in tears. Mother wondered whether she urgently needed to use the bathroom, but it seemed worse than that.

'Do not open the door,' she said again. This time Mother heard her. Rafiq turned his head to look at her. Behind her, through the windows, a bright light shone. It was dusk now, surely, but a fierce light was shining in the street.

'Turn the radio off,' Father said. It had been talking in a low voice, an illegal radio station, but probably harmless. 'Turn it off. Spin the dial.'

Afterwards, they disagreed on some things, but one thing they all agreed on was that the grandmother had said, 'Do not open the door,' long before the sound of hammering had started. They agreed, too, that it was then Rafiq had said, 'I go to my fate,' and had laughed, not knowing what was about to happen.

'Do not open the door,' Mother said to Father. The noise of hammering on the door of the house shook the floors.

'I have to,' Father said. 'They can see that we are here.'

There were faces at the windows of the salon, peering in. Father was right. There was nothing that could be done. Sharif went to the door, his face set.

There were two men at the door of the house. A bright set of lights blazed in the street behind the open gates, and more men. The two men were in uniform. One was a subedar; the other, who took charge, was a young man with pale skin, shy-looking and scholarly, his hands delicate around a baton of some sort. His uniform was very clean and pressed. He and the older subedar both stepped into the house.

'I am Captain Qayyum,' the officer said. 'I am here to search your house.'

'You can see who is here,' Sharif said. 'My mother and father; my daughter; my wife; my two younger sisters and my younger brother; my colleague and superior; my grandmothers.'

'And who else?' Captain Qayyum spoke in Bengali; his language was hoarse and stumbling. The subedar by him paid no attention when he or Sharif spoke. It was clear he did not understand or speak the language.

Mother stepped forward and enumerated the servants in the house at present – the cook, the houseboy, the housekeeper, the gardener and the gatekeeper, whom they had dealt with and brushed aside. Captain Qayyum's eyes went over each of them in turn. He seemed bored and uninterested in Sharif, in Father, even in Professor Anisul, who was sitting at the back of the room reading a dull book. He came finally to Rafiq. He looked so innocent, his head roughly shorn, his hair fallen about him on the towel and onto the white sheet on the floor. He looked like a child; the blisters on his neck could have come from anywhere.

'He is your son,' Captain Qayyum said to Mother. 'You are washing his hair.'

'No,' Mother said. 'I am cutting his hair.'

'Yes, cutting – cutting – his hair. You are cutting his hair. Why?'

'It is not safe for a boy to go out on his own in Dacca these days,' Mother said. 'His hair needed cutting and so I am cutting it. I cut my daughters' hair, too.'

It was not clear that Captain Qayyum understood what Mother had said, although she had taken the trouble to speak clearly and slowly. The subedar stepped forward and said something. He spoke in Urdu. Father shuddered. He had always said that he would never have that language spoken in his house. Both grandmothers looked up, their attention caught by strangeness. They had known what would happen.

'I am taking him into custody,' Captain Qayyum said. 'It is just a routine questioning. He will return to you within an hour. Come along.'

'Where are you taking him?' Mother said.

'To a police station,' Captain Qayyum said. 'It is nothing serious.'

'Which police station?' Mother said. She stopped herself adding more; she could see that if she suggested a police station, for instance the one in Dhanmondi, this thin and nervous Pakistani officer would agree.

Captain Qayyum hesitated. 'We are returning to the Ramna police station,' he said finally. 'Madam, please do not worry. He will be returned to you in no time at all.'

For a moment nobody moved. Then the subedar took some action. Engaging the suspect's father with his eyes, he moved forward briskly, taking the pinking shears from the dining-room table. He seized Rafiq's head in a firm grip, and there, in four movements, sliced off some chunks of hair, randomly, from four places on Rafiq's head. His littlest sister screamed and was silenced. The subedar dropped the scissors without troubling to close them, on the floor. Rafiq stood up. There was no question what these people could do. The four places on his head where the subedar had applied the scissors were bare, ugly, and at one point the scissors' blades had cut into his skin; a shine of blood was beginning to gather along a line on his scalp.

'Come along,' Captain Qayyum said. His face remained kindly, polite, sympathetic. 'There is no need to bring anything. He will not be with us long enough.'

They took Rafiq firmly, marching him between them. Mother half ran towards the door, but there, in the hallway, collapsed. The Pakistanis shut the door of the house and, with a final tocsin and clang, the steel gate of the house on the street. Sharif came for his mother, lifting her up and taking her back to the sofa. She was moaning and making a noise of weeping, her sounds of grief still suppressed after a month of enforced silence.

'No,' she was saying. 'No, no, no ...'

'It may be as they say,' Father said. 'It may be that Rafiq is back with us within an hour. He has the strength to say nothing. They don't know where he was.'

'They know he was away,' Mother said. 'They know that he was returned. You,' she pointed at Professor Anisul. 'Who have you told? You cuckoo.'

'Professor Anisul has been here all day,' Father said. 'I am sorry, my old friend. She does not know what she is saying.'

'Someone has told them. One of the Friendly Ones. You – you said you had to go out on your own. Who was it you were telling Rafiq had returned?'

She was pointing at Sharif. He had no words.

'Mother, Rafiq is my brother. I went to the flat. I saw nobody.'

'Why did they not take you for questioning? Did they know that you are on their side, the Friendly Ones?'

'Mother,' Nazia said. She went up to her and laid a hand on her arm. 'Mother. Sharif did not betray his brother. He could not.'

'Who else?' Mother said, moaning. 'There is no one else.'

But Bina looked up at the door of the salon. They were standing with Ghafur and the housekeeper. Bina had known. Dolly should have known, too. Feluda would have worked it out in a moment! Ghafur and the housekeeper and Khadr, too, they had worked out that little-brother was back when they had got up and started work, and discovered that in the night somebody had needed to eat eight eggs, and that now little-brother's door was closed and the room darkened. Khadr not being there – it was like an admission of guilt. He knew who he had told. Bina whispered to Dolly, and Dolly's eyes grew large. In the market Khadr had said – oh, you poor stupid Khadr with your smiling clever friend from another kitchen – had said how nice it was now that little-master was back from his adventures. Had said, Oh I mustn't say more. The smiling clever friend had gone back; had said to his master that someone was returned from the war, was going to go on to the war. That master had been a Friendly One, to inform Captain Qayyum. Bina felt quite proud of herself for this piece of Feluda-like deduction. It was lucky that Captain Qayyum had promised to return little-brother from questioning in an hour. When he came back, Bina would be absolutely sure to advise him to leave the house and not come back until he had won the war, and not to trust Khadr with any important secret. Everyone would definitely realize that now.

6.

Mother went out in the morning with a tiffin-pail of food and a change of clothes for Rafiq. She needed some persuading, but Khoka the night-watchman went with her for her own safety. She refused to let Father go with her. This was a task for a mother to undertake. When she came back it was after seven at night. She called for tea.

'Listen,' she said. 'This is what happened. I went with Khoka to the police station that Captain Qayyum indicated to us. He told us that my son was being questioned at the Ramna police station. Khoka and I went there in a rickshaw. We saw so much on the way. Half the city is destroyed. We saw bodies lying in the street, and everywhere signs in Urdu, buildings burnt out. Outside the Ramna police station there were women, seated, their faces covered with veils. I thought they were cleaners and domestic servants. I went up the steps into the police station and there at the front desk was a Pakistani army officer. He did not look up as I came to him. I said to him that I wanted to speak to Captain Qayyum. He said that Captain Qayyum was not there and he would not be there.

'I could not know what next to say. Captain Qayyum had said to me that he was taking my son to Ramna police station for one hour. That was not true. I dreaded to ask the next question – is my son here. The officer asked me why I was asking. "Mother, why concern yourself?" he said. "Look what I have for him," I said. The officer said that if I handed over the food I had brought, and the razors and the shirts and the soap, he would ensure that they reached my son.

'Another officer came up and said, more briskly, yes, my son was in the building and he was being very well looked after. I did not believe that this second officer had heard me enquire about my son by his name. I asked him who I was talking about. He responded by saying that no one was being held there for a long time, that my son would be returned to me soon. I turned to the first officer and handed over the food and the parcel of razors and soap and the packet of shirts, and I said that I would return tomorrow if my son had not been released by then. He seemed confused by this. "Madam," he said. "There is no need for you to come back here. He will be released soon."

'Khoka took me away, and I covered my face. My son would be very ashamed if he knew I had cried in public. We went down the stairs outside the police station and I saw that the women, some of them, were dressed in good clothes, one or two had even a handbag. They were women like me. I stopped – Khoka almost pulled me away – and I said to one, "What are you doing here, sister?" She looked at me and said, "Where else should I go, sister? My husband was brought here and my three sons. And this is the only place I know to go to."

'I saw the terrible future for me. I am going to sit on the stairs outside the Ramna police station and wait for Rafiq. But he is not there. Is he in the cantonment, or in some house behind high walls? And all the way back we saw houses which have been burnt. The tailor Father uses, it is burnt out and destroyed; the bookshop where Rafiq was such friends with the owner, destroyed, burnt to the ground with all its neighbours; and I could see down the street where Murtaza's house is, where my oldest friend's husband lived, and it is not there. Against the walls there is blood, as if people were lined up against them and shot. I saw seven-eight bodies in a heap. Tomorrow I am going out again and I will ask again where my son is, and I will take more food for him.'

7.

'Mother,' Nazia said, one day in August, 'yesterday, Khadr asked me if there were any news about Professor Anisul's housekeeper.'

Mother stopped what she was doing. She was sorting through the scraps of cloth and lengths of thread in the mending drawer. She liked to do this from time to time; everyone reached into the drawer and took out what they needed without leaving it in an orderly situation. Very soon the drawer was in a mess. Mother liked to sort it out twice a year or so, and afterwards she would say to Nazia and the girls that that was how it should stay. The pieces of silk and cotton that had such a lot of use were in neat piles, separated by colour, by Mother on the sofa.

'I haven't heard any news,' Mother said.

'He asked me if she had gone to Gazipur,' Nazia said. 'He said he thought that she had been wise to return to her family in these circumstances.'

Mother laid her hands down, palm upwards, on her knees. She raised her head and looked, despairingly, at Nazia. 'He can't go,' she said. 'We can't go on without servants.'

But at the end of the conversation, Mother and Nazia decided that, if he wanted to leave them, he would be allowed to leave them without anyone complaining.

It must have been September, months after Rafiq was taken. Mother had continued going to the Ramna police station, to the gates of the cantonment, and demanding news of her son. She did this every day, accompanied by Khoka. Father said nothing. He would not go with her. Hope, according to Father, was what would drive a man insane. He watched her go in the mornings, and sat down in his chair to read a book, or he went to his study to prepare, he said, a case that had been suspended. The door to the study was shut and Father was left to be alone with his thoughts.

Seven times the Pakistani police had visited, demanding to search the house. They had only once taken anyone away. On that occasion, they had taken an interest in Professor Anisul's elaborate drawing of a bridge, and had taken it away, and him with it. On this occasion, they returned Professor Anisul within three hours, unharmed. They kept the drawing of the bridge, to Professor Anisul's disgust and anger. 'They seemed to think I was a spy, or a saboteur,' he said. 'But how could I spy or sabotage something that does not exist, that I drew on paper?'

Sometimes, these days, women came to the gate to beg for food. They were those who had lost their homes, their families, their livelihoods. Father said that what could be done for them should be done for them. They did not ask for anything much: they asked for the water that rice had been boiled in. Father said that if more was given to them, then they would be giving more than their neighbours; if they gave more, the gates would be broken down and the house ransacked by a mob. The eight widows who came to the gate every day were given the water that rice had been boiled in, and sometimes a spoonful of dhal.

Nazia came back one day from a walk to the lake. She needed to be out in the last of the monsoon; the catastrophe of the falling water made her feel again, made her conceptions reach out in a different direction. The grandmothers sat inside, but they had chosen chairs close to the window onto the garden. As the rain fell, they looked up often from their small tasks, from grinding paan in their little bowls, from sewing or mending, from the occasional secret needlework they practised and gave as presents. Out there the monsoon was roaring; through the window the smells of grass and earth and trees and clean water poured. Their faces shone; they had nothing to say. Nazia knew what they were feeling. When she walked to the lake under her father-in-law's second-best black umbrella, her skirts decorously hitched out of the mud, she could have sung. Once, she had been a small girl who had run through the rain, soaked and splashing in puddles halfway up to her knees, screaming with ragamuffins. She could have jumped into the puddles even now.

The Pakistanis were said to hate it, didn't know how to fight in it.

Khadr let her in, hissing and puffing at the state of her; however she tried, she could not keep quite clean.

'Madam, please,' Khadr said, pointing in affected despair at the clean floor. 'Your shoes! The mud on your skirts!'

'Three inches deep in mud,' Nazia said happily. 'Like Elizabeth Bennet.'

Khadr, grandly, paid no attention to this. Nazia went into her room and changed her clothes, wiping her ankles clean with a wet cloth. Khadr had heard of Hitler, but not of Napoleon; he had heard of Feluda, but not of Elizabeth Bennet. He had been a night-watchman, just like Khoka; now he felt that anything that revealed his lack of education must be passed over, like a rude word from an old person. He would not ask for elucidation; he would give a vague smile, as if of pity, and start to talk about something else.

When she came out, clean and with her hair neatly brushed, Khadr was still in the same position she had left him in. 'Sir is here,' he said.

'Who?' Nazia said.

Khadr gave a superb gesture, a kind of circling wave of the hand, as if launching a cricket ball underarm in the direction of the salon. There, seated with his back to the door, was Mahfouz. He sat unlike anyone else in the family, his hands locked behind his head, a thoughtful way of sitting. On the sofa at the far end, the grandmothers sat with Sadia, talking quietly. At the sound of Nazia's chappals clapping, Mahfouz got up.

'I didn't know you were here,' Nazia said.

'No,' Mahfouz said. 'It is so disappointing when people say they will come, and then are somehow prevented. I thought we would just come.'

'But no one is here!' Sadia called.

'Father thought he would pay a visit to his friend Mr Khondkar, I believe,' Nazia said. 'He took the girls – they get so few outings, poor things, and they leapt at the chance. Also, he has sugar-coated biscuits that little girls like. Who else? It seemed quiet, so Professor Anisul went to see how things are at his house. That seems safe, but he worries that his office at the university might have been broken into and his possessions destroyed. I say to my husband, what about your office, but he just laughs and says we will find out what has happened there in due course.'

'Where is he now?'

'Well, he's with Mother,' Nazia said, steadying her voice. 'They go to the police station each day to ask about Rafiq. She used to take clean shirts every day, and they accepted them, but then after a few days she asked if she could have the shirts back for washing, and what they gave her back were the clothes she had brought in, still in the brown paper packaging. The tiffin pail she brought in, they gave that back to her. I suppose they ate the food themselves.'

'I am so sorry about your brother,' Mahfouz said.

'About brother?' Nazia said. 'Thank you, brother.' It was a small formal exchange, meaning nothing. 'When did you hear? It must be six or seven weeks since they came for Rafiq.'

'Oh – I think … I'm not quite sure. It was …' Mahfouz lifted his eyes to the ceiling, raised his hands to his head. Over on the sofa, Sadia had stopped talking to the grandmothers.

'Things are so difficult,' Nazia said. 'He hadn't been here for a day when they came for him. Thanks to a Friendly One.'

'I am so sorry,' Mahfouz said formally. 'A Friendly One?'

'Yes, a Friendly One,' Nazia said. 'Patriots, brother – those who say they love their country, people who would sell their neighbours, people who …' Sadia had laid a hand on the hand of a grandmother to silence her; she was tense and listening. She knew that Mahfouz had made a false step.

'Well, there are so many organizations,' Nazia said. 'A new one every day. We hear only rumours, and more rumours, and things people have misheard in the street, and I don't quite know, even, how you heard about Rafiq being taken.'

'I told my brother,' Khadr said. He was bringing in a tray of tea and biscuits. He set it on the small table. 'That must be how Sir heard about the facts of the case. I told small-brother when I saw him in the market. I was buying eggs and he was buying eggs.'

'What do you mean, your brother?' Nazia said.

'My mother's small-son,' Khadr said. 'Small-brother, a very very good boy.'

'Oh, I see,' Nazia said, attempting an air of studious vagueness. 'Oh, yes, I remember.'

'It was when we married,' Mahfouz said bravely. 'Khadr's small-brother came to us to deal with the extra work. And a very good thing he is.'

'That must be it,' Nazia said, smiling warmly. 'I so hate it when I can't work out connections. It is so nice to think that Khadr and his little brother can let each other know how things stand with each of us! Thank you, Khadr. That will do.'

'Well, that must be how it was,' Mahfouz said. He leant forward and poured a cup of tea for himself; poured a cup of tea for Nazia. She took it, and they began to talk about Aisha – she was small to be taken out to Mr Khondkar's, but she could behave herself, and it seemed a shame to leave her out.

'Well,' he said finally, 'I'm afraid that we must think about going. It is such a disappointment not to see the others.'

'Yes, indeed,' Sadia said, getting up from the sofa. 'We will perhaps give you some warning next time.'

'You could send a message to Khadr through his brother,' Nazia said lightly. She knew now how Rafiq had been sold. It was not the fact of his imprisonment that Khadr had shared with his brother, as he remembered. It was the day that Rafiq had returned from training camp, and the brother had gone home and shared the news with someone; someone very close to the Friendly Ones. The Friendly Ones had reached out. Within the hour, Captain Qayyum had been at the door. The Friendly Ones, Mahfouz had said. What are they? She looked at him, his smiling face, his performance.

'It won't be long now,' she said, showing them out. 'I don't believe this war is going to last much longer. Then we'll have our independence, and be safe from all this.'

Sadia gave her a sharp glance.

'And then you will be able to come and visit whenever you like,' Nazia said.

'I'm sure it will end, one way or another,' Mahfouz said. There was nothing else he could decently say. He did not hope for Bangla Desh. He sat among people who believed that his brother-in-law should be shot alongside the Friend of Bengal.

She said goodbye to them, and closed the door, but in a few seconds there was a knock again. It was Sadia.

'Did you forget something?' Nazia said.

'Just a word,' Sadia said. 'You have a moment, sister?'

She walked ahead, turning right and opening Father's study door. Sadia had never been in there unless at Father's express invitation, if he was in there himself. It was strange to walk into the dustless seriousness of the dark, book-lined space with her sister-in-law. There were two armchairs to the side of the desk, where Father liked to sit with his juniors. Sadia sat down in one of these chairs, motioning Nazia into the other.

'You think we did it,' Sadia said immediately. 'Gave them Rafiq's name.'

There was no point in dissembling. 'Yes,' Nazia said. 'Yes, I do.'

'You don't understand how important this is. For you –'

'Sister,' Nazia said. She was astonished.

'Listen,' Sadia said. 'You should stop talking as if Mahfouz is a traitor.'

'Did he not do what we think he did?'

'Traitor is a word anyone can use,' Sadia said. 'What are people who go into the countryside, train to kill the government's soldiers, plan to overthrow the government, plan to destroy the country? What are they?'

'You're talking about our brother,' Nazia said.

'What is more important?' Sadia said. 'My brother or my country? Mahfouz is not a traitor. And Mother – she must stop going every day to shout at the officers.'

'You might as well ask her to stop breathing. She has to ask where her son is. Is he dead? Have they killed him?'

She meant it as the questions that Mother bore at the front of her brain, but Sadia said, 'I don't know. I don't know how you could find out.'

Nazia was seized with rage. 'You must be able to find out. Ask your Friendly Ones.'

'Don't talk about it. I'm asking you as your sister now. If you want to stay as you are, stop going to the police station. Soon the war will be over and people will have to pay the costs for what they have done.'

Nazia gripped the arms of her chair. She pulled herself forward. She could have pushed her face into her sister-in-law's. 'Don't you understand? No Bengali is ever going to give up fighting now. Your government would have to shoot every one of us. The war is going to be over, soon, but it is going to be over when your people are beaten. And they will be beaten. What will you do then? You will have to pack your bags and leave. Your Mahfouz will be put on trial for what he has done. He will be hanged if he has done what we think he has done.'

'Some things are more important,' Sadia said. She stood up, brushing herself down. 'If you want everyone in this house to live, you will accept what God has delivered to you. You have no idea what love means, what love will do.'

Sadia left.

Nazia sat in the chair and collected herself. She would say nothing of this to the others. She would observe that Sadia and Mahfouz had visited; that they had sat with the grandmothers; that they would visit again soon, when things were calmer. Once or twice, Sharif had observed mildly that Sadia had never been the same as the rest of them. Her play and her fantasies were never the same as theirs, in childhood. She was the only one of them not to chase, not to play wild games of capture, but to sit in a corner of her room with small possessions to play at shopkeeper. What was the joy in that? little-brother Rafiq used to ask, with his incredulous bored expression – he could be dragooned in to be a customer or a warehouseman for two minutes before he was off with his wooden pistol to pretend-shoot Mother, the cook, the boy next door with yelps and screams. When Sadia grew up she would own a shop for materials and cloth, for silks and cottons, her assistants unrolling them and saying, 'Two taka the yard, madam, makes twelve taka,' and taking the real money in exchange. Her eyes would grow bright. She had seen that the sort of people who sold things were not the same people who wrote things, who argued things, who were doctors and engineers. In the end she had watched her husband selling her brother. The things history will do at the bidding of love, standing on one leg and waiting for the witless command to come.

8.

They had been waiting for days for this, clustered round the radio in the sitting room. In the end the news came, announced by Radio Calcutta. The Indian troops had crossed the border. They were participants in the war of independence. The Pakistanis were surrendering as they met the greater force. The Indians, joining with the Mukti Bahini, the brave Bengalis fighting in the country, were meeting with no resistance. In a matter of days they would reach Dacca.

'The war is over,' Father said, looking up. 'And now ...'

'They will be gone,' Mother said. 'And my son –'

'The war is over,' Sharif said.

The day before, Khadr had told them that he wanted to leave, to go to his family. Nobody had put up any objection. Khoka could become the new houseboy, with a little training.

9.

It was the next day that Professor Anisul woke and decided to leave the house. The war, after all, was over. These good people had been very kind, but it was hard never to be able to leave the house alone, for a walk, without anyone telling him that it was too dangerous. He had always liked his walks in the city. It was how he had often had his best ideas. In the previous months, he had been obliged to sit inside for the most part, drawing fanciful projects like the glass bridge, the cantilevered tower, the floating road on pontoon sections. He would have done better if he had been able to go outside and walk for two hours, making his mind up. His hostess had looked up at him repeatedly the one time he had tried to walk up and down the salon to think something out. Professor Anisul was not always very good at working out what people meant by the expressions on their faces. In this case he had stopped walking up and down. He had worried, to be frank, that in fact his hosts found his presence something of a bore. But he could not have gone anywhere, once he had moved in. They had really been very kind. He would think of a suitable present to give them now that the war was quite over.

He opened the gate and walked into the road. Nobody was there. This was unexpected – he had rather thought there might be celebrations everywhere. The trees, painted white up to knee-height, were in some places torn and shattered. Some of them were ripped up entirely – one lay across the road. Some of its branches had been sawn off. Perhaps for fuel, gathered by poor people. Professor Anisul, however, could not see how traffic was expected to drive down this road if the trunk of a great tree was lying across it. Unexpectedly, a house no more than five from his host's had been destroyed. The gates hung open, and the house was gutted by fire. The windows were empty, and around them, the walls were blackened with soot. Inside, Professor Anisul could see shapes, as if organic; they were burnt furniture and possessions.

It was a very pleasant day; the sun was not too hot, and the skies were clear. Everywhere there was a smell of burning and of spilt petrol. By this point, there were always rag-and-bone men, pavement barbers, street jelapi-fryers, stationers with a barrow, boys selling a dozen ancient books; the servants of families going about their business, and perhaps two or three people like him, enjoying a morning walk in the agreeable air. But there was no one. There was not even a rickshaw idling, touting for custom. He expected that was because of the tree blocking the road. He could not see why everyone was not out celebrating. Perhaps they were. It would not be the first time he had failed to find out about a general festivity.

Now that the war was over, he supposed Bangla Desh was a reality. East Pakistan – something would have to be done about that. The East Pakistan University of Engineering and Technology could hardly limp on under that name. Professor Anisul had never been very enthusiastic about the creation of an institution called EPUET, and time had done very little to modify his views. It should not limp on under the name of the Bangla Desh University of Engineering and Technology. BADUET. It sounded perfectly ridiculous. (By now Professor Anisul had reached the edge of Dhanmondi. Now there seemed to be some men standing about, at the edges of street corners. Of course there would be some people around – he did not know why he had doubted it.)

This morning, he could walk to the university. He had a lot of exercise to undertake, after so many months cooped up. And he would think on the way of how things had once been. He had taken his own degree at Dacca University – an excellent institution, a historic institution, as good in its own way as Calcutta University, or any university you might name. And he had started teaching there – the Engineering Faculty of Dacca University. A splendid body of people! Of course they had gone on being a splendid body of people, even after the government had decided in its wisdom that they should acquire institutional independence, run their own budgets, and be part of something entitled the East Pakistan University of Engineering and Technology. Professor Anisul had been introduced to a lawyer friend of his neighbour once, four whole years after the change. They had been on an evening walk round Dhanmondi lake. His neighbour had said that Professor Anisul was a professor of engineering at EPUET – a blank look – at the East Pakistan University of Engineering and Technology; the neighbour's friend didn't believe he had come across it himself. If this revolution achieved anything, it would restore things to their proper place in the world, under their proper names. Professor Anisul wondered whether that entire run of shops, now burnt out, with a small group of men standing in front of them bearing guns, would in the end be worth restoring and rebuilding. Perhaps they would simply knock them down and build something new in their place.

A man had separated himself from the small group, standing at the corner where a narrow alley ran off the main street. He stepped forward into the street, and waited as a single rickshaw wove past. It was the first one Professor Anisul had seen since leaving his host's house, and he watched it go with interest. Perhaps it was just the grid of Dhanmondi that everyone had abandoned. Probably Old Dacca was as crowded and noisy as it ever had been. He had been a little nervous – you heard such stories! It was only when the man approaching him spoke that he could feel quite safe.

'Professor Anisul,' the man said.

Professor Anisul looked at him carefully. He had never been particularly good at faces, but in a moment he realized that he was being greeted by his host's son-in-law. He had shown a lot of interest once, when road building had been under discussion. He had had his own ideas about how to increase capacity, and the young man had contributed intelligently. He fished for his name – but it would not come.

'My dear young man,' he said. 'A pleasure to see you. What are you doing out of doors? There seem to be very few people about.'

'We were merely ensuring the safety of those few people,' the young man said. His name was Mahfouz – it came to Professor Anisul now. He turned to his companions and called, 'It's Professor Anisul Ahmed.' He appeared to stress the word 'Professor' – a mark of respect, no doubt, which was good to hear.

'Professor Anisul,' one called back.

'From the university?' another called. 'A professor from the university?'

'I very much hope so, soon,' Professor Anisul confided in his friend's son-in-law.

'An intellectual,' one of the men shouted. Perhaps there was something less respectful in that. Simple people often found it difficult to understand what scholars did, and made a little mockery of them.

'There is so much damage,' Professor Anisul said. 'I am sure that a structural engineer will be able to contribute so much to the nation's future.'

'Were you going towards the university?' Mahfouz said. 'There must be more of your colleagues gathering there.'

'Yes,' Professor Anisul said. 'I believe there will be. There is the physics common room on the third floor of the old building of Dacca University. People often congregated there, quite naturally. I expect that now there will be a few people there, just to share news and to see what there is to be done. You see, a lot of us have not been near the institution for months. Now that these events are over, I am sure that many colleagues, like me, simply want to get on with things.'

'I see,' Mahfouz said. 'But is it not a very long distance for you to walk? From here to Dacca University?'

'My dear boy, no,' Professor Anisul said. 'It is a pleasant day. It is safe now that the war is over. I would very much prefer to walk. I was looking forward to seeing the city, seeing what needs to be achieved, and to take in some fresh air.'

'I am not sure that the war is quite over,' Mahfouz said. 'There may even be danger here and there. I think I must insist, Professor – I am going to ask my friend and colleague over there, who has transport of his own, friend Abdul, if you please …'

A short man, scarved about the head, black-clad, raised his face. His expression was tranquil, undisturbed, unemotional.

'My friend, you have your vehicle to hand, do you not? I think it is down there, in the yard along the small street, two streets to the right, then left, then left again, is it not? Friend Abdul, this is Professor Anisul. He is a great treasure to the new nation now arriving to take charge of us. Take very great care of him, I beg you. Take him down to the yard where your vehicle is parked. Take him wherever he wants to go. He did not know how unsafe this city still is. Take very good care of him. I am going,' Mahfouz said, turning to Professor Anisul, 'to say good-bye to you now. But I think we will go to the university, too. To make entirely sure of your colleagues, up there in the physics common room, on the third floor. But it would be sensible for you to go with my friend Abdul. Goodbye, Professor Anisul.'

Professor Anisul had always liked Mahfouz, but he was surprised that he now gave him a gentle push on his back towards the man Abdul. The driver did not seem like a very educated or polite man. It was just as well that Mahfouz had stressed that Professor Anisul was a man of distinction and intelligence. For some reason Abdul did not lead the way down the narrow alley that was going to take them to the vehicle that had been left out of the way, in a yard that must be behind a house or a business of some sort. Instead, he gestured to Professor Anisul to go first. He would follow immediately behind. It seemed unusual to Professor Anisul. After all, he had only Mahfouz's instructions – rather complicated – to go by to reach the vehicle. He expected that if he went in the wrong direction, however, the driver Abdul would set him right. He could not remember, in fact, ever having been in this little warren of streets. It surprised him that somewhere so unknown and dark and narrow should exist a few hundred yards from places he had known almost all his life, and with the close sensation of the driver Abdul walking a foot or two behind him, he went on, looking about him with some interest at the unfamiliar scenes, as if into a close-built labyrinth.

CHAPTER ELEVEN

I.

Business was quiet, for spring. Everybody who worked at the estate agent's had a theory about what drove people to decide to move house. Stuart had been there for two years, his first job straight out of college. He said it went back to when the human race lived in caves. People just buried themselves in for the winter, wrapped themselves in bearskins, slept eighteen hours a day between October and February, and then when March came, bingo.

'What do you mean, "bingo"?' Carole said.

'They come out,' Stuart said, 'and they look around them and they say to each other, it's spring, must be making a move. It's in the genes.'

'Oh, the genes,' Carole said. She'd been an employee there for twenty years. A mere humble employee, she liked to say. It was a family firm, Lydgate's of Sheffield. It was still run by Graham Lydgate, whose office was in the back of the shop. The profession had changed in those twenty years. Stuart fancied himself as a bit of an impressionist, and she'd heard him do Mr Lydgate and one of Mr Lydgate's favourite expressions. '*We*,' Stuart-as-Mr-Lydgate would say, stressing the word as if the important thing was that changes were happening to them, to the Lydgate family business, 'are moving in uncharted waters.' She could be rather grateful for Stuart's Lydgate impression, since it made an occasional change from him eternally doing Denis Healey, saying, 'Silly Billy,' and, at any professional setback or disaster, mouthing, 'Ooh, Betty, the cat's done a whoopsy,' which was that programme on the idiot box that Carole frankly couldn't endure.

Lydgate's wasn't one of those city-centre agencies with branches everywhere. It had been in Ranmoor for decades. The shop was on the same side of the street as the church, between Mrs Rose's bakery and what everyone said was the best French restaurant in Sheffield, if not in Yorkshire. (A little local pride exaggerated things here, perhaps.) On the other side of the road, in the roads leading down the hill towards the Porter Brook and the park, there were at least two houses that Lydgate's would never be requested to place on the market: the two square mansions, each handsomely – ideally – surrounded by three acres of lawn and flowerbed, assigned by the university and the church to the vice-chancellor and the bishop respectively. (Bish and VC didn't get on, it was said, and the vice-chancellor's wife bought her bread and cakes from Gateway supermarket, according to Mrs Rose next door.) There were plenty of other big dark stone houses to be getting on with, though once people were in one of those, they tended never to move again. Not 'mansion', Carole thought: Gentleman's Residence would have the right ring.

The business was not what it had been twenty years ago. There was more seriousness about the money. When she'd come into it, there was something quiet and second-choice about it as a profession. 1956! Then, she'd worn a hat every day, without fail. It would have been unusual, to say the least, to see a university graduate like Stuart start work there.

She'd seen them come and go, the Stuarts of this world. They were brought in on a warm wind, set down gracefully, full of ideas that Carole had heard before; and between three and five years later the warm wind picked them up again and deposited them in some other office, full of the same ideas. But the thing she certainly knew was that there was a little flurry of interest, infallibly, when the weather improved in springtime. Sometimes people did the spring-cleaning, and even a bit of decorating, then just looked at it and thought that wasn't enough. Some years it seemed as if half of Sheffield spent January and February thinking about packing up and moving, and the first week in March, at the latest, through the door they came.

This had been one of the years when the partners had decided to use the quiet time of December to redecorate the shop. Smarten it up a bit; a new red carpet; new desks and lamps and a lick of paint. The shop in Ranmoor had the full treatment every five years. Graham Lydgate had complained things had gone up so since the last time. 'I'm inclined to query this estimate,' he'd said to Mr Norris, the painter-and-decorator. But people would want to buy their houses from an estate agent that looked like a dream of soft carpets and gleaming glass, of bright clean walls and comfortable modern furniture without fuss or dust. It had to be done and it was done.

'I just can't understand it,' Carole said. 'Always, always, always they pour through the door come the last week in February. I feel like somebody who's organized a birthday party and no one's turned up.'

'People don't know what things are going to cost in a year's time,' Stuart said. 'They're going to sit tight. In any case, I've got a family this afternoon, wanting to view.'

'What's their price range?'

'Fourteen to eighteen,' Stuart said. 'Mr and Mrs ...' he looked, making a business of sorting through the papers on his desk '... Mr and Mrs Sharifullah. They've just arrived in this country. Quite young.'

'Mr and Mrs how much?'

'Sharifullah. I've got some houses in Lodge Moor to show them, and that cottage in Acre Avenue I thought might suit.'

'Don't show them Acre Avenue unless absolutely nothing in Lodge Moor suits them. Where are they from?'

'Somewhere hot,' Stuart said. 'India. I think. No, Pakistan. No, I'm not sure.'

'They'll not go for Lodge Moor, then,' Carole said. 'It gets the full blast of the north wind. We can't sell them Acre Avenue – we'd never hear the last of it. Acre Avenue, they're our neighbours down here in Ranmoor. What does he do, Mr ...'

'Mr Sharifullah. It's Dr Sharifullah in fact. Not a medical doctor. He's going to be teaching at the university. I've not met them – they came in yesterday after you'd gone for the day and I was out showing the house in Stumperlowe, a waste of time that was. Mr Lydgate met them. Said they were very nice.'

'Well, I suppose it could be worse,' Carole said. 'My cousin Susan, she's got an Asian family living opposite her – this is in Crookes but she says Broomhill. They're very nice, according to her. He's a pharmacist, run a chemist's in Manor – someone's got to. You can't pick your neighbours but you can't blame people for wondering.'

'Wondering what?' Stuart said. He had something approaching a smirk on his face.

'Oh, you know what I mean,' Carole said. 'I'm going to get on with chasing up the printers. Don't pretend you don't know what I mean. I don't think you can complain if you live in Lodge Moor. I suppose they'll want to know about the schools if they've got family. They're very nice, some of them, I suppose, but I'd not be wanting to live next to them myself. Does that sound ... It's the smell. Not them, but it's what they eat. It's all very well once in a while, but you won't be wanting to sit down in your garden and smell that drifting over morning, noon and night. I'm sorry, but that's just how I feel.'

'And for that reason,' Graham Lydgate said, 'it'll be you that I've asked to show some houses to Mr and Mrs Sharifullah, Stuart, and not Carole here. That must be them now, look, getting out of their car. There, that's not too bad, is it? She's not in a sari with a cardy on top, at all events. I told you, he's a very respectable professional man anyone would be happy to have as their neighbour. And their little girl, charming. Carole. Look. Charming. And here they come, our only serious customers for the day, if you don't count that gentleman at ten a.m., which I frankly don't, so, everybody, that means you, Carole – And here you are again, Mr and Mrs Sharifullah, or should I say, Dr and Mrs, a pleasure to see you again and so punctual. And this is?'

Mr Lydgate lowered his hand in the direction of the small girl, in a neat tartan dress, a pink ribbon holding her hair back. Mrs Sharifullah, a very new and shiny black handbag on her arm, visibly restrained herself, tensely.

In a moment Mr Sharifullah – Dr Sharifullah – barked at his daughter, 'Where are your manners?' he said. 'Shake the kind gentleman's hand. Say you're pleased to meet him – this is the gentleman who is going to find us somewhere lovely to live. There. Good girl. She knows how to behave.'

'Just a little shy,' Mrs Sharifullah said.

'Very understandable,' Mr Lydgate said.

'You see,' Carole said later, 'they can speak English as well as they like, none of that sing-song, but they'll never be English, will they? No English father would have spoken to his daughter like that when she was a bit slow with you, Graham. As soon as they're behind closed doors, he'll be beating his daughter with a paddle, and the wife, too. She knows her place, you could tell.'

'Carole,' Graham said, 'you're entitled to your views, but as long as Mr and Mrs Sharifullah and their tribe are customers of ours, I would be very grateful if you would shut your cake-hole on the blessed subject. Say those things in front of the wrong people and you'll find yourself tarred with the brush of a racist.'

Carole stared. 'Racist? How can I be racist? I was talking about them. They're Indian, aren't they? I wasn't talking about black people at all. Racist, indeed.'

'Be that as it may,' Graham Lydgate said. He did hope that the Sharifullahs weren't going to be difficult and protracted customers, nevertheless.

2.

Who would have thought – Nazia said, with some amusement, in the evenings, when Aisha had been put to bed and they were reading the newspapers in the lounge of the Hallam Towers Hotel – who would have thought that moving to a new country was as complicated as all that?

Sharif would laugh. He saw the point – he always had. There was such a relief of tension in the decision to move to England, to come back to Sheffield, that the endless meetings and applications and issues had the capacity to astonish them. They hadn't the faintest idea, any of these people they were meeting, where Nazia and Sharif had come from, or why. They all had a cousin in a keep-fit class who had neighbours from India, very nice people called Banerjee, or a difficult name that the speaker wouldn't attempt. Or was it from Uganda they had come?

Nazia did think that one day she might explain why they had come here. There was a lady in the black sandstone building in the centre of the city, the council's education department. She had paused when naming the school where they were going to live. Would it really suit Aisha, she wondered, before suggesting a school that would take a two-mile drive, anyone could see. 'No,' Nazia would have liked to say. 'We didn't come here because we thought the schools might be better. We came here because we couldn't see any kind of future for people like us in the country where we were born.

'Yes,' Nazia might have gone on. 'Kind of you to ask. The country's called Bangladesh – at least, that's what it's called now, has been for the last five years.'

To the GP who registered them, now that the house in Lodge Moor was bought, she would have wanted to say a few things, too. He hadn't liked it that she was moving to England pregnant. 'It wasn't in the plans,' Nazia would have said. 'I don't know what happened. Perhaps it was moving to England. And stability! Did I mention why we decided we had to move? It was

Bangabandhu being murdered. The Friend of Bengal? The man who founded our country? They broke into his house and they killed him and all his family.

'What's that got to do with … Well, I suppose we looked at the sort of people who are in charge now, and it didn't seem to us that – I know! It sounds terrible! But you should see those colonels and generals and those people in charge. You might be interested to hear my brother's in general practice in Bombay. A public-health specialist. He's doing very well there. Emigration, it's in the family.'

Or to the people from the Home Office – the permission to work had been granted, everything was in order, thanks to the university, so she did not quite know why they had to have an interview with the authorities. She supposed one day they would start the process to lose the new green Bangladeshi passports and gain solid old blue British ones. He was very interested in what family there was remaining out there, even in Rumi's details. She was not going to write to her brother Rumi in Bombay and suggest that he should up sticks and move to Sheffield to start his illustrious career all over again. She had to explain this.

'There is my husband's mother,' she had said. 'His father died last year. She wouldn't come to England. And two sisters, in the middle of their education.'

'How do you know your husband's mother would never come to England?' the little man had said, shuffling his papers in their drab-blue folder, not looking either of them in the face. He had accepted that Nazia would be talking on behalf of Sharif, who sat there still, not contributing.

Nazia would have liked to answer that question honestly. 'Look,' she might have said. 'My husband's brother was taken away from her by the Pakistanis and probably tortured to death. His mother went to the police station every day for a year or more, long after the Pakistanis had been thrown out. She knows he must be dead. His body is somewhere in Bangladesh. She doesn't know what happened to him at the end. Do you think anything on earth would get her to leave the land where younger-son's body is lying before she knows where he is and how he died? Do you think anything would persuade her to come to the country where the son-in-law responsible for his death now lives in peace and prosperity?'

But she did not say any of that. 'No,' she would have liked to say to the kind receptionist at the hotel. 'We do have relations in this country, in fact. My husband's sister, her name is Sadia. Her husband is Mahfouz. They live in London, I believe, but we don't see them. They moved here in 1972, to live with an old uncle who was already living here.

'Why did they move here? I think they thought if they stayed in Bangladesh, Mahfouz would be sent to prison or shot. My husband's brother was killed, as I mentioned, and Mahfouz arranged that. His name was Rafiq. Mohammed Rafiqullah. Like my husband's name is Mohammed Sharifullah, but he is called Sharif. It's complicated, I know. We think of Rafiq every day. And there was a nice boring old man who lived with Sharif's parents, he was killed as well. He was just a professor at the university. He was in Sharif's department, not his boss, but his friend, in fact. He was Professor Anisul! Silly old man. What was the point of killing him, shooting him in the head in a butcher's yard and leaving him there? Well, ask Mahfouz what the point was.

'No, there was a war. It was a war of independence. It was in 1971 – didn't you hear about it? No? You've always longed to go to India, though, and see the Taj Mahal?'

They were good people. She didn't say any of that.

'Here we are,' Sharif would say, when they were alone together, in his doleful way. 'Among the savages.'

'It's not as bad as all that,' Nazia said. 'But the government changed, and Mahfouz and Sadia escaped here. And then the government changed again and we escaped here too. We're exactly the same.'

'Except that we haven't killed anyone,' Sharif said. 'Those people –'

'I know,' Nazia said. Those people were now in charge, the ones who had killed every writer, every poet, every academic, every professor they could lay their hands on, in those last terrible days in 1971. Those people were now going to be running the University of Dacca, deciding where budgets were to go, deciding what would be taught and who would be teaching it. 'So here we are, among the savages.'

In his little office, the little man from Immigration shuffled the papers in his blue folder again and said, 'So your husband's family, if I can get this straight – there is a mother, who you say wouldn't move to England, and two younger sisters. These are all in Bangladesh. Anyone else?'

'My husband's younger brother is dead,' Nazia said quickly.

'And so not of interest to us,' the official said. 'And no other brothers or sisters?'

'No,' Nazia said. She and Sharif had agreed this, and she could stick to it. He had two sisters, not three, and no brother-in-law at all, until Dolly or Bina should decide to marry.

3.

After dinner, in the lobby of the Hallam Towers Hotel, Nazia looked up from her knitting – it was more for something to occupy her hands than to produce anything, and she was only emitting a scarf in purple and green stripes, at best. They had been half watching an English couple with untouched glasses of what must be brandy in front of them, their eyes bright, their hands running up and down the other's thigh, and when they talked, they brought their lips to the other's ear and whispered. The woman clapped her hands to her mouth in a performance of shock and astonishment; she smiled with satisfaction. Soon they would go upstairs. Nazia put her knitting down and looked, sensibly, at her husband. He was reading a novel by Alistair MacLean; he lowered that in response.

'What about love?' Nazia said. 'It seems an awful waste of time to me.'

'Oh, you're there, are you?' Sharif said. 'Taking advantage of it. It won't be much longer.'

'What do you mean?' Nazia said.

'It won't be much longer that Aisha goes to bed before we do,' Sharif said. 'Only a very few more years and she'll be going to bed when we do. No more hours between goodnight-Aisha and lights-out.'

'I suppose so,' Nazia said. 'But I don't see –'

'You said you didn't really know about love. They know about love.'

'Those two?' Nazia said, looking at the amorous couple on the sofa. 'I don't think they know anything about love. I think it's just what they call it.'

'We know what the secret of love is, and it's not the hearts and flowers, the chocolates and kissing type of love. Is that it?'

'I was thinking about Sadia.' She had not mentioned the name of Sharif's sister or her husband since the day they had been told, four years before, that Sadia and Mahfouz had left the country and moved to England. Mother had told them this; she had told them in a blank, neutral, un-expanding way, and that had been the end of it. Father had not mentioned her name for the whole of the rest of his life. 'I was thinking of the things that love made Sadia do.' She and Sharif, their love was tea at blood temperature.

'You'd prefer Grandfather and his two wives. I think they were told they were to marry him and to take their dowries, that he was a good person and would not hit them and would lead a distinguished life.'

'But in the end that was love too.'

'I don't know,' Sharif said. 'Look at those people. It's like a fight. They can't keep their hands from each other – Look, look where she's going with her right hand!'

'Husband,' Nazia said, with some amusement.

'And they're going,' Sharif said. The flushed pair had picked themselves up, and now with a key jauntily swinging from the man's right hand, they walked hand in hand towards the lifts. Margot the receptionist looked up from behind her counter, a paper in her right hand, and smiled in an artificial, disapproving way. 'I don't believe they've signed for their dinner.'

'That isn't love,' Nazia said. 'There's another word for that.'

'Or perhaps they signed when they were still at the table. That must be it. There's too much going on about love here,' Sharif said. 'Have you noticed? All their books are about falling in love. Has she found the right man? Is the right man going to marry the right woman? Does the man investigating the crime have a happy marriage, are they in love, are they still in love, how does he show it – my God it goes on. All that worry, and a lot of going on about love. Not this.' He waved Alistair MacLean. 'This one, not so much.'

'People are going to ask whether we're still in love,' Nazia said composedly. 'After thirteen years or whatever it is. We had our honeymoon period, and then Aisha was born, and then it was all about her.'

'What about the Lump?' Sharif said. 'I hope they notice the Lump and come to the conclusion that something must have caused it. I don't know whether I want to call it love. Love was the thing that got my sister to stand by her husband when he killed Rafiq – as good as killed Rafiq. It sent Mother off to stand outside the Ramna police station day in and day out. She would have been better to be a cat with a missing kitten. She would have wandered about for a day, or two days, looking for the kitten that wasn't there any more.'

'When I die,' Nazia said, 'I want you to be utterly and completely destroyed by misery. When I die in childbirth, perhaps, of the Lump.'

'It might be you that's destroyed by misery,' Sharif said happily. 'I might die first. And Aisha growing up in all of this.'

'There's nothing can be done about that,' Nazia said. 'She is going to see it all, all her little friends that she doesn't know yet talking about love, and thinking that is all that matters.'

'Let us decide that love is not what I feel for you and love is not what you feel for me,' Sharif said.

'I'm sure you felt love for me once upon a time,' Nazia said, with tranquil pleasure. 'Not enough to arrange to have my brother killed and then expect me to go along with it.'

'Your brother was in Bombay,' Sharif said. 'It would not have been at all easy to arrange. For Mahfouz it was straightforward. Rafiq was close at hand. Look what love does! It makes me talk about Rafiq, and it makes me blame my sister.'

'If you are killed by the Friendly Ones,' Nazia said, 'I promise I will go through the correct procedures to address the wrong. But there are no Friendly Ones in Sheffield.'

'These people,' Sharif said. He made a small gesture at the lobby: the woman they had termed Madame Brezhnev, the small old couple who resembled each other so, today's gentleman with a briefcase, the family on a celebration, and all the rest, including the head waiter, who they thought was called Ian, and the receptionist Margot and her husband, the one who looked like a pale fish, now coming into the lobby as he did every night, to collect her. Fishface, there with his car keys. 'If they knew what we were saying, how they would stare.'

'Well, we don't need to say it again,' Nazia said.

Sharif looked at her with relief. He could not say what was in his mind when he thought of her, and the Lump, and of love. How could it be that he had felt only excitement and promise when the last one was born? His mind contemplated the Lump, and it filled with terror and possible disasters. The child, yet to be born, might decide to stand in the eaves of a house and from above and behind a tile might fall, slicing its head in half; a child not yet born seeing a balloon in the road, running out, hit by a fast truck and its father behind on the pavement; a child underneath darkening skies, letting go of its father's hand and being struck by lightning, struck dead in front of him ... These thoughts of catastrophe filled Sharif's mind. He dwelt on disaster, as if he knew that the child would be born but would not live long. His failures were many. The last one could be taken back, that was the thing: Aisha was born in England but was not meant to stay there. The Lump that was coming to be born would be born in England and would stay in England and the disasters that were about to happen – ah, there was no escape from them with a passport, none at all. They would speak in English and have Sharifullah as their surname, an ordinary unchanging English surname. After that it was up to them.

4.

The university had been wonderful. They had sorted everything out and had virtually initiated the idea of Sharif returning to Sheffield. Sharif had always said with joy that Sheffield University's faculty of engineering was, as far as he was concerned, the best faculty in the world. They had found – almost created – a readership for Sharif in material science. He could not believe it when the letter came from his friend Roy. After the usual chatty business about family and the hiking club and university politics, he had wondered whether Sharif had ever thought of coming back. They had collaborated on three or four papers in the last ten years, and were quite close to getting a publisher for a book introducing undergraduates to material science. It had all been done by correspondence so far, but the book would get done much more quickly if they were in the same place. The university might produce a post for Sharif and do all the heavy lifting, as Roy put it, about immigration and other dull things. A senior lectureship, he thought, or, with a fair wind behind the proposal, a readership.

Sharif went to tell Father, and without a moment's pause, Father said that he would sell the house in Old Dacca and give them the money to move to England. Sharif stared. The house in Old Dacca was a rambling, shabby old thing that nobody lived in, but that Father had inherited and never did anything about. He explained to Father that, along with the heavy lifting of immigration, the university had proposed that, for the first two or three years, they could live rent-free in the warden's house around the student accommodation.

'No,' Father said. 'It is not necessary. If you do this, you must not start as the object of charity. If I sell the house in Old Dacca, you can buy a house in Sheffield immediately. I don't want my son living on a university campus like a zookeeper.'

If there was some memory in Father's mind of what had happened to people living on university campuses three years before, he did not say. Sharif thought it was unlikely that the family living in the warden's house at the university in Sheffield would be dragged out and shot.

The house was sold; the money was transferred; and Father died, one Saturday afternoon while the girls were reading to each other, the sunlight outside dappling the lawn under the little orchard. He raised his hand to his head; he called for Khadr – but Khadr was long gone – he said he was struck by a great headache, perhaps he needed to lie down. A wet towel was brought and placed over his forehead, and in half an hour, while Mother was just deciding that a doctor should be called, he died. He was only fifty-five. In the circumstances, Sharif made no claim on the percentage of the estate he was entitled to: he settled it on Mother, to enable her to go on living where she had always lived.

The money from the house sale was eight thousand pounds, in English money, with their savings. They could buy a pleasant house with four thousand pounds of deposit on a mortgage. They would furnish it in England, slowly, piece by piece. Nazia thought she would take the two good carpets and a box of Bengali books. That was all. English beds were so good! And English chairs and sofas – but not all at once. Sharif had persuaded the university that, rather than pay for the shipping of furniture, it would be more useful if they paid for them to stay in a good hotel for six weeks while their house was bought and prepared. How long could it take to find a house?

On her first day in her new home, Nazia went to the front window and looked out onto her street. The road was a cul-desac, an extended half-circle of similar houses. 'I live in Sycamore Close,' Nazia said. 'Number seven.' Out of the window, she could see four houses in yellowish brick, each with a front garden. Three were close-cut grass with some kind of flower – a rose growing up a pole, a bed of something white and pink, a little circle of what must be tulips in the centre of the lawn – and the fourth, strangely, had a miniature mountain range, a pile of rocks with heather arranged artistically over it. The houses were similar; the large, bright windows were shadowed with net curtains, and in the upper room of each house, a dark shape behind the net curtain must be a piece of bedroom furniture of some sort – a dressing-table? She wondered how her house would look from the other side; dark, empty windows, or a lightbulb hanging unadorned in the empty space. The glass shook with a blast of cold wind outside, a mutter of drum. Against the back of her hand a breath of the cold air came. There were no bars on the windows. The expanse of glass knew that nobody was going to throw a stone through it. Now they were in England and they would have to put away the things that had kept their minds going for so long.

Aisha had been walking about the house, now that it had been decided which bedroom was hers and which Mummy and Daddy's, and which would, in the end, be the new baby's when he or she was a little older. She had wanted the bedroom at the front, looking out. Now she thundered downstairs and ran to her mummy.

'There's a lovely wardrobe, with a shelf I'm going to save for shoes,' she said. 'And my books can go on the shelf over where my bed's going to go. They won't fall off in the night. When is my bed coming?'

'That's what we're waiting for,' Nazia said. 'They said some time today. But it might not be until this afternoon. They can't phone us. We're waiting for the Post Office to connect us again.'

Sharif was going around the house, bleeding the radiators one by one. It was something that gave him a lot of pleasure, the hiss and whistle of approaching catastrophe, the rise and rumble of the water within and, just in time, the turn of the key and silence from the safely enclosed metal block. He had learnt how in England, before. What was the water inside like? Pond-like and green, or with an unearthly clarity and glow? The water rushed up to Sharif's key and, with an engineer's sureness, he locked it just before anyone could find out. She would have liked to stand by her husband as he lay on his side on the floor, waiting for him to ask to be passed the slightly larger Allen key for this one. The central heating was oil-fired; she hoped it would be as reliable as the vendors had claimed.

'What are Bina-aunty and Dolly-aunty doing now, do you think?' Aisha said.

Nazia turned and gave her daughter a kiss on the top of her head. 'They're probably finishing their dinner just about now, and asking Granny if they can get down, because Bina-aunty's going to have work to do from her course, and they're probably saying to each other, I wonder what Aisha's doing now, over there in England.'

'Why are they eating their dinner?' Aisha said. 'It's only – Oh, I remember, it's different, the time in Dacca, I keep forgetting.'

'Don't you remember when we got off the plane and it was five o'clock in the afternoon in London and we'd been on the plane for twelve hours, but it had been nearly lunchtime when we got on?'

'I sort of remember,' Aisha said gravely. 'But I just thought it was a little bit strange, like other things when we got off the plane. Look, Mummy – who's that?'

It was a mother and daughter, emerging from the house almost opposite. They were dressed in light spring clothes, the mother in a thin and pale green cotton raincoat, open at the front, the daughter, who must have been about Aisha's age, in a flowery dress with white patent sling-backs. They shut the door behind them. Aisha and her mother must have been visible from the street, because the girl pointed at them in their window, saying something to her mother. The mother looked, screwing up her eyes to make sure of seeing; Nazia hesitantly raised her hand in some sort of greeting. But the mother turned her head away, and the pair scurried off. The daughter looked behind her as she went, allowing her hand to be taken by her mother.

'I thought they would bring a cake over to welcome us,' Aisha said. 'That's what happened in Nancy Drew. They took a cake over to the new neighbours, but the new neighbours wouldn't –'

'That would have been in America,' Nazia said. 'I don't know that people bring cakes round in England.'

'It's because they haven't seen a van with all our things in.'

'Maybe,' Nazia said. At some point the neighbours would realize that the house was filling with deliveries, that they could now come round and say hello. She wondered whether it would be with a cake, or not. From upstairs a triumphant hiss, like a factory whistle, crescendoed, formed a note, was abruptly silenced. If the van from the department store would only arrive, they could all go to bed; the beds, the brown three-piece suite, the coffee-table, the two bookcases, the dining table and six chairs, the desk for upstairs, the bedside tables – really, Nazia could not remember it all. It had been such a burst of purchasing, she felt now she need never go into a shop ever again.

5.

Aisha had been going to school for nearly three weeks when she was invited to her first party. She came into the sitting room one afternoon, having dropped her satchel at the end of the stairs. Nazia had some forms spread out across the new Swedish coffee-table; it was not ideal to work on, circular and segmented into three glass slices by polished maple. But the desk they had ordered for the upstairs office had not arrived yet. It was a slow race to the finishing post between the man who kept promising the desk, and the Post Office, who seemed surprised that she might want to have a telephone in her house at all. She was trying to work out what needed to be supplied to the council for the regular payment of rates, and looked up at her daughter with pleasure and relief.

Aisha hovered. She had run from the bus and had been running all day; her warm smell was milky and girlish and something bland and meaty Nazia could not identify, the smell of food from outside, the food that the school gave them that Aisha had said straight away she really liked. She had a piece of paper in her hand, and stood like a pupil in the head teacher's office.

'How was your day?' Nazia said. 'Nice day at school?'

'Can I go to a party?' Aisha said. 'A girl at school asked me to her birthday party. It's on Saturday afternoon. Mummy, I don't know what I've got to wear to a party. I can't wear …'

Strangely enough, Aisha put her face in her hands. It might have been an adult performance of despair, done to amuse, but her shoulders began to judder. Nazia should have felt relieved. She had ignored the half-expressed advice of the office worker that Aisha would feel more at home at some other school where (Nazia concluded) new arrivals could be dumped, where Urdu was heard in the playground and hopes were not raised. Three weeks before, she had taken Aisha to the school that was nearest, the one that was normal to go to. She had sat in the upstairs office of the headmaster, a man no older than Sharif, and had watched his eyes go from one of them to the other, rubbing his hands in what might be enthusiasm and, surely, speaking a little more slowly, a little more loudly about the large family at Latchworthy Middle, about Class 2 Mg and lovely Mrs Morgan, about welcoming Aisha to that family and helping her feel at home (*at home*, as if it were a rare and probably unfamiliar idiom to Nazia, who suppressed the irritated reflection that she had a first-class degree in English literature and had written her dissertation on Dryden's tragedies). He had made no allusion to their being anything but English until almost the very end. 'Are

there any special dietary requirements we should be aware of?'
he said.

'No, no,' Nazia said. 'She eats anything.' They had no
particular religion. With a cheerful and not a lingering look,
Nazia had let Aisha go and walked back towards the exit. She
could not dawdle or peer too much, but it did appear to her
that every room she looked into was a roomful of English children. She corrected herself: white children. This was not a
matter of nationality, but of race, and in time she would be
British, Sharif would be British, Aisha would be British and
certainly the Lump would emerge as brown as any of them but
would be nothing but British from the start, whatever humanity
surrounded them.

Only three weeks later at least one girl in her class had
decided she liked her well enough to invite her to her ninth
birthday party. Nazia wondered she had ever doubted it. Her
daughter was a little pet in the family, a little love to half the
doctors' wives of Dhanmondi, with dozens of friends her own
age, the judges' twin granddaughters, the daughters of the
professor of physics, who had married late, the little girl called
Rita, the one called Baby and the other called Sweetie. Perhaps
Sharif had been right: people only saw the colour of someone's
skin from a distance. With a start, Nazia realized that she had
been doing what she had forbidden herself to do, comparing
the past to their life here, in the slowly filling house in Lodge
Moor with the wind whistling and banging against the windows.
In her arms, her daughter was still crying, and all she was crying
for was that she didn't think she had a dress to wear to her new
friend's party.

'There's plenty of time,' Nazia said, rubbing her shoulders.
She took the invitation from Aisha's hand; it was a piece of
paper with balloons and fireworks on it, and Aisha's name,
misspelt as 'Ayeesha' by someone called Wendy. 'Daddy will
drive us into Sheffield, and we will buy you a lovely new dress
for the party. I don't know – maybe I can persuade Daddy to
buy me a new dress to wear to it as well?'

'Mummy,' Aisha said, detaching herself, 'you're not supposed to come. It's Wendy's party.'

'But they're expecting Wendy's friends' mummies and daddies too, I should have thought,' Nazia said.

'It's not like that here!' Aisha shouted. 'You come and you leave me there and then you come back later and take me away again. That's what birthday parties are supposed to be like!'

Nazia checked herself. Birthday parties in Dacca had been all mixed up; in the worst of them, she remembered, the children had sat timidly on sofas while the fathers engaged in dull conversation about grown-up things, and because there were sweets and it was somebody's birthday, it was called a children's party. Of course things were not like that here.

They had fled from the military dictators, and now she saw they were justified in doing so: their daughter's worries were that they might not get a children's party right. Safety.

And then the invitations started to flow, one almost every week for Aisha. One day she came home with three separate invitations, going forward almost a month into the future. It was so nice that she had friends, and that Susan, Marian and Katy were including her in their weekend lives. It might be that she was the first person they had ever met who did not look like them; they would remember her. Nazia knew what it had been like to be that age, and when the second invitation arrived, she took Aisha to the shops again, not telling Sharif, and bought her two other party dresses. One of them was in denim, but very smart, and Aisha had begged for it; the dress in Cole Brothers that Nazia had thought lovely, a very sweet gingham dress with puffed lace at the shoulders, Aisha had pulled a face and had only tried on at all under duress. Aisha had two beautiful salwar khameez in silver and pale mauve. They would probably never be seen again.

'Do you think she had a good time?' Sharif asked once, as she returned one Saturday afternoon from one of these parties.

'She had a lovely time,' Nazia said firmly. The mother had smiled so sweetly, saying goodbye to them, and Aisha knew how to behave better than her parents did. She had picked up a set phrase at goodbye, 'Thank-you-for-having-me', though Nazia thought that she said it with too much feeling, not rattling it off sourly, like the other little girls. The rest of the guests departed in twos and threes; the mothers seemed to know each other, had been to school with each other, to drop in and out of conversations that had started and been suspended days before. Aisha left with her mother, not looking back, holding the slice of birthday cake wrapped in a paper napkin. 'Did you not eat a slice at the party?' Nazia asked, but Aisha shook her head. Everyone asked for a slice to take home. Sharif had once picked up Aisha. In truth, he later admitted, he was concerned that Aisha was the only one to be picked up by a mother on foot. He had put on his tweed jacket and a tie, and driven off in the new Vauxhall. But he had been greeted by a look of such horror and humiliation on his daughter's face, suspended in a world of mothers and daughters, that he never suggested it again. There was no escaping the wrong thing, or so it seemed. Nazia had found herself isolated from the other mothers, not just by her pedestrian arrival and departure, and was held at arms' length by polite smiles and the carefully enunciated compliments to little Aisha, how charming she was and how happy they were to have her. Dismissed. It would take time, she knew, and driving lessons. It would have been just the same – Sharif's point again – if a white German family had moved into a house in Dhanmondi and expected their children to be included in everything.

Now Sharif's daughter appeared to be the most popular member of the family there had ever been, but of course he would want to make sure that she took some pleasure in it. 'The first we hear about any of these girls,' Sharif said, lowering his voice, 'is when one of them sends an invitation. Are they truly her friends? I hope things are all right for her at that school.'

'Well,' Nazia said, 'it's her birthday next month. She can have her own party.'

'No mishti doi and no jelapi and no biryani and no fish to eat …'

'I know,' Nazia said, amused. 'Imagine a birthday party without any fish. I am going to ask my daughter to tell me what her party should consist of, and I am going to do it absolutely correctly, to the letter. I am ahead of you by some distance.'

'They could play kumir danga, at least,' Sharif said. 'I used to adore kumir danga, I longed to be the crocodile. I was so good at it. They would love it.'

'Let them have their own little games,' Nazia said. 'If Aisha heard you talking about kumir danga or shaat chara or any of those old street games, she would be mortified. They can play pass-around-the-box if they want to.'

'Pass the parcel, I believe,' Sharif said, laughing.

6.

It had taken a number of months, but the Post Office now assured Dr Mohammed Sharifullah that the telephone line at number seven, Sycamore Close would be connected on 9 April. They might have said reconnected, since the previous owners had disconnected the same number before moving out. Dr Sharifullah himself was under no doubt that they merely had to perform a simple step. Nazia said that they ought to insist on being 'Dr' Sharifullah to the Post Office. Dr Sharifullah had thought it would be more effective to mention that his wife was pregnant. But 9 April came, and 9 April went, and still the telephone produced nothing but a dull enclosed silence when picked up.

The next morning, Nazia sent Sharif and Aisha off after breakfast, and determined that she would, without fail, take the 51 bus down to the Post Office in the centre of Sheffield and demand to know what was happening. But she was just about to put her coat and hat on when the unexpected happened: a curious, repeated warble, like a drowning bird. It was, astonishingly, the noise that the telephone would make if it ever worked.

She picked the receiver up – looked at it, a foot from her face – brought it suspiciously to her ear.

'Hello?' she said.

'You're supposed to say your number!' the voice at the other end said. 'In this country, you answer and you say what your number is!'

'Who is this?' Nazia said, amazed. 'Not Rekha? Is this Rekha?'

Rekha laughed, her big gurgling laugh. 'Of course,' she said. 'Am I your first telephone call?'

In the months they had been waiting for the telephone to be connected, Sharif had sometimes tetchily asked who they had to telephone in any case. Recently, Nazia had been able to answer that it would be useful to be able to telephone some of these mothers, to ask what time it would be appropriate to collect Aisha. But at first and for a number of weeks Nazia had only been able to answer that it would be nice to be able to telephone the people who were supposed to be delivering the beds, or the three-piece suite, or the television, and nicer still to be able to telephone Rashed and Rekha, over there in Manchester.

Rashed and Rekha had been in England for years now. Nazia remembered their wedding in Dacca, but they had left very soon afterwards; Rashed, like her brother Zahid, had been a solicitor but now worked in local government. Rekha, now, had trained in England as a librarian. They had been good friends to Nazia and Sharif when they were here before, Sharif finishing his doctorate and Nazia having her baby at the same time, more or less, as Rekha having her second. Little Bobby was already in school, a beautifully turned-out child who would never deign to muddy himself or even run for a bus. People said that your life was changed by having children, and of course it was, but the alteration in routine and interests was surely complemented by a more outward-facing change, that you felt admitted to the part of the world that knew what it was to feel responsible for another soul.

Together they moved onwards with their babies, Rekha sometimes offering advice or reassurance, Nazia feeling protected and a little superior and saved from selfishness. Rekha had become huge with Fanny and afterwards remained plump, puffing up the stairs, a sweet little yellow bun of a person where Nazia had bulged, neatly, containedly, then melted back to the person she had been. Once a month they tried to see each other, Rashed and Rekha, who had a car, a white Morris Traveller with picturesque wooden insets, lumbering over the Pennines. Baby Fanny was on Rekha's lap, Bobby in the back seat. They had been happy times, sitting in the dank sitting room of the flat over the newsagent's, crowing when Fanny took her first steps across the carpet (or were they? Was Rashed in his kindness just making sure that they felt special in their cousins' lives by witnessing this?). Fanny and Aisha would always be great friends, there was no doubt about that; they were second cousins, and they sat up, side by side, and embarked on their own parallel courses of investigation.

Nazia had managed to call Rekha two or three times since they'd arrived, from the phone box at the end of the road, and they had exchanged postcards, too, but she had looked forward to this conversation – a real one, over her own telephone.

'... and a television set, and a radio for the kitchen, and, oh, you can't imagine, so many things a house has to contain,' Nazia said. 'We hardly brought anything from Dacca.'

'I don't blame you,' Rekha said. 'When we came, Rashed's mother insisted on us bringing everything, and the shipping cost a fortune, and it was all wrong when it finally arrived, and – Well, that was fifteen years ago and I don't think we've got a single thing remaining. It's all from English shops now. Rashed's mother, in every letter she asks whether her father's buffet table is still as beautiful, but we gave it to Oxfam years ago when we bought a nice new unit. Polished mahogany, it was just – oh, you can imagine. How are your neighbours?'

'It's so nice to speak to you,' Nazia said. 'The neighbours love Aisha – well, their children do, it seems. She's always going to birthday parties.'

'I know!' Rekha said. 'Those birthday parties. They are the curse of my existence. Every week, an invitation for Fanny, an invitation for Bobby, every week a present or two presents to buy – the awful junk! But this is what I was telephoning about. I don't know how it is, but there isn't a party this week, on Saturday. And I said to Rashed that we might come over and visit you.'

'Oh, Rekha,' Nazia said. 'You don't know how happy I feel about that. You'll be so horrified when you see me, too. I'm twice the size that I was with Aisha.'

Nazia would not treat them as the source of memory and nostalgia. In Dacca she and Sharif had enjoyed their long, languid, nostalgic conversations about catching the number 51 bus, of going to Cole Brothers, of the wind biting just at Barker's Pool outside the City Hall, about faraway Sheffield. Now Nazia could step out of her own front door and walk to the number 51 bus stop, and one would be along in a moment to take her into town. In a month, Sharif had calculated, they would be in a position to buy a new car, and she could start learning to drive. They would not reverse the situation, and now start discussing what they missed about Dacca. Rekha and Rashed and Bobby and Fanny were part of this new world, and they were part of the best of it.

'I can't wait,' she said, when Sharif and Aisha were home. 'It was so nice to hear cousin's voice on the telephone, and so near-sounding. Do you remember cousin Fanny, Aisha? You were such friends when you were tiny.'

'Mummy,' Aisha said. 'Caroline's having a party. I said I would go. I promised.'

'But, Fanny, child,' Nazia said. 'You see Caroline all week, and Fanny you haven't seen in years. Your cousin!'

'But I promised!'

'Well, that's quite all right,' Sharif said, in his generous way. 'I have the perfect solution. It's unfair if there's a lovely party going on and you can't go to it. So I'll phone – no, Mummy will phone Caroline's mummy and ask if it would be all right if

Aisha came to the party with her cousin Fanny, since she's going to be here. Bobby won't mind staying on his own, I'm sure.'

'That would be perfect,' Nazia said, clapping her hands. 'That solves everything. We'll come and pick you up at five, and all the boring grown-up talk will have happened.'

Aisha had acquired an expression of complete horror. Her knife and fork were frozen in mid-air. 'Mummy,' she said. 'You can't do that. No one ever brings their cousin to a party. They would think you were mental even asking.'

'They would think –'

'They would think you were mental,' Aisha said. 'Oh, you know what I mean, crazy, mad. Please don't.'

'Well,' Nazia said. Her daughter was in a position to instruct her in detail about correct behaviour. 'Shall I phone Caroline's mummy and explain that, unfortunately, you can't come?'

'No, Mummy,' Aisha said. 'I've got to go. I've promised Caroline.'

'So,' Sharif said slowly, but there was a hint of amusement in his voice at these tiny dilemmas, 'you don't want to take cousin Fanny and you don't want to stay at home to spend time with her here? You want to say goodbye to them and go off on your own to your friend Caroline's party?'

'Please don't,' Aisha said, almost on the verge of tears.

'Don't you think that poor Fanny would be very upset that you don't want to spend time with her?' Nazia said. But she felt that even in asking Aisha's opinion she had taken an important step. Aisha, strangely enough, won this competition over the course of two days, and even stranger, Rekha and Rashed humbly accepted the decision. It really didn't matter, Rekha assured them. Everyone understood. So they came over as early as they could; they had lunch together, shouting and laughing and not agreeing at all about anything, not even whether this was hot weather or not. Bobby delighted them with his beautiful manners, saying that he was simply delighted to meet his cousins again after such a time. And Aisha went upstairs and put on her new party dress and came down to be admired. Her father took her off, a gift-wrapped cube in hand, and came back to find Fanny reading a book in a corner. He made a fuss of her and soon it was all right. It was a lovely day.

7.

There were eleven houses in Sycamore Close. Three on either side of the road where it ran straight, and five around the wide circle that it bulged out into at the end. They knew the other four houses in the circle. There was the older couple, and there were the parents with the daughter who had peered into the house on the first day. Next door, to the left, there was a family with two teenage daughters – one Sunday afternoon one of them had stuck her head out of the window and shouted into the quiet street, 'I hate you!' Who? Perhaps she was saying that she hated Sycamore Close, Lodge Moor, Sheffield, or England. Or perhaps she was shouting at her mother. To the right there was a single man who had an executive job of some sort; his shoes shone brilliantly, his suit was pinstriped, his briefcase was black and plastic, with a leather finish. He had a small dog, a white one with an intelligent face called Rosie. His was the only household in the close that had a servant of any sort, an older woman who came twice a week and let herself in, apparently to clean. For some time Nazia wondered whether this woman might be the man's mother.

They had reached the point of nodding and smiling when they left the house at the same time as another household. Most of them nodded and smiled back. Some of them pretended not to see – well, there were always going to be the friendly ones and the ones who looked away. Even to the friendly ones they hadn't quite managed to introduce themselves, however, and Nazia wondered whether it was because of that that the friendliness appeared to be dying away as the weeks passed. Once she caught the husband in the older couple pausing as he unlocked his car, staring for a good twenty seconds at their house with a cross frown. He shook his head, a performance of disapproval, before getting into his car.

The mother of the teenagers was leaving the house at the same time as Sharif one morning. She was unlocking her car, sleepless worry on her face, and came across to the little wall that separated her front garden from Sharif and Nazia's. It was perhaps her standing there that made him see all of a sudden the cause of the disapproval: the grass on her side of the wall was trimmed neatly short. But on their side, they had done nothing to the grass or to the garden since they had moved in, now three months ago, and it was long and unruly. The mother of the teenagers gestured downwards.

'We shall have to do something about it,' Sharif said. 'It's getting a little out of hand.'

'I think people sometimes forget,' the woman said, 'that it isn't like choosing an ugly wallpaper for your own house. It can have an impact on your neighbours in a direct way. The weeds!'

'Oh, I see,' Sharif said. 'Well, yes, I do see. I am sorry. I'll do something about it immediately.'

'There is so much to do when you first move into a house,' the woman said, in a conciliatory way. Perhaps she was one of the friendly ones, after all.

'Yes, indeed,' Sharif said. He might have said something now about the noise that came from her children's bedroom. He raised his briefcase – brown, leather, soft, the same briefcase he had had for years, since he was a PhD student – to show her that he had something to do and somewhere to go. 'I think we're getting there. If you could recommend the name of a gardener …'

'A gardener?'

'… that would be – I'm not a gardener, I admit.'

'Most of us do our gardening ourselves,' the woman said.

That evening, he mentioned it to Nazia, and she thought that the important thing was to cut the grass in the front and the back garden. It was an expense, but they might need to buy a lawnmower. It was irritating, having just had all the expenses of buying a car, but the alternative was to have the utter disapproval of their neighbours for ever. Where to buy it from? Did Cole Brothers sell them? Or was it those places called garden centres? Sharif enquired from his colleagues in the engineering faculty, and discovered where garden centres could be found, what the different lawnmower models were, and how to decide between them – he liked the sound of a lightweight Flymo – and how to keep your lawn green and neat. It turned out that his English colleagues were all enthusiasts, and knowledgeable. 'Mind you,' Dr Smithers said, 'you won't have to buy yourself a hosepipe to water the lawn just yet, not this year. They're talking about a ban on that and asking you to reuse bathwater. Have you thought about a strimmer, to tidy up the edges?'

The lawnmower was a big success. Nazia and Aisha came out to the front porch to watch Sharif hard at work. He had read the manual carefully, at the dinner table, making little frowns and pencil marks in the margin. Then he came out and opened the garage door. The boxed-up mower was opened, and the parts laid out. Sharif checked them carefully against the instructions, ticking each one off, and then set to work. He was not sentimental about the tools in his toolbox; he had not brought the household tools from Dacca, and these were almost as new as the lawnmower. In an hour, the lawnmower was assembled. He placed the lightweight mower on the edge of the front lawn, and returned to the garage to plug it in. The device started immediately, cutting smoothly. He experimented, swinging the mower to left and right in widening half-circles, but then decided that the best way was the old-fashioned way of walking up and down in parallel stripes. It was fascinating to Nazia and Aisha to watch him at work with his sleeves rolled up. He explained about the cord of the electric mower; he had been told that there was a risk of running over it, unplanned, and severing the connection dangerously. He went over the lawn twice, as he had been advised; once lightly, and then more aggressively. There was that beautiful smell, the odour of cut grass that he remembered from home, from Dacca. It was like the smell that arose when the rains first fell on grass, but one that could be made, not one that must be waited for. The rule, Dr Smithers had said, was not to try to cut more than a third of the length of each blade of grass with each mowing. The mowing took twenty minutes, and then twenty minutes again. At the end, the lawn was heavily strewn with cut grass, and now Sharif went back to the garage to fetch the rake.

The wife who lived opposite had been watching too, and now she came across, smiling. 'My husband will be ever so pleased,' she said. 'He's been wondering for weeks – when are those new people going to do something about the grass?'

'Yes,' Nazia said. 'We were continually putting it off.'

'Much longer than that, and you would have had to cut it with a scythe. That's what my husband said. I suppose the next thing you'll be wanting to do is perhaps weed the flowerbeds,' the woman said, her smile dropping. 'Or maybe you'll pay someone to do that for you.' So she had discussed it with the mother of the teenagers. Now she turned away and bustled back to her house without introducing herself. The flowerbeds in the front were not as trim as they could be; some of those plants had no right to be there at all. And Sharif was quite enthusiastic, now, about the garden: he went down to the garden centre the very same afternoon, saying he was going to plant some tulips. But the season was wrong, and he would have to come back after September, he learnt. Nazia had managed to get back into the house and into her bedroom, closing the door behind her, before she started to cry. It was the tone of the woman's voice that had done it.

Aisha's birthday was in June, four weeks before her school broke up for the summer holidays. It had not occurred to either of them that what they needed was a holiday. Nazia's babies would be born in July. Mandy, her midwife, had observed with a jollity that must have been meant as encouragement that she was having twins, how about that? She had distinctly felt two skulls and two bottoms. In Bangladesh, they would probably have gone to the village for a month to show the children off. Aisha's holiday suggestion of Spain (her classmates' preferred destination) would have to start next year. This year, they were going to stay at home in an unplanned way, and perhaps drive out during the day, to see the countryside. Nazia might be able to manage a birthday party for Aisha, to say thank you to all her friends who had been inviting her along almost from the beginning.

But Aisha at first was not very willing. They were astonished. Of course she must have a birthday party! But they had made the suggestion at the dinner table, and Aisha in response gestured downwards, at her plate. 'Oh, Mummy,' she said. 'I can't think of anything more boring. I really don't want to have a birthday party. Just me and you two and maybe Caroline – she could come to the pictures or something.'

But there had to be a party! There were so many debts, and so many people had been so kind to Aisha that they had to be asked back. Nazia promised Aisha that she would absolutely definitely not have the twins in the middle of the party. She could see that that would be a worry to poor Aisha. Sharif reassured her that no grown-ups would come, no one from the engineering department, no one from Manchester, no one apart from as many friends as she wanted to ask.

'Eight,' Aisha said. 'You have eight friends to a party.'

She spoke promptly, and now that it was agreed upon, she began on the instructions. Her thoughts and memories came haphazardly, and over the next day or two Nazia kept reaching for the pad of paper to make notes of what an English birthday party consisted of.

'Chipolatas,' Aisha said.

'Chipolatas, what are they? I never heard of them.'

'Sausages, cooked but cold,' Aisha said. 'You have to have chipolatas! And a gift bag and –'

Nazia was unsure, but she went on: 'And a birthday cake? Surely you want a birthday cake?'

'Yes, a nice one with a theme, or perhaps just with icing, very very lovely, with roses on the top. Then you give people a slice and they take it home in a paper napkin. You don't eat it there.'

'Yes, I know!' Nazia said, triumphant. She knew perfectly well: at every party Aisha had been to, she had emerged from the throng bearing a slice of cake wrapped in a napkin, tenderly, like a present, the gift bag dangling negligently from a finger.

'And you get to play games,' Aisha said. 'But they aren't the games that you play in the playground or normal games or anything like that. They're pass-the-parcel with a present inside.'

'Oh, yes, I know,' Nazia said.

'But at Charlotte's there was a present on every layer so everyone got something, that was lovely,' Aisha said. 'And her dad taking the needle off the gramophone. We haven't got a gramophone! How are we going to play pass the parcel? And the gift bag. In the gift bag you have to have –'

'We will arrange it all,' Nazia said. 'And what other games?'

'Hide and seek, maybe, and musical chairs, and once we played consequences, but you need pens and paper for that. And then there's birthday tea with chipolatas and vol-au-vents and – and – and … There might be a magician but he was rubbish, he was boring, I don't care about him. Oh, Mummy, what am I going to wear? I need a new party dress.'

'All in good time,' Nazia said. 'You're sure about the magician? Was that at Susan's party? We could find a different one.'

'No, I don't want a magician, it was boring. I could see the bird up his sleeve from the beginning.'

And in fact it was a great success. It was from that afternoon that Nazia's great friendship with Sally Mottishead started, her first English friendship. They were so nervous. Sharif had been persuaded into buying a gramophone for the occasion – coming so soon after the lawnmower, he needed some persuading – and of course they had had to buy five records, too. There was Mozart and Beethoven and *The Carnival of the Animals* and some more classical music played on a Moog synthesizer and the Beatles. And two pop singles, too, Demis Roussos and Elton

John with Kiki Dee singing 'Don't Go Breaking My Heart', which they could have with the Beatles if the girls wanted to dance. It was so hot the day of Aisha's party! The ice-cream was going to stay in the freezer right until the last moment, and Nazia had made a red raspberry jelly rabbit on a bed of green chopped-up jelly (lime) for grass. Sharif had been astonished when he saw that, the night before. Where on earth had she got that idea from? The answer was *100 Ideas for Children's Parties*, bought from Hartley Seed's the week before. It had been full of wonderful suggestions. Chipolatas turned out to be sausages made out of pork. Aisha had insisted. Chipolatas were delicious and the *sine qua non*, as Sharif put it, when they discussed it later. Well, they would serve sausages made out of pork, and Aisha's grandfather would turn in his grave. 'I'm going to eat one,' Sharif said dauntlessly. 'I think I had pork in the canteen once without really noticing.' And there was a schedule of games to play, and a table where presents and cards could be deposited. Aisha was standing at the window saying, 'It's three o'clock, it's three o'clock, I told them to come early, I know no one's going to come at all,' when a purple Astra drew up and out popped little Caroline, and Julie, who lived only three doors away from Aisha's best friend; they didn't much like Julie really. Caroline's mother came out too, to say hello to Aisha's mummy and daddy – it was so nice for them to meet properly! And Caroline and Julie were through the door and exclaiming at Aisha's and their own party dresses just as a second car was pulling up in the close, negotiating its way past Caroline's mummy manoeuvring out. Aisha had gone for a very pretty sort of aquamarine, with a butterfly pattern on it, and white sling-backs. This second car must be Susan. Already Aisha was showing off, and they could hear Elton John and Kiki Dee starting up on the new gramophone. Their house was charming, Susan's mummy was saying, as she came up the path, with Susan almost running ahead, and, my goodness, when are you due? This summer, everyone told them, was the most glorious anyone could remember, and all the little girls who came to Aisha's birthday party would remember it for ever. It was the social climax at the end of term. Sharif and Nazia stood there smiling as the parents came up the path with their little girls, being friendly, and in Nazia's case aching terribly about her swollen ankles and legs. The party was right in every single detail: she was quite sure about that after lengthy study and consultation. Both she and Sharif were wonderfully excited, too, about the surprise presents they were giving their lovely daughter. They were sure she would love them: a junior chemistry set and a harmonium, on which she was going to love to play those old tunes she had always enjoyed.

CHAPTER TWELVE

I.

Most of the university's buildings were clustered around the inner parts of the western suburbs. The central buildings formed a plaza, or piazza, on either side of a dual carriageway; the stately red-brick palace that was the oldest part, the 1950s expansions of library, student union and Arts Tower, with its famous modernist paternoster lift. For most of the faculties, however, the mansions of the Victorian rich had been acquired – very few people since the Second World War had been able to envisage living on that kind of scale, and the houses had often been very good value for money – and restructured into offices, teaching rooms, research facilities. The music faculty was up a very grand road in Broomhill, the former billiard room now an electronics studio and recording space. The engineering faculty had been placed in an immense blackened mansion, the interior parcelled out and opened up, a substantial modern extension replacing the conservatory for more practical purposes of demonstration and experiment. The garden had, it was said, once been six acres. The university had not seen the need for its engineers to stroll about in a leisurely manner between classes, more's the pity (this was Sharif's colleague Steve Smithers's view). Instead they had got their new lecture hall and workshop space built, a little car park, and the rest of the land had been flattened into a pitch and handed over to the university's sportsmen. Lectures at the back of the building were often conducted to the musical accompaniment of whistles, shrieks, cries of pain and yelled profanity, as a football match took its impassioned course.

Sharif loved the faculty. It was a magical place for him, the fantastical ornamental building that had loved his mind. It might have forgotten him when it had sent him back with a doctorate, but had not: it had sent out a modest sort of request and welcomed him back with a morose, abrupt greeting that was how Yorkshire engineers expressed joy. Welcomed him back with a readership and, three years later, a professorship. The promotion had recognized his introductory book on material science with Roy Burns and, true, was offered in order to compete with a formal approach from Imperial. But it needn't have happened. There had been a point, a year in, when the head of department had called him in and said that students had been complaining that he was too abrasive, that he seemed to turn everything into an argument, that he never said, 'I see what you mean.' Sharif was more worried that he would be sacked than expectant of promotion to professor. He was very young for the title, he believed, and now he had a place in the car park.

The place in the car park was by the steel-mesh fence circling the football pitch. He parked the blue Ford Capri and locked it. There were some boys kicking a ball about on the pitch. There was no adult in charge. It was half past eight in the morning. Had the boys of the neighbourhood just found a way in? It was no concern of his. He turned and walked towards the faculty. A teenage boy's raucous voice called out behind him: 'Look at that Paki!' it shouted. 'Look at that fooking Paki with his fooking car! Paki Paki Paki!' Sharif walked on. He would not turn.

He had heard the word before. When he was a PhD student here, he had heard himself and Aisha referred to as 'the Pakis over the newsagent' by the butcher opposite. He had paid no attention and he paid no attention now. He went into the faculty. The pigeon holes were in the same room as the faculty secretary, Mrs Browning, who was frowning at her electric type-writer and gave only a cursory response to his 'Good morning.'

'The children on the sports pitch,' Sharif said.

'The ...' Mrs Browning said. 'Oh, I'm sorry – I was miles away trying to work out what this word's supposed to be. If only everyone had such neat handwriting as you do, Sharif. What was that you were asking?'

'Do you know there are children on the sports pitch? Isn't it just for university use?'

'It's some sort of social-welfare idea they've had,' Mrs Browning said. 'I'm actually ahead of you there. I thought, That's not right, and phoned up the central admin. They've allowed three schools to make use of it during the week. Do you think that could be "Nonterriers", is that a word?'

Sharif went over to look at a letter in Steve Smithers's handwriting.

'Nonferrous, I think,' he said.

'Nonferrous,' Mrs Browning said. 'I wish your colleagues would take especial care to write difficult words clearly. Those children, I think they're from Gower. That's a school. Their sports lesson starts at nine, but they make their own way up here, apparently.'

'I see,' Sharif said. 'Is it going to be every Wednesday, do you know?'

He put it from his mind and certainly did not mention it to Nazia. The twins were nearly four, and exhausting presences, even now they had a big garden behind their stone house in Hillsborough for them to run about in. Nazia liked the Hillsborough house more than their last one, in Lodge Moor. There had been two or three days together, both winters, when there was no possibility of leaving the house, so deeply had the snow fallen. There was, too, the question of the neighbours in Sycamore Close, some of whom had never made any effort to greet or speak to Nazia or Sharif, even the single man next door with the little white dog. 'You just have to accept it,' Sharif said. 'There are the unpleasant ones, who you wouldn't want to know in any case. And then there are the friendly ones. It's always going to be the same.'

And certainly, down here in Hillsborough, the neighbours were more open. Nazia's best friend Sally Mottishead knew some people who lived opposite, and they had introduced them to quite a lot more. When, two months after their moving into the house in Hillsborough, Sharif's little sister Bina arrived, they had been able to take her round and introduce her to half the neighbourhood. She was going to marry this year, and move to Cardiff where her husband-to-be, Tinku, the son of one of Father's student friends from Calcutta, was an industrial chemist. Then the fourth bedroom could be reserved for one of the twins when they grew a little older, or kept for guests. It was impossible to imagine anyone in Myatt Road shouting, 'Paki,' at them, or even thinking it.

The Wednesday following, the same boys were kicking a ball about, and again their attention was drawn by Sharif getting out of his car. He wore a neat tweed jacket and polished brown shoes; a countrified checked shirt with a plain brown tie; his hair was thick and black still at thirty-seven; he was tidy and healthy-looking, his hands small and plump, his face open. He looked, surely, like a professor of material science at an English university, the joint author of a first-year university textbook for students that promised to be indispensable and highly profitable. 'You'll find everything you need to know about ceramics in Sharifullah and Burns,' people were already saying to each other. Here, with his neatly shone shoes, was Sharifullah himself. His skin was unmistakably that of a person whose ancestry was from one part of the world. He did not think many people placed very high importance on that when they met him. But today, and last week, boys preparing to play soccer on the football pitch had shouted the word 'Paki' at him, and laughed when he had walked away towards the safety of the building at a slightly faster pace than was perhaps natural.

He looked Gower School up in the departmental phone book, and noticed that it was in the same postcode as Wincobank, where last year, with the first of the royalties from the textbook, he and Nazia had bought two nearly adjacent terraced houses for almost nothing. They were going to renovate them and rent them out to students. He made a note of the school's general enquiries number, and in his office began to dial it. He hung up, one digit short. There was nothing to be said, and he could not imagine that they would say anything to the children that would have any useful effect.

This time he would say something at home. Wednesday was his heaviest day for work: a lecture and a seminar, and in the afternoon, when they were not supposed to teach by agreement with the Students' Union, Sharif was 'at home' to any student who wanted to drop in. Today, too, one of his PhD students had to be seen to talk over some questions of properties on the nano scale – that was not a chore: that was something potentially rather exciting, Sharif felt. But it meant he did not get home until half past six, and Nazia and Bina were almost at the point of putting the shepherd's pie on the table without him.

He wanted to ask the question as soon as he came through the door, but Nazia would know that it had a cause, and that would affect the answer. He came in, and the boys were sitting on the stairs, as they liked to. Their faces lit up on seeing their daddy. In the sitting room, music was playing: Aisha's latest pop band, a man who performed with a white stripe across his face and a pirate jacket on. Nazia came out of the kitchen to greet him, and Bina behind her. She scolded him that the boys could not wait for ever for their dinner and she had been on the point of putting the dinner on the table without him. Bina, a nice humorous presence in the house, pouted in amusement behind his wife. Sharif asked what was for dinner, although he knew; Nazia said that it was shepherd's pie with peas. 'Did you hear that, boys?' Sharif said, raising his feet delicately over their heads as he went upstairs. 'Shepherd's pie with peas and ketchup.'

'We know, Daddy,' Raja said, but with pleasure and excitement. It was their favourite meal.

He let the conversation go its way. Bina had gone to the library to borrow some books with Nazia's ticket; she had taken the boys with her. Nazia had gone over to Wincobank to see how the building works were going on. Sally had come with her again. The kitchen at number eighty-two was looking very nice, and she really thought – Sally thought so too – they could put some furniture in number fifty-seven. They would have student tenants there by September. Joe was a real treasure – he'd suggested today that she'd find it would work out cheaper to get him to make and fit cupboards and shelves, rather than buy them from Habitat.

This was perhaps Sharif's chance to ask the question that had been in his mind in a general way.

'What do you think they think of us?' he said.

'Joe and the boys? I think they like me very much,' Nazia said. 'It's my project, after all, and they're getting paid for it. I don't know what they think of you.'

'The English. The whities. When they look at us, what do they see?'

'The whities?' Bina said. Her nephews, seated side by side on the opposite side of the table, raised to shepherd's-pie height with cushions, looked at her brightly. They had learnt to recognize and enjoy the first stages of an argument brewing: that was their main claim to being Bengali. It was in the blood.

'The whities?' Nazia said, and she began to laugh.

2.

She went on laughing. She could hear it in her throat, coming up and choking her, like bile. An aura of heat and glowing colour was in the room, radiating out from the table with its peculiar burden. What did they think of us what did they think of us. She laughed. A woman passing a remark and walking away. Out there the gaze and the hidden opinion. There they were and they were like no one else. A man in his office behind his desk asking a question and looking at them with distaste, the crinkle in his lip. What did they think of us. This man at the table looking at her, who was he who was he. She laughed. He was married to her. She said the word to herself *marriage marriage marriage* and then the word for what she was, *stri stri stri*. Wife. The gaze falling on her and on him and on those around the table, the children they had together, the big one the medium one the small one the other small one.

What did they think of us.

She was laughing. They looked at them from the outside of that house and the outside of this house. They were not like them. They had come here but why had they come here. To be the topic of interest. The room was full of heat and a light that came from the table, green yellow. They had come from somewhere but that somewhere had gone now. They could not go back, they were looked at there and they were looked at here.

What did they think of us.

What did they think of us.

She was laughing and laughing and out of her it came an ugly ugly noise and they stared and she did not know how to stop and outside there were people who had been born here who stared at her and said why are you here what are you thinking look at you and look at your children and. Out there somewhere there was Brother. There was Mahfouz she knew his name and he was stared at and they said to him why are you here but no one would they ever would. They could see that difference and that was enough and they would never be part of any of this. She laughed and laughed and laughed and laughed.

3.

Later that evening she spoke to Sharif. She had gone to bed and he was in the bathroom attached to their bedroom, washing with the door open.

'I don't know what happened,' she said.

'You were overtired,' he said. 'It happens, sometimes.'

He took those fifteen minutes at the table to himself, to consider alone. He would never speak about the episode again. He had asked how they were thought of, and the laughter she poured out was the laughter of one with a knife to their throat. Anisul had laughed like that when he turned and he saw what few seconds remained to him. He was sure of it.

The next Wednesday he drove into the car park with a firm idea in his mind. The children from Gower were there. He made a small performance of shyness as he got out of the car. They would not shout if they thought he was likely to turn round.

'There's that fooking Paki,' one cried out. Was it the same one every time? 'Paki! You fooking Paki in your fooking shirt and tie! Fooking look at the little Paki!'

Sharif turned. His expression was forcibly mild. He walked up to the fence. The children stood exactly where they were, not moving and not quailing. They had the right to this land: that was what was in their minds. He had not looked at them closely before now. There were seven of them. The one who, he thought, had shouted was short and sharp-featured, with very dark hair that stuck up at the back and paper-white skin. They all wore shorts and T-shirts; one or two wore those drapes of wool around the ankle called legwarmers.

'Did you call me a Paki?' he said.

'Paki's come over,' the boy shouted, with something like affected glee. The others were less sure.

'Did you call me a Paki?' Sharif said again. 'I am not a Paki. I am certainly not a Paki. If anything, I am a Bangi.'

'You're a Paki,' the boy said, but not shouting now, speaking with derisory contempt to Sharif on the other side of the fence. 'Look at you in your shirt and tie.'

'That is because I teach at the university here,' Sharif said. 'And I am not a Paki. If I were Pakistani, I could understand your shouting "Paki" at me. I would not like it, but I would understand it. Do you know what I am? My country was Bangladesh. I have more reasons to hate the Pakistanis than you do. They ruled my country for twenty-four years. They robbed us. They forbade us to speak our own language. When we voted for one of us to run the country, they annulled the election. They murdered people I knew and loved, and they murdered my brother. How old are you?'

'Paki's asking how old we are,' the sharp-featured boy said. He was intelligent-looking. He could have done well. The other children were dull in their faces. They had no spark or interest; they could not even walk away through self-awareness. Towards them was coming a larger person, a grown man.

'It was only ten years ago,' Sharif said. 'You weren't born then.'

'Fook off,' the boy said, and some of his friends started to laugh. 'I'm fooking fourteen, I am.'

'I'm fifteen,' another boy said, his hair almost white, his jaw square, like a hero's, his eyes empty of anything.

'There was a war,' Sharif said. 'I had a brother two years older than you. You would have called him a Paki too. But he wasn't a Paki. He was fighting the Pakistanis and they took him away. We never saw him again. My mother never knew what had happened to him.'

'Ay, but if he were in war, fighting as soldier, like,' a boy offered from the back.

'They tortured him,' Sharif said. 'The Pakistanis tortured him and they killed him and he was much the same age as you are. So I am not a Paki. You can shout out at me and call me a Bangi. But do not call me a Paki. Do not call me a Paki.'

The man was here. He was brisk and ginger and thirtyish; he looked as empty as the boys. His head was shaved around the back and sides and his shoulders bulged from the sleeveless T-shirt he wore. 'Are you talking to my boys?' he said. 'What do you want with them?'

'I am not talking to your boys, as you call them,' Sharif said. 'They shouted inaccurate abuse at me and I was correcting their inaccurate misapprehension.'

'You little bastards,' the man said, but affectionately. 'What they bin shouting?'

'They called me a Paki,' Sharif said. 'I am not going to be insulted when I am parking my car at my place of work, and your boys –'

'They called you a Paki? It's not exactly wrong, though, is it?' the man said. 'Are you Pakistani? I don't see there's much wrong with –'

'I was explaining precisely what is wrong with what they were shouting,' Sharif said.

'If you called me a Brit –'

'I don't care to be called what they called me,' Sharif said, with a level gaze. 'If you are in charge here, you will see it doesn't happen again.'

'I'll see they don't indulge their animal spirits in your direction again,' the man said un-seriously. 'They're good lads. This is our first team. They'll be looking at trials for clubs in two years.'

'You should teach them how to read,' Sharif said, walking away. He was not quite sure what the man meant. He understood that it was a world of no significance that he spoke about, in which his boys would in any case fail. 'That,' he turned his head, 'would be of more benefit to them than the ball in the net.'

'Hey!' the man was shouting, but Sharif went on walking, into the faculty. He walked with a certain buoyancy in his stride. Those children would dream of football and kick balls around until they could kick balls into nets six or seven times out of ten. Then they would fail in their dreamt endeavour and would have to be sent off to learn how to read. Sharif knew that they could not read, or not much. No person who could read looked like that, so animal in the gaze, either docile or blankly raging. They didn't know what they were here on earth to do. That was the future for the English.

There was ten minutes before his first student, and he could hear the shouting and whistling from the pitch behind the building. He picked up the telephone and dialled an internal number. In four minutes he had extracted a commitment from the registry that they would speak to the headmaster of Gower School and extract a number of commitments in turn, before the school was allowed to use the university facilities again. Sharif put the telephone down. He had ruined a child's life – somewhere, one of those sharp-featured boys in the crowd had a talent with the unlettered ball and an instinctive understanding of the spatial dimensions of a trajectory that needed no marks on paper. A dog could catch a thrown ball, after all. The brilliant moron, somewhere in that crowd, would have to do without the support of the university's facilities, and he would fail in life because of it. Sharif was glad. And in a moment Mr Wentworth and Mr Tan knocked on his door, and he welcomed them in and began to explain, yet again, about ductile fracture equations.

4.

How had Nazia's friendship with Sally Mottishead come about? She was her first white friend, she believed – the only one she would say anything to as if she were talking to a sister, without restraint or worrying about the effect it would have. Now she felt, indeed, that she talked to her in ways that she did not talk to Bina. Sally had offered to take the children and look after them overnight when they had driven to Heathrow to collect Bina. It would be a lovely adventure for them, she said. And there were seven at home: what would three more be, especially since two were so small and really only halves of the same small one anyway?

A kind of shyness, it turned out, had sprung up between her and Bina, the shyness of five years and the gap before adulthood. The small untidy person, just recognizable as Sharif's little-sister, had fallen asleep in the back seat of the car after her long flight. They had come home to the surprisingly quiet house and put her to bed. In an hour Sally Mottishead was there with the three children, holding the hand of one each of the twins, Aisha walking in a very ladylike way up the Hillsborough path, wanting to make a good impression on Aunty Bina, as Sally observed from behind. Nazia had melted with gratitude, and made Sally a cup of tea.

At first the mothers and the daughters had been an indeterminate mass, all much the same; the daughters, glimpsed in their finery on Saturday afternoons and hardly to be identified with the small figures in brown and mustard and navy blue hurrying into or away from school on weekdays. The mothers, too, had a kind of careful finery for those Saturday afternoons, and for the longest time Nazia could not be sure which was which. There was the mother with an amber brooch whom she pictured surrounded by an arbour of white clematis; the mother in a cottage with the flagstoned path running up to it in a disorganized, charming, overgrown way; there was the mother whose garden gate had a sunray pattern and whose house had no net curtains, the one who was plump and jolly in a red party dress, who laughed a lot when she was saying hello, somehow laughing at a point beyond Nazia in exactly the same way she would laugh beyond someone she didn't know and didn't know how to engage with. That last one was Caroline's mummy, Nazia knew for certain.

Where had Sally Mottishead fitted in? Her daughter was Sam, short for Samantha, and Aisha must have gone to her party. It was incredible, but Nazia had no memory of walking up to the Mottisheads' astonishing house that first time. It was a fantasy of turrets and chhatris, balconies and encaustic-tiled buttresses smothered by a forest of Himalayan rhododendrons. From the road you could glimpse only the princely peaks of the house, red-tiled and story-like. Nazia had met Sally when Sam had come to Aisha's birthday party. Therefore she must have taken Aisha to Sam's birthday party, because she knew that Sam was only invited out of obligation – Sam was not one of Aisha's intimates, for deplorable reasons to do with breathing through her mouth when she read and always being the first to put her hand up in class. But she had no memory of taking her there. Sally was one of a crowd of mothers for most of that summer. It was only at Aisha's own birthday party that she had extracted herself with a galumph and a breaking of the rules that Nazia thought she had understood. After that, Nazia started to recognize the other mothers, to tell them one apart from the other and to want to talk to them. But Sally Mottishead was first.

'You're last on my round,' the woman had said, bustling the small, staring girl with straight black hair and thick glasses up the path. She herself was short, packed with purpose, intense with amiable exertion. 'It's one of those Saturday afternoons. The twins had a party to get to and my little one's got a party to get to, it's his first one. This is right, isn't it? You're expecting our Sam? I dread delivering the wrong one on days like this. I've got six but the other two, one's old enough to get himself where he wants to go and the other's with his dad and a pair of binoculars on the moors, he doesn't get invited out much. There you are, Sam love, in you go, got your present. I'm just about beat. I'm Sally Mottishead, we've met but you might not remember, shall I come in, just for a moment?

'The thing is,' Sally Mottishead went on, coming in and following Nazia into the kitchen, 'I've reached the point where the side room at a children's party where I don't have to do anything, that counts as a nice restful experience. I'll miss them when they're gone, but since I'm going to have to set off collecting them again in an hour, do you mind if I just have a bit of a sit-down? Are you settled in by now? When did you move in?'

Sharif, in a neat and festive bow-tie, took over the running of the party, beginning with a round of pass the parcel. It was not his métier: the supervising of games was better left to Nazia, with her strict sense of fairness and sharp eyes for cheating. As it was, Sharif became aware that some of the players were clinging for far too long to the parcel, and one little girl opened two layers in succession. They had put a small piece of make-up in each layer for the little girls, and by the time the game finished, the girls were just comparing their finds. The party was safe for a good fifteen minutes and Sharif could supervise it from behind his newspaper. In the kitchen, Sally Mottishead was telling Nazia about everything. The house they lived in was mad, but there was no alternative – it had been Martin's mother Wiggy's house, and now Wiggy was getting on a bit, she welcomed Martin and Sally and all the kids. Nine bedrooms, thank the Lord.

And Sally's children – there were six of them. Too many. How had it got out of hand? Sam and the twins, two years older, and the little one who was at his first party this afternoon. He didn't want to leave his mummy, even though they were all the children he saw every day at school; she'd had to push him in but she expected that he was all right now. There was William, who was out birdwatching with his dad, and there was George, who these days called himself Spike. He was out and about and she hoped it wasn't glue-sniffing in the park. The thing was …

Before long Nazia was as deeply involved in the doings of the nine people from Wiggy to little Simon, down there in their piled-up heap of a house, as she ever had been in the lives detailed in Dolly's beautiful hand arriving once a month from Dacca, the pale blue paper always carefully used up to the last before being folded into an envelope and a stamp placed on it. Sally always had something ridiculous to tell, some hopeless disaster that had been set off by delinquent George, or Spike, or her husband Louis. Louis was the professor of ancient Greek, of all the completely useless things, Sally always said. At least if Sharif was an engineer he'd be able to put up a shelf or – or – 'Or bleed a radiator,' Nazia shyly supplied. Whereas Louis, the one occasion that they had all gone to Greece together because he had a lecturing job to a tour group, had been completely unable to communicate with any locals. Ancient Greek, not modern, it seemed. Wiggy lived upstairs, painfully deaf and refusing any kind of hearing aid. Sally thought she had a false idea that they were huge and ugly, a pink plastic box on the side of your head. 'Anyway, she hears whatever she wants to hear, so

best not go on about it,' Sally finished up. At the far end of the
sitting room, Wiggy, an austere figure in a plain black dress with
white cuffs and a collar, drew her beaky face up and emitted a
pained smile from the depths of winter.

At first Nazia had worried herself over Sally's unfailing stories
of disaster – 'You'll never guess what's happened' – and by the
way she had of treating Nazia as an old friend who could be told
anything. Almost at once Sally had explained, without being
asked at all, that the reason she wore her hair in a remarkably
unflattering perm was just convenience. 'When you've got six
children, a husband and a mother-in-law to get ready in the
morning, you don't want the sort of hairdo that's going to take
an hour to put together, and it's not the end of the world if you
don't wash it either. I thoroughly recommend it.' Nazia had
spent years in friendship with women without finding the
slightest need to confide in them anything to do with the hair-
style she wore.

Soon, when the phone rang before ten, as it did most days of
the week, it was Sally, begging her to bring a bit of amusement
into her life because the alternative was a morning shouting into
Wiggy's ear and then a little light carpet-beating. Sally must
remember very well, from five separate occasions, how very
boring the last month or six weeks of pregnancy could be. Sally
would pop round, or if there was some task that needed doing,
she might pick Nazia up on the way. 'Your friend Sally,' Sharif
would say, in an amused way, and it was astonishing how
quickly the connection had expanded into a proper friendship,
of intimacy and confiding. At first Nazia wondered why she
minded so little that it was mostly intimacy and confiding in
one direction. Sally never showed interest in the part of their
lives that had lain before and outside Sheffield. In fact, it was a
pleasure to be treated by Sally as someone whose history was too
commonplace to go into.

For the first time, on meeting Sally, Nazia stopped feeling
that she must look outwards at the ways this place did things,
that she was about to be tested on what she had observed. The

fierce obligation on her to observe was matched, in general, by the hope that no observation or curiosity would meet her in response. When you failed, they looked at you, took you in, observed what you had done. It was like the moment when they had handed over a harmonium and a chemistry set to their daughter, and her daughter's friends had looked, interested, furrowed, concerned, and had found polite things to say about them before looking and smiling at Dr and Mrs Sharifullah, the parents of their friend Aisha.

Had Sally Mottishead been listening at all? One day Sally asked if Nazia cooked what she called 'Indian food' at all. Nazia agreed that she sometimes did, and Sally, without waiting for anything more, recommended the Indian grocers on the London road. Nazia knew that shop. She had driven past it. She would never have gone into it. On either side of the name of the grocery was a green Pakistani flag. She let Sally's attempt to be helpful go without comment. In fact she found her detachment a pleasant rest.

Before Sally, the expression of interest in Nazia and her journey had been universal, stumbling, and led always to an impasse in conversation. All the other mothers had commented that Nazia and Sharif had only just arrived in this country, was that right, and went on to ask where they had come from. When Nazia answered 'Bangladesh', conversation soon dried up; they quickly moved on with a smile and a wave. They had expected, at worst, India. To come from a country so new and which might have called to mind (she believed) only famines and floods dictated a place below all social levels. That Sharif was a professor and their family had been lawyers and academics as far back as anyone could remember was only confusing. Perhaps they should call themselves 'Indian' in the same way that Sylhetis running 'Indian restaurants' here did. It would make things easier.

Sally Mottishead had not done that at all. Sharif at first could not endure, he said with precise asperity, her egotism. Nazia challenged him. He explained that not only did she never ask anything about their history, their relations, or about anything that did not have a precise echo in her own life, like children, schools, the university administration bearing down on husbands, or the buying of furniture. She had the egotistical habit of referring to people known to her but not to her inter-locutor by their first name. 'Mildred's got a carpet just like this one,' she had said vaguely, that first afternoon, walking through the hallway. Mildred had, in fact, turned out to be her mother-in-law's best friend from school, who lived in the Cotswolds. Sharif had a point, whether the person that Sally was referring to was one of her children, a friend, a relation of some sort or, once, a character on a radio serial that Sally was addicted to. But it did not matter. Egotism accepted the world as a single admir-ing gaze. With her, Nazia did not see herself from the outside, a small lost confused brown person with a face that in repose fell back into a scowl. Sally had hardly noticed that Nazia was any different from anyone else she might meet. A thick veil had fallen over the past, and the pair of them sat in each other's kitchens and talked about house prices, the vandalized phone booth at the corner of Coldwell Lane, Mrs Thatcher, Wiggy's latest, anything. In England, Nazia was getting to like coffee as a drink.

'Is she always here?' Sharif said at the beginning, but he was glad of it the day in August when the twins were born. For ever afterwards, Nazia knew the one thing that would stop Sally talking. She treasured it. It was her waters breaking on the lino-leum in the kitchen. She had been on the verge of saying to Sally that she thought her contractions had started when –

Well.

Sally had been through it five times, and once with twins. She tried to phone Sharif, but with no answer put Nazia in the car and was straight down to the hospital. Aisha was out for the day at her friend Alison's, and after they got to the hospital, Sally was so good, phoning Alison's mum so that Aisha could stay there for tea. Afterwards Nazia didn't know what she would have done without Sally. The twins came so fast. Sharif was only just there in time, laughing and half in tears to hold his sons. Sally had retreated outside; she waited to make sure everything was all right, then went off, saying over her shoulder that she'd done exactly the same thing for Karen when Karen had her second girl. Who Karen was, they couldn't say.

5.

And now – she couldn't see how else to put it – they were rich. She had been in charge of business since they came to Sheffield. At first she had thought that, perhaps when the twins went to school, she would apply for a job – teaching English literature, after she had got the qualification. But by the time the twins were old enough, she was being kept quite busy. The two houses in Wincobank she and Sharif had bought with the first year's royalties on his textbook were renovated, let to students, and in two years had produced enough rental income to buy two more houses in the same street. She renovated them; let them to students; put the rental income on one side. In five years they owned eight terraced houses in Wincobank.

The income from Sharif's textbook carried on coming in, too. That went into a separate account, the twice-yearly royalty cheques from the publisher mounting up. For the longest time Nazia had been satisfied with the interest on the account. Then the government announced that it was selling off a public utility. Nazia applied for shares: she was granted a few. The following year another utility was privatized. Nazia applied for more shares: she was granted a few. The next day she went to Manchester, by train, to meet with a stockbroker, and wrote a cheque for twenty thousand pounds to invest in a range of stocks and shares. On the way back from Manchester, looking at the high, wet-shining walls of the trench cut by railway companies through the hills, she was light-headed, appalled, in shock, as if she had divested herself of a great weight. She told herself the twenty thousand pounds was gone; she should forget about it.

Burns, who had co-written the book that made all this money, had dedicated his half of it to his father, who had been an engineer too. Sharif had not told anyone what he was going to do. When the final copy arrived, she saw that it was dedicated to *Professor Anisul Ahmed of Dacca University (1926–1971)*. Her eyes filled.

They lived on Sharif's salary quite comfortably. And at first timidly, sceptically, then with a little more confidence, they spent money. They bought a new television and a video recorder, then a second video recorder in the more popular format – for years, Sharif would maintain that Betamax had been the superior technology. The house in Hillsborough had a perfectly nice kitchen and two perfectly nice bathrooms; they came out and were replaced by glossy structures; a power shower; a bidet. By this time Nazia had replaced eight bathrooms in Wincobank, eight kitchens in Wincobank; she knew where the bargains could be found, and she knew all the mistakes that could be made. There was a microwave, and a barbecue for the garden, and a big American fridge and a separated hob and grill and oven. There was a new bed for them and the loft was converted into a playroom for Aisha and the boys.

Steadily they spent and steadily their Manchester money grew, untouched. Nazia bought a new winter coat for herself and a new winter coat for Sharif every 1 September. She bought a carpet, a beautiful large carpet, from the Oriental Rug Shop. It was twenty times what such a carpet would have cost in Dacca and Nazia did not care in the slightest. One day she took the boys to their favourite place to eat, Uncle Sam's Chuck Wagon, where they liked to eat burgers as big as their heads and what they called 'fries'. Afterwards, they went for a walk down Ecclesall Road. She had never got over Father's injunction that you should never overeat, but if you had eaten to excess, you should always take a walk around the Dhanmondi lake, once or twice round. There was no Dhanmondi lake, but they walked down the Ecclesall Road and there, in the window of a gallery called Philip Francis, was a painting that she simply loved. It was a wooden chair in a room with sunlight pouring through it and a grey-purple shawl on the back of the chair. You could see that the walls were thick and the window was small, and it was very hot outside. She stood with the boys as long as they could bear it. And the next day she put on her best dress and persuaded Sharif to come with her straight from work, so that he, too, would be carefully, professionally dressed. They had never been in an art gallery where you could buy the paintings before. They asked about the painting; they were told some things about the painter; they asked what the price was; they paid it. It was a disappointment to be told that they had to wait two weeks until the end of the exhibition, but when the time came to pick it up, Nazia found that she had been thinking about it every day. Nazia had had the whole house redecorated only three months before, and luckily the colours in the painting were just right in the sitting room.

Since Sally had been a great help about all the Wincobank houses, negotiating and arguing and discovering what sort of rent they could ask, there was no point in pretending that she didn't know what money they earned from that source. 'A new hairdo, I see,' she might say airily, or 'I wish I could afford a new sofa at the drop of a hat, but anything goes straight away on children's shoes and Jif. Exciting things like that.' The hair was exactly as it always had been, and the sofa was in fact eighteen months old when Sally first made a comment on it, a great success from G Plan, oatmeal in colour and immensely comfy, but not new.

She was with them in Hillsborough one day, in the kitchen at the front of the house, when the telephone rang. It was quite a frequent occurrence now. Nazia picked the phone up, and in a moment she was speaking across the world. This was Mrs Sharifullah – this was Nazia, yes – the unfamiliar voice announced itself as Samir Khandkar. They lived next door to Sharif's parents in Dhanmondi.

'Is Dolly all right?' Nazia said. For ever afterwards she would never know why she had asked that. She put it down to Sally Mottishead standing there like that. Dolly was all right, but Samir explained that she didn't feel she could come to the phone, and had asked him to call England. Sharif's mother had died, quite suddenly.

'Just like his father,' Nazia said. And then it was done. She could have been putting the phone down on the country she was born in.

'Do you phone Bangladesh? I expect you do it all the time,' Sally Mottishead said. She followed Nazia into the hallway, holding her mug of coffee. 'Wiggy would have a fit. She got in a bate once because I called London before six when the rates go down.'

Nazia was standing there, her attention elsewhere.

'What is it?' Sally said.

In five minutes, Nazia had agreed that she should not break the news to Sharif that his mother had died over the telephone, but should go immediately to the faculty. It was one of Sally's practical, thoughtful moments. Sally led the way into the faculty and found Ada Browning in her office. Ada's assistant took Nazia into the inner office for some privacy, bringing her and Sally a cup of tea, and Ada went to fetch Sharif out of his lecture. She returned in a few minutes to say to the students that Professor Sharifullah had had some bad news, and that the lecture today was cancelled. The way they filed out was a disgrace, in Ada Browning's eyes. She had a good mind to ask that Desmond Baker, the one who caused all the difficulties round here, whether he'd like it if people cheered and sang a rude song when his mother died.

It had been a mistake for Sally to drive Nazia to the faculty, since she had to drive the pair of them back. They could have sat in the back together, as if Sally were their chauffeur, but Sharif did the polite, inconvenient thing of sitting in the front and asking Sally polite questions about how Martin's student recruitment was going – he'd heard they'd dropped the language requirement. It wasn't until they got home, Sally dismissed with thanks, her kind offer to pick up the twins at home time accepted, that they could talk at all. The conversation was efficient: it had to be done with before the end of school.

'Dolly will have to come back with us,' Sharif said calmly. 'There's nothing for her in Dacca any more. I thought Mother would last longer.'

'She's only twenty,' Nazia said. 'I can't think of Dolly, twenty.'

'I don't see why she can't finish her degree at the university here,' Sharif said.

'She's not on her own, is she?' Nazia said.

'We should phone Samu Khondkar,' Sharif said judiciously. 'That was the surgeon with the collection of butterflies. He had a son called Samu, a fat little boy. She must be with them. It was kind of him to phone, an awful job.'

'Strangers,' Nazia said dazedly. She could not remember any Khondkar, any collection of butterflies. For a moment she envisaged a man in a room, his head swathed with flying creatures, a fat little boy like a cupid among them in the air. 'We are here and Bina is in Cardiff. How would Bina know?'

'I will telephone Bina now,' Sharif said. 'I expect that light blinking on the answering machine means that she or Tinku has already tried to call us. And then I will go immediately to the travel agent and book flights to Dacca for you, and for me, and for Bina and for Tinku. Aisha. What do you think about Aisha coming, at least? We will be too late for the funeral, but there are always things to be done.'

That evening, Nazia sat with Aisha in her bedroom and told her about poor Nani. It was very sudden, she said; it was best for Nani. She had been very sad since what had happened to Rafiq-uncle. (Aisha now was only two years younger than Rafiq had been when he disappeared – when he was killed, they must think.) It was very sad that now she would never know what had happened to him, or be able to bury his body. She had been very sad since Nana died, too, and now it was all over for her. Tomorrow, they were going to go to Dacca, Aisha too.

'Mummy,' Aisha said. 'When did Nani die, exactly? What time of day? Was it yesterday?'

'Why do you ask?'

'I just want to know what I was doing when it happened. Was she in her house?'

'Do you remember it? The house, Dacca?'

'Of course I do,' Aisha said. 'I was eight when we came back here. Are Raja and Omith coming?'

'I think they're too young,' Nazia said. She picked up the green-haired plastic troll sitting against the pillow; set it down again. 'I've spoken to Mrs Mottishead, and, this is so kind of her, they'll go and stay –'

'Mummy,' Aisha said. 'I'm telling you. Don't leave them with the Mottisheads. You don't know what you're doing.'

Nazia stared. 'What is this? Less of the drama, please. Just because you've fallen out with Samantha. It's very kind of Mrs Mottishead to take them in.'

'They mustn't,' Aisha said. 'Mummy –'

'It's not a matter for discussion,' Nazia said.

6.

It was only yesterday, Aisha felt like saying to her mother. But her mother thought she was popular. There was too much to start explaining now. Mummy hadn't even noticed the sticking plaster on her fourth finger.

Mummy had dropped her at the bottom of Darwin Lane in the mornings. There was no need to drive right up to the school gates, and everyone would think she was spoilt if they saw it. Almost everyone else got the bus to school. It was raining, and underneath the trees lining the road, it was dismal, dark and dripping fatly onto Aisha's umbrella, like the stroke on a drum. Ahead of her there were some little ones, and just beyond that three figures she recognized. She slowed down, but somehow

Samantha Mottishead knew she was there. She was flanked by
Alison and Katy. They used to be her friends. They were still her
friends: just the sort of friends that were always horrible to you.
They were waiting for Aisha to catch up.

'It's this afternoon,' Samantha Mottishead said. Her voice
was croaking with excitement; her horrible face was lit up with
what she knew and what she had planned. Her glasses were half
the size of her face, and because of her long-sightedness,
enlarged her almost colourlessly pale eyes in her white flat face,
like a fish that lived in the dark. The mothers felt sorry for
Samantha Mottishead because of what she looked like, her dark
hair parted in the dead centre of her skull, falling to a cloud of
split ends somewhere two feet below. She had not had her hair
cut in five years because, Aisha believed, she thought she drew
some of her power from it. 'It's this afternoon it's going to
happen. It is Wednesday afternoon. My powers are
approaching.'

She had seen the looks on the faces of the others as they went
on, through rain and in the shadows under the trees, in quiet
ordinary interiors with the curtains drawn, in neat gardens.
What did Samantha Mottishead believe about the powers she
claimed for herself, when her voice dropped into that bestial
deep wail? She had started alluding to them months ago,
perhaps even a year, and by the time she came out with it and
said she had *powers*, the group did not laugh. The others might
believe Samantha, and a serious secretiveness took hold.

There was almost no one that Aisha could talk to about it.
Mummy was such friends with Mrs Mottishead, and she felt
that if she tried to say anything to the others, it would get back
to Samantha. Samantha looked at her in her own way; she was
searching for a person to cast out, and Aisha was on the edge of
the group. She only spoke to Fanny, when they came over for
their monthly visit; they were allowed to sit upstairs or to go out
for a walk, these days. Fanny thought it was hilarious. 'She
sounds mental,' she said. 'There's a girl like that in our school.
The boys throw conkers at her.'

The afternoon was devoted to sport, and you were allowed to undertake sport of your own choice, self-supervised. Four of the boys went off to the swimming-pool; others formed two five-a-sides; the keen girls played a hockey match, a football match, or a pair did their best with the school's pitted tarmac tennis court. The sports mistress had been persuaded by Alison and a couple of the others to let five or six of them go off jogging. The morning's rain had cleared; it was only damp and cloudy now. They left the school in their shorts or tracksuits, theatrically stretching and raising their knees and even performing short sprints down the drive; they even ran in a manner of speaking down Darwin Lane. But now they reached the bottom and walked the half-mile to Samantha Mottishead's house. At the beginning of the walk, it was only Samantha Mottishead who was silent, a dark island in the middle of their noise. The silence spread; by the time they reached her house, no one was talking.

The Mottishead house was not like anyone else's: it hid its towers and rooftop pavilions away behind a jungle. Once inside, you could not understand it, and afterwards, it was impossible to remember the shape it had exactly. In other houses, the things that could be moved stayed in the rooms they were ordained for. The plates went from the kitchen to the dining room and back again; the clothes went on a tidy circular journey from bedroom to wearer to laundry basket to washing machine to ironing board to bedroom again. In the Mottishead house, you could feel a hard prod in your back as you were sitting on the sofa, and it was somebody's toothbrush. Once Mrs Mottishead's bra had been draped over the back of a dining-room chair. And there were books everywhere, in the kitchen and bathroom and even in the porch. Nobody ever tidied Samantha's bedroom. They trooped upstairs and she carelessly pushed her old clothes and things to the back of the room, staring at each of them, daring them to say anything. She had not opened her curtains that morning and she left them shut now.

'They're all out,' she said. 'Except Granny. She's probably sleeping. She won't bother us.'

'What's that?' Alison said, pointing at something behind the bed. Aisha would not look.

'We need to start straight away. Or there won't be time. You have to do what I tell you and not to argue. You see? Understand? Now. You need to sit in a circle,' Samantha said. 'It won't work without.

'I discovered this,' she went on. 'I found this through my powers. Sit. Sit.

'*Little Tommy Tucker sang for his supper …*'

Aisha knew that Samantha had not found this through her powers. She had found it through watching the same old film on the television, last Saturday afternoon, a film about summoning up ghosts. She had silenced the group nevertheless. They were in a circle, cross-legged, just as Samantha had ordered, and Samantha's head now fell backwards. It returned to upright slowly. Samantha's eyes had rolled back in their sockets, the blank of the whites terrible behind the enlarging lens. Her mouth was hanging open.

'Who is it, who is it, who is it?

'*Kadapatazaxou, tiddy-otty-gilly-quash, pabaranagoofin, graaaar …*

'I feel your presence, O great one …

'I feel you, now command us, ask us for what you want …'

It was stupid and ridiculous, what Samantha was doing, but Aisha had never felt like laughing. If Fanny was here, she would have had somebody to encourage her into laughing, but these others, they were serious, even frightened by Samantha's special voice and her made-up language. Did they believe she had powers? That she was summoning up the dead? It was impossible to know without making the precise observation that would expel her from the group.

'Yes,' Samantha was saying, as if listening to a detailed set of instructions. 'Yes. Yes. I hear and understand. Yes, from the dark one, I hear and understand and obey.'

Downstairs there was a small noise, a thud of something falling to the floor. It was probably only the old grandmother's book sliding off the arm of her chair, but it made Alison shriek.

'He comes, he comes,' Katy moaned, joining in. 'I hear his dreadful footfall.'

Samantha's eyes slid back into place. Her mouth closed. She focused with disdain on Katy. 'You hear nothing, foolish one,' she said, but in her normal voice. 'He does not make himself heard to just anyone. I have my instructions from him. He has asked for something, one small thing. He wants the life force of the dark one, as he calls her, just one drop … of *blood*.' A wavering hand was raised; a finger extended; and it moved around the circle slowly before stopping where Aisha knew it would stop.

'Forget it,' Aisha said. She pulled her hands away from Katy on her right, Marian on her left. 'I'm not your dark one.'

'Oh …' Samantha said, a sigh diminishing into a deflating noise. 'Oh … so small a thing … a drop of the life force … If you disappoint him …'

'If you disappoint him, he will grow *angry*,' Katy said, singing the last word.

'I don't care,' Aisha said. 'I'm going.'

But somehow now Samantha had sprung forward like an angry dog, and Aisha found her legs being gripped. Samantha's bare knees rammed her shoulders to the floor. Get off, she started to shout, but a hand was in her mouth. She could not breathe.

'Fetch the knife,' Samantha said. 'And the bowl. So small a drop, it will not hurt, and a drop of the life force from the dark one, from the dark continent, from far away, her black blood an offering to the one we all serve …'

'Don't,' somebody was saying, in real terror, but now Samantha was reaching out her left hand to where somebody was passing her a Stanley knife.

Not my neck, not my neck, Aisha was trying to say. But the hand in her mouth was firm, and the blade of the knife was, surely, against where her jugular vein ran. Could Samantha be as stupid as that? She was holding the knife there; the cold of it against Aisha's skin.

'So fine and delicate,' Samantha said. 'And a drop of the life blood, a gift for our master.'

'Not the neck,' someone said.

'No,' another voice said. 'Not the neck. The neck isn't necessary. It is only the blood we want. A little prick on the finger will do.' Had somebody new come into the room? It was a voice to be obeyed, it appeared. The knife left Aisha's neck; in a moment her hand was picked up. She tensed; a short savage pain at the end of her fourth finger, and then fierce pressure.

'Blood! Blood! The life force!' Samantha was crying, and got off Aisha's shoulders. Aisha raised herself. It seemed to her that the door to Samantha's bedroom, behind her, closed. Samantha was clutching her hand, and pressing blood out of it into a little Chinese tea-bowl that Katy was holding. She was pleased to see that some of the others were looking at Samantha with real dislike.

'Get off me,' Aisha said, pulling her finger away and sucking it. 'If you ever – ever –'

'And now,' Samantha intoned, ignoring what Aisha had said, hunching with a performance of glee over the few drops of blood in the white and blue bowl, 'now the real magic can begin. I call upon my powers. Descend! Descend!'

The afternoon was over. For another half an hour, Samantha Mottishead waved her arms in the air and muttered syllables. She performed a dance of her own invention, all undecided gestures and songs she was making up; she announced what she was about to do was a mime of gratitude to the Sun, but explaining that Night was better. In the end she cast a spell, raised up above the others in the only way possible, by standing on her bed with the rainbow-patterned continental quilt, and lifting the bowl with Aisha's blood in it to her mouth. Aisha did not believe that she had drunk her blood. Her finger really hurt. She had sucked it and sucked it. That Samantha Mottishead was going to get her an Elastoplast. She could walk out: she thought she could get further by staying with her arms folded and putting on a sarcastic expression.

'What's that spell going to do, Sam?' Alison asked, when Samantha Mottishead had finally collapsed on her bed. It was true: she had not explained its purpose.

'It's a curse unto death,' Samantha said, getting up. 'It is the most powerful curse a witch can cast, against those who stand against the bond of love between witches, and the acolytes of witches.'

'Are you –'

'Yes,' Samantha said. She raised her grubby hand to her throat, clutching it. 'I am now a witch. I am a white witch, and I use my powers for good, against the forces of evil.'

Aisha said nothing. She would leave with the others, and go home instead of going back to school. If she went in first thing, yesterday's clothes would still be on the peg in the changing room where she had left them.

7.

In fact the twins had behaved very well on the long flight to Dhaka. The stewardess had managed to find them a pack of colouring-in pictures with crayons, and a little magazine with games to play. There was, too, the excitement of looking out of the window, and they were good at taking their turn to sit on Mummy's lap, though they were getting rather big for that. And the excitement of dinner on a tray, full of strange little things like butter wrapped up in a square in foil and salt and pepper in sealed paper twists! Bina-aunty had told them a story after dinner, and Tinku-uncle had kindly swapped places so that they could sit either side of her. Mummy had not told anyone, but at the last moment she had put Mr Rabbit and Doopstop the bear into the hand baggage. (It was lucky that the two favoured totems had been put through the washing machine only last week: Raja had been trying to get the bear he had named Doopstop to eat some cheese squeezed from a tube, and the toy had looked and smelt very strange afterwards.) Sharif had told her not to create excitement by producing them before bedtime. He believed he could let the twins go off to sleep and then gently place Mr Rabbit and Doopstop the bear next to their owners, Omith and Raja respectively. That would be a comforting and nice way to wake up in this very strange place, a metal tube hurtling eastwards through the air.

Sharif wished there was something that would help him. He had had his own Mr Rabbit, a small brown bear called Butter, but Butter had been through the wars and was probably in a tea chest in somebody's cellar. The arrangements had occupied him: the tickets, Tinku and Bina, the yielding to Nazia's sudden decision that the boys must come too. Now they were all on a plane together, and there was nothing to do for a whole long day. When the stewardess came, he refused any food, taking only a glass of water, knowing he would regret it later. There had been a bad moment at Heathrow when, in the crowd at the departure gate, he thought he had seen them. But the man had turned, and it had not been Mahfouz after all.

Nobody had said anything about Mahfouz and Sadia. Ten years ago, when Father had died, they had been informed. But they had not responded. At the time everyone had said that Mahfouz, safe in London, would not dare set foot in Bangladesh again. He would be seized by the police and thrown into jail before he could reach home. That might have been the case in 1975: certainly Mahfouz and Sadia had not made an appearance at Father's ceremonies. It was clear to Sharif, however, that things must have changed in Bangladesh. The Friend of Bengal was dead; he had promised that wrongs would be righted; and now there were no elections and no freedom, and the country was being run by a general who would welcome Mahfouz and his kind with open arms. Sharif, in seat 12F, his family around him sleeping, brooded in the little tent of illumination cast over him by the reading light.

And now finally they were there. They queued up for Immigration, Bina taking Raja's hand and Nazia Omith's, and, in a crowd behind Sharif, listened while he answered the many questions, respectfully responded to the officer's salaam, his careful but peremptory offering of sympathy when he heard the reason for their visit. How dirty the hall looked, and how dim the lighting was, as if a transparent veil of brown had been cast over everything. Somewhere an amplified voice fell into distortion and crackle, wailing its way to an abrupt conclusion. The smell of wet earth penetrated this ramshackle building, as if through widening cracks. It was long familiar to Sharif and to Bina and to Nazia, but Raja was going as far as to hold his nose. His twin was vastly amused by this, and of course copied it; it was not a bad smell, though, just an unfamiliar one. Sharif looked at the filthy rim of the immigration officer's white cuffs, the thick line of dirt running behind the man's neck on his white collar, and restrained himself from moving backwards six inches.

The baggages were delivered, and had to be searched. They were small enough bags; most of the clothes they had packed were mourning clothes in white. A book that Tinku had brought was confiscated – it was nothing so very dangerous, just a silly-sounding novel, but it had a girl in a swimsuit on the cover, holding a gun. Their attention was held by the women's and Aisha's toiletries; at one point Tinku was on the verge of stepping forward angrily, but Sharif restrained him. These men must be allowed to go their own way, greeted by a cheerful, smiling, submissive face. Sharif, watching their dirty hands go through his wife's carefully folded white saris, made a vow to himself: he would not leave this country without his little sister Dolly. She deserved better than this.

The seven of them were out of the building, finally, and in the hot blaze of Dhaka. They would need two taxis, and Tinku and Bina took Aisha with them so that the twins would have one parent each to entertain them. It was needed, because after half an hour, the traffic, which had been heavy and slow, came to a complete halt. The air was thick with black smoke from exhaust fumes; Sharif shut the window against a BRTC bus – battered, its side flaking patches of paint and showing whole stretches of rust – whose exhaust fumes were being directed into the car.

'What's the problem?' Sharif said.

'Perhaps an accident, brother,' the driver said. 'Always an accident, the traffic stops. And then the other days, if there is a hartal, you daren't go out, you lose a day. The strike, the big strike. The hartals! Where have you been? They hold the city to ransom. Every week, twice a week. And the other days an accident stops the city. Look at this.'

'What can we do?' Sharif said.

The driver spread his hands in a gesture meaning 'nothing'. It was so hot, there in the back of the car. Raja was raising and lowering his whole arm to his face, theatrically, letting himself tense, then flop down again. His twin was showing interest and in a moment, Sharif knew, would start to imitate him. By the side of the road there was a large sign, it was –

'That sign, it's in Bengali. What's happened?'

'What else should it be in?' Nazia said.

'The signs – they were all in English,' Sharif said. 'Weren't they?'

The car was stationary. Somewhere, probably only twenty yards ahead, was the car with Tinku and Bina and Aisha. The heat inside the car was immense, and the smell of the traffic fumes choking.

'Omith wants to go to the toilet, Mummy,' Raja said.

'Omith wants to be a very good boy, and sit and wait for a very short time,' Nazia said, with evident exasperation. 'I wish he wouldn't do that.'

'What? Mussolini?'

'He just says something that his satrap is supposed to want, and then before you know it, the satrap's taken it on board and he confirms the statement.'

'I want to go to the toilet, Mummy,' Omith said.

'As if on cue,' Sharif said. 'But there are strange mystical facts about sets of twins, you know. Who is to say that the satrap's desire to micturate could not have conveyed itself through telepathy to the mind genetically nearest?'

'I want to go to the toilet, Mummy,' Omith said.

'I'm really not in the mood for this,' Nazia said. 'It's not even funny any more – there are just orders in the form of suggestion and then the satrap obeys. A distraction is called for. Look, Omith, look, Raja – I spy with my little eye something beginning with C.'

'Car,' Raja said. 'I want to go to the toilet, Mummy.'

'Your turn, Omith,' Sharif said. 'Look, we're moving!'

The driver started the car; took the handbrake off with a crunching groan; drove forwards eighteen inches; stopped again. He turned the engine off.

'It's your turn, Omith,' Sharif said commandingly.

'I spy,' Omith said. 'I spy … I don't know.' Raja turned to look at his twin, leant over and whispered something to him. 'I spy something beginning with L.'

'Lorry!' Raja said immediately.

'That doesn't count,' Nazia said. She had always, as long as anyone could remember, been a great one for fairness, the one given the task of dividing a dish into fourteen.

'This is bad,' the driver announced. 'When an accident like this happens, it could stop us here all afternoon.'

'What are the police doing?' Nazia said.

'The police,' the driver said neutrally, dismissing the comment.

'Mummy, I want to go to the toilet,' Omith said.

'He really does,' Raja said.

'You can't go now,' Nazia said sharply. 'You'll just have to wait.'

And all around them was the country that had started them off. Sharif tried not to look at it in any particular way. The old beggar making his way between the stationary cars, a filthy white rag round his head, bent over his stick, his arms thin as biros, his bloodshot eyes weary with their asks being refused; the rust on the side of the bus in great patches; the thick stench of petrol fumes clogging the air; the new signs in Bengali by the side of the road that had somehow already sustained dents in the metal and smears in the painted letters. This was a new country, Sharif told himself, and things would not go right immediately. He had looked at things like that for many years and had found nothing so very wrong in them. His eyes were trained by the neat streets of Hillsborough and Lodge Moor and by the clean surroundings of Sheffield University's faculty of engineering. They were places where people would stare if you scrunched up a piece of paper and dropped it. Once, he had seen a lady walking her dog pause behind it, drop to her knees and scoop up what must be a log of excrement in a plastic bag, to carry away, rather than soil the public environment. And the English did not think of Sheffield as a beautiful city, either.

'If the boys want to wee,' he said, 'I don't see why they shouldn't get out to wee. The traffic isn't going anywhere. No one is going to care.'

'I don't want to wee,' Raja said. 'It's Omith who wants to wee.'

'You can do your very best to wee if your brother's going to,' Sharif said judiciously. 'We aren't going to stop more than once. This is your one opportunity.' He explained to the driver.

'They mustn't go against the side of my taxi,' the driver said.

'Of course not,' Sharif said, and then, performing a fine degree of contempt for the country he had come from, he took first the Herr Kommandant outside to piss, and then the Rural Proletarian. The Kommandant wanted to piss after all. There was a hole in the road, just there, that would do to piss in, so nobody's paintwork was affected. Above them, the passengers on the BRTC bus behind the open grille looked down with interest at the little group. For a moment Sharif thought he might piss, too, to give them some more entertainment. From the moment they could talk, the boys had been referred to by him and Nazia after their roles, Raja to command and Omith to obey, and the names changed daily: Caesar, Mussolini, Bose the Great, Mrs Thatcher, Colonel Reginald Dyer, the Last Viceroy of India, the Managing Director, the Zamindar with the Whip: the Unknown Soldier, the Rani of Jhansi, the Urban (or Rural) Proletarian, the Prussian Army, Poor Winston Smith and the Backbench Rebellion. One day they would catch on, and their vocabularies and points of reference, Nazia observed, would be colossal. In the meantime they could be talked about without their recognizing what was happening. It took something like three hours to clear the blockage and arrive at the house in Dhanmondi – a rate of about two miles an hour. What the accident was that had stopped them like that, they never discovered.

8.

Bina and Tinku and Aisha were standing outside the house. They had clearly just dismissed the driver, and their suitcases were being dealt with by the houseboy and the security guard. The house had a dozen loudspeakers on its roof at least, a pair of silver metallic lilies at each corner, and from them a crackling voice was trumpeting in Arabic. Something from the Koran. Sharif had not been to the mosque in years, but he recognized the holy scriptures when he heard them.

'This isn't Dolly,' Bina said. 'Dolly wouldn't put up loudspeakers that you can hear four streets away.'

'At Daddy's funeral,' Sharif said, 'we just had two boys from the mosque reading in the grandmothers' room with the door open. You could go and listen if you wanted to. That was very nice.'

'That was lovely,' Nazia said. 'Who's done this?'

'Mummy would never ...' Bina was saying, and Tinku was encouraging her not to go on. It was a funeral, after all. They had turned up from England and would not start complaining about the arrangements. But Sharif knew, with some dread, who it was who had made these arrangements, had ordered a dozen loudspeakers to chant the scriptures from the roof. Those people had, like him, just landed from London before taking the arrangements away from poor Dolly, insisting that what Mother would have wanted was to amplify the Koran all over Dhanmondi for three days. And now his intuition was confirmed because through the gates came a plump, prosperous-looking Mahfouz: older, greyer, fatter, and with false teeth glittering like confident lies, his mouth spit-wet shining out of a full long grizzled beard. His arms were spread wide as if to embark on an embrace. Behind him was what must be Sadia, but her head covered, only her face emerging from the tight-wrapped scarf. She was pale, thin and very old-looking, as if she had not eaten properly for many years. She stood back, her eyes lowered. Bina and Tinku, then Sharif submitted to the embrace. He approached Nazia. She bundled the children behind her, and something in her eye kept Mahfouz's embrace very short.

'Dear brothers, sisters,' Mahfouz said. He had a smoker's voice, croaky and breaking, though he and his beard did not smell like a smoker. 'How good to see you, though – you will want to change as soon as possible, of course.'

'Where is Dolly?' Nazia said, ignoring the reproach that they had not travelled in white. 'I want to see Dolly.'

'She is inside,' Mahfouz said, but addressing his comment to Sharif. 'Dolly and I – we have already been talking about her future. There is so much to settle.' But there was Dolly, just coming out in her plain white sari, her arms held high for her brother and sister. It had been ten years since Sharif and Nazia had seen her, and she was now twenty. They embraced quickly, and with Nazia holding her in grateful affection, they went inside for the children to meet her. Above, the loudspeakers spoke of gardens in a harsh, syrupy, cracked, Chittagong voice, the voice that Mahfouz had hired for this particular afternoon.

'They turned up yesterday,' Dolly said, in an urgent whisper, to Nazia. They had found a quiet corner of the familiar sitting room, unchanged for twenty years, apart from the touching little detail that Mother had framed the photograph of the twins that Nazia had sent last year and added it to the collection on the sideboard, in pride of place next to the photograph of Rafiq. Mahfouz had made himself scarce, not trusting things to go beyond a regretful greeting and a performance of loving kindness. Sadia, however, was still in the kitchen, making demands. 'Samu said that I must inform Sadia at least. Mother was still going every week to the ministry to ask what the news of Rafiq's story was. Mother would never have agreed to have Sadia's husband in the house again. But Samu said, quite rightly, that he and she had been informed when Father died, and they had not responded and they did not come. So this time I thought there was no harm in it. But they arrived and straight away ...'

Dolly gestured upwards at the noise of amplified prayer.

'Straight away Mahfouz has been talking to me about what I should do. He said within ten minutes of stepping into the house that he knows a very nice man in England who would make a very good husband for me.'

'Oh, Dolly,' Nazia said. 'I don't want to think of Mahfouz's idea of a good husband for you.'

'He said he was a little older than me, but that he had a good business, that his family was well respected, that they came from Sylhet but were decent people, very religious – Nazia, don't let me marry someone like that.'

'There is no question,' Nazia said. 'You will not have to marry anyone Mahfouz chooses for you.'

'I think it was a dry-cleaning business, what they call a launderette, that this man owns. I haven't seen Mahfouz since I was eight years old. I don't want his choice.'

'Has Samir been helpful? Samir – he's the Khondkar son who informed us, isn't he?'

Dolly brightened. 'Oh, so helpful – he is so kind. I didn't know if you would remember him, he was so little when you went. Well, no littler than I was, but still.'

'I remember Khondkar-nana's fat little son. Is he still so fat?'

'No, no,' Dolly said. 'Samu was never so very fat and he certainly isn't fat now. When it happened I ran out of the house, not knowing where I should go or who I should speak to. Ghafur came after me, saying, "Madam, madam" – he could not endure that I should run in the street looking for people. He sent his boy to the Khondkars', and Samu was at home. I do not know what I would have done without him.'

'Dolly-aunty,' Aisha said. She had been sitting with the twins but now wandered over in her brilliant white mourning sari to listen. 'When did Nani die? When exactly?'

'Aisha, please,' Nazia said. 'This is not an adventure from Feluda for you to interrogate poor kind Dolly-aunty.'

'It's important, Mummy,' Aisha said. 'When was it?'

'Well, it was in the morning,' Dolly said. 'Aisha-darling-child, you can ask your Dolly-aunty anything you like. I am so happy to see you again. It would have been two days ago now. It must have been about half past nine, certainly after breakfast. There was a sound from downstairs – a noise Mummy was making without meaning to. And I came down without delay, but she was gone, just like that. Quickly, like when Daddy went.'

'Just like Daddy,' Nazia said, dazed with mystery.

'She had keeled over on the sofa. It was so fast. I can't even remember the last thing I said to poor Mummy. It was probably something like "I wish Ghafur would learn how to make toast properly," because, you know, he still has such a habit of burning it and not even scraping it afterwards. When I saw her like that I thought for a moment she was looking for something down the back of the sofa.'

Aisha had been working something out. 'Is that – that would have been half past three in the morning in England? Is that right? Mummy?'

Nazia batted away the irrelevant question. It was not like Aisha to be so inconsiderate.

'So what are you going to do?' Nazia said. 'Where will you live while you finish your degree?'

'Oh, the degree,' Dolly said. 'I haven't been to the university for weeks. It's been closed down, temporarily, and it will soon be back to normal, or so they say.'

'Dolly, that can't be right,' Nazia said. 'What are you going to do? Where will you live?'

'I thought perhaps I could go on living here,' Dolly said bravely. 'I don't need to keep on all the servants, perhaps just Ghafur.'

'Oh, Dolly,' Nazia said. 'Sister.'

'I don't know what the alternative is, unless I marry the man Mahfouz has in mind for me. Look, we need to greet people.'

Some people had come through the door; a married pair, as young as Nazia and Sharif. Dolly said it was Mummy's dentist – her new dentist, not old Raychaudhuri, a nice man. Sadia emerged to greet them, and after a moment's hesitation Nazia and Dolly went forward, encouraging Aisha to come with them. The dentist had heard about it, and wanted to say what a very charming and elegant lady she had been, what a sad loss it was. In a while they were offered tea and sweets and other things, and they stayed for half an hour. By that time there were other people – the Khondkars, with Samir, a brother of Mahfouz and his wife, a poet Mother had known and liked, and others. All this time Sharif was tensely aware of his sister Sadia. She had not gone when her husband had gone. She was decisively talking to those who had come to pay their respects, looking them levelly in the eye. She had not come when Mother died. Now things had changed in this country, and she and her husband felt they could come back, and talk. She looked very ill. He watched her as he talked to a retired civil servant, a keen amateur of folk art, whom Mother had always liked to see on her lakeside walks.

After an hour he went outside onto the veranda at the back of the house. The noise out there was tremendous. There were

six men, he had established, in the upper rooms, taking turns
with the verses from the Koran, and their devout utterances
were being amplified from every corner of the house by the
pairs of silver trumpets. He waited. In two minutes, the back
door was opened: Ghafur, cowed, stood there holding the door
in a servile way; Sadia sailed through in her brilliant white
headscarf.

'Brother,' she said. 'How was your journey?'

Sharif bowed his head.

'Your boys are so charming,' Sadia said. 'And Aisha, so
grown-up. We have two children now, you know. They are so
clever and hardworking, I am sure they will do well.'

'You must be very proud of them,' Sharif said dismissively,
rattling it off.

'And I am told you don't live in Dhaka any more,' Sadia said.
'I had no idea.'

'We left the country nearly ten years ago,' Sharif said. 'We
live in England now, like you.'

'We must –' Sadia said, but Sharif looked at her directly. He
made his eyes go blank as paint. He could feel them freezing
over as if they were looking at nothing, at a blank white wall.
Within the house there was a clashing of dishes in the kitchen,
the sound of cutlery being washed. No food was to be cooked,
but neighbours had brought round dishes, and Ghafur and the
other boys were serving the contents to the guests, as discreetly
as possible.

'I must go in,' Sharif said.

'Brother,' Sadia said. She gathered: she came to the point.
'We are only here for four days, then we must return to England.
There is a matter we must discuss while we are here. I am sorry
to bring it up directly.'

'Go on,' Sharif said.

'It is the estate,' Sadia said. 'How is it to be divided?'

'According to the usual division,' Sharif said. He would not
say that he was proposing to give his share directly to Dolly, if
she wanted to go on living here.

'Quite so,' Sadia said. 'But what does the usual division mean here? Is it divided between four of us, or among five? Do you see my difficulty?'

'I had not thought of it,' Sharif said.

'What happened when Father died? You see, I was not here – we were not able to come. Was a share set aside for Rafiq?'

'Yes,' Sharif said. He hardened his heart. 'I see your point, sister. You want to know if little-brother has been declared dead. It is true – his body was never found. Unless I am mistaken, Mother went on hoping to the end of her life that he somehow survived, perhaps in a Pakistani jail. She would not have applied to have him declared dead. So in 1974 he would have been assigned two parts of Father's estate, held in trust. I see your point. If he has not, in the meantime, been declared dead, then I quite see. You would be entitled to one seventh of the estate. But if it is accepted by the law that your brother – that Rafiq – came to his end some time in 1971, then you and your husband will be entitled to one fifth. A significant differ-ence. I see why this is important for you, sister. By all means. Go and establish the death of your brother in the eyes of the law, and go and profit from it. He was seventeen years old, sister. He was seventeen. He was seventeen when he met his end.'

'I know how old he was,' Sadia said. She looked terribly old, and ill, and it now struck Sharif that he might never see this sister of his again. He could spare her now, or he could say the thing that needed to be said. She had brought it up. Mahfouz, the coward, had wiped what he had done from his mind. If it was safe for them to return to Bangladesh, it was safe for them to be met by the family. And perhaps – Sharif could hear Mahfouz's voice explaining patiently, over the long night unwinding at thirty-three thousand feet – the time had come for his wife to raise this question with her brother.

'Where are your children?' Sharif said. 'Are they here?'

'Yes,' Sadia said. 'A boy and a girl. They are good children. They are with Mahfouz's mother and father today. They hardly speak Bengali at all! Do you know how it is, brother? We try so hard, and yet –'

'I know how it is,' Sharif said. 'As to the other matter –'

'I'm sorry if what I said upset you, brother,' Sadia said.

'No,' Sharif said. 'I am not upset. My emotions are quite in order. I will look at the question with the lawyers. Perhaps we can lay Rafiq to rest, and then the financial consequences will follow. He was tortured to death. That must be the truth of it. I do see that you and your husband would be anxious to draw the financial benefit from the death you brought about, after all.'

'How can you –'

'And if I ever see you or your husband again, after these days, I promise I will strike you upon your face with the flat of my hand. If you ever try to interfere with the lives of my sisters, I will find you and strike you upon your face. I promise you that on the grave of my brother, on the place his body rests.'

9.

Against his sister's protests he finished what he was saying, and closed the door in her face. The salon, to his surprise, was now nearly empty. At one end, there was Dolly, sitting with the twins, he was glad to see, talking earnestly and with some evident pleasure. The only other person in the room was a boy of sixteen or seventeen in a white robe. He had been lifting a small silver box from the sideboard, a little treasure of Mother's. Now he put it down again and began to walk out of the room.

'Who are you?' Sharif said. 'Brother, can I offer you anything?'

The boy kept on walking, saying something over his shoulder that Sharif could not catch or, perhaps, understand. In a moment he was out of the open front door of the house and away.

'Did you see that, Dolly?' Sharif said. 'I think he was about to steal Mother's silver snuffbox. Boys, go and find Mummy, straight away.'

The twins got up, good as gold, and made their way towards the dining room – they seemed to know exactly what was where in the house.

'I thought he was one of the readers Mahfouz arranged,' Dolly said. 'But there are so many people turning up. I should have put all the valuables away. Where is big-sister?'

'She's gone, I believe,' Sharif said drily, hoping that this was so.

'I expect she'll come back before much longer,' Dolly said. 'I've been making friends with the boys! I have to say – I simply adore Omith, he is my favourite relation of all, I believe.'

Dolly had always amused him, and he focused all his trembling attention on the sister he still loved and cared for. The boys had been taken off by Ghafur to see the workings of the kitchen, and the others were asleep upstairs, exhausted by the flight.

'What is this?' Nazia said, coming back. 'Do you have favourites between my boys, Dolly?'

'I must say I do,' Dolly said. 'Omith is especially sweet. Raja, he thinks he's in charge, doesn't he? But I think it's Omith you would like to trust and to rely on in the end.'

'What nonsense,' Sharif said, pleased. 'They are only seven years old, Dolly.' To the world outside, Raja and Omith must seem like two halves of an apple, different only in the way that halves of a symmetrical form were different. He never understood the confusion others sometimes had about them: he thought it showed only a lack of time spent with them, or a lack of observation. Even when they stomped, chanting a rhyme, about the house, one was doing the stomping, the other was imitating the movement. Omith never ran first; he always waited half a second after his brother had started. In the end, like him and Sadia, one boy would turn left, and the other would turn right.

'They're quite different,' Nazia was saying. 'If one of them's been naughty, I know which of them to interrogate. It's useless asking Raja. He always says, "Omith did it."'

'The flowerpot that got kicked over,' Sharif said. 'They still haven't had their punishment for that.'

'If Mahfouz and Sadia have gone,' Nazia said, 'I really don't think I can carry on with this noise, and it must be even worse from outside.'

'Oh, we can't stop it,' Dolly said. 'It would upset sister so much. Brother went to such lengths to arrange it all, and he was so shocked to hear that there was no amplification last time.'

'Well,' Sharif said, 'I think if we just left one pair of loud-speakers working, people would still hear it and still think it was very nice that we are doing our duty by Mother as they walked past.'

'Sharif will do it so neatly, everyone will think most of the loudspeakers failed,' Nazia said.

'If they think anything,' Sharif said. 'At least we will be able to get some sleep tonight. Now. Before I do that, let us talk about your future, little-sister.'

At the end of the three days, Nazia and the children flew back to England with Bina and Tinku. Sharif stayed in Bangladesh with Dolly. What happened to Mahfouz and Sadia, they never knew. Those three days, they expected to see him come through the front door, already complaining that there was something wrong with the loudspeakers. The readers themselves made this complaint, and were ignored. Sharif regretted that nobody would see the very neat job he had done of making the connections look frayed and, in the first place, incompetent. No one would suspect industrial sabotage, as he remarked to Dolly, once it was all over. On the second day, a letter came for Dolly in Mahfouz's handwriting, among all the other letters. She set that one aside from the letters of condolence, and some time later Sharif saw it unopened in the polished brass wastepaper basket underneath Father's old leather-topped desk.

He had a number of tasks to carry out before he could come home, and the faculty had given him two months' compassionate leave. First there was the question of Rafiq's death. He had to concede that his existence had to be left as it was. There was no 'Captain Qayyum' on record, though Sharif was certain he had remembered the name the officer had given as he took his brother away. There was no Mohammed Rafiqullah recorded as a prisoner anywhere. In the circumstances, he set about agreeing the provisions of the will and the distribution of the estate. It was straightforward: Father had left his possessions in good order – he had sorted it all out at the same time as selling the house in Old Dhaka for Sharif's sake. Mother had preserved what she had, not touching Rafiq's share, not really needing what Sharif had made over to her. The remains of the estate – Mother's property, the house in Dhanmondi, some land in the village and more savings than they expected – could be divided into seven. Two parts for Sharif, two nominally for Rafiq, one each for Dolly, Bina and Sadia. It was the law. Sharif proposed to divide his second part into three, and hand two of the parts to Dolly and Bina, so that they had the same as him. If Sadia and Mahfouz wanted to claim a fifth of Rafiq's inheritance, now sitting in trust as far back as Father's death, they would have to take steps to prove his death, and they would have to accept that they would enrich her brother and two sisters, too.

'I am so glad that my children are growing up in England,' Sharif said to Dolly one night. 'I promise you, when I die, Aisha is going to get one third, and Raja one third, and Omith one third. Absolute equality. This one-part-two-parts for the daughters and the sons is such nonsense.'

'Poor Sadia,' Dolly said – she was so soft-hearted. 'I wish things were a little easier for her. She must have loved Rafiq too, in her way.'

Sharif snorted. He quite enjoyed these evenings with little-sister. She had been so small when he left, her favourite reading was Feluda and the comics at the back of Daddy's newspaper. It was pleasant to sit with her, nearly adult, and talk seriously without a pair of small thugs kicking the back of the armchair, without the phone going constantly with requests for his daughter. They were safely back in Hillsborough.

All this might have been achieved much more quickly than it was. There were constant hartals, general strikes, in the city, and during those days, it was impossible to get anywhere. The lawyers' offices were closed, and no taxi driver or rickshaw-wallah would have risked the wrath of the mob that had demanded a general withdrawal of labour. The only way to get about, Samu said, was to persuade a friend with medical connections to lend them an ambulance. But Sharif was priggishly shocked at this. An ambulance that could have saved Mother might have been occupied by a Mrs Rahman, using it to visit her widowed sister for tea.

Samu was a clever chap, who was not at all troubled by the way Dolly blushed and ran for her brother's cover whenever he entered. He cajoled her, made flattering references to her, smiled in her general direction, and finally asked her a very easy question. He was good at drawing her out. Sharif liked him a great deal, but he was proving a tiresome difficulty. Dolly was not, for any reason, to marry before she had finished her degree, but it had taken her three years to finish the first year of study, what with the university being constantly closed down by the government. She could hardly live here alone with Ghafur cooking for her. But would she leave Bangladesh without Samu? Sharif embarked on his project, and instructed a lawyer to undertake the measures that would enable him to travel back to England with his unmarried sister. There was no reason why she could not do her degree at the University of Sheffield. Furthermore, if Samu was serious, he would wait for two years, and then he could join her and marry in England, or she could return to Bangladesh.

He rehearsed these arguments in the back of taxis and rickshaws, travelling from government office to lawyers' chambers and solicitors' rooms before speaking about it with his sister.

'How can you say that?' Samu said, towards the end of one evening. He had been their guest for dinner and had enjoyed the chicken curry, the bitter gourd and the little fried fishes they sometimes had; they knew now what pickles and garnishes he liked, and a small array of dishes was set out by his place on the table – the long, dark mahogany table had sometimes seated sixteen, and the three of them clustered now at one end. After dinner, Samu had requested a record of Beethoven, the 'Archduke' trio. It had been one of Father's favourites; the record had been bought, with several others, on Father's last trip to England in 1968, and Samu had heard it, and loved it, on many evenings here. 'There is nothing in our music to compare with Beethoven. We just have to accept that our music never advanced to that level of sophistication, that degree of ambition.'

'I disagree, my dear fellow,' Sharif said. He leant back in his armchair, scratching his chin as he talked. 'A work of art is not like a piece of engineering, subject to certain immutable physical laws. It carries the conditions for its own judgement with it. The standards by which Beethoven is judged are the standards that Beethoven created. If you tried to judge a song by Tagore by those standards, it is regarded as inferior. But the excellence of a song by Tagore is to be judged by the standards that the song created. By those standards, Beethoven must be regarded as full of errors and ugly of proportion.'

'But, brother!' Samu said. 'This is all cultural relativism. If we are to claim that we deserve the first prize in some areas, worldwide –'

'Such as?' Dolly put in. She and Samu sat side by side on the long oatmeal-coloured sofa, she knitting a blue-and-green sleeveless pullover in a complicated pattern; the four balls of different-coloured wool orderly in her lap. She was shy at first, and then, as her Samu engaged her and confronted her with things she could not agree with, she spoke up like her mother's direct daughter.

'Such as film. We are agreed, are we not, that the Bengali film is the highest utterance of the art? Even Western prize juries have accepted this, handing their prizes to Satyajit Ray humbly. Why not accept that Beethoven is at the pinnacle of that particular art form? Why must we suggest that a little song by Tagore is the equal of the Ninth Symphony, the Missa Solemnis, the – the "Archduke" trio?'

'This is abject nonsense,' Sharif said, with some energy. 'This is what your grandfather the babu would have said to gratify the Englishman, to pretend to admire the German dead a century ago.'

'Ah, but we are not talking, are we, about what is truly loved?' Samu burst out. 'We are talking about what is truly great. Take the "Grosse Fuge". It is universally admired but considered harsh, difficult to love. Should we therefore dismiss it in favour of a popular hit?'

They enjoyed Samu's company immensely, Sharif as much as Dolly. They had not half done with Beethoven when Samu declared that it was midnight, and he must be off. Sharif walked the dear fellow down to the gate of the house. It was a beautiful night, and Samu said he would walk the short distance home. Dolly was still in her chair when Sharif came back into the house. He dismissed Ghafur, busy tidying up, and sat down again.

'There is no question of Mahfouz's gentleman any more,' he said. 'The one who owned a laundry.'

'Ah!' Dolly said. 'Is my sister so little to be trusted? There is no question of such a gentleman. There never was.'

'But I think we must talk of Samu,' Sharif said. 'He is a splendid chap.'

Sharif went on to explain the difficulty, and made his proposal. It was hard for Dolly to listen to. She had envisaged only a world with her and Samu in it. Like an inept novelist, she had set out only the meeting of twin minds, the beautiful things the two of them would say to each other, and not given any thought to where such things would take place. From time to time Dolly said, 'But he will forget all about me!' and her eyes started to shine with tears. Sharif had a single, unchanging point: if Dolly abandoned her education for the sake of love, she would come to blame the man she had married. This country – Sharif had to make the point – it was what they had all fought for, but now, it was a country more like one in terminal decline than one at the beginning of its life. The education would only eventually be provided by Dhaka. Education; or Bangladesh. Samu was not in doubt. 'Samu will not wait,' Dolly said. She hunched forward at one end of the oatmeal sofa. 'He will marry someone else, and I – I – I will be stuck with the man that Mahfouz found for me, in England somewhere. Oh, brother, please …'

In the morning, Sharif put on his best clothes – a blue jacket, a white shirt, a decorous, restrained tie in a dark orange with circles on it – and went to call on Samir. They took a rickshaw to the gardens around the Lalbagh Fort, and walked around that interesting historical monument seven times. The rickshaw-wallah waited patiently for them for over an hour. The little flowers that bloomed in the beds around the park were a lovely cloud of pink and white; in the corners, in the niches on the old red stone walls, pairs of lovers sat, discreetly exchanging their promises. Sharif and Samir walked amicably, like two old gentlemen with walking sticks. Sharif started by saying that he had reconsidered, and that perhaps Samir was right to praise the ambition of the Western classical tradition. Samu responded by saying that Sharif, too, was right, that they had no means of judging a work of art other than by the standards established by a particular culture. Which, for instance – to take another example – was the best fish? Hilsa, koi, pabda, rui, bhetki – how to decide? Or the English halibut and plaice and mackerel? They began in high good humour with each other, and after they had gone on to talk of other matters, bought each other a bag of chotpoti from the roadside vendor who waited outside the iron gates to the Fort, and ate, sitting companionably next to each other on a wall. They had turned in the previous hour into a pair of students, irresponsible and hungry.

10.

At the end of that summer, Sharif returned to England with his youngest sister, Dolly. A bond that he would support her had been supplied to the British High Consulate in Dhaka, along with statements of his income and professional standing.

With some negotiation, Dolly began her degree at the University of Sheffield. She thought it best to start from the beginning, so patchy had her course in Dhaka proved. In three years, she finished, and was thought unlucky to have missed out on a First. She lived all that time in the spare bedroom in Hillsborough, with a trip once every six weeks to visit her sister Bina in Cardiff, along with her husband Tinku and their clever baby Bulu. She made three friends at the university, girls called Farna and Karen from London, and another with very bright red hair called Annie, who was Welsh.

In 1987, a month after Dolly finished her degree, Samu arrived in England. She went to meet him at the airport, Sharif and Nazia coming along with her for moral support, hanging back to allow them to say hello for the first time in three years. Aisha had wanted to come, too – she was at the end of her first year at Oxford, and her plans to travel to Italy with friends had been put off until August – but Sharif thought it would be best if she stayed at home with the boys.

Everyone in their different ways had worried about this meeting, whether it would be the same after all these years. But Samu came through the departure gates pushing his two big suitcases on a trolley; there he was with his careless hair, his baggy blue pullover and old tweed jacket, and his expression that turned from anxiety to shining delight, like a coin being flipped over. It was the sight of Dolly, strange to say, that had done it.

They married in October, and settled in Peterborough. A year later, they had a daughter. They called her Camellia. Sharif laughed when he heard the name; he smiled, however, in a quieter, more occluded way when Dolly said it had always been her favourite flower. She hoped the bush was still there, in Father's garden.

The next year, both cousins, Aisha and Fanny, graduated from their universities. Fanny was in disgrace: she only got a 2.2 from Manchester. But Aisha got a First in modern history from Oxford. She was the only one from her school who had got into Oxford or Cambridge that year. Now she was planning to go to Cambridge to do an MPhil in international relations, after spending some months as an intern at the United Nations. One of Sharif's friends at the university, Steve Smithers's near-neighbour the professor of law, Jeremy Chang, had helped to arrange that. It meant a stretch in Geneva from November to April.

In the wake of Aisha's degree success, Nazia had to comfort her great friend Sally Mottishead when she wondered what she had done wrong to deserve such children, when you looked at Spike and now the twins, totally off the rails, and she had no idea what had gone wrong to make Samantha like that; when you looked at Nazia and her clever daughter, you really wondered … Nazia smiled sympathetically. Spike had been lucky not to be sent to prison the year before. She doubted that Aisha ever gave Samantha Mottishead a moment's thought, these days. They had been quite friendly at one point. To reward Aisha, they took a villa in Umbria for two weeks that summer. Feeling sorry for poor Fanny, they asked her along too: Rekha wanted to punish her by refusing to let her come, but Nazia and Aisha prevailed. It was a perfect holiday. Always afterwards, everyone remembered it not by the trips to see anything historic, or the beauty of the countryside, but by the twins deciding that they would use the two weeks to learn to juggle. They stood on the terrace, all afternoon long, throwing one, then two, then three, then, in the end, four balls in the air. It was very impressive.

'When we go back home,' Nazia said to Sharif, 'I want to look for a new house.'

'Not again,' he said. 'We only moved –'

'Ten years ago,' Nazia said. 'I'd like to move to the house where we are going to live for the rest of our lives. We've been long enough in that house with the noise of Mrs Selden's television through the party wall. I want to move to a nice big house in Ranmoor. That's where I want to live.'

Together they watched the boys throwing their bright-coloured balls into the air. Aisha and Fanny had gone for a walk, in search, Nazia suspected, of the handsome owner of the farmhouse, an Italian nobleman. They were good girls, but she would not say anything to Sharif. The weather had been beautiful: deliciously hot but dry, not humid at all, and a pleasure to sit and eat outside in the evenings. This part of the earth was richly forested, the layers of foliage thick and dark over the soaring hills, the sky an intense and pure blue. The scents of a high Italian summer would stay with Sharif, and the sounds of crickets scratching in the late afternoon, the wild threadlike screams of birdsong in the early morning.

'I'm so pleased they'll have some skill in life,' Sharif said, meaning the boys. He was not exactly agreeing to Nazia's proposal, nor dismissing it. 'They could run away and join the circus when they fail their O levels.'

'GCSEs,' Nazia said. 'They do GCSEs now. O levels are historical curiosities, I believe.'

Towards the end of their holiday in Umbria, an unexpected event occurred. They were driving back late on Saturday night from dinner in Assisi, a restaurant recommended by the Signor, as Fanny and Aisha termed him, giggling. The dark country roads had been empty, but tonight they could see that in laybys or just by the side of the road, cars were parked. Once or twice a light was on in a car, and a single man was sitting in it, smoking to protect himself against the mosquitoes, waiting for something. There were no people on the roads. They could not understand what could lead these men to sit in their cars, in the middle of nowhere, buried in the forests, so late at night. They reached the farmhouse, said goodnight to each other, and went to bed.

It must have been six in the morning that they were woken up. A huge noise of artillery broke out – it seemed almost at once – of gunfire all around the house. Later that day, the Signor would explain the cause of it. This Sunday was the first day of the hunting season, and many keen hunters slept in their cars in the forest, so as to be able to start shooting at six in the morning. There were many casualties on this day, every year, so numerous were the hunters, and so keen to shoot at any movement in the bushes. But that explanation would come in some hours. At six that morning, Sharif and Nazia woke with a shock, and were in each other's arms in a moment, Nazia making the noises a small animal might make, stifled, terrified, and them bundling each other out of bed to – where? Nazia's eyes were wide and screaming, silent. It was five long minutes before Sharif could get to the point of realizing that this was not the place he had last been woken by gunfire outside the house; it was five minutes more before he could say to his wife –

No it's not happening not here please not again where where where no

– that the terror was unfounded. It had not happened yesterday and there was no reason to think that it was anything to do with them. It was deep in both of them, that reaction of the legs to the sound of gunfire. 1971. That day in Umbria, deep in the much-shadowed forests that lined the hills twenty miles behind Assisi, they discovered what had stayed with them and always would.

Two days later they packed their suitcases and began to drive, the long journey back to Rome. It had been a wonderful holiday, they all agreed. The day after they returned, Nazia went to an estate agent and asked about houses in Ranmoor. Perhaps that noise of gunfire in the forests just by the house in Umbria had revived in her a strong desire for bricks and mortar. For a wall around them. Her budget would stretch to eighty thousand pounds. In six months, she had found the perfect house for them, and Sharif indulgently agreed. Three months after that they decided to hold a small party to celebrate, now that the new house seemed to be in order. The last thing they did was to paint the front door a new colour. The twins decided on the particular shade of blue, a dark policeman-like blue, perfect.

CHAPTER THIRTEEN

I.

Nearly four months had gone by since the weekend Enrico Caracciolo had spent with the Indian girl and her parents. He had hardly seen her afterwards, and in early June he had returned to Sicily to work on his thesis, the shutters of his parents' house closed against the great heat.

Enrico was certain that his thesis would form the basis of an entire rethinking of the subject. An earlier version had been greeted by his undergraduate tutor at the University of Catania as a stupendously original synthesis of intellectual models. He did not believe that a master's thesis on its own would reshape the subject and change the minds of politicians and professionals across the globe. He had therefore applied to Cambridge to progress to a PhD, and his doctoral thesis would be a fuller example of the idea he had only sketched out at master's level. After all, had not the *Tractatus Logico-Philosophicus* formed Wittgenstein's doctoral thesis at that very university? And had it not, indeed, changed the entire discipline of thought until Sraffa, an Italian (Enrico's thoughts went on, ambitiously), had persuaded Wittgenstein of his fundamental mistake?

The university insisted that the thesis be delivered in person, and Enrico did not trust the Italian postal service in any case, so he returned to England for four days with the two copies of his thesis in his hand luggage. During those days in Cambridge, he tried to meet the academic who, he had decided, would supervise his PhD thesis, but Dr al-Maktoum did not answer the note he sent, and when Enrico succeeded in reaching him on the telephone, Dr al-Maktoum sounded surprised. It would not, unfortunately, be possible to meet with Enrico in the next two days.

Enrico's thesis was an application of Marxist structures to the global relations of nation states. In it, he dismissed the old models of first world and third world, or colonizers and colonized, and proposed instead a division of the world's nation states into *bourgeoisie, petit bourgeoisie, intelligentsia* and *proletariat*. The role of the intelligentsia-state, for instance Sweden, is to educate the proletariat-state, for instance many sub-Saharan African states, into a state of mind in which the overthrow of the bourgeois-state, for instance the United States, is not only contemplated but a reality.

Twice during August, he met Dr Salaparotti who had supervised his undergraduate thesis. Once they met at an evening party at his aunt's country house in the mountains, once at an ice-cream stand in the centre of Catania. Dr Salaparotti was eating a watermelon granita, Enrico a double scoop of chocolate and raspberry, an original combination. Dr Salaparotti had moved on from ice-cream combinations to assure him that his thesis, too, was remarkable for its originality, and could only impress more with the addition of greater detail, which, no doubt, the MPhil thesis had supplied. He looked forward, in due course, to welcoming a Cambridge PhD to the faculty in Sicily. Enrico said nothing: he believed that his destiny was elsewhere.

At the end of August, the results were posted to Enrico.

Enrico made a telephone call to his Cambridge supervisor, Dr al-Maktoum, on the day when, the letter had informed him, supervisors would be available to discuss marks and comment on work. He made the telephone call from the office of Dr Salaparotti in the faculty of law, a large, high-ceilinged room with a number of electric fans buzzing, looking out over the handsome Renaissance courtyard where the new students were congregating. Dr Salaparotti sat on the edge of the desk, looking at Enrico with an expression of disgust, one corner of his mouth slightly raised – the disgust was for the narrow minds of Cambridge, bigoted against original applications of classical Marxism. Dr al-Maktoum informed him briskly, in his high-pitched, yawing, feminine voice, that his thesis applied a historically unfounded model to real-world experience where it made no sense. Furthermore, many of these points had been made repeatedly to Enrico in the course of his work, during every single meeting with the supervisor of his thesis, and it was impossible to see that any cognizance had been taken of any of these comments or, indeed, of what the events of 1989 across Europe might mean for a Marxist analysis. There was no possibility of his being accepted for a Cambridge PhD. Enrico asked what, in that case, were his options for progressing?

'You could try to get a job outside academia, or one that did not concern itself with relations between nation states,' Dr al-Maktoum said. 'I think a post in local government somewhere would be quite suitable, so long as no policy-making was involved.'

When the telephone was put down, Dr Salaparotti wordlessly handed Enrico a letter he had received. It advertised a conference to take place in London, on the new Europe 'after Communism', and invited submissions for papers from specialists in international relations. It would take place in late October.

There would be no better place to display his big idea before the important minds of the academic world, and to invite them to bid to host Enrico's PhD thesis. He sent in an application, and a summary of his MPhil thesis, describing himself, with Dr Salaparotti's consent and subterfuge, as a research fellow of the University of Catania.

2.

The conference was taking place in the humanities block of Islington Polytechnic. The briefing package had stressed that the campus was not within walking distance of the Islington underground stops, and that colleagues who were planning to make their own arrangements for accommodation should look at bed-and-breakfasts in Chigwell, Theydon Bois or Woodford. Enrico was staying on campus. The buildings were square and bleak, either glass-fronted with rusting metal frames, or solid barracks where graffiti had been allowed to take hold. The grounds were pleasantly grassy, with the occasional island of trees and stunted flowerbeds. His room was in one of the glass-fronted buildings, and the winds whistled through what he discovered too late was a cracked windowpane. He shivered all night on the damp, narrow mattress.

Registration took place in the morning from nine thirty in the barracks. Enrico looked around him at the dining hall, but those having breakfast were not familiar to him. They did not look like academics at all, but like prosperous businessmen, and the noisy tone of their conversation suggested they had been acquainted comfortably for many years. He went with his bag of notebooks and papers as soon as registration started. There was a good-looking, well-dressed woman in the bony English style just settling herself behind a desk, getting a series of folders out of her bag. There was a smell of onions frying, which had been in his room, in the canteen, and in the humanities block to the same degree.

'Right,' the woman said. 'Just hold your horses for two more minutes and I'll be all set.'

The meaning of her words escaped Enrico, but he understood that she was almost ready to deal with him.

'And here you are. Now. Who are you and where's my list? Ah – here it is. Your name, please? Nice journey?'

The conference did not begin for another hour, so Enrico sat down on one of the benches underneath the noticeboards. The woman busied herself with her papers, muttering as if Enrico had gone away. From time to time she shot him a hostile look over the top of her folder. He inspected the programme, which he had seen before, and the list of participants, which was new to him. He saw only one name from Cambridge, a name he was not sure he recognized. He had hoped that Dr al-Maktoum would be coming: he did not anticipate his changing his mind about admitting Enrico, but he looked forward to Dr al-Maktoum observing the acclamation, the depth and engagement of the questions afterwards.

In bursts, the other participants started to arrive. With the second of the arrivals, a woman with unbrushed hair and a green woollen dress, the administrator engaged in some amused and reproachful mockery. With the others, Enrico was pleased to see, she was just as dismissive and unhelpful as she had been with him. A gentleman from the University of Alexandria tried to start a conversation with Enrico. Someone who had been on the course with him at Cambridge, a middle-aged Englishman, an ex-army officer, sat down next to him on the bench.

'Are you giving a paper?' the officer said.

'Yes, this afternoon,' Enrico said contemptuously. Why come to a conference without reading the programme? The man was an idiot.

'I did rather better than I expected,' the officer said. 'In the exams, you know. I thought I'd scrape a pass but – well, it was a touch better than that. Thrilled.'

'Congratulations,' Enrico said.

'The thing is,' the man continued, 'I really only did it to give myself a year off. My boss wanted me out of the way. You remember I work in the City? For a merchant bank?'

'I thought –'

'Left the army years ago,' the man went on. He must be used to this. In seminars, he had started comments with the words 'In the armed forces', even putting his hand up in lectures to make objections in the same terms.

'Olu Adetokunbo, my boss you know, he actually suggested the sabbatical himself. Get the old bugger out of the way, I thought, then suggest retirement. I wasn't far wrong, as it turns out. I won't bore you. But I'd thought I'd do it as a pleasant diversion, then come back and inflict a lawsuit on them. I don't have a paper to give, alas, I wasn't prepared. But I hope to make useful contributions from the floor. What's your paper?'

Enrico told him.

'Oh, aye,' the man said, not very curious. 'It's still interesting you, then? I saw there's another of our friends here. She played her cards very close to her chest.'

'What do you mean?'

'Well, you wouldn't have thought – well, here she is. Heroine of the hour.'

Afterwards, Enrico examined his conscience and was quite clear. He would not have come if he had known that Aisha Sharifullah was coming. He didn't know how he could have missed her name on the list of speakers. She wore a bright red coat and, underneath it, a short grey dress; in a kind of nod to student existence, her shoes were black, heavy and thick-soled, like toy versions of the boots that builders wore. She inspected the pair of them without surprise.

'I saw you were coming,' she said briefly. 'What's up? Bill al-Maktoum told me I should come to this, give a summarized version of my thesis. What are you talking about?'

'Not speaking,' the officer said, and at the same time Enrico began to give a version of his paper.

'That sounds great,' Aisha said. 'I'm on this morning. I wouldn't bother coming, you must have heard it all before.'

Enrico watched her go. He knew her work; he would ask a devastating question; he would make this conference, full of the thinkers of the future, sit up and pay attention. She had nothing but the citation of particular cases, Cambodia against Bangladesh against Afghanistan against South Africa, all meas-ured against a new innovation called War Crimes and another one called Reconciliation. She talked about people who had shot other people, talked about them by name without any acknowledgement of historical necessity, which must be more important than one death here and one death there. There was no understanding of class in her work, and no understanding that nation states might fall into antagonistic and rivalrous social classes, too. And the example that came up regularly in her work, that of the place she came from, Bangladesh, she was too personally invested in it. Of course the English, with their love of the person they happened to know and the story they had once heard, would reward that.

'She's a splendid girl, Aisha,' the army officer said. 'I thought you two were seeing each other at some point?'

'Not actually,' Enrico said. He began to roll up the sleeves of his old pullover.

3.

A girl Aisha had known at high school was at the conference, oddly enough. She had gone into immigration law after Manchester University. Unlike Aisha, she was working, and her firm had given her a couple of days off to attend the conference. Julie had come down by train, but since she was going back to Sheffield, she gratefully accepted the offer of a lift from Aisha in her new red Fiesta. Almost all the way – certainly beyond Leicester Forest East service station where they stopped for an awful sandwich – they laughed about poor Enrico. Julie had never met him before: she frankly couldn't believe that Aisha had ever been serious about someone like that. Aisha said it was a weekend at home that had put her off him.

'Not the mark he got,' Julie said. At the conference, that second morning, Aisha had listened to the paper she had already heard summarized repeatedly, over cups of coffee in Cambridge cafés, in seminars that Enrico had monopolized, in his room late at night ... There were no questions afterwards: Enrico had apparently taken that as a sign of people being overawed rather than kindly looking away from a car crash.

'I'm always going to ask to see a man's academic work before I go out for dinner with them in the future. Actually, I think I'm off men for the foreseeable future.'

'Very sensible,' Julie said. 'I shook his hand. It was wet – I mean actually wet, not just a bit damp. What were you thinking?'

'There was a certain Signor in my past that I longed for. I thought all Italians would have a bit of Signor in them.'

'Ah, well,' Julie said. 'What are you going to do now, then?'

'I honestly don't know,' Aisha said. 'I didn't expect to do as well as I did in the MPhil.'

'That paper was brilliant,' Julie said loyally. 'I was on the edge of my seat.'

'I've got an internship sorted out. A friend of my dad's leapt into the breach. Someone had to drop out and he phoned on just the right day, apparently. Down at United Nations in Geneva. I did one before I did my MPhil and this other one came up. After that, I don't know. Perhaps I'll do what you do.'

'We wouldn't have you,' Julie said. 'You'd show us up.' But in fifteen minutes it emerged that Julie was coming to Sheffield for the sake of a client of her firm, a piece of pro-bono work. They were borderline illegals, living on top of each other, a dozen and a half in the house and doing odd jobs for building contractors. Julie was going to see them, sort them out, put them on some kind of footing.

'I should come along,' Aisha said. 'Offer my expertise.'

'What expertise?'

'We're immigrants,' Aisha said. 'I know what it's like.'

'In what sense,' Julie said, 'are you an immigrant? You were nearly head girl.'

'My mum and dad are from Bangladesh and I grew up there and I came to England in 1976. It's only fifteen years ago. In what sense am I not an immigrant?'

'Your dad came over to be professor of engineering,' Julie said. 'That's not the same as what we're talking about.'

But she agreed to take Aisha to visit the men. It occurred to Julie, too, that some of them, at least, were also Bangladeshi, and if there was a problem with language, Aisha could try to translate. The easiest thing, Julie said, was if they went straight away to the men's house in Burngreave. She'd just told her mother she'd be along some time today.

Aisha had very little idea where Burngreave was in the city. The Wicker was the limit of her knowledge in that direction, and it came as a shock to the system when Julie directed her to turn off from the usual route from the motorway before they reached the city centre. There was a landscape of shops boarded up, or made secure with wire over the windows, and betting shops and dank pubs. They turned off the main road at Julie's direction, and there was a gang of children trying to climb a no-entry sign, the one on top of the pile being pushed up by the others, his arms wrapped round the pole. There were a few cars in the road, and the occasional house had a neat front garden. Most were paved over. Julie directed her to stop at number seventy-six. The curtains sagged at the front windows, drawn across, and in the front garden was the rubbish of many weeks.

'Some of them will be sleeping,' Julie said. 'They're either sleeping or they're working. My man's expecting me, or said he was – he's working nights at the minute. That's how they get eighteen in a house, there's beds for six or eight at a pinch, some sleeping now, some sleeping when the other lot go to work, a couple between jobs who just sleep when they see an opportunity. God knows when they wash the sheets. Or wash themselves.'

The man who opened the door had been woken up; his hair was tousled, his face open and bewildered, as if roused from a dream of a different, warmer, greener and less-peopled place. From him, or from behind him, came a wave of a smell, of the uneasy sleep of eighteen men after labour. He looked at Julie, his innocent face waiting for them to start, and looked at Aisha. He was young, perhaps no more than twenty.

'This is one of the ones who struggle with English,' Julie said. 'Over to you. Tell him that we're here to see Anis and he needs to go and wake him up.'

'Good morning,' Aisha said in Bengali. The boy responded, repeating her words, but awkwardly. She repeated what Julie had said, but the boy looked at her blankly.

In the end he repeated, 'Anis,' and then something that Aisha could not understand.

'He doesn't speak Bangla,' Aisha said. 'I think it's something from the north he speaks. I'd just be shouting at him.'

'Anis,' Julie said to him firmly. He turned and went into the house ahead of them, going upstairs one step at a time, like a tired old man, holding on to the banisters. The smell was over-powering in the house, and she led them past two shut doors into the kitchen. It was surprisingly clean, with almost nothing out on the work surface, kitchen table or sink. There were padlocks on each of the cupboards. 'I thought it was all the same, your language.'

There were steps coming down the stairs. The boy went into his room and shut the door. He had answered the front door because he was nearest. An older man, perhaps in his thirties, who had made an effort to brush his hair and to put on a shirt and trousers, came into the kitchen. His eyes lit up when he saw Julie.

'Hello, Anis,' Julie said. 'I've brought a friend to help out, as you see.'

'Hello, Julie!' Anis said. 'And hello to you, madam, very honoured.'

'I'm Aisha,' Aisha said, dropping into Bengali. 'Where are you from, brother?'

'I am from Chittagong,' Anis said. 'But now I am a citizen of the UK, thanks to my friend Julie. I have been here for four years, to my shame without papers, but my friend Julie is regularizing my position.'

'How do you live?' Aisha said.

'I work,' Anis said. 'I was working on a building site and clearing away rubbish, but I was no longer needed at that job ten days ago. I arrived at the place where I was meant to be each morning, and there at the correct time, but the van driven by Michael that had come every morning at the same time, that did not arrive. But I have found another job in the last week, a job emptying a house where an old gentleman died, and the owner of the firm has told me that he will use me again because I worked very hard and we finished the job on time.'

'Good, good,' Aisha said, and translated all this to Julie, who had been asking, 'What's he saying?' all the way through.

'I don't suppose he's got any records of any of this,' Julie said. 'Payslips, hours worked … No, forget I asked.'

'But why can't he –'

'There's a lot of why-can't-he in this job,' Julie said. 'We'll have to go with what we've got, and on to the next one.'

Anis watched their conversation patiently. When it had finished, he said, 'I would like to make you a cup of tea, madam, and for Julie as well.'

'Thank you, that would be nice,' Aisha said, and with a look of relief and pleasure, Anis rose. From his pocket he took a set of keys, and unlocked one of the cupboards.

'Is he making us some tea?' Julie said. 'He always asks, I always say no, thanks. I don't want to put him to any trouble. You can see the struggles he's got.'

'You've got to accept hospitality,' Aisha said. 'My mother would never talk to someone who refused it. Drink his tea.'

In the cupboard were two mugs on one shelf and another on the upper shelf. From signs of duplication such as two bags of rice, it looked as if the two shelves belonged to different tenants. From the lower shelf, Anis took three teabags. With an unnecessary number of journeys between table, cupboard, sink and kitchen work surface, he filled and boiled the kettle, made three mugs of tea and added dried milk and sugar from the cupboard, not asking for any variation. Finally he took three digestive biscuits from the packet and placed them on a small plate. Aisha reflected that if he had a teapot he could probably have managed with two teabags. But there was no teapot. She sipped the strange-tasting tea with Anis's eager eyes upon her; she took a biscuit from the plate.

'Why did you leave Chittagong?' Aisha asked.

'I came to England to join my brother,' Anis said. 'The university closed and it had been closed for some time. It was best to come to England. I wanted to study but I could not study, so I worked in a job my brother found for me. It was near Derby, an hour from here, and then another job in Chesterfield, and so it went on. When I heard what the job was paying me I thought of it in taka and I thought that I would save nearly all of it to do my degree at the university. But, alas, sister. The cost of everything is so much greater here. Even small-small packet of food. And living here in this house, it is already eighty pounds every week, which is how much in taka?'

'How many of you are there, paying eighty pounds a week?'

'Sixteen,' Anis said. Aisha made a quick calculation. The landlord in receipt of sixteen times eighty pounds times fifty-two, call it fifty, would have made the money in one year to buy the house that her parents had just bought in Ranmoor. She doubted that this house was worth more than ten or fifteen thousand pounds. She wondered what her mother's income from the houses in Wincobank was, with four students in each, everyone with their own bedroom. The landlord probably owned several houses just like this one. There was no reason for him not to buy another with the profits from the previous one every two or three months.

'Who is your landlord?' she asked, when she had translated Anis's explanation.

'My brother Quddus,' he said simply.

'My father says "brother" to anyone who speaks Bangla, pretty much,' Aisha explained to Julie. 'Brother, who are the other men in this house?'

'They work hard,' Anis said. 'I want to get a job in the post office, a good, respectable, safe job. But I need to have a permission to stay in this country. I have been in this country seven years now and I have not been a problem to this country. Once I was very ill and I tried to get better and I went to Boots the chemist and they told me I had to go to a doctor. And I went to the doctor and he gave me some antibiotics and it was cured. I went to the doctor in the hospital because they would treat me without looking to see if I had a number of permission, which I do not have. That is the only time I have been to the medicine and the only time I have been to something that costs money. The property taxes are paid by my brother who owns this house and the income taxes are paid by the men who employ me and I am not worried by that. Can you tell me when I will be English? Are you English? Did Julie help you to become English?'

'I was born in England,' Aisha said simply.

Afterwards, as she drove Julie back to her mother's house on the borders of Crookes and Broomhill, where the elm trees shaded the road and a stately stone house acted as a branch library, the children's books upstairs, where the shops were open, selling meat and fruit and birthday cards and posters and dry goods and newspapers and books and flowers and wine and shoes and clothes for old and young and children, selling everything in profusion – she watched them come, the shops, and she knew they complained about their prospects and it could have made her cry. Anis would never step through the door of any one of these shops. They talked about it, in a way.

'I don't know anything about that sort of thing,' Aisha said. 'It makes me feel so lucky.'

'Lucky, how?' Julie said.

'I didn't have to do any of that,' Aisha said. 'My mum and dad – they just came over because my dad got a job at the university. And my grandfather sold his big house in Old Dhaka that no one lived in so they could just buy a house here. And we'd been here three years when my dad just went out and bought a video recorder.'

'A video recorder? Didn't he have to buy a TV first?'

'Oh, you know what I mean,' Aisha said. 'Those men, they've got nothing.'

'They've got a video recorder,' Julie said. 'I happen to know there's a TV and a video recorder in the front room where the guy who opened the door sleeps on the sofa.'

'Well, it's not ...' Aisha said. She couldn't explain what she felt. 'They didn't have to share a house with anyone and they didn't have to put a lock on the kitchen cupboard against someone stealing their teabags. We just came here and my mum handed her credit card over to Cole Brothers immediately. It's class, not race, divides people.'

'It's fine,' Julie said. 'Do you think an Englishman would have got your dad's rightful job as the professor of engineering? Do you think that if he hadn't come, using up, I don't know, twenty thousand pounds of English people's money every year, there'd be space for five more people like Anis to come and be ripped off by builders to pay them four thousand a year each, tops?'

'My dad wasn't paid that much when he got here,' Aisha said. 'It was 1976 we came over. He wasn't a professor then, either.'

'Anyway,' Julie said. They were arriving at Julie's mum's house; half of a pair of big stone houses with a huge rhododendron bush by the front gate. Julie's dad had scarpered five years ago, was living with a girl he'd taught at school out in the Peak District, and now Julie's mum had been looking out for them. She was standing with delight at the front window, holding her unruly dachshund Eccles up, like a fat writhing sausage with legs, trying to make him wave with his ginger front legs.

'How long are you here for?' Aisha said.

'Just while Friday,' Julie said, putting on a joke-Sheffield accent. 'I'm reet thraiped wi' struggle.'

'I've no idea what that means,' Aisha said. 'I'll be off – give me a ring if you're at a loose end.'

'Oh, come in for a cup of tea,' Julie said. 'My mum'll be thrilled to see you – "your clever friend", she always calls you.

You know,' she said, seeing that Aisha wasn't to be tempted, 'it's the women I worry about. When the men get a bit beyond the Anis stage, they come and see you to say they want a visa for their wives. And the wives come over and they can't speak a word of English and they never learn. They just disappear into the back rooms and the kitchens and they just look out of the window and that's it.'

'Not all of them,' Aisha said. 'My mum –'

'I'm not talking about people like your mum. She's not done down by the class struggle. Listen, thanks for the lift. I'll see you.'

And then, quite soon, she was home. It was home for a while longer. Then she would go out into the world, as people did, though perhaps not as Anis had, at the mercy of a man he called his brother, a man called Quddus making £1440 a week from that house alone, somewhere in the region of £75,000 a year. She had always been good at mental arithmetic. She would not go out into the world like that. In a month or two her parents' house would stop being 'home', but for the moment, she pulled into the driveway of the new and barely familiar house, and her mother was already opening the front door with poor old Raja in tow, she looking delighted, as if it had been weeks since Aisha had gone away, Raja – who should, surely, have been at school – making a performance of grinning and waving at his sister. I have no idea how we deserve this, Aisha said to herself, smiling and waving back. Then she remembered that her mother was being especially nice to her since that business of writing a stupid letter to the son of the man next door. There was a lot of sympathy and advice to get through in the weeks before she went off to Geneva for the internship, the second one she'd had.

4.

At first when Ada Browning had arrived there, the engineers had all seemed the same. They had had their bright faces and their air of ingenuity; they dressed in nylon-heavy ways that academic engineers liked; and at some point they had all lost the ability to observe a woman. After a time she had started to register the differences between Bob and David, between Phil and James, and the differences were not all to do with age. She had been there twenty years and as soon as she had been able to identify him, she'd never got on with Steve Smithers. It was all to do with treating you like a grown-up, she believed. She had always liked Sharif, on the other hand, because he didn't come into the office and start picking up things and putting them down again before getting round to asking her a favour. He came in and he asked a question and then he went away again.

So after thirty minutes of the Steve Smithers treatment, she was quite pleased to see Sharif through her door.

'You don't by any chance want to change your office, do you?' she said.

'Me? No, I don't think so,' Sharif said, puzzled. 'If it's absolutely necessary I will, but –'

'That's quite all right,' Ada said. 'That solves a problem.' Now she could go back to Steve Smithers and tell him, with regret, she had explored all possibilities and for the moment there was no office available for him to move into. 'What can I do for you?'

'I didn't know that you knew my next-door neighbour,' Sharif said. 'I saw you visiting him yesterday. I didn't realize until I saw all of you, arriving in black.'

'Oh, you're living next door to Hilary Spinster, are you?' Ada said. 'Poor Celia. She was really my friend. I knew her years back – my first must have been born at the same time as her fourth and we kept in touch. She was a friendly soul. It was only the end of the week before last. I phoned him up and he said she was too ill to have visitors, and then his daughter phoned on Monday to tell me that the funeral was yesterday.'

'There were plenty of people there,' Sharif said. 'We never met her, unfortunately. I think I saw her being brought home about a month ago, and then last week an ambulance came for her. I suppose that was her being taken into the hospice.'

'I suppose so,' Ada said. 'It was a strange event. They've got four children but I don't believe the boys came. It was only the girls. I don't know what happened there. There's a girl who's practically middle-aged now, she's got four or five children, and a much younger girl, very shy and upset she was.'

'One of the boys was there,' Sharif said. 'I think it was the younger one.'

'Anyway. It was nice to say goodbye to Celia, though I think she had a rotten old time with that Hilary. Very supercilious and angry. Short men, very difficult, in my view. How is he as a neighbour, thus far?'

'Oh, very pleasant, very pleasant,' Sharif said, and then he was off.

Raja and Omith were having the same discussion they had been having for weeks now. The television set was on, and making an awful din, but the boys were ignoring it.

'Why would you be satisfied with the maze that someone has designed for you?' Omith was saying. 'You can't change it. You just have to go round and round it. After about a week you work out the right strategy for that maze and then there's no reason why you can't get to level fifteen at least, barring stupid mistakes.'

'You don't want to waste your time designing mazes,' Raja said.

'But you don't have to design the maze just for yourself,' Omith said. 'What happens if – Listen, the Japanese guy who designed this, what if one of the mazes he tossed aside, I like that one better? It's gone, isn't it?'

'Where's Mummy?' Sharif said. He had heard all this before. It was a game that the boys were addicted to but found infuriating – they were constantly discussing ways to improve it. Sharif had heard so much about it, and still he had no idea at all how to play it – a maze and four enemies chasing the player, it sounded like.

'She went out,' Omith said.

'Where?' Sharif said, but that was beyond the boys' knowledge. When she came back, in ten minutes' time, she had been on her annual trip to Marks & Spencer to replenish her boys' underwear – a regular habit, not conducted on a particular date, but once a year to buy six pairs of pants each for Sharif and the twins. Already a sceptical eye had been cast over their underpants drawers, and the six worst pairs thrown out; six pairs of white Y-fronts for Sharif, which he had worn since the 1960s, six blue underpants for Omith and (a recent innovation) six white boxer shorts for Raja.

'I think we should invite him for dinner, or something,' Nazia said, when the purchases had been handed over and exclaimed about. 'I don't like to think of him alone. The children came for the funeral and now they've gone away again.'

'The elder son didn't come,' Sharif said.

'That's terrible,' Nazia said. 'I think it would only be kind to send him a little note saying that he would be welcome here for dinner any time he chooses. I don't know why you're laughing, Raja.'

'I was laughing at Omith's pants,' Raja said. 'They're like the pants you'd buy if you were a professor of engineering and seventy years old.'

'I think they're very nice and very suitable,' Nazia said. 'And your father isn't seventy years old. You're not to laugh or fight when Dr Spinster comes round for dinner, or you'll be in serious trouble.'

Sharif said nothing. He was thinking of his recent liberation. It had demonstrated to him that you need not, after all, engage with people, and need not say goodbye. Was there any need to say hello? For ten years, he had been going to have his hair cut in Hillsborough, a small concern with four chairs. The barbers were three Greek Cypriot brothers and their cousin; they had come here after the division of Cyprus, having lost their house and land in North Cyprus when the Turks invaded. It made him sick, Tommy the barber confided, to think of the plates still there on the table, still with food on them, where his mum had left them, grabbing the kids and a few clothes. They had thought they would be back in a few days and the mess could be cleared up then. That was the best part of twenty years ago. Sharif had been a customer for a decade, even though it meant submitting to the mockery and abuse of Nick and George, the two elder brothers. 'Got millions of starving relatives out there, ain'tcher?' George would greet him, meaning Bangladesh. 'Fuck me, what a fucking mess. Whatcher going to do for the Maharajah Fauntleroy today, Tommy, you cunt?'

'Do something about your fucking language while we've got the fucking Princely States in the chair,' Nick would say.

Sharif had once, years ago, made the mistake of asking them if they would mind not using the F-word and the C-word; he just hated them being volleyed over his head. Sometimes the haircut he went in with was better, honestly speaking, than the haircut he came out with.

One day he went in, saying to himself, 'If George calls me a cunt three times, just three times, I shall leave and never come back.' And he did. George was, as if on cue, in an unusually venomous mood that day – something to do with the football team he supported. Sheffield United or Wednesday came to his rescue by making a fucking hash of the job and losing four–one at the weekend to Leicester City, leading George to observe that not every cunt gave a fucking shit, like our little brown friend here. Sharif had paid with a beatific smile, quite unaffected by the volleys of abuse. Perhaps Tommy knew what was going to happen: he gave an embarrassed smile, a clap on the back. Sharif said goodbye as if he would see them again in a month's time. He drove home, pausing in the driveway of the house to examine himself in the mirror and confirm that it was a terrible haircut. Then he never went back. The Hillsborough lot might have given his disappearance a moment's thought, or they might not.

There was a great deal too much bother about saying hello to people and saying goodbye to people. Obligations. It had taken him ten years to understand that he could walk away from Tommy and his kind without saying goodbye. Now Nazia was laboriously erecting obligations and habits towards their neighbour. It seemed unnecessary to Sharif.

'We would be much better off not knowing him,' he said in the end.

'What do you mean?' Nazia said, staring. 'He's our neighbour. We know him.'

'Let's not,' Sharif said. 'Let's just say hello when we happen to be getting the car out at the same time. Let's just be friendly but not friends. He's old and his wife's just died. Now we've started having Christmas, are we going to have to invite him round for that?'

'He saved my life,' Raja said. 'Look.' He pulled down his shirt collar. 'Look, I'll always have this scar. But you could be weeping over my grave if it wasn't for him.'

'You weren't going to die,' Omith said. 'I don't think you should keep going on about it.'

'Let's just be friendly,' Sharif said. 'Not even his children like him. They couldn't wait to be out of there after the funeral.'

'It's true he didn't ask us to the funeral,' Nazia said. 'I think we ought to. If he doesn't want to then he doesn't want to, but we've made an effort.'

'The making of effort!' Sharif said. 'What lives are warped by the making of effort! He is an old English doctor! He lives on one side of us! Shall we have to have the people on the other side, too – Jennifer and Clive of India? And their horrible children?'

'They aren't very friendly,' Nazia said. 'Clive just said they'd been to India on holiday and then walked away. And Jennifer's said nothing at all. There are people like that, and then there are the friendly ones. Dr Spinster's wife has just died and he's all alone in that house. I think it would only be friendly and neighbourly to ask him if he would like to join us for an ordinary family supper in the middle of the week.'

'Oh, very well,' Sharif said. He'd known it was going to end in this way. He could have let it decline of its own accord. Hello, Dr Spinster. Hello, Professor Sharifullah. Your tulips are looking nice. Is that a new car? I meant to say, about the rubbish collection. Oh, and I should really have thanked you properly for that thing you did for my son, whatever it was. It's very nice to see you. There would be no hello and no goodbye, and when either of them stopped paying attention the relationship would drift off harmlessly. He would not have to care about anything like the neighbour's dead wife.

But Nazia had her way and a note in an envelope was dropped through the letterbox next door. He came round immediately, Nazia said, and said it was very decent of them and how would Thursday suit? That seemed perfect to her. She made something unpretentious, a shepherd's pie that the boys would like and not make faces over, and maybe just ice-cream from a tub afterwards? He left it up to her. It might only happen once.

5.

'Well, this is very nice of you,' Hilary said, stepping through the door with a bunch of yellow tulips in one hand and his raincoat over one arm. Since it was a sunny evening, and he was only coming thirty paces, he could have spared himself the outer garment. 'I think I lived next door to the Tillotsons for thirty years, and they only ever invited me into the house at Christmas, for drinks. I bet they drove a hard bargain when it came to selling the house.'

'Come through,' Sharif said. 'Nazia's here and I expect the boys will be down in a minute.'

'It's just shepherd's pie, nothing special,' Nazia said.

'Oh, my favourite,' Hilary said, without enthusiasm. 'You've painted the sitting room, I think. Didn't they have a sort of wallpaper along that wall? So you've really settled in. Is your daughter not around today?'

'It's just the boys,' Sharif said. 'Aisha did an internship after her master's and now she's working for a sort of charity.'

'An NGO, it's called,' Nazia said. 'To do with the education of women.'

'Oh, that would be a good idea,' Hilary said. He sat down. 'I wonder if she's come across my daughter. The younger one. She works for a charity, very worthwhile, very serious, medical supplies to Africa. They do a lot of good work, a lot of fatal diseases in Africa don't kill a lot of people annually, don't attract much attention but it's quite possible to deal with them. That's her line. I don't know what the alternative to large amounts of aid is for these places. It might be quite possible to eradicate a disease. We got rid of smallpox, after all.'

Sharif was quite enjoying this. He had been firmly instructed not to engage in anything resembling an argument with a man whose wife had died a few days before, so he merely said, 'Would you like a drink? Dry sherry?' The bottle had been purchased, as well as six glasses, two days ago, and then, as a second thought, a bottle of gin and some tonic water. It was lucky that Hilary said, 'Well, I'm not a great sherry drinker, but I wouldn't say no to a gin and tonic, if you have such a thing.'

If he had requested anything more complex, they might have been stuck. Sharif had practised. He went to the kitchen, and put some ice in two tumblers. He took a sharp knife, and carefully sliced a lemon, placing one piece in each tumbler. From the fridge he took a bottle of tonic water that had been chilling, and placed everything on a tray. He took it, concentrating, into the sitting room where the drinks cabinet sat with its two bottles.

'Some dreadful old bags,' Hilary was saying. 'They're constantly coming round with a lasagne they've made, or a fish pie or even a beef stew, wrapped in foil. There's no getting rid of them.'

'Oh, I'm sure they mean well,' Nazia said.

'Yes,' Hilary said. 'Yes, they probably do.'

Sharif took the bottle of gin. This was where his knowledge gave out. He was quite proud of doing all the preliminary steps, but how much gin and how much tonic did you put in the glass? He did not feel that he could ask. He had probably gone too far now to admit inexperience. With a sense that his two grandmothers were watching him with horror and incredulity, he played it safe: he half-filled Dr Spinster's glass with gin, and filled the other half with tonic. For himself, he put only a very small amount, a millimetre or two, into the bottom of the glass. He would get used to English quantities of alcohol over time, he expected.

'Doesn't your wife want anything?' Hilary said. 'Well, thank you very much. Here's to you. My goodness, you've put enough gin in that. You like a strong one, do you? My wife was exactly the same. I've got a weak head, could hardly ever drink more than a glass or two. You couldn't tip a bit of that away and fill it up with tonic?'

'We're not very expert with drinks,' Nazia said. 'We didn't grow up with alcohol in the house, either of us.'

'Oh, of course,' Hilary said.

'In fact,' Sharif said, coming back from the kitchen with a corrected version, blushing rather, 'I didn't have an alcoholic drink at all until after my daughter was born.'

'I'm amazed you liked it,' Hilary said. 'A habit better not acquired if you've escaped it thus far, in an old doctor's view. What were the circumstances?'

'It was a mistake,' Sharif said. 'It was my faculty's summer party – I'd only just arrived and they said I must come, with wife and daughter, and there was a fruit punch to drink, which I drank in one – it was a hot day – and Nazia was just handing a glass to Aisha, my daughter, who would have been about eight, and Ada Browning saw and flung herself at Aisha. Of course you know Ada. She mentioned.'

'Oh, yes,' Hilary said. 'She was a friend of my wife's. I can't remember how. Does she work with you? Is she an engineer? It is engineering, isn't it, your field? Splendid woman, everyone always says.'

'No, she's the faculty secretary,' Sharif said. 'Actually, she came to our housewarming party last year, the one where you – Ada. She's what we call a mother hen.'

'Squatting warmly over the fledgling engineers, hatching out, squawking from time to time. I quite see. We all need one,' Hilary said. 'So you drink alcohol now – and your wife? I won't ask about your daughter, though she must be old enough by the laws of the land.'

'I hope it went well,' Nazia said abruptly. Sharif saw her point: they seemed to be stuck on the question of who drank alcohol and in what circumstances, like remote acquaintances who could think of nothing to discuss but what was immediately in front of them. 'Your poor wife's funeral. These things are so difficult.'

'Yes, indeed,' Hilary said. 'I can only say I'm glad it's over.' Nazia smiled and returned to the kitchen; what she needed to do was not at all obvious to Sharif. 'And all those people my wife was such friends with,' Hilary went on, 'in the book group and neighbours. Excuse me, I don't mean … Blossom, my elder daughter, she was a great help, she remembers who is who, but I can't, never could. When I was still dealing with patients, I often wanted to say, "Now you, I remember your cyst in great detail," but them, their names, what they were like as people, no. I expect,' Hilary went on, turning back to Sharif with an almost audible crunch of good manners, changing points, 'I expect you feel much the same about students.'

'Yes,' Sharif said. 'Yes, that's right, really. Will you excuse me for one moment?'

In the kitchen Nazia was looking with general concentration at the glass door of the oven. Inside, the shepherd's pie was warmly lit, like a singer on late-night television, a star singing of sentiment that had been got up for the particular purpose.

'I think it'll be another half an hour,' Nazia said. 'This is nice, isn't it? I hope the boys come down soon.'

'I'm sure they're playing one of their games,' Sharif said. 'Shall I go up and fetch them?'

'No, they'll be down soon,' Nazia said. 'Leave them in peace.'

He had nothing to do in the kitchen, so with some dismay went back into the sitting room where his boring next-door-neighbour sat. It was incredible to Sharif that he could not admit to his wife of twenty-six years that he had always thought it was a mistake to ask the English round, and that they couldn't both go hiding in the kitchen. He was going to challenge her for saying, 'This is nice, isn't it?' when the old man had gone home.

The old man was still sitting there. 'Another drink?' Sharif said.

'No, I'm fine, thank you,' Hilary said.

'Your daughter's in international aid, you said.'

'Yes, indeed. Been doing that for a couple of years now. She seems to like it. I suppose you would enjoy a job if you felt that it was doing some good in the world. I must say, I can't see how the rest of the world is going to manage unless we hand out large sums of money to them on a regular basis.'

'Well ...' Sharif said. He paused. He went on, 'I don't know about that.'

'Really?' Hilary said. 'You think there's an alternative?'

'Actually, I think aid is a problem in itself,' Sharif said. 'I think it creates some problems that wouldn't exist without it.'

'Such as?'

'Well, I come from a part of the world that receives large donations in aid, and it just doesn't do it any good at all. It's keeping a terrible government in power, for one thing – they can rely on the Western billions when they can't run the country effectively. And it promotes the wrong sort of people! Those people who just make the case for more aid and then hand it out and then ask for more aid – they've no idea how to make anything or build anything or create anything. They just –'

'But hold on,' Hilary said. 'The principal fact about your country, as far as I can see, is that everyone who has an idea about any of those things legged it years ago. All those entrepreneurs and bright sparks, they're over here or in America making money. You would have to be mad to stick around in Bangladesh.'

'Nonsense!' Sharif said. 'Nonsense! We came over because of an opportunity and because things looked particularly bad, but I can tell you, not everyone feels as we do. I had a brother who died fighting for independence, and I know, I am certain, he would have stayed and improved things where he was. But you can't build a country on aid! It is just inviting people to steal it, to say, "You don't need to do anything, just rise effortlessly to the top and then reward yourself with a million or two lost to inadequacies in book-keeping." Frankly, Hilary, I doubt you know what you are talking about.'

'Well, I'll let that go,' Hilary said, with some heat. 'But really – not to stick on Bangladesh – what chance do most of these countries have of raising any kind of income? Their revenue collection is catastrophically incompetent, probably damaged by a recent civil war. They have no access to the sorts of loans that the government here can rely on.'

'Oh, excuse me,' Sharif said. 'I don't accept that. If an African government chose to issue bonds, it could start on a very small scale, but when adventurous investors were rewarded, they could do it again, asking for more, and before you knew it, we would have a rock-solid economy in Central Africa raising billions through the bond market every year. And no need to come running cap in hand to Western governments and Western charities so that their people can have rice in their bowls! I really despair.'

'It sounds wonderful but, frankly, this kind of utopian thinking – the issue of bonds? Come off it.'

'I utterly refute the label "utopian",' Sharif said. 'That is just what cynics say to people who are offering a real solution, an unorthodox solution, it's true, but ...'

He looked up. In the doorway were his two sons, side by side. They were smiling. The sight infuriated Sharif. He and their neighbour, Dr Spinster, were talking of serious matters! They were discussing the future of the world with serious intent, and for two teenage boys to come in with a superior smile on their faces – two teenage boys who talked about nothing but silly games.

'Go and help your mother,' Sharif said. 'I don't think supper will be long. The facts of the matter, Hilary, are quite simply that …'

6.

Much later, Sharif was helping Hilary into his raincoat. It turned out to have been not such a bad idea: at some point in the evening it had begun to rain. No one had noticed: Hilary and Sharif had been shouting at each other over the dining table.

'Well, thank you very much,' Hilary said. 'I've very much enjoyed myself. Do you know Imran Khan? The chap who replaced me at the surgery?'

'No, I don't think so,' Sharif said.

'I'd very much like to return your kind hospitality,' Hilary said, turning and smiling at Nazia, his cheeks flushed and his eyes bright with searching out moral, intellectual and logical failings over the last hour or two. 'But I won't inflict my cooking on you. I wonder if I can take you out for lunch in a pub – I was going to suggest asking Imran as well. I'm sure you'd get on.'

'Hilary,' Sharif said, with solid certainty, 'I would very much enjoy that. Fridays are always good for me to skip off early.'

As soon as the door was shut behind Hilary, Nazia said, 'I told you. What did I tell you?'

'I had a very nice time,' Sharif said sheepishly.

'Well, that's not the point,' Nazia said. 'I told you – I made you promise – Boys, go upstairs now ...'

'Mummy and Daddy are going to have a row now,' Raja observed to Omith as they filed upstairs.

'A discussion – we are going to have a *discussion*, child – Sharif, I made you promise you wouldn't start an argument. What did I say? No arguments. His wife only just buried! I cannot understand ...'

'He very much enjoyed it,' Sharif said. 'And I think he made some interesting points about aid helping with diseases. But I still think he is wrong in his overall ideas.'

'Well, if we're going to turn to that, I have to tell you ...' Nazia said, leading the way back to the sitting room.

7.

Blossom thought she would visit her old father. They hadn't seen him last Christmas, or the Christmas before – to be honest, she was rather afraid that it had been nearly three years since she had laid eyes on him, though of course they spoke on the phone from time to time. He had been invited to Lavinia's wedding, but had pleaded old age – it would just be too much for him at eighty-two, and he would prefer to send a truly splendid present. Nobody believed the excuse, and the truly splendid present was a cheque for a hundred pounds. Lavinia had spent it on a huge cooking pot and a jam thermometer, and made sixty jars of jolly nice raspberry jam with, strangely enough, some tarragon giving it a liquorice-y tang. All the wedding guests had had a jar sent to them with a kind note from Lavinia and Jeremy. Blossom wondered whether Lavinia had bothered to send one to Daddy, explaining what she had spent his splendid present on.

Clever Josh had read Greats at Oxford, and poor old Tamara had only scraped into wretched Exeter to read English – what a hole that was, everyone agreed. You constantly had to explain to clever people that you meant Exeter the frightful university, and not Exeter the excellent college at Oxford, too. Still, Tamara had been persuaded to cling on and get her amazing 2.1 before going back to where she'd spent her gap year and where she longed for, Brisbane. Tamara had had an extra year, compared to Josh, but they were graduating at the same time – Greats was a four-year course, or school, or whatever you were supposed to say about Oxford. It was so sad that Leo didn't know, but perhaps this was one of the things he would not have wanted to know above all. Just before Tamara headed back to Australia, perhaps never to return, and Josh went to law school to become a solicitor, Blossom thought it would be extremely nice for them both to come up to see Grandpa. Poor Grandpa, living on his own, never seeing anyone.

'I don't give a flying fuck for poor Grandpa,' Tamara said, in her drawl, over the breakfast table. 'I'm not going. Send Josh. He likes that sort of thing.'

'I hope when you're old and alone and sad,' Trevor said – Trevor was nine, and she was widely agreed to be insufferable, 'I hope your children and nieces and nephews refuse to come to visit you.'

'Oh, shut up, you little beast,' Tamara said. 'I notice that no one's suggesting you get inflicted on poor Grandpa, and I can well understand why. Anyway, I'm going to be in Australia when I'm old. Actually, I'm going to die being eaten by a Great White Shark while I'm surfing, before I'm forty with any luck. Josh can go.'

'I'll go,' Josh said. 'I don't mind going.'

'Well, there you are,' Blossom said. She could not wait, sometimes, to see the back of her daughters.

They arrived in Sheffield just before four, and they were expected, but there was no answer at the door. 'This is too bad,' Blossom said to Josh, and she got out her mobile phone to telephone in case he was asleep; they could hear the phone ringing inside the house. 'I should never have given my key back to Daddy. I can't remember why he said he needed it.'

But they had been there only five minutes when the lady from next door, the Asian mother who had been there for nearly eight years, appeared on the other side of the fence. 'He's with us,' she said. 'Would you like us to send him back? Or would you like a cup of tea over here? It might be quicker if you came over to our house.'

'He's not being a nuisance, I hope,' Blossom said, leaving her suitcase in the porch and walking with Josh to the gate and back again up their drive – it was Sharif, the husband, she remembered, but the wife … Ah, Nazia. That was it.

'Not at all,' Nazia said. 'It's been their day for lunch in the pub. They love it, him and my husband, and Imran Khan, the GP, you know. They always ask me if I want to come and, strangely enough, I always have something very important that can't be put off until later. Dr Khan's gone home but those two, they've been having a lovely time.'

In the hallway, the first thing that greeted you was a large photograph in a silver frame of an old gentleman and, underneath the walnut table on which it stood, Blossom's father's unmistakably tiny shoes, beautifully polished. She took the hint, noticing, too, that Nazia was in her stockinged feet, and told Josh to do the same. From the other room she could hear her father exclaiming energetically, 'Nonsense! Nonsense!'

'They got on to Princess Diana, I believe,' Nazia said, opening the door. 'Probably about two hours ago. It's still going on. Hilary, look!'

Rather than furious, Hilary turned to Blossom and Josh with a look of great pleasure and excitement. Sharif, the husband, was pacing up and down by the long window into the garden, and turned to them in something like surprise.

'You're early, my dear girl,' her father said, but without asperity. 'And Josh, look! Sharif, I can hold my head up in public – I have a descendant as clever as your children at last. Josh got a First in Greats, you know.'

'That sounds wonderful,' Nazia said. 'I wish I knew – Well, very well done.'

'It's what they call classics at Oxford,' Josh said, then, remembering that he sometimes had to simplify still further, 'Greek and Latin. Ancient history and philosophy too.'

'Sharif's boys graduated last year,' Hilary said, now getting up and coming to embrace his daughter and grandson. 'They turned down Cambridge, went to Manchester to read maths. They wanted to study with someone there. Golly! And Aisha, their daughter, of course, she's busy now with –'

'Hilary,' Sharif said. 'It's bad enough us boasting about our children without you doing it as well, particularly when we want to hear all about Josh's plans. Please, sit down. A cup of tea?'

'What were you talking about when we came in?' Josh said. 'You sounded so …' He struggled for the word: the word was perhaps 'unusual'. He had heard his grandfather before when he was disagreeing with people, or venturing to egg their disagreement on, but his voice had always risen in pitch and twittered about, waiting in the upper reaches for someone to contradict him. That contradiction had never come. To the rest of his family he was someone to whom one said, 'I expect you're right,' and walked away from. Once, Josh had come down to breakfast in the house next door and found his grandfather so itching for a fight that he had turned the radio over to a piece of classical music, just so that he would have to listen and would not be able to barrack and heckle. He had always danced up to opposition and then, faced with a tactful retreat and 'I expect you're right', found himself lowering his fists. They had, surely, heard him now saying, 'Nonsense! Nonsense!' with real vigour, rebutting someone who had in turn put his case.

'They were talking about Princess Diana,' Nazia said. 'I heard enough and left the room. I don't know why other people's emotions should be regarded as authentic or inauthentic. It seems like what philosophers would call a category error.'

'I wasn't precisely saying that,' Sharif said. 'My wife misunderstands the point I was making.' His wife left the room to make the tea. 'What I was saying was that people had been coached by the media to feel what they felt for a living Princess

Diana. They were performing the emotions that we all saw, no doubt, but they were unaware of performing them.'

'Well, that seems very unlikely,' Hilary said. 'I saw the television pictures of those mourners last year. They seemed overjoyed to be able to weep in front of the cameras. They knew perfectly well that what they were feeling was insincere. You know where they got it from, of course.'

'What do you think?' Sharif said, turning to Blossom. 'Your father and I, we've been talking about this all afternoon.'

'I thought it was terribly sad,' Blossom said. 'A mother as young as that, killed with two quite young sons. It must have been awful for them.'

'Yes, but,' Hilary said, 'did they really feel sad?'

'Of course they did!' Sharif said. 'They would have – they would have …' He trailed away.

'I certainly felt sad,' Blossom said.

'Aunt Blossom said she cried,' Josh said. 'She did cry. She stayed inside in the morning room with Trevor and watched the funeral on the little television in there. They cried all day. I went out with Thomas. We went riding. We didn't see anyone else out of doors all day.'

'Well, there you are,' Sharif said. He smiled brilliantly. 'I would say that there is something very interesting going on in this country, something to do with a relationship to emotions. I have seen mass emotions at work: I am not sure what their end necessarily is.'

'Exactly,' Hilary said. 'Those people weeping outside the palace and in the Mall, they weren't English, most of them – they were African or South American or Spanish or something of that sort. An interesting change in this country. You know what a West African funeral is like – everyone works themselves up into a passion of weeping and wailing and tearing of the hair over the course of a week. They're not acting exactly, they're inhabiting the roles ordained for them. Then the next morning they wake up and they never give the dead person a moment's thought, ever again. You know what I'm saying is correct.'

'No, I don't,' Sharif said. 'I really don't. Apart from the child-ish way you bring up a culture I'm quite certain you know nothing about –'

'Oh, believe me, I've seen plenty of West African weeping in my years in the NHS,' Hilary said.

'Be that as it may,' Sharif said. 'The fact of the matter is that grief is a proper, analysable state, probably involving an imbal-ance of bodily chemicals. If you scraped up the tears of a bystander at the funeral of Diana, Princess of Wales, and those of – of – of a brother mourning his sister and analysed the nature of the fluid, you would find very little difference, if any. These tests have been done – tears of grief are significantly different in make-up from tears of onion-peeling, or tears of laughter.'

'You quite misunderstand me,' Hilary said. 'I was not ques-tioning the sincerity. I was distinguishing between real grief, and superficial grief, briefly experienced and quickly dismissed. The fact is –'

'Is that true?' Josh said. 'That onion tears are different in make-up from tears of grief?'

'Yes, certainly,' Sharif said. 'A very interesting experiment. I don't know how it was achieved.'

'They certainly feel different,' Blossom said, sitting on the arm of the chair. 'Onion tears and tears in the wind and tears of laughter even are watery – the serious sort just trickle down slowly, like jam. I wonder why that is.'

She was wondering, strangely enough, about her brother's tears. She had seen them only the night before. It was in the last episode of *Our Mutual Friend*. He'd been terribly good, Hugh. He had cried buckets, very convincingly. What would it take to scoop up Hugh's tears, to bring them to a laboratory, to find out whether his emotions were real or not? It had been years since she had seen him, and on that occasion she had been watching his happiness, and not quite sharing in it.

In the end Josh was sent next door to take the suitcases in, and Blossom hung her coat up and sat down properly. They stayed for tea and (resisting Nazia's invitation) only just failed to stay for supper too. Blossom gazed, awestruck, at her father's vigour and brightness and dash.

The next morning she was down early for breakfast, and John Prescott was on the radio. She observed experimentally that she didn't know why such a talentless buffoon was in the cabinet; but her father first said that he expected it was something to do with keeping that half of the Labour Party onside, and in a moment that he was sure she had a valid point. She was frustrated. It was fifty years too late to start arguing with her father. If she had known what an effect it would have on him, with what joy he rose to meet spirited contradiction and being rebuked with the word 'Nonsense!' she would have persevered long ago. They had tried to tame him, and had only caged him. Now he was monogamous in his arguments: he saved them for Sharif and, whatever she found to say about John Prescott, she would only be greeted with a magnanimous pat on the head.

'I'm sure you're right,' her father said in the end, passing her a jug of milk for her tea.

She poured it, giving him what she regarded as a withering look. The look contained a sitcom rebuke, one that did not need to be uttered. If she had spoken it – but she was not at all the person to say these things, to pose hands on hips, to sum up half of the human race in a scene-ending foot-stamp as the canned laughter rang out – it would have been this: 'Men!'

'Yes,' she said instead mildly. 'I don't think I've ever had much time for the deputy prime minister. I suppose it keeps him out of trouble.'

8.

The boys came back from California in 2004. Everyone thought they were crazy – they were at the centre of things there, the centre of the universe. They had lived in a pair of white houses five minutes' walk from each other with a swimming-pool in the back garden – *backyard*, they refused to say. How could you leave that, and the HQ with a trampoline in the lobby for anyone to go and bounce on when they wanted to think? The fact of the matter was that the business was profitable and would grow, given a fair wind, but it just wasn't what Raja and Omith really wanted to do. They peered over the garden wall from where they sat, listening to accountants with their ties off trying to be mellow but money at the same time, talking about monetizing the BTL, and they thought about what they were doing. It had been an idea and a half, getting people not just to buy things from a website, like an old-school catalogue, but to give them the choice of selling them on, buying things new or second-hand, saying next to them what they had thought of them. 'This is really going to fuck with the British Home Stores, innit,' Raja had said at some point.

But bloody hell – they'd been doing it now for like four whole years since they'd left England. Four. Years. It was basically anarchy, but it was still selling things. Yawn. One day they had just looked at each other, out there in California, and they had seen that they didn't want to be doing this. They'd been fending off offers for the company since before day one. One Thursday, they utterly surprised someone who was making an idle offer by saying they were interested. The venture capitalists moved in, the lawyers moved in. The boys cashed in. All of a sudden they were back in London with their friend Martin, who they'd always known felt the same way that they did, and to everyone's surprise, they had bought a games company with twenty employees in a warehouse in Hoxton. That was what they wanted to do: make games. And then play them.

Raja bought a flat on the river at Vauxhall, in a building forty storeys high, from which you could see the Houses of Parliament, all of that. He liked pointing his finger at Big Ben and pretending to be an evil mastermind with a laser gun, going to take over the world once he'd blown it all up. The flat had four storeys, and Raja honestly didn't know the name for that – duplex, triplex, but then, fuck knows. Quadruplex. Tetraplex. There was a floor of his flat he never really went into. There was stuff in it. You could see Omith's house from the terrace of the flat, two white stucco houses in Pimlico next to each other. Omith had bought one, then a week after he'd made himself known, the neighbours on one side had put theirs on the market and he'd bought that too. Might as well. He'd knocked them together. 'Didn't want to live next to a brownie,' Omith remarked of the pompous old couple, with what truth not even he knew. Martin had bought a Bengali supermarket in Brick Lane and pulled it down. He was keen on architecture: the house he was building on the site was based on unbuilt plans by Louis Kahn for a Connecticut villa, a luminous cube of polished concrete. All the light was going to pour in from above; the windowless cliff would face the street. In the meantime he was living in his mum's house in Dulwich, the one with a Barbara Hepworth in the front garden. He'd given it to her for Christmas – the Barbara Hepworth, not the house. She hadn't wanted to move from where she'd lived all her married life and, anyway, the Barbara Hepworth, to the rage of the planning authorities on the council, was as tall as the house. It had cost more, too.

Perhaps they weren't so crazy to flog it and come home with the money. The glitches in their original website, the ones they'd known all about from the start, did for it in the end when something much better came along. Of course the new owners had done a lot to try to fix it, but by that point Anybodys.com was a worldwide joke. You wouldn't buy anything off it, so nobody did. Down in Hoxton the catalogue of games ticked away, selling nicely. It was an aficionados' label, passionately enthused over by people who, like Raja and Omith, didn't think they had done anything much other than play games for the last twenty years. Sqrrrxkl*briiii – that was theirs, you brilliantly couldn't ask for it in WHSmith's, and only the real obsessives (the DICSHONNARI you got to in the twenty-ninth level on the shelves of that abandoned pet-shop on the left) knew that the * in the name of the game was pronounced with the plop you made with a forefinger in your cheek 'and the second r is silent'. Two years after the takeover, Fuck That was launched. (You couldn't ask for that in WHSmith's either, or at least you couldn't at first). It was brilliant, profane, brutal, investigative, exploratory; it was set in a beautifully intricate African war zone. You could kill the tiger leaping at you or – with a complex series of actions – you could trap it, tame it, teach it to be dependent on you over the course of a dozen games, anaesthetize it once it had got to the point of loving you, curling its big head up in your lap – oh, and it's bitten your cock off again. The tiger and your cock were only a collection of pixels. Still, that fucking hurt. Start again … and it's curling its big head up in your lap, you're anaesthetizing it, you're taking revenge for the last game by castrating it, you're letting it bleed to death, you're selling the tiger penis to the punters in the brothel you've earlier taken over by main force, it's the greatest aphrodisiac, and they're queuing out the door, so …

It could go on for ever, or so the awestruck players thought. The detail in the pixels – the texture of the bricks and the sand and the exploding flesh and blood and sinew and fat and skin and brains. There was a decrepit bookshop in one village in the game with exactly five books on its shelf for sale, novels. You could pluck the novels from the virtual shelf and open them, and you could actually read the five novels while fighting off the rebel forces outside. Omith had commissioned five novelists to write a novel each for the purpose. They'd done it for five thousand each. Worth it for the publicity when some player discovered that particular corner, and there were lots of particular corners. There was, too, the decision you could make to play or replay the game in FIRST PERSON (you see the world),

SECOND PERSON (look, look, that's you and I'm your companion who mustn't die), THIRD PERSON (look at the little man running) – the huge comedy of it.

'There aren't any tigers in Africa,' Omith said, several times a week during development, every single time they got to the tiger. Everyone would get to the tiger, it was on like the second level, except that they didn't talk in like levels – that was like 1999 – it was *cool*, a word that always made the boys laugh with its self-disproof.

'That's what's so wack,' Raja said. 'They won't misunderstand us, you feel me? You put like a lion in and it's, you know …'

'Simba,' Martin said.

'Simba. They're going to think that the people who made this and put a tiger in Africa, they're American and thick and don't give a shit about the rest of the world. The real rest of the world. Ruddy Nora, these people are thick as shit, there's tigers in Africa in their ruddy game, good job they've got no real power, because for aye they would, you know –'

'Just drop a bomb on it because, who the fuck knows, there's probably like tigers there and that's like really really dark, you know?' Martin's voice rose at the end like the girlfriends he'd got through in Palo Alto. They cracked up.

'You've got to stop getting hung up on, like, stuff,' Raja said to his twin. 'Don't you remember what Daddy said about Anybodys.com?'

'"I can't believe my sons don't know where the apostrophe should go in the name of their business,"' Omith quoted.

'We all know where the apostrophe should go,' Raja said. 'Up yer bum.'

'I saved your life once, you dickhead,' Omith said.

They liked going up to see Mummy and Daddy in Sheffield. They almost saw them more often than they saw Aisha, who only lived in Brixton in a handsome Regency house in an impossible setting – she was almost always away, out of the country, sorting out the education of women here and there. 'She's away getting burgled,' Raja used to say to Omith. It made him laugh. It was one day in March that Omith mentioned it to Raja, and Raja told Martin that they'd be unavailable from Thursday night to Monday morning. This had happened before, but this time Martin said, 'I've never met your mum and dad. Are they like old-school?'

'What are you like?' Raja said. 'Old-school – you mean like saris and big beards and shit? Turbans, motherfucker? No way, bruv. They think it's like *totally appalling*, what we do, but they'd be reassured if they met a nice boy like you.'

'Man, that sounds epic,' Martin said. 'Let's close down the office. Give the underlings some, like, holiday. Give them a hundred quid each and a first-class return ticket to Brighton. Five nice crisp purple twenties. They'll like that.'

'It sounds *cool*, bruv,' Omith said, with contempt. 'You do that, they'll be wondering what you're gonna do with their position when they come back on Monday, is it still there, you hear me?'

'We'll send them off to Brighton on the Friday and when they come back on Monday they'll see that we've painted the office. How about that?' said Raja.

So while all the underlings went off to Brighton with a return ticket and a hundred pounds each to be spent on lunch or slot machines or weed or anything, Martin drove Raja and Omith up to Sheffield. Martin was a restless, enthusiastic car buyer, and the car he turned up in was a Citroën DS, a beautiful grey lacquer over it, the great sweep of it somehow grand and suburban at the same time. The hydraulics, like a swan puffing itself up in mild menace, worked in a quiet, luxurious way; Martin had had the whole thing restored, and the upholstery replaced in brilliant yellow leather. French post-war cars were his thing, the more suburban the better: he had a 2CV with a hard-to-source original *Atomkraft? Nein danke!* sticker in the back, a heartbreaking turquoise Simca, a first-generation Renault 5 and other curious joys from the experimental designers' studios. After a month it seemed to him that the 2CV was too immaculate. He took it out and drove it, quite gently, into a wall, after which it had quite a satisfyingly authentic dent in the front. Perfect. In the luxury line, he had one of the last of the Delahayes, kept like all the others in garages in Herne Hill: that was a beautiful monster, taken out very rarely for a cruise round the block on a Sunday morning. No one else had ever heard of Delahaye. Martin confided that the weight of the thing was enough to make you wonder whether it would ever get to the top of the hill. For most everyday purposes he had a Merc, like everyone else, but the trip up to Sheffield was a jaunt. He picked them up in the grey DS with the yellow interior.

There was no one there to greet them when they arrived. Their father's car was in the garage, suggesting that he was in the vicinity. Raja let them in with his spare key, calling out, and though the house was still warm with their presence – a newspaper tossed on the side table, a pair of plates and glasses wet in the sink tidy – it was empty. They hadn't set the burglar alarm.

'He's probably just gone out for a walk,' Raja said. 'This is what produced the geniuses behind the hit games Fuck That and the sequels, Fuck That Shit and Fuck That For A Game Of Soldiers.'

'We're not calling it that,' Martin said, not for the first time – the third issue in the series was a long way into development and still had no name. 'Oh, my God, look at this!'

He was on his knees by the fireplace, his hands lovingly over the line of twenty-five or thirty box sets of classical music. 'Look at all this vinyl. God, I want to play with it. Whose is it? Has he just bought it all?'

'It's my dad's,' Omith said. 'No, he's had it for years, why?'

'Look at this,' Martin said. 'This set! The youth orchestra I played the horn in when I was a kid, we played the Brahms third symphony. I'm not kidding, I've got to play this.'

Like all their father's acquired LP box sets, the one that Martin had settled on still had its layer of protective plastic on. He had half a dozen favourite LPs, had had them for years, playing one once a month, enjoying and always pointing out the same enjoyable moment in the first movement of the 'Emperor' Concerto. The box sets had crept into the house – had he been the member of a record club at one point that sent him such things? But he placed them on the shelves in their protective wrapper, proudly, a little shyly, and never opened them, never quite ventured away from his half-dozen favourites. The CD player, a Christmas present from Mummy ten or fifteen years ago, had a dozen CDs to choose from, but still it was the LPs and their short-winded vinyl burden that pleased their father, once a month.

'What the hell are you doing?' Omith said. 'That's my dad's.'

Martin had torn off the plastic wrapper, and was now leafing through the records. 'There's no point in owning records if you're never going to play them,' he said. 'This is a fantastic set – I don't think you could get it any more.' Omith went out to fetch the bags from the car.

'He's going to waste you,' Raja said. 'Those are his records – if he wants to keep them wrapped up in plastic and never play them, that's his biz, bruv.'

Martin was putting a record on the turntable. 'This is the third symphony – it's incredible, the way it starts. Listen to this.'

'You'll need to turn it on,' Raja said. Martin had lowered the needle onto the disc, and the symphony began with a slow rising whoop.

'Isn't this amazing?' Martin said.

'My dad's here,' Omith called from the front door. They left Brahms behind and went outside. There was no sight of Sharif, but his voice could be heard, perhaps from twenty yards down the road behind an elm tree. It was raised.

'… was justly believed to be there. Of course everyone believed Saddam to be aiming at constructing WMDs. The intelligence was perfectly reasonable. It seems to be wrong, but it was entirely reasonable. No one should have refrained from action on the off-chance that it might not be correct.'

'On the contrary,' another voice, an older, posh English

voice, said. It must be the retired doctor who lived next door. 'If there was any possibility that it might not be correct, they should not have started invading another country. And the truth is they wanted to find a threat far too much. They'd always regretted not carrying on to Baghdad in 1990.'

'Yes, that was a mistake,' Sharif said. 'If only we had carried on and defeated the tyrant.'

'There are too many tyrants in the world,' Dr Spinster was saying, and now they were coming into view, walking a few steps, pausing to harangue the other, walking a few steps more. Dr Spinster had a walking stick, but he did not seem to have very urgent need of it; he was using it to wave around and make a point, even to stab Sharif in the chest. 'Sometimes you have to shrug and deplore and sit tight, or face the facts – there are millions of people out there who are going to suffer from your high moral stance, and are going to get on a boat and see if they can't come and live in your country. Take your pick. Their lives are going to be dreadful either way. Look, it's your boys. Hello, young man – where's your brother?'

'He's here,' Omith said limply.

'Are you playing some music?' Hilary said. 'It sounds heavenly. We've been having a walk down to the post office and back – I saw your father leaving and asked him if he'd get me some stamps, but then I thought how very lazy of me, so I walked down with him. We've been putting the world to rights. Back from America for good, then? I'm ninety next year, you know. Fit as a flea. My successor Dr Khan inspected me from topknot to shoe sole last month, said he'd be out of a job if everyone was as fit as I am. He wouldn't mind, though. I remember from my own days as a quack peddling magical thinking, all those middle-aged folk turning up and saying they were tired all the time. What a bally waste of everyone's energy. I'm nearly ninety! I'm fit as a flea! When I get tired all the time, shoot me and put me out with the rubbish.'

'We'll see you later, Hilary,' Sharif said, with resignation. He felt that he had not had the last word, and looked forward to bumping into the old man some time over the weekend. He wondered what that music was, and saw that somebody had opened a box set. He thought of saying something, but these were his sons, and their friend. He smiled, and sat down in the second-best armchair.

Nazia came back around six. She was already complaining before she was through the door about the tenants in Wincobank that Aisha had persuaded her into. Why couldn't she have stuck with students? It was all very well saying that new arrivals from the developing world were more in need of accommodation and Mummy had ten whole houses: why not let two of them to workers at a reasonable rate? It had sounded perfectly sensible, and Aisha's friend Julie had been a great help in finding solid individuals, then impressing on them how lucky they were. She had given way to her children, yet again, and taken meek instruction from them. For three years it had gone perfectly: the Sylhetis and Afghans who had turned up were reasonably decent and clean. Something had gone wrong with the current mixture. Two of them had taken to importing into the house English girls, who came and went at their own pleasure. She had had to ask another one to leave when she found he was smoking heroin in the house. To her horror, today one of the quieter members of the house had phoned her to say, in distress, that his bed was broken. When she went round there, she found that it had been jumped on repeatedly until the frame shattered, and innocent Qasim in tears, blaming Shakur in the room next door – there had been fights in the past. She told Qasim, who worked nights in a chicken shop on Abbeydale Road, that his bed would be replaced in short order. The lavatory, she noticed, was in the state a pig would leave it in. Shakur's days as a tenant were numbered. She never thought she would say it –

– she said, coming through the front door of her house –

– but this lot were more trouble than four student houses combined. Then she exclaimed. Her boys! Hadn't she expected them? Well, yes, but it was nice to pretend to be surprised by her favourite boys, wasn't it? The Wincobank saga could wait. And this must be Martin! She had no idea what she was going to do to entertain her sons' rich friend. Perhaps they would enlist Hilary.

'We'll miss him when he's gone,' Sharif said, over dinner. Nazia had made a real effort, had cooked a chicken biryani but also had done a Thai-spiced dish of four mackerels, roasted asparagus in garlic and sea salt, some scallops and a brilliant salad of her own invention with a dressing she'd seen on television, only improved.

'Pa, don't talk about him like that,' Raja said. 'He looks OK. He's got another ten years in him, I reckon, fifteen, easy.'

'Your father isn't talking about him dying!' Nazia said, standing behind Omith, serving him. 'What a thought. No, he's selling the house and moving into a smaller place. Going! He just wants some more money. He's finding retirement more expensive than he planned for. Anyway, he'll get five hundred thousand pounds for that house, I would say, and he'll get a very nice flat for half that.'

'I'm amazed,' Raja said. 'I thought he loved it here. Just because of money? What are those seeds on the salad – like frogspawn or something?'

'It's passion fruit, wretched boy,' Nazia said, very pleased. 'Does your mother have to put up with this sort of stuff from you and your sister, Martin?'

When dinner was done, it was nine; they did not want to go to bed, of course. Nazia went to the bookshelf in the sitting room and extracted a volume. She could feel her husband's eyes on her back. It was a volume of Feluda, an old collection. They must have bought it some time in the 1980s, been sent it as a present. She had loved Feluda, and so had the boys. The book had a particular smell. She raised it to her face and sniffed: a smell of damp and mottle and a warm hot iodine humidity, steel-edged. It was the smell that things that came from Dhaka had. For a moment she had thought about reading to them from Feluda, just as they had in Dhaka thirty or more years ago after dinner. But it would not do. She slid the volume back onto the shelf and turned, smiling.

'Your family,' Martin said later. They had cosily reconvened before bedtime for a chinwag in their jim-jams in Raja's little room. They sat cross-legged, Martin and Raja on the bed, Omith swivelling round in the captain's chair that Raja had chosen for his desk when he was eleven years old. They were enjoying the mucking about – here they were, three boys in their jim-jams, having just played a couple of rounds of Tetris, and the three of them with something like half a billion dollars between them in the bank. Martin had produced a baggy and they'd done a line each on Raja's old desk – it gave Omith a queer feeling to think of it, and he only did it to be sociable, ever. 'Your family,' Martin said. 'They're mental.'

'Mental how?' Raja said. 'They're all right.'

'Well, what's that about buying vinyl and keeping it safe in the plastic? That's mental. And that food, it was nice, but what was it? Do they eat shit like that like every day of the week? And you know what, that thing your mother does, right, at that dinner we just ate. When you sat down she stood up and went by you and served you, like she was some waitress or something. Is that because you're rich now?'

'No,' Omith said. 'She's always done that, even when we were like ten years old. It's just what she does. She did it to you, too, but that was different, you're a guest.'

'It's the fact she gave us a fish head each,' Raja said.

'Yeah, I saw that,' Martin said. 'That's disgusting.'

'It's because we're so rich,' Omith said. 'We get the fish heads now. My dad always got the fish heads before. The serving when she stands next to you, that's always happened, nothing new.'

'I don't get it. You told my mum to do that, she'd hand you a book by Germaine Greer, saying read that before I cook your dinner again. And your mum, right, she ain't no servile downtrodden type otherwise. Your dad too. He's saying stuff to you like, if I heard it, I'd say, "Yeah, you got a point, bruv", move on, nothing to see here, but you just started arguing with him and everyone didn't seem to care. I know you ain't got an opinion about Iraq and Tony Blair, bruv, that was all to have a ding-dong with your dad, and he like wanted it. It's mental round here. I love it.'

'They were going to tarmac the whole back garden last year,' Omith said disloyally.

'Yeah, that's cool,' Martin said, cracking up. 'I saw they've got like three rows of plants in pots out the back, all of them flowering, man. That's brilliant. Tarmacking the back garden, I feel you.' It wasn't even true, but Omith thought he might as well say it, the stuff about tarmacking gardens that the white kids always believed the brown kids' families were planning. He didn't know what was wrong with having rows of flowering plants in pots in the garden. That seemed a good idea.

'The thing is,' Raja said, 'they're maybe a bit like that because my dad, right, he had a little brother who got murdered when he was like seventeen. You get to hear a lot about little-brother Rafiq if you hang around here long enough.'

'And he was murdered, right?' Martin said. 'That's cool. I don't know that I ever met no one who had a murder in their family, like not that close. Who murdered him – was it like gang stuff?'

'It's a long time ago,' Raja said. 'Ask my mum. She'll ask you to leave the house for not respecting us and little-uncle Rafiq who got done in. That I want to see.'

'Man,' Martin said, disappointed.

9.

When they returned to London, Omith instructed his lawyer to write to Dr Hilary Spinster of Sheffield. He investigated the recent house prices in the street where Dr Spinster lived and his parents lived, and now asked his lawyer to offer to purchase Dr

Spinster's house for £650,000 in cash. (This was the maximum house price reached by properties in the street, plus one hundred thousand pounds.) He made, however, an unusual offer. If Dr Spinster wanted to remain in the house, he would be very happy to offer him a permanent and irrevocable tenantship, without requiring any rights of inspection or access to the property, for the sum of one pound per annum. The offer was made by his lawyer on behalf of an anonymous buyer. In time, a typewritten letter from a machine of shaky tendency was received by Hunt, Hunt, Branksome and Newburg saying that Dr Spinster was asking his grandson, Josh Spinster of Brigham, Townsend and Self (solicitors, a parenthesis in wobbly blue biro in the margin clarified the wobbly typescript), to investigate the legality and soundness of the offer, and subject to his advice, Dr Spinster would be prepared to accept this offer with thanks and some puzzlement.

'I don't know why you wanted to be anonymous,' Raja said. 'You ain't gonna be anonymous, neither. They'll work it out. I'd want a bit of gratitude, to be honest. Acksherly I'm gonna look modest. Take the credit. I bet Ma was thinking of installing him in one of her houses in Wincobank, too. She could do with the fifty quid a week, I reckon.'

'It's the thanks I can't be doing with,' Omith said honestly. They were in Omith's Pimlico house, a hired decorator's symphony of oyster and cream and highlights of orange; a pair of muddy green Nikes lay on the white rug waiting for Omith's housekeeper to tut over them.

'And what's going to happen when he dies? You're not giving it to his children, are you?'

'No way, man,' Omith said. 'I'm selling that motherfucker when Dr Hilary exits. Or I'll give it to Ma and Pa to keep their recipe books in. I don't know.'

'Well, I can't really understand why you're doing it,' Raja said.

'He saved my brother's life once,' Omith said.

10.

They were good boys: Omith and then, separately, Raja phoned their mum before she would have heard about the bombs in London. They were OK; they weren't hurt; Aisha was in Sri Lanka and perfectly OK. It was a beautiful morning and Nazia was in the garden with a book. She probably wouldn't have known about the bombings until she heard the one o'clock news. She phoned Aisha in Sri Lanka on her mobile – she thought it was probably justified, just this once – and told her that everyone was safe and she was thinking of her. Aisha was between meetings and sounded calm; it was only afterwards that Nazia realized hers was probably the third, at least, phone call she'd have had. She'd been phoned by her brothers, one after the other, before Nazia had got to her. 'Of course we're in Sheffield, so we're not in any danger,' she said absurdly.

She had thought, however, that with that she had been spared, and it was only the next day, watching the horrible news, that Sharif turned to her and took her arm – laying his hand on her forearm in an awkward and unfamiliar gesture.

'Hugh Spinster,' she said, repeating what the television news had just said.

'I saw him come out of the house this afternoon,' Sharif said. 'He was just sitting there without moving. What a thing. I must go over.'

'What can you say?' Nazia said.

He patted her arm; he tried again and now squeezed her hand. He got up. 'Whatever there is, it must be said. He can't be alone.'

'Those bombers – those men – the murderers – they were –'

'Whatever they were.'

'They weren't …'

'Say it,' Sharif said, seeing the necessity – seeing the historical necessity, it might have been. 'Say it. Just once and then never again.'

'They were Pakistanis,' Nazia said.

'I know,' Sharif said.

'They were …'

'That's enough now, Nazia,' Sharif said. 'That's enough historical wrongs.'

'OK,' Nazia said. She had said what she needed to say. Sharif left the house. It was for him to go round to Hilary, his friend, and tell him whatever it was that needed to be said, in the house that had been his and now was his only by the forbearance of his neighbours' children.

CHAPTER FOURTEEN

I.

Mr Benn had been admitted six days ago. He had been placed in the Carnation Room – a pleasant room, but not one with a view. It looked out over a scrap of garden, a red-leafed maple and an ivy-covered old wall, then the sober eighteenth-century roofs of respectable south London. He was beyond the point of appreciating the view. The doctors had taken a view of his likely progress, and he was now following the pathway they had anticipated. At first, the bed had had to be changed every eight hours, at the beginning of each shift, to keep him comfortable. By the fourth day, he had sunk into a calm unconsciousness, his breath shallow and rattling, his movements tranquil, like someone summoning another with a languid raising of the hand. His face had been drawn tight with pain; now it had relaxed with the support of morphine, and his eyes fluttered under the lids as if watching something very interesting go by. He had passed into a world of painless confusion and warmth. His bed had been changed that morning; it would not need to be changed again.

Often patients had crowds of visitors, who needed to be managed and asked to wait. Mr Benn's only visitors were his two children. He was sixty-two, though the dying have no evident age: so often, they look like the dying, their cheeks sunken and their skin pallid and glistening. Leo had seen men born less than thirty years ago who, on this bed, looked just the same. His children were simple-looking, bewildered rather than grief-stricken. Mr Benn had been brought in the first day by the daughter riding in the ambulance with him. She was a girl with a white-blonde bob and a flush of pink in her white face. She was wearing what she ordinarily wore, a neat greenish sweater and a knee-length tartan skirt with black stockings underneath. There was something old-fashioned about her as about her brother, and something indelibly youthful, as well. The son had followed two hours later, and had come directly from work; his black shoes shone, and his grey suit, his white shirt, his blue patterned tie were all neat without being anything out of the ordinary. He, too, had brilliantly white-blond hair, an old-fashioned cowlick, his head nearly shaved round the sides. Probably his father and his grandfather had gone to work looking very much the same. Today, they had greeted each other in Reception, modestly, before the sister had led him upstairs. She had merely reached out her hand and squeezed his, before they went upstairs to sit with their father. Now the last hours had been reached, and the brother had arrived for the last time.

They were quickly brought cups of tea. They were sitting side by side, next to their father's bed, and the daughter held her father's hand. Sometimes she called out her name, 'Judith. It's Judith,' and sometimes her brother, in shyer tones, said, 'And Kieron. Can you hear me? Kieron's here.' It was strange that he was called Kieron, a name so redolent of 1980s babies. He should have had the name of a minor royal, George or William or Henry. They called their names as if throwing something to keep a drowning man afloat, or to give him something to clutch on the journey to come. They only left the room when the doctor arrived and took them off to explain what was happening, and what was likely to happen. Dr Solomon explained these things well, with kindly sympathy, and was very clear that their father was no longer in any pain or distress. The end would be very peaceful. The brother held his sister's hand; the sister looked away when one of the orderlies came in with more tea. She was wiping her face, not wanting anyone to see that she had been crying.

Leo had worked at the hospice in Clapham for twenty-one years, and in that time had seen thousands of people die. He should know what it was like by now. He had seen people reacting in rage, by bursting out in laughter, which they could not understand, in silence, in tears that came in floods or the smallest trickle, by marked embarrassment as their relation lost control of him or herself and died in front of them, perhaps as they were being told an interesting story. He had been thanked and blamed and coldly dismissed. Some people went on sending him Christmas cards, with a reminder, in brackets, of the name of the person he had helped to the end of their life. Here, the higher medical professionals were impotent and useless. It was those who were tasked with nursing and cleaning and taking measurements and bringing cups of tea for visitors who mattered, especially to patients who had come in for the last time.

The mystery of Death had been before him steadily for twenty-one years. Like everyone in the same position, he averted his eyes and managed to find something joyful, even, in the work he did. He did not contemplate suffering and he did not dwell on the process, but on what must be done now, at this moment. Only sometimes did the realization of what was happening come to him in the way that it must come to the relations, who were probably seeing a person die for only the first or second time in their lives. He had never seen a person close to him die in this way, not intimately, patiently waiting from beginning to end. From time to time he reflected, as relations did, on the last event of a particular type in the life: the last meal was half a small bowl of chicken soup, defeating the moribund after half an hour's effort; the last time that their sheets were changed under the living flesh registering as a solemn and serious event, since the next and final time their sheets were changed would be for the viewing of the body; the last thing they said – and what fuss there was about last words – was often 'Nurse', or merely 'Thank you.' If Leo thought about it, it would strike him as *very nice* that the last emotion of a person's life was gratitude, and that it expressed itself in such a *very nice* way, whatever the person had been like. *Very nice*: he had once known that you could be more precise in your vocabulary to explain what had happened, but over the years he had come to appreciate the solid, banal, universal worth of two words that everyone could say, and that everyone, at some point, almost always did. 'Thank you, Doctor,' the simplest said. (They hardly ever distinguished between the highest dignitary and the simpler sort of nurse or orderly, like Leo.) 'That was very nice, at the end.'

His shift finished at two. There was a principle that you merely left work, not saying goodbye. He did not believe he would be seeing Mr Benn and his children again when he returned to work at six the following morning. This was a difficult thing for families to accept, that one member of staff was just the same as another member of staff. Leo himself understood that this was not the case, and that some colleagues were lacking in warmth, understanding or kindness, but it was not for him to compensate for that. He had often heard a daughter say to her husband, or a wife say to her children, 'That's Leo. He's one of the friendly ones.' When he had first started there, he had sometimes seen that a patient was within an hour of their death, and had stayed beyond the end of his shift. Then it was explained to him that that would not do. He slipped away; the nurse just coming on duty took charge of the patient's last moments.

There had been a note in his pigeon hole from Mr Ghosh, the manager of the hospice, asking if he would come to see him at the end of his shift. At first, long ago, these notes had made him nervous. For a long time now, however, they had appeared when Mr Ghosh needed Leo's help in a difficult matter. He had worked there much longer than anyone else.

Mr Ghosh made his importance plain, however, by continuing to type on his desktop computer when Leo entered. Leo sat down and waited patiently. After a while Mr Ghosh said, 'I will be with you in a moment,' and carried on with what he was doing. In the end he turned away, gave a brief smile and said, 'Now. What can I do for you, Leo?'

Leo was used to this tactic. 'Actually, you asked if I could come to see you.'

'So I did. Now. What was it? Ah, yes. I don't know if you heard, but we were preparing for a visit from our MP.'

'I hadn't heard,' Leo said.

'It was going to be quite informal, just her dropping in, finding out what we do. I hadn't announced it just yet because she said at the time that, of course, it depended on the result of the general election. Well. I thought she was just speaking for form's sake, but it seems not.'

'They've given her a peerage, haven't they?' Leo said. He was aware of his hands tensing in his lap.

'A sort of consolation prize,' Mr Ghosh said. 'A very nice one, of course, to be called Lady Sharifullah. I don't think anyone thought the election result was a reflection on her personally. In any case, we were in touch with the new MP's office, but unfortunately he doesn't think he can find us a date for some time. So we went back to Baroness Sharifullah. She's coming – delighted, she said. She said there was no reason now for her to wait until December. She doesn't want any fuss, just two or three people to tell her about our work, what we need, that sort of thing. She's coming next Wednesday. I'd like you to take charge of her, talk her through everything.'

'I don't think I can do that,' Leo said.

Mr Ghosh brushed that aside. 'You just have to do the usual tour you give dignitaries, but a little less pomp. No one else needs to be warned – if it's good enough for our patients, it's certainly good enough for Lady Sharifullah to cast her noble eye over. Actually, I'm being unfair. She's supposed to be perfectly nice. She was chief executive of an NGO about women's education in Asia.'

'She's from Sheffield,' Leo said. 'Like me.'

'Well, there you are, then,' Mr Ghosh said. It seemed that Leo had agreed to host Lady Sharifullah. Did they say 'Lady Sharifullah', which was absurd, tea-party-on-the-lawn, or did they say 'Baroness Sharifullah', which suggested a serious place in the legislative programme? Neither of them could quite decide. And now Mr Ghosh turned back to his computer. 'I'll let you know some more details tomorrow.'

2.

Leo had bought his house in 1995. The housing market had sunk over the previous years; selling his first flat, he had escaped negative equity, but only just. (A strange way of putting it – he had sold his flat for five thousand more than he'd bought it for.) The house he lived in now, between Clapham and the Battersea bit of the river, had cost him £90,000, which was three times the salary he had reached at the hospice plus a little bit. Now, his salary was about a fifth higher than it had been, twenty years ago, and his house was worth a million pounds or more. 'I want to be a millionaire,' he imagined himself saying in the 1980s, what he would have thought of that. No one he worked with at the hospice could possibly have afforded a house within walking distance, not even Mr Ghosh. He wished that the careful respect with which people treated him was down to his work, his length of service, his reliability. He was afraid that it was down to the fact that he had been able to buy a house near the park in 1990.

'So much for my vow of poverty, obedience and obscurity,' he imagined himself saying to an imaginary friend, one who would smile and shake his head ruefully. 'If I sold the house in Kandahar Road, I could buy my dad's mansion in Sheffield and have enough left over for a top-of-the-range caravan.' The imaginary friend shook his head ruefully at Leo, the SW11 millionaire. It was so ordinary a dilemma.

Rubilynn was in the kitchen, cleaning, when he let himself in. The sound from the sitting room meant that she had collected Sandy from the infants' school and set him down on the sofa, which was wrapped in protective clear plastic, in front of the television. The tinkle and the calm voice proceeding from there were the programmes he had gone on liking. Leo liked them too: they soothed him, if Sandy let his dad take him on his knee and they watched them together. Rubilynn hardly looked up: she was scrubbing the sink with bleach.

'You had a good deep clean yesterday,' Leo observed by way of greeting. 'It's not necessary to do it every day.'

'It's good to do it every day,' Rubilynn said. 'We do it at work twice a day, very clean. Sandy likes it.'

'The house is lovely and clean,' Leo said. He didn't think that Sandy cared either way.

'Thank you,' Rubilynn said, but without turning round and without any pleasure or gratitude in her voice. Leo knew why.

'Are you going out tonight?' he said.

'Your friend – he's coming here? Thursday night, he don't come last week, so this week, he's coming? Tonight I *am* going to spend time with my sister. Sister in Vauxhall.'

'She's not really your sister, is she, Rubilynn?'

'She's my sister, she was very kind to me,' Rubilynn insisted.

'That's not what we mean here when we say "sister", is it?' Leo said. He despised himself for his meanness towards his wife, and yet he went on saying these things.

'She's my sister,' Rubilynn said. South London was full of sisters and brothers, uncles and aunts, at a pinch cousins; it had taken Leo some years to realize that, for the most part, Rubilynn meant only that she harboured adequately warm feelings towards a person who came from the same place she did. 'Your friend is coming tonight, what time?'

'I don't know,' Leo said. 'Probably after work.' That was Leo's polite fiction in turn, the suggestion that Tom Dick had a job that he did during the day. It was probably the English equivalent of Leo calling him his brother.

'I'm going soon,' Rubilynn said. 'Sandy comes with me and when I go to work I leave him with my sister, sleeps there. I collect him tomorrow morning when I am finished, take him school.'

'And I'm working tomorrow from six,' Leo said. 'And all weekend. So perhaps Monday we can sit down together as a family? I'll get something nice to eat.'

And now Rubilynn turned round, peeling her rubber gloves off: she gave him the look of concern and gratitude that was never far from her eyes. 'As family,' she said, and a sweet and lopsided smile appeared as if from nowhere. She was not cross with him; she was cross with the sense of duty and humiliation that insisted on having Tom Dick round to visit for an evening twice a month, every other Thursday night. The duty and humiliation preceded Rubilynn and took, somehow, precedence over her. Rubilynn did not understand, she said nevertheless, why they had to have anyone else. There were the three of them and they were happy in the little house. Nobody else was needed. Leo actually had a sister – a real one – who lived fifteen minutes' walk away, only five minutes' walk from the hospice, in a grand white stucco house by the Common. He had seen her in the street and she had looked at him, disbelieving, as if he were a ghost. He had walked on with his wife and his baby son. For Rubilynn, the aunts and the uncles and the brothers and the sisters and the cousins were needed, it appeared. But Rubilynn did not have it in her to say, 'I hate your friend Tom Dick. I do not believe that you like him. Let us close the door to him for ever.' She must have felt that that was bringing Leo to the point of making a choice. Her view of herself in his life was always provisional, Leo knew, despite Sandy, despite everything.

As a family: Leo thought he would have time after work on Monday to go to Gerrard Street and buy some stinky tofu. It would make Rubilynn clap her hands to see something she liked so much, that made Sandy's eyes widen with horror and that Leo could only ever force down. Stinky tofu was his first clue to what Rubilynn guarded carefully, her story. It was still almost his only one. He had hardly seen the small round nurse when she arrived, ten years ago. It had taken him ages to get her name right, and he had actually appealed in the end to Mrs Roy, Mr Ghosh's predecessor-but-two, to make sure that he was in the right area. She was silent and smiling, efficient and tidy; if Leo had been asked, he would have thought she was Filipina, but without much concentration. It was with astonishment that he now remembered a time when he could hardly have distinguished Chinese from Japanese, Burmese from Thai, Filipino from Malay at a glance. She listened and smiled at what others said; she did not proffer any information. Only once, when somebody was making a cheese toastie in the kitchen, did she pull a face.

'Don't you like cheese?' Leo said – he was there with his mid-morning cup of tea. 'Is it too smelly for you?'

He blushed to think, now, that that used to be the way he spoke to foreigners. The first normal thing he had said to the woman who he was going to marry was 'Don't you like cheese?' as if explaining what that smell was. Of course anyone would know what cheese was. And in a moment Rubilynn was explaining, haltingly, but in little bursts of enthusiasm, that where she came from there was something called stinky tofu, so good, but no one liked it at first. She would never bring stinky tofu into work! But you could not buy it in London. Leo was tactful then, or was conscious of drawing the limits of enquiry tight, and he did not ask where she came from. But he believed that you could buy anything in London. He went to an internet café on Clapham high street and did a search. He learnt that stinky tofu was something that was popular in Taiwan. He went, therefore, to Chinatown, and in the first supermarket he went into he found that they were prepared to sell him some. He had no idea how much to buy: he settled for half a pound.

The next day he had presented it to Rubilynn. She gazed at him, astonished. She did not have a beautiful face: she had the reassuring face of somebody's mummy, photographed when young. He explained that he had been tickled by the name she had mentioned, and had wanted to seek it out.

'Did you try it? Did you like it?' Rubilynn wanted to know, but Leo had not. She had offered some to him, but he said he had just eaten – there was a Gorgonzola-like smell from the plastic bag that he shrank from, in fact. Rubilynn would take it home, that evening. Her sister – she did not eat stinky tofu: she did not like it. Rubilynn was going to be so happy, eating stinky tofu here!

In his mind afterwards he had a story of a poor Filipina girl who had to grow up in Taiwan, who escaped from there as soon as she could. It touched his heart, as made-up stories so often turn back on their creator and touch the heart. They had married four months later. It seemed to Leo to be the right thing to do. There were only the two of them, and five friends – nurses, mostly – from the hospice. He decided not to invite Tom Dick, although by then Tom was already visiting him twice a month, every other Thursday. It was very nice. Rubilynn produced a big white dress with a veil; she looked swamped and nervous in it, and relieved when it was all over. When she wrote with a pen on the form that her place of birth was Taipei, Taiwan, Leo was overcome with the magic of it, the beauty and certainty of his knowledge of her. Afterwards she moved into Leo's house. It was full of Leo – he had been there for ten years – and there was so little of her to make room for. Every time something needed replacing, he promised himself, a kettle, the curtains, the carpet, she would be given permission to choose it, and make his world hers. He would not say any of this to her. It would just happen. His marriage became another of those things that he deserved and would live within; his job, his solitude, his single friendship with a man he did not like. There was no week of the year that he did not think about what he had done to Aisha Sharifullah in the summer of 1990. His cruelty.

Tom Dick came round at half past seven, almost on the dot – some wildlife programme was just starting, and Leo was almost glad of the excuse to turn it off. There was something atavistic in Tom's sticking to conventional mealtimes as times to turn up, as a decadent society preserves the performance of ritual obeisance long after it has stopped possessing any meaning. The cargo cult was evident in what Tom was holding: two square pizza boxes from Domino's round the corner. He must have rung the doorbell with his elbow. He would not eat more than a slice, if that; almost one whole pizza would be left behind with the unfailing observation that there was nothing like cold pizza for breakfast. It had never been eaten; Rubilynn would never have allowed either of them to eat anything that had been brought to the house by Tom Dick. But the polite fiction was preserved by Leo eating one of the pizzas, hot, and throwing the other away, cold.

Tom Dick looked terrible; grey and exhausted, his eyes brilliant and his gums showing in the pulled-back smile. His hair was wild and upright, his crumpled shirt open over an old black T-shirt; the slept-in appearance was forgivable in a man of twenty-two, but Tom Dick was Leo's age. He was fifty-seven, or perhaps fifty-eight.

'Come in,' Leo said. 'Is that pizza I see?'

I am doing something good, Leo said to himself. I am doing something good.

'It was tonight, wasn't it?' Tom Dick said, stumbling over the words in his haste. 'I'm sure it was tonight we agreed. I got a text from you, was it, I don't know, yesterday, saying are we on for tomorrow night, and I'd forgotten but I'm quite pleased, I was pleased to get it because you know I had a date, I had a date planned for tonight but it fell through. I won't bore you with the details. So that was nice, to get your text and think, OK, yes, that's a nice idea, great, good old Leo.'

Tom Dick appeared to be reaching for his pocket while still holding the pizza boxes. Leo reached forward smartly and took them from him in the nick of time. Tom Dick extracted his phone as if nothing had happened.

'Yes, here we are. You sent me a text and it was yesterday. I got a Four Seasons and a Quattro Formaggi, is it, I hope that's OK. I thought I'd leave you to get something to drink.'

'I can get you a beer,' Leo said. 'But you're going to have to make it last, Tom.'

'Oh, that's fine, that's fine, perfect, I don't ask for anything,' Tom Dick said, now humbly shedding his shoes and kicking them to one side of the hallway. He had learnt that this was a shoeless house and now did not need to be asked to remove them. As always, Leo could not help seeing Tom's trainers, worn and dirty and, most of all, size thirteen, next to the neat, shining and tiny array of the shoes of three tiny Spinsters. 'Just one beer and then I'm happy with water from the tap. What's our movie tonight? Do we have a movie? I really fancy a movie and a pizza and maybe a beer, one beer. I can't help thinking, I was thinking only tonight or this morning or maybe yesterday,' Tom Dick said, coming into the living room and looking about him wildly, 'I was thinking – Listen, this is important, I want to say this, but first I'd better just, well, as it were, go to the loo.'

'You know where it is,' Leo said. He set down the pizza boxes on the table; he went into the kitchen and fetched two plates and two sets of knives and forks; he extracted two beers from the fridge, opened them and poured them into two glasses. He sat down to wait.

Presently Tom Dick returned. 'That's fine that's better,' he said, sitting down. 'Oh a glass of beer. Well, just the one, perhaps.'

'Tom, I've told you before,' Leo said. 'I can't have you doing drugs in my house.'

Tom reached out. He was on the verge of touching Leo's knee with his great hand, in reassurance or sympathy; it hovered; it withdrew. 'I wouldn't do that to you,' Tom Dick said, his eyes rolling.

'You've just done it,' Leo said. 'I'm not an idiot. I have a child, you know. A child lives in this house, you understand?'

'I was thinking,' Tom Dick said. 'I was thinking about – this was yesterday – I was thinking about the first time we met. Not the first time we met obviously, that was when we were maybe like twelve, or whatever, but the first time – do you know – the first time we met when I had made up my mind to do the right thing. Do you know what I'm referring to?'

'Yes, Tom,' Leo said resignedly. He had heard this before. Tom often brought it up: it was the moment he drew many morals from; he remembered it quite wrong.

'It was just one day and everything had gone wrong. I was sitting in this place and around me there were people who I didn't know and would never see again. I just saw them. They were naked, some of them, but it wasn't until this moment that I really saw them, I saw them! I just understood that I shouldn't be with people who I'd met twelve hours before in Soho, I should be with people who, you know, I knew, I'd been with for years. And then I just saw you in my mind and I thought about all the things I'd done to you, all the bad things I'd offloaded onto you, do you know what I mean?'

'Yes, I think I do,' Leo said.

'That's it, you understand when I talk,' Tom Dick said. 'And I realized that I was afraid of stuff happening to me, you know, *stuff happening*, and so I created it, I made it happen, and I made it happen to other people, I made it happen to you. So I left that place, I went to St Pancras, I bought a ticket, I got on a train. I thought I would drive but then I thought I was high, I would kill myself, I would fall asleep on the M1. I knew exactly what I had to do. I got the train, I went to your house. Your parents' house. I don't know what I wanted to say. But then you were there and you were getting into a taxi and you were driving away and I was just standing there, I was too late. I thought I was too late. I just stood there trying to make up my mind. I waited until those others came back and I got them to give me your address in London. I followed you home! I must have done. And then at first you didn't want to talk to me.'

'No, Tom, I didn't,' Leo said.

'My life was so terrible, it was terrible,' Tom Dick said. 'I looked you in the face and I saw a man who was looking at me with death in his soul, who wanted to shut me out. Do you remember? You were there in the door of the place you lived, where it was … I don't know where it was. I was living with my mum I think … It was that place you lived in before. Do you remember? And then I looked at you and you saw me. You sort of gave way, you saw what you had to do, and there it was, you forgiving me already. And you said, "Come in." Do you remember? I'll never stop thanking you for that. After that I was OK, I was really OK. After everything I'd done to you. At Oxford and everything.'

'Yes, Tom,' Leo said. 'I remember. It's fine. You don't have to say thank you all the time. We're friends now. What do you fancy? An old movie? Something foreign? A blockbuster? Something arty?' Wordlessly, Leo reached out and took a wodge of tissues from the box on the table. He had placed it there before Tom Dick arrived. He passed them to Tom Dick, who wiped the tears from his eyes and from his sweaty face, and blew his nose. They watched *Singin' in the Rain*. Half an hour before the end, Tom Dick excused himself and went to the lavatory, where he probably took some more drugs. His puzzlement at the complexity of the film, his invulnerability to anything that might be meant to make him laugh, was almost tangible. The film came to an end; Leo stood up and said goodnight; Tom Dick stumbled to the door and left.

Leo returned to the sitting room. Before tidying up, he watched his favourite part of the film again. It was everybody's favourite part of the film, the part where Gene Kelly danced in the rain. Earlier, Leo had not been fully concentrating on it. As it had started, Tom Dick had recognized and understood the famous music, and his brow had unfurrowed: he had given a sweet, boyish smile of recognition. It unfurled across his face. The smile on Tom Dick's face: it was the smile of beatific joy, before he had ever felt the need to pretend in the face of the world. Then, Leo had enjoyed looking at Tom Dick's absorbed, sweet smile; but now his concentration was on the film. He enjoyed it a lot. Sometimes things were really good and everybody agreed. You did not have to seek out things that were unheard of. Often the best things were like a bank-holiday Monday with your wife and your delighted child on the front at Bournemouth. That had been a very good day, a day of kindness to others. It was what men lived by. He remembered that he must organize Rubilynn's birthday treat, now only three months away.

Leo put the pizza boxes in the bin, and took a new yellow sponge-wipe from the unopened packet underneath the sink. He went to the downstairs toilet, and, after trying the window-sill and the little bookshelf, determined that Tom Dick had used the top of the lavatory cistern to chop up and snort his drugs. He poured bleach onto the sponge, wiped the surface, then wiped it again with hot water and dried it with toilet paper before repeating the whole sequence. He took care not to brush any crumbs into the crevice at the back of the lavatory cistern, and afterwards washed the floor around the lavatory with the same care, with the same sponge in case any fragments had fallen to the floor. Afterwards he let the hot tap run over the sponge for five minutes, before taking it out to bury it in the outside bin. Leo had long ago concluded that there was no point in trying to separate what love did from what you did out of penance. Love was not only what you felt like doing, and for him it had not started with that.

3.

The office still made Aisha laugh. It was so much like an American funeral parlour, with its perpetually renewed flowers, pale beige carpet and air of tactful dignity. The twins' idea of what a lawmaker's offices should look like. It was gloriously convenient, there was no doubt about it, but the feeling of the hushed suite of offices, a room outside for the PA and another, slightly larger, attached for a pair of interns was not very comfortable. She couldn't think in it. It was incredibly kind of Omith and Raja to commit to paying the rent for the next ten years, and even kinder of them to devote so much energy to finding it in the first place. After three weeks there, she had asked Veronica if she would move her desk into the main office, as she called it. The interns could move to Veronica's old office. And the interns' office ...

'Let's use it as a meeting room,' Veronica said. 'You won't always want me around when someone important wants to talk to you. Or – I know – let's not shift at all. Let's just keep the doors open and you move your desk closer. Then we can chat or we can shut the doors and not chat.'

'Oh, God,' Aisha said. There was no getting round it. She was now officially very grand. They'd been open-plan at A Woman's Place with a meeting room for private or difficult conversations. In the House of Commons she'd shared a wood-panelled office with Sean, an MP from the same party, plus Veronica, plus Sean's assistant (his wife), plus coming-and-going unpaid assistance, plus whoever came to drop in and perch on the edge of the Pugin desk and shout at them, like a party whip. It had been quite jolly. Now the twins had intervened and offered to put her somewhere where she could actually do something. She'd agreed without thinking too much about it.

The boys hadn't thought about it at all, it turned out. They'd just stared in horrified incomprehension when she'd thought to tell them that she'd of course have to declare their generous gift in the Register of Lords' Interests (Category 6, Sponsorship). It was too late. The connection between her and them had been made. She might as well become a director of Fuck That Games and let the red-tops do their worst.

Today she was on one of her visits. It was a visit that had been set up in her previous life, when she was finding out about everything and everyone in the constituency. Now she had no constituency she was concentrating on her interests and projects, but the hospice had said she was still very welcome, and Veronica thought, Why not? Baroness Sharifullah did not think that she was going to tell a hospice that her interest in their work had stopped sharply – 'Don't say "stopped dead", Aisha, please,' Veronica had said – on the morning after the general election of 2015.

The taxi drew up, and Aisha got out. The hospice was converted out of half a dozen tall nineteenth-century houses, a glass box constructed in front of the main entrance. There was, happily, no one there to greet her, and she went inside.

'Baroness Sharifullah,' the receptionist said. 'Yes, indeed. We're expecting you. Leo was here a moment ago – he'll be showing you round. Here he is.'

Leo was a very short, grizzle-haired, square-faced man with nervous blue eyes, flickering from side to side. She shook his hand.

'This way,' he said, leading her towards what had been the back of the house; it gave way to a modern extension with a glass roof. He didn't say anything as they walked, not even asking if she had had a good journey. (Perhaps he knew that she had only come from Westminster.) They went into a meeting room, and she shook Sanjay Ghosh's hand – she had met him before, a decent sort, a bit keen on the bottom line. Lady Holloway was there as well, a Tory peer; she greeted Aisha like an old friend, and soon it turned out that Sheila Holloway, as Ghosh referred to her, was chair of the Friends organization. She lived just a street away, she explained. The man called Leo ran through the history and functioning of the hospice in a couple of minutes: he went through its funding and its financial situation, all the time looking down at a folder that, Aisha could see, he did not really need to consult. She knew all about these shy people who had all the facts. He handed over to Ghosh, who went on to outline what they needed to expand. The demand for their services was such, Ghosh said, that users could only very rarely be admitted more than two or three days before their eventual death. Aisha nodded: she understood. A few words from Sheila Holloway about their fundraising and their fêtes, a warm embrace from a woman who, as far as Aisha knew, she had never spoken a word to, and she was handed over to Leo.

'You don't remember me,' Leo said, when they were on their own.

'I knew it was you,' Aisha said. 'I was sure it was you. It must be –'

'Oh, twenty-five years,' Leo said. 'At least that. You'd just finished at Cambridge, hadn't you?'

'I can't understand …' Aisha said.

'They're still living in the same place, then?' Leo said. 'Your mum and dad? Are they well?'

'Still well,' Aisha said. 'Still living there, next to your dad. He's going to be a hundred in two months, isn't he? We're all going to the party for it – I wouldn't miss it for the world.'

'I never thought,' Leo said, 'I never thought I'd bump into you again.'

'Why do you say that?'

'It seemed best. It's bad luck we're meeting again now.'

'Oh, kay,' Lady Sharifullah said. But then she engaged. Her eyes lit up, not with happiness. 'I don't know why you would say that.'

'Because,' Leo said. It was as if a flicker, the temptation of superiority, crossed his face. 'Oh, I don't think we really want to go into that.'

'Yes,' Lady Sharifullah said. 'I suppose we left each other in rather an awkward way. You telling me what I should have done and me wanting to say all the time that I didn't feel any of that stuff I wrote in that letter. I had just made a mistake.'

'Well, there's no point in going over it,' Leo said. 'We're all so pleased that you've come to see our work here. Let's just forget about the bad-luck element of it.'

'Actually, you know,' Aisha said, 'I thought you were going to be nice to me. But when you say that … It makes me feel – how do you think it makes anyone feel, being spoken to like that? You ought to think twice before you say things like that to anyone.'

'It's not meant to be rude,' Leo said. 'It's just how things are. It's lovely to see you again. I'm really happy to see you again.'

'Except you wish it hadn't happened,' Aisha said.

'Don't take it to heart,' Leo said. 'It's nothing to do with you in particular.'

'What do you mean?'

'You in particular, I meant,' Leo said.

'And people like me, you mean?'

Leo stared. She could see that he was in a conversation he had not understood and had not engaged with, and he blushed. Whether or not he had meant to dissociate himself from anything, he now had no language to explain himself.

'I've heard that before – don't take it to heart. It's nothing to do with you. It's all to do with me, who, by the way, has done nothing wrong or unusual. I'm not challenging you. Do you know what it's like, being an immigrant?' Aisha said. 'You know the word. Don't flinch when I say it. I was an immigrant. I came here when I was eight years old. That's old enough. I'll tell you what it's like, being an immigrant. It's like having a knife held to your throat and being told that if you do exactly what they tell you to, then they'll take it away and you can be allowed to be friends with them again. Never knowing whether you've said the thing that is going to bring the knife to your throat. You probably haven't said anything. The knife is at your throat and slowly someone is going to take it away. That's what it's like. Don't tell me it's lovely to see me when you did what you did. That was like a knife to my throat. That letter. Don't tell me you'd prefer never to see me again and expect me to smile.'

'I don't think that was anything to do with what I said,' Leo said. 'I'm not that sort of person.'

'I don't think you get to decide whether you're that sort of person or not,' Aisha said. 'I think it's for the people who you make suffer to declare what you are.'

'I'm actually not going to go to my father's party,' Leo said. 'It's best not.'

'You've got your own reasons,' Aisha said. She pulled at the silk scarf at her neck, tightening it.

'My life's down here now. I don't go up there at all.'

'When was the last time you were up there?' Aisha asked. She breathed. She could feel herself letting kindly interest back into her voice. There was no reason for her to lose her temper. Leo was a long time ago and she would walk away from him in five minutes.

'That would have been when I last saw you,' Leo said. 'Twenty-five years ago. I don't mean to be dramatic. It's not important.'

She digested this.

'My dad's still there, then,' Leo said.

'He's amazing,' Aisha said reprovingly. 'Are you really not going to go up there for the big jamboree? It's going to be amazing. Didn't you know? Surely you knew.'

'I'm really out of touch,' Leo said.

'Well, you'd have to be, not to know that your dad's going to be a hundred years old in two months. He's really looking forward to it. My mum and dad, they're organizing the whole thing for him. They love it. Everyone's going. You've got to come.'

Leo smiled and shook his head.

'What?' Aisha said. 'What does that mean? They're all coming. Your dad's tortoise is looking forward to it no end. Do you even know that Gertrude's still going strong?'

'Is she,' Leo said.

'Your dad was talking about giving her her own blog at one point,' Aisha said. 'Do you know what a computer whizz he's become? He's the king of below the line, my dad says. He's always getting kicked off the *Guardian*'s comments. A hundredth birthday – it's to say goodbye.'

'Are you living in London, these days?' Leo said. She turned and looked at him. Her memory of him had been, until this kindly sentence, of being spoken to as if from above by a man hardly five feet tall, specific and sharply limited. She had remembered his identity and the summer during which they had spent time together, in the car, driving him backwards and forwards to the hospital – who was it who had been ill? Was it Raja after his throat had been cut open to save him? She forgot. It was this kindly sentence and others like it, produced in writing a quarter of a century ago, that had sent her out into the needy world. She was a peer of the realm and a well-known public figure, and she was being talked down to by a nurse in a hospice as if she had made some awful incontinent blunder. He was going to overlook what she had said for her own sake. She had written him a letter, twenty-five years ago, and he had responded in exactly the same generous way. Her mind produced, without effort, a couple of phrases she had written with girlish abandon. A patch of sore skin had been touched again, and she winced.

'Yes,' she said. 'Yes, I am. It's been extremely nice. Thank you so much for finding the time to show me round. I really appreciate it. I won't disturb Sanjay to say goodbye, if you could just ...'

She walked to the tube; was back in the office by one thirty with a sandwich. She thought she would phone Nihad.

'No!' Nihad said. She was at work; she handled the publicity for a very successful football team. She'd shut herself away so as not to have to deal with anyone for half an hour. It was a pleasure to hear Aisha's voice, she said. 'You're literally the last person to say, "Is that Fanny?" to me. You know, you're lucky to get me. They're announcing a new coach for the juniors downstairs as we speak.'

'You've got to pretend to be interested.'

'I am literally counting the days until retirement,' Nihad said. 'Just a few more months – just ninety-six months – and then there's a carriage clock and I'm selling up and buying an estate in Poland. Umbria. Wherever. What's up, your ladyship?'

'You'll never guess who I met this morning,' Aisha said.

'Who have you met today? I'm literally not guessing.'

'Here's a clue – his dad's going to be a hundred years old in two months.'

'Prince Edward. I really don't know.'

'Come on, Fanny, it's the son of Mummy and Daddy's next-door neighbour. You know. Dr Spinster who leapt over the fence and cut Raja's throat and saved his life that time – you must remember. He's going to be a hundred.'

'And you met his son. Spare me.'

The list of Fanny's men was short, and consisted of Matthew, the man she had met on her course at university and who had been the root cause of her 2.2, the disgrace. Perhaps Aisha's was longer, and harder to remember in detail. The list began with girlish enthusiasms; the last two or three were guarded, doubtful, hedged round with obvious scepticism. The very last one had been another MP, God save her. She had examined those recent men sceptically, rigorously, thoroughly, as if they were novice budget proposals full of unjustified assumptions about growth. By the time she had finished reminding Fanny about Leo, the impact of their meeting had somehow gone.

4.

All week Josh had been in a state of dread and excitement. The event happened once a month in the club under the railway arches. He at once longed to go and hated the thought of going. He did not really want to go. But he knew he would go.

He had broken the rules, he knew. On Tuesday, he had sent her a text message asking if she was going. The response had come back in seconds. She wrote in capitals, WHO IS THIS? HOW DARE YOU. DON'T YOU EVER FUCKING PROPOSE ANYTHING TO ME, YOU SCUM. And then silence. He accepted it humbly. The rules of the game could extend beyond the hours OYK was open, once a month.

All week, he had thought that she had dismissed him, that he had broken the rules and was now cast out. The game had lasted for two years and was now over. He thought of going on his own, but she would be there: she would look at him in real, not performed, contempt, as an amateur who just didn't know how to play, and then ignore him. He had blown it. But then on Saturday morning the text came. He was to be standing at Old

Street roundabout at nine p.m., shirtless, wearing his slave's collar and his leather trousers. He must await his betters.

He did it. They made him wait for an hour as traffic roared past and he drew the attention of Hoxton party-goers. He had slicked down his hair and put on sunglasses. If a partner saw him here, surely, too, they would think it could not be Josh: Josh certainly didn't have a two-foot panther tattooed on the side of his ribs. Josh – boring Josh, who always wore a vest and lived with his mummy? No.

It was after ten that a white Nissan drew up; the window was rolled down. She yelled at him to get in. The black man she called Saveloy was driving. Josh got into the back and she carried on talking to Saveloy as if they were still alone. Josh accepted this humbly. She was talking to Saveloy about what they were going to do to their runt, dwelling on it lovingly. Saveloy was a huge presence in the car, a matter of cubic metres filling the space. He had made the atmosphere in there – thick, soup-like, intoxicating. He had mastered it at her command, and had been instructed to be silent. 'Sav went to the gym last night, didn't you?' she said. 'And you didn't shower afterwards. And you ran to my house. More sweat. It's three days now since you washed, Sav. And that T-shirt you've got on. What's that, Sav? What's that all down the front? It's cum, isn't it, Sav? We used it to wipe up your cum. And then you put it back on. Oh, you spilled some poppers on it, too. Oh, Saveloy, you stink.'

Josh waited.

'That's right, Sav. You've got a new hole to fuck. You're going to take the runt, aren't you, and there in front of everyone at On Your Knees. I've got a little something for him. Have you seen what I've got for him? I've got it in my bag, to tie on with little ribbons, little ladylike ribbons, and then master him with it. He won't like that, not one bit. And then when I'm done with him, I'm handing him over to you. Little straight boy. He doesn't like being fucked, does he? It's just a fucking hole to you, isn't it, Sav? You'll do it if I tell you to. Little runt. He only sent me a text this week. Against orders. He's got to learn his lesson.'

They left the car streets away. She fastened a lead to the collar round his neck, and, there on the street, turned and kissed him deeply. There was a pill on the tip of her tongue: he swallowed it gratefully. She handed the lead over to Sav, filthy, his T-shirt stained and ripped, and in a stately procession, Sav behind her in her four-inch heels, he, the runt, humble behind Sav, they walked to the club. The cars passing hooted; the faces in the back averted, hilarious, incredulous. He stripped at the cloakroom; Sav stripped; she watched as they put their clothes into black plastic bags: and she led them into the once-monthly gathering, under the Vauxhall railway arches, of the club Josh had always dreamt of, a club called On Your Knees. Faces turned to them, and the events of the hours to come began to unfold.

The morning after his OYK nights, Josh could always count on being in an unusually optimistic and cheerful mood. He had the largest bedroom in the house, and when he woke, around eleven, could hear movement and conversation from downstairs. He stretched, luxuriantly. For two or three pleasant minutes he contemplated the paintings in his bedroom, one hanging on the wall at the foot of his bed, a Polish painter's thoughtful imitation of Pollock, fifty years old; another on the wall behind the walnut chest of drawers, a portrait by Meredith Frampton he had found mislabelled in an auction in the nineties. He liked his room; it was his own and nobody else's. The leather trousers were neatly folded on the walnut chair; his boots lined up. He felt surprisingly good and, making a deep and satisfying intake of breath, got up and reached for his white dressing-gown. His back stung, but not too disagreeably; the whip had been produced at some point last night. He had been out of it. He felt the full mystery of sex in the aches and satisfactions of his body.

Mummy was downstairs. She was talking to Thomas. Breakfast had been finished some time ago, but they were sitting over its detritus; Thomas had evidently cooked a sausage and some bacon for his aunt, some scrambled eggs. Thomas was following the resolution that he had confided in Josh some

weeks ago, to be good to his aunt. Mummy was bright and
smiling, telling Thomas about an adventure that Deborah had
had on her way over last night. They'd planned to spend
Saturday night in front of the telly, watching *The Voice* and then
Casualty.

Deborah was Mummy's friend from AA; Mummy had relied
upon her to speak to whenever things started to look unpromising, five years ago at the whole beginning of AA and the twelve-
step programme and the new resolutions, five years ago when
Mummy had lost her job and had had to move into Josh and
Thomas's house in Hackney. They had gone down to Brighton,
leaving Mummy under the care of Aunt Blossom in Clapham
for a few days, and had cleared out the incredible state of the
house down there, a house out of Kienholz. How had Josh let
it get so bad? Thomas kept asking, but Josh couldn't say. He
didn't know that it was his to keep good or let go to the bad.
They cleared it up and filled two skips and paid off the mortgage
arrears – fortunately only three months; it was so sad, the tiny
scale of the debts that were threatening to overwhelm Mummy.
When it was empty, they painted it white from top to bottom;
they threw away the carpets and polished the floorboards. The
bathroom and kitchen would have to do. They handed it over
to a local estate agent and let it, unfurnished; the income from
the letting, a pleasant family called Kawabata, was Mummy's
income for a long time, until she found a job teaching English
as a foreign language to businessmen, three days a week.

There had been no alternative to them taking Mummy in at
the time. Thomas had agreed. They had bought the house
knowing it was too big for the two of them – it had been astonishing, what you could buy in Hackney even in 2005 with Uncle
Stephen's millennium gift of £250,000 each and a mortgage on
a pair of young professional salaries. Perhaps they had envisaged
some different future at the time. The temporary solution of
giving Mummy a bedroom and looking after her while she was
at a low ebb had turned into a permanent one. Thomas had
even stopped saying that he didn't see why Aunt Catherine

couldn't be taken in by Mummy and Daddy, his mummy and daddy, in Clapham.

There was no doubt about it: Josh was now a middle-aged man living with his mother. There was no space in this life for a woman, so he resorted to trips, once a month, to a club where what he wanted was catered for and exactly supplied. What Thomas was proposing to do was not at all clear to Josh, or to anyone (he had asked Aunt Blossom). The girls came and went: sometimes he had periods of spending most of the week at the current girlfriend's flat. So far none had stuck.

Mummy was talking; Thomas gave Josh an agonized smile as he came in.

'He must have been already old, or what I thought of as old, when I first met him,' she was saying. 'I don't think he was quite retired, but there was talk already of him retiring, I'm pretty sure. Josh's dad gave me such an explanation on the way up – what I was supposed to do, how I shouldn't be afraid, if he said something awful how I should just smile and talk about something else. I can't believe he's going to be a hundred.'

'You're not going to Grandpa's party, are you, Mummy?' Josh said.

'Well, of course I'm going,' Catherine said. 'I had an invitation, like everyone else. It's very nice of Grandpa to think of me.'

'I think it was Sharif who thought of you,' Josh said. 'I don't think Grandpa's doing anything.'

'Well, it was very nice of Sharif,' Catherine said. 'I really didn't expect to get an invitation at all. I was only Hilary's daughter-in-law for five minutes back in the 1980s and then I disappeared from the family album. I haven't seen him for thirty years. I can't think why they've invited me.'

'You don't have to go if you don't want to,' Thomas said, grinning. 'It's only going to be a massive Bollywood-style party. Those neighbours are organizing the whole thing.'

'Oh, I think I will go,' Catherine said. 'It's during the day so Deborah and I can go up on the train, stay a couple of hours, toast Hilary with a cup of tea, then get on the train and come down again.'

'You can't bring Deborah to Grandpa's hundredth birthday,' Josh said. 'He doesn't want to meet people from – well, he doesn't want to meet new people.'

'Oh,' Catherine said. 'I suppose not. I don't know who I'm going to talk to. I'll just go up on the train, stay a couple of hours, toast Hilary –'

'I thought you'd drive up with us,' Josh said.

'I couldn't do that,' Catherine said. 'I've bought the ticket now in any case. I thought if I bought it now it would be cheaper. Do you know how much it was? I almost bought a first-class ticket, it was so cheap. I only paid …'

They let her run on. After a time, she finished talking; she looked around her as if she were not quite sure where she had been all this time, and gave Josh and then Thomas a bright, brilliant, insane smile. Explaining all the while how she was going to fill the rest of her day, she washed up her plates and cup before leaving the kitchen and going into the sitting room. Thomas watched her go.

'I've reached the point where I don't know whether it's break-fast or lunch I'm eating,' he said.

'You could invent a new meal,' Josh said. 'You could call it – hang on a minute, I'm almost there – *lunst*.'

'I was going to have some of that sticky toffee pudding from Friday night, only cold.'

'You do that,' Josh said. 'You could fry it first, like cold Christmas pudding.'

'What time did you roll in, then?' Thomas said.

'No idea,' Josh said. 'Let me look. It'll be recorded on Uber.' He got out his mobile phone, in the pocket of his dressing-gown. 'Four forty-three. I must have been back about half five.'

'My God, the life you live,' Thomas said. 'The life you live once a month, anyway. I had a drink with Ellie and then she said she was tired and she had files to go through today, so she

went home. I came home and had a wank. That was the high-
light, to be honest. I thought afterwards I might as well have
stayed in and watched *Casualty* with Aunt Catherine and
Deborah the Dipso. I'm quite into *Casualty* at the moment.
There's a story about two brothers who are both doctors, only
one's good and the other's evil.'

'Sounds brilliant.'

'What were you up to? No, don't tell me. Being whipped and
pissed on by dominatrixes. That place you go – I bet it's full of
other solicitors, too.'

Josh looked up sharply. Thomas was, as far as he knew, the
only person who knew about OYK or any of this. He had told
him once because he couldn't stand nobody knowing, and he
knew Thomas wouldn't care.

'Why do you say that?' he said.

'What? Full of solicitors? Obviously it's full of solicitors.
Who else would it be full of? Vets?'

It had been an unlucky comment. The thing that had
happened last night was not supposed to happen. There was a
moment when the outside world and the secret world had
touched, not in a performance of humiliation, but in a couple
of words. A man in a mask had been circling, watching; Josh
was tied to the bench, an old-style school pommel horse, his
head pouring with sweat. There were others, too, walking
round, prowling, muttering encouragement, perhaps waiting to
see if it could be their turn. This man in the mask was walking
around him for ten minutes, maybe more. At one point he
squatted, his face right next to Josh's; Josh had the hot smell of
leather from the mask. He just said 'Hello, Josh,' in a quiet
voice that Josh could identify and could not identify. It was
from a place other than this place. He had not thought about it
until now, but now he examined it, it seemed to him that it was
a voice he knew from the week, from the office. Someone he
worked with had seen him at OYK.

'What are you going to do?' Thomas said.

'What?' Josh said.

'God, stop snapping at me,' Thomas said. 'I'm just asking what you're doing about Grandpa's party. Are you driving up? I thought you were supposed to be organizing the whole thing.'

'Sharif's doing most of it,' Josh said. 'I wouldn't know who to invite, even. Grandpa's already given me a hard time about not knowing how to get in touch with Daddy.'

'I bet Mummy knows where your dad is,' Thomas said. 'She just isn't saying.'

'I don't think so,' Josh said. The leather face, its inexpressive features, bent down. When he closed his eyes in dread he could smell it again, an inch from his face, and hot with glee. He made an effort. He thought of other things.

5.

Thomas let himself into the house in Grafton Square. He kept a set of keys, given to him as he was the nearest child. Tresco, blond-dreadlocked, was capering round burning men in a field in Somerset most weekends, and otherwise in his and Daphne's farmhouse outside Wells with half a dozen children running round trying to kill each other; Tamara was in Brisbane making a success of her beachfront boutique; Trev was in Wales producing inedible goat's cheese with her sixty-year-old lover, Alison, and campaigning to save the planet. Thomas wasn't sure, but Trev might not be speaking to any of them at the moment, either. The last time he'd seen her he had been trying to say goodbye in the square of the town that was nearest them – why had it been there and not at Alison's square house up the lane? – and Alison had evidently thought they'd been saying goodbye long enough, and had come over, her big eyes staring, her long grey hair draped over her bosom in a way that maybe in 1975 had been alluring, and had embraced Trev from behind, her hands placed on Trev's breasts in a direct way. 'See you soon,' Trev had said, in her newly gruff way, and Alison had stared and said, 'Not

too soon, maybe. Sell well. Make money.' Before Thomas could
say anything in response to this, Alison had forcibly turned his
sister away, and they were off in their jeep. Thomas didn't understand why people had to be like that when they knew that he
was an estate agent. Mummy had probably looked at all her
children, far away, and fended off her thought that it would be
best to give the key to their house in Grafton Square to Josh
before entrusting the third and least of her children with it.

To his surprise the only person home was an Indian man,
barefoot and in a T-shirt reading 'XBOX' with white jeans. His
hair was in a beautifully constructed quiff, two inches high, and
he squatted on the floor in Mummy's sitting room with a square
metre of paper in front of him. The paper – some kind of plan
– was held down by two champagne glasses at each corner, an
empty bottle and the little bronze of a lizard that Mummy kept
on the side table. The Turkey carpet that almost filled the room
had been in Mummy's morning room, the smallest downstairs
room in the big house, Thomas remembered. The painting
above the chimney breast was the Guercino from the dining
room that they all had to be so careful of and not flick food at.
Who was Guercino? Thomas had no idea. He had only had the
name drummed into him. He was as ignorant as one of the
ducks on Clapham Pond, he knew.

The man looked up and smiled, a big warm bright smile, and
scrambled to his feet. 'I know you,' he said. 'You're one of
Blossom's sons. Are you Josh?'

'Josh is a cousin, really,' Thomas said. He could hear his voice
growing superior, snubbing, posh.

'Oh, well, I don't know who you are, then,' the man said.

Thomas introduced himself.

'I'm Omith. You don't remember me, I don't suppose. Your
mum's just gone out to get something to drink. We finished a
bottle, her and me and your dad, who then went out for a walk.
She'll only be a moment. She went to Oddbins.'

'I'm surprised she had anything in the house to start with,'
Thomas said. 'You take pot luck round here if you turn up

expecting a drink.' He remembered that there was a time when, quite apart from the contents of the cellar, for splendid occasions or merely for investment and resale at some later point, there had always been a case of champagne or two in the buttery, probably left over from a dinner party or birthday or something of the sort. There had always been a couple of dozen bottles of the sort that now lay empty, holding down the corner of the map.

'Oh, I brought that,' the man Omith said. 'I know they like it.'

He spoke guilelessly, but now the sound of the key in the lock was heard, and in came Mummy, looking as ever as if she'd been dragged through a hedge backwards. Now that Daddy was so mystical and forgiving all the time and at one with the universe, she didn't have anyone even to comb her hair for. Josh said she looked like the White Queen; Thomas thought she was sixty-two, and could be eighty. As if to confirm what Omith had said, the bottle she was clutching, its paper waving off it like torn pennants, was only prosecco rather than the august gift now pinning down a map.

'Hello, darling!' Mummy said, embracing him. 'I didn't know – Goodness, did I forget? Were you supposed to be coming for supper tonight? There's not a thing in the house. I'm so sorry, darling. It's probably written down on a piece of paper somewhere under a pile of other pieces of paper.'

'No, I just thought I'd come over,' Thomas said. 'It was either that or spend an evening in with Josh and Aunty Catherine.'

'Oh, well, I can quite see that,' Blossom said, turning to Omith. 'We have a difficult sister-in-law. Ex-sister-in-law, but of course she's Josh's mother, lovely Josh, so we have to bear her in mind. Of course you know all this – you sent her an invitation to Daddy's party.'

'Well, I knew the name, it was on a list,' Omith said. 'Just half a glass, perhaps. That would be lovely.'

'They didn't have anything really nice cold,' Blossom said. 'So I got prosecco, which is quite as nice, really. I do hope that's all right. Omith's been a perfect angel, taking charge of everything. We're just talking about the seating plan.'

'The seating plan?' Thomas said. 'We're sitting down, are we? I thought it was just a garden party.'

'It would be best if Daddy sat down. And of course people are not as young as they were. Heavens, even I dread a party, these days, if I know I've got to stand up the whole time. So Omith and Raja, so sweetly, said what about a lunch, we could easily get a table for forty in the back garden, so that's being hired, and the cooks are coming in in the morning and cooking cold salmon mayonnaise and cucumber salad and Eton mess for dessert. The caterers are under strict instructions not to mix the Eton mess too early. It's so exciting, don't you think, darling?'

Thomas was filled with rage. He hardly knew these people, and here they were, taking charge for his grandpa's hundredth birthday, paying for it, turning it into a vulgar, ostentatious spectacle, no doubt, taking all the credit for it. Those people! They were all the same. He knew about this Omith now, splashing his money about and showing off. Turning up with bottles of Krug on a Sunday afternoon, getting on Mummy's right side. The worst of it was what Josh had told him a few years ago about the ownership of the house itself.

'Well,' he said to Omith. 'That sounds very exciting. And you must do whatever you think would be best. It's your garden, after all. Grandpa just happens to live in it.'

Omith's amiable, inexpressive, pleasant face made no reaction at all to what Thomas had said. Blossom made a great pretence at not hearing any of it. 'And the vice-chancellor's coming. He came to Sharif's retirement party last year – Sharif, you know, Daddy's neighbour and Omith's father – and he and your grandfather got on like a house on fire. It turns out that your grandfather delivered one of his sister's babies, or saved it from croup, or something like that, I forget. He's coming and Mrs V-C. I've put him between Grandpa and Omith's sister Aisha. She's very grand, these days, you know, she's in the House of Lords. I will say this for Daddy, he's been really good at making new friends in the last twenty years. He hasn't closed himself down at all. Who would have predicted – your mother and father, Omith, they're so good to Daddy. I know I ought to know, but where are you from in the first place, your family, I mean?'

'My mum and dad were born in Bangladesh,' Omith said. 'But they've been here since before I was born.'

'How interesting,' Blossom said. 'I must ask them about it. I don't think I ever knew exactly where they came from.'

'Who's Sally Mottishead?' Thomas said, getting down on his knees and inspecting the seating plan.

'Oh, poor soul,' Blossom said. 'That's the wife of a professor at the university. She threw herself into good works when her daughter committed suicide. That was very sad. Poor girl. The good works took Grandpa in somehow. I put her next to Alison, Trevor's Alison. I'm sure they'll find plenty of things to talk about. Global warming. And I'm putting all the little ones at their own table, look, all of Tresco and Daphne's, so sweet, and Ada Browning's granddaughter really wanted to come because she wanted to see a man who remembered the First World War, she said. She's doing it for a project at school. So adorable. I just couldn't bring myself to put her right.'

'Well, that sounds enchanting,' Thomas said. He had deliberately used an absurd word. His mother had not looked at him or even registered who he was. She was talking for the benefit of this man Omith, the richest man they knew. And Omith, barefoot, cross-legged, smiling as if from a stage to an audience of interns he would never meet, would just sign the cheque at the end of it.

She registered his sourness. 'Oh, darling, it'll be lovely. And, look, we've put you and Ellie here next to Omith's brother Raja. He's such fun, you'll get on like a house on fire.'

'Oh, good. You remembered Ellie.'

'Well, of course, darling,' Blossom said. 'Of course we remembered Ellie. She came here for dinner. She said she couldn't eat onions just as I was serving her some onion soup.

Of course Ellie must come. There won't be any onions, especially for her.'

'Oh, look,' Thomas said. 'You've got a place for Gertrude. That's Gertrude the tortoise, I suppose.'

'Not really a place,' Blossom said. 'We thought we'd put her in a glass case and let her have a lovely meal with everyone else for once. She's getting on, too, you know. She must be sixty. They go on for ever, tortoises. It's been ages since I've had any involvement in a really lovely party, it really has been.'

'And you're going up, what, the night before? Do you want to pool cars?' Omith said. 'I'm sure we'll all have spaces.'

'Oh, I don't think we want to put anyone under an obligation,' Thomas said. 'What about Uncle Leo? Is he expected? Have you left a space at the table for him?'

'No,' Blossom said shortly. 'We're not expecting Uncle Leo. And I don't know what's got into you, but since you've obviously arrived with the intention of being as unpleasant as possible, I'd be grateful if you would take it out again, whatever's got into you.'

'No trouble about the lifts,' Omith said, getting up and putting his sandals on – Paul Smith, Thomas noted. 'Just let me know if you change your mind. I'd better be off, Blossom. Lovely to see you.' It was as if he were refusing to rise to any kind of challenge, merely smiling and performing his own friendliness, and in the end paying for everything. If Thomas had been Mummy, he would have sent the vulgar sod out to Oddbins with instructions to get some more bottles of Krug, no messing about. If they were going to have to put up with this lot, then they might as well take full advantage of their money. He prepared to go on being as unpleasant as he possibly could, whether this man Omith was there or not.

'I really –' Blossom said, when she came back in.

'Mother, you really can't ask people where they come from,' Thomas said. 'Just because they're brown. It's terribly rude.'

'Nonsense,' Blossom said. 'Omith didn't mind a bit. And if we're going to talk about being rude –'

'Well, I don't know,' Thomas said, talking very fast. 'It's poor Grandpa's birthday and the people who are organizing it are the Asians next door. And they're inviting everyone they know and everyone they're related to, it looks like. Who is this Rekha? No idea. I just don't understand what you think it's going to be like for poor Grandpa.'

'Poor Grandpa is thrilled someone else is paying for it,' Blossom said, talking over Thomas. 'Take it from me. And Omith and Raja are so sweet and kind, I just don't know what you think you're doing, being rude like that. Rekha is a simply charming lady, actually. What do you think Grandpa thinks? We see him once a year and I don't know when the last time was you made the slightest effort, and he'd be all on his own if it weren't for Sharif's family. I really think they're the best thing that ever happened to him. I can tell you, I wasn't ever going to have poor Grandpa living in the carriage house.'

'They go for three-quarters of a million, those carriage houses now,' Thomas said. 'We sold one last spring.'

'Well, we'll make jolly sure to hang on to it,' Blossom said. 'We've got absolutely nothing else, let's face it. I don't think you should expect to inherit anything very much. You could all get together and sell the Guercino. But I don't suppose it really is a Guercino and I don't suppose they ever appealed to very many people. We've got no plans to move but this house is part of our retirement plan. If we need to move to a semi in Wimbledon and live off the proceeds, so be it.'

'Well,' Thomas said. He wanted to say the very nastiest thing he could possibly say. 'Let's all very much hope that there isn't another house-price crash, or anything. That would be really bad luck for you, wouldn't it?'

'Oh, do shut up, you beastly toad,' his mother said. 'You really are the bally limit.'

6.

For almost as long as Leo had been married to Rubilynn, he had made an event out of her birthday. It was, in fact, only at their wedding that he saw her carefully filling in her date of birth, and realized he did not know when her birthday was; did not know, either, the names of her parents or her place of birth. Every piece of information came from the point of her pen with trust and surprise, and a magical solidity. He had been right about Taiwan. But he had not known that it had been her birthday only four weeks before. He did not say anything. It occurred to him only as he watched his new wife write her details down that he had been running a terrible risk in marrying a foreigner who, investigation would quickly discover, he knew almost nothing about. After that he made a careful note of the date, and determined that he would make a big thing out of her birthday.

There had been some early failures, but what Rubilynn truly enjoyed were musicals with some dancing in them. Leo enjoyed them, too. A straight play with a star from *Friends* had been a smaller success, though Rubilynn had loved *Friends*, had clasped her hands together when Ross actually came on stage, only forty feet from their seats; a much-praised revival of Stephen Sondheim's *Merrily We Roll Along* (without dancing) had not, he thought, been a success at all. She was polite and subdued, gracious afterwards. She hadn't loved it and, actually, neither had he. For a couple of years he had thought that a long-running resident of the West End would be a good bet, but those had not been a great success, either. *Chicago* had been going for ten years by the time he had presented it as Rubilynn's great annual treat, and it was tired, the dancers now getting on, plump round the middle. After that he pulled himself together, and made a greater effort. He thought Imelda Staunton in *Gypsy* last year had been an immense success; it was so funny and touching, the songs were wonderful, you could enjoy the dancing and laugh a little at it too. It was one of the shows that Rubilynn had enjoyed the most, he thought. This year he was not sure: it might be *Aladdin*, a new Disney musical, which would be slick and undemanding and certainly enjoyable, or it might be the more adult choice of *Funny Girl*, which was happening at the same lovely theatre that *Gypsy* had been at. It was a hop and a jump from the Savoy Grill, where they had their supper beforehand. That was Rubilynn's idea of a beautiful restaurant, and it was Leo's idea, too. He had heard her, days afterwards, telling Sandy all about it, from the beautiful napkins you found folded on your table to the delicious tiny cups of coffee two hours later. It was only once a year, after all, and the four hundred pounds the evening cost was, he thought, worth it. The evening was looked forward to and looked back on, and some of them were in the mind years later. He loved his wife.

Tonight he was upstairs, sitting in front of the old computer, thinking about love. He was on the verge of buying two tickets for *Funny Girl* for the evening of Rubilynn's birthday, which happened to be a Saturday. The website had warned him that it would hold the tickets for thirty minutes; now it was informing him that the period would expire in two minutes. He did nothing. It was possible that Rubilynn had had her own views about whether she should marry him; views based not on practicality and sense, which had prevailed, but on her own feelings and her assessment of his. He had thought it was a good idea to marry a kind, rational person so that he could improve her life, and to bring home to his own sense of self what it was that he had to fulfil penance for. But it was Rubilynn who had paid the cost, in the end, for his determination to pay compensation for his father's marriage. She deserved a marriage where her husband did not have to tell himself all the time that he loved her. The truth was that now, after fourteen years, his love had become a comfortable thing that inhabited the space reiteration had made for it, like a dog treading down its spot in the grass, night after night; her love, however, was what it had always been, a degree of esteem, respect, and an understanding of what the alternatives might be. He reminded himself that he loved his wife and that, after all, marriage was not something that took place in a silvered hall, swift with art-deco figures, as an actress filled her lungs and sang about the passion she was paid to simulate.

Sometimes, not often, it came to him that he had been married before and he had had a son whom he had gazed over as he gazed now at Sandy. It had not been the same. It appeared to him that he had been drunk, most of that time, and sex-crazed. That was certainly over. The last time he had had sex with a woman who was not his wife was at a time before he had met the woman who was now his wife. Somewhere in this large world there was that son, too, who had a brother he knew nothing about.

The time was over. He would have to log in again and see if the same tickets were available. Downstairs the goodwill created by the dinner as family was warmly subsiding. They had liked the roast chicken and the very elegant salad of mango and halloumi and pea shoots that he had got out of Nigel Slater in the *Observer* at the weekend; Sandy had said that he liked it, it made his teeth squeak, but really what he had liked best was the effort of elegant arrangement on the plate and the *chic* of having a 'starter' at home; he was an exquisite, solemn child who could spend hours arranging his possessions to his visual satisfaction, who would have gone to school in a bow-tie if they had let him, his brilliant shiny sweet-smelling hair always just so. Most of all Rubilynn had been thrilled by what she must have known was coming, a little dish of stinky tofu that he had been to Gerrard Street to buy. They had never quite agreed on the right place to eat stinky tofu in a meal, and seemed to have settled on a sort of plate of cheese. That, and a macaroon in three surprising flavours for Sandy and a fourth (coffee and black pepper) for Rubilynn, to make a gesture towards something sweet and final. The lovely dinner as family he had promised. There was no reason for anyone to think that he was anything but a good, responsible husband and father, who would never lose contact with his child and never tell his wife as she was dying that he wanted to divorce her.

Instead of reopening the ticket website, Leo opened his email account. He quickly typed in Aisha Sharifullah's address. He had looked it up earlier – she hadn't given it to him. He knew that the address was an office address, that whatever he wrote would be read by an assistant and perhaps not read by Aisha at all. He wrote to what he had, aisha@aishasharifullah.org.

> Dear Aisha,
> It was lovely to see you a few days ago. I feel that we did not have enough time for me to say what I meant to say to you.

He wrote, 'I don't want to leave our encounter incomplete', and then rolled back, deleting it. He didn't think she would know what he meant, and the statement was vague and confused, the product of him not quite knowing what he wanted to say. He went on:

> I made a mistake twenty-five years ago. I think if I was replying to the letter you wrote me then, I would now write something very different. I would very much like to meet again.

He signed himself 'Leo (Spinster)', although his address was leospinster@hotmail.com and there could be no confusion. Before he logged out, he changed the password on his email account. He went downstairs, forgetting about what he had done. Sandy had been allowed to sit up and have dinner with them, a special treat to make him feel grown-up, and he had managed beautifully, not spilling a drop of gravy down his clean white shirt, nibbling his passion fruit and chilli macaroon in tiny, neat, crumbless bites. Now it was time for bed. 'You've been busy,' Rubilynn said, but her eyes were shining. She thought he had been arranging her birthday treat all this while.

He smiled, the good father and husband, and picked his child up. He put him into his pyjamas, tucked him up, then read to him from chapter six of *The Wizard of Oz*, a book they had read together at least five times, which made Sandy's eyes widen every time they got to the Cowardly Lion. He was scared of the Cowardly Lion, more than the wicked witch or the flying monkeys, even though he knew and remembered there was nothing to be scared of in the lion's roar. The first time Leo had read the book was last year, to Sandy. He himself had only ever seen the old film. He had enjoyed the book as much as Sandy had. He didn't remember ever having read a story to his other son. That had been a mistake, surely. They reached the end of the chapter and Sandy lay down and shut his eyes. Leo left the night light on, a shadow-pattern of giraffes and elephants circling his son's little bedroom, and went downstairs. His wife had switched the television on, and was watching a programme about home improvements. She turned her face to him with a large, grateful smile. If Aisha wrote back in the way he had invited her to, he would leave Rubilynn and leave Sandy, and that would be the end of things.

In the morning, there was already an email in response:

Dear Leo,
It was sweet of you to write to me. Veronica, my
assistant, saw it and forwarded it – she thought, from its
tone, that you were probably expecting a personal
response from me. As I'm in Osaka and between
meetings, I'm responding straight away. I would give you
my private email address to write to in future, except
that – well, I'm just not going to.
  It's sweet of you, too, to think that I might want to
reverse years of experience and say things that I probably
didn't mean very seriously at the time, twenty-five years
ago. You see, Leo, I laid myself out in all my girlish
ardency for you and, in return, you gave me a very
grown-up lecture, saying, in effect, 'Grow a skin.' Well, I

have grown a skin; I think I know what human beings
are like, a little bit more. The world I went into, I saw
things that you never want to see, heard stories of the
ways people can treat each other and still think well of
themselves. It hasn't been good for that girlish ardency.
Do I mean ardour? I think I do. I think I'm thinking of
skin cream when I write 'ardency'.

So thank you, but I am going to decline your kind
offer, whatever the offer was. I'm sure in a week's time,
you are going to regret having made the offer, whatever
the offer was. You would regret it whether you
abandoned your wife and your little boy and ran off with
me for a week of passion in the Seychelles, or if, as seems
likely, you stay with them, having been turned down by
the girl you used to know, who is now a hardened old
bag of fifty. So best not. You see, as I said when we
talked, we immigrants, we never again trust people, not
one hundred per cent. They are always going to hold the
knife to your throat, to insist that you say that you're
best friends for ever. We are always going to be hard to
love. Our sense of timing is not all it might be.

Yours as always
  Aisha

PS You see, you aren't going to your father's one
hundredth birthday. That might have something to do
with it, too.

PPS Veronica will see this too. She sees everything, in
fact.

PPPS You should come to Osaka. The food – it's
amazing.

7.

On the afternoon before her father's one hundredth birthday, Lavinia Housman was standing in what seemed like a howling gale, begging her son to get back into the car. It was not a howling gale: it was the steady flow of hundreds, perhaps by now thousands, of cars hurtling past, inches away, at top speed. Perhaps Russell could not hear her.

In the car her husband, Jeremy, sat in the front passenger seat. He stared forward. He would not get out. Lavinia shouted and pleaded. All the time in her head was the conviction she had never got far from since the day Russell had been born that he was not as good as other children. Not less virtuous, just not as good, like the bunch of grapes nobody would pick off the shelf if they were given the choice. She had seen him emerge and be handed to her and instantly she'd had the feeling of dread she'd always had when forced to meet a stranger. She knew it was her duty not to give this belief the slightest public airing. But she looked at other children and they had all seemed much better at it than Russell ever would be. He was like the children in the Royal Family that nobody has ever heard of, as if taken to one side, defectiveness tacitly admitted.

Now he looked as green as a grape himself. He had, indeed, been about to be sick; that was why they had pulled over, at his announcement. It had been a mistake to let him get out. The traffic was terrifyingly close, and Russell had a bad sense of where his body was at the best of times. The fumes must be making him feel worse. It would have been better to have sat in the back with the windows open.

'Darling,' Lavinia shouted. 'Please get back in the car. It isn't safe here.'

'I'm not getting in the car,' Russell shouted. The skirts of his long leather coat flapped like a great black bird in the wind of a passing lorry, a foot from him. 'I feel sick. I hate you.'

'Please, darling,' Lavinia said. 'We can talk about this later.'

She was aware of how ridiculous they must look, how scripted in their comedy: a very short fat woman with cropped grey hair and a party dress, an obese teenager in a black leather coat and black eye make-up. A junior Goth being shouted at by his mum at the side of the motorway. She had put her second-best party dress on; she wanted to arrive well dressed, not a vicar's wife in last decade's Laura Ashley smock. But that was the spectacle they were presenting now to the passing traffic. Please, God, don't let his father get out, Lavinia begged. Adding the comedy of a fat vicar in his dog collar would make the whole thing perfection in a driver's glimpse.

'If you get back in, we'll be at a service station in no time,' Lavinia shouted. 'We'll sit down and you'll feel much better.'

'Only if you give me back my phone,' Russell shouted.

'Darling, it was looking at your phone that made you sick,' Lavinia shouted.

'It's *not* having it that makes me sick, you cow,' Russell shouted. He stamped his foot in its heavy boot; for a moment, Lavinia felt faint as she saw how he might so easily lose his balance, fall into the slow lane with his head under the wheels.

'Just half an hour without it. Looking out of the window. Then we'll be at Grandpa's, almost.'

'I hate you,' Russell shouted. Was there some ritual repetition about the quality now? Was he winding down? But then he remembered. 'You made me stop just when I was about to finish a level.'

'It'll still be there later on,' Lavinia shouted. 'Please, Russell, come back into the car. You're really frightening me now.'

'You don't understand,' Russell shouted. 'It was level 746. I've been stuck on it for weeks. I nearly got it and then you made me stop. I hate you.'

'Please, darling,' Lavinia shouted. 'I know you love Candy Crush Saga, but you were going to be sick.'

'*You* make me sick,' Russell shouted, 'when you just interfere, you horrible fat old bag. I hate you.'

But then, strangely enough, having made his point, he went over to the car and opened the back passenger door on the side of the grass verge. He looked at his mother with contempt, as if she were dawdling. With some terror, Lavinia went along the road-ward side of the car, half opened the door, slid in with relief. She breathed.

'All's well that ends well,' Jeremy said. 'There we are. And off we tootle.'

Lavinia concentrated. If she started driving along the hard shoulder she would probably find a gap big enough to slip into. She loathed motorway driving – she actually hated driving in any case, even in their quiet bit of Penge. She should not be doing this. She knew that Jeremy was perfectly capable of driving. When he had been diagnosed with diabetes five years before, there had been no suggestion that he needed to give up driving; even when he had been put on insulin, two years ago, having failed to make the slightest change to his health or weight, the suggestion had only been that he measure his blood sugar before setting off. But he had thought it unwise. 'My dear girl,' he had said – and how these fluting pomposities had started to grate on Lavinia, 'it is those sudden collapses, those abrupt blackouts that frighten me. What should happen if I were at the wheel with you and dear Russell in the back when one of those petits-mals should strike me? One shudders to think.' To Lavinia those petits-mals looked very much like her husband taking a snooze at short notice in the afternoon, just closing his eyes and having forty winks; surely one didn't snore during a blackout. But he had not driven since.

'There!' she said, having inserted herself into the flood of traffic. She would be all right now. Russell had, as a matter of emphasis, picked up his mobile phone and was, almost certainly, playing the game he was so addicted to. In two minutes he would consider that he had made his point, and set it down.

'It was level 746, apparently,' Lavinia said. 'That was the cause of the trouble. The significance of it!'

'Thank Heaven for small mercies,' Jeremy said, seeing that she was inspecting her son in the wing mirror. 'At least the wretched boy has turned the sound down. I simply couldn't bear that music.'

Three months ago, Jeremy had had a suggestion from his bishop. It was known that he spoke German – the relic of his degree. The bishop had noticed that he and dear Lavinia had now been in Penge for ten years. They had done awfully well; the bishop had so much enjoyed the fête he had come to with Mrs Bish two years ago. A tombola and a coconut stall! A competition for constructing scenes from current affairs in vegetables (the resignation of Ed Miliband in green beans, pumpkin and a disconcertingly well-carved potato the acclaimed winner)! A Horrifying Spectacle tent which you paid 50p to enter to see Lawrence Llewellyn-Bowen, the real one, in a velvet armchair. And (the bishop's favourite, to tell the honest truth) a Guess the Weight stall with a cake, a guinea pig and an obliging curate to guess at. Awfully charming and *entirely* like a country fête, but in Penge. The bishop *immensely* appreciated the efforts that Jeremy and dear Lavinia had put in, and their success in greatly increasing attendance on Sundays and making the church a *wonderfully real* focus of the community. (There had been folk-music concerts, as well as the occasional string sextet playing Brahms on Saturday nights; one was popular, the other closer to Jeremy's heart.) But had they ever considered moving on?

The bishop was a cosy old poppet, hopelessly over-promoted; he was grateful for any kind of signs of life below him, and happy to agree with whoever had last voiced an opinion. It was impossible to say definitively whether he was evangelical or not; he was clearly delighted to have been elevated to be Bishop of Wandle, and had, genuinely, no ambition to go any further. For these reasons he was popular in the highest ranks of the Church, and his very occasional requests for favours were usually granted.

Had Jeremy ever thought, perhaps, the bishop went on, of a parish outside England? They were unusual posts, each very much of their own, and very much requiring someone of initiative. It was terribly important not to create scandal, despite the lack of close daily oversight. It wouldn't do for the bishop in charge to arrive from Gibraltar to find half a dozen teenage rent-boys lolling about the vicarage, entertaining themselves in *frightful fashion* by smashing priceless antique plates ... at least, *not again*. (Jeremy had heard this story of misbehaviour in a historic European parish in some detail; he nodded sagely.) So, naturally, when the bishop had heard about this coming vacancy, he had thought immediately of Jeremy and, of course, dear Lavinia. Where? Oh, hadn't he said? It was Salzburg – the Anglican vicar of western Austria. Of course, Vienna looked after itself. Very pretty, the vicar's house in Salzburg, an eighteenth-century palace, but naturally one wouldn't need to live in the whole thing. The Archbishop of Salzburg had been awfully unlucky not to have been made an elector back in the old days, and now they really had more palaces than they knew what to do with. One of which was ours, now, incredibly. Inconvenient number of bedrooms. Ideal for hide-and-seek on rainy days, or Sardines – did people still play Sardines?

Jeremy told Lavinia about this offer when they were alone in the vicarage, a three-bedroomed yellow-brick construction from the 1960s with windows that could do with replacing; Russell was out on a Saturday afternoon, hanging around with his three friends. She would always remember that when he said the name of Salzburg, she leant forward and clasped his hands in hers, out of joy. It would make everything all right; it would justify everything; it would mean so much to Jeremy, to be surrounded by beauty and intelligent, charming people, to have friends who were musical, to listen even once a month to the music he loved so much, played at the highest possible level. 'Do you think it's a serious proposal?' she said eventually, keeping her voice as level as Jeremy's. Jeremy thought that it was a serious proposal, or else why mention it?

With Jeremy's agreement, she told Russell after a week. Jeremy was not in the house. 'I hate you,' Russell said. 'We can't go to fucking Austria. What am I supposed to do? Learn fucking Austrian?'

'They speak German, darling,' Lavinia said. 'You'd pick it up in no time.'

'Don't you know?' Russell screamed – he had gone from nought to top decibels in eighteen words. 'The system's completely different there. I can't learn all that stuff and then learn it in a foreign language. I'd fail every single exam and I'd have no friends because no one could talk to me. You're always wanting to destroy my life. I hate you. This is your idea, it's you that wants to destroy me. Always, always, always. I fucking hate you and I'm not going. I'm going to live with Blodwen's parents. They're cool. They wouldn't ever go to live in fucking Australia.'

'Austria, darling,' Lavinia said. But at the end of four weeks, in which Russell had, if anything, escalated the hostility and beastliness and, at one point, actually hit his father for the sin of calling him 'old chap', Jeremy had felt obliged to go to the bishop and tell him that, having discussed it with his family, he felt it would be too great a disruption to his son's education.

'How did he take it?' Lavinia said.

'It is fair to say,' Jeremy said, without levity, 'that he could not believe it. He was literally incredulous. He had not a shred of belief in what he was hearing. And so things come to an end, and the gates of Salzburg are shut to us.'

'Oh, darling,' Lavinia said. 'There will be other chances. There really will. And it's only four years until beastly Russell leaves school and we can do whatever we like. Think of that. We need never see him again.'

'Don't,' Jeremy said. 'I wish I could ...' but at that point he had shaken his head, and Lavinia was horrified to see that he was actually crying. 'No one is ever going to –' he got out, before the tears got the worse of him. It was so unfair: he had been offered an eighteenth-century palace in a beautiful Austrian city with a Brahms sextet playing with perpetual kindly rapture in an upper room and, like a gift in a fairy tale, it would be offered only once. That was it. Beastly Russell.

Now they were at the motorway service station, and parking the car.

'Look at that blind man,' Russell said. 'How can he get here if he's blind? He can't drive a fucking car, can he? That's just stupid.'

'He's not blind, darling,' Lavinia said, out of habit, without looking.

'Are you calling me a liar?' Russell said. 'You didn't even fucking look. Look, that blind man over there with the dog.'

There was, in fact, a blind man in the car park, standing irresolutely with his patient dog sitting by his side.

'I expect somebody has driven him here and he has momentarily separated himself from his friend,' Jeremy said. 'He can hardly have driven here himself.'

'When they shit,' Russell said, 'I mean, when guide dogs shit, because every dog, right, they shit the whole time, what are the blindies supposed to do? Do they just stop and wait, do they think that the dog's stopping for a reason, like there's a danger around, or do they see that the dog – ha-ha, I said does the blind person see, that's funny – do they get that the dog's stopping to have a shit? Because if you don't pick up your dog's shit in the street the Old Bill's going to be after you. But if the blindie, right, if he works out that his dog's having a shit and he gets out one of those bags, he's like blind, and how's he going to pick up the shit, he doesn't know where it is? Is he just going to feel around until he finds something warm? Because that's like disgusting.'

'Oh, you depress me so much,' Lavinia said. 'Every single time you open your mouth, you depress me.'

The telephone in Jeremy's lap rang. It was Lavinia's, but he answered it.

'Yes, it's Jeremy, I'm afraid … Hello, Blossom – how lovely to hear from you. Are you on your …'

He listened intently to what was being told him, with infrequent 'Yes, that's probably right' and 'Well, yes,' and 'That sounds exactly …' In a couple of minutes, as they were getting out of the little car, he handed the telephone to Lavinia with a smile, and began to wave at someone walking fast, but separated from them by a hundred silver cars. It was, in fact, Blossom herself.

'I saw you,' she said, when she was still thirty yards away, calling out of sheer joy. 'I was so astounded I couldn't quite believe what I saw – my little sister out on the hard shoulder and her son, too, waving their arms. I said to Josh – here's Josh, he's travelling up with us as well – I said could that possibly be Lavinia? What on earth? And in the end, he said why don't you go to the next service station and call them, and if they need breakdown assistance, we can organize it from there, and if not, then we can just meet up. Very sound advice, very rational as always. I don't know what we would – Well, hello, Russell, and hello, Jeremy, and hello, *you*. Of course we were travelling up today! You knew we were!'

Lavinia embraced her sister, not conventionally, but warmly, knowing that Blossom, in the end, was what she had. She had recognized her sister from hundreds of yards away, in fact, almost before Jeremy had started to wave at her. There was a space in the universe through which Blossom moved, and Blossom's movements were most special to Lavinia. She was the only one still standing. Of course Blossom had recognized her in return, infallibly recognized her in a moment passing at speed. There was no one else who could fill the space allotted to Lavinia.

'Well,' Lavinia said, 'let's go and have a cup of tea or something.'

'And afterwards,' Blossom said, with every appearance of enthusiasm, 'we can swap the passengers. You can have Josh and Thomas – here they come, they can't believe it either – and I'll have lovely Russell. No, just the three of us – Stephen couldn't come in the end and boring old Trev and her friend Alison, they're coming under their own steam. Is that quite all right, Russell? I do hope so. Now, darling ...'

Lavinia trotted after Blossom. She could feel herself warmly preparing to be funny about beastly Russell over a nice cup of tea. Behind them her husband was saying, 'I'm sure Mummy didn't mean it, but you have to admit, old chap …'

8.

Omith and Raja and Martin were nowhere that mattered, and were in the same place, talking. Or in old-school terms, like real-world terms if you trusted the assumptions inherent in the words *real* and *world*, Omith was on the twenty-seventh floor of a tower in Toronto. Raja was in a hotel in Athens. Martin was in the first-class lounge at Qatar airport waiting to change planes. Private jets were bullshit, they'd all agreed. You could save an incredible amount of money if you flew commercial, and the auditors and shareholders would be thrilled with you. Martin preferred to fly with Qatar because the first class had not just a separate lounge but a whole separate building, glistening with white and glass surfaces, the air inside chilled to the bone, and everyone was just … politer all the way through. They were talking about something Martin and Raja said they got and Omith was insisting he didn't get and thought there was nothing to get.

Just watch it again, bruv

I watched it. I aint watchin it again bruv theres nothing there to get

Old man talking

Yeah yeah and whose forty next March

I get it. Just watch it again bruv

Fuck how much do I have to do to get you to shut TF

Just do it or Im pulling the plug and Mart and me we're talking and thats the end of it bruv

Right koooooool

They watched it again, all simultaneously, the comments from Raja and Martin coming thick and fast. There was something in the tone of Raja's enthusiasm that made Omith think that he, in fact, did not get it; he only thought that he should get it; he was worried that there were fifteen-year-olds called Mustafa or Amber or David or Jonelle or Bobby or Anaconda who were watching this, transfixed, seeing the thing they'd been waiting for all their lives in it, the perfection of entertainment and wit and –

He didn't even know. Was it supposed to be funny? Did Mustafa and Amber and David and Jonelle and Bobby and Anaconda split their jolly old sides when they watched this stuff? Or was it just Raja, pretending to laugh, alone in the hotel room in Athens, where he had gone to buy a Cycladic figure from a dealer, laughing because he couldn't think of another response to convey? Omith didn't know. They watched the thing. It was soon over.

A girl of perhaps eight, a black girl with pink ribbons in her hair and big eyes, had, just before the clip started, run up in the direction of the camera. She said, breathlessly, 'Seventy-two.' You wondered, too late to examine, whether something had been done to adjust the size of her eyes when the eyes held and mutated into those of a small boy, rebellious on a rocking chair, who said, in tones of disgust, 'Sixty-*three*,' raising his hand, which focused and turned and went into black and white, an old film of a super-sweet girl with blonde hair and ringlets who said, 'Fifty-five,' before the word FIN was printed in screen-sized letters and it was over. It took seven seconds from start to FIN.

That was like the future

Did you see when she said 55 and you thought man that's Shirley Temple saying it the wrong

This ones better than that prime one

The one that goes 2 3 5 7 10

With the old woman Thatcher is it going the 10 the wrong

I don't get it

Cos it got to be 54 this one only NOT and maybe like 11 in the old woman Thatcher is it one only NOT.

Don't you fullstop me asshole

I tell you if you pay a cent more than 25 mil for those jokers in Chicago you aint no kin of mine

Chill bruv they aint gonna need more than 19 max

WILTH but the fuck is Shirley Temple is it IDK and the kooool kids who like this they aint never heard of her neither so this is like sadface

Ye well stick with what you know and is happy with bruv like your board of halma and ludo and a nice game of chess

Ain't argue with 276 mllion in three days bruv

I don't get it

YAWN

I like it when it says FIN at the end because it goes off like a fish going off or something

Man that French means End you is kidding me right

Ye ye I got you there you thought I was like stupid or

There was a sound in the real world. Omith looked up and the accoutrements of the room swam into his consciousness. The long pale oak table, the huge screen hanging on the far wall, the remains of the corporate coffee and Danish and four types of water, tap, still, Badoit, old-school sparkling. The view of Toronto out of the window. The people were from Chicago, but they'd had to meet in Toronto: Raja and Omith had gone on holiday to Iran in 2012, basically to buy a carpet. They were assuming that they weren't going back to the US any time soon, now this new guy off of *X Factor* was in charge. The Chicago lot could come to Canada. It was a beautiful day; the lake sparkled to the horizon. There was a smell of new furniture and blond new carpet; an opulent meeting space, hired by the hour. These people had made all their money since October; there was nobody for him to talk to within ten years of his own age, apart from the lawyers.

For a moment he could not think what the sound in the room was. It came from his bag, a music case with a horizontal bronze rod, forty years old, containing nothing but his tablet and the very first model of iPhone, a retro antique. The sound that rang out was the Nokia theme tune.

It came to him that somebody was telephoning him on his mobile and expecting him to talk to whoever it was. This was unusual.

'Mummy,' Omith said into the phone.

'There you are,' Mummy said. 'Where are you today? That was a very unusual-sounding ringing tone.'

'Canada. Toronto. It's twelve here. Beautiful weather.'

'Oh, yes. I remember. Have you met up with your cousin Camellia? She's getting married to a boy called Henry. He's a dermatologist, isn't he?'

'Mummy, she lives in Vancouver.'

'You're not cancelling on poor Dr Spinster, I hope.'

'No, no, no,' Omith said. 'I'll be there. Don't you worry. What's up?'

'Oh, I just wondered ...' Mummy said. 'It was really only that I ...'

Seeing you tomorrow, Omith typed, as he listened to his mother.

What tomorrow

The hundredth birthday man we promised at Sheffield yo

Yeah man can I come I'm back in England can be there in like half an hour

NO.

Tell Martin fuck off

See you tomorrow be there by 2

Easy bruv

'What is it, Mummy?' Omith said.

'Where's Raja?' Mummy said. 'Is he there? Can I speak to him?'

'No, he's not,' Omith said. 'He's away too – Mummy, don't panic, he's much closer than me. He'll be back tonight probably and with you in the morning first thing. I'm not supposed to tell you where he is because it's too much of a clue. He's buying someone a little present.'

'I'm not going to rest until I get it out of him,' Mummy said. After a few more exchanges Mummy said she would see him tomorrow and hung up. He didn't quite know what she had wanted. He warned Raja.

Ye its ringing now the phone MAAAAAN

and logged off. He would be done with these people in a couple of hours. They were only pretending to be difficult, pretending to be exquisitely, plutocratically specific. That boy with his water: 'Half Badoit half Evian, Madison, please.' It cracked him up. He wasn't even going to trouble Martin and Raja with the details; they had agreed to start at seventeen and be happy with twenty, and if they wouldn't accept twenty-five at the outside to just walk away. He'd told Raja that he was confident of being accepted with nineteen; in fact he thought their price was probably twenty-two, which he'd be happy with. The sun was shining! Relax! The plane was on the runway with its engines running, practically. He started to watch the thing again: 72, 63, 55. It made him feel old, not getting stuff. Soon his time would be over, and his days devoted to Pac-Man and Fuck That, Cluedo, Ludo, draughts and shit.

Nazia finished speaking to her other son and set the phone down. She should have told the boys why she was phoning them. But it made no sense. She had never quite taken to mobiles; she used hers only when she was mobile, and when she was in the house, she used the old cordless phone. The music from the sitting room started up, the theme tune to the television news. It was the reason why she had phoned the boys, and phoned Aisha before either of them. Aisha had been on the motorway; she would be here in an hour or two. She went into the room where Sharif was standing. He looked sick and solemn; he went on watching. The film at the head of the news was what it had been on the one o'clock, when they'd first seen it. Since Sharif had retired, he had always made a point of watching the one o'clock news: today it had rewarded him.

They had last seen Mahfouz and Sadia at Mummy's funeral. That had been in Dhaka, in 1982. They had tried to take that over, and had even had some kind of plan for finding a husband for Dolly. (They had phoned Dolly and Bina too, as soon as they had seen the footage; the children could wait until later.) They had come and slipped away and never been seen again. They were in their lives: there was no possibility for Sharif that the woman who was his sister could disappear from his mind for ever and irrevocably, and Nazia thought often of Sadia, speculating about where they were, what had happened to their boys. Now these questions had probably been answered.

The piece of film was short. The cameras were positioned outside a suburban house, which, the voiceover of the reporter announced, was in Nottingham. It was tidy and clean; the front garden had long since been concreted over, and the curtains were drawn tight. The voice explained that this was the house of members of the family. It was a question of two boys, one twenty, one only sixteen, who had run away to fight. 'The boys were last seen in Turkey in the company of their uncle, a seasoned jihadi,' the reporter said. 'They were initially suspected of travelling to Syria to fight for so-called Islamic State. Now it is thought that, in the company of other fighters, they have travelled to Dagestan where a new front in the increasingly global battle of terror is opening up. Their families had this to say.'

The front door opened and a man in late middle age came out. Behind him were two women in full veils, who advanced a little, then turned sharply at a word from the man, and went back inside. There was no question as the man came towards the camera to speak. It was Mahfouz.

'Please don't let one of those women be my sister,' Sharif said. 'I could not stand it if I thought she had taken to wearing the jilbab over her face.'

There was more than one reporter at the gate, and they called out to Mahfouz.

'Where are the boys?' one shouted. 'How do you feel about them going to join a terrorist organization?'

Mahfouz spoke. 'My son and my nephew have gone abroad —'

'Nephew, how?' Nazia burst out, just as she had done before, at one o'clock. Bina and Dolly had not been able to enlighten her; they had no idea that any of Mahfouz's brothers had come with their sons to England, which was the only explanation. Wouldn't those sons have been too old? It looked as if Sadia had had another child in the 1990s. But how could that be? She would have been fifty to have had a twenty-year-old son now, and fifty-four if the sixteen-year-old were hers. Had someone – Mahfouz or one of his brothers – taken another wife? It seemed the only explanation.

'Quiet, Nazia,' Sharif said. The nephew and son had gone abroad to work for an Islamic charitable organization, helping refugees. There was nothing sinister about any of this, Mahfouz said. The elder had left his wife and two young children in the care of the family until he returned from this important mission. On the one o'clock news, he had gone on to say that this was just the usual anti-Islam position of the media and especially the BBC, but this part of what he had said had been cut for the six o'clock news. The report came to an end and the news moved on to the next item. Ronnie Corbett had died today.

'They went to – where did they go to?' Nazia said.

'They went to Dagestan,' Sharif said. 'I had to look it up. It's by Azerbaijan. Russia. Southern bit of Russia.'

'Who are they?'

'I don't know,' Sharif said. 'They had two children when we last saw them. It can't be them. It could just about be their children, I suppose.'

'No, the news said it was his son – Mahfouz's son. They were very definite.'

'You've got to warn Dolly and Samu and Bina and Tinku that there's to be no talking about any of this at Hilary's party tomorrow. And Rekha and Fanny too. We can talk about it later.'

'But how could Sadia have another child, so old? I can't understand it.'

'They're all breeding like rabbits,' Sharif said.

'Sharif, please,' Nazia said. 'Don't talk about them like that, even now.'

'Those are Father's grandchildren,' Sharif said. 'All those grandchildren. What did we do that none of ours ever settled down?'

'They settled down,' Nazia said. 'They could not have better lives. They have everything they could have. They don't want anything else. They're not off fighting for religion in Syria or wherever those places are. They're not wearing the veil, or making their poor wives wear the stupid veil.'

'But Mahfouz's children, they marry and they have children of their own before they're twenty-one,' Sharif said. 'That's something they can understand, out there in the rest of the world.'

'We did nothing wrong,' Nazia said. 'It just hasn't happened for them. They've got each other, too. Don't start pitying our children. Nobody else would.'

'I wondered ...'

There was a long pause in the room. Outside a blackbird began to sing in the early-evening light. The marquee in Hilary's garden, a lovely white silk with absurdly festive pink pennants, shone above the fence; the measurements supplied by Raja had been absolutely accurate, and the marquee filled the garden. Inside, there would be forty golden chairs around a single table; perhaps twice that number had wanted to come, too. Beyond the marquee, in the last stretch of lawn, you could hear men calling to each other as they erected a wooden frame. It was supposed to be a surprise for Hilary and the guests, but at the end, the back flap and the front flap of the marquee would roll up: a band on Hilary's patio would begin to play, and a series of military-grade fireworks would begin an unforgettable display. Tonight, on the eve of the celebrations, the evening was melting into a beautiful indigo night with the last day of Hilary's one hundred years, and a man who must be Sharif and Nazia's nephew was shivering in a tent in the desert, working out how to kill the infidel, how to establish the Caliphate and its theatrical executions on the steps of town halls, as the benign and yet murderous power ruling over the cities of London and Sheffield, of Edinburgh and Manchester, of Cambridge and Oxford, where a home had been made for students of the Koran for three hundred years, or so Sharif had once been told. The things he knew! The things that the children and grandchildren of his father had ended up doing!

'I know what you were going to say,' Nazia said. 'You were wondering what Rafiq would be doing now.'

Even after fifty years of marriage, his wife could surprise him. His train of thought was so clear to her, they could run through old arguments in abbreviated form, going from start to finish in seven minutes flat.

'Yes,' he said. 'Rafiq was crossing my mind just then. I don't suppose we'll ever find out what did happen to him, let alone what he would have done.'

'I'm forgetting what he looked like,' Nazia said. 'I'm forgetting all of it. When I think of him I just think of that photograph, not what he was really like. I can't remember any more what Daddy's house looks like. And it's all changed anyway.'

'I don't know whether it's time or space that does it,' Sharif said. 'Made the changes in us.'

'What do you mean?'

'We're so changed. But I don't know whether we're changed because it was fifty years ago. Or because it's thousands of miles away. Perhaps we were changed when we got off the plane in 1976. Hilary is the same as he was and Rafiq is the same as he was. They didn't go anywhere.'

'If I'm a hundred years old,' Nazia said, 'and they write to inform us that they have Rafiq's body, I am going to go there and bury him properly, with dignity. If I'm a hundred. I don't care.'

'Do you think he would be here, too? With all the rest of us? He would be sixty-three this year. No age at all. I just can't imagine it.'

'He would have stayed. He would never have gone, given up like us, run away. Once you had fought for the Delta, you wouldn't settle for this, I don't suppose.'

'Perhaps not,' Sharif said. 'I can't imagine what his life would have been like. I can't think of him with a wife and children and grandchildren, telling stories about his days in the Mukti Bahini. He knew he was going to die, I suppose. The only thing is that he was thinking of a death with a bullet through the skull on the battlefield, dying gloriously. He never saw action. It was just Captain Qayyum and his sort, knocking on the door in the middle of the night. That man who took the scissors and sliced at Rafiq's hair. I wish I hadn't seen that.'

'Don't think about it.'

'Anyway, it's Hilary's day tomorrow. We don't have to think about Dagestan, or Mahfouz, or any of that. You were right.'

'Right about what?'

'Phoning them. But not telling them. That was the right thing to do. Is that Blossom in Hilary's garden? She sounds like she's handing out instructions. Should I go over there? I'm supposed to take the cake over in any case.'

Blossom had arrived with Russell about half an hour before; she was a strong, confident driver, who saw no reason why she should obey the speed limits if it meant spending an extra half an hour in the company of her nephew. That nephew was now crouched on the floor of the sitting room, the patio doors open. He had not removed his long leather coat, and his rounded squatting back shone in the evening sunlight, like an infected cyst of huge dimensions. He was peering into the eyes of Gertrude, who was having none of it. Behind him, Father was standing, trying to see what Blossom was doing.

'Daddy, stay where you are,' Blossom called back. 'There's no need for you to come. And Lavinia and Jeremy and Josh and Thomas are going to be here any moment. You're going to need to let them in. Daddy, stay where you are. There. What did I say. Russell? Go and let your mother in. Russell. Russell. Russell.

I can't believe,' she said, to the three men from the party organizers that Omith had found, 'I can't believe that my nephew, who's fifteen, is letting my father totter off to open the front door. Wretched child. My father was born during the First World War, how about that? He's earned the right not to do anything any more, I would say.'

'He's looking good on it,' one of the men, the handsome mixed-race one, smoothly said. They were a Manchester firm, astonishingly efficient and emollient under Omith and Raja's beadily assertive commands. 'It's not often you see someone who's as fit as that who's even eighty. My old gran ...'

Blossom listened for three more patient sentences.

'But that stage,' she reverted, 'it looks dangerously close to the marquee, in my opinion. What we absolutely don't want is for the marquee to go up in flames because of a few sparks. When we had fireworks at my old house in the country, the fireworks were at least a hundred yards from anyone. This can't be more than twenty.'

'Twenty-five,' the other man said, the older, grumpier one. 'We measured. It's well outside the recommended minimum, it's perfectly safe.'

'We do this all the time,' the mixed-race man said, whose name, she remembered, was Ralph. 'Over in Manchester, footballers and their wives, they order the maximum size of marquee, fill the garden, then the maximum possible fireworks display. We're used to the minimum requirements. Believe you me, these people who are new to their own money, we say no to them all the time if they want to let off a really massive effect. You're fine as you are.'

'Lavinia, darling,' Blossom called. 'Stop hugging Daddy and bring Josh out here for some expert opinion. What do you think? It looks terribly close to that flapping silk to me. Even if it doesn't go up in flames, will they even be able to look up and see the things going off in the sky?'

'What's the weather supposed to be?' Josh said, coming out and holding his grandfather by the arm.

'Perfect,' Lavinia supplied. 'The weather's continuing unbroken for at least five more days, apparently.'

'Well, I don't see why we need a marquee at all,' Josh said. 'Why don't we take it down and have dinner in the open air? It'll be quite warm enough.'

Hilary said something, pawing a little at his grandson. He looked anxious. Josh asked him to say it again.

'Grandpa wants the marquee,' he said resignedly. 'Omith went to a lot of trouble, apparently, and now Grandpa wants the marquee for his birthday. He's never had one before. Forget I said anything, Grandpa. You'll have the marquee. It all looks lovely.'

'It will all be absolutely fine, sir,' Ralph called, in a hearty, consoling, unconvincing way.

And really Hilary felt fit as a flea. He was going to be a hundred the next day! How about that? There weren't many around who lived to be a hundred. If they wrote his biography, they would say, 'Hilary Spinster's remarkable life began during the First World War: he lived to see ...' What had he lived to see? Bloody Jeremy Corbyn as leader of the Labour Party? That moron running America? For God's sake, that would be forgotten soon enough. An independent South Sudan? Hadn't been there, didn't know where it was, even. It was all so uninteresting, what had happened recently. If only the dear old Queen would die soon, they could say that he lived into the reign of King Charles III, or King George VII, or whatever he was going to call himself. People always remembered that sort of thing when wars and political leaders faded from the collective memory. On *Pointless*, his new favourite TV show, those idiots could hardly remember the name of the chancellor of the Exchequer from twenty years ago. (Lamont. Or Clarke. He tested himself.)

'If I wrote my own biography,' he said to the grandson holding his arm. Which one was it?

'You should,' the grandson said. 'It would be very interesting.'

'"Nothing matters very much, and most things don't matter at all,"' Hilary said. 'Know who said that?'

'Lord Salisbury,' the grandson said. 'I do know, as it happens. Before even your time, I would say.'

His name was Josh, Hilary remembered. He was the one Blossom had taken in. There were others, too, and great-grand-children. They'd overcome the Spinster curse: they were all at least five foot six, five foot seven. One of Blossom's children had six children! He looked terrible, that grandson, with his hair all in a mess, a lot of dreadlocks, and blond. Ridiculous. And the wife! His children were wild but amusing. Did these grandchil-dren here now have any children? The one who was supporting him, now helping him back inside – Josh, the nicest of all of them, going a bit grey round the edges. And the one with a sour, disapproving expression reading the *Radio Times* in an armchair, Thomas. And the other one who was poor old Lavinia's only contribution, still wearing his leather coat, looking like a mass murderer, whose name was Russell. Fat as a pig, too. None of them – not a single one – had ever become a doctor. What a shower. But look at Hilary! He was a hundred and he had forty people coming to his dinner tomorrow! There weren't many people who remained as popular as him into three figures. Off the top of his head Hilary couldn't think of any. The Queen would be glad to be sending him a telegram, if anyone had remembered to organize it. There weren't many people left who were actually older than the old dear, these days.

'I've lost a lot of people along the way,' Hilary said to Josh, as he was depositing him in the armchair.

'Do you want a cup of tea?' Josh said. He didn't seem to have heard what his grandfather had said. 'I was just going to make one for everyone.'

'I said, I've lost a lot of people along the way,' Hilary said again.

'Well, that's true,' Josh said. 'But you don't need to think about them today, or tomorrow. What's done is done. You've nothing to regret, in the end.'

It was true, what Josh had said in his calm and level-headed way. Hilary had organized all of that. When Josh's father had disappeared in the way he had, Hilary had decided that Josh had to be taken care of. And he was taken care of. The mother wasn't up to it. Was the mother coming today or tomorrow? For some reason Hilary thought she was. The father wasn't. He hadn't seen the father for many years now. He might be dead. The other son was dead, wasn't he? That had been sad. Things had gone wrong. Perhaps some of those things had been caused by Hilary. He could admit that now. It was too late to do anything about any of that, and he could honestly say that if the possibility arose to share the truth with another, to clarify matters before it was too late, he would now take a long look at the situation and consider whether anything, in the end, was to be gained by making a frank statement of the truth. Sharif had lost a sister in the same way. Hilary forgot the details, how that happened, but he'd definitely lost a sister in the course of things. Sometimes people walked away, and sometimes you did not have the last word you had craved so. As Josh said, what was done was done. Nothing mattered very much: and most things didn't matter at all.

'Who's coming today?' Lavinia's husband said, pulling up a stool. He was plump and grey-haired; his eyes were catlike, triangular, a little sad if you didn't know how amused he was at things. Reminded you of someone. He was sixty himself, and his father-in-law's encounter with old age was something he might be expected to share. 'And who's coming tomorrow? I know Blossom will have sorted out all the sleeping arrangements in a very expert way.'

'Aisha came today, I know,' Hilary said. 'That's Aisha next door. She was supposed to be coming today. Their boys are coming tomorrow. They're coming from the ends of the earth! Sharif said he was going to bring the cake round this afternoon – I can hardly wait to see what they've decided on. He should be here by now, I would have thought.'

'How thrilling!' Jeremy said. 'And the others – Blossom's

children? I know that it was too far for Tamara to come, all the way from Australia, alas. Russell, please stop doing that.'

'Yes,' Hilary said. 'It was sad that she couldn't come. But the boy's coming, Tresco's coming, with all his children. They're sleeping in their campervan, I hear. And the little one, her youngest, the one who lives in Wales – Celia. Celia's coming with her friend who she lives with.'

'Celia?'

'Yes, my granddaughter Celia,' Hilary said. 'Blossom, your youngest daughter's coming, isn't she? Celia?'

But Blossom, who was just coming in for her cup of tea, looked at him, head cocked, a little touch of sadness in her eyes. 'It's not Celia, Daddy,' she said. 'You're getting a bit mixed up. It's Trevor. She's coming with her friend Alison.'

'Oh, Trevor, of course,' Hilary said. How had he made such a silly mistake? Called her Celia? He had promised himself he would not mention his wife. She had been dead for so long now, and it had been the cause of such trouble afterwards. It was really best not to bring her name up, as he had for the last twenty-five years. It was better not to talk about any of the people who couldn't be here, and there was such happiness all around Hilary today and tomorrow, he promised himself again that he would not.

It was lucky, then, that the doorbell rang. It was the same chime that had always been there; Blossom had arrived not long before, and it shocked her with its vital reminiscence. But for her father it was not a shock. He heard it all the time, and had been hearing it for the last fifty or sixty years, all the time he had been in this house. He leant forward in his armchair. Below him another animal made the same forward gesture with the same long wrinkled neck, the same disapproving expression that was always used to conceal pleasure. It was a visitor, asking for admittance in a polite musical clangour.

'There you are, Gertrude,' Hilary said, but really for everyone else's benefit. 'There's Sharif from next door. He's bringing the cake.'

'Is there a cake?' Lavinia said. 'Oh, my God. I knew I should have thought of it. I just assumed …'

'There is no need to punish yourself,' Jeremy said. 'There is no need whatsoever. There is a cake, you see. And that is wonderful Sharif from next door, bringing it for us to admire, but perhaps not eat, not just yet.'

'But I should have thought of it!' Lavinia said. 'Or brought a cake for eating purposes? Heavens – isn't anyone going to get the door?'

Of course it was Josh who got up, in his trim and elegant weekend garb. He made himself useful. He walked to the door full of his certainty that he had made himself useful without being thanked most of his life, and now he would carry on. He looked forward to seeing this new stage in the celebrations of his grandfather's birthday. But he opened the door and it was not Sharif there, and nobody with a cake. There was a small round woman, perhaps Filipina in appearance. Her hair was brushed down firmly into a neat black helmet; she wore a bright pink suit with black brocade around the lapels. She might be going to a wedding, and the tiny boy by her side might be a page boy. Josh's heart went out to him, dark and big-eyed in his suit; they did not fit him, his best clothes, and the brilliant white shirt and red bow-tie hung loosely about his neck. The little boy looked up at Josh and, judging from his expression, he did not know yet that there was nothing here to be frightened of. The lady started to explain. She had come ahead because it was so difficult to park. Their drive – the Spinsters' drive – it was quite full! It had even been hard to find a space in the street. Leo had thought it best to drop Rubilynn and Sandy at the gate. They hadn't met. This was Sandy. As for the lady – 'I am Rubilynn,' she said. Leo, she explained, was parking the car. He would be here in a minute or two, no more than that.

Champel, 9 May 2016

ACKNOWLEDGEMENTS

Some details of Rafiq's story and experiences are taken, with humility and honour, from a great memoir of the Bangladeshi war of independence, Jahanara Imam's *Days of 1971*, and from Anisul Haque's beautiful novel about her, *Ma* (*Mother*). A poem that Sharif recites is a national favourite by Rabindranath Tagore; his favourite novelist, Shahidullah Kaiser, is also one of mine. Kaiser was murdered by Pakistanis in the closing days of the war of independence in 1971, as part of a concerted project to kill as many writers, thinkers and creative spirits of the Bengal nation before it could be founded. No Pakistani has ever faced justice for the genocide they planned and individually carried out between March and December 1971. The name of the officer who took Jahanara Imam's son away to torture him to death was, as here, Captain Qayyum. Captain Qayyum may still live in protected retirement, untroubled by his deeds during the Bengal monsoon of 1971. I would not shield him with a change of name.

Many thanks go to my first readers, who made very useful suggestions: Tessa Hadley, Nicola Barr, Delwar Hussein, my agent Georgia Garrett, my editor Nicholas Pearson and, above all, Zaved Mahmood.

The plot of the novel has been quite consciously taken from *The Winter's Tale* and from *Eugene Onegin*.